THE FUTURE OF HISTORY

VOLUME I

~

ON MINDS, MACHINES, AND MONSTERS

THE FUTURE OF HISTORY

~

VOLUME I

~

ON MINDS, MACHINES, AND MONSTERS

~

BY
BRIAN RODRIGUEZ

ISBN 978-0-6151-7139-5

Printed in the U.S.A.
First American Edition, December 2007

I dedicate this book to my wife, RaeLena, without whom I would have never found the determination or motivation to finish.

This is for you, my dear. I Love you more than any words could ever express and thank you for your unending patience.

CONTENTS

PART THREE ~ OLD WORLD - NEW WORLD

PART ONE

BEGINNINGS

1 Clear Vision

JUST CALL HIM TAYLOR. Everybody else did. He actually preferred it over his first name. In fact, from a very early age, when anyone called him by that name, Robert, he found that he didn't like it at all. To hear that name almost made him cringe in pain, thus giving the idea to those he knew a way to really irritate him. To those who didn't know him he was Dr. Robert Taylor, or just Dr. Taylor, though for obvious reasons he preferred the latter.

When looking at him for the first time, one would always take note of his startling light blue eyes. On his face these were his most prominent feature, and no matter who was doing the staring, as everyone always did, this was what caught and kept the attention of those he met. Later, if the effect of his piercing stare had worn off, an onlooker would probably notice his small thin nose and his straight, light-brown hair that just touched his shoulders. He had what many people called a baby-face, and he would occasionally use this baby-face in conjunction with his one-of-a kind stare to his advantage – helped him get practically anything he wanted – though he had to do this very rarely. He was far too smart for that.

Taylor was considered tall, at 6'4", but being small framed he appeared lanky and weak, though nothing could be further from the truth. So, standing shirtless in front of and staring at his 120 inch PlexView screen, all of these features, from his young and innocent looking face to his slightly pinched frame, were clearly evident as he commenced his morning with a cup of coffee and a widening grin.

This screen that he was staring at was an electronic and modern version of a giant televised window, for Taylor resided a large building, and where he lived there weren't any windows to speak of. So the PlexView was Taylor's modern way of viewing the outside world, and he had for the last few weeks spent every morning looking out over the massive city in which he lived, ever admiring its towering buildings. His smile continued to grow as he glanced at the corner of the screen noticing the date: July 17th, 2457. A feeling of contentedness quickly washed over him. He had celebrated his eighteenth birthday just the day before, and now that he thought about it, everything in his life seemed to be perfect.

Gradually turning his head, he continued to survey the tall buildings on the screen. Taking a deep breath, thus revealing more ribs than what might be considered healthy, he sighed. Taylor enjoyed this morning ritual – sipping his coffee, his blue eyes wide, taking in the gleaming sunlight as it reflected, in varying degrees, off the glass, steel, and stone that was the Los Angeles Metroship.

This city, like all Metroships, was densely populated, and had been built upon centuries ago when the population of the world had decided to condense itself to a few hundred massive and agglomerated cities. The LAM, or Los Angeles Metro, had well over 2 billion people tightly packed into a few thousand square miles and Taylor marveled at how well the whole of it functioned, much with the aid of technology and ingenious planning.

He watched as transport crafts full of people lifted high into the air before fearlessly falling back into the mass of tall buildings with their targets in sight. Greatly amused in seeing this happen over and over again all around the screen, it often reminded him of flies buzzing hungrily around a large table of food.

With a wrinkled brow Taylor stepped back and stared at the PlexView in concentration. As if obeying his thoughts, the image panned up and down and side to side until it fell on a huge towering structure. At a massive five-hundred-fifty stories, Taylor was now staring the tallest building in the city; nearly double any of its neighbors.

He knew this building very well, with its four wings, North, South, East, and West, built in the shape of a cross, and its matching towers atop each one. These towers, as if they were four sets of spiraling stairs reaching higher and higher into the sky, were of different heights. North Tower was the tallest, followed by West, South, and lastly East; the shortest. To Taylor, this building was one of the greatest architectural masterpieces of the city and he stood for a moment, impressed at how it overpowered anything and everything else in the skyline.

If its height alone didn't get the attention of anyone approaching the city, the structure's pure white marble exterior would certainly do the trick. The bright reflective color could be seen from all of the city's borders without the help of any visual aid.

Taylor's smile suddenly waned. Looking around his apartment, he heaved a great sigh in noticing its quiet, and in his opinion, all too empty and tidy appearance. He turned back to the screen. Staring at these towers every morning he was always filled with the same simultaneous and yet conflicting emotions. With one deep breath for the great freedom he felt, then another for the loneliness that it brought him, his heart ached for the laughter of children. His life suddenly wasn't as perfect as he thought it was just a moment ago.

This massive building he was staring at and to which he always attributed these conflicting emotions, was called the EduCorp Towers; named for the company EduCorp that resided inside. In staring at it from a distance Taylor filled with a rush of memories he had experienced when he lived inside its sterile walls. Some of these were recollections of his training as a child and the constant watch that a team of scientists had over him at all times. Other memories were focused on his own students. Now that he worked for the company that was responsible for teaching him everything he knew, he had six young scholars all his own to teach, train, and mentor. He loved these children with all his heart, and it was with a great pain that he made the decision to move out of The Towers and physically distance himself from them.

With another sigh, he turned and stared at his all but empty apartment. It had so much space – so much room for these children – and yet at the moment it was barren, filled with nothing more than a few boxes, a minimum of furniture, and the bland color of its lonesome walls. Walking to the far end of his living room, he reached into a small metal box. Pulling out a picture of their six young faces and chaotically strewn bodies in a playful pile, he closed his eyes and smiled.

Shaking his head at the image, Taylor began shifting his stare back and forth from the screen to his apartment, to the picture, and back again. In his mind, everything was for the best. He had to move here to satisfy the adoption requirements so that he could gain custody of these children. With any luck this cold and silent residence would be filled with their laughter in less than a month.

It would be at that time that EduCorp would relinquish its adoptive rights, and the children could have their custody transferred to those who applied for it. Taylor had applied to adopt these specific children by name several months ago, and he would settle for nothing less than to be given parental rights to them, complete and unquestioned – all six of them. He had already consulted some of those on the EduCorp Council and they assured, being as the children were his students, that he was by far the best candidate to complete their outside care. With this, Taylor knew that the pain of moving away from his students, children that he had grown to love so very much, was only temporary.

He concentrated again on the PlexView screen. A moment later it zoomed-in to the side of The Towers where he had pre-set it to go on his command, thus eventually landing on six small windows on the 484th floor of West Tower. These windows, unlike the myriad of other glass panes on the side of the building, were those that had been colorfully decorated by his students. These were their rooms, and in looking at them he could see a horribly conversed reflection of their confined lives.

Once the screen finished its adjustments Taylor touched each window and whispered their names: "Aspen, Grace, Caitlin, David, Orion, Johnny" Three boys and three girls – a perfect set in his mind.

He placed his counting hand flat on the screen in its middle and turned a heavy gaze over his empty apartment. It was large, cold, quiet, and boring, a complete contrast to the windows on the screen and the children that lived inside. Thinking this only filled him with an even greater sense of impatience and of being alone. He took a deep breath. Yes, in a month they would be his – permanently, and he would not feel as empty as he did at this moment.

Taylor knew from his learnings years ago that EduCorp, the place where he was raised, and where he was raising his own students now, was the only company in the world with the right to adopt children. This was for the purposes of advancing the company's Virtual Reality Training and Education or VRTE. This company, bestowed with the title of parent for tens of thousands of children, was responsible for creating the virtual reality programs that taught the world, and while both of these responsibilities were granted hundreds of years ago, the company had remained unwavering in its goal of improving the education of the planet. Even still, it could only do this with government sanctioned experiments on its adopted students.

Indeed, many of the experiments and projects that went on in The Towers were simple and benign to the children: a better history program, a more accelerated math curriculum, a condensed language course – these were quite common alterations and experiments that would have to be thoroughly tested before being launched on the world's population. And these were considered, by almost all standards, simple updates and upgrades, but the experiment that trained Taylor, named *Prodigy*, and the experiment that he was using to train his own students, *Prodigy II*, were both highly aggressive and highly unorthodox.

Taylor's training program, *Prodigy,* was designed by EduCorp to push a student as hard and fast as possible, from birth, in the hopes of creating an individual who was the most advanced in academics – in essence creating the smartest person on the planet. Needless to say, it was clear that by the age of 13, and with more than 10 PhD's, Taylor and *Prodigy* had well exceeded EduCorp's expectations.

It was no surprise to EduCorp then, that when Taylor decided to start his own project, he too, focused on an aggressive idea, and with *Prodigy II*, he devised a training program that offered his six students their only possible way of having a normal life; a life he had given to them and been a part of in so many ways.

Taylor shook his mind of the thoughts of his work, his ground-breaking training, and of his job. In just a few more weeks his experiment, his *paid* reason for being with these children, would be over – and they could live with him as their father!

The teen gazed around at his empty apartment, squinting at it, trying to focus on the future, to pull images of what was to come into his mind. He wondered if he could get a flash of his children running through it: laughing, playing, and *living* like they never could in the company building. He turned to look at the screen again and, without warning, his head pounded with a searing pain. A white flash blurred his vision then... the pain was gone.

Looking out across the vastness of the city, Taylor saw the same six windows on the screen, but whereas he could just a moment ago identify each room by the different dressings and decorations they had due to the child that resided inside, now there was nothing, each room – empty!

He concentrated and the screen zoomed further in on the first window. The room was clearly deserted and with the dressings pulled, he could see absolutely nothing inside. Gradually he forced the image to pan over. This eventually showed each room to be utterly barren.

Taylor was confused by the sudden change of the windows. His heart pounded quickly as he realized that his students were no longer in the rooms he had sent them to the night before. The children's rooms had apparently been cleaned out and were now unoccupied. But, then again, now that he was looking at the rest of his apartment, even it was completely bare. It seemed that in just a moment all of his possessions, or what little there was, had completely vanished and yet this all happened while he was standing in the middle of the room. How could he not have noticed it! He quickly shot his eyes back up to the screen.

With the PlexView having landed its focus on the last window, it was here that Taylor noticed something sitting on the window sill. It was a clock. He zoomed in to see if he could recognize it. This proved of little purpose, for Taylor was certain that this timepiece didn't look the least bit familiar to him at all. He zoomed in on it further so that the image became so large that the light green characters offered an eerie iridescent hue to the whole of his apartment. Lowering his head, he grunted loudly, half in anger, half in relief. What was most peculiar about the clock wasn't the fact that it was the only thing in an empty room. It was the fact that the time and date were all wrong. It was showing 10:24AM March 23, 2458.

Taylor opened his mouth, laughing an almost uncontrolled laugh.

"I'm having a vision, that's what this is." he said aloud to reassure himself. "This is a vision of the future." He turned back to look at the clock with its large blinking numbers and he concentrated to make the screen zoom out and view the six windows again.

But what does this mean - he wondered. Judging by the absence of possessions in his apartment, he wasn't living here, and it was obvious that his students weren't in their dorm rooms either. So where were they?

Amid his thoughts Taylor gazed through the PlexView and, quite quickly, the six windows grew very dark, only brightening up with the occasional flash. With his face lighting up for a split second, Taylor snapped at attention and forced the window to zoom out, showing the Los Angeles skyline the way he had seen it before.

His face screwed up in confusion against the dull glow of the screen. This new view revealed something peculiar happening in the sky above. The sunlight he had been enjoying earlier was now obscured by clouds billowing fiercely in the sky. With bright lightning that sparked between them, the churning vapors offered ominous flashes that Taylor was all too curious to watch. Then, to his surprise, the clouds gravitated to a single location where a swirling started to take place. If Taylor didn't know better he was sure that what he was seeing was the start of a tornado. *But that couldn't be* – he thought. *The new Weather Control System would never allow such a thing!* Yet, to his amazement, this billowing cloud formation continued to swirl and dip into the air, in plain sight, above the center of the city, beside The Towers.

Come to think of it, even the city looked different. It was almost unnoticed against the dark clouds in the sky, but several of the tall buildings were actually giving off their own dark puffs into the air. Taylor zoomed in on some of the structures and saw with wide disbelieving eyes that many of the buildings had broken windows and cracked facades. Panning around quickly, he was amazed to see that nearly every building in the city was in some state of despair.

Taylor looked around on the screen hoping to see something that might explain this, but couldn't find an answer. He zoomed the screen back to a view of the whole skyline and whereas at this time of the morning he could expect to see thousands of transports zipping through the air, now he only saw a few, and they were all moving with the same general direction – away from the city's center.

Looking at this massive city, it seemed nearly deserted. The wide sidewalks showed almost no activity with practically everybody gone. Taylor panned the screen and pulled back to the broad skyline. Seeing this large city, which was usually wrought with activity, now so quiet and inactive, he filled with a great curiosity and a sense of foreboding. Then, quite suddenly, his eyes were distracted by something.

A white flashing dot forced its way through the center of the cyclonic cloud formation, and Taylor watched as it made its way between several of the buildings, illuminating the EduCorp Towers with each flash as it descended into the heart of the city. Then, a large white flash filled the screen forcing Taylor to hold up his arm and block the light. This bright burst remained for a few seconds before subsiding, at which time the floor shook uncontrollably. Taylor suddenly realized that the strange feeling he had in his chest was a growing fear unlike anything he had ever experienced.

"What was that – what's going on?" he uselessly muttered; his heart pounding in his ears.

He was confused and panicked, but his eyes stayed glued to the screen. He now watched as, in the center of where this bright object had fallen, buildings crumbled and bent inward. He forced the PlexView to zoom-in so that he could clearly see the activity. He watched with a tenacious curiosity as objects and debris were sucked into the center of this bright phenomenon. As if watching it at half speed, he saw the EduCorp Towers crack at their bases and topple over, falling at an odd angle toward the ever present light beside the base of the building. *All those children!* He thought in horror.

Zooming out to a wider view, he watched as several transports that were flying across the screen came to a stop and, trying as hard as their engines could, started squirming uselessly in an attempt to escape some unseen force. Finally, horrifically, the transports were dragged in like everything else. Taylor could see the panic stricken faces of those inside the transports that were largest on the screen. Wide eyed and fearful, they were screaming; pounding the windows as their craft slowly moved away and out of sight.

The rumbling under Taylor's feet continued to build until it was so extreme that the PlexView glitched, then cracked and lost the image.

Bah – Boom...

A massive exploding noise forced Taylor to turn around. He gasped at seeing that the other side of his apartment was now nonexistent and when he looked out he could see this phenomenon, or rather the effects of this phenomenon, off in the distance. In its center was the bright light that seemed to consume everything its force could pull in. It was growing fast, getting stronger and stronger. Taylor grabbed his own churning stomach. He had a shifting feeling that made his body want to fall toward this thing and he was sure that, had his apartment had furniture, it would have been pulled away into this wrenching force.

Falling over, Taylor grabbed hold of an outcropping of wall, knowing that it would only temporarily prevent the inevitable. The length of his body eventually became parallel to the floor as he was being pulled hard to the center of this insatiable phenomenon.

He concentrated on keeping his feet on the ground, but with all his might, it didn't seem to work. He looked between his sideways dangling legs and could see other people, both from his building and others, getting pulled into the center of this – this thing.

On his way inward, one man's head was struck by a large block of concrete debris and Taylor was certain that if the man wasn't dead, maybe he was lucky enough to be knocked unconscious before getting annihilated by whatever it was that had so ruthlessly planted itself at the center of the city.

Taylor's eyes shifted to a woman, a brunette, who managed to keep hold of a railing in the distance. He felt his heart pain as he saw her lose her grip and fall, then watched in terror that, as she approached the edge of this gravitational distortion, her physical shape stretched into disfigurement while she screamed in pain.

Taylor; happy at becoming a teenaged-adult only moments ago, was now terrified. He grunted, in an effort to improve his grip, but the wall he was holding onto began to crumble and break free. He was falling inward! He yelled, though he knew that it was useless. The rushing noise around him caused such a deafening pain in his ears and he was sure it would be impossible for anyone to hear anything at all in the surrounding chaos.

Just as he was about to reach the edge, the event horizon, of this phenomenon and most certainly suffer the same fate as the woman he had just witnessed, he felt a hand on his shoulder. It was pulling on him. He could feel the grip, soft and yet strong at the same time, and it took a great deal of effort to pull his head up from the strong gravitational force that was trying to consume him. Finally able to see it, noticed that it was a small hand, a child's hand, but there was no body attached to it. It continued to pull, harder and harder then, without warning, Taylor felt an excruciatingly sharp pain in his head.

2 City News

WITH A WHITE FLASH Taylor opened his eyes and sat up in bed. His heart was racing and he was completely drenched in sweat. His flannel style bottoms sticking to his skin made him feel very uncomfortable. He turned, dropped his legs over the side of the bed and dipped his head low. After a spell of dizziness, a great throbbing came to pound in his brain. He had just experienced, without a doubt, another night vision. What he had dreamed was a view of the future or a version of the future and from what he had seen and felt it terrified him to think that such a thing was even close to a possibility.

He stood, his whole body aching, and with a slumping walk, he made his way into the living room of his apartment, feeling comfort in the few items in contained. For him, they were an anchor – telling him that what he was seeing was indeed real.

He focused on the PlexView – turned it on and started surfing channels, his entire sweaty form shining brightly against the flashing images in front of him. He paused briefly at Channel Omni-View LA, where he could get a bird's eye view of any point in the city. This was the channel he always used – apparently even in his visions – to get a full view of the Los Angeles skyline. In seeing the darkness of a cloudy night that covered the city, he slowly relaxed with the feeling that everything was normal, whatever that was.

Continuing to turn the channel, he lowered his head in anger and frustration. It wasn't uncommon for Taylor to have visions. He was after all a postcog and precog. That is to say, he could experience visions of events past, and premonitions of events yet to come.

Indeed, EduCorp's virtual reality training had, nearly four centuries ago, helped mankind to evolve several extra abilities or powers or gifts, as they have been called all three. At first these were thought to be a side effect. Now, though, and with the global distribution of EduCorp's virtual training programs, a full 99.99% of the world was Telepathic. Only one in ten million, however, possessed any extra gifts beyond this, and Taylor, in addition to having these Precog and Postcog powers, was also an extremely talented Telepath, Telekinetic, and Cyberkinetic. All of these gifts made him one of a kind on a planet of over 350 Billion people.

He stood in front of his PlexView with a building anger against himself over the fact that his sleep had once again compromised his ability to control his visions. While Taylor could easily control his pre or post visions during waking hours, it was often that sleep caused his mind to lend itself to dreams of either. Most often the visions Taylor picked up were inconsequential to him, but this last vision – it was definitely different.

It was troubling. So troubling in fact, that the teen felt he had to distract himself by nervously flicking through channels on the PlexView – biting his lip and rocking on his heels. He changed the channels cyberly. That is to say, he was using his cyberkinesis; a power that let him control wireless devices with his mind, and when he felt he was paying more attention to the screen than the thoughts in his own head, he finally he stopped the viewer on a channel.

Taylor felt instantly that he recognized the female newscaster on the screen. She looked very familiar to him, but he was unsure where he might have seen her before. With barely a thought he turned up the volume.

"This is Shannon Lombardo for LAM Late Night News – We give you the latest breaking news straightforward and straight up! It's 2:30 in the morning, thanks for watching. Our top story this half hour is on GC President Andrews – who announced late yesterday that he is committed to solving the GCSPD's fumbling efforts at creating the faster than light drive engine in the next five years. He has declared a willingness to dedicate whatever resources necessary in this effort. I don't know about you but, at 200 years and nothing to show for it, many think this long running project spanning 5 GC administrations is completely foolhardy – myself included. Still, however, the President feels it necessary to drill it into our brains that this effort, while still a complete failure – is still worth our wasted time."

"Now – on to a division of the Governor's Council that always comes out on top! The Evol Crew! This small group of the GC has tracked down and apprehended yet another elusive and powerful criminal. The suspect: a cyber, who allegedly stole vital data from the GC Special Projects Division, centered in the DC Metroship. It has been reported that three of the five-member Evol Crew were needed to apprehend the suspect and that fortunately, no injuries were reported in the arrest. While neither of these statements can be confirmed by independent sources, I'll be the first to say – it hardly matters. At least they know how to get the job done!"

Taylor listened to the newscaster as a large video caption appeared next to her head. He watched as the suspect was taken into custody, followed by three individuals draped in capes and hoods; one in red, another in black, and still a third dressed in green. Nearly everyone in the world recognized the Evol Crew – who, while their faces have never been revealed, were easily spotted because of these colored uniforms.

The GC, or Governor's Council, was *the* governing body over the Metroships of the world. With each Metroship having a *Governor,* there were a total of 548 Governors on the Council. An extra five Governors, the Evol Crew, represented no Metroship at all. They were actually security liaisons to those who possessed more than just standard telepathy. Taylor, himself, viewed these members of the GC with an almost celebrity status, and he concurred with their receiving such fantastic praise for a job well done.

Muting the channel, Taylor turned his stare to the metal box across his living room. Indeed everything did seem to be back to normal, but as Taylor would come to realize years later, things never were what they seemed in his life. And so, with his shining form bare in front of the PlexView, the teen jerked then doubled over in pain. His head suddenly filled with images of the vision he had woken from just a few minutes before. His eyes dulled from a bright white flash, and just as it died down he could make out a child standing amid his memory of an empty apartment.

The teen whipped his paining head around from the PlexView, and his eyes flashed to a vision of his apartment being ripped to shreds with the barely discernable image of a child there in his mind. With this realization a sense of fear and panic filled his every thought.

Then, all at once the painful vision was gone. With his thoughts clear again, he bolted from the living room to his bedroom, willed the lights to come on and, although it was still very early in the morning, he knew he had to get to EduCorp immediately. He had to see his kids!

It was often that Taylor referred to his experimental subjects as his own, even if on paper he was nothing more than a project leader. This title did little to fully describe the relationship he had with these children. On countless occasions they referred to him as their father, or "dad" and while he always smiled before taking time to correct this error, it filled him with a great sense of pride that they considered him such. And why not, he had worked with them for over five years, more than half their life, and so much history bound them to him and the reverse. To him, it was clear that they were more than just his students, in his own words, they were his "kids", and now, at this moment, he was fearful that one of them was in trouble.

So he minimally readied himself, grabbing only his wallet and large trench coat before tearing for the door. Then, suddenly, he felt another shock inside his head. So unexpected, so painful was this piercing pain that it caused his legs to buckle. Using a nearby wall for support, he closed his eyes and, with the flashes of a few images, he could see that this same child was reliving his vision again. He saw his apartment in the half destroyed view he had dreamed of. He caught glimpses of others who were falling victim to the destruction he had seen. He didn't know what was happening, but he was certain that he didn't like not having control of it.

After a moment, when the images and pain subsided in his head Taylor made another effort for the door, which opened for him at his willing it to, and he headed for the lift, which had already found its way to his floor and was waiting, doors readily open for him. Yes, when in a pinch, being a cyberkinetic definitely had its advantages.

While descending Taylor was attempting to *will* a late night transport to the pick-up station outside his apartment building when, "Aaaahr…" once again, he saw flashes of the same vision, and with an intense pain he grabbed his head with both his hands, hoping that a little pressure would alleviate his suffering. He steadied himself on one side of the lift watching the numbers slowly decline in a blur of imagery and haze. When he reached the level of the pick-up platform the doors opened to reveal a successfully called transport. It was waiting for him with door open and a few curious, late-night commuters complaining about the unscheduled stop.

Taylor exited the lift and entered the transport so fast he barely had time to notice that it had started raining outside. As such, his forceful entry startled those who were squinting through the nighttime downpour to look outside. Willing the transport to leave, he stood full upright and shook the chill of the night off before taking his seat.

With the craft climbing through the air another flash of images pained Taylor's thoughts. He winced, letting out a shriek of agony, instantly causing those in the transport to look alarmed. One of them, noticing that the teen was still dressed in his nightwear, grumbled angrily "What the hell's wrong with you? You high on somethin'?" This man was thick, with a large jaw and a square face, very muscular, and very wet from rain and, by the smell of the air, a good deal of sweat.

Only barely catching these words through his pain, Taylor immediately stared up at the man in anger. Then, looking around the transport, his eyes met only a few others that were staring at him, mostly out of fear. His ears perked as he could hear a few of their stray telepathic thoughts in his head.

A woman at the back of the transport with light blonde hair was thinking "He isn't acting high. He's in pain. What's wrong with him!" with a simultaneous thought that he was "a strange and yet attractive man." The muscular square faced man was now looking at him in disgust, "Serves him right; stupid junkie. How does it feel when you've had too much huh, how does it feel?" He could feel this man's anger. It was as strong as his pungent odor that saturated the transport, yet, given the situation, Taylor couldn't understand why the man was so irate.

Taylor looked away hearing another woman in his head, "I think I know him, I've seen him before," and on turning around he noticed that this woman, a brunette, was the same that he had seen in his vision earlier that night. It amazed him to see that, when her face wasn't screaming in fear or pain, she was actually quite beautiful. For only a moment amidst this mind-splitting flashing in his head he thought of the irony that only a few moments ago he had watched her pained face, yet here she was staring at him with the expressions in reverse.

The brunette shifted her stare to the large muscular man – with a sour face, she reached into her pocket and pulled out a small bottle of perfume that she sprayed quickly in the middle of the transport. Taylor wanted to thank her.

With the images and pain subsiding yet again, Taylor took a moment to gain his composure. Holding his knees and looking around the transport, he knew that everyone was staring at him. He stared back at each one trying to figure out their thoughts, but couldn't. This seemed strange as he heard everything they were thinking only a moment ago. They glared at him in fear, in confusion, and impatient for an explanation. He offered none and just sat quietly.

His mind rolled over the thoughts of those in the transport; their reactions, their faces. What always bothered Taylor when he was in a public situation like this was his inability to determine the age of those around him. Growing up in EduCorp, he could easily look at the youths in his presence and determine their ages; a ten year old girl here – a fifteen year old boy there, but now that he mingled in the general population, figuring the age of his peers had become much more difficult. But it had been this way for centuries.

The Methuselah Virus, a virus that Taylor learned about when he was only two years old, was a genetically engineered virus designed to rid the world of all major diseases. It was created under the auspice of improving the human genetic code, making us impervious to many of the illnesses of the past. Well it did exactly that, and more. Due to the miracle of genetic manipulation, people now lived to be over two hundred, and, for a good one-hundred-eighty years of their life, they didn't look a day over 25. So even though Taylor looked around at a transport full of young adult faces, the truth was that they could range in age from 18 to 198, and neither he nor anybody else wouldn't know the difference.

He hated this inability to age someone on sight, unlike when he was growing up, and while, right now, he'd rather ignore everyone around him, he kept glancing up at the large muscular man, feeling a thick menacing stare. It was as if this huge oaf was measuring the teen's every detail.

"You got a problem!" the large man said stiffly.

Taylor said nothing, keeping his head down, he slipped his hand into his coat pocket, pulled out his small black wallet and opened it to reveal his I.D. to the large man, hoping it would make him back off.

"Yeah – I've seen those fakes – you can't fool me!"

Taylor grinned almost to the point of laughter. *Could it be that this man was really that stupid?* Under any normal circumstance this large, gruff individual, whose foul nauseating odor offended everyone in the transport, would be very oppressive to someone of Taylor's small frame, but Taylor was different. The teen looked down at his ID that clearly showed 4 emblems lined on the side – white, black, red, and green. Each was for his registration as a person that possessed his unique powers. It had to be modified to have all the emblems, because, in the world, everyone else who even had such an emblem, only had one. He, however, had white for being a pre-cog, black for being a post-cog, red for a being a cyber, and green for being a telekinetic – or kinetic for short.

Seeing Taylor's smile, the large man grumbled sourly, "There somethin' funny?"

He stepped ever closer to Taylor, casting a shadow over the teen's seemingly weak frame. Taylor continued to stare at his ID, eventually having to wipe it of drops of sweat that had fallen from the man looming over him.

"Nothing is funny sir. Now if you don't mind I would like to finish this ride without you dripping your stinky sweat all over me!" With these words the large man's eyes grew wide and he started to back off while quickly reaching for his throat. The man was terrified, and in his movement he eventually sat himself down, or rather fell into a seat at the far end of the transport. Taylor smiled, realizing that everyone else was absolutely confused at what was going on. But then again, they hadn't seen the teen's ID.

Taylor didn't like using his powers on people, unless, of course, he really felt that they deserved it. In this case, he was losing patience fast. His frustration over the thick man forced him to look down, trying to avoid eye contact with any of the other passengers. Eventually he closed his eyes altogether, hoping to keep from distraction. His worry over his students was swelling, and he wished the transport would hurry up. He fidgeted, staring up at the ceiling – then out the window, watching other transports move quickly by. He hoped o find any kind of distraction that would help pass the time and keep from getting into more trouble with any of the other passengers.

No such luck! Taylor's nervous behavior and halfhearted focus on the buildings that whizzed by was broken by an unexpected interruption. A man, a short, very thin, almost emaciated man that Taylor hadn't even noticed before, braved the thought to sit next to him and, in a soft whisper, asked the teen a question.

"Hey, buddy, are you alright?"

Taylor sighed. He was starting to shake his head for a no, but instead opted for a "Yeah, I think so..." to keep from attracting too much attention. This was a lie for at any moment he felt that he'd either throw up from the competing smells hitting his nose or pass out from another attack of visions. He could feel them pressing into his brain – images he was trying to keep out.

"Are you sure...?" pressed the thin man, who at this point put his hand on Taylor's shoulder in an attempt to comfort. This seemed to help for a few seconds, but quite quickly the kind gesture wore off its welcome, having the adverse effect of making Taylor feel very uneasy. The teen very quietly slipped his wallet back into his pocket and watched the thin man's hands suspiciously.

Unexpectedly an agonizing cry filled the transport. Taylor almost didn't even recognize his own screaming voice, and with the others staring at him, he finally quieted, clenching his teeth and grunting horribly. His head was exploding with more images from the same terrifying vision. This time the pain was a lot stronger. He felt like his brain was going to burst. He stared up amid flashing images of his apartment and views of the people and transport around him and could see the fearful expressions on the passenger's faces. Curious of what they were thinking, he opened his mind to theirs.

Normally this would allow Taylor to hear more of their stray thoughts, if there were any, but, at this moment, that's not what happened. His mind didn't pick up their stray mental meanderings – instead, he unwillingly offered them his own thoughts – or rather – his broken visions and the pain that accompanied them.

All around Taylor the passengers were wailing in agony, and Taylor was certain that the uncontrolled pain he himself was feeling caused the transport to show signs of uncontrolled cyberkinetic influence. The inside lights flickered and with jolts and unexpected movements, Taylor knew that the stability of the craft was clearly compromised. The teen realized immediately that he had to concentrate, but the pain seemed too great. He couldn't get control of his powers.

He closed his eyes, took a deep breath, and focused hard on the images that kept flashing into his head. If he wasn't able make them stop, he could think of nothing better than to just take them on – fully. He concentrated on the vision, emotions, and pain penetrating his brain, trying to forget that the craft around him was shaking, and by the feeling in his stomach, he could tell that it was rapidly descending.

Then after a moment, his vision grew dark, and his body – cold.

3 Commuter Vision

WITH YET ANOTHER bright white flash, Taylor found himself standing in his apartment again, and in front of him were four ghostly transparent figures: two men and two women. He shook his head with a smile, realizing that he had somehow mentally brought those in the transport with him. He could only barely make out each of their faces, but when they spoke, he could understand them perfectly.

"What is this place?" asked the brunette woman snapping her head around frantically.

"Yeah, where the hell are we." grumbled the large muscular man.

"This is where I live," snapped Taylor sternly, and with these words the four blurred and transparent figures that were lined against the bright skyline of Los Angeles turned and stared at the teen with disbelief.

"Your place? That's bull," growled the muscular man. "We were flying through the air just a second ago!" The man then turned around and stood square and threatening in front of Taylor, "Now I'm going to ask you one more time. Where the hel..." He reached to grab Taylor by the throat, but this effort was useless for his hand passed right through the teenager, and instantly he, the large man, became so frightened that he stepped back behind the others. All eyes were again directed at Taylor.

"All I know is that you are definitely in my apartment," Taylor said with a soothing calm look between the others. "And the better question to ask isn't where you are, but when you are. Right now, here, it's March of 2458, and this is a vision I had of the future just earlier tonight." Taylor made very strong efforts to keep his voice tranquil - almost monotone. This had the singular effect of calming those around him and with a few slow and gentle nods it was clear that he was successful in subduing them into understanding.

The brunette snapped her head up at Taylor, wide eyed and mouth gaping. "I know who you are!" she declared stiffly. "I read about you in an article on the Net. Yes, yes I know you. Your name is Taylor, Rober..."

"Dr. Taylor" the teen cut in to keep from hearing his first name fully.

"Sorry," she said with a false apology turning to the ghostly figures around her. "Well anyways, he's only eighteen – got something like twelve or thirteen PhDs or something like that." She was now speaking very blandly as, behind her, the city was growing dark with overcast and flashes of lightning.

"Fifteen!" He said dully, half wanting to brag, half wanting to correct.

"Hhmm," she huffed. "And he's the only one in the world that's got all five powers." She said this in the voice of an almost accusing whisper and as Taylor looked around he could tell that at least two of those in his small audience were actually impressed by this bit of information.

"Listen," said the large man stepping out from the four of them, "I don't care what you are, or what you can do, I just want to get the hell out of here, and go home."

"I wish I could help you," started Taylor "but even I have no choice now but to wait this vision out."

"Vision! This is bull crap, I don't see any vision, I just see some empty apartment, and a big freakin' window!"

"Actually," corrected the very thin man in a soft and squeaky voice. "This isn't a window at all. This is a flush-mounted PlexView 120... Oh, wow, how cool!" he added in excitement putting his hand on the large image, yet ill aware of what it was showing. "You said you live here, but – where's all your stuff?"

"Whatever, string-bean," murmured the large man under his breath, but Taylor had more encouraging words

"That," Taylor interjected in response to the man's inquiry, "is a very good question. As this vision is nearly a year in the future, I can't say where my stuff is, the – strange – thing – is..."

Taylor found himself distracted by the formation of another person in the vision; a small person, a child, and he thought instantly of his students. Could this be one of them?

"Johnny!" he called aloud – but there was no response. "Caitlin!" he persisted, but he just received the same ignored behavior, and as he continued to call out the names of his other students the blonde haired woman spoke out with great curiosity.

"Who are these names you're calling?"

Before Taylor could respond, the question was answered by someone else. "His students," said the brunette. "I read about them in the article. He has six students currently under his watch. They're quite gifted, just like him. In fact, the article criticized him" she continued, nodding in Taylor's direction, "for not pushing the training of their powers; something about wanting to be the only one, or something like that."

Taylor gave the woman a hard, angry stare then turned to continue attempts at getting the attention of the new child in his vision. He even went so far as to walk through its transparent body a few times, but there was no response.

Then, with a flash on the screen, all six of them, including the image of the child, raised their hands to cover their eyes. The ground shook fiercely and Taylor turned away from the screen. He stared nervously at the wall that he knew would soon disappear. "You might want to hold on to something," he said in a soberly stern voice as he himself stood beside the half present child in the center of the room. He had already decided for himself that it was pointless to hold on to anything because he knew what this vision was to bring.

The confused looks of the transparent figures around him quickly changed to stares of fear as the rumbling floor and walls forced the PlexView to fracture - *again*. Eventually they all moved quickly to find a safe place to hide. Taylor himself watched as his apartment creaked and cracked around its walls and ceiling before tearing itself apart. Everyone, except Taylor screamed loudly from fear.

Whether out of concern or curiosity, Taylor's ears again perked from the random and uncontrolled thoughts of those in his presence and, surprisingly, it was the large man's emotions that caught his attention most. The feelings and thoughts that were emanating from this man were of a strength that Taylor had rarely experienced. As such the teen's eyes were torn between watching the ghostly childlike figure at his side, unwavering in its position, and this man, whose feelings were not of fear, nor of despair at what he was seeing, no – no, they were of regret.

All seemed to be going exactly as Taylor had expected until he heard an abrupt scream and a thud as the brunette woman behind him fainted. She had just witnessed her own demise and obviously couldn't handle seeing her own death in vivid reality. With her being unconscious, the thin man and the blonde woman held her arms with their free hands to keep her from falling in. Taylor could see that, even though the others were transparent, they were still suffering from the effects of the phenomenon at the center of the city. Their discernable fear filled faces consumed Taylor with shame that he had brought them with him.

Simultaneously, Taylor and the image of the child at his side both fell toward the light. It was just at the moment of lifting off his feet and flying inward that Taylor turned around and focused on the muscular man. His thick hands were holding desperately onto a sink spout in Taylor's kitchen, and in looking at him, Taylor was again sensing the strong emotion of regret that just poured from his meaty soul. With an unintended concentration on these thoughts, Taylor's eyes met a white flash that devoured the whole of the world around him. With a painful thud he felt his body fall on solid ground in a rush.

Looking around, he saw that he was no longer in his destroyed apartment, and that his four compatriots had indeed followed him to this new place and time, though they were still only a ghostly silhouette of their real selves.

"What the hell are we doing here?!" voiced the large man in a curiously loud and demanding fashion – so much so that Taylor was instantly suspicious.

"Do you - do you know this place?" Taylor asked cautiously, realizing that this man was in fact, fully formed and opaque.

"'Course I know this place," he said with a sour biting attitude, "I live here!"

Taylor could smell the stench of truth in the air, and with the understanding that he had in fact moved from one vision to another, he searched for a calendar of sorts to tell him when he had transferred to. His eyes fell on many tale telling items, an old brown couch, riddled with patches, a kitchen that was kept clean and tidy, despite its well worn appearance, and ah, yes, an inset digital calendar on the wall.

September 30th, 2457.

"Well," Taylor said in a bland voice, "we've apparently moved from that awful vision to another," and he continued by telling all the new date of their arrival.

"With any luck I might be able to concentra..." Taylor started, but was distracted by a strange series of noises from a different room. Slide – then thud, slide – then thud. He turned to investigate, but was cut off by the muscular man.

"Oh, I don't think so! This is my home – and you're all very much unwelcome here!" The man was planted in front of Taylor, shaking his large square head and the teen understood. It would be quite improper for any of the group to go moping around this man's residence without his permission. Taylor turned and waved the three followers back into what was undoubtedly the living room.

With a jerk, the large man gasped in fear from something that had grabbed his leg causing all to turn around and see what was going on. Even Taylor was shocked to see, of all things, a person – a bony young woman, dressed in a white hospital gown was crawling on the floor. With breaths of fear, the now unwanted visitors, Taylor included, watched as she coughed and spat up blood. Low, incomprehensible moans filled the air as she turned her face up and glared at the muscular man. Looking down at her smoky white eyes, Taylor felt a chill run up his spine as the girl struggled to speak a single word at the large man. "Daddy," she spewed in a dull, hissing whisper.

The large man dropped to her side, turning her over. It was at this time that Taylor realized this suffering girl was near, but had not quite reached, adulthood. The man howled as he leaned over and pulled the girl to his chest. Though they looked the same age – it was clear that this was, in fact, a father daughter pair, and once again, Taylor found himself irritated at the difficulty in aging someone on sight.

"Oh, no, no, no..." the thick man wailed in great emotional agony. "No, no, no" he continued even louder, rocking her in his thick powerful arms, "This can't be!"

"Who is..." Taylor started to ask, but an answer was snapped quicker that the question was given.

"My daughter, idiot!" he shouted, eyes welling with tears. He struggled to lift her up, but her muscles were convulsing uncontrollably. "Well, don't just stand there," he added, "Help me – e – e"

Taylor knelt down, "She's overdosed on HaloFix. She needs medical attention."

The large man looked over at Taylor with a fierce scowl on his face, "That's not it, it's something else!" he shouted. "It's something else!"

Taylor shook his head at the girl's trembling body, "I'm a doctor – and I've seen enough of them to know an H.F. O.D. when I see it."

To everyone's astonishment, when Taylor reached to grab one of the girl's arms, his hand simply passed through her. The teen had only just now noticed that he was translucent like the others – a mere ghost of himself.

"I – I can't DO anything." Taylor said nervously, "We're in *your* future now!

You're the only one that can do anything here!"

The man barely had absorbed these words when finally, after a horrible gagging struggle, the girl stopped moving. Her flailing arms and legs went limp. All eyes moved from Taylor to the girl. Her color disappeared as she coughed and sputtered her last bloody breath. Her chest no longer moved, and her bubbling mouth ceased to produce any new red froth. "Why, why, why" the large man sobbed and wailed loudly, holding his lifeless child carefully, "why would you show me this...?" he continued, turning an angered stare to Taylor.

The teen took this accusation style question in stride as so much more was making sense to him now. He knew that the girl was obviously the victim of an overdose of HaloFix. All the signs pointed to it, even if the large man denied it. It was clear, too, that earlier, on first sight, this muscular man thought Taylor was a junkie, just like his daughter. *That's where all the hate was coming from,* Taylor rationalized. This accusation may have been misplaced, but it's not like the teen's behavior and appearance in the transport lent to the contrary. *Yes, it was all making sense now*. This large, hard working man, in watching his daughter's slow deterioration, must have harbored a horrible hatred for anything having to do with drugs, addiction, users, sellers - everything.

"So, how long has it been?" Taylor asked.

"Wha... Huh..." The man sobbed, looking through thick tears up at Taylor, who was leaning over, putting a falsely placed hand on the man's shoulder.

"How long have you known about your daughter's addiction," Taylor asked in a louder accusing voice before adding, "while you did nothing about it." Taylor's voice was harsh, and the others stared at him with surprise over how he could address someone so much larger than himself in this way.

"But she's not addicte..." the large man started, but Taylor cut his words short.

"You're holding your daughter in your arms. She's dead. Addicted or not, as *you* say, this is what will happen in less than three months unless you do something about it."

The large man looked up at Taylor, now with an expression of pain and fear, "You don't think I've wanted to. My wife and I, we raised a good kid, a smart kid, and she's going to get better, I know it. She's going to get better."

"I hate to break it to you big guy," Taylor pressed blandly, "but if something doesn't change here, and quick, this is going to be your future, and hers, and there's no way out."

The buzzing and chatting that had ensued between the thin man, the brunette, and the blond all stopped in an instant with the blond raising her hands, "Wait, wait, wait – so this future," she asked looking between the others "this future that we see here – isn't set?"

"None are!" Taylor answered. "Most times a precog can effect change in their future if they want, but the easiest way to make an uncertain future more definite is to do absolutely nothing to effect change." He stared down at the large man with a lecturing gaze, and on finishing these words he leaned over. Placing his hand on the large man's shoulder again, both realized that there was true interaction here as Taylor's limb was now physically opaque. It was felt by the large man, making his emotions run even more rampant than before. He sniveled and cried uncontrollably as Taylor watched everything slowly slip into a smooth and bright dissolve of color. This vision was finished.

4 Saving Johnny

SOUNDS OF RAINDROPS filled Taylor's ears as a plain palette of dull colors blended in from a flash of white light. He blinked his eyes a few times and noticed that the transport, now with full stability, was waiting with its door wide open at the front steps of the EduCorp Towers. He reveled in the moist, fresh – very fresh smelling summer air. With blinking eyes it was clear that the others were all coming 'round. The large man jerked his head around fiercely and with a deep sigh Taylor could see that he was shaking off a great sense of relief. It was clear that the large man quickly realized his daughter wasn't yet dead. So, with a returning sense of purpose, Taylor moved to step out, but just as he was just at the point of getting a face full of rain a large adult hand grabbed his thin adolescent arm.

"Hey – uhm kid? I – I'm sorry for what I said earlier," the large man said softly, "I – I..." The man paused and took a deep breath. "Thank you." The man now had real tears welling in his eyes, "If no one else says it to you tonight – Thank you for sharing one of your gifts with me. You – you've just saved my daughter's life."

Taylor shook his head at these words, seeing how hard it was for the man to speak them, and he looked at this massive individual in a completely different way. "Sir –" he said very formally looking at the large firmly gripping hand.

"Please. Call me James." He interrupted in what was the kindest voice Taylor had heard from him all night.

"Listen – James, I've only shown you one possible future – it isn't set, and it might not happen, but just know that saving the life of your daughter is all up to you. Me – I've got someone to save here." Taylor said this waving his free hand at the towering building behind him. The man, now known to Taylor as James, lowered his head with a nod, released Taylor's arm, and kept a watchful eye as the teen stepped out of the transport. This was a good thing as it turned out, for Taylor had just taken his first step outside when, once again, he felt a rush of pain that caused him to stumble to his knees on the wet concrete.

James leaped out and grabbed him, trying to help him to his feet, but the man could only watch with great concern as Taylor was shaking stiffly and rigidly, his eyes rolling in his head, and his jaw opening and closing, though little sound came from his mouth. It took a good deal of strength for James to hold Taylor upright, and finally, after nearly a minute, the teen's body relaxed and he seemed to return to normal.

Politely shaking free of this muscular, smelly hold, Taylor moved to the entrance of The Towers. He was certain, now more than ever, that one of his students, and he had a pretty good idea which one, was somehow trapped in this horrible repeating vision of the future.

Looking up at The Towers as he went, his face full of rain, Taylor heaved a sigh at returning to his former home. He willed the large glass doors of the Edu-Corp lobby open and as he entered he bid James a thank you and goodnight nod before swiftly walking across the marble floor. He nodded with quick recognition to the night security guard, and took West Tower's lift to the 484th floor, where his children resided.

On exiting the lift he ran down a long corridor, curious that all seemed so quiet. *Well, it should be quiet* – he dismissed – *it's barely 3AM.* He slowed to a quick walk, taking in every possible detail, eventually making a left turn at the end of the hall. He skirted by dormitory doors, looking in each one through their small glass windows. The children all seemed fine, asleep, asleep, asleep, asleep, asleep... and, only at the last door did his heart explode with emotion.

"Johnny… Of course, Johnny!"

Looking through the dark window with only a glint of light coming in over his shoulder, Taylor could see two small bare feet hidden under the dormitory bed that were shaking as if something between a shiver and convulsion. He took a quick step back from the door, staring at it in concentration. It opened quickly, and he sprinted into the room, willing a dim light to turn on.

Crouching to look under the bed, he called to Johnny. The boy did not answer. He called again, but still there was no response. With a furrowed brow and a surge of telekinetic energy he threw the bed across the room.

He reached to quickly grab and hold the boy, but the very moment he touched the child's arm another series of horrific images hit him. Now his being so close to Johnny caused Taylor to feel a pain in his head so strongly that he nearly lost all control of his abilities. Lights and computer terminals in the room flashed at random, objects in the room started to rumble and a few small novelty items on a nearby shelf flew across the dorm, breaking on the wall.

Taylor immediately focused on trying to control his powers, despite the pain in his head, and quickly distanced himself from the boy. Immediately after, the sharp twinges subsided and he thought to try again and help the child before him. Looking down over his sweaty, convulsing student, Taylor took off his trench coat and wrapped the boy in it while struggling to keep control of the boy's movement.

It was clear to Taylor that Johnny was in some kind of shock. His eyes were moving wildly under closed lids and on his face was an expression of pain and terror. After making sure to keep from any physical contact, Taylor pulled him close and held him tight, hoping to calm the involuntary shaking.

This wasn't easy as the boy, while young, still had strong muscles to contend with. That, coupled with the will he needed to try to work through the painful images still being shared, made the experience all the worse.

Taylor closed his eyes, forced himself into a deep meditation, and offered a soft "Shhhh…" while rubbing Johnny on the back. As the time passed the entire room slowly started to pull itself away into a bright blinding light...

Taylor was now deep inside the vision with Johnny, and to his slight relief he could see that the premonition had only just started its newest cycle. But Taylor was annoyed and panicked at the idea that this was still the same vision that he had been seeing painful parts of all night long.

The teen rocked on his feet while scanning the room, eventually landing his eyes on the city as seen through the PlexView. It was difficult for him, looking around at his empty apartment, to shake the feeling of absolute loneliness that had consumed him the first time he had this vision. With a deep sigh, Taylor felt someone grab hold of his hand; the small set of digits slipping into his palm to weave delicately between his own fingers. Closing his eyes, he could already see Johnny's shining young face with bright blue tear-filled eyes before actually staring down and looking at the boy.

Stripes of cool shiny trails, tears that had already worked their way down the boy's face by way of crying from pain were clearly visible. Taylor bit his lip. In looking at this face that he loved so much now in such an insurmountable amount of agony, he had to exercise total self control not to let his own empathy and emotions get the better of him.

Taylor knelt down and spoke to Johnny in a soothing voice. "Hey big guy," he started, wiping away some of the boy's tears. "Whatcha doin' here? You know what's gonna happen. Why don't you leave?"

"I c – can't." murmured the boys soft, desperate and sobbing voice.

"What do you mean 'you can't'" asked Taylor as he watched the formation of clouds just above the city, exactly as he remembered.

"I don't know…" the boy said, looking down as if ashamed, "I would a thought this'd be over by now, but I just keep coming back here and..." the boy paused and heaved a sobbing wet breath, "I just don't know why!"

Like Taylor, Johnny was now growing fearful of the approaching future as they both looked out across the view provided by the screen. With a bright flash, the tall and short silhouettes of the two held their hands to their eyes to block out the light as once again the floor began to rumble. The two stood there, it seemed, as a sign – a symbol of the approaching and unavoidable conclusion of this vision.

Taylor rubbed the boy's shoulders to comfort him, "Johnny, you need to let me get you out of here. You can't keep doing this. You can't handle this much pain!" Taylor looked down, and in a forceful tone he offered a more personal plea – "*I* can't handle this much pain. We have to get out of here, now!"

Johnny simply nodded with raised eyebrows, then lifted his shoulders to match with an 'I don't know expression' on his face.

"What do I do?" the boy asked in frustration.

"Just think of something happy – someplace better than here. Think of anywhere but here. Okay!?"

"But, Dad, the only place I can think, is to be with you. That's all I've been thinking," the boy whined.

Taylor felt so pressed for time that he wished he didn't have to explain so much. But he could see that Johnny was in a very delicate state, and so he offered as much patience as he could.

"Well, yes, this is where I live. But it is not the where that counts, it's the when." He could see that there was a slightly confused look on this young nine year old face, and all Taylor could think to do was explain. He was, after all, a teacher.

"Think of something you *did* that was fun – any vision of the past would be better than this. Come on now – just think – something fun!"

Taylor blinked as the PlexView turned off, having lost its signal. The end was very close and as they both realized this time seemed to slow to a crawl. Taylor now pressed the boy now sternly. "Think of anything – ANYTHING, ANYPLACE, but here. Think – concentrate!" he bellowed in desperation.

One might mistake that Taylor had a personal fear of what was going to happen to himself, but this wasn't at all the truth. He had no fear for himself – he knew that in visions there was no real danger. What he, in fact, did fear for was the wellbeing of his student. He was fully aware that any amount of pain he could feel would be nothing compared to his having to watch the pain and agony of a child that he loved.

Taylor looked down and saw that the boy was trying hard to find someplace in his mind that would be suitable, his tongue sticking out a little and massaging his sucked in lips. He looked up from beneath his tilted brow and messy light brown hair offering a slight smile. "I think I've got it!" the boy shouted.

Just as these words slipped out of the child's mouth Taylor's apartment tore itself open in a rush, exactly as it had several times before. The teen grabbed Johnny, holding him tight in a firm embrace with one hand and held the same outcrop from the first vision with the other.

With a whisper in comparison to the surrounding noise, Taylor screamed in the child's ear, trying to instruct the boy in his arms, "Come on Johnny! Think! Think!"

After a few seconds of holding the boy, with all of this chaos around him, Taylor's body jerked with a harsh sensation of pain rushing through it; a pain that he couldn't explain. Through every limb and every nerve, he felt an insane mind-crushing pain that seemed to come out of nowhere. His ears were equally met with the pain of the boy in his arms, who was squirming from his own sense of unidentifiable suffering. This made it nearly impossible to hold the boy and still keep a firm grip on the outcropped wall.

Taylor, distracted by the boy in his arms, looked at the child's face. Johnny's eyes were transfixed on the phenomenon or rather they were set on the many people who were meeting their demise by it, and when Taylor noticed this, he grabbed hold of the boy's head, forcing him to look away. The pain that the two were feeling ceased immediately.

With a terrified sense of understanding Taylor realized what was happening, and why. All through his morning journey Taylor continued to see not only images of this vision, but also feel a great pain that came with it. His reasoning for this; Johnny was somehow absorbing and feeling the pain of those that he watched die. *Had the child found a way to tap into the feelings of others in his vision?* Taylor was baffled by this, as he had always thought it impossible to bond with those in premonitions of the future. They were, after all, only impressions of the possible future, not the reality of the future.

With a knot in their stomachs and dizziness in their heads the two moved toward the disturbance at the center of the city when their anchored outcropping of wall had given way. All Taylor's efforts stayed focused on holding Johnny and reminding him to mind his thoughts. "Think of that better place. Think of that happy place." In his mind he tried to do the same. He prayed that this would work, for he could sense the terror not only in himself, but also in the child in his arms. It was this child's fear that pained him greater than anything the physical world could do, and inside he was desperate for the whole thing to be over.

With a sharp and excruciating agony, both he and Johnny were consumed by the edge, the event horizon, of the disturbance. Taylor tried with all his might to ignore the moment of pain in his legs as his only thought was to be someplace better and to take Johnny with him. He could hear the boy's screams and couldn't help but let out his own wail of sympathetic agony and tears to match.

While the pain may have lasted only a mere second, it seemed like ages to Taylor, and finally, desperately, with a white flash, everything disappeared.

The cries in Taylor's ears melded into an odd sound, a happy sound – the sound of children's laughter. He was looking up at a bright blue sky and he could feel a prickling against his ears and head. He was lying on a bed of grass. His ears perked as suddenly the sound of laughter stopped. Still held tightly in his arms, but shaking and weeping, Johnny was clutching Taylor's neck so hard the teen was having trouble getting the boy to let go so the two of them could take in their new surroundings.

Taylor eventually coaxed the boy into being peeled off before they both stood up and looked around. With an all too wide smile, he saw his other five students standing in a small circle, each with their own perfect grin. He returned the favor, but the children were, it seemed, frozen. Concerned that they were motionless and not breathing, he stared at them one by one: David, Aspen, Orion, Caitlin, and Grace.

Taylor was reminded, just now, of how each one looked different from the other, and yet in some way they still shared the same features. And why not, the six of them, Johnny included, were brothers and sisters, though not by coincidence, and it it was indeed quite the job Taylor had to be teacher, trainer, and parent to them when their ages were so unnaturally close together. Johnny, at nine, was the youngest while all the others were ten; five brothers and sisters all born in the same year. It was an oddity that had initially confused Taylor when they arrived at EduCorp five years ago.

He glanced around at them again, and upon turning to the last, Grace, he knelt down to take a closer look.

Now nose to nose with her motionless and stiff body, Taylor touched her and it felt as though she were a hard statue. Her limbs were so firm it felt as though she was, indeed, made of stone and he was sure he had never seen anything like this before in any dream or vision. He stared at her with their faces less than an inch apart. He was gawking in confusion and curiosity at her, but had to smile at her bright green eyes and short, crew-cut blond hair – the picture perfect tom-boy!

Blinking her eyes, she surprised him, nearly making him fall on Johnny.

“Is he alright?” she asked in a plain and inquisitive matter.

Behind him he could now hear the newly animated voices of David and Orion. “Is he good to play?” – “We need a fifth person!”

“What happened to him?” sounded the curious voice of Aspen from behind, and in a few moments the five siblings were all crowding in on the two of them.

Suddenly a shrill voice of bossiness commanded, “Make way! Make way! Give ‘em room to breathe why don’t you?!” This came from its usual source, Caitlin, and in looking at her Taylor couldn’t believe what he was seeing. She was dressed in the most unusual mix of clothes he had ever witnessed. While the others were clearly dressed in simple jeans, colored tees and the like, she was a colorful mismatch of clothes in strangest assortment. Why, he had looked at her a moment ago and he was sure she wasn’t dressed so oddly, but now – here she was – it didn’t make sense.

Looking at her though, he could not help but laugh, and with the children all being so happy, Taylor himself was filled with a fantastic joy that he could only explain as being his future emotions. Looking around at the beautifully curious faces of his students, he was quickly coerced to let Johnny go.

“He’s – eh – He’s okay. I’ll just leave him here with you – to play.”

With a resounding cheer they all rushed on Johnny, who was quickly on his feet. It was clear that they hadn’t noticed their brother’s mournful face, and as Taylor’s eyes were now washing over with a bleaching white, the boy’s sad blue-eyed expression was the last part of the vision he remembered.

In the quiet dormitory Johnny’s shaking had slowed to nonexistence and his face relaxed to a plain sleep. With the two still having their eyes closed, tears streamed down both their faces. While Taylor’s were from a sense of relief and happiness, Johnny’s were from great pain and suffering.

Taylor opened his eyes and let out a slow, almost weeping breath. He lifted Johnny off the floor and kinetically replaced the bed in the dorm before laying the boy on it. Johnny’s resting finally resembled normal sleep.

Standing up, Taylor stretched from tiredness and left the dorm. He walked down the hall some twenty feet to an M-Gen panel where he pressed several buttons to activate the unit. A soft humming noise let him know that the machine was performing its required task. While he waited, Taylor stared at the M-Gen, marveling at how a single device had completely changed the course of history and the face of the entire planet.

The concept of the M-Gen panel had existed for over 250 years. It was the foundation of the world's economy, and, simply put, it ridded the world of poverty, need, resource shortages, and any problems with pollution. Right now, however, Taylor was using it to convert water into energy and energy into any form of matter, but not just any matter. Here he was generating a few modern conveniences. And so, after a few seconds, a light beeping noise, which echoed very noticeably in the dark hall, let him know that it had finished.

He opened the panel and pulled out two plates of sandwiches that he took back to the dormitory. A moment later he returned, but this time he concentrated on the panel, cyberly forcing it into action. Waiting for the beep, he pulled more items out of the panel, turned it off, and returned to the dorm.

Inside this small room he laid out the items that he had retrieved from his second trip to the panel: a thin self-inflating mattress, a flat bed-sheet, and a thermal blanket. After a mere minute his makeshift bed was complete and he sat on its low soft cushion. With great pangs of hunger, he ate one of the fresh plates of sandwiches.

It was common knowledge that the extensive use of any evolved powers resulted in a great deal of hunger. This was strictly due to the amount of energy required to keep the brain at such an active level for so long, thus having the unfortunate side effect of depleting the body of its much needed nourishment.

When Taylor finished his plate of food he stood up, went into the dorm's bathroom and grabbed a paper towel, which he soaked using the basin. He then gently laid the moist paper towel atop the second plate of sandwiches being careful to make sure that some of it was still visible from Johnny's point of view. Taylor was sure that, at some point during the night, the boy would wake and be hungry. This food would be waiting for him and with any luck the wet towel will have prevented the bread from drying out.

With minutes passing slowly, Taylor now lay quietly on his makeshift bed. He smiled, happy to be where he was – not in an empty apartment, or a smelly one, or an odor filled transport with strangers – no – with his kids – where he truly felt that he belonged. In looking up he could see one of Johnny's hands hanging over the side of the bed. Taylor grabbed the soft limp fingers and massaged them gently. In this dark and now calm room Taylor ached from the boy's former pain. Feeling the ultimate in empathy, he quietly whispered, "You're too young for this… much too young."

5 The Enigmatic Sphere

THE FOLLOWING MORNING, after only a few more hours' sleep, Taylor woke next to Johnny's bed having nearly forgotten the events that lead to his resting at this location. He sat up; raising his weary body with one hand, grabbing his slightly throbbing forehead with the other, and was grateful that he hadn't dreamt any visions during the last few hours. With this thought in mind he turned to the boy by his side.

Looking over the peaceful child who was resting quietly above his covers, Taylor smiled. Sitting on the bed beside the boy, he was careful not to disturb the child's rest. He put his hand on the boys back and with a soft rubbing he felt that the child was warm to the touch. It was with concern that Taylor then closed his eyes and concentrated, forcing himself into the boy's thoughts.

After a moment Taylor sighed with a smile. Eyes opening, he whispered, "a dream."

Indeed it was a good dream, or vision rather, for the boy was still in the company of his brothers and sisters; happily playing in what Taylor could tell was a vision of the past. Oh, it was quite an amazing thing that all of Taylor's students were in some way also gifted beyond standard telepathy. Johnny happened to be both a precog and a postcog, and it was clear that, last night, Taylor and this boy happened to tap into the same strange and terrifying view of the future.

Looking over Johnny, taking in his quiet, resting, nine-year-old form, Taylor felt now more than ever that he should be given adoptive custody over not only this child, but his five siblings as well. He, Taylor, had readied himself for the possibility of instant parenthood in so many different ways, not the least of which was his move away from The Towers. And even though teaching these children was his job, it was quite some time ago that he considered their care and parenting more than this. Now, he considered them his life and purpose.

Taylor was always overjoyed when he thought of the luck he had of being in charge of these six beautiful, mostly well behaved, and exceedingly intelligent children. All other assigned caregivers at EduCorp had ever only been given charge of a maximum of five subjects. But, as these six were related, he insisted to the Council that they be kept together as a family.

His requests were obliged and so here Taylor sat, as caregiver, project-leader, and supervisor over them.

Staring at Johnny in the quiet dorm, Taylor felt his heart skip a beat. With the close of *Prodigy II* he worried at quiet times like this that everything was up in the air and was terrified that the children might be taken from him; his fledgling family separated into different homes before it ever had a chance to start. But how could they – these kids love him just as much as he loved them, to say nothing of their bonds with each other. And he was the only one with the ability to care for them in every possible way. His powers, like theirs – his relationship with them – his history with them – his understanding of them – it was undeniable.

Taylor lowered his head with a sigh. He always troubled over these many things when he thought of the fact that his experiment was nearing its end. He had all but ignored the one other direction that his student's lives could take. They could always be kept in the care of EduCorp for additional experiments and testing.

No! – Taylor resounded in his head. Keeping them in the walls of this company was too much like a cage, and he desired so much to see these little ones stretch their wings without the restricting confinements of their current daily routine. He constantly daydreamed about the many possibilities that lay before them in the outside world, all the while he could be their father in nearly every sense of the word.

Absent mindedly looking down at Johnny again with these many, many thoughts running through his head, Taylor noticed a few flashes of light from the door window. His concentration on the boy and his deeply felt worries were broken. He could tell that there were other workers making their way up and down the corridor. A quick glance at a nearby clock told him that it was now 7:33 and that, in some official way, Taylor was over a half-hour late for work.

A face stopped in the corridor and stared in on Taylor from the outside. The teen stood, but before he could properly compose himself, a tall man with light blonde hair and a small mousy nose entered the room in a rush.

Taylor instantly recognized this figure through the bright light as Dr. Jaylen Wess his project assistant. He and Jaylen, or Jay as Taylor called him, had been friends for years, despite their age difference; Taylor's eighteen to Jay's twenty-eight. Taylor stared up at the man, barely able to make out the look on his face due to the shining light from behind. With Jay's shifting stance, though, Taylor could see enough of an expression to know that his partner was looking for an explanation for what was going on.

"What the hell dude, we've been lookin' all over for you. Where the hell've you been? You're late! Dude – this is so not cool!" In his usual fashion, Jay spoke with a broken California-Classic accent. The man was always nervous about something, and always fidgeting. To Taylor this was an endearing quality that only occasionally became irritating. This morning was turning out to be one of those times.

"Shhhhh…," hissed the teen, motioning to Johnny, who was still sleeping, "and mind your language." There was a short pause that Taylor took advantage of to lightly massage Johnny's back again. "Now what do you mean 'Late'?" he whispered harshly, both confused and irritated at the same time. It was, after all, only every morning for the past five years that the two started each day with a few hours of simulations and tests on the classes that the children were to have that day. This was the stuff of loathsome tediousness that Taylor only did out of a sense of diligence and excessiveness to protect his students. It wasn't required at all, so he was absolutely baffled at Jay's terseness. Why should today be any different than any other day? Why should he be considered late?

"I'm not late?" Taylor insisted before feeling at that instant that he had somehow forgotten something. Looking up, he questioned, "Late for what?"

"Laaaaate, dude!" bellowed Jay in an extended and annoyed fashion. He thrust out his arm and handed Taylor a small file of papers and a memory module, "Don't you remember? Like, today's our annual presentation, you know – the Council – Duh! We're supposed to be there at 7:30 – This is so bogus - I've had to leave a message with 'em just so we could delay our freakin' spot."

Taylor's face jerked to stare at the papers, and raising his hand to his forehead, he gasped. "Oh, crap! I forgot! I – Jay, I am so sorry – I totally forgot about – ugh – completely forgot! I've been here all morning. I..."

"And what's up with that?" Jay pressured. "I mean, like what are you doing here? Is he alright?"

I'll tell you on the way," Taylor said while slipping on his trench coat, "let's get going, I don't want to make things any worse than they have to be by showing up *too* too late." and with this the teen gave a gentle rub on Johnny's head, leaned over, and offered a soft whisper in the boy's ear. "I won't be too long. You just sleep now." He lifted himself off the bed and made his way to leave the dorm.

It was only just at this moment that Taylor's foot suddenly caught itself in a strange set of cables that nearly tripped him. He hadn't noticed these on the floor before, and they certainly didn't fit with anything else in the room.

Following the strange grey metallic wires back to their source with his eyes, Taylor spotted an odd chrome-colored sphere the size of a large cantaloupe sitting on the floor in the corner of the room. His curiosity was instantly peaked.

He squatted in front of the sphere, staying completely still while staring at this strange object. Behind him Jay was now venting strongly for the two of them to leave. Even still, Taylor felt compelled, with his friend's voice washing away in a deadening silence, to grab this thing and figure out its purpose.

The room seemed to shrink ever smaller as Taylor reached out to touch the silver orb, and while there was only a small part of his brain telling him he ought not to mess with things that weren't his, something was forcing his curiosity to new heights. He put his hand on the orb with a full flat palm and the instant his brain could register its cold smooth exterior everything washed away into blackness.

In that darkness he heard a light clip-clop noise, yet he wasn't able to see anything and all he could feel was the orb in his hand. He took a deep breath and, uselessly closing his already obscured eyes, he concentrated on the sphere while desperately trying to get a better grip on it, now with both hands.

In a rushing blur he was dropped into a long hallway as if through the ceiling. With hazy vision he recognized this hall as any one of many that lined the entire EduCorp building. The sphere was in view and it was being carried, quite quickly, by someone – someone wearing gloves. Taylor forced his mind to look up so as to see the owner of these hands. He was immediately confused at this, for when his gaze turned upward, what should have been the image of someone's face was actually nothing more than the flat color of skin. There was no nose; there were no eyes or mouth. He couldn't see any distinguishing marks to help him determine who was carrying the object at all. But the clip-clop noise he had heard before was definitely this person's resounding steps down the tiled corridor.

This person, whom Taylor couldn't even identify as male or female, turned and a nearby door opened. This was a dorm room and it was clear to Taylor that the person hadn't paused long enough to offer a proper security scan, so it was strange to see the door open so easily on approach. This person, Taylor reasoned, must have used some kind of remote override.

Taylor knew instantly the dorm that was entered. It was Johnny's, and with this understanding his mind spun as to who this person might be, and why they were messing with one of his students. He scanned the person over to see if any of the rest of their body or uniform might show a sign of who they were. This proved useless; for the only thing he could figure out was that he couldn't figure anything out from what he was seeing.

Inside the dorm Johnny was sleeping peacefully and quietly, unaware he was about to be disturbed. The faceless person leaned down towards the child, who was in a moment awake with eyes that were instantly wide with fear. With no time to react the intruder grabbed the boy's arm, using a hypodermic gun on it. The child fell back to sleep almost instantly, telling Taylor that some kind of tranquilizer had been used.

The only thing that matched Taylor's anger at this point was his terror at what happened next. The faceless image set the familiar sphere, which Taylor was holding in reality, on a nearby counter and pressed a small button that Taylor had not noticed on the object before, but it seemed to show itself quite clearly now.

One by one small several small wires slipped like tiny snakes out of the sphere's sides. They found their own way to the floor with no help, but then they started working their way up Johnny's bedside. Taylor felt a chill run through his body as he watched the ends of these wires flower into strange suction cup like receptacles with a fine needle that pulsed in and out of their center.

The wires, with their new ends, had taken positions all around the top of Johnny's head while he lay helpless and unconscious. Taylor felt just as helpless to do anything about it by watching through this vision of the past. He felt himself jerk as the wires, with a simultaneous attack, jumped for a different spot to attach to on Johnny's head. It was clear to Taylor that the ends of these snake-like wires were now forcing their needles inside the boy's brain.

Filling with such anger and frustration as he had never felt before in his life,

Taylor's emotions actually changed the way he viewed the vision around him. It was as though someone had slipped a red filter over his eyes, for everything shifted to a deep crimson shade. He noticed this and reveled in the fact that everything around him had substituted for the red and angry face he would have had if he actually had a body. In this vision he did not, and he shifted his now altered perspective towards the face of Johnny's perpetrator. He stared at this person, faceless as it was, and he imagined creative ways of how he could hurt him or her if he actually had the use of his powers.

The intruder turned to leave and the door opened without anyone being near its control panel. Taylor noticed this and, with a raised eyebrow, he had a strong suspicion that he knew at least some small part of what was going on. He followed the unwelcome guest out of the dorm, talking at it despite the fact that he knew the person could neither hear nor see him in any way.

"So, you're a cyber too!" the teen muttered in a groaning voice. "I don't know who you are, or what the hell you're doing with my kids, but I will find out and when I do…"

He continued shouting threats, uncontrolled in his anger, as the unknown person walked down the hall, leaving the sphere behind. It wasn't until something grabbed what could have been his shoulder, if he had a shoulder to speak of, that Taylor felt his mind being pulled away. Suddenly his vision slipped into a deep black abyss…

"Come on, dude! We have to go. NOW!" heaved Jay sternly. Taylor, blinking quickly, took in his surroundings. The light from the dorm door window reflected off the sphere and shot straight into his eyes, causing him to squint. He grabbed and winded the cables around the enigmatic object much like a ball of twine, and as he neared their ends he was careful of their sharp points. He then wrapped the sphere in the sheet he had used on his inflated bed the night before, eventually tucking the cloth ball under his arms with the presentation files before putting on his trench coat and leading the way out of the dorm and down the hall.

Walking toward the lift adorned with this very out of place trench coat, Taylor heard the beep of an M-Gen panel on the way. Opening it, he pulled out a lab coat, data pad, and some clothes to change into, which he planned to do while riding to the top of East Tower.

Jay, realizing Taylor's convenient use of cybering, simply added a "Good Thinking!" comment as they stepped into the lift, whose doors happened to be wide open, waiting for them. On stepping in Jay smiled, "When you do stuff like that – man – it's so cool!"

Taylor didn't always use his powers to make the chores of his life easier; in fact most of the time he preferred not using them. In his mind this helped him stay on a level playing field with his co-workers and others who might otherwise believe that any of his successes were due to these gifts. There were other times – many other times, however, when he felt it necessary by either timing or emergency, to use those powers, and when times like that came up he had no problem using a few tricks that always impressed anyone who was around at the time. In this regard Jay was no exception.

On their way up to the Council Chamber atop East Tower, Taylor and Jay pursued a pathic, which is short for telepathic, conversation whereby the younger described to the older what had happened the night before. This included his very eventful journey to The Towers and the painfully repeated vision that Johnny kept pushing into his brain.

Conveying any message was always faster and easier when done pathically, and because Taylor was such a gifted telepath, he could also communicate with images and full experiences rather than just the minded words peppered by emotion. On the teen initiating this pathic link though, Jay scrunched his eyes and gripped his own forehead, waving a hand as a signal that the images and information were coming too fast for any kind of comprehension.

The teen responded quickly, slowing his pathic expressions, and after offering a complete account of the night's events, he broke the link and the two engaged in vocal conversation.

Taylor spoke softly, yet firmly, "I still can't believe it. He was reliving that nightmare over and over again. And he was feeling so much pain. It's unlike anything I've ever done. You know – well, you probably don't know. When I have a vision, if it ends badly, I'll either slip off into another vision, or another dream, or – well – nothingness. He just kept at it! I can't be sure, but I think this – sphere has – something to do – with it all."

Taylor was talking and pausing repeatedly in his attempts to slip on a clean shirt and slacks along with a lab-coat, all pulled from the M-Gen panel. "It's clear, though," he continued, "that something forced that vision to repeat over and over in his head." He now picked the sphere up off the floor and held it firmly under his arm.

"So, that thing's the culprit?" Jay asked, pointing at it in disbelief.

"Not sure. It's an easy assumption. And it's what my gut's telling me." Taylor paused and pulled the *thing* out of its cloth wrapping. Holding it at fingertip ends he examined it closely, taking in its every detail.

"You know what's strange though?" Taylor said inquisitively, "Johnny was still having that vision even when it wasn't attached. When I found him he was under the bed, and still cycling through the vision – the boy was clearly in shock."

"Detached itself," Jay repeated in confusion. "Dude, whaddaya mean, '*detached itself*'?"

"Jay, there's a lot more to this thing than meets the ey..."

"Ahhhggg. That bugger's alive!" Jay squealed as he noticed some of the tentacle-like wires move. Jay even reached out and put his hand so close to the sphere that one of the wires jetted out for one of his fingers, offering a deceptive needle that nearly poked him.

Taylor could not help but laugh. "See, I told you!" he sniggered before rewrapping the ball.

"This is all just way too crazy." Jay said waving his hands quickly as he spoke, "You know, Little J. linkin' to those in his vision. Kid's pretty special in my book. I've never heard of anyone hookin' up to some Joe in a vision before."

Taylor responded quickly, adding to Jay's obvious excitement. "I know, I know, unheard of is right, and believe me, I'm a one-of-a-kind 'unheard of' whose never done it myself. And remember, the whole time he was in those visions he was trying to link with me from across the city, pushing *their* pains into my head, and there was nothing I could do about it. I wasn't even sure what the heck was goin' on."

Jay's face, with wide eyes, couldn't hide the fact that his mind was thinking hard. "Wow – Little J. connected with you like all the way 'cross town – that's wild man! Hey, could you ever – I mean did you ever – do – stuff like that when you were his age?"

"No. I tried a couple of times, but my pathic thoughts always got tangled up with others' who were between me and my target. I was too young to weed out the noise." On finishing his words, Taylor could see a curious, questioning stare from Jay that he felt compelled to respond to. "Oh, sure I can do it now with no problem. It just takes discipline and concentration. But I wouldn't've expected Johnny had enough of either to do what he did last night!"

Taylor, noticing that they only had a few more seconds before reaching the designated floor, decided to slowly shift the subject, "I have to say, though, there are too many factors to try and give a sure explanation of what happened last night, far too many factors. I mean, what I saw just now, back in Johnny's dorm, I couldn't even figure out who it was put this there."

Jay shot a look of concern to Taylor, "Hey dude - you gonna rat this out to the council?"

Taylor looked at him with surprise and spoke with a voice to match. "What makes you ask that? Of course not! Our project's been perfect so far, and I am this close –" he said now speaking with his hands, "this close – to having those kids be mine. I don't want anything to mess that up! I've just moved into some huge empty apartment just so we can all be happy – happy and away from this place. You know how much I love those kids. I can't even put into words how much... I've saved their lives. I named them. I was able to communicate with them when no one else understood them. If this comes up, it could change everything. Do I want to mention it? Of course not!"

The look on Jay's face was half between apologetic and frightened, and in seeing this, Taylor sighed. "Listen, if any of this comes out – well – there's likely to be an inquiry, and that could change everything. I could lose out on gettin' the kids. You know, in a few weeks we can bring it all up at our final review, if it even turns out to be something worth mentioning."

"Hey dude, it's all good, just chill out – I was just wonderin', you know, why bring that oversized marble in the first place?" Jay acted as if to fearfully prod the object under Taylor's arm. "The council's probably gonna say somethin' about it if you don't."

Taylor pulled the sphere out to stare at it cautiously. "Well, I figure, if someone took this thing into Johnny's room, then there's at least one other person who knows about it, and in case that someone is here..." the doors to the lift opened and with the two exiting, Taylor continued in a whisper while tucking the sphere back under his arm. "If that someone is here, then this thing might just come in handy."

Taylor turned, noticing Jay's uneasy face, "You aren't going to say anything, are you?" This, to Jay, was more a command than a question.

"Dude – you're the boss – just chill – I got your back!" He said with a sideways grin.

Taylor nodded with confidence, "That's right. Just stick to the presentation the way we rehearsed it. Everything'll be fine!"

Taylor then thought about Jay's words, *you're the boss!* He smiled, knowing with certainty where Jay's head was at. Jay often said these exact words during their project and Taylor found the expression a perfect declaration. Perfect because, despite the ten years difference in their ages, there was a deep understanding – a bond between the two of them. Taylor was better educated with three times as many doctorates as his counterpart, and had a forced maturity that made him much wiser than his years. This is not to say that Jay was either stupid or immature, despite Taylor's annoyance over his dialect, no – the teen was simply more qualified to make in-charge decisions when his emotions didn't get in the way. And so, in walking into the massive council chamber, it was Jay that questioned in his own mind if that was the case now.

6 Council Chambers

THE THIN CORRIDOR from the lift to the Council Chambers was lined with a few bench seats, potted plants, and curved cherry wood panels that widened as they walked from the lift, but then narrowed as they reached the chamber entrance. To finish its look, when Taylor and Jay reached the oval corridor's they came face to face with a set of large marble doors. Taylor opened these cyberly, waving for Jay to enter, and on walking again, the teen was warmed over by a fantastic wash of sunlight. Being at the top of East Tower, he and Jay were greeted by the bright July morning sun. Taylor himself felt a great rush as he took in the impressive view of the city skyline through the huge slanted glass windows that comprised nearly all of the ceiling and walls around the room. Only pausing for a moment, he proceeded forward, working hard to maintain his composure amid the awe that filled him from head to toe.

As the two approached the long gray metallic table where the council usually sat, Taylor noticed the informal state of the Council itself. Some were turned in their chairs looking out over the city, enjoying the magnificent view. Some were chatting with each other, either verbally or pathically, discussing the many topics of their expertise. Taylor, in his history at EduCorp, had wondered many times what it would be like to seat one of the chairs on the Council.

It was this small group of nine, with its eight members and one leader, that directed and controlled the many experiments being conducted at EduCorp. What they were doing, in fact, was pacing the advancement of education around the world. While Taylor understood the power they possessed, he also knew that they each had a great respect for their positions and that none of their decisions was ever taken lightly.

Taylor noticed that, as usual, the council members had small illuminated crystal placards in front of where each of them sat. These labeled each of the eight departments of Education, Training, or Development that they represented. From the left, he mentally read them in order: Physical Training, Language Education, Historical Education, Social Development, Mathematics Training, Science Education, Evolutionary Development, and Neurological Development. Taylor set his eyes in the middle of the large table. The ninth council chair, the leader, was the only one who didn't have an illuminated designation. He controlled all meetings, and watched over each of the different departments. As their leader, he could overrule the decision of any one council member, and almost always was available to preside over and control the council meetings.

Drawing ever closer to the table, Taylor and Jay listened to the echo of their feet on the marble floor in this room that measured several stories high. The noise quickly caught the attention of the council and each one either quickly sat, or turned to face forward in their seat. Some had smiles – others had frowns – and at this moment Taylor wished the two of them weren't running so late.

With cautious steps he and Jay separated to reach a pair of opposite ended podiums located on either side of the long council table with Taylor taking the left and Jay, the right. Tapping their microphones to ensure proper function, a rhythmic echoing rumbled through the chamber before quieting, forcing everyone and everything to become awkwardly silent.

The council leader stood and spoke with a loud echoing voice – one that seemed to surprise even himself. "Welcome, Dr. Taylor – Dr. Wess." Then much quieter, "We've been expecting you. You are, of course, several minutes late..."

Taylor tried to interject with a plethora of apologies, but the council leader ignored this effort, rolling out his words as though he had been thinking them over for some time. "...and while this is something we frown on, it seems that – eh – *most* did not mind. It gave us a chance to take in such a beautiful view of the city this morning."

The council leader, who was now uselessly pointing out different sights of the city from such a towering view, was Dr. Jesse Ellington. At 190 years, though he looked like a simple, clean-cut and attractive 25-year old, he had served in each of the Council's head positions at one point or another and to Taylor it was only fitting that he was now in charge of all of them.

But amid his thoughts on the council leader, Taylor noticed that in the man's speaking, when he mentioned the word "*most*" just now, his eyes cast a sideways glance towards a woman sitting to the far right of the council table. Taylor recognized this woman, Dr. Hathaway, in an instant, and his face soured just as quick. She wasn't staring at Taylor for the moment, but then again, considering their history, he had a pretty good idea why. If two people could be defined as begrudging enemies, the relationship between Taylor and Dr. Hathaway was almost exactly that. *But why? Why was she sitting in the Evolutionary Development Chair?* As far as he knew, she had not worked for EduCorp in five years and if there had been a change in the council lineup he would have certainly heard about it.

As the seconds passed his stomach clenched due to mounting nervousness.

He tried to distract himself by listening to Dr. Ellington, but it was no use. With each moment the elder took he grew more irritated. *How could this happen? How could she of all people end up in a Council Chair?*

With a cough from the female council member to his immediate right, Dr. Ellington got back on subject, "Oh right! Right you are, Dr. Young, enough about my favorite restaurant, that is Bravada Italiano!" He said this looking intently amongst everyone at the table with a wide misplaced smile, "eh – anyways – back to you two! You are, eh, here to report on the progress of the *Prodigy II* experiment are you not?"

With a sense that his voice might fail him, Taylor leaned forward, "Yes – eh – yes sir."

"Good, good, good. Love those kids – wonderful kids! Is, uh – Grace, is she still insisting on looking like a boy?"

Taylor looked up with confusion thus expressing a long drawling "uhhhh" before being interrupted.

"Oh, it's alright, boy, I'm just curious of her uh – social development," the man said this with a strange emphasis on his words. Taylor nervously nodded with a faux smile. He could see Dr. Ellington jabbing Dr. Young in the side, all the while growing an even wider smirk on his face. This did nothing but force Dr. Young to wear a playful frown – she was, after all, the chair for Social Development. Event still, could it be possible that Dr. Ellington, who was distantly in charge of over a hundred thousand students, actually remembered one of Taylor's own? He quickly dismissed any doubt, knowing for a fact that his students were, indeed, very special.

Dr. Ellington coughed, smiled and sighed, "Aahhhh, before I ask you to begin, I would like for the council and the presenters to take official note that we will have a Governors Council member here to oversee the presentation. Also, as you may have noticed Dr. Taylor, Dr. Wess, that in place of Dr. Richardson, the Evolutionary Chair will be held by Dr. Hathaway this morning."

As the words spilled from Dr. Ellington's mouth a side door to the chambers opened allowing a tall thin man wearing a scarlet red cloak to quickly enter the room. With his head dipped low no one could see his face for the dark mysterious hood that was clearly part of a very strange, yet instantly recognizable uniform. The man walked across the front of the table eventually making his way to an empty chair at the far left of the room behind the Council's table.

Dr. Ellington merely nodded to the man, but Taylor had a completely different response screaming in his head. *What – that – that – that's a member of the Evol Crew!* He'd recognize that uniform anywhere. The teen watched the man with an eye of absolute scrutiny as he pulled his cloak around himself and sat at the side of the chamber. Taylor sensed that the man was impatient – patting his own arms, tapping his feet – it offered up to Taylor that he was, in some respects, a real person.

Taylor was bubbling over with giddiness at being in the same room with someone so famous – if not infamous. His mind was spinning and with all the commotion going on in his head he barely had the thought to register the last part of what Dr. Ellington had said.

Dr. Hathaway – subbing in the Evolutionary Chair – how did that happen? Suddenly a wonderful opportunity for Taylor to show himself off to a bit of GC royalty had turned horribly sour! He could clearly remember the last time he and Dr. Hathaway had seen each other. They worked on different projects for EduCorp, and, upon the arrival of *the gifted six*, as the children were known then, the two had fought equally hard to get them instigated into their own training programs.

Changing Taylor's life, and that of his students, he won that struggle years ago and Dr. Hathaway seemed more than just a little upset at the decision. Indeed her pride was so far damaged from being bested by a thirteen year old that she took assignment away from EduCorp completely. Over the last five years, she had been working for the GC, or so Taylor had heard. But he had hardly given her a thought since she had gone and now, apparently, she was working for EduCorp again. Seeing her here, in that chair, Taylor sickened. *How could she just walk right in to such a prestigious position – it just wasn't fair!*

Taylor gritted his teeth, listening as Dr. Ellington finished introductions by listing the other Council members and their respective departments. Taylor himself had aspired to sit in either the Evolutionary Chair or the Neurological Chair, and he worked very hard to impress the council members in these departments, both of whom he had great respect for and a long running history with.

Respectful or not, at this moment he found himself eyeing Dr. Hathaway and becoming very uncomfortable. He walked into the chambers fully ready to give his presentation with confidence and now, knowing that a once competing enemy was sitting in a supervisory position over him, this self assurance was rapidly fading.

He heaved a heavy sigh, set the cloth-wadded sphere on the floor by his feet, and quickly readied himself to give his presentation. With any luck, everything would go smoothly and the sour emotions of events long past, much less the whole topic of the sphere and last night's tumultuous hours wouldn't even come up.

Looking down at the podium, he inserted a memory module into a short slot on its left, and tapped three small buttons; one labeled 'dim windows', another labeled 'dim lights', and a last one labeled podium spotlight. In sequence, the polarized crystal latent windows grew opaque with a very dark shade of bluish black and the lights, while sensitive to the ambient brightness, lit up at first, then dimmed immediately, offering only the blue hued dot where the sun shone brightly outside. Then, in this almost pitch black room, a spotlight shone over Taylor, forcing him to become the absolute center of attention.

Realizing his singularity, Taylor quickly activated the memory module, causing holographic images to display at his right – dead center in front of the council. He then spoke with a forced confidence that seemed out of place for the meager beginnings of such a simple presentation.

"The first part of our presentation is a brief history of our experiment – so bear with us as some of the information is redundant from last year. That being said, here goes the neighborhood." Taylor took a deep breath, and was barely able to see a grin on Dr. Young's face through the light beaming over him.

"As you may recall, there were very tragic circumstances surrounding the arrival of our six *Prodigy II* students. The crash of their transport on the tower's landing platform not only left them in near death states, but it nearly killed me and dozens of others waiting for their arrival."

The holographic images in the dark chamber showed archival footage of what had happened those years ago, and, with the council gasping at the impact, Taylor stopped the video and continued to address his superiors. It felt awkward seeing himself in the holographic image with the transport stopping only inches from crushing him while here he stood in the flesh, but he spoke in a manner that hid these emotions.

"After their injuries were repaired, the children were comatose, and it was believed by *some* that they might never wake." At this point Taylor offered a narrow sideways glance at Dr. Hathaway, but he could only just tell that she was forcing her eyes to stare at the unchanging holographic image, not offering any sign of hearing Taylor's strongly placed emphasis.

Waiting out this short pause, Taylor continued. "After four weeks they all woke within seconds of each other and, strangely enough, had no memory of who they were, or of each other even though genetic tests could confirm that they were all brothers and sisters. They had no language or basic communication skills and their education was years behind others in their bracket – some might remember my original statement – Taylor pulled up a clip from a speech that he had given the council years ago and paused the playback after a key line on which he wanted to focus. 'It is as though they're newborns.'

Taylor immediately started speaking again without missing a beat. "And it was this quality that set them apart as perfect candidates for the *Prodigy II* experiment." On saying this, Taylor heard something between a snort and a grunt that came from the Council's table, and he knew that he had finally hit a nerve with Dr. Hathaway. *Now* he was getting to her, and while it pleased him to do so, he never paused, even for a moment, to wonder if he should play with fire in such a flammable environment.

He eyed her with a grin and continued, slightly louder than before. "*Prodigy II*, developed by myself and Dr. Wess, was designed to help students who were behind or underdeveloped in their Educational or Neurological training. This accelerated and modified program was based on the original programming of the 'Prodigy' experiment, and its goal was to help off-grid or undereducated children in the hopes of giving them a chance at reaching normal or even excelled education levels."

Taylor looked at Jay and nodded as a signal for him to continue with the presentation. The man responded quickly. Offering no pause or break, he pushed his own podium spotlight button just as Taylor turned his off.

The holographic images changed to show pictures and profiles of the six *Prodigy II* students were revealed as Jay spoke to the council. "What we hadn't counted on was these kid's awesome powers. I suppose it was a good thing they were put with us – 'cause we got them under control, in record time. To date we've taught these kids right up to where they should be, and dude – lemmie tell you – that was no picnic." Jay paused and gave a nod to the GC member, who was still hiding enigmatically under his red hood.

Taylor coughed, letting Jay know that he needed to calm down and just present.

"Yeah, uh, right!" Jay continued. "We expect that in the next few weeks they'll have surpassed the general pop and with their final tests scheduled and soon to be completed, our experiment'll be done! Now as we all know, the important thing here isn't the beginning, or the end, but the steps that it took to achieve this awesome goal that counts. So let's get to it and look at last year..."

In continuing, Jay outlined the course for the children's past year of development as designed by the system that Taylor and he had put together. Now in prior years it was Taylor, as project leader, who usually handled the major body of presenting to the council, but as this experiment on which he and Jay had been working was coming to its end, it was Jay who insisted to do the presenting this year. This was in the hopes that he, Jay, would be noticed; maybe stick out in the minds of the council. There was, of course, the possibility that after the experiment, he and Taylor may still work together on the same project, but as always, there was the possibility of their separation. In this case, with any luck, if Jay had left a good enough impression on the council, he might be offered a lead position in his own experiment. It made the man nervous, of course, to think of the weight that was being placed on his words and the demeanor in which he presented them, but just the same, it was something he wanted, and Taylor, with great understanding, was happy to allow him to do it.

But as this part of the presentation was just getting under way Taylor suddenly felt very strange. Standing in the dark beside his podium, and as if without control, he thought of Johnny and the vision they both had experienced the night before. The images were simple, and the thoughts were shallow. He shook his head and looked at Jay. He tried to focus on the words of the presentation, attempting to distract his mind from those immediate thoughts that were trying to get inside his head. Nothing seemed to work – his brain was pushing everything away – focusing not on the now, but on his memories and thoughts of the previous night's vision. Suddenly – with a shock, his body jerked and his view flashed to a bright blinding light before revealing the most bizarre of scenes...

Glancing around, Taylor was standing in the middle of what looked like a barren muddy wasteland that had been heated to a humid saltiness by the overhead sun. Looking beside himself, he saw a sign that read "Los Angeles Metro Park". The sign had been twisted and abused in such a manner that it was barely readable. With a warm breeze the strong salty ocean air became ever more present – but why the smell of saltwater? In looking down Taylor could see fish and crabs at his feet. But he wasn't at the beach. Why, if that was the metro park sign, then he had to be at least twenty or more miles away from the coast. *This didn't make any sense?* He thought hard on this for just a moment, trying to figure it out.

His mind then quickly flashed a few familiar images that he had seen before of the destruction of the city – he didn't know how the images were coming into his head, but they actually made sense of the world around him. He could see the buildings crumbling as they had before – all of them being pulled in to the center of the dying city. Then – with a rush of watery aquatic chaos – a massive wave several hundred feet high washed over the remains, bringing with it an accumulation of mud and underwater life. Then, with a pop and a final bright flash – he was standing back beside the metro park sign.

Now the world around him did make sense – the force of that disturbance reached far beyond the city – even out into the ocean – pulling water over the land like a drowning blanket. With clarity coming to him from these horrible visions, he looked around and understood that, even though the buildings that normally stood there were hundreds of stories tall, there was little to no debris after their destruction. The brightly lit disturbance had practically sucked everything that the city was made of out of existence.

Taylor quickly jerked his head in every direction. All around him there was a deep rumbling noise, the wind picked up, and suddenly he was cast in a massive shadow offering him a welcome and yet oppressive shade. He looked up, trying to see what was overhead, but the image contrast of brightness to dark was so extreme that he couldn't make out anything. Soon the great swirling of debris and mud around him made it difficult to see at all, but he knew that whatever was above him was looming ever closer.

Then, from beneath his feet, Taylor felt several muddy hands reach up and grab his legs. The fear that rushed through him was immeasurable. He had certainly never seen anything like this before! He was quickly filled with the terrified emotions of his future and present self. The dirty hands struggled to pull him into the earth.

With his eyes bouncing between the ground and whatever was overhead, Taylor wasn't sure which he should fear more; being crushed from above or the unknown pulling at him from below. This hardly mattered, for in a moment, the hands were successful in pulling him down so far that his neck was level with the ground, and though his hands were still flailing to stay above the soft wet earth, one final, harsh tug forced him into total darkness.

He had landed on his feet and instantly he heard muffled voices amid the even saltier air of his new surroundings.

Was he under the city? What was going on?

All at once he heard the horrible sound of a howling gurgling growl. He whirled himself around to see the source of the noise but slipped on the mud under his oddly bare feet. Falling backward, he got a face full of light from the hole he had fallen through.

With a white flash the windows of the council chamber bellowed with morning glow and it was clear that while Taylor had experienced another vision, Jay had completed their presentation, utterly unaware of what was happening to his friend. He, Taylor, was himself looking about, trying to get his bearings and gain composure. He listened to Jay's words, still feeling very disoriented.

"So that wraps up one totally awesome year," his partner said half excited, half rehearsed, "In a couple of weeks we'll be wrappin' this baby up and giving you guys all our files for a final review. Ha – and after that, this crazy guy over here's hoping to adopt…"

Taylor pathically let Jay know that he, yet again, had another uncontrolled vision and he needed a little filling in.

Jay stopped his words for only a moment, and in response, mentally informed his partner that all seemed to go well, and that he, Jay, was just about to prompt the teen for a closing statement. With a nod Taylor waited for the right moment before turning to the council to speak.

"As you can see," Taylor chimed in confidently, "this experiment is showing itself to be a complete success, and, indeed, these children will be ready for release into outside care," he paused, thought for a moment, and added, "hopefully my care."

With nods between the two of them, Taylor and Jay agreed that their work was done and the presentation was over. Taylor spoke again with a slightly cheerful tone, "With nothing else to say, this concludes our presentation, I hope we have provided you with a clear idea of the progress our project has made, and where it's headed. At this time I would like to open the floor for any questions."

A voice from the middle of the table rose out of the quiet. It was Dr. Young, of the Social Chair beside Dr. Ellington, and someone with whom Taylor had an enduring friendship since the earliest days of his training. Knowing it was her, he exhaled a sigh of relief from his quickly abated nervousness.

"I have a question about what will happen after your experiment." She stated in a conflictingly smooth, yet loud voice. "We are all aware of your application for custody of these children, and your age not being a secret, I have to say; you are very young to take on such a huge responsibility."

With these words Taylor's face slightly soured, and Dr. Young quickly recanted, "Oh, I have confidence in your work here, don't get me wrong, but I think we, the Council, need a little convincing before we simply hand over the lives of these six beautiful and gifted young children. So, now I ask my question. Why, when you are so young, do you want to take on this demanding and enduring task?"

Considering the department for which this woman was in charge, and the fact that he knew her on a personal level, he swallowed his pride and understood her need to ask this question. While he might normally feel insulted by the insinuation that he was in some way incapable of this lifestyle change, he knew that Dr. Young only had his and these children's wellbeing at heart. Indeed, years before, he had consulted with her on numerous occasions to help him develop the Social aspect of the *Prodigy II* experiment. Her assistance helped him to not only complete his work, but it gave him a great respect for her and her position.

With a deep breath, he found his mental footing, and gave the best answer he could to her question.

"My request for adoptive custody is *not* the subject of this presentation," he opened, offering her a gracious smile and a nod. "But just the same, I am more than happy to entertain this question with an answer." He gripped the podium lightly as his mind passively thought of his students and his life at The Towers.

"It should be clear to *nearly* all here that I, while under *Prodigy,* exhibited advanced development in ALL areas. This included mental maturity, and my own advanced social development. For this reason, though I was only thirteen at the time, I was given charge over these children, and given charge over my own experiment. There are privileges that have never been given to one of that age. And with these great privileges granted," Taylor continued with an increased volume and confidence, "I have not only demonstrated responsibility far beyond my years, but I have suffered the horrible side effect that comes with caring for such an infectious group of kids. I have fallen in love with them."

Each of the council members, save one, was impressed, not with Taylor's words, but with his passion a passion that he knew he could only convey with pathic fury. Seeing and even feeling their reactions, he continued with a loud pounding in his ears. "I have helped these kids with everything from their homework, to their fights with each other, and I don't have to tell you how interesting that can be. And remember, I had to teach them how to go to the bathroom – at age five – five mind you." Taylor heaved a sigh. "Those kids are my life and I would be lying if I didn't say it would be for my own good as well as theirs to have this adoption go through."

At this, several of the council members smiled and talked between themselves, and Taylor was glad, relieved even, that he could lay his emotions on the table so plainly, and so truthfully.

Finishing his from-the-heart soliloquy and thus answering Dr. Young's question, Taylor was happy to see and hear a general approval from the council. Taylor dared to glance over at the red-hooded man from the Evol Crew and found that even he was nodding his scarlet hood. Sure he wasn't facing Taylor, but it was still a good sign. In looking at him, however, Taylor suddenly did a double-take on this man cloaked in red. Even though the teen couldn't see his face, the man, just now, seemed familiar to Taylor. It was something in his size or shape. Had he seen him before? If he did, he certainly didn't know from where. Taylor bubbled inside with irritation over what he assumed was a failing memory. He stared at the man, taking in his bright red cloak that seemed all the more annoying to look at in the sunlight.

Then, in waiting for a response from the council, Taylor watched as Dr. Ellington's face broadened with a wide smile. This filled the teen with a hope that the presentation went perfectly and that, with any luck, he had guaranteed his chances of becoming the newly adopted father of his beloved students.

7 Arguing with Dr. Hathaway

IT SEEMED AN ETERNITY before anything more was said, and only after this long pause, and a noting cough from Dr. Young, did Dr. Ellington haphazardly and gingerly stand up.

"Oh, right… eh – if there's nothing else. Gentlemen, you will find our review of your presentation and the data you have supplied to be complete within two days time. If I might be so bold, I think you'll like what the council has to say, but for now I offer a simple 'thank you very much for your hard work', and we look forward to your final report next month. I might also like to add that you've done a fantastic job with these children. They and this company are in your debt." With a simultaneous standing, *seven* at the table rose with Dr. Ellington for his final words, "Dr. Taylor, Dr. Wess, thank you, you are dismi…"

"I have a few questions, sir." Spoke a voice from the right of the table.

From the look on his face, it was clear that Dr. Ellington was both surprised and displeased at this mild interruption. His response was almost immediate. "Uh – what – I'm sorry. Were you sleeping just now, or were you just not paying attention Dr. Hathaway?" Taylor and Jay, while also surprised at this tardy interruption, smiled to the point of laughter over Dr. Ellington's snapping reprimands, they were, in fact, used to this kind of biting rhetoric from the man, for he could be just as severe as he was playful and lighthearted.

Dr. Hathaway's face shifted to a look of apology, "Oh! Sorry, sir. I've just been going over my notes, and I wanted to confirm a few things before my interrogation."

"Interrogation!" Dr. Ellington scoffed. "I will remind you, Dr. Hathaway, that you are here only as a substitute for Dr. Richardson, and as you are speaking on *his* behalf, don't forget to respect the position that you now represent and do not come here hoping to settle some personal vendetta – we all remember what happened in these chambers five years ago – and to put it simply – none of that should influence you as a temporary member of the council. Moreover, these are employees of EduCorp, and as such, just like *you,* they have the complete confidence of our company. When a presentation is completed here, we do not interrogate our staff unless there is some form of gross negligence. After *this* presentation, I am *sure* you will agree that no sign of such negligence exists!"

While Dr. Ellington shifted in color from anger, Dr. Hathaway did so from embarrassment, and it was clear that she had not expected such a rapid verbal lashing from her superior so quickly. "Yes sir. I understand, sir. Let me rephrase. I have a few *questions* that I would like addressed by our presenters."

Taylor felt his heart sink. He was hoping that after all Dr. Ellington's scolding she might just sit down and shut up. He, of course, had no such luck and her tenacity was unyielding.

"Firstly, and I only ask this out of curiosity; have you noticed anything unusual with your subject's gifts or – eh - powers recently?"

Hearing this question, a sudden rush of excitement leapt through Taylor's body. *Did she know about what went on in Johnny's dorm the night before? Did she have something to do with it?* The room must have warmed up at least ten degrees with Taylor's sudden nervousness. But wait, this was what he wanted. He forced himself to calm down, and with perking ears he listened hard for any stray thoughts from Dr. Hathaway, and worked even harder to keep stray thoughts from pathically leaking out of himself. *Maybe she did know, and maybe he could hear the truth out of her!*

"Uh – no ma'am. Nothing about their powers has been, as you say, 'out of the ordinary'. Unless of course you mean the fact that they are fully developed so much earlier than the standard popula…"

"No, no, no, that's not what I mean. Let me be more *specific,"* she said insultingly. "During the course of your experiment, have any of your subject's powers been so erratic that they could cause neurological damage?"

"Well sure, in the beginning, when they first woke up, but in recent months – well – no. Their powers have been monitored, trained, and under control for years now; nothing dangerous or out of the ordinary."

"Oh! *Really?!*" she said haughtily, "Well, I thought the test you ran last night spoke volumes to the contrary. So, tell me Dr. Taylor, why is it that these results were not brought up during your presentation?"

Taylor found himself confused and oddly terrified at the same time. "What test results. What are you talking about?"

"These test results," she said gruffly while simultaneously pressing several buttons and inserting a memory drive at her station. The lights dimmed and everyone in the chamber watched a holographic display of the extreme brainwave activity that Johnny was giving off the night before, as indicated by the timing index beside the graphic representations. As this was revealed Dr. Hathaway pointed out the areas she knew would be most troubling to the council.

"Here – we can see that the precog spike is so high – it's as though the subject's brain and body couldn't tell the difference between vision and reality. And here," she said pointing to another peak, "we can see a huge telepathic spike – one so strong it ran the risk of burning out the pathic synapses. I find this all very disturbing Dr. Taylor, and I was *hoping you could explain.*"

There were several murmurs and vocal outbursts after the holographic display went dark, and with the lights coming back on Taylor felt as though things were turning for the worst. He pulled at the collar of his shirt. Was it him, or was the temperature still rising with the morning sun. He felt a frustration wash over him and with this came the suspicion that he had been set-up.

With a deep breath the teen's anger overwhelmed him. "So you lied!" he hissed strongly.

"Excuse me?" asked Dr. Hathaway in a melodramatic tone. "Council members do not lie!"

Taylor stared at her with a furrowed brow. "Well, at least that much is true. YOU are NOT a council member. And you did lie, just now, when you said that you were asking this question *'out of curiosity.'* If you want to ask me something, ask it outright and get to the point!"

Comments could be heard at the council table as Taylor achieved creating a flustered and irritated Dr. Hathaway. She huffed and snapped her stare from the Evol Crew member, to the council, and back to Taylor again.

"*YOU* are diverting from the point of my question, to which I still expect an answer. Can you explain the erratic brain activity in subject 2675A? More specifically, can you explain why subject 2675A almost died during these night visions?"

Questioning and confused stares came from the council as Taylor boiled over with anger. As far back as he could remember Dr. Hathaway never referred to his students by their name – she always used either the word *subject* or their EduCorp I.D. number – so impersonal – so cold. Feeling he couldn't stand it any longer, he exploded.

"Johnny." He shouted, causing a silence to fall over the chamber.

"Pardon me?" jerked Dr. Hathaway confused by this name.

"Jonathan Kristopher Louis Matthews." Taylor said, both loudly and firmly, "That is his name. If you want, call him Johnny. He likes it better, but he is NOT a number – he has NEVER been a number – he is a child – a person, and has more compassion at the age of ten than you could ever hope to possess!"

Taylor shifted in front of his podium, and he nudged the sphere with his toes – something he'd practically forgotten about in his anger against Dr. Hathaway. With a quick thought, he realized something he hadn't thought about before.

The sphere! It was transmitting Johnny's brain activity. That's how she got the recording – that's how she knew – she put that thing in his room. But how could he prove it?

With absolute silence in the chambers, the council stared at Taylor with surprise over his outburst, but he was more relieved having figured out at least some small part of the mystery of the night before. Taking his breath, he looked at Jay who was almost panting in panic, tapping his fingers nervously on the podium, then, with more words from the council table, Taylor's stare snapped back to Dr. Hathaway.

"That's the second time you've diverted from answering the question. Well – that's fine. If you can't answer my question, or put my concerns to rest, I have no choice but to motion for an inquiry into your project."

"An inquiry?" Taylor shouted across the room. He thought his heart was going to fall through the floor. She mentioned an inquiry, which, for EduCorp, was one of the most disgraceful actions that can be taken on an experiment. More than this – the idea of an inquiry, a metaphorical slap in the face, threatened his ability to adopt his students. Taylor nearly took on Jay's panting fit of nervousness; his mind aching, barely able to handle such horrible thoughts.

He looked around the room in a panic, and with his eyes falling on the wadded up cloth at his feet he took a deep breath. With a rush, an idea – a plan – worked its way through Taylor's brain.

"Fine," he shouted, half to Dr. Hathaway, half to the rest of the murmuring council, "If you have to know, I'll tell you." He reached down for the sphere, mumbling as he did so, "It's not like it's a big deal anyways!"

Taylor looked up at Jay with a slight smile, but it was no use. The man was ill aware that his partner was staging a way to get out of this mess and as such he scrunched up his face in bewilderment over Taylor's confusing grin.

"This device," Taylor said loudly, while carefully holding up the cloth covered silver orb for all to see, "records neural patterns. It was used on Johnny last night while he was asleep and just this morning, and only just this morning, we discovered that there are possible side effects to using this machine. I took it from Johnny's dorm just before we came here, and after this presentation I was planning on running some diagnostics on it."

This was a carefully worded truth, for in fact, it was a neural recorder, it was used last night while Johnny was asleep, and Taylor was going to run diagnostics on it after finding out that it was the cause of his disturbing visions. So, indeed it was a stretched truth, but it was the truth Taylor knew and it was the best way out he could come up with. He looked over at Jay, who was as baffled as ever. But Taylor, offering a wide eyed stare of understanding, linked pathically with his out-of-the-loop compatriot, hoping to show what he was trying to do.

Jay smiled and nodded, adding to the conspiracy, "Yes, I, yes" he said loudly and repetitiously, forcing the entire council table to turn their synchronized heads in his direction, "I, I've already got those diagnostics lined up to figure out what exactly went wrong. This whole thing – it's why we were late this morning."

Taylor had to smile – still all truth, still no lie – and still dangling bait for Dr. Hathaway to try to devour.

Her eyes grew large. Her face tense with anger, she shifted to a bright pink that made Taylor want to laugh. Looking at her, he thought she might explode, physically, all over the place.

"But you didn't – you couldn't. I was – NO!" she stammered.

"I'm sorry," shrilled Taylor, "No – what?"

"No, that is not a sufficient explanation. I require more infor…" At this point Dr. Ellington and Dr. Young both gave a stern look to her and pathically pulled her attention. She could see that they were each shaking their heads in disapproval. "Sorry," she apologized, and it was obvious that it annoyed her to do so. "We, the council, require more data and information on this matter before it can be closed.

You're keeping information from us – and that is something worth investigating. If you keep something like this hidden during your annual presentation – what other secrets does your *Prodigy II* experiment hide? I think we should call a vote!"

Taylor's mind spun. He could see that Dr. Hathaway believed herself as having the possibility of winning this argument. As she turned to the council waiting for hands, waiting to see who agreed with her and who didn't, Taylor noticed a red bobbing out of the corner of his eye. The Evol Crew member was actually nodding, agreeing with this action. Taylor felt sick. It was only when he lowered his head, staring down at his data display and mindlessly reading what was on the podium that a smirk widened on his face and he spoke to the council once again.

"Excuse me," Taylor said stiffly. "Dr. Hathaway, Council, let me be the first to tell you that you will get all the data you need – at our final presentation in four weeks, I'm certain you will see that this singular fluke was nothing more than a side effect, the result of a machine's incompatibility or malfunction in dealing with such a far evolved human mind. When you see our report, at that time, I am sure you'll agree that there was no permanent damage done and therefore no inquiry necessary."

"Four weeks! Excuse me?" Dr. Hathaway squealed, "We are not asking for this information at your leisure. We are asking for it now and you are required to give it to us in your report, here, *today!*"

She had become so heated that her neatly placed blonde hair had started falling out of place as she hammered on the table, "This is *your* presentation, this is *your* experiment, and therefore it is *your* responsibility to offer a complete report for this meeting!" At this point it was clear to the entire council that Dr. Hathaway was making this a personal vendetta, and Taylor knew that in her anger she was ignoring the limits of her position and what she had been warned about early on by Dr. Ellington.

"If I might ask the council," Taylor said with a sly smile before adding, "*and* Dr. Hathaway, to please read the title of the report on your screens." He waited a moment, and could hear a few consenting "hmmms" and "ohhhhhs," and Dr. Ellington and Dr. Young exchanged glances and offered a little chuckle after reading the header.

"You see, everything is fine," Taylor cooed, "and now that *that* is all cleared up I wou…"

"Cleared up, I don't see how that cleared anything up… what are you babbling about?!"

"I was hoping I wouldn't have to explain this." Taylor said with a shining arrogance, "Dr. Hathaway, would you be so kind, and to *completely* read the title for this morning's report."

The woman turned the brightest shade of red that Taylor ever thought he had seen on a person, and with a fuming voice, she vented across the table, "I don't take orders from you. You're just wasting time! I can't believe you – still as arrogant as ever, you little sh..." With a just-in-time cough, Dr. Ellington once again caught the eye of Dr. Hathaway, but this time, when she looked across the table she could see that all of the other council members were looking at her as though she were some strange creature they didn't understand.

Dr. Ellington gave her a look that, to Taylor, signaled a pathic connection, after which, she looked down at her data display and huffed, "Fine I'll read the damn thing!" She then heaved a deep breath and blandly trudged the lines off the page, "Annual Report on *Prodigy II: Accelerating the Development of Underdeveloped Minds*." Her disdain unwavering, she continued, "Scheduled date of Presentation July – 17 – 2457 8:30AM" Dr. Hathaway then read the next line in her head and paused. It was clear to all that she now saw the flaw in her argument. Taylor though, watched eagerly as all the color slowly drained from her face. Finally, she flopped out the final line on the cover page, "Data Set: July-11-2456 to July-10-2457"

She slumped down in her chair, offering a pouting look to the table in front of her and a bewildered expression to the Evol Crew member across the room and it was this look, this stare, that most interested Taylor.

Jay, in watching all of this – from the arguing, to the reading, to things turning horribly personal, to the final relief – now stood back to bask in the glow that was a shining Taylor, who looked back at his friend with a smile, sending a quick pathic message.

"Let's see if we can't wrap this up!"

Jay nodded, realizing that this perfect moment was over, and stiffened to a professional address of the council.

"Ahem" Jay started, "Well – we did our job – we gave our data – you like it – we pass – cool. If there isn't anything else…" Taylor, nearly opened his mouth to speak, but Jay still had more to say. This had the immediate effect of causing Taylor's nerves to hit edge. "I've got something else to add," the man continued, "and let me be very, *very* clear on these things." He turned a menacing stare to Dr. Hathaway and Taylor knew by Jay's tone and look that the man had dropped his California-Classic dialect in lieu of a more professional one.

Taylor panicked! *What was he doing? What was he saying?* Taylor's heart thumped an uneasy rhythm. Usually when it came to impromptu presentations and speeches, Taylor was always in control Jay – NEVER! Now, to hear the man speak words that had never been rehearsed, it filled him with trepidation.

"In all seriousness, I've worked with Taylor for over six years now," Jay breathed somberly, "and I've watched him not only perform medical miracles on these children, but I've watched him give them the hope of what might be a normal life. He has shown them that even though they have no family outside of their own kinship, there is someone out there, or rather right here, who cares enough to want to bring them into his life." Jay paused and turned to the rest of the council, "Dr. Taylor – Taylor, as I have seen it in the way he teaches them with such passion – he loves these children. He loves them so much you can be sure that if any part of this experiment had a chance of hurting these kids he'd rather just scrap the whole thing, losing his job first, before harming any one of them. He works tirelessly, over a hundred hours every week – and he does this out of love – not for his job – for love.

To entertain any doubt of this love and his care for these kids – well – it's – it's – *it's just not cool*!"

Taylor felt himself warming over yet again because of Jay's words. Never, in his time at EduCorp, had he heard the man say more than what was necessary to the Council in any meeting – he was always too nervous. Taylor could only assume that now, Jay was saying, in his mind, what was necessary and nothing more.

"So, is there anything else?" Jay spewed out at Dr. Hathaway as if spraying her with acid. "Come on, doctor, is there anything you might like to add?"

"Ooooh! Never mind! Go on then." heaved the angry Dr. Hathaway, and at this point it was clear that Taylor had, once again, won another victory.

After a long pause, during which time much of the council was looking between Dr. Hathaway and Dr. Taylor, it was Dr. Ellington who stood up. "Well, wasn't that exciting?!" he voiced playfully.

There were a few dissenting groans and coughs, at which point Dr. Ellington laughed, "Ah well, if there's nothing else, you may go Dr. Taylor, Dr. Wess. We will await your reports and experimental closings scheduled for – eh – August 14th, at 11AM *sharp*." He said this word with emphasis and a grinning stare at Taylor.

The teen returned the sentiment with a smile and the council leader thereafter directed his attention to his immediate subordinates. "Our next presentation is not scheduled 'til nine-thirty. We have at least a good twenty minutes until then, so I am recommending a fifteen minute break. We will reconvene at that time."

With a slight hustle and bustle in the chamber the two presenters readied themselves to leave. Sweeping past, an angry Dr. Hathaway rushed by the podiums, making her way to the chamber entrance and down the long corridor to the lifts. Taylor looked up and pathically told Jay to finish packing things up. He wanted to have a final word with Dr. Hathaway before she had a chance to get away.

He followed behind her and just as the lift doors opened to allow her to enter he concentrated quickly to force their closing. She offered a violent huff of anger and started pounding the manual "open" button beside the door. The button, however, didn't work as Taylor was concentrating to keep the doors closed, allowing the two of them an opportunity to talk.

"Having troubles with the lift are we," Taylor said smugly. Dr. Hathaway looked at him with very disapproving eyes. "Is there anything I can do?" he falsely offered.

"*You*" she turned, solidifying her evil stare, "have done enough already! I don't need *your* help."

"I haven't done anything doctor; I've only protected that which was mine."

"Yours – Yours! Those subjects aren't yours, they're the company's, and if I can help it, it's going to stay that way. I can't believe you. You think helping them is gonna make a difference. You think the government really cares about how well they're educated, or your little experiment? You're so blind! Those children aren't ever going to belong to you! Not with their powers!"

Taylor blinked. He could feel anger rising inside him. It was clear that he had, indeed, triumphed over her today. But she was still in a more powerful position than he and, as long as Taylor had known her, her threats were never empty; maybe not well thought out – but never empty.

He heaved an angry breath, "You stay the hell away from me and my kids. I warn you now, accepting all consequences, if I ever catch you near them *again*, there'll be hell to pay – and after that you'll have to answer to me!" Taylor now stared at Dr. Hathaway with extreme telepathic concentration. With his ears perked, he was hoping to pick up any stray thoughts that might offer themselves after the bait he had just laid out.

To these glares she offered a contorted face of confusion, then a smile, "I'm sure that the Council will be more than happy to read my report on your threats. Huh, answer to you! That – will – be – the – day!" she said with a rhythmic pounding of the 'open' button.

During her words, Taylor couldn't hear anything pathically, and with her final push of the button he reluctantly released the door.

Dr. Hathaway looked relieved at being offered a way out of this confrontation and she stepped into the lift, but the doors did not close.

"Uhhhaaagh! What's wrong with this damned thing now!" she growled, now pounding buttons inside the lift.

"Mind your language Dr. Hathaway – there's nothing wrong with the lift. I'm just not finished with you – *yet*."

"You know what," she said loudly as she could now see Jay approaching Taylor from behind, "You, the both of you, are doing nothing but get in my way. You think helping those six little freaks is gonna make a difference in this world. Ha! Don't you ever wonder why they're so special? Why they're so powerful? Why they're so young, and yet so evolved? You just don't get it. I was ready for them – ready and waiting – but you and your stupid little experiment stood in my way. Now, I guess I'll just have to wait my turn. But that's alright. I'll get them soon enough..." These last words were said with biting disdain, forcing Taylor to grit his teeth.

After hearing this statement Jay looked at Taylor with annoyance. The man's arms were full of papers, memory modules and the mysterious sphere wrapped in cloth and he was clearly frustrated at having to wait for this conversation to end.

"Come on, Taylor, aren't you done with this chick yet?" he said shrewdly as papers fell behind him out of one of the files he was holding.

Dr. Hathaway, with her jaw dropping at this statement, unknowingly spewed her final words of the conversation. "Done with me?! Done with *me*?! He's not done with me. I'm done with hi…"

SLAM! The lift doors closed on her final word and with a breezy air of satisfaction Taylor murmured with nearly a laugh, "I'm almost done with her."

The teen kinetically helped his counterpart with the mass of objects that had fallen to the floor. And while Taylor lifted these papers, the sphere, and the memory modules all into a nice stack that now floated in front of Jay's face, he, Jay, stared at the numbers above the lift door. He couldn't help but notice that the lift was moving rapidly up and down several floors over and over again, at a notably faster rate than a normal lift would go, and most certainly not in any way that made sense.

"Dude, you're evil!" Jay said with a haughty smile. Taylor beamed, and just to see if what he was doing was actually working, he made the lift come all the way back up to the top of East Tower. With its rise, the two could hear screams coming from the doors in front of them, and for a split second, Taylor opened the lift. Inside, a ratted, tattered, and disheveled Dr. Hathaway, was lying in the back corner. Taylor and Jay offered an arrogant smile, waved their fingers with a polite goodbye, and the doors closed again. They could hear the screaming restart as the lift descended.

"You know" Jay said softly, "as sweet as this is, and believe me, this is pretty damn sweet, I do think that's quite enough!"

Taylor, almost overcome with surprise, looked at his friend with a smile. "Oh, I quite agree," he said with a laugh, "I'm not doing anything now. The lift's under normal operation. I think she's screaming because she's afraid of the motion completely."

"Chick's got some major stress issues, and you, my man, you're just wrong." Jay said while pushing the lift request button.

Taylor lit a wide smirk, "Only a little, and only to those who deserve it. Besides, she needs to know who she's dealing with."

With a light beep another lift came to their floor, and as Taylor entered and turned around to face the long corridor and open Chamber doors before the lift closed itself off, he felt satisfied with what he accomplished that morning. Turning to look at Jay, he put a hand on his friend's back just as the doors closed. "Thanks for that!" he said softly.

"Dude - What?" Jay replied with a false annoyance.

"You know, what you said back there. It really meant a lot to me, and it's good to know that someone out there's got *me* covered once in a while."

Jay gave a smile, offering a jab to Taylor's side, "Like I said, I've got your back, and besides man, it was only the truth, only the truth."

As the lift descended Taylor was filled with a sense of contentedness that he had such a true friend in his life, even if he sometimes felt that Jay was his only one. And so, with a downward stare at the data-pad in his hand, the teen slowly filled with memories of a time when his having such a friend wasn't always so.

8 Truly Alone

TAYLOR, OR ROBERT STANLEY TAYLOR, as he was named through EduCorp's alphabetic naming system, started his youth not knowing the details surrounding his birth or anything about his family. He did know, however, that after his fifth birthday he would be granted level six accesses to the EduCorp's computer archives and that in these protected files he would be able to find information on both and thus learn about his family history.

Under the Prodigy experiment Taylor reached critical understanding at an unprecedented three months. This is a point when EduCorp determines a child fully able to learn and communicate through language. This couple with a continuing of his advanced neural development allowed him to start what would become a relentless set of virtual courses at the infantile age of six months. Understandably, it was from this point that the boy's development curve shot up like a rocket.

In an attempt to match this steep learning curve the EduCorp Council decided to accelerate his computer access as well. Taylor often felt that this was one of the best perks of being in his particular experiment. But he also felt he was learning at a much faster rate than what they prescribed for his computer access. He was scheduled to complete his eighteenth year of equivalent education at the age of four, so why should he have to wait an additional year for this greatly anticipated level six access. He had, after all, only just turned three, and with his life as it was, waiting was the hardest thing for him to do.

In November of 2442, after that third birthday, Taylor *re-learned* in his North-American History Class that EduCorp was the only company in history to ever be granted the ability to adopt children.

"This adoptive power was granted in 2075 with the idea in mind to help the company experiment on its students in a completely controlled environment for the development of their Worldwide Virtual Training and Neural Development Programs..."

Through the monotonous sounds of the virtual trainer who was teaching the class, Taylor only half listened, instead opting to doodle playfully on his desk. Because much of this information was common knowledge, he found that to just let the VRT helmet force the information into his brain was far easier than to simply pay attention.

The virtual instructor continued, “At the same time, the Child Education, Safety and Protection Agency or C-E-S-P-A (pronounced sespa), was also created with the sole purpose of reporting and acquiring data on the many experiments devised and set in motion by EduCorp and its subcontractors and making those findings public...”

On hearing this Taylor dropped his virtual pencil and suddenly sat upright with full attention. He looked around, and as there weren’t any other students in this class, there was no one to notice his quick change of behavior. He now listened intently as the instructor went on about CESPA.

“This organization works hard on behalf of the government, collecting data, monitoring students' progress, and noting any discrepancies or dangers that might present themselves to said students as a result of the company’s experiments. Today they are the eyes and ears of the Governor’s Council inside the EduCorp infrastructure.”

Continuing to listen, it was with full delight that Taylor learned about how this organization was government controlled, and required to make all of its findings on the experiments of EduCorp a matter of public record.

Instantly, through this newfound knowledge, Taylor had an idea.

Outside the class, in the real world, Taylor was sitting in a large auditorium style room, surrounded by over a hundred chairs, and while he only occupied one, he was the full class for that session. At three-and-a-half, he was larger than he should’ve been at that age. Something about the advanced training forced his hormones out of balance, and thus he grew a few years beyond his age. Fortunately, the many project leaders over *Prodigy* worked together to find a way to keep his hormones in check so that by the time he was five, he didn’t look twenty. So here, in this massive room, sat a boy of three with the body of a six year old. He wasn’t moving, nor saying a word. No – he was just breathing, quietly absorbing as much information as his brilliant brain could handle, all as part of the experiment that spawned his every bit of knowledge.

Only one other person was in the room with Taylor, and this was his supervising instructor, or S.I., whose job it was to merely sit and watch the children or child, as it was in this case, who were being trained. This instructor, like many Taylor knew, hated this one person class – it all seemed too boring, and while teaching a larger class might be more interesting, the fact that Taylor’s classes were so much shorter made the S.I’s that much more irritated, believing the class a waste of *their* time. Taylor had become quite accustomed to being treated poorly by his S.I.’s for this reason, and, were it not for his advanced maturity, their bluntness might have forced him to tears on several occasions. But Taylor was too smart to let these *nobody’s,* as he called them, ever get to him.

Inside the helmet he waited impatiently for his class to finish, and when it did, he practically ripped the training visor from his head, and his eyes squinted from the bright surrounding light. He didn’t mind this so much as he bid his supervising instructor a quick goodbye in the hopes of storming out of the classroom. He almost made it, but was quickly caught by the arm and it was with great irritation that he had to stop and wait while the S.I. took a minute or so to read his vitals.

"Argh. They were right about this kid," the S.I. spoke sourly of Taylor, as though the boy couldn't hear her. "Useless. I don't know what good it does to just train one child – just useless – not even a proper data set. Ridiculous! Just ridiculous!"

The young an impatient Taylor was forced, quite roughly in fact, to take his place next to the examining wall by the even more impatient S.I. He waited as a small white rod shot out near his heels. It slowly moved up his legs and back with a bright scanning light. It then rounded on his head, which always took longer than the rest of the body due to intense neural checks, before proceeding down his front. He felt himself rocking in his sneakers, patting himself on his thighs impatiently as the machine finished the last of its scan. It then displayed a report on the wall nearby where the S.I. viewed it over carefully. Not waiting to hear the results, which he was sure were "normal", he shot out of the room in a rush.

"Okay – uh – Robert, we're fini..." the observer started to say, but as she turned all she caught was the door closing behind him. The S.I. hardly minded this, for she knew that this would be the one and only time she would train the boy, and she had her own "more important" work to be getting on with. So, like so many other S.I., she interpreted Taylor as a one-time speed-bump in an otherwise simple daily routine.

All down the hall Taylor's mind was overwhelmed. Had he found a way of looking up information about his birth and about his parents; something that was outside the dreaded Level-Six-Access-Required EduCorp Computer Network? The idea thrilled him beyond words.

He ran so fast, he had bumped into several people on the way and on finally entering his dormitory he immediately grabbed the data-pad from the nightstand next to his bed. Tapping it in his completely darkened room brought an onslaught of light and color he was hardly ready for. He pressed the WSN logo in the upper right corner of the screen and as a result, the letters animated to show the full name of the "Wireless Super Net," ready for surfing.

With a prompt blinking in front of him he typed out his search attempt, "Prodigy" onto the pad using the touch-screen. It was only just after hitting the "Search" button that he realized this was too broad of a request. To his irritation and expectation, this request resulted in over a billion results, and immediately he changed his search string to "CESPA". This yielded two large web databases followed by a host of related sites and links. The first of these major databases, as expected, was the EduCorp files. He was certain that at some point he would be required to enter a level six access code to search the information here, and as such, he moved straight to the second link. This was the CESPA homepage – bingo!

Taylor felt a rush flow through him as he tapped the logo and eventually navigated to a list of the many experiments that had been logged over the last 367 years. He noticed a second search cursor, and it was here that he knew typing in the Prodigy name would yield a more defined result.

He did so, and indeed there was only a single folder named Prodigy in the entire database. He tapped it and immediately located files dating back nearly 10 years. While he would have loved nothing more than to just zip through these to find information on his parents, he thought better of it and started with the earliest data instead.

The files were sorted by type and Taylor could see that the database was comprised of the three basic file formats: Text, Graphic, and Video. Taylor organized them by date to ensure that he didn't miss anything, and started reading the text and watching the videos to see what he could find...

In 2433 EduCorp scientists and instructors, under the quiet direction of GC President Andrews for one of his first decisions in office, designed a project whose purpose it was to advance a child's education and mental maturity as rapidly as possible; possibly even pushing dangerous levels of neural development in order to complete this goal. This project, named "Prodigy", was met with a great deal of positive feedback by the GC, but was received with skepticism by those within CESPA and even EduCorp itself.

The methods and overall design of the project were completed in record time, and all looked well for the insertion of infant subjects into this newly developed training program until, much to the frustration of the GC, it was shelved on January 22nd, 2435.

In the final stages of acceptance, the experiment met with objections by the EduCorp Council. More specifically, the objections came from the council chair for Social Development: Dr. Young. It was arguments from her that eventually convinced the rest of the council to abandon the project.

Taylor clicked an audio link here and listened to the words of this *Dr. Young*, who he instantly decided he didn't like very much, and when her words were finished, he continued reading more online text...

"While we may be able to advance a student's learning and development by leaps and bounds, in the end if there isn't a world ready to accept them, we will have achieved nothing but the creation of friendless outcasts who will always find it difficult if not impossible to fit in. More to the point - we should ask ourselves - just because we can do something - does it really mean we should?"

Backed by EduCorp CEO Dr. Gerald Isaacs, this was the single arguing statement that eventually convinced the rest of the council to follow suit.

Biding their time for a few years, President Andrews convinced the Governor's Council to overrule this decision citing specific

legislation surrounding the control of EduCorp by the GC. To the surprise of many at EduCorp, it became apparent that legally the GC can not only shut down programs it deemed inappropriate or negligent, but it could also force programs into effect if decided by a majority vote.

With this precedence in place, the GC pushed for the initiation of *Prodigy* on June 27th, 2439, and on July 17th GC President Andrews hand-picked the child that would be the sole subject of the experiment. This child, coded subject 1275A and named Robert Stanley Taylor by EduCorp, was initiated into the experiment within hours of his birth.

Taylor flattened his short, helmet-disheveled light brown hair into its usually perfectly combed form and in reading this information the boy dropped his hands back to the pad in front of him. He immediately noticed the lack of detail in telling how he was chosen or where he came from, but still felt a sense of pride in knowing that he was actually picked by President Andrews, and noticed further down on the page that his name was highlighted; a clickable button he could use to find out more about himself.

"Hmmmm. I wonder what CESPA thinks about me?" He whispered this with a smile as his bright blue eyes glistened hungrily in the glow of the data pad amid his otherwise dark room. *Well, there's only one way to find out.* He tapped his name and found that the resulting data page contained hundreds of reports, a few video links, and photos. Taylor was having trouble reconciling with the fact that so much of his life was available for the public to learn about. Indeed he felt special having seen so much effort to document his life's detail and made a mental note to see if other students from the company had this much data reported on them.

Scrolling down the never ending list of files and piecing together what he saw, practically every moment of his life had been covered by either text, picture, or video, and so much so was this that Taylor started bubbling with annoyance, realizing that every moment he believed to be at least mildly confidential, was actually made available to the public in one way or another.

He shook this awkward feeling off and scanned the pages for information on his family. Here, in a database that was all about "Robert Stanley Taylor", he was sure to find something on his parents.

He noticed a link on the first page that defined his parents as "unknowns" and when he clicked on this word he found that the definition of "unknowns" was anyone who lived off the information grid; subsequently having no name or identity that could be tracked. His heart sank. If their identity could not be tracked, then there was no way he could find out anything about them.

He stiffened up as he looked down at the data-pad. He clicked on the "back" button, returning him the page he'd been looking at before, then back even further until he was viewing the details of the Prodigy experiment. There had to be something. A name, a date – something!

He continued reading the text files.

> **Robert Taylor's neural development began almost immediately after his being picked by President Andrews and his delivery to The Towers. By the time he was five months old tests showed that he was ready to accept his first Virtual Reality Training, or VRT, session.**
>
> **By the close of his first birthday Taylor's advanced education was in full swing and showed no signs of problems, or slowing down. With all other development programmed to match his education Robert Taylor showed maturity that exceeded his age, and education level. To date, these factors are combining to help him become the prodigy that the experiment has been looking to create.**
>
> **The scientists at EduCorp couldn't be happier with the development of young Mr. Taylor, who the staff affectionately calls "Little Robbie".**

Taylor winced at what he read. Indeed the staff *had* made a habit of calling him "Little Robbie" and he hated this, for it wasn't out of affection, but more out of spite that he had been granted this nickname – a contradiction of his size to his age.

He continued to peruse the online pages only to find that there was little to nothing about his origins and that everything seemed to center around *Prodigy* and its predictable success. He did notice, however, a "Prodigy Timeline" link that caught his eye at the bottom of one of the pages. He clicked it and was directed to a simple chart showing the stages of the Prodigy program. Due to the long term chronology of this project, the last few years of the experiment, those in which Taylor was an actual participant, spanned only a fraction of the chart near its end. At the start of this section, however, Taylor noticed an arrow marking his birth; July 16, 2439. His heart leapt.

On tapping the link this excitement turned to anger as the blinking yellow letters of "EduCorp Lockout" flashed across the screen intermittently with red letters of "Level 6 Access Required". The web-link showed at the top of the screen that the CESPA site was now trying to access the EduCorp internal network.

Frustrated to the core, Taylor threw the pad across the room, shattering it. After the moment's anger, Taylor heard a beeping at his door. This beeping, along with a red light at the top of the door, signaled that there was a request for entry and, as Taylor did not have any friends, he knew that this would have to be one of the overseers in his experiment. "Come in!" he heaved insolently while sitting quite plain and exposed in the middle of his bed

As the door slid open he sickened with both shock and surprise. Dr. Young, a member of the EduCorp Council, the same he was just reading about, was standing at his entrance. He had seen her before when he was interviewed by the Council a few months ago. Indeed it was most unusual for a child to be directly interviewed by Council members, but as he was in a most unusual project, it seemed to suit the council to change its standard practice.

She did not look any different than he remembered her. She appeared young, to suit her name, with long blonde hair that she always kept tight in a ponytail behind her head, light brown eyes, and she was tall – very tall. Taylor would later discount this, realizing that his own lack of height offered a false perspective. Still, at the time, she appeared towering. He remembers, at one point looking up the current Council members and had read that she was just over a hundred years old, and while he understood how this was possible, it frustrated him that telling how old an adult was could never be done by their appearance. He looked at her and this whizzed through his mind with the same thought that he himself did not fit in appearance either. As irony would have it, he looked *older* than his year.

Dr. Young's smiling face was greeted with a screwed up angry one from Taylor, and her grin widened all the more when he quickly replaced this unwelcome expression with one of surprise.

She looked around at the extremely tidy surroundings and was impressed with how neat someone so young could be, especially someone who was so much younger than they really looked. Her eyes then caught the destroyed remains of the data pad sitting in one corner of the room, and she offered a soft "Hmmm." She could tell that he was watching her every move and thought it best to try to break the ice first. "May I have a seat Mr. Taylor? I have something I need to show you." She said in a soft melodic voice.

"Sure, but what are you doing he…" he started, but was immediately interrupted.

"I was coming down to see how some students from my own division were doing." She motioned for Taylor to sit next to her as she continued. "But as I came down the hall, I could see a reckless little boy running so fast, and he cut me off as I was walking. Let's just say it peaked my curiosity what this kid was up to.

"So..." snapped Taylor in a rude fashion so quickly that he had to awkwardly continue, "I mean, so what do you want to show me... exactly."

She looked at him with a plain expression – no smile, no frown, just a soft stare. "Well, I feel the need to talk to you, but I'm not sure how to say what I need to..." she offered a short glance around the room, and continued. "You are looking for information on your family. This I know.

"But how..."

"Let's just say that I know, and leave it at that..." she said, interrupting him again.

She continued to look around the room in what was clearly an awkward moment; then her eyes fell on the broken data pad again. She reached inside her white lab-coat and pulled out a new one which she slipped to the quiet boy at her side. "Here, you'll probably need a new one of these then..." She said this as she nodded to the broken one in the corner.

Slowly, shame started to well in Taylor over his actions. This was a feeling that he wasn't at all used to. Granted, he could always go to an M-Gen panel and request a new data-pad, but for a member of the Council to know that he had somehow recklessly destroyed one on his own was all too embarrassing.

He looked down at the pad she had given him and saw that it was displaying the same page he had been looking at before. It was blinking the security restriction screen and at that instant he knew that she had a way of linking to his data pad and seeing the pages he had been viewing. He stared at her, his face shifting between confusion to anger.

"We council members have so many resources available to us," she said softly. "I was curious what had you so excited so I talked to your last S.I.. She told me what your last lesson was, and it gave me a pretty good idea what a smart kid like you was probably up to."

She reached around him, patted him on the back, and soothed the back of his head with a light rubbing through his hair. "So you want to know the truth do you?" she asked with a slight grin, and bit by bit, when he looked into her light brown eyes, he felt his anger, his embarrassment and all the rest of his emotions melt away.

"I just wanna to know if anyone out there even knows I'm here or even cares," the boy said in a pathetic tone. "I've talked to some a the other students, and they all say they've got family outside the company; waiting for their experiment to end. You know... aunts, uncles, and grandparents, and such, but I don't know if there's anyone out there for me. I don't know anything 'bout my family and I've gotta wait another two years before I can even try 'n' find anything out." As he spoke he could feel a sad desperation well up inside him so much he started to tear, but turned his head so Dr. Young could not see.

"Well, maybe I can fix that," she said almost cheerfully. "I must say, I think we underestimated your ability to learn and mature so quickly..."

He looked up at her and watched as she placed a thumb in the bottom right corner of the data pad he was holding. The screen instantly recognized Dr. Victoria Young's print, and offered access. She then tapped a few other buttons on the screen before handing the pad back to the boy.

"I've given you access to just these pages. You can look them over as much as you like, even come back to them later. They've been released to your access only."

She gave him a squeezing hug from the side, and stood up. "I'll leave you then, if you'll be alright."

For these last few seconds Taylor was truly at a loss for words. This had to be the kindest gesture anyone had ever done for him, and he didn't know what to say in gratitude. In Taylor's chest, he felt such a welling of emotions that were so rare to him; as rare as the personal touch and attention Dr. Young had offered.

"Yeah, I'll be fine," he muttered down at the screen. He looked up and offered a "Than – ks!" but the door to his room had closed behind Dr. Young in the middle of his speaking, and he didn't know if she had heard this final word.

Not knowing exactly what he should do next, Taylor gave in to his ultimate curiosity and tapped the folder that had restricted him before. When it opened, he saw that only a text file and a picture was held inside, and while he was somewhat disappointed, hoping to find much more, he would take what information he could, and feel grateful for it.

On tapping the picture, he saw that it was of a baby, obviously himself just after birth. It was taken so near the time of his birth, in fact, that those around him didn't have time to wash him properly. This was of no matter to Taylor as he quickly closed it and opened the text file thereafter. It was some kind of medical report or journal; simple to read, and to the point:

```
IMPORT FILENAME:  RST232-AA1        REPORTING PHYSICIAN: XXXXXXXX
SUBJECT NAME:  UNKNOWN              AGE:  Unknown   GENDER:     Fe-
male
REPORT DATE:  July 16, 2439         REPORT TIME:  06:47PM
-------------------------------------------------------------------
Subject brought in unconscious, pregnant, and in labor - also un-
responsive to external stimuli.  Subject found in the North Los
Angeles Forest 10 miles beyond the North Wall.  She is badly
bruised, but no signs of foul play can be detected at this early
stage.  Complete medical scan shows no signs of disease or inter-
nal damage.  Severely elevated hormone levels suggest a geriatric
pregnancy.  All I.D. markers offer no data as to who she is.
REPORT STATUS:  OPEN
-------------------------------------------------------------------
REPORT DATE:  July 16, 2439         REPORT TIME:  09:23PM
Subject is aging at a highly accelerated rate as her hormone lev-
els continue to rise.  Methuselah has completely lost its hold.
My only option is to deliver the baby.  The mother is not expected
to last the night.
REPORT STATUS:  OPEN
-------------------------------------------------------------------
REPORT DATE:  July 16, 2439         REPORT TIME:  10:48PM
Delivery was successful.  I have delivered a very, VERY healthy
baby boy (4.7 Kg/ 57 cm) by cesarean.  Initial scans show no signs
of genetic defects, and on first sight the baby's blue eyes seem
almost unnatural, but may fade over time.  Searching for allele
markers has offered no positive I.D. for a known paternal link.
The mother continues to age rapidly.  Her death is inevitable.
REPORT STATUS:  OPEN
-------------------------------------------------------------------
REPORT DATE:  July 16, 2439         REPORT TIME:  11:57PM
As expected, the mother of the newborn died at 11:49PM due to
Natural Causes; her remains have been labeled for processing.
REPORT STATUS:  OPEN
-------------------------------------------------------------------
REPORT DATE:  July 17, 2439         REPORT TIME:  12:30AM
```

```
President Andrews was here! Amazing, among a room full of new-
borns in the claim nursery, he has hand-picked this child to be
the only student in a very radical training program, code named
Prodigy at EduCorp. The boy, immediately numbered 1275A and named
Robert Stanley Taylor, is set for transfer first thing this new
morning. I hope all the best for him in his new life.
REPORT STATUS: CLOSED        GENERATE NEW CASE SITE RST232-7EAL
```

On reading this simple text report Taylor's heart ached. He now had little more information than when he started. But at least he knew the truth about his mother and thus one small mystery had been solved. She was dead.

He did not feel angry or remorseful about his mother's death. Indeed, Taylor felt that, considering the circumstances, his life was pretty good. He could have died that night or the following morning, but because she was found, he had a home, so to speak, and was geared to become the smartest kid on the planet. All things considered, if he had blessings to count – there would be many.

After taking a few minutes to think on what he had learned, roll it over in his head, and even play out that night several times in his brain, Taylor stood up, walked over to his shattered data-pad. Rummaged through its remains, he found the memory module it had contained. He knew the chips were designed to be nearly indestructible, and, on finding it, he slipped it into his new data-pad. Tapping a few buttons on the screen, the picture and text file were quickly saved on the chip and with one last button pushed, the screen went blank.

Taylor forgot how dark it was in his dormitory without the data-pad being on. With a shiver from the cold air in the room, he felt a sudden isolation. Being with Dr. Young such a short time had left quite the impression on him, for he immediately wished she were still there by his side.

His mind started fumbling through memories of the last three years. It was here, in the cold corporate embrace of this facility – this company, that he lived a life of education and training. With each of his one-person classes, where all eyes were on him and everywhere he went he was the center of attention, it truly hit him, as though he had never realized it before, that everyone he saw in his day-to-day wasn't really seeing *him*. They were looking through him, seeing only what he represented – *Prodigy* – an investment – an experiment, worse than this, he felt as though he were only a number – a collection of statistics – not a person, not a child. And those he dealt with were always impatient of the program and, not seeing any purpose in it, they treated him with instant condescension. This was always there, always there – and yet it never bothered him before. But now something aching churned inside him. It was now, for the first time in his life, that Taylor – who was always the center of attention – truly felt alone.

9 Gifts

THE FOLLOWING MORNING, with a rush of white cloth, three lab-coats swished down a long corridor, hands waving and voices talking over each other in verbal confusion.

"What do you mean 'he's gone telepathic'? He's not but just turned three." asked one voice. This was Dr. Harrison, the scientist in charge of Taylor's neurological development. He, himself, was not telepathic, which made him somewhat rare. He was a short man showing a lot of forehead, with light brown curly hair and a crooked nose. The man had the appearance of someone who was very smart; a truth *usually* realized whenever he opened his mouth.

"Just what I said, he's gone telepathic. He can communicate *with his mind.*" Said another voice loudly, pointing at charts with the initials RST at the top corner. This was Dr. Richardson who wasn't scheduled to be an active part of *Prodigy* for another nine years. This man was apprised of a recent development in the experiment and decided to interject himself into its workings immediately. His field of expertise: Evolutionary Development, which really meant Telepathic Development, as that's really all the experience he had with evolved abilities, gifts, or powers – as they could be called all three with the complete understanding of what was meant.

Dr. Richardson was tall and thin, with a long face that stopped abruptly, giving him almost no chin at all. He had long black hair that was pulled back into a ponytail.

"I'm not an idiot you know." retorted Dr. Harrison, "I know what telepathic means; I'm just a little confused."

"Well, all I want to know is how this could happen?!" spewed a female voice. It was Dr. Young, fuming with anger and fear at the same time. She had consulted with Dr. Ulrich, who was in charge of Taylor's social development, and, at a ripe 198, was also very ready for retirement. Dr. Young convinced the man, just the evening before, to respectfully step down from his position on the project, allowing her to take his place. As such, from Dr. Young's talking with Taylor and being around him for only a few minutes, she had instantly become quite fond of the boy, though he himself did not yet know it.

"By looking at his charts," started Dr. Richardson, "the best I can guess is that his accelerated training has somehow triggered early telepathy."

"That's your *guess*, is it?" sneered Dr. Harrison quickly.

"Well of course it's a guess. I've only been on this project for about twenty minutes and I can't be certain of anything 'til I have a chance to get up to speed."

Dr. Young was walking much faster than the others, and on entering the lift she fumed, "Is there any way that we can *undo* this, Dr. Harrison?"

Before the intended had a chance to answer, Dr. Richardson immediately snapped, "What for?!! So he's the youngest telepath the planet's ever seen! What's the problem?!"

"I would expect a response like that from *you*, but my question was directed at Dr. Harrison." she said coldly.

"Well, umm…" started Dr. Harrison looking worried, "Unfortunately not. Every attempt at controlling a person's pathic abilities with neural digression has resulted in severe brain trauma. The government has tried... but no, they didn't work – no – never mind."

"Don't never mind me – go on, what didn't work?" she pressed.

"Well, I was doing a little research a few weeks back and I read an article that said the GC's trying to develop ways of digressing a person's telepathic abilities, you know, to control criminal telepaths. Anyways; it said all efforts have been unsuccessful, horribly unsuccessful. In each case the treatment caused a chemical imbalance in the brain so severe that it resulted in a complete memory wipe. They still can't figure out why it's happening. Even still, the telepathic ability remained. The project was a complete failure. I couldn't even say if they were on to something, or so far off base that they may never get it right. I just, I don't know!"

"Hold on now!" Dr. Richardson heaved, offering a harsh stare to Dr. Young. "You don't wanna bring outsiders in on this do you?"

She turned her head and gazed at the digital numbers counting downward, "No, and besides, it obviously wouldn't've worked anyways would it?"

"Listen," said Dr. Richardson, "I don't see what the big deal is. So he's telepathic. It doesn't make sense why we should want to undo this little miracle."

"Miracle!" snapped Dr. Young, looking sternly up into Dr. Richardson's eyes. "This is by no means a miracle, doctor. You seem to have forgotten your own field. Controlling telepathy takes time – remember? Oh, that poor child!"

She rotated her jaw slowly in irritation as Dr. Richardson lit a grin. "This must be somebody pretty special – to have you wrapped around his finger so quick..."

"Ohhhhh" she heaved, whirling her head around in a blond wash of color, "Of course he's special, but that's not the point. In the next few hours, if he is not put in pathic confinement, he'll start communicating with every telepath around. If they start communicating back, he'll have to listen, whether he wants to or not. Not to mention emotions – if he's not careful, he could start feeling tons of things that just won't make sense to him – fear, love, hate, anger. Oh, this is horrible!"

"Calm down, calm down," Dr. Richardson breathed softly, putting his hand on her shoulder, "So we put him in confinement until he gets trained, what's the big deal?"

She pulled her shoulder from his grip, and at this point Dr. Harrison was the one to offer a voice of reason, "She's right, it is a big deal. You have to understand, all our pathic development programs are designed for teenagers. We don't have any protocols for training a three-year-old..."

"Or a six year old for that matter," Dr Young cut in.

Dr. Harrison nodded, "Right, right! If we tried to use our current programs, we could cause irreparable damage to his brain, and I for one won't risk it. We've worked too hard – too hard..."

Dr. Richardson's face went pale as he realized the error of his thinking. It was quite clear to him now that if they couldn't find a way to either undo Taylor's telepathy, or find some way to train him on how to control it, then he could be forced to stay in confinement until he reached an age where it would be safe to do so.

"What about modifying the training program? Maybe we can teach him how to, you know – do it slowly – gradually." asked the now concerned Dr. Richardson.

"Well, I suppose it could be possible," said Dr. Young, looking down at Dr. Harrison and searching his face for some affirmation that there might be a slow solution to the problem. He furrowed his brow with a look of uncertainty, "The best thing we can do right now is to talk to the boy. See what's going on, inside his head... Ah, here we are..."

With a "ding" the lift doors opened and the three of them stepped out into the quiet dormitory corridor. All seemed fine until Dr. Harrison nearly tripped on something at his feet.

"What the hell!" he said as he turned and saw that one of the technicians, a female, was lying on the floor unconscious. As he knelt down the other two quickly turned to see what was wrong.

Dr. Harrison felt for a pulse and offered a sigh of relief that the woman was still alive. He looked up at the other two. "Mind your thoughts, you two. If what I'm thinking is true, you'll have to watch what you think around here." and with this Dr. Young and Dr. Richardson nodded before continuing down the hall.

Other doctors and technicians were lying about, unconscious, and as the three approached Taylor's dormitory they could see a dim light coming from inside. They peered into the door window and saw the boy holding a data-pad in his hands. He was tapping away at some game, completely unaware of the state of things outside his room.

Dr. Richardson motioned to offer a retinal scan to the security console at the door but Dr. Young stepped in his way.

"Let me go in first. I saw him just yesterday. He knows me, and if we have to confine him," the woman said with lowered head and a worried tone. "*If we have to,* I want to be the one to tell him." She watched as the two men nodded, and in looking between them, she offered an idea of how to occupy their time. "Just stay out here – try to revive the others. If I need you – I'll let you know."

With this, Dr. Young turned around to offer her own retinal scan and when the door opened Taylor's eyes shot up in quick surprise and he offered an instant gleaming smile under his bright blue eyes. She returned the favor and looked about the room. As usual, it was extremely neat and, remembering the last time she was there, she was happy to see that there was no shattered data-pad in the corner.

"Oh my gosh!" he said excitedly. "Am I glad you're here?"

"Really!" she replied in a slightly nervous tone, for he had leaped up and practically pulled her arm off to get her to sit next to him on his bed. "Uh – ouch – oh – sweetie, why is that?"

"Well," he answered before taking a deep breath and started rambling at high speed, "'Bout an hour ago I started hearing voices in my head, and it was just after my last class, and I didn't know what it was, and so I was trying to listen to what they were saying and before I knew it the voices got so loud, and they weren't making any sense, and I started feeling nervous, excited, worried – all kinds of things – before I knew it my head started to hurt, so I made the voices go away because they were way too loud, and I..."

"Slow down Robert, slow down." she said, and with good reason. His speed made it nearly impossible for her to make sense of anything he was saying. More than this, she could tell that he needed to heave another breath of air.

"Taylor!" he said loudly, and with her tenseness Dr. Young flinched at the outburst. "Call me Taylor, there are so many Roberts, Robbies, Bobs, and Bobbies around here; I want to be different."

Dr. Young smiled at these words thinking inside her own head that this boy had long ago achieved being very different from any of the other students, even if his name was a common one. "Okay, *Taylor,* go on then," she said, "just tell me slowly, a little at a time, please."

"Well," he started again, "I just finished my last ND (*neural development*) session and I came back to my dorm." He offered a pause and a breath, "I was sitting here playing 'DrexoBlaster' when all of a sudden I started hearing voices inside my head." Pause – breath. "They were soft at first, then they got louder." Pause – breath. "They got so loud that I thought my head was going to explode." Pause – breath. "So many voices – and strange feelings, I didn't even know why I was feeling the way I was feeling." Pause – breath. "It was strange – the voices were so loud my head started to hurt and I didn't know what to do!" Pause – breath. "So I closed my eyes and concentrated really hard to stop the voices inside my head." Pause – breath "And I – I did it, I stopped the voices."

"You stopped the voices?" asked Dr. Young, forming her own suspicions about not only what he was saying, but what he had done without knowing it. She had concluded that Dr. Harrison was right and she made quick efforts to mind her own thoughts.

"Yep, all by myself. You know? I think I'm telepathic, and I think those voices, well they must've been other people's thoughts," he said in a half whisper, smiling at her. He reached over and grabbed her hand softly, and she, sitting next to him, staring into his hypnotic bright blue eyes, found it impossible to be angry at him, or even blame him for what he had done. He had unknowingly knocked out what would later be counted as twenty one EduCorp personnel with one huge telepathic blow, and while in any normal circumstance this might require some form of legal or disciplinary action, it was clear that this instance was no normal circumstance.

"Telepathic – that's what you think, do you?" she asked falsely with a smile, "Well, tell me, Taylor, if you're telepathic, and you can hear people's thoughts, and they can hear your thoughts – I want you to tell me what you've been thinking since I walked in this room?"

He turned a bashful stare down to his data-pad and cocked his head to one side. Dr. Young could clearly see that he was blushing. "Come on now, be honest. When you saw that it was me, and since I've been here for a bit, what have you been thinking?"

"Well," he said in a soft, almost false baby voice, "I was happy to see you."

"And…" she pressed.

"And I've been thinking how pretty you are," he continued, turning his eyes up to her, then quickly back down to his data-pad in embarrassment. "You know, I think you're the most beautiful person I've seen in my whole life." Now the blushing seemed to have rubbed off because Dr. Young was now filling with color.

She suddenly snapped at attention, "You've been thinking that this whole time?" she said brightly.

"Yeah, since you walked in."

"Funny," she said with confusion, "I didn't hear those thoughts."

"Well of course not! I wouldn't want you to hear that. It's private."

"Well," she said with thoughts whizzing through her head, "Think of something, with your mind open to me, and we'll see if you really are telepathic." She looked over her shoulder, happy to see that neither Dr. Harrison nor Dr. Richardson was looking in on her and the boy.

He stared at her in concentration. Inside her head she could hear a small whisper of his voice; it seemed to get louder at times, and weaker at others; a true tell tale sign of a telepath struggling with their new gift. Still, she could still hear all of his words when she concentrated on them.

She could hear his voice telling her what he had done in the day, and every now and again, a flash of images would enter her brain, showing how he had been playing video games. She could see his adorable face. Even when he was concentrating on just a game, she thought he was such a ham. Then she could feel the genuine elation he had when she herself had walked in the room. She smiled and laughed at this, amazed that the boy could already project not only emotions, but images as well – something only the most naturally gifted telepaths could do.

The images she was seeing quickly changed. His thoughts had moved to the day before; the moment when she left his dorm. He was conveying the words 'thank you' over and over in his head, and, in watching her own self leave his dorm, she felt the loneliness that consumed him after he read about his mother. With his sadness washing over her, her smiled waned and she rubbed her hand on the boy's back.

Taylor stopped his telepathic contact with her, and he offered a look of concern,

"What's the matter? Is something wrong?"

"Huh!" said Dr. Young as she shook herself to attention, wiping away a quick tear, "oh, nothing." She then gave a laugh. "That was wonderful. That was amazing. That was…"

The door to the dormitory shot open and Dr. Richardson and Dr. Harrison stepped in.

"Is everything alright?" asked Dr. Richardson. The two of them had quickly taken places at the end of the bed, staring at the two sitting on it.

"Oh, everything's fine! Fine!" she said trying to hide her borrowed emotions. She turned to Taylor and spoke very formally. "Taylor – he likes to be called Taylor now because Robert is too common – Taylor, this is Dr. Richardson. He has been brought into your program to help your telepathic development."

Taylor instantly showed a look of confusion, and at this expression Dr. Young explained.

"We knew about your telepathy over an hour ago, but we didn't want to tell you anything, or lead your hopes in the wrong direction until we got a better picture of what was going on."

Taylor nodded his head in understanding and, taking a cue from Dr. Young's previous formality, stood up to greet his guest. "Nice to meet you sir." he said stiffly, drawing out a smile on Dr. Richardson's face. Through his smile though, this man looked between Dr. Young and Taylor, his mind filled with dozens of questions.

"So, eh, what's the verdict?" he asked nervously.

"Well," said Dr. Young with a smile, "I think we'll have to do some tests to be sure, but unless I'm mistaken, he's already learning to control the telepathy on his own. He can project thoughts and hide them at will, which is the first step for a…"

"What!" exclaimed Dr. Harrison, "How can you say that after what you saw outside?"

Taylor, again with a face of confusion, turned to Dr. Young for answers. "Outside?" he asked in a nervous voice.

"Well, Taylor, honey," she said in a very soft and maternal voice while offering a harsh look to Dr. Harrison for blurting out such delicate information. "You don't know it, but all the technicians that usually run around outside – they're all out cold. And best as we can tell, you knocked them out when you tried to stop the *voices* inside your head. You must've hit them with some kind of pathic wave and, well, sort of shocked their brains into submission."

A dreadful panic consumed Taylor and this clearly showed on the boy's face. "But I didn't. You know I wouldn't… Not on purpose… I didn't know…!" He was now looking at all three of their faces for some explanation of what sort of trouble he was in.

"Taylor, dear, don't worry. We don't blame you – and you're not in any trouble – any trouble at all. We just need to make sure that you can get these abilities under control before we continue your training."

With a quick thought Dr. Richardson walked around Taylor's bed and squatted in front of the boy. "How 'bout we try a few exercises – right here and now – to see how developed your telepathy is – like a test!"

Dr. Harrison hummed a nervous negative tone, but Dr. Richardson waved for the man's silence. "It'll be fine – fine – stop worrying!"

He stared at Taylor expectantly for an answer.

"Uhh – a test?..." Taylor repeated nervously, "Okay – I guess."

"Now I am going to think of something, and I want you to tell me what it is that I am thinking."

Taylor nodded with understanding and Dr. Richardson sat in silence for a moment.

After a few seconds Dr. Richardson nodded, "Anything?"

Taylor looked bright eyed, "I got loads of stuff!" he said excitedly. I saw the two of you, walking down the hall beside me. I was tall – much taller than I am now, and I was afraid. I felt very afraid. There were bodies lying around, they're all wearing white lab-coats. They look – dead!" Taylor's eyes filled with terror. "Did – did I do that?"

"Relax Taylor," soothed Dr. Young, "I've already told you, you just knocked them all out. They'll be fine." she put her hand on his shoulder to comfort him, but he seemed a little overwhelmed from his telepathic sense of fear from Dr. Richardson.

Dr. Young glowered angrily at the man, who only nodded with a smile. This offered to her that the boy was correct in assessing the man's thoughts, but she was unhappy that he had nothing better to offer the child.

"Alright, Taylor, let's try that again." Dr. Richardson said this almost cheerfully, as if completely forgetting what the boy had experienced. "I am going to think of something different and I want you to tell me what it is."

Once again Taylor nodded and they started at each other in silence.

After a few moments Taylor looked very confused. "I couldn't hear or see anything. Are you sure you were – uh – actually thinking anything."

Dr. Richardson clapped his hands together under his chin with a smile. "Of course I was," he said with almost a laugh, "I was thinking of different things, yes. But I wasn't projecting them, so therefore you couldn't read them. It was a test… and you passed."

Dr. Harrison now looked between Dr. Richardson and Dr. Young with an awe-stricken smile. "It seems that our boy here has yet again amazed us all. Phenomenal! Well, I think after a few tests we might be able to develo…"

"Slow down – woah – that's too much stuff." Taylor said both loud and so unexpectedly that Dr. Young jumped.

"What's the matter Taylor!" she snapped fearfully.

Taylor rubbed his temples, and, looking up at Dr. Harrison, he pointed. "He's thinking so much so fast. He's so excited, but I can't get everything that's going on... Slow down."

"What!?" spewed both Dr. Richardson and Young at the same time. They were sitting on either side of Taylor, but leaned away so as to turn and look at him with disbelieving eyes. "What do you mean, *he's* thinking so fast." scoffed Dr. Richardson. "He isn't telepathic."

"Well then," started Taylor, "how come I can hear him. I mean right now I can hear his thoughts in my brain. He's so excited – the thought that someone can read his thoughts… no his mind... no – no, stop. Stop. Make him stop. Make *it* stop."

"What's going on?" shrieked Dr. Young loudly, snapping her eyes between Dr. Richardson and Taylor.

Dr. Richardson stood up immediately. "You!" he said pointing at Dr. Harrison, "OUT!" He then turned to Taylor and Dr. Young, "You two, stay here." In that moment both men then left the dorm in a rush.

Inside the room Dr. Young's mind filled with curiosity. "What happened just then – between you and Dr. Harrison?"

Taylor looked up at her with a face of confused fear, a look that somehow still seemed adorable on the boy.

"Well, I could hear his thoughts. He seemed excited at first that I could, but then, just after I said I could, he wanted me to stop. But I didn't and he didn't know how to stop me. He got frightened that someone might know what he was thinking and he couldn't do anything about it. He wanted me to stop, but I didn't. I could have stopped, but I didn't." Taylor now looked up at her with a face welling with tears. "I hope he's not mad at me."

"Oh, it's alright Taylor. It's alright – everything'll be fine!"

The boy instantly filled with so many emotions that in his chest he felt like either his stomach or his heart was going explode, or both. Little by little he could feel those emotions leaking out by way of tears and sobs that he was at a loss to explain.

Dr. Young gave him a quick squeeze. "What's wrong?" she asked, hearing his sniffles by her side.

He looked up at her. "What do you think?" he snapped in an almost sarcastic tone.

She slowly listened in on Taylor's thoughts. Hearing his concerns, she wrapped her arms around him and rocked back and forth. "It will all be okay You know we have so many bright people working here, we'll figure something out. You just wait. Everything will be just fine."

Taylor could hear her words, but for some reason he did not feel comforted. In the last few hours he had gained a new untrained and reckless ability and in that time he had already knocked out several innocent people and intruded on the thoughts of one of the EduCorp Council Members without his permission. This wasn't good at all, and he was afraid.

"Taylor," whispered Dr. Young, "I think it best that you stay here. I'm going to go into the hall. I don't want you to try to do anything pathically unless we say that it's okay – okay"

He looked up at her with tears in his eyes, offering an "okay" in response.

She stepped to the door; it opened, and just as she was about to leave a quick, "Hey!" was shouted across the room. She looked back at Taylor with a smile.

"Can I get something to eat? I'm starving," the boy asked soberly.

She smiled and left without a word. Moments later she came back with a plate of cheese and crackers that he started to eat the instant he could get his hands on them.

Stepping through the door of the dormitory to leave again, she picked up a quick pathic thought inside her head.

"You're still the prettiest one here!"

She paused and looked over her shoulder. Both of them were now smiling, and with her face flushing from the compliment she had just received, Dr. Young left the dorm for what would be the last time that day.

Keeping her smile, she approached the other two council members who were waiting outside and it was obvious to her that all of the technicians who had been revived earlier were eyeing the door of Taylor's dorm with suspicion and fear.

"Listen people, there's nothing to be afraid of," barked Dr. Young stiffly to the crowd of idle lab-coats. "He's the most advanced child here, you all know that. So wouldn't it stand to reason that he could become the youngest telepath too?"

In the calm wake of her words she listened in on their thoughts. She could feel the presence of fear. All around her she sensed that these people didn't really care for the boy and that what had just happened only made matters worse. She narrowly eyed the group and with a loud and fierce voice she shouted at them. "Get back to work, all of you. You have things to do, so do them!"

In an instant the room was filled with a rush of talking and motion as all of the experimenters, observers, and scientists continued working on their respective projects with Dr. Young watching to make sure that her orders were being followed. In her observations her attention was quickly distracted.

"I wouldn't know where to begin with that kind of project!" said Dr. Richardson looking at Dr. Harrison.

Dr. Young turned from the now active technicians to address her contemporaries. "What kind of project?" she asked curiously.

"A project," whispered Dr. Richardson cautiously, "to develop Pathic, Kinetic, Cyber, Pre, and Post cog powers all at the same time."

"What – I don't understand – Why would you..."

"Believe me Dr. Young, if it were any other student, on any other day, I would ask myself that same question." interrupted Dr. Richardson. But that's not the case, and today is a page in the history books for sure.

"Doctor, you're not making any sense," she scowled, yet still whispering.

"Well, let me explain it this way. A moment ago, when Dr. Harrison and young Mr. Taylor were linked in telepathic thought, I noticed that the doctor here had lifted off the ground some inch and a half. Mind you I only just barely caught this and I knew I had to get him out of the room."

"Since then we've been going over his neural recordings from this afternoon. In comparing them with the other known special cases we can see decisive peaks in each of the five known areas of evolved powers."

"What?" beckoned Dr. Young in disbelief. "That can't be!"

Dr. Richardson tapped a panel by Taylor's door and instantly the grey matte surface darkened to reveal deep digital display that brightened to show a digital display of Taylor's neural patterns.

Dr. Young was awestricken to see that there were five peaks in his neural pattern that were labeled for each of the five evolved powers.

"This has to be wrong." She said quietly.

"We thought so too," said the men in awkward unison.

"But if this chart's right," she said nervously, "then he has the potential to be stronger in all of these powers than any who have come before him. Why didn't you notice this before?" She asked, turning an accusing stare up to Dr. Richardson.

"Well, it's not like we've got a lot of these brain patterns to compare to. In fact, we've so few on record I had to look these up in archives. And if I have anything to say about it, he *will* be the strongest eh – everything – on the planet!"

Dr. Young gave him a dismissive stare and turned back at the screen. She glared at it, and it seemed that the different colors used to represent each peak slowly washed over her in a rainbow of both excitement and concern. She would be curious to see how a child might develop with such abilities, and yet, she was worried for Taylor's well being if he could not learn how to control these powers just the same.

Slowly she tapped each of the peaks with her index finger one by one until she reached the last and placed her hand flat palmed on the screen with a realization of what she had to do.

"Doctors – I think this qualifies as an Article 897 – don't you agree?"

The two men stared at her, and while a smile grew on Dr. Harrison's face, Dr. Richardson's darkened with dissatisfaction. They both rolled over what she had said and considered what it meant as she pulled her hand from the panel and started tapping the five peaks over and over again.

10 A Second Visit

TAPPING THE NAMES of the five students he would be training in less than an hour, Taylor lit a smile. He was filled with an excited anxiousness. And he wasn't the only one that felt was warming over with fantastic pride on the lift ride down from The Towers. Between the two, it was clear that Taylor and Jay were both in a glow over how well they had performed at their presentation. More than this, Taylor was absolutely full of himself over how he had *handled* Dr. Hathaway.

The two shifted as the lift changed directions to move from East Tower to West Tower, all the while, Taylor was busy watching his data-pad bring up the names of his students and show what each one was to learn for the day.

With another change in direction, this time pushing the lift upwards to nearly the top floor of West Tower, Taylor suddenly felt lightheaded. He wavered and steadied himself by holding the sides of the lift. Jay perked with signs of concern.

"What's the matter? You alright?"

"I – I'm fine. Just got a head-rush. Just need some rest. It's – it's oay." Taylor wasn't sure if this was a lie or not, but as he stared at the data-pad in his hand, his vision became blurred and slowly he watched without control as the pad left his hand and fell to the ground. This image was shortly followed by a quick view of the lights at the top of the lift, then a thud.

Taylor now had nothing in his sight but a wash of bright white. This lack of image eventually gave way to the view of an earthen hole through which a painful amount of light was coming through. He quickly realized that he was lying on his back and he looked around to see if he could recognize where he was as it was apparent he wasn't where he last remembered being. But this effort to gain his bearings was short-lived and incomplete as, in a mere second, his shoulders and head were being held and grabbed by several pairs of hands. He would've panicked if his eyes weren't so quickly met by familiar faces, and his ears met with clearly identifiable voices all around.

"Is he alright?" asked one voice.

"I – I don't know?" answered another, which was then followed by an "I told you it was a bad idea."

His students were talking over his head. He sighed with relief, breathing the familiar salty air he instantly recognized from his last vision. He tried to speak, but when he opened his mouth, nothing came out. Terrified, he rolled his head side to side and understood that while his face was trying to give expressions of pain and discomfort over his restraint, he wasn't being acknowledged by those around him. Taylor could see all six of his children looking down at him. They were very dirty. Their clothes, a strange light pajama-like outfit, hadn't been cleaned or re-generated in days it seemed, but to his relief, they each seemed completely unscathed. Taylor's heart skipped a beat with the realization that all of his students *did* exist in these recurring visions of the future, and what's more – they were all fine!

Yet again, however, this vision was different from any he was used to. He seemed unable to move in it at all. He watched as the children talked amongst themselves and, despite his efforts to communicate, they offered no sign that he was doing anything to get their attention. To his surprise, he realized when he looked up at his six students that he was now being held down by no-one, and yet still he was pinned to the ground.

Then, he heard a strange yet recognizable noise, something between a howl and a growl. This strange animal like call repeated several times with increased volume until it was ear piercing and deafening. To listen to it sent a chill up Taylor's mud covered back.

"We've gotta wake him up." Johnny said in a frightened voice.

"Well what do we do?" asked Aspen nervously.

It was with perfectly clear vision, and a gripping expectation of pain, that Taylor watched Caitlin take control of the situation by kneeling on his chest. She raised her flat-palmed hand and he knew what was coming next.

With a quick pain across his face Taylor could tell that he had been slapped, but at that instant his eyes opened only to see Jay looking down on him. Taylor was lying on the floor of the lift and the pain on his face continued into the reality of his own true flesh.

"Did you – just – hit me?" he asked, lifting himself off the floor.

"Uh – yeah!" Jay said with a half smirk on his face. "You were going all nutso on me; kept rolling your head around, calling the kids' names, askin' why they couldn't hear you... really strange. Dude, when your head started smackin' the wall I had to do somethin'."

Taylor now thought to himself that, come to think of it, his head did have the extra pain of being pounded a few times. "Huh – uh – well, thanks," he said, rubbing the back of his head. He was at a loss for words.

"Dude – d'you have another vision? What was it?" asked Jay while helping to steady Taylor between two walls of the lift.

"Yeah, uh – same as before – it was really strange though." Taylor answered calmly. With these words they both stood, staring ahead, and, for a split second, the ride could have continued as if nothing had happened.

Most of the time Jay felt inadequate to ask Taylor about his visions; he thought that Taylor was his own best expert on the subject and that if there need be any concern on the matter; Taylor would know his own limits. This, however, was not one of those times. The man stared at Taylor expectantly, and the teen, while watching the numbers slowly ascend, caught Jay's glowering face out of the corner of his eye.

"What's wrong?" Taylor asked without looking away.

"Oh, nothing. I just – well – come on! Dude, you gotta understand. This is all a little weird." Jay spoke with a calm uneasiness and it was clear to Taylor that his friend was worried.

"Listen," he replied while still keeping his forward stare, "I'm already planning on running some tests on myself. I'll do it while the kids are training, that way we'll keep schedule."

"Good!" said Jay with a definite sound of relief, "But there's something else..." With this Taylor turned to see that the nervous look on Jay's face had not changed.

"What is it?" he asked, now irritated at the unwanted attention he was getting from his friend. His nerves were on edge, and the last thing he needed to do was explain away something that even he didn't have answers to.

"Well, it's about these visions."

"Yeah! What about them?"

"Well, come on man. Don't you think you should warn someone, like the GC or somethin'? I mean, dude, you've seen billions of people die. That's not just something you forget, is it?"

"Listen," started Taylor, "and I know I've told you this before, so here it is again. The first few months that I had visions of the future, I always got some crazy death, destruction, and chaos view of it here and there. I was three and a half the first time it happened. For a child at that age it was horrible, and I was terrified. I was also naive – naive in my understanding of how the whole precog thing worked. I warned everybody told everybody they were going to die! Then days would pass and nothing would happen. Some of my visions would even contradict each other, and I would end up confusing those I had told."

Taylor continued to speak, all the while Jay kept trying to "but, but, but..." his way in.

Still, Taylor persisted. "What *I've* come to realize is that through the day to day thoughts decisions of our own government and even the tiny intricacies of what any common Joe does, I could see the possibilities of horrible endings to our way of life *if* the wrong choice was made or if the wrong chain reaction is started. Sure I saw great visions of the future too – but I definitely got the *bad* with the good."

Jay finally stopped pressing, lifted his eyebrows and nodded in understanding.

"What *you* have to realize," continued Taylor, "is that all visions are only possible. Definite visions don't exist – they can't it goes against how precogs work." Taylor now stiffened his face. "Now, I am very guarded about what predictions I reveal to others. My being right more than wrong helps improve my credibility as a good precog. The only reason why you happen to even know about this vision is because it is having a direct effect on our project."

"So what if this 'possible' starts to become 'definite'?" pressed Jay.

"Not that *that* would ever happen, but if it did, the kids'll be the *first* to know... – oh – and you too." Taylor quickly lit a sideways grin.

The lift reached the floor of the dormitories, the doors opened, and it only took a few seconds for their attitudes to change. Between the two of them, Taylor and Jay's entire focus was now on the children. More specifically, they had a mutual understanding that tests needed to be run on Johnny to see if any damage resulted from the early morning's visions and trauma. Because of this, and his sense of responsibility Taylor instinctively approached Johnny's dorm.

"I don't think so buddy! You deal with the other five, I'll deal with Johnny." Jay said, raising a hand to block his friend's path. "You've been with him enough. It's best if the two of you had a little space. I'll take it from here."

With a nod from Taylor, Jay added, "It'd do you some good to pay attention to the other brats once in a while! Give *them* a little attention!"

Taylor scrunched his face in frustration and tried to stammer a protest but said nothing coherent. He instantly felt accused of being preferential, and while this might be a little true, it bothered him that anyone else might notice.

Taylor's shallow thoughts on this matter were quickly broken by Jay's continuing words. "Hey Kid! Tell 'em how the meetin' went this mornin'. They'll definitely get a kick outta that!"

Taylor nodded, shrugging off the name "Kid," and with a feeling of displacement he realized that this was one of the few times he had ever been given a real order by his counterpart. What's more was the look Jay gave him. It was as though Taylor had no choice but to do as he was told. Taylor smiled – knowing that Jay was only saying, again, what he felt was necessary. He gave his friend a warm handshake and a quick hug with a pat on Jay's back.

"Here, take this thing." Taylor said on separating. He was holding out the sphere he had for the most part, kept tightly under his arm. "See if you can find anything out about who made it and where it came from."

Jay took it very carefully, making sure that none of the cloth wrapping had come undone. He then turned and walked to Johnny's dormitory door, offered his retinal scan and walked in, all the while being watched by Taylor, who had his own concerns.

"What the hell, man!" Jay shouted at the door's entrance.

Taylor, having turned away for only a second, jerked his head back at these words. He saw Jay standing in the doorway with a look of shock on his face. Instantly Taylor had a backwards sense of déjà vu, for it was only earlier that morning that Jay had stood in the exact same doorway and said the exact same thing.

"What is it?" the teen asked quickly while at the same time moving to stand behind Jay and look into the room himself.

The whole dorm was in shambles. All of Johnny's possessions were scattered across the room. The bed and mattress had been turned upside down, and, as it seemed, this was done while Johnny was still on it for the boy was lying unconscious underneath the mess. The two bumped shoulders as they both tried to rush in.

Taylor grabbed the boy and with a quick look over the child's arms he could tell that Johnny had been tranquilized again. He stood, with the boy still in his arms, and handed him to Jay.

"Take him outside," Taylor said in an angry, but somehow calming voice.

Jay did as he was told, and the door of the dormitory closed behind him with Taylor still inside.

It was only a minute's wait before Taylor exited the room and waved for Jay to enter with Johnny still in a warming soft sleep in the man's arms.

On stepping in Jay was impressed, but not surprised to see that the room had been picked up and put in proper order in record time.

"Dude, did you cog your way to see who did this?"

"Yeah - same person I saw before – no face – no nothing!"

Jay shook his head, "Well, whoever it was, it's clear what they were doin'." With wide eyes, he pulled out the cloth wrapped sphere. "They were looking for this. Man, they were trying to cover their tracks. I'm sure of it!"

"Oh, absolutely!" said Taylor confidently. "I don't want you to let either of these out of your sight!" He motioned between the boy who was lying on a now properly situated bed and the wrapped sphere in Jay's hand.

"I'm changing the dorm's security settings," Taylor said coldly. "From now on the only ones who can enter any *Prodigy II* room will be you, me, and the kids."

"Stay with him 'til he wakes up, then start your tests. No – wait! Find out what they used for a tranquilizer ASAP. I don't want any side effects and it might give us an idea of who did it."

Taylor was giving orders again. He was now comfortably in charge, and with yet another nod from Jay, he exited the dorm only to stand right outside the door. He stared at the retinal scanner. With absolute concentration he forced lines of computer code to light up on the display screen just beneath it. Changes to this code were being made so fast that, were it anyone else, there would be no time to even see, much less understand the modifications.

Taylor, as a cyber, understood it all perfectly and as such, he was carefully reprogramming the machine so that any efforts to open the door without a retinal scan would result in a complete shutdown of the entire floor's power grid. He also recoded the scanners to only allow a very, *very* select group to enter. So, with the last changes in place, and telling the other doors to perform the same modifications, he tilted his chin up, turning the screen off.

"There, that should do it!" he said confidently.

Taylor then walked to the security desk that watched over the lift doors. These, along with the nearby emergency stairway, were the only entrances to the floor. Taylor smiled at this narrow wooden piece. To call it a proper security desk was something of a joke, for it consisted of an autonomous robot, all in shiny white exterior armor, standing a towering eight feet tall behind a simple wood barrier that separated if ever needed. The robot was molded to be part of the wall where it stood so it could scan and store a log of all those who gained access to the floor either by stairs or by lift. If at any time it needed to subdue an intruder or control a student (neither of which had ever happened as long as Taylor could remember) the robot was equipped with non-lethal, and lethal means of action.

Taylor approached this electronic monstrosity and, with furrowed brow, started scanning its security log, actually reading the information and security logs inside his own brain. The robot twitched and flinched inside the wall, but this ceased once Taylor was finished. As he might've expected, his search for answers or any kind of information came up empty. The robot had suffered a critical power failure both the previous night, and some time just over an hour ago. Taylor knew from his earlier vision that the perpetrator was a cyber and that having this power would make a stealth entry very easy.

Taylor jerked his stare back to the robot. Editing its internal code, the electronic guardian twitched and jerked even more uncontrollably than before and, when Taylor was finished, it relaxed to find every part of itself fitting smoothly back into the wall. Uselessly, Taylor smacked and rubbed his hands together as if he had performed a difficult task of manual labor.

"There, perfect!" he whispered. Inside the robot he had changed the code in such a way that now, should the robot suffer another critical power failure, it would silently reroute its battery backup to the corridor's retinal scanners, and notify Taylor's personal com-tracker of the problem all before completely shutting down its own wireless communication.

Now why didn't I think of that before? Taylor questioned to himself as he turned away from the robot and walked back towards Johnny's dorm. He glanced into the door window and saw that Jay was still sitting on the bed beside a sleeping Johnny. The man was quickly tapping a data pad, presumably working while waiting for the boy to wake up.

Taylor turned away and walked to the other dormitory doors. Now on his own, he made his way, one by one, to the other five rooms and pushed the call buttons located near the retinal scanners. Above the doors a bright yellow light glowed to show the request. After completing these requests, he stood between dorms one and two, Aspen and Caitlin's, and stared at the wall opposite their dorm doors. He pushed a small red button there, forcing a console with even more buttons to reveal itself. With the push of one of these new buttons a long panel on the wall, spanning from the floor to the ceiling, started to shrink and bow out from the side of the corridor. In a mere second the protruded panel offered a level, cushioned seat that Taylor took and waited.

While he was sitting he felt his hunger pain him, and he realized that with all he had done so far this morning he could do with a little snack. He obliged this hunger with a 'Protobar' from a nearby M-Gen panel. He didn't leave his seat to get this new bit of food. No – he merely cybered the M-Gen down the corridor into operation, then kinetically made the bar fly across the hall and into his hands.

This little candy-bar like food was designed to replenish the body of what it needed after the excessive use of any powers and with only a few bites Taylor was quickly relieved of his hunger. He grinned with a fidgeting rocking of his leg, overcome with an impatience to see his students. He had only left them less than twelve hours ago and yet he already missed them so very much. With his visions, his presentation, and the chaos of the night before, he wanted to see them as soon as possible – to know that they were alright. He knew, in his heart, that they were fine, but to see them, to talk to them, it was always his best way to know for certain.

But to talk to them, he wasn't sure if he should tell them everything at once or keep what had been going on to himself until he had figured out the truth.

Eventually deciding to play it by ear, Taylor looked at his own legs for more unending moments until, with a soft hiss, his eyes looked up to see the opening of the first door down the corridor.

11 Lining Up

AFTER ONLY A FEW SECOND'S WAIT Taylor observed the countenance of a short, muscular boy with dark eyes and long light blonde hair which was only partly pulled into a ponytail that snaked its way down the middle of his back with the rest of his hair. This was David, or David Elijah Fuller Matthews, and though he was the shortest of the six, even among his sisters, he still, like the lot of them, had a relatively thin frame. He was the thickest, though, because of his insatiable appetite, and was that morning dressed in a loose white button shirt and blue jeans. Each morning, without fail, this boy was the first of the six to be ready and Taylor was certain that this was because he was a kinetic, short for telekinetic, and used this ability to help himself ready every morning. Taylor had himself, often used his powers to say, put on his shirt at the same time was lifting up his own pants, and he could imagine David doing the same just to save time.

David stood in front of Taylor to offering a "'morning" greeting. Taylor nodded and lit only a hint of a grin from the side of his mouth before throwing a quick punch in the direction of David's head...

Abusive – hardly. Taylor had, long ago, taken several classes, both physically and virtually, in self defense, believing it to help his clarity of thought and develop better control over his many abilities. When David found this out for himself, he, wanting to be like his teacher and father figure, did the same. With the two of them being similarly trained, they would often offer sudden punches and kicks at each other as a way of initiating quick sparring sessions.

So as he expected, though he was ready to hold it back, his fist was blocked kinetically, and as such the two jumped to positions opposite each other in the corridor. They started throwing a series of punches and kicks in what was quickly an all out effort to try and get a first hit. All moves were blocked, some physically, others kinetically, and at one point the fighting stopped with Taylor staring at David with a curious and confused look.

The boy was crouched on the ceiling like an upside down lizard in a cage, with his ponytail hanging just low enough for Taylor to hastily reach up and grab. With a firm tug David protested. "Hey! Owh! No Fair!"

The boy released himself from the ceiling, spun around and landed on his feet like a cat, before standing at full height. Taylor responded with a smile. "Tuck it in your shirt – that'll keep it under control!"

The boy, offering a pouting frown, complied with blonde kinetic flair. The ponytail was pulled up by an unseen force before tucking itself quickly into the boy's shirt – no hands required.

The two started sparring again and after about a minute they stopped in response to the opening of a dorm door beside them. Taylor gave a quick bow to David, who returned the favor, and the boy quickly ejected his own seat next to Taylor.

"I'm impressed!" Taylor whispered with a grin.

"You should be!" David retorted with a sufficient degree of arrogance to widen Taylor's smile even more. He couldn't help but scrub David's head in response.

Looking up at the new addition to the corridor, Taylor and David noticed it was Aspen that had disrupted their little fighting session. Aspen Barré Christine Matthews, with her long, bouncy and naturally curly brunette hair, thin figure, and always immaculate form, had always taken the role of princess in his class. Taylor looked behind her and into her dorm. It offered the bright colors of flowers and rainbows that seemed to match the dress she was wearing. She walked over to create and sit in her own seat, but she didn't offer a single word or even a nod of recognition to Taylor or her brother.

She was also a kinetic and, as with David, Taylor was sure that she too used her abilities to help herself ready in the morning, but due to the fact that she was female and all the detail that she put into her morning ritual he expected she would always follow in a short second behind David.

Taylor leaned over, looking past David. "Good morning Aspen," he said in such a way as to point out the fact that she had ignored the two of them.

"Good morning father." She responded in a mimicking tone.

"Uh – It's Taylor, honey," the teen whispered in correction. "Is everything alright?"

"I'm fine. Everything's fine." she snapped, making him understand the exact opposite of what she said. He was confused at the attitude. Of all of his students Aspen was always the happiest, and most cheerful. She could walk in a room of kids and make everyone smile – the girl practically glowed with radiant energy, but this morning was obviously different and he worried over what might be troubling her. He would've pursued the matter further, but in the possibility that it was something she preferred to keep private, he thought better of asking in front of her brother.

With a quick hydraulic hiss, three sets of eyes snapped up as the next door opened, revealing dark, pitch-black walls. Immediately emanating from the room was a screaming, deep, dark melody that Taylor recognized as Grace's favorite band, "Alphabetic Anarchy." The song being played, horribly titled "D is for Death" made Taylor cringe and he had often debated whether he should, or had the right to, interfere in her music listening habits. Still, he covered his distaste with a faux smile.

The girl stepped out of the room wearing black jeans and a sleeveless black T-shirt. Her light brown hair, much to Taylor's disapproval, was kept in a short half inch crew cut style. Grace, or Grace Holly Isabelle Matthews, was a Cyber, and despite her name, grace seemed to be the furthest word from her being. She was a tom-boy, to use an old phrase from centuries past. She was tall for her age, thin and muscular, but most notably, she was a polar opposite of Aspen. Harsh and insulting, she always had biting chides for her siblings at every opportunity. Interestingly enough though, none of them minded, as the abuse usually came with an air of comedy that they seemed to appreciate – and related as her way of paying positive compliment and attention.

As Taylor watched her leave her dormitory, cyberly turning off the music as she walked, he caught a glimpse of something in her hands. *Some gadget or trinket no doubt* – he thought to himself, and sure enough, when she sat down, offering a head tipping nod to her siblings, she was holding a metal object that he could tell was the result of her own creation.

The girl was extremely gifted with machines and had taken extra virtual training in mechanics, physics, and engineering whenever she had the chance. This, Taylor was certain, was what caused her to shift away from being the cute feminine little girl he remembered only two short years ago. His eyes gravitated to the object in her hands. It had the shape of a ball, a few inches in diameter, mostly white, with a few colored panels around its sides.

"What's it do?" he asked with a note of reservation. Indeed, ever since she blew up one of her dorms by mistake, he was always afraid of the answer he might receive from this question.

"It's a dog!" she said indignantly.

"Does it work?" David asked, ignoring how she had answered Taylor.

"Duh, course it does, *loser*!"

David quickly closed his mouth, nudging Aspen for her giggles.

"What kind of dog is it?" Taylor asked out of curiosity, and there was a small part of him that doubted the fact that such a small object could contain, or be called a "dog" in any way.

"It's my own mini version of the K9-2600 model."

Taylor smiled at the mention of this robot, for he had recently acquired two of them for the current day's class.

"Well come on, let's see it!" Aspen insisted. Secretly, though Taylor was aware of it, Aspen envied Grace for her technical talents.

Setting the ball on the floor, Grace stepped back. She offered it a focused stare, causing it to immediately pop out four legs and slowly eject a head and a thin antenna of a tail. The small unit looked around and slowly walked up to Taylor, who found the device to be much cuter and more attractive than the K9-2600 model. But then, unexpected to anyone, the little tin pooch barked a loud roar that was almost deafening and certainly not expected from something so small.

"What!? I used Digiphonic 2500 speakers!" Grace replied playfully when she saw the look of pain on everyone's face in the hall.

"Dude, that's so cool!" David said before getting down on all fours to look the metallic pup in the eyes. Grace barely lit a smile before forcing the unit to shut down.

"'T's not *that* great," she said dismissively, "I've got tons of upgrades I could do, buuuut, I'll prob'ly just scrap the whole thing."

Aspen instantly offered protests over her sister putting all that efforts to waste – "I like it – if you don't want it – give it to me! I'll take good care of it!" she said affectionately, as if it would make a difference to the robotic toy.

Grace barely had time to appreciate this comment when the next dorm door opened, revealing Orion; a tall, skinny boy with slick, short, jet-black hair topping a thin gaunt face that offered a boorish expression. He was the tallest of the six, standing a full five feet at ten years old. He stepped out of the room stiffly. Wearing a white button up shirt, necktie, and grey slacks, Taylor sighed as the boy walked mechanically to his seat, which had created itself at the child's mental request. Why this boy always dressed the same each day Taylor would never know. It was as if the child was in uniform even though none was ever required. Still Taylor knew that somewhere inside that tight necked exterior, there was a real boy just aching to get out and have some fun. In the child's hand was a data-pad which he immediately put up to his face and, without even acknowledging his siblings, he dove into a flight simulator game that Taylor had referred him to several weeks before. But Taylor could see that the boy's shoulders were high, and that he was very, very intensely focused on the game.

"Come on big O' relax – it's too early to be so stiff!" Taylor insisted as the child settled himself at the end of this growing lineup of his siblings.

Orion Phillip Quentin Matthews spoke very little and, second to Grace, was always judgmental of his brothers and sisters. Best as Taylor could tell, he was his own best friend in his own little world. Taylor supposed that what irritated him most about Orion was how the boy's behavior was so much like himself at that young age, for when Taylor was even younger than Orion, he would often judged those of his own *age group* harshly for their inferior maturity. All he would have to do is listen to Orion for a few minutes to understand that the boy had a matured attitude, and while Taylor respected this, it still annoyed him.

He, Taylor, even went so far as to consult with Dr. Young on how to break the boy's habit of social isolation, but all efforts seemed useless. Taylor debated in his own mind if it was right to try to effect too much change on Orion, thinking to himself how difficult it is to get someone to change without changing who they are or who they are to become.

Nonetheless, Orion frequently judged his siblings by how they decided to have fun, and what they considered to be fun, without ever having any fun himself. On the rare occasion that he would break free of his shell and actually *play* with his brothers and sisters they would be so amazed by this that the boy would quickly become the children's new center of attention.

Taylor looked at his lineup of students and realized that he and the children were sitting, waiting for a good several minutes before the silence was broken. It was Taylor, who stood in impatience.

"What's taking Caitlin so long?" he asked rhetorically as he walked up to her door. This wasn't the first time she'd been late in the morning, and Taylor knew that he would have to move things along himself if they were ever going to keep schedule for the day.

Taylor cyberly activated the com feature of Caitlin's dorm door's side panel. With a flinch all of the other children sat upright as the entire corridor filled with blaring music. The four children plugged their ears, offering excruciating looks of pain on their faces. From what Taylor could tell, the music was classic turned modern; it was a piece that he recognized, but couldn't put his finger on its exact title. Then, with a few familiar high pitched notes of the clarinet he caught the tune in his head. It was Rhapsody in Blue, Gershwin. At over five hundred years old it was one of Taylor's own favorite pieces.

He turned his head to the other four and yelled. "At least she has good taste in music," but he could see that they were not amused.

He took a step to the side and placed his hand on the door of the dorm. The music made it difficult for him to concentrate, but when he did, it subsided and the outside hall could clearly hear the ranting voice of an unhappy girl.

"You always do this to me! I'm almost ready. I'll be out in a minute."

Taylor pulled his hand away from the door and spoke into the com. "Caitlin, how many times have I told you? You need to be on time. To be punctual is the first sign of respect..."

"Oh, that reminds me," she interrupted arrogantly, "how did your meeting go with the council this morning? Unless memory fails, I could've sworn that you were running a little *late* yourself."

"Oh, now she's done it!" Grace said with a smile, as if she delighted in her sister's troublemaking.

Taylor turned a frowning stare to Grace, and in doing so, he noticed his other students. He took in their somewhat fearful expressions with delight. The children all knew what Caitlin had done, and they knew that there was going to be trouble.

Nothing frustrated Taylor more than his students using their powers against him. Keeping the com active, he again placed his other hand on the door. Within seconds, wails of "stop" and "no" and screeches of anger and frustration were heard in the corridor. Shortly after – a ten year old girl stepped out of her dorm wearing an odd assortment of color and fabric.

Caitlin, or Caitlin Diane Elizabeth Matthews, was a postcog, and the price she paid for using her powers to get a *one-up* on her guardian was comical. She revealed herself wearing a pink skirt over blue jeans, yellow blouse with outer orange tank top, and a black hat with a red rose. From head to toe the last thing the children noticed was her mismatched shoes and socks. The dead silence in the corridor gave way to the children's uncontrollable giggles, and even Taylor was amused at his quick and creative dressing technique.

Caitlin offered a screeching growl of frustration and stomped her way to take her place at the end of the four person line.

Taylor followed her stomping trot and after she sat he kneeled to look at her eye to eye. "You are going to have to wear this all day," she instantly offered a face of protest that would've been accompanied by words, but he spoke loudly to cut her off. "AAAND if you don't want me to dress you like this *every* morning, I suggest you do two things. First, I want you to be on time. No, strike that, I want you to plan on being early from now on. At least ten minutes. You knew I had my meeting, and that I would be picking you all up at ten. Here it is, fifteen after, and we have a schedule to keep. You know that each minute you waste is less time you get to spend at the park today."

Taylor watched as Orion turned and offered a punch in the arm to her sister. He gave the boy a glowering stare that told him not to interfere, but when he looked back at Caitlin he was more interested in the details of what his eyes were seeing. He had just noticed only now that she was wearing the same outfit he had seen in a vision before. Yes – when he pulled Johnny out of that last horrible vision of the night and he saw all of his students in the park, this is what she was wearing.

He offered a small grin at her, and she falsely grinned back. This offended Taylor and he instantly snapped, "Second!"

She jumped with a start, and he continued, "If you ever, outside of class time, decide it appropriate to use your powers against me, you will find that I will return the favor from here on out. You are all old enough to understand that you," he said as he turned to glare at the small group, "will be held accountable for your actions."

"And third: If you…" he continued but Caitlin interrupted with a sassy over-tone, "*You said two things, not three…*"

"I know, dear," Taylor said softly, "I'm improvising. And third: If you are re-lying on your powers to show you the past, know all your facts before you act on what you see. I was late because I did not sleep well, and I did not sleep well because I spent a good part of the morning taking care of, Johnny."

Caitlin's eyes widened with fear as her face turned to his dorm room door. "What's wrong with Johnny – what's going on?"

Taylor smiled at this emotional sentiment. Caitlin always looked out for John-ny. That is not to say that the others didn't. But it seemed to Taylor that there was some kind of special older sister-younger brother bond there that didn't quite exist between any of the others. Maybe it had to do with their shared gift, that was a good guess, but it was only that – a guess.

"He isn't coming to class today." Taylor responded. "He had some problems last night 'n' Jay's giving him some tests to make sure he's okay" As Taylor said this he could see concern fall over all the children's faces.

"He's going to be fine. Just fine." Taylor reassured with a degree of certainty in his voice that no-one would doubt, and he quickly decided to stand up and move things along by talking and walking.

"He was having terrible visions and could've hurt himself." Taylor said blandly before turning a thin eyed stare to Caitlin, "That's why he's not coming to class this morning and that's why I was late for my meeting – the results of which I will discuss with all of you later."

Caitlin's face offered a look of apology to Taylor, and slowly she and the other children became worried over their brother's condition with David being the first to inquire.

"Can we see him?!"

Taylor was, really, a big softie, and seeing the eager faces of his students he knew they all wanted to see their brother. He would almost always give in to their requests if their faces offered just the right expressions, or their voices hit just the right tone, but this time he had more than a few reasons to deny this request.

"No, he needs some rest – and to be alone." Taylor replied in a soft yet definite tone. "Jay is working with him to make sure there's no permanent damage. I think it best that this be uninterrupted. Johnny'll be joining us later I'm sure. Now let's move it along, we're already behind schedule."

With these words Taylor and the five kids, like a family of quail, walked the corridor in a short line. With a right turn, then a left they made their way to their first training classroom. All the while, Taylor was sweeping his eyes from side to side looking at the walls and floor. He always took pride in how clean EduCorp was, and at the same time he was always looking to improve this by keeping an eye out for anything out of the ordinary. Today was a good day though, as nothing in the halls caught his attention.

So, standing at the door to classroom W484E, Taylor tapped the side control panel, offered his retinal scan, and within a moment his request to enter was granted.

12 Showing Off

WITH THE GROUP ARRIVING so late to their first class, it was quickly apparent that their tardiness couldn't have worked for the better, for the previous session of students weren't yet finished. With the door open and a roomful of teenagers staring in their direction, Taylor and the children stepped into the large auditorium-style classroom wondering why they were being laughed at. Taylor could see that the last few of the hundred member class were still being scanned while the others waited. This was a group of fifteen-year-olds that Taylor's students often had occasion to follow, and so it wasn't without a few waves and smiles that his own students recognized and interacted with the others despite their age differences. Still, Taylor was taken aback by so many of them laughing almost uncontrollably at his small group. It didn't make sense – until he noticed a few of them pointing. They were pointing – at Caitlin.

They sniggered and chortled away, but a couple of the girls in the class, those who considered Caitlin their friend, did not. They quickly grabbed her by the hand and took her to the top of the classroom, which offered high seats at the back; the perfect place for Caitlin and these two friends to hide – for a while.

The trainer for the previous session, the tall and thin faced Dr. Swanson, with her shortly cut auburn hair and ghostly pale skin, was perceived as so cold that even her own regular students had trouble warming up to her. She had the look of someone who was always nervous, and always upset, but Taylor had accidentally caught a pathic glimpse of her emotional core once, and he knew that inside her deceiving flesh was a woman who was begging for more. If it was more out of life or more out of love, Taylor wasn't sure, but he knew she had a fire inside that he was certain few had ever noticed.

She started filing her class into four equal lines and was nearly ready to escort them out of the room, and it was in this effort that she was by no means slow to the fact that there were two students missing from the teenaged mass before her. She called to them with a befitting shrill tone.

"Jessica Kate, Lisa May come down here right now – we're ready to go – we can't keep Dr. Taylor's class waiting," she shrieked in her laughingly best efforts at a strong and commanding voice.

Three heads popped up from behind different seats at the top of the class. Jessica, Lisa and Caitlin, the last of which was now showing bare shoulders, were looking at over a hundred sets of eyes that were all on them and immediately Caitlin dropped her head behind the seat again.

"You too Caitlin, get down here, right now!" Taylor shouted, but it did little good. The other two girls dropped their heads behind the seats again, and a rustling swelled from the back of the room.

Taylor turned to his teaching counterpart with a smile. "Dr. Swanson would you be interested in a demonstration of kinetic and cyber powers for your class."

She was very familiar with Taylor's abilities, and was instantly flattered at the offer, wanting nothing better than to show him off to her class.

"Oh, absolutely, I think they'd love it," and she turned to her body of students. "Class – class," she squeakily continued. "Now pay attention class. We're going to get a little cyber and kinetic demonstration. So listen up!" She paused, took a deep breath, and continued. "Now class, there are only one in ten million in the world who can do anything beyond telepathy. None in the world has more than one of these extra abilities – except our Taylor here. So you're all going to get a treat as we watch what he can do."

Taylor wanted to correct Dr. Swanson over the fact that Johnny did, in fact, possess two abilities all on his own. But, Taylor, decided against this as the boy was not there, though the teen was sure that if the child was there his lab-coat was sure he'd be getting a little tug, egging him on for the correction. With a deep breath and an aching in his chest, Taylor missed not having the boy there to see what he was about to do.

Taking position at the front and center of the classroom, Taylor motioned for his own students to get behind him and stay close in case there was any panic or confusion. This being done, he raised his hands into the air. This lifted the three girls, yelling and screaming, from their hiding spots and levitated them above the class.

Taylor didn't have to use his hands for any of his abilities save his cognitive ones – and it was only for show that he often utilized them as a way of offering a clue of what he was doing. So, with this useless act of showmanship, he grinned at hearing the oohs and ahhhs from the class. This was a grin that quickly faded though, as he saw that Caitlin had only just put her shirt on straight before she was forced into the open. He was annoyed see that she had properly dressed herself, defying his orders of the morning's discipline. *Wasn't it made clear that what she was wearing was supposed to last all day?*

Taylor tilted up his head and focused on the clothes that were left behind the back seats of the classroom. He levitated these articles to float right beside the three girls.

"Oh this is going to be fun!" he half whispered to his students as they were all laughing at the floating bodies in the air. "Caitlin," he spoke loudly, "I thought I told you to wear those clothes all day." He offered a pause for her response, and when there was none he continued. "Now I'll have to change you back, right here and now, in front of all these students."

"You wouldn't dare!" she bellowed insolently with arms folded in anger.

"Oh, I would." he said, and he looked at Dr. Swanson who was shaking her head with strict disapproval at the idea. He offered her a wink and she lowered her head in fear of what was about to happen.

Taylor looked back at the three floating students and, holding one hand in the air as a show of keeping them in their place, he pulled his other hand to the side...

SNAP

The lights went off. Within a few seconds the familiar wails of "stop", "no" and a new one "not again!" were heard as the class offered giggles at the idea that Taylor could cut out the lights with the snap of his fingers and was good enough with his kinesis to work in the dark.

SNAP

The lights came on and everyone could see that Caitlin was floating above the crowd, dressed the same as she was when she entered the room. The same, that is, except for the last touch. Floating up from behind the seats where the she had changed, a hat came swishing towards her head. After a flailing of her arms and a shaking of her head, Taylor was finally able to put the hat where it belonged – firmly on her noggin.

Cheers came from the class at this display of telekinetic control and Taylor turned his head to look at Dr. Swanson. She was shaking her head with a grin, offering a mix of praise and disapproval at the same time.

Turning his head to the larger class, Taylor grinned. "It's not over yet."

Still holding up a hand as if to keep the three in the air he took his free hand and pushed it outward with a flat palm. Sound of sparks could be heard from the sides of the classroom and all watched with bated breath, including his own students, as the auditorium seats quickly folded themselves to the back of the classroom with a loud crushing noise. These folding seats were remote controlled, and Taylor was, indeed, cyberly manipulating them, forcing them to compress. He then pulled the same hand out and pointed at a door at the side of the classroom that immediately opened and the larger class could see the insides of this storeroom they had never before seen opened. For his own class, however, Taylor had always accessed this storeroom to pull out individual seats that his students would regularly use.

To do this task, he twisted his hand in a funny fashion, curled his fingers, and pulled his hand back strangely. Again, this action was all useless, but offered showmanship on his part, and in doing this he had kinetically forced, with a loud screeching, six chairs and a desk to slide out of the storeroom, frightening some of the larger class until everything had positioned itself into a nice circular group.

To finish, Taylor raised both hands into the air and split the floating group of three girls in two. Caitlin was slowly and gently set in one of the chairs he had just pulled out; the other two were placed with their well entertained classmates.

With more cheers of praise even Jessica and Lisa smiled because their embarrassment was small in comparison to the attention they received as a result of being held by a telekinetic grip.

Satisfied that her class of an even hundred was now complete, Dr. Swanson lead her students from the classroom and as this group left the other four children stepped from behind Taylor and sat in their respective seats. These youngsters, despite their own talents and abilities, were all in awe at what they had just seen. Never, as far back as any of them could remember, had they seen Taylor use his powers like that before. He always used the auditorium switches and remotes to control the seats and physically pulled out the chairs and desk himself. Only on rare occasions, did he ever use his powers in front of them, and even then, he only did very small gestures – move *a* chair – open *a* door. Often he preferred that the children help – physically – with the chore of getting ready for class.

Yes, it was obvious that with two of his students being kinetics, and two being cybers, they could use their own powers to do these tasks just as well, but Taylor had always discouraged showing off to avoid questions and standing out too much.

"Okay class," Taylor said in a formal tone as he watched the last of the fifteen year olds exit with Dr. Swanson following behind, "today's lesson…" He paused. The moment the door closed, he and his students let out small bit of laughter. "Who starts a class like that anyways?!" he asked rhetorically while shaking his head. He was never so formal with his students. He knew that, as a form of protocol, he should be, but this was one standard that relished in breaking.

"Dude, that was so cool – 'specially when the chairs crunched to the back! That was so awesome!" David said loudly spinning his head and his long hair around in excitement.

"I especially liked it when you put the hat on Caitie's head!" giggled Aspen, jabbing her sister in the arm. Caitlin was the only one who seemed at all displeased about the comments. She was stubbornly forcing herself to look angry, even though Taylor could tell that she too enjoyed some of what she had seen and been through.

He smiled and laughed with the children for a moment before continuing in a semiformal tone. "Ahhhhh, even if I saved time by getting this room ready myself, we are running late, kids, so – eh – why don't we just get started."

Orion, who had hardly said a thing all morning, quickly snapped at these words. "But you said you'd tell us about your meeting!" the boy pressed as he watched Taylor use an access panel at the front of the classroom.

"I know, I know," Taylor pleaded as he watched a large rack push itself out from a wall in front of the students. "I'll tell you all about it 'n' answer any questions when class is over."

Pulling six Virtual Reality Training or VRT helmets off the rack, and handing them to the children, he pressed on. "Right now I've got questions of my own that need answering – so helmets on!"

With this stiff command there were moans of distaste that Taylor both expected and ignored. "Helmets on!" he playfully growled.

Donning a helmet himself, Taylor watched with impatience as one-by-one each student pressed a green button on the side of their headpieces. In series they were given retinal scans so the units could verify who each of them was. Then, after the scans were complete, the helmets zipped a strange series of sounds as they resized to each child's head. Finally, with a series of beeps and clicks the appropriate software was downloaded into the helmets through an antenna that pointed from the back of these helmets.

This was all performed in a mere thirty seconds, from the scanning to the resizing to the downloading, and while the system itself was quite efficient, it was an eternity to someone of Taylor's eager disposition, and he sighed with relief as the children's visors simultaneously lowered over their eyes.

He watched each of his students slowly relaxed their entire body and thus the neural training began. Unlike classroom style training, this type of class did not allow that the visors should emit any of the usual flashing bits of light from their edges. Any evolutionary session was actually an advanced form of neural training and development – helping to hone the pathways that improve control over one's evolved powers.

When Taylor was satisfied that his students were well into their training, he initiated his own helmet. The helmet scanned his eyes with a bright bluish purple light, and with a quick zip it pulled itself tightly around his head – almost uncomfortably so, and he adjusted one of the straps to manually loosen it from under his chin.

With his eyes following the visor as it lowered over his vision, Taylor was eventually in total darkness. On activating, the helmet gave him an initial view of the brain activity of his five students. He monitored these, over a period of a minute or so to ensure that their neural activity was normal. He then controlled the helmet by focusing on it cyberly, initiating several tests on himself, as he promised Jay he would, to see if there was any explanation as to why he was having these uncontrolled visions.

Much to his disappointment, the tests resulted in everything being normal. Indeed, most might expect that normal was a good thing, but Taylor understood that if the computer couldn't find anything out of the ordinary, he was no closer to getting an answer to the mystery of his random and uncontrolled visions than before. Frustrated, he decided to consult the huge mass of human knowledge through the SuperNet and thus navigated cyberly inside the helmet to pull up the main WSN screen. He immediately discarded this screen, showing a picture of President Andrews with the caption – *Andrews Administration spawns more advances in science and technology than any other in History.* Another article on the page detailed the capture of a Cyber criminal, and judging by the picture in view, Taylor recognized the story as the same one he had seen the night before on the news.

"Big deal!" the teen muttered under his helmet as he mentally pushed through to a search screen so he might surf the web for some much needed answers.

Since being a cyber, Taylor loved surfing the web – in his mind it was really like surfing – he glided smoothly from one screen to the next – searching for one bit of information – then another – then anther – on and on. What was he looking for? Answers – answers that, apparently, didn't exist. He couldn't find anything that came close to resembling the mysterious sphere he had discovered in Johnny's dorm earlier that morning, and in searching the PNVC – the Precog Network for Vision Confirmation – he saw that no one had experienced a vision showing the destruction of Los Angeles – or at least none that were the same as his and Johnny's. After many minutes of useless searching he grumbled in annoyance and continued bouncing around the net until, after feeling he had exhausted all of his known resources and still coming up empty, he wiped away the external network and focused on the EduCorp internal systems.

Eventually Taylor found some of his own planned courses and initiated a neural development session for himself. These sessions were designed to help improve and develop the powers he possessed. In his mind he reasoned that if he couldn't find answers, the least he could do is spend his time wisely by completing something useful.

It was true that at eighteen Taylor had already taken all the courses EduCorp had designed for his powers years ago, but he wasn't satisfied with this. No – he wanted more. He wanted to better himself – to perfection if at all possible. With this in mind he quietly, that is to say secretly, developed his own advanced programs to continually push his many evolved powers. He never really asked if this was okay by way of the council – but as he always stayed within the company's safety guidelines – he figured what they didn't know wouldn't hurt them – or him.

He changed his virtual display to show the six brainwaves of both himself and his students, making it easy for him to be trained while observing the trained.

With a yawn, Taylor could feel his lack of sleep from the night before pressing down on him and this session had grown so wearily long as over an hour had crept by. Neural development classes normally lasted for over three hours – but Taylor had scheduled this one to be cut an hour short, and in realizing that he still had nearly an hour to go, he felt his eyes grow heavy and bored at watching the unchanging brain patterns of his students. He felt his eyes nodding and his mind wished for either the extreme of something exciting or the calm of sleep.

Then, with a jump inside his helmet that forced his body to stiffen upright, Taylor shouted out with the realization that one of the students was showing an abnormally high peak in their neural activity. Instantly a wash of guilt washed over him for having the thoughts that just passed through his brain.

13 Trouble in Class

"CAITLIN!" TAYLOR SHOUTED, thus naming the student whose brainwaves had become so horribly erratic. The child was showing extreme spikes in the range of precog abilities, confusing Taylor because as he had ever seen, she had never displayed any real talent as a precog.

Inside his visor Taylor enlarged her brainwave display. It expanded to consume his entire view and show, without a doubt, that there was a strong, glowing peak in the precog area, followed in a very close second by a peak in the telepathic range. The two spikes were ebbing in a synchronous dance of dangerous levels, making Taylor very nervous. He quickly returned Caitlin's neural display to normal size and to his ultimate frustration now all of the students were displaying the same throbbing neural peaks; one in the pathic area – another in the precog area.

Panicking, Taylor immediately disengaged their neural training – hoping this would eliminate the peaks. At this, Taylor heaved a grunt of anger. After watching through his visor that the training had cut itself short, the extreme brain levels still persisted. With the thought of doing so and the simultaneous pull of his visor he disengaged his training and quickly tore the helmet from his head.

"Dude, What the hell's going on!?" yelled a surprised voice as, unexpected to Taylor, Jay had just entered the classroom.

"Where the heck'd you come from?" Taylor spewed in a frightened voice as he rushed over to his students.

"Lab L - I just finished my tests with Johnny! What's going on here!?" Jay pressed in an insistent voice as he watched Taylor, who had quickly taken to pacing between the students, putting his hand on their heads one by one. Jay could instantly see that, by the look on Taylor's face, something was wrong, and Jay could see that the children were each flinching in such a manner that definitely as not normal. As the time quickly passed both men grew more trepidatious, and eventually Taylor looked to Jay with a stare of extreme distress. But Jay was still none the wiser to what he had walked in on.

"Come on man, would ya just tell me what's going on...?" Jay shouted, now overflowing with frustration.

"I don't know! They're *all* peaking in precog and not just a little. They're maxing out!" Taylor was talking very loud, and showed that he was even more frightened than Jay, and *that* was really saying something. In walking from one student to the next, the Taylor persisted in trying to reach them by putting his hands on each of their heads. "I don't know what's happening... Damn it, I'm not getting anything!"

Taylor pulled his hand off David's forehead with a wiping aggravation. "It's like their minds are somewhere else – I just – I can't get through!"

"D'you red-line their training?" Jay asked

"Of course – was the first thing I did, but it obviously didn't help!

Taylor was now so terrified, so panicked, that his face swelled a crimson red and his hands started to shake. He had never been locked out of his student's thoughts before – not when they were passive. Something was definitely different, and being unable to really know what was going on, Taylor had no idea what to do.

Jay, with a heaving sigh, went to Taylor's desk and snatched up the VRT unit. "Dude, here!" he said quickly. "Put it on! If you can't get to them from the outside, maybe you can do it from the inside."

"Don't waste my time! They're trapped inside their own heads – I can't just break into their brains with that – it's just not possible!" He pushed the helmet back at Jay, jabbing it into the man's chest while offering a pained stare that clearly showed the teen's despairing frustration.

Jay, in his own way of panic, looked at Taylor with fierce eyes. Jay was about to say something but his words failed him, so he slowly turned his back on the teen. Barely holding the helmet in one hand, Jay stared at the children, and bit by bit he was washed over by his own, more sobering, thoughts.

In Jay's hand Taylor's helmet started beeping a warning as the children's peaks were pushing ever higher levels. It was this noise that forced a memory into the Taylor's brain. In that instant, the teen remembered something deep within his many mental archives, and with a quick snatch he reached out over the desk, his long arms just able to seize the helmet from Jay's grip, making the man turn around in surprise.

"What, what?" Jay repeated quickly in confusion – "But I thought…"

"I've got an idea!" Taylor said shoving the helmet back onto his head.

In activating the headpiece, he quickly saw the same strong neural signals emanating from the children, but, to his relief, they had stabilized at five percent above the red level indicators that Taylor himself had long ago deemed as the critical high. This meant that while their brain activity was extreme, it wasn't necessarily life threatening. He pushed these five neural monitors out of his way with his virtual hand and forced a menu to appear in front of him that he used to navigate cyberly with lightning speed until he found what he was looking for. With a sigh of relief his eyes caught a familiar filename and he immediately downloaded a program that he started to describe to Jay with rapidly spoken words in the real world. True, Taylor wasn't able to see Jay at all, but he knew that the man could hear him just fine.

"I can't believe I forgot about this! Arrrh I'm so stupid. Remember – *Fly on the Wall* – the program I did over four years ago?"

"Sure – but – that's for virtual classes – not for visions or neural training."

Taylor shook his helmeted head. "Actually, I don't think that'll matter much. If they're sharing the same vision I can still jump in and I just might have a chance to pull them all out at the same time."

"Are you sure about this," Jay asked apprehensively.

"Of course not, but it's worth a try. After all – it was your idea!"

Taylor could hear protests from Jay that *this* wasn't his idea, but Taylor was busy with other things. Quickly and with a deep concentration, the teen was recoding the program to work with multiple targets and modified the search parameters to specifically find high end pre-cog signals. Inside the visor this code was spraying itself and changing itself across the screen so fast that Taylor's body, in the real world, was twitching with edginess. Eventually he finished and tapped a few final menu options with his virtual hands until he reached the one that mattered most.

"Initiate!" Taylor whispered this in the classroom while at the same time tapping the menu button. Meanwhile Jay, who was scanning the children's vitals, turned his nose up at this as it was the only noise made in the room for several minutes.

Instantly the teen felt a rush as the menu before was pulled away so fast and with a bright flash of light he saw nothing but an intense white. Then, after a few seconds, his virtual display showed him that it had honed in on one… two… three… four… five… signals. He had expected at this point to be pushed into the same vision with his students, but the computer persisted. It had detected a sixth signal; a signal that Taylor felt confirmed that Johnny was mentally trapped with his brothers and sisters.

With a swirl of bleeding color Taylor was standing, again, in the middle of a barren wasteland where once stood the great city of Los Angeles. He could recognize this scene in an instant as he had so recently visited it in his last vision.

So with familiarity, he felt a chill from the passing of a shadow over him as once again a loud dark object loomed overhead. As expected, it lowered itself closer and closer until Taylor could hear and feel the rush of moist salty air being blown in every direction. Then, to replay what he had seen before, Taylor was again firmly gripped by several hands that were pulling at his feet. His heart was pumping, and he lost all control of thought, his mind giving way to the shock of his future fear – even though he knew – *he knew* that these hands belonged to his kids.

With a great thud of earth and mud around him Taylor was pulled into the same underground cavern that he remembered. He looked around, but something was different. He was still standing – not lying on his back – not fallen and unable to get up. He looked around and, with an instant smile to his expression, he could see the beloved faces of his students; David, Orion, Caitlin, Aspen, Grace, and, to his expectation, his eyes met the tired and somber stare of little Johnny.

"What are you all doing here?" Taylor asked in a quick and stern voice, looking between the children. "And what are *you* doing here?" he added looking straight at Johnny. The boy looked up at him with a shameful expression that contrasted his now *glowing* blue eyes.

"We can't talk now we have to run," the child said stiffly.

Taylor looked at the boy in confusion and became mesmerized by the bright color of the child's eyes. In response, Johnny quickly shook his head. "Run!" he shouted with a fear Taylor had rarely seen on the face of any of his students, and with this in mind, he knew they should heed the warning.

Instantly Taylor directed the six of them down a dark concrete tunnel having almost no light, and it was only with a strange sense of telepathic radar that they were able to navigate the dark passages without running into any walls. Taylor had no idea where he was going, and while Taylor was grateful he had found his kids so quickly, he also had a great fear building inside him that he, at first, could not explain. Then, without any sense of where it had come from, they all heard a loud growling howl that echoed through the chambers. Taylor recognized this sound as the one he had heard before in his previous vision. In the midst of this animal like noise he could hear breaks in the pattern of howling. It sounded more like barking. *Were those dogs?* He wondered, but his mind was too distracted by his focus on his surroundings and feet to worry over what it was that was chasing them. No, to just keep moving was the important thing.

The group quickly passed a side chamber that they did not enter and for unrealized good reason. After skipping its entrance Taylor could hear the same howling noise coming from inside and while he was curious of what was making such a horrific sound, he wasn't curious enough to stick around and find out.

Then, with a rush of thought, the teen instantly started shaking his head. He had to remind himself of his purpose for being in this vision. He called to his students, whose quick running steps he could hear in front of him.

"Hey, I came here to get you out of this place – come on – slow down!" he said shouting into the darkness. After a second or two he could tell that they had slowed their pace, as he was now catching up to them, practically running them over when they had come to a stop.

"Everyone, hold my hands – come on – just – just hold my hands – that's it – I've got a way to get us outta here."

"How can you do that?" asked Orion with a sound of disbelief.

"Just trust me" Taylor said in a heaving voice. "Just hold on."

One by one they grabbed hold of Taylor's hands, three to each, and when this was done he concentrated hard on his VRT helmet back in the reality of the classroom. He focused on forcing it to disengage the *Fly on the Wall* program. This would, Taylor hoped, bring them all back to a state of normalcy and reality.

Not a moment too soon did this effort prove itself to work, for they all started lifting off the ground and shifting out of this virtual world just as Taylor heard a loud crashing noise. Whatever it was that was chasing them – it had crashed through the ceiling of the winding tunnels and through the shifting perspective and the onslaught of light Taylor was only barely able to get a glimpse of what it was that had been on their tails.

They were dressed in some kind of squat armored uniform. I*t must be military,* Taylor thought. They probably had dogs with them, he reasoned. Maybe they were engineered smart animals that could actually talk to each other.

Taylor purged his mind of these thoughts and turned his stare upward and focused on pulling his students out of the vision. He could tell it was working for they were gliding upward through the concrete cavern, but with a jerk and a high pitched scream, Taylor could tell that a weight was released from one of his arms. As he turned his head he could see that Caitlin had lost her grip and was hurtling through the air at a wall of earth and stone. She hit it hard and rolled to the ground while the rest of the group melded through the ceiling of the cavern, and into the bright light of day. He couldn't turn back. Not now!

The wash of sunlight was pulling them into the brightness of release.

The white quickly extinguished to reveal the darkness of Taylor's VRT. He pulled it off, and just in time too, for it had shorted out with the intense activity he had just put it through. He looked around the room and could tell that four of his students were coming round very fast. The program had, for the most part, worked. Clearly, however, Caitlin was still trapped in the vision.

She's more than trapped, Taylor thought in a panic. *She's unconscious, and about to be attacked by whoever it was that was chasing us!* Taylor felt his heart pump so hard and fast he thought his head was going to explode. He shot out of his chair and crouched next to Caitlin's. She showed no signs of arousal and this, Taylor knew, meant that she was in trouble.

She started twitching in her chair and flinch, causing Taylor's heart to ache. His fear got the better of him and his emotions quickly turned to a bleary eyed anger. He looked around for any ideas on how he could just pull her out of her nightmare.

With a fierce stare of determination, he pushed a slowly waking Orion out of his seat, and took the boy's place beside her. He put on the child's helmet and located the modified *Fly On the Wall* program in record time. He initiated the program, hearing mild protests from Jay in the background...

Taylor didn't care what the man was saying. He was more relieved that in far less time than before, he entered the vision and the cavern, arriving at no better place than with Caitlin at his feet. She was unconscious, but still breathing. He tried to move around her and pick her up, but as he made this attempt, he felt his hands and his head hit something hard, something unseen, and something big. He was initially confused by this unseen object in his way, but after slowly *feeling* his way around it he realized that this thing must be one of the military persons that had been chasing them all down the tunnels a few minutes ago. He stepped back in fear, but realized soon enough that this person was frozen. Getting a grip on his thoughts, he remembered the vision he had the night before, where his students were all frozen, except for himself and Johnny.

"Hmmm," he mumbled aloud as a way of confirming his realization of what was going on, but he was still confused as to why he and his students could make out a blurred image of this person before and yet it was invisible now. He jerked his head away and started tending to the unconscious child nearby. To this end, he worked his way around *the unseen*, using his hands every now and again, to get his bearings on its position.

When he had a good, full hold of Caitlin, he looked her over and was happy to see that, other than scrapes from her fall, no other physical harm was done. Looking up, he focused again on releasing the program so that he and Caitlin slowly lifted and shifted out of this virtual vision.

While this happened Taylor had a thought and quickly turned around to face the invisible person nearby. As the virtual reality slowly melded away, and only for a brief moment, Taylor was able to again see the strange short armored uniform of someone that was clearly ready to attack.

Taylor's heart jumped as, at the last second of their transition, the uniform came to life and continued to rush on the rock wall that was near where Caitlin had fallen. The hit was with such a force that debris came crumbling down from the ceiling above and Taylor realized that, had things been offset by a mere second, Caitlin would've been crushed.

With a consuming white that faded to pitch black, Taylor pulled his visor off and fell out of the desk to Caitlin's side. He then lifted her helmet off, slowly feeling her arms and hands for muscle movement.

Nothing.

Taylor shook her, slowly at first, then more violently, trying to wake her up. Her arms started flopping with the efforts and Jay looked at the pair with a shifting face of anguish. Taylor heaved a deep sigh before looking up at his partner – "still nothing."

He scanned her quickly with a handheld version of the wall scanner that was typically used on the children after a class. In an instant he realized that she had no neural patterns to speak of – she was, in fact, brain dead.

"Caitlin. Caitlin, honey – Caity – CAITLIN DIANE ELIZABETH – you wake up right now!" he called to her over and over, his voice becoming more desperate with each effort as he pushed himself to tears. At a final moment of fear, he picked her up out of her seat and kinetically pushed all of the other chairs and desks out of his way before sitting down in the middle of the classroom, the girl still in his arms.

Jay, during all the commotion, was completely at a loss of what to do or say. Remarkably, while Jay was usually the first to panic, the man's resoluteness seemed to stiffen when he knew it was needed. So, seeing his partner at an emotional end, he thought it best to gather the other students and take them out of the room. Walking toward the exit with the children, who were still very much disoriented from their revival, Jay had a very different set of thoughts running through his head than those he mused over shortly after leaving the Council Chamber that morning. He was now certain that the termination of *Prodigy II*, and therefore his job, was close at hand.

Standing at the classroom door, Jay turned for only a moment to gaze back at Taylor. The teen was a pathetic site, holding a child that he had forced to dress so oddly, and was pleading and apologizing for it being done.

When the door opened the sound caused Taylor to lift his head to the departing group. But in the doorway, he noticed a boy standing there with his head hung low. It was Johnny!

"It's not over yet!" the child said in an unnaturally deep and loud voice. The boy then slowly walked in the classroom, not acknowledging Jay or any of his siblings, who had snapped up their heads to look at Taylor. Ignoring all, the boy headed straight for Taylor and Caitlin. Johnny crouched down beside Taylor, who was still distressed and holding Caitlin's hand. Taylor looked into Johnny's eyes and immediately the fear and anguish he had been feeling started to ebb. The teen quickly reached out and pulled Johnny close, giving him the best comforting embrace he could. The boy returned the favor, but then pulled away. The boy the then put hands on the sides of Taylor's head so as to force the two to stare at each other, eye to eye. The boy was shaking his head offering a subdued expression of *no*.

"It's not over..." Johnny said in a whisper, pulling Taylor's hand over to rest it on Caitlin's head. "You can still bring her back," he added softly.

Taylor looked at Johnny in confusion, and only after a long pause did the teen nod in understanding – a memory entered his brain, and when he saw a small twitch in the girls arm as she lay there calm and delicate, he came to understand what it was that he had to do. He stared at Caitlin and, as if overflowing with love, he smiled, pulled her close, and concentrated hard on the girl that he was, so far, unable to rouse.

While Johnny stepped away, Taylor closed his eyes. He forced himself inside her thoughts, using every bit of effort he had inside himself. As he did this he could hear sparks in the classroom. All of the electronics were going berserk and the desks were shaking horribly, clanging hard against the ground. Taylor could tell he was losing his cyber and kinetic control, then everything went black.

In the classroom, after nearly a minute of this chaos, Taylor finally opened his eyes. With Jay by their side, the other students had come back to the center of the room and formed a circle around the pair, waiting to see if Caitlin would be okay.

After opening his eyes, Taylor just sat there, staring at Caitlin as he held her in his lap. She was lying motionless with smooth breathing and a slow rhythmic heart-rate, but he wasn't sure if what he had done actually worked.

Kinetically snatching the hand scanner from the wall again, Taylor activated the unit and slowly moved the wand up her body. He started her feet and progressing upward, noticing on the wall that the wand's data was being transmitted to a large screen.

When he got to her head he leaned over very close to see if he could find something with his eyes that the scanner might miss. He passed the tip of her lightly freckled nose and over her twitching eyes. It was at this moment that her eyes opened wide, and he could see a great fear in them. Her irises were large, but quickly contracted due to the scanning light. She immediately began to convulse and screech in terror, at which point Taylor quickly used his kinesis to hold her arms and legs as stiff as he could.

"Get – Get away – Father! – Get – Get! Father!"

"Shhhh" Taylor offered in a soothing whisper, "you're alright. You're safe now, your back home..." It only took a few seconds for Caitlin to finally calm down, and when she did she closed her tear-filled eyes, took a deep breath, and opened them again, offering a soggy smile.

With Taylor's emotions as they were, he had no choice; he leaned over, grabbed her and lifted her to an embracing hug.

"I'm glad you came back..." she whispered in his ear.

He smiled with a light laugh amid his own tears. "Of course I came back. I had to make sure you weren't getting yourself into trouble – right?" He turned his head and stared with a smile at four half curious, half nervous faces around him.

"Where's Johnny?" Taylor asked in a soft tone, noticing that the boy was missing from the group.

"Johnny?!" asked Jay in surprise. "He's in Lab L – I told you that's where..."

"No. No. He was right here, just a minute ago." Taylor barked in response to this belligerence.

"Noooo." responded Jay in a patronizing two tone. "Come on dude, he was never here." At this point the other students stood in confusion and started staring back and forth between Taylor and Jay.

"No, No!" persisted Taylor, "You were leaving. You opened the door and he was standing right there – right there! You stopped and he walked right by you. Hell, he was the one that told me. He told me not to give up – that I could save her!"

"That's so bogus – not what happened at all!" said Jay with a widening smile to contrast the confused thoughts in his head. "The kids and I were leaving, and when the door opened, you said 'it's not over yet'; caught us all by surprise the way you said it, then you said it again." The children all nodded around Jay, corroborating his story. "Then you said 'you can bring her back' and I think we were *all* confused by that one, but the kids thought you were talking to them, so they all came over. They, eh – thought you had something else up your sleeve." Jay then smiled and half laughed. "And you did, you brought her back."

"No! No! No! Now wait a minute. I saw him here. I saw Johnny right here, I touched him, gave him a hug and everything. He was the one that said I could bring her back..."

It was at this time that Taylor paused and thought for a moment. "When I spoke before, you say I said 'you can bring her back." not 'I can bring her back.'?"

Jay looked at him with raised eyebrows of thought, then nodding, he offered the answer. "You said 'you', not 'I'."

Taylor laughed and shot a confusing smile at Jay. "He was inside my head. Johnny was inside my head, and when he talked, I talked." Taylor spoke with a weak confidence in his voice and this did nothing to reassure Jay that he made any sense.

"That's crazy man! He made you refer to yourself as *you*?" Jay spoke with a tone of understanding and great disbelief. "I - I think I get it now. But..."

Taylor simply beamed. "I don't know how he did it. I don't care. All I know is that right now everything's fine." He pulled Caitlin in for another huge grinning hug that she seemed all too happy to receive.

On releasing her, he could see the stares of his other students. They looked relieved, but at the same time, Taylor couldn't mistake their questioning eyes. They were expectant of an explanation over what was going on. None of them had ever experienced a vision of the future. This included Caitlin, who had only ever had visions of the past. Taylor could tell by the looks in their eyes, that they weren't at all happy with the idea of having a power that could be so dangerous.

"I see the looks on your faces," Taylor started, "and you're right. I think it's about time I explain what's been going on here." He then motioned for the class to take their seats again as he kinetically repositioned the chairs and desks, even bringing out an extra seat for Jay. But Jay was far too busy scanning the children from head to toe, working desperately to make sure that they were all fine. Only when he finished these scans, each time giving Taylor an almost giddy thumbs-up, did the man finally take his seat which, it was quickly realized, was far too small for his large frame.

"Don't you think it's a little late for you to be spilling your guts out now?" Grace said in annoyance.

"Late!" snapped Taylor quickly. "Absolutely it's late. But it's better late than never. Now listen, I know that this is all very strange – and scary. Especially considering what happened to Johnny last night, but I don't want you kids to panic."

As Taylor spoke and his eyes stared over his able bodied students, he couldn't help but let a relax wash over him and relieve the panic he had just been through.

So, with his mind slowly settling, he continued, "I'll do my best to put your mind at ease, but even I can't explain everything, as even I don't understand it all. But, I don't want to keep secrets – so here goes..." Taylor then looked around at his small class. With a deep breath he readied himself to tell them everything he knew, and he felt so relieved. Even though everything was going so wrong just a few minutes ago – right now – everything was perfect and, in a way, he felt as though he had returned to something so familiar – being a teacher.

14 Flexing Mental Muscle

TAYLOR LOOKED INTENTLY at each of his students as he explained the events of the early morning hours and what had transpired in Johnny's dorm, and he could tell by the looks on their faces that they were all concerned for their younger brother.

To their questions of whether he was alright, Jay chimed in and told the children that basic scans of Johnny's brain and body were both normal, so, at least for now, everything seemed fine.

Taylor then continued by explaining that "a strange device," a reference to the sphere, was found in Johnny's room and that he, Taylor, was certain that this object was somehow involved giving Johnny the vision he had experienced the night before.

"Cool, where's it now?" David asked, and while it was rarely that he did so, the boy was listening dutifully to Taylor's every word, his head propped on his hands above his desk.

Taylor frowned at the word cool, then turned to Jay who offered a quick "It's in lab-room L with Johnny. I haven't had a chance to run any tes..."

While Jay was talking, Taylor jumped up and proceeded to run out of the room and down the corridor. Everyone else in the class was confused by this quick departure and after a few minutes, during which time Jay sat uncomfortable and confused in front of the curious eyes of his students, Taylor returned with the sphere. It was now contained in a cylindrical plex container.

"Just as I thought," Taylor said, offering a scowling look to Jay. "This thing attached itself to Johnny again! And I know – *I know* that explains his and – uh – you guys' visions." He said this with an accusing stare to Jay, who simply shrugged his shoulders in apologetic response.

The students crowded around Taylor's desk, and watched as the sphere, which had detected their presence and tried ejecting its small wires at them. This caused an almost eerie tapping noise to emanate from the cylinder. As it seemed, this object had its own personality, for after a few seconds of tapping and flicking its cables around wildly, it seemed to realize that it was in some type of confinement and threw what Taylor was sure looked like a tantrum. The containment cylinder shook violently with the motions of the sphere inside and the tapping quickly turned into loud banging noises as the sphere attacked the sides of its prison with its needle-like probes.

"Take this back to the lab," ordered Taylor, who was barely able to keep a good hold of the sphere with his hands. "Put it in a containment locker, and bring the cart when you come back." By the sound in Taylor's voice, it was clear he was still upset that Jay had left Johnny alone with the sphere. All Jay could do in response was lower his head in shame as he grabbed the cylinder from Taylor and exited the classroom.

Taylor watched as Jay struggled to keep a steady hold of the containment cylinder. Watching the sphere leave the classroom suddenly reminded Taylor of Dr. Hathaway. Jay, who was practically out of the room, seemed to pick up on this half pathic thought, and he rounded on his heel, offering a quick series of pathic worries.

"Does she know what just happened to Caity?"

"Would she tell the council?"

"Are they on their way right now?"

"Slow down," interjected Taylor through Jay's thoughts, "Even if she got a recording of all that just happened, I'm sure the council would be more interested to know the details of the vision rather than the fact that this machine had once again, forced an adverse reaction on the children. We've already established that."

"Come on man, the council's got a right to know what's going on. Dude – if somebody's gonna tell them it might's well be us." Jay insisted pathically.

"And what should we tell them?"

Jay looked at Taylor and, had the man been several years younger Taylor was sure he would have shrugged his shoulders in an "I don't know" fashion. Instead Jay gave a look that made his eyebrows to all the work.

"Dr. Hathaway wouldn't instigate any more than she had to – it would draw too much attention. She could get into real trouble if she's involved, *as I'm certain she is.*"

Taylor shifted his stare to a more submissive expression. "Listen – give me 48 hours. Let me find out all I can about what's going here. The last thing we need to do is give a report to the council that sounds completely insane. Besides, telling them anything now would also prove that we withheld vital information during our presentation this morning. That's tantamount to telling a lie!"

Jay backed his head in surprise; he hadn't thought about that. But then again, they didn't lie – they merely worked the truth around their words and the facts.

"If I can offer a good enough explanation for what's been happening," Taylor continued, "and I've got proof to back it up, then there's a chance we could avoid an investigation."

Jay nodded his head. "Two days," he said pathically and his look quickly changed as if he was asserting his control on the matter. Taylor then looked at his watch as a show of checking the time.

Interestingly to Taylor, though, as he looked at his watch, he was filled with a deeply rooted sense that in far less than two days things would be changing drastically in his world – but he wasn't sure how, and this feeling fleeted the moment he noticed the pressing stares of his students.

"In the meantime," Taylor pathically continued, trying to ignore the faces David was making at the sphere in the cylinder, which had for the moment become far less active. "In the meantime, let's try to keep things running normal for the children. I don't want them to panic over what might happen if things should turn for the worst."

"Are you finished yet?" spoke a child's voice in the background of the voiceless conversation, forcing Taylor and Jay to break their telepathic link. "Yeah," whined another voice, "are we going to just sit here all day and stare at you two giving each other funny looks or what?" Aspen and Orion both were offering very impatient looks, and, when glancing around the class, Taylor and Jay both offered very awkward and exposed expressions, realizing that their conversation had, indeed, lasted long enough.

"Right," said Taylor. "Go on. Go get the cart, and make sure" he continued in a louder voice as Jay walked away and down the corridor, "you put *that thing* in a place where it can't get into any trouble."

He turned to the class as the door closed, "I think that the Neural Development side of today's class is done," he said, offering a caress of Caitlin's face before slipping the class a sideways smile and continuing, "now for the practical side."

There were a few confused stares between the students, "Practical side?" they all questioned in unison.

"That's right," Taylor replied with a pained expression at having them bellow the same thing simultaneously at him. "We've offered our data to the council for your progress last year and, so far, haven't heard anything negative, so I think the next step is to start some practical sessions for your powers."

Now typically, when it came to the common talent of telepathy, neural development and practical sessions were instant and simultaneous due to the fact that fledgling telepaths could easily communicate with each other through their new-found gift. This common ground on which most of the planet now sat offered nearly everyone this easy avenue of training, learning, and practice. With any of the other four powers, however, there were no true forms or designed protocols for how to train the brain, how to improve the control and use of these abilities. Much of this was due to the rarity of anyone who actually possessed those powers. Taylor became well aware of this in his research, design, and customization of the *Prodigy II* experiment for his students. So, to compete with this lack of protocol, he had already put into play a series of quick one-on-one demonstrations and training sessions with his students whenever he had the chance.

Taylor himself had, of course, been trained at EduCorp to use his own powers quite well, but he was matured beyond his years, and it seemed as part of the nature of *Prodigy I,* that all aspects of his training should reach the highest levels possible, including finding what limits, if any, his evolved powers would have. With his own students, however, it was decided shortly after their inception into *Prodigy II* that because of the nature of that program and the condition of the students; prudent control and a general sense of what Taylor understood as *neglect* should be exercised with regard to their powers. The idea was simple – don't harvest the fruit and eventually it will wither away. Taylor had an instant disrespect for this order, an order to neglect training the children to use their powers. With this also came a general disrespect for the department chair, Dr. Richardson, who issued the order.

Taylor very quickly decided to ignore that order, believing in time, that he could simply explain to the council that their abilities were developing on their own and that there was little he could do to stop it. In turn, privately teaching these children to harness their abilities seemed the wisest choice because without the training, they had a greater chance of harming either themselves or others by accident. So through this effort, in Taylor's one-on-one sessions he would ask for some short display of his abilities and see how far the child in question had progressed since their last session. He would take copious notes on the results of these demonstrations and do his best to integrate the data into his neural development training. Still, however, Taylor had never instigated any formal, physical training in the classroom or any way by which the children could really push themselves.

Considering how close these children were to being released, Taylor had decided weeks ago that after this last presentation to the council, it would be a good time to put their abilities on the table – train them how to control and when to use their powers. He had already seen so many small displays of this on a daily basis, so bringing that into the classroom seemed the next logical step, and with this in his mind, and the start of his first practical session about to begin, Taylor continued to address the class.

"With the exception of today," Taylor said loudly before softening his address, "because I've already worked it into the schedule, your school sessions will now be *extended* to make time for a full hour of this new practical development course." He scrunched his face after saying this, fully expecting to receive groans and complaints at even the slightest hint that their workload was going to increase. To his relief, however, he received a more than warm reception to this change.

"You mean," started Aspen with a high tone of excitement. "You mean now you're going to really, REALLY show us how to use our powers?"

"Absolutely, and in time I want you to show each other what you've got – what you can do – nothing holding you back."

"So now we can use our powers whenever we want?!" David said as a half excited question to which Taylor held up his hand with a slight sense of nervousness.

"Eh – in the classroom – sure!"

Coming belated, Taylor now heard the groans he was expecting earlier as the children were all clearly irked at the idea of still being restrained. Despite this noise, Taylor thought silently in his mind for a moment. He understood their feelings quite well for he, as a young and extremely powerful student, found that being unable to really let loose with what he could do was a lot like being in a cage with an enormous amount of bottled up energy. He looked around at the faces staring up at him and created an image in his head of his six children all in cylinders like that mysterious sphere. Cramped in the fetal position, and convulsing inside, just dying to stretch their limbs. Yes, not being unable to really let loose and push their powers to the limit felt a lot like that.

"Fine," he snapped, forcing the five of them to flinch. "Here are the rules!" At this point the children quickly cued to an upright position, fully hanging on Taylor's every word. "I won't put any limit on the use of your powers in public as long as you stick to the following: YOU MAY NOT," he said loudly…

"Harm other people,

Harm each other,

Harm your teacher" and at this point Taylor jerked his head to imply that he was referring to Jay. "Unless, of course, it is a clear matter of self defense there will be no reason to break or even bend these rules."

Taylor was about to continue with the class when he thought better of it and added, "And just because you're not hurting someone does not mean you can 'play with them," he gave a strong stare at David and Aspen, "and you cannot change the natural function of any public service machine." He turned and gave the same stare to Orion and Grace.

He then turned to Caitlin, "And you..." he looked at her and thought for a few seconds, "don't get too nosey." She giggled and Taylor scanned his students looking for a reason to stop the lesson dead. They were all nodding, though somewhat unconvincingly, in acceptance of his stipulations.

"Your powers make you very special. You all have your I.D.'s with the special insignias on them – well, those actually mean something – and it means that you still have to obey the laws that restrict the use of your powers and that there's a great deal of responsibility in using those powers. So I expect that these rules will not be a problem!"

Taylor finished this verbal contract with a firm and menacing stare – at which point his eyes were met with several nodding heads.

"Now over the next few weeks we'll be going through lessons that I designed myself. And I will do my best to explain to each of you, the abilities you possess and the reason for the day's lesson. You will also notice that I will be showing the use of my own powers a lot more. I can only hope that in showing you what I can do, I'll also show you some of the things you can do, and how far you can really go."

Eager looks of anticipation were glaring at Taylor and, as if with perfect timing, Jay entered with a cloth covered cart. He wheeled it before class and Taylor, with a small flit of kinetic effort, caused the simple cover to fly up into the air, across the room, and hang itself on a VRT helmet hook on the wall.

"Now, kids, we have brought you several carefully thought out items that we will use to test and benchmark your powers. But first I need separate you into pairs." When he said this, a resounding "huh" came from the group and it was clearly obvious what their confusion was. There were five students, "You can't make pairs with only five of us." stated Orion very matter-of-factly.

"Well, there's no doubt about your math," Taylor said while staring the boy down. "I plan on being the sixth person."

Taylor knew, with the group as it was, that defining the pairs really wasn't necessary because the children's powers pretty much did that already, but he decided, as a matter of protocol, that he should still call out the names so that the kids didn't try to mess up his already laid out plan for the day's lesson.

"Now, Orion, Grace you'll be the first pair. Aspen and David, you're the second, and Caitlin, I'm with you."

The teen walked up to the cart and grabbed a handful of small items. "First thing's first," he said holding them out, "When you use your powers it can take a lot out of you, so I want each of you to eat a *Protobar* before we get started. Now I got 'em in all flavors, so come and take what you like."

He walked between the students and, with each grabbing their flavor of choice, they started eating.

"I hope none of you is too picky about what you eat," Taylor said as he eyed Aspen through a sideways glance. "We'll be eating one of these at the start of each of our practical sessions.

After about a minute's wait, Taylor held out his arm. "Now, Orion and Grace come on up here." Despite how simple this request was, when he turned to look at the two now chocolate faced children, they were shaking their heads fearfully. "Come on guys, all I want you to do is stand right here." Taylor pointed at a spot right beside him.

With lazy, whining protests, the two reluctantly got out of their seats and walked slowly to the center of the room – each punching and pushing their partner as they walked. "Geeze!" Taylor said testily, wiping their faces with the sleeve of his own lab-coat. They were reluctant to receive the attention, which only made Taylor laugh.

"Now Jay has been kind enough to order through the M-Gen Network, these robotic K9-2600s – they weren't cheap – so be good to them."

Jay walked up to the cart and pulled out two small, odd, mechanical objects that Orion thought looked all too much like a set small metallic beach balls. Jay set them down and pushed a small blinking button on the tops of each of them. Instantly a strange clicking noise resonated through the room, and with the sounds of mechanical servos and actuators, the metal balls sprouted arms and legs that eventually supported the remaining *bodies* to a point of standing on all fours. Thereafter a head slowly emerged from each of the bodies, and an antenna sprouted from the backside, mimicking a real-life tail.

"Now everyone here knows that both Grace and Orion are cybers." Taylor said loudly in a lecture style. "Let's define what that really means."

"Oh, come on!" Grace said harshly. "Everybody knows what that means!"

"Yeah – Duh," added Caitlin.

Taylor, expectant of an outburst, turned an arrogant smile to the two girls, put his finger to his mouth, offering a soft "shhhhh!"

"Oh, sorry," Caitlin apologized, but Grace merely frowned.

"Being a cyber obviously means that these two can control machines." Taylor continued, putting his hands respectfully on Orion and Grace's shoulders. "They can control all machines and computers as long as those devices receive, via electromagnetic waves, information from the outside world."

"It is a strange thing," Taylor continued, "but the minds of cybers have found a way of receiving and transmitting electromagnetic signals that instantly match and adapt to the requirements of their targets. These signals carry the most basic of binary functions. In the right combinations, which aren't too hard for a cyber to decipher in an almost rudimentary fashion, these signals can force a machine to do as they wish."

"Jay, if you please."

Jay pulled from the cart a small control pad. On it, he pushed a series of buttons and levers, thereby commanding one of the robots to move. It walked forward clunking weakly with each step.

"Jay, make it sit up," commanded Taylor, "you know, like a dog would." Jay responded with difficulty; making the robot slowly slump down on its hind quarters with a clunk. It then awkwardly raised its front body into the air and, one at a time, pulled its front legs upward so as to mimic the way a real dog would normally sit-up.

"That was horrible." Taylor said in a false condescending tone, "What took so long?"

"The controls, man." Jay said. "There are so many freakin' buttons. It's a pain."

"Right you are, right you are... Now, Grace, I want you to make the other robot do exactly the same thing, but I want you to concentrate. Concentrate hard, and see if you can get it to do it like a real dog would."

She turned her head to Orion and sneered, "Easy."

Looking at the other robot she stared at it for only a fraction of a second before it took two steps forward and quickly assumed the same pose as the first. The movements of her K-9 unit were simple and lifelike. She then offered a quick wink to her nearby brother, and the class all watched as the K-9's rear antenna, scanned back and forth; offering what was unmistakably the look of a wagging tail.

"Very nice. Very nice." Taylor said with a beaming expression.

"So, Orion, I'll let you pick a task you want your robot to do... tell us what it is first, then go for it."

He looked around the room for an idea, and eventually the perfect task came to mind.

"Excuse me – Jay, can I see that remote for a second."

Jay looked at the boy with surprise and handed the unit to him.

"Now Orion," interjected Taylor. "You're supposed to use your kinesis for this, not the remote."

Orion looked from under his jet black hair and gave Taylor a sideways, still slightly chocolate latent grin. The boy threw the remote across the room, called the word "fetch" and instantly offered focus to his robot. It sprang into action and galloped smoothly and seamlessly across the room, like a true animal. Then, at the right moment, it jumped high into the air and caught the remote magnetically with its beak.

When the robot landed it walked back to the children, who greeted it with applause.

"You were supposed to tell us what you were going to do!" said Taylor with a tone of disapproval.

Orion sneered, "I said 'fetch' didn't I?"

Taylor threw up his hands. "Okay, whatever." He found it difficult to do anything but give-in after seeing such an impressive display of cyber abilities.

Orion took the remote and offered a sideways smile at Grace, "Your turn!" he said and he quickly threw it into the air again. Thinking fast, Grace sprang her robot into action, but, to add flavor, she forced hers to do a back-flip in its jump to catch the remote. More cheers were heard from the others while Taylor fiercely shushed the group down – all the while keeping a wide grin on his face from the positive energy that had circulated the room.

"Now that was very impressive." Taylor said to the both of them, as Aspen handed him the remote.

"Jay..." he called in an arrogant tone "Think you can top that?"

"Dude, are you kidding..." he said and he started offering movements that resembled some odd robotic run, making the students laugh.

"Now, Aspen, David, it's your turn," Taylor said and he motioned for the other two to have a seat. They quickly responded by forcing their robots to jump onto the cart. Half way through the air though, the K9's had retracted their arms, legs, and heads so that they thudded into the cart as a solid metallic lump exactly the way they were before Jay had removed them from it.

David and Aspen stood up as the others took their seats. It had been plainly obvious to the group that each of the pairs was designed to match abilities and while it needed no announcement, Taylor worked to keep the rhythm of the class.

"We all know that David and Aspen here are kinetics." Taylor said in a matter of fact way. "So I've brought simple weights for them to work on."

Taylor then turned to the cart and after a few seconds several small metallic objects started to float across the room and set themselves in front of the two students.

They both giggled as they could see that these weights were so small in size. Why, each one couldn't possibly weigh more than a few ounces.

"Dude, they're like totally small!" David said with a smile. "Honestly, like, that's the best you could do?"

Aspen giggled as well and in response Taylor lit a grin.

"Laugh if you want, you two, but these are no ordinary weights. They are electronically controlled."

Taylor was now speaking very haughtily as, in series; light popping sounds could be heard from the weights followed by several loud bangs that resonated through the whole room.

"The popping that you hear," explained Taylor, "is the instantaneous fusion of the material at the weight's center. The core then becomes so dense that its gravitational force is increased to a much higher degree, thus inducing the loud bang of weight against the floor."

"Hmmm" offered David with a nod of understanding.

"That's right, these things may look small, but the heaviest of them is over two thousand pounds, and in a moment you're both going to raise them from the floor – if you can."

The whole class was now staring at these little units, mesmerized at the idea that something so small could reconstitute itself at such a heavy weight.

"Right now," said Taylor so loudly that he surprised the class, who listened as he continued much more softly. "Sorry – uh – right now there isn't to explain how the power of telekinesis works." he said looking at each of the young faces around him. "Kinesis, the short term, is the ability to move objects with one's mind. But how is it that this can be done? While most around the world understand how cybers work, kinesis remains a bit of a mystery. It is clear to the scientists here at EduCorp that, in ways unknown and unobserved so far, kinetics have the ability to manipulate the gravitational and electromagnetic attractions of specific objects – this includes particle masses that are shapeless such as air and water. Again, they haven't quite figured out how the brain of a kinetic does this, but it is one of the most powerful and handy gifts when used frequently, and with control."

Finishing this short explanation he turned to David and Aspen, offering them a nodding signal that they should try to lift the weights.

David bowed to his sister, "Ladies first!"

Aspen stepped forward and stared at the several weights. Figuring she didn't want to be such a show off like Orion or Grace, she opted to lift the smallest weight first. She was able to raise this object, weighing a mere pound, high above the ground with ease.

On seeing this Taylor quickly decided to chime in. "Good! Why don't you take turns; work your way to the heaviest?"

David nodded at this, took his turn, and in this fashion the two children continued until they reached the heaviest weight. Aspen, with a deep furrow of her brow, worked very hard to lift this final weight into the air, and with nervous looks from her siblings, she was able to do so, even though the weight wobbled precariously back and forth.

Those around her offered gasps, which Taylor followed with a singular applause as an offering of congratulations.

"Unless I am mistaken, you're the first ten year old in the world to lift 2000 pounds all on her own, with no outside or mechanical assistance. I should've got the press here to see this one..." He said this jokingly, but just the same, he could have been serious, and no one in the room would have thought the worse of it.

Seeing how hard his sister had worked, David took a deep breath and stood in front of the same weight. He concentrated with all his might while at the same time having an almost pained expression on his face, and eventually he forced the weight to shift and move. As the seconds quickly passed, the boy continued to push his mind further into focus in an attempt to lift the object into the air.

Taylor, whose eyes were on the weight itself, noticed that its top button had slowly started to compress. He stood, ready to call out in an effort to break David's concentration, but it was too late.

With a pop the button was fully pressed, and, as if a canon had shot it off, the silver weight flew straight into the air, crashed through a light fixture and went on into the ceiling.

David's horrified expression was quickly hidden as he leaned over and buried his face in his arms and a swish of blond hair. Taylor, on the other hand, immediately used his own kinetic abilities to make sure that the falling debris avoided any contact with the students who were sitting below.

When silence finally returned to the class from the commotion and calls from the other students, Taylor addressed his students while also using his powers to clean up the mess.

"David," he started, "You were trying too hard. I saw it – while your mind was trying so desperately to handle the weight, you started pressing the activation button. My apologies," Taylor continued lightly, "but I didn't have time to warn you."

During Taylor's words a nearby storage closet opened up and out from it rolled a strange unit that none of the students recognized. Taylor on the other hand, had used it several times; namely to clean up Grace's many experimental messes. This device looked something like a pyramid on wheels, and Taylor kinetically placed it just under the area that had been damaged by David's kinetic efforts. He pressed a few buttons to turn the unit on before cyberly controlling it.

"This," Taylor said looking at his students, "is a ReConstructor 5000."

With simultaneous callings Taylor heard the questions of "What does it do?" and "How does it work?" at the same time.

Taylor grinned at his curious watchers. "This machine scans a structure for damage then uses its internal M-Gen to repair any discrepancies."

Taylor then looked intently at a side display, and, focusing on its readout, fed commands directly into the machine from his own brain.

"It works by analyzing reference schematics that can be either scanned or digitally transmitted into its database. In this case, we are going to use the EduCorp archives to get a picture of this room as a reference."

Taylor continued to stare at the display, "Got it!" he said aloud, and shortly thereafter strange lights started beaming from the top of the machine. The children watched in awe as the lights moved all around and focused on the nearby floor, and thereby consumed the fallen debris. After a few seconds, the beams moved straight upward and started de-replicating and re-replicating the light fixtures and ceiling that had been damaged. After a moment, a strange beeping suddenly emanated from the pyramidal unit.

"As could be expected," Taylor said, looking over five curious faces staring at him with very thought-thick expressions. "It found a foreign object in the ceiling. It's going to remove it, and re-replicate it here on the floor.

"Must be the weight," said the very somber voice of David.

"You can't be so hard on yourself," Taylor said as we he walked over and squatted in front of the boy. "It's a mistake anybody could make..." he paused and thought for a moment, "well not just anybody, it takes a special person to shoot a blunt piece of metal into the air like a rocket just with their brain, but still, it's easy enough to fix, and when I'm finished you'll never know anything ever happened – so relax!"

Instantly Grace stood up in mild protest. "That's how you cleaned up my room so fast! But you said it took hours – you said it took loads of paperwork – you said..."

"Hey, hey hey" Taylor cut in, and he knew that while she was acting angry, she was really only playfully frustrated at discovering what had been an obvious ruse.

"I made you believe it was hard so you'd really *really* think before making any more messes or explosions – I didn't want it to be a regular occurrence."

"How'd that work out for you?" Grace replied sassily, to which Taylor only smiled and shook his head. He turned to walk back to the machine, which had signaled its completion. It was at this time that the teen suddenly picked up a stray thought emanating from David's mind which he instantly felt compelled to reply to.

"Don't worry so much about the fact that Aspen beat you... By the time you're finished with your training, you'll be so much more powerful than you are now!"

Taylor looked around at his students, who were offering faces of disbelief, "Trust me!" he said and with this he raised his hands. Simultaneous with this action a popping noise could be heard which signaled the fact that the newly replicated weight had been reactivated and immediately thereafter all of the weights lifted from the floor.

"That's over six thousand pounds!" whispered an awe stricken Orion. This instigated a series of 'oohs' and 'ahhhs' before Taylor decided to up the ante and he turned his head to concentrate on the cart, the ReConstructor, and just about anything else he could see that wasn't attached to the floor. Before long there were dozens of objects floating in the air, and Taylor, not breaking a sweat, turned to his jaw-dropped, flabbergasted students. Whatever you can do now with your abilities... in a few months you'll be able to do a whole lot more!

15 Caitlin's Power

WITH A CAREFUL RELAXING of his kinetic efforts, Taylor slowly lowered the many items he had raised into the air so that they delicately returned to the floor, at which point he received a well deserved, but small applause. The teen then motioned for Caitlin to come to the front of the class. She, albeit thrilled with what she had just seen, quickly lowered her head with a look of obvious contempt.

"What's the point?" she whispered in a pout. Taylor smiled at this, with a hidden understanding.

Her post-cognitive ability was something Taylor termed as *passive*. By his own definition, a passive ability is one that "cannot effect a physical, measurable change in a person's surroundings." Under this definition telepathy barely qualified as more than a passive ability, and precog and postcog abilities were strictly passive.

"The point is," said Taylor, kneeling in front of her "You have a gift to see things that others cannot."

"Aaaaaannnd!" she said irritatingly.

"And, as I have told you many, many times before, knowledge gives you more power than any physical or active ability." Taylor now looked between all of his students with a harsh lecturing stare that ended on Caitlin's frowning face. She huffed and folded her arms in front of her while forcing Taylor to shake his head in an almost playful gaze.

"Fine," he said softly, "I'll ask for the rest of the class to help me." Taylor was hoping that this would force Caitlin into action, but she persisted in her angry stance; arms folded, eyes blandly scanning the classroom, as she chewed her own tongue indignantly.

"Well," Taylor said quickly, "let us begin." Out of the cart floated a tray that eventually rested on Taylor's ready hand. The children all stared curiously, seeing that the tray had several brightly colored cubes on it.

"On this tray I have ten different cubes," Taylor spoke softly as he paced in front of his students, who each stared at the tray intently, confused that, considering the large scope of the previous tasks, this was something so small.

"I want to know if any of you can tell me which one of these cubes has the letter *C* underneath it."

The children looked between each other with understanding. It was clear that none could simply pick a cube and be right unless they had some kind of insight; Caitlin's sort of insight. The children turned a cautious stare in her direction. She whipped herself around angrily – ignoring her brothers and sisters almost out of spite.

This is not to say that Caitlin was being overly rude – or difficult, - well *maybe* difficult. But in her heart and in her mind she always envied her brothers and sisters for their powers, regarding her own as nothing more than a waste. Even at that moment, in her mind, she tossed around the idea of lifting heavy weights, operating robotic canines and the like as being so much more impressive than just picking out a stupid block.

The children, impatient for any kind of response from their sister, turned back to the tray, and it was Grace that pointed to the first cube.

"That one!" she said loudly, pointing to the one painted a deep emerald green.

"Are you sure - because if you are wrong, I have already arranged that instead of going to the Los Angeles Metro Park, we could spend the rest of the day cleaning the EduCorp halls, from floors 250 to 275. – So you might want to really think about this if you're going to condemn everyone to a day of hard labor."

Suddenly a quick "Oh great! *Toddlerville* – I don't think so!" popped out Grace's mouth, and she immediately retracted her hand from the tray, as did the rest of the students who were all now very unsure of attempting guess on this challenge. They each turned their stare to Caitlin, who was ill aware of the attention she was again receiving.

Caitlin, her curiosity rising, did eventually turn to the others for a fleeting moment, and Taylor, seeing her stare, immediately pressured the other four. "Well, come on. If someone doesn't guess quick I'll just call a forfeit and you'll still clean the halls."

Caitlin suddenly envisioned the five of them walking the halls; David and Aspen using their telekinesis to do the cleaning, and Orion and Grace manipulating some cleaning machine with their minds, while Caitlin herself would be stuck with a bucket and a primitive scrub brush to do hard manual labor. She could see herself somewhere in those 26 floors of children younger than her, all surely making fun of her appearance and her work. She could see this clearly in her head as if looking at pictures out of some Grimm fairy tale.

"Well fine," said Grace quickly, "if we have to pick one…" and she raised her hand to point at the tray. The other students however, decided to rush their hands on the tray to do the same and quickly Taylor pulled the tray away.

"Only one pick," he said quickly, "That's it."

Taylor glanced out at Caitlin, and whether out of interest or fear, she whirled around, offering him a harsh stare from beneath her hat...

"Oh, fine," she said loudly, "you win!"

She huffed her way over to the small group, and with Taylor's beguiling smile, she found it hard not to return this with a grin of her own and a light laugh. As irritated as she was, she had to appreciate his well laid plan of trapping her into playing along.

With the other students standing around her, Caitlin placed her hand over the tray, hovering about an inch above the cubes, and closed her eyes. The others looked between themselves and their sister in thick curiosity.

Caitlin suddenly grabbed David's hand and as if he had no control to do so, he grabbed Grace, who grabbed Orion, who grabbed Aspen, who finally grabbed Taylor. They were all now hand in hand with their eyes tightly closed.

Everything was completely black, then, in a flash of color, the group found themselves standing in a room whose center had the familiar looking cart. Beside it Jay was sitting at a table, placing the many colored blocks on the silver tray. He had put them all in place then, looking between them, he picked up the red block, grabbed a paint brush, and proceeded to carefully paint a black letter "C" on it. He blew on it softly in an attempt to dry the paint before replacing the cube carefully on the tray. On seeing this David and Aspen both sneered aloud in the class at Grace for she had chosen the wrong block.

Jay stood and proceeded to carry the tray to the cart when, something startled him.

"How's it coming?"

It was Taylor, who had entered the room without Jay noticing, and with this quick question, had frightened the man to the point of jerking his arm, stumbling and dropping the tray of blocks.

"Dude! Don't doooo that!" said Jay fretfully.

The Taylor of the present, along with the children, could not help but laugh.

"You know," said the Taylor of the past, "we're all going to get a kick out of that when we see it again later!"

Jay ignored the comment and slowly picked up the blocks and carefully placed them on the tray *again*.

Suddenly, with a quick rush of darkness, the entire group felt itself being pulled from the vision, and in a rush, they were dropped back into the reality that they had left only a moment ago.

Caitlin pulled her hand back, opened her eyes and looked up at Taylor. All those around her, along with Taylor, were slowly reviving and when Caitlin knew that she had Taylor's attention she, without pointing, or gesturing in any way, simply opened her mouth to speak.

"The red one." she said boorishly.

Taylor, set the tray down on one of the nearby desks and with a quick bit of kinesis the ten pieces turned themselves over to reveal that the red block, as expected, had a black letter "C" painted on its bottom.

"Now for the explanation!" said Taylor.

All of the students rounded on their desks and took their seats while Taylor made his way to the center of the group.

"Postcogs have the ability to see things in the past because of one simple fact. Every living thing on this planet survives by the presence of electronic impulses that rush constantly through their bodies. Where these pulses come from, and where they go when we die, that's a point for theologians to discuss – and most certainly isn't the point of *this* class.

What is important for this class is to know that every thought, every emotion, every sight and sound that we experience and even so much more that engrains itself in our subconscious – all of it is registered by these electronic impulses. A postcog's brain has the ability to pick up on a trail of these thoughts and impulses because no matter where we go or what we do, we usually leave a residue of these behind."

"Usually through touch, a postcog can ride these residues back through time to specific event, or even a series of events of when those impulses were first experienced. With enough concentration the postcog can control the *when* of what they see – but usually only the strongest or most recent impressions are what they get first."

Caitlin squirmed in her seat with discomfort. All during this lecture her siblings were constantly staring back at her, as if trying to find out what it was that made her brain function so differently. She stuck her tongue out at Aspen and Orion on more than one occasion to keep their stares on the teacher and not herself.

Continuing the lecture, Taylor cyberly dimmed the lights and brought up a video presentation on one of the walls of the classroom.

"The discovery of post-cog abilities has lead to one of the most radical changes in human history: a true way to determine guilt or innocence without the *opinion* of twelve men or women to decide the outcome."

Taylor attempted to continue, but was interrupted by an outburst from Orion.

"This is old school."

David continued, "Yeah, we learned this a long time ago."

Taylor stopped the video in frustration. "Yes, I know you learned this a long time ago. What I am trying to teach you, and show Caitlin, is that her ability has caused legal changes and ramifications that have helped the human race to better itself. So listen up, do not interrupt, and maybe... just maybe, you'll learn something today that you didn't learn from your virtual teachers."

Taylor quickly continued the presentation, "Anyways – before the discovery of postcogs, crime was at an all time high. The planet had not yet condensed itself into the 554 metroships that it has today, and, being spread all over the planet, we were causing damage and chaos not only to ourselves, but to the fragile world on which we lived. And it was nearly impossible to really tell who was doing wrong because we only had physical evidence that could circumstantially point to wrongdoers – not offering any jury or judicial system the confidence of knowing, for a fact, who committed a crime."

"When the United States Government did finally decide to use witness protected postcogs to track down criminals and determine guilt or innocence, crime declined at a rate never before seen. Those who did wrong by the law would have their guilt determined by a pair of postcogs. The decision to use two separate postcogs helped ensure redundancy and improve definitive confirmation. As a result, the decision of the court was definite. No guesswork. No appeals. The visions of the past were absolute – and seen exhaustively several times over to ensure completeness."

"Violent crimes all but disappeared within a year of utilizing the post-cogs, and with a retrospective use, the culprits of crimes committed long ago were sentenced and punished, while in many cases their convicted, innocent counterparts were pardoned and released."

Aspen spoke up, curious of this part of the lecture. "But I don't understand. We can know how a crime *was* committed, but how does that prevent future crimes? I don't get it! Wouldn't that be a precog's job?"

Taylor smiled, happy to engage his student's question. "We'll talk about precogs later – but to answer your questions from the post-cog side, think of it this way. If you knew that there was no crime you could commit without being caught – no wrong that you could do without being found out – and with ABSOLUTE CERTAINTY you would be punished... would you still commit the crime."

Taylor watched his five students shake their heads fiercely, and he was glad to see this, despite the next part of his lecture.

"Ahhh. Even though we now have absolute justice, there are still those that choose to commit crimes. The population of the world is now nearing 320 billion people, so it should be no surprise that, statistically, some will still waver and break the law – even committing unspeakable acts of violent crime. Granted, it is a very minute percentage, but it is still there."

Taylor again saw that his children were shaking their heads, and he stopped a video he had pulled from archives which showed a series of headlines defining some of the worst crimes over the past one hundred years.

"Well, that's just stupid – I mean *why don't* we just use precogs to prevent the crimes before they happen?" Grace asked condescendingly.

Taylor glanced at her, the reflection of one of the headlines, "Murder!" printed on her forehead. "Well, Grace," started Taylor, "there were those out there who thought of your idea, but, unfortunately precogs don't work in the same way. When a precog sees the future, it isn't a definite future."

At this point Taylor looked over at Jay and they were both reminded of the conversation they had exchanged just over an hour ago.

The teen walked over to the cart, ready for this question, and ready with an explanation. He pulled out, of all the least interesting things, a long string from it.

"Take this string," Taylor said, seeing a trolling face on his students, "Come on kids – wake up! Let's assume that this string is time."

He showed it to the class and they could all see that it was a simple piece string about a foot long. Taylor took an end of it between his fingers and pulled at it, separating it until it was nearly half unwound.

Holding it in the middle, at the point where the string was just undone he spoke again. "This is where... er... uh... *when* the past is," at this point Taylor stroked and pulled at the end that was still a single line of string, "we only have one history, only one definite route. This is where postcogs can look; into the past with definitive truth. He continued, now focusing on the part of the string that was unwound and had several frayed ends. "In the future, the further you go the more infinite possibilities exist for a line of events or different paths for the future."

He continued, now pulling the string between his fingers and twisting it quickly, "As we pass from past to future, these many lines must converge into the one true present to create our one true history."

He stopped winding the string about two inches from its end, and handed it to Grace. "So, if a pre-cog can look into the future, which future are they looking into? Is it the one where the crime in question is committed or the one where it is not?"

"Oh, I get it!" Grace responded, now nodded her head with understanding.

Taylor continued, now talking to the rest of the class. "It is true that sometimes precogs can get a definite view of the future. It is as if parts of future events have already wound themselves together before we got there. While these definite views of the future can help to determine what might happen next, the Government had long ago determined that if there was even the slightest possibility that there could be an alternate future for a case or crime, they would never use pre-cogs to determine anyone's guilt or innocence."

Taylor turned to the clock and saw that there were only ten minutes before class was to end.

"Well, I think that about does it for toda... yes Caitlin."

The girl had raised her hand eagerly into the air, obviously with a question bearing on her mind.

"I have a quick question," she stated obviously. "Is there any way that you can control having a vision in your sleep? I get them sometimes, and sometimes they're scary. I didn't want to say anything, but I haven't been getting very good sleep these past few days, and I was wondering..."

Taylor slowly showed a look of understanding. This must be the reason she has been having trouble getting started in the morning. It didn't excuse her using her power against him, but it did explain a lot. He sighed with a deep breath, and wished that Johnny could be here for these words.

"The best thing that you can do, sweetie," he replied with a genuine look of concerned affection on his face, "is force yourself into a vision that would be more pleasant. Allow a better vision to wash over you before you fall asleep and it will work its way into your dreams. Over time, you can learn to control your visions better, but it is never absolute."

He thought for a moment then continued, "Lately I've been having trouble controlling visions myself, even when I'm awake." Some of the class looked alarmed at this. They had never heard of their teacher having trouble with his powers. It struck the group of them, the idea that he was fallible, with a sense of awe.

"It's true." Taylor said in seeing their frightened expressions. "In the middle of the presentation this morning , right in front of the council – I'm not kidding. S'the same vision we all had about an hour ago. I had it again in the lift on the way to the classroom. I can't explain it, but it just goes to show that some gifts can come with their own curses."

Caitlin did not seem comforted by this, but she nodded her head as Taylor repeated a simple mantra. "Good visions before you go to sleep. That's the trick."

With a look at his watch, he knew that it was time for the class to rise and begin their scans. With the students rising, he quickly motioned for the desks to put themselves away and for the auditorium seats to return to their extended positions. As such, with scratching and sparking sounds, everything obeyed his command, all the while the students were being scanned by Jay near the wall.

Taylor stood and stretched almost giddily. "Okay kids I want you to go back to your dorms and grab what you need or want to bring with you to the park. I don't want any funny business, and if I hear any trouble... Well, let's just say there's always *Toddlerville*!"

The classroom door opened and the five children quickly ran down the halls.

"Walk – you crazy buncha heathens!" Taylor yelled after them, almost laughing. He turned to Jay, who was scanning up and down the vitals of the children, and decided that he, Taylor, should take a stroll to see how Johnny was doing. Taking one step out the door, he felt something hit his chest with a light thud. In looking down, he was nearly blinded by a bright light and after a moment's focus he could see that it was a scanning wand held by Jay, who was shaking his head.

"Alright, alright… fine!" Taylor said in irritation. "But make it quick."

Jay pressed a green button on the wand and started up the back of Taylor's heels, worked his way up the small of the back, the shoulders, over the head, down the front and to the feet again. Here he stopped.

"Dude, you need some new shoes big guy," Jay said with a smile.

"Huh!"

"Your shoes; one of them's got a hole in it!"

Taylor lifted his foot and saw that, indeed, there was a small hole that he couldn't explain. While Taylor was busy looking at his feet, Jay plugged the scanning wand into the wall computer, after which he motioned that Taylor should see the results.

They both stared at the screen with interest and a bit of cathartic understanding, for it showed that Taylor had apparently suffered a small puncture to both his heel, and the side of his chest, just under his arm.

Upon raising his forearm this was confirmed by seeing a small hole in his lab-coat that was in line with another hole in his shirt, and a small pinhole in his skin that, for some reason, didn't pain him at all.

"The sphere!" Taylor said quickly. "It was the sphere!"

"How?" offered a confused Jay, "When?"

"Think about it!" Taylor persisted, "During the presentation I set the sphere down at my feet. It got me then and gave me that vision. And again in the lift, I was holding it under my arm it probably got me then too – that explains everything. It must have been the sphere giving me those visions."

"So…?" said Jay not sure what this really meant.

"So I've got to run some tests, my friend. I need to see what that sphere is all about. I – I'll see you at the park..." Taylor said, then quickly exited the classroom and made his way down the hall. Jay would have tried to stop him, but the man was sure that there was no use. Realizing that he had a cart that needed to be returned to its supply closet Jay re-entered the classroom and re-exited it, lightly guiding the cart down the corridor all the while complaining miserably about the fact that he had to spend time alone with the children.

It wasn't that Jay didn't like the children. In fact he cared for them very much, and he loved watching them play. He was just uneasy about spending any time with the children without Taylor's presence. When this was the case, it seemed inevitable that one of two things would always happen: their powers would either get each other into trouble, or they would get him into trouble. In either case, he felt that Taylor was best at handling the situations they got into. He held better authority over them and kept them under much better control.

Putting the cart away, he continued down the corridor to eventually see five wide-smiling students lined against the wall opposite their dormitories, waiting to be taken to the park. He quickly walked past them speaking loudly,

"Come on, let's go – let's go!"

They stared in confusion, "Where's father?" Aspen asked indignantly.

"*Dr. Taylor* will be working with Johnny. He'll catch up with us at the park. Now come on! Let's not waste any more time!"

With this, the children swiftly made their way to the lift and Jay followed shortly behind. Crowding in, the doors closed and with their shutting Jay caught by reflection what he thought was a shared smirking look between David, Aspen and Grace. As the lift made its way up to the landing pad level Jay felt his nerves on edge and his stomach turned from more than just its descending sense of inertia.

16 The Young Employee

THE SUMMER MONTHS of 2452 brought more than just their fair share of heat to the citizens of the Los Angeles Metroship. Amid these arid days came the unexpected arrival of six young and gifted children in the most bizarre of events in EduCorp history.

Taylor used every possible excuse to never go outside due to the staggering temperatures that had been exceeding 110 degrees for several weeks now. One might think that, as a newly turned thirteen-year-old, he would've taken advantage of these hot days to go out and have as much fun as possible at the Metro Park of Los Angeles, or, simply transport himself all around the city and see as much of it as he possibly could. As a teenager, though, Taylor was most peculiar. He worked; he actually had a job, and holding positions in two different divisions at EduCorp kept him quite busy, thus preventing any outward excursions into the massive city that weeded around at the feet of The Towers. Ah, the perfect excuses he needed to remain indoors, keep cool, occupied, productive, and thus turn his work into the fun he needed.

Indeed, with his many degrees, doctorates, and certifications, Taylor found it difficult to choose a single department in which to work when he was allowed and offered employment at EduCorp two years ago. In his training and growth, he held a great desire to help people in any way possible and it was this desire that molded his two decisions; to take a post on the EduCorp Emergency Room staff as well as a second job in the "Education for the Underdeveloped" branch of the Experimental Education Department.

Initially the boy was met with a great deal of resistance, particularly in the Emergency Room, due to his size and age. Many of the more seasoned physicians and surgical doctors found it hard to trust or rely on such a young counterpart. Just the same, through a period of long, hard hours, Taylor proved himself to be more able and capable than any of those he worked with.

As to his other position, Taylor spent all of his spare time developing his pet project, *Prodigy II*. He reviewed, tweaked and improved the protocols for this experiment hour after hour and day after day. He would then submit these protocols for approval, and thereafter submit their improved revisions, even if none were requested or required by the council.

It wasn't until one afternoon on August 2nd that Taylor took a deep breath at his desk with the realization that had seen little to no sunlight or fresh air for several weeks that summer

Sitting at his desk, mulling over news articles on the SuperNet about how horrible of a job President Andrews was doing this year, his eyes caught sight of an article mentioning an increasing number of strange sightings of unidentified crafts flying over the forests outside Los Angeles. Always entertained by the notion of U.F.O. sightings, he'd of clicked on this article to read more, but a new graphic blotted out most of the screen, annoyingly asking the teen if he wanted to buy some strange device that was designed to help keep the body cool while out in the scorching summer heat.

Instantly the idea popped into Taylor's head that he had indeed not been outside in quite a few days because of the high temperatures and he decided it was time to check the weather. Tapping away at the data unit mounted inside his desk, he eventually read a line of numbers showing what to expect for temperatures over the next couple of days.

"Hot – Hotter – Hot – Blistering!" Shaking his head, he looked up as the door to his office opened, thus breaking his weak focus on what he quickly dubbed *the heat wave report*.

"Jay! What's up?"

The man, who looked no different at twenty-three than he did at twenty-eight, had huge tale-telling eyes framing an almost bursting smile. It was obvious that Taylor's new guest was being consumed by some shallow secret he couldn't wait to divulge.

"Oh, not much..." said Jay falsely. Taylor offered him a disbelieving stare.

"Dude – I' been waitin' to tell you all morning. There's a report 'bout some kids found just north of the city." He said this with all intentions of peaking Taylor's interest to match his own and it was immediately clear that his efforts were successful.

"Kids – What kids? North of the city? You mean like outside the city?" Taylor's face had finally pulled itself away from Jay and started tapping away at his desk's display. Without saying a word, it was clear to Jay that he had indeed spawned more than a bit of excitement in Taylor over this news. To say the least, Taylor had completely forgotten about the weather reports or the news articles he had just been looking at.

"Is that what you mean; outside the city?" Taylor asked again.

"Exactly! And their off the grid!"

Taylor exhaled a sigh and with barely a cyber thought, he turned off the desk's display. "Off the grid! Wow, this – this – this is good news – very good news. When can I see the..."

"Hold on, little man. There's more. There are six of them, three boys and three girls. They were found unconscious just outside the north border. They haven't been revived yet." With this comment Jay could see Taylor's look of disapproval. "They can't figure out what's wrong with them." Jay explained.

"Unconscious..." Taylor's face offered a shifty look of concern.

"Yeah. At first the ERR-Crew thought it was heat exhaustion, but cooling them off and restoring their water balance didn't seem to work. They're showing stable brain activity, so it is up in the air right now what the problem is."

"When are they due to arr..."

"Two hours... right now they're in transport quarantine, waiting outside the wall." Jay said quickly cutting Taylor off.

"Two hours! We've got to get ready." Taylor snapped, his eyes growing wide. "You grab the kits. I'll fill out the applications for experimental custod..."

"Already done!" Jay said with a sideways smile. At this point Jay found it strange, as he often did, that he would take orders from, and that he worked so professionally with someone who was not only ten years his junior, but was also, in all visible estimations, still a child.

After quickly grabbing many different boxes, units, bits and parts of equipment, the two rounded on the exit to Taylor's office only to meet up with Dr. Weston when the doors opened for their departure.

"Just where do you think you're going?!" he asked gruffly, staring down at Taylor.

The teen had a great distaste for the large, thick, man. Dr. Weston was the new EduCorp Emergency Room supervisor, and Taylor found that the way this man forced himself onto others as the "Boss" of the E.R. by dictatorship rather than leadership only caused more problems than solutions.

Taylor looked at him unblinking. "I'm headed to the landing pad, Why, is there a proble..."

"Oh no you're not! You've got to cover for O'Connor's shift in the E.R. His son's birthday's today and he asked for the time off weeks ago." Dr. Weston paused to look at his watch, "I *just now* decided to let him have it off, and put you in his place."

Jay looked at Taylor and with a quick pathic message told the teen that Dr. Weston had read the same report as Jay about the kids' discovery just a few minutes ago down the corridor. Jay showed Taylor an image of the two men standing side by side reading the report with Dr. Weston grumbling and obviously thinking inside his thick skull.

Taylor felt his anger building. He had seen how Dr. Weston, over the past few weeks, had made things so much more difficult for others in the E.R., but he had not experienced any of this *treachery* first hand. Thinking on how he himself was now about to be forced into the ways of Dr. Weston's methods of control, Taylor gritted his teeth in annoyance and frustration.

Seeing the displeased look on Taylor's face, Dr. Weston took advantage of the moment to make him feel that much worse. "Oh, what's the matter, did you have something else planned! Well too damn bad! Now get your scrawny little ass up to the E.R. and get to work! O'Connor's shift's to start in five minutes."

Taylor felt his telekinetic control slipping as he watched Dr. Weston's quickly panicking face slowly slide away from him and out the door, and, with the sound sparks behind him, it was apparent that he was also losing his cyber control as well.

With a swishing and a boom, the door to Taylor's office slammed itself shut in Dr. Weston's face. This happened as more of an accident than intentional for at that very moment the teen was startled by a hand that had gripped his shoulder.

"Dude, calm down!" Jay said in a soft but stern whisper. "I'll greet the transport. You go to the E.R. and do what you've got to. Hey, they'll have to go to the E.R. when they show up anyways, so you'll probably see them there."

Putting his hand on his forehead, Taylor slowly ran his fingers through his longer, but not yet fully adult length hair. He took a deep breath and stared at the door fiercely with his ultra light blue eyes, angrily willing it open again.

He could see on the other side a startled and somewhat unnerved Dr. Weston. "I'll be in the emergency room if you need me!" he said to Jay as he walked past the large Dr. Weston and several onlookers who noticed the commotion. The teen continued to the lift, and willed it to take him to level 165, the infirmary and Emergency Room floor.

When the doors opened he saw and greeted only one other physician, an attractive sandy blonde, who he had only ever met in passing at shift changes. Now, it seemed, he would be working with her for a full shift.

He checked the charts and saw that there wasn't anyone in for treatment, and that, in fact, there hadn't been anyone there all day.

"It's been a snore fest all morning," said a high pitched female voice. "Only thing I've even heard that's interesting is those kids they found outside the city!"

"Huh," Taylor said turning his head up from the charts. He saw that the other physician, Dr. Reed by her nametag, was walking toward him.

"Well then why the hell did Weston have me come in for?"

"Because it's your turn." she said softly, not at all surprised by his language.

"It's *my* turn?"

"Oh yes," she continued shrilly, "It's your turn to be irritated, alienated, and pissed off, just like everybody else."

"I didn't know we were takin' freakin' turns!" Taylor said in a frustrated huff as he sat at one of the E.R. desks.

"So what's your story?" Taylor grumbled curiously.

"Well," she started, "you're looking at it. I've been here twenty hours so far, and I have another four to go before I get off."

"Twenty-four hours! A twenty-four hour shift! That's unheard of! So unsafe – for you and your patients!"

She shook her head, "I know, I know. But at least right now I haven't any. And I can't believe I still have to put up with this. I've been here nearly two years. I'd quit, but I need this job. God, if I knew there was something else out there for me, I'd of left yesterday before this whole horrible fiasco, buuuuat," she offered a long and tired yawn, "but I've applied everywhere else, and it seems that there is little place for young practicing physicians when so many out there are saturating the field."

Hearing this made Taylor think for a moment, and though he might have thought better of it, he felt he had to ask. "How *old* are you?"

"Oh," she said, looking over from a data display on a nearby wall, "I'm 20!"

"Quite impressive!" said Taylor over his desk, now taking an extra interest in this person that, until now, he'd hardly ever noticed.

"Not as impressive as you…" she beamed. "I mean you're only thirteen, and you've got a two year record that's not only spotless, but it involves some of the most complicated procedures."

Taylor felt himself blush a little, and looked away before really taking in what he had just heard.

"How do you know abou..." he started to ask, his head snapping almost harshly in her direction.

"Oh, I've heard all kinds of things about you, but rather than take other's word for it, I looked you up myself." She continued to talk at him while looking at several images on the display, "I must say, your record and your *reputation* speaks for itself."

Taylor lit an instant smile, but was filling with an irritated curiosity over what was keeping Dr. Reed's diligent attention on the screen in front of her.

"What are you doing?"

"Oh! Sorry. I'm checking the logs."

"Uh – Okay – why?" he asked with the air of someone who was being nosey – and he knew it.

"Well, it's a great way to see what procedures have been done before. It gives me a chance to see how lives are really saved – and how things are done in the real world. I mean you can get all kinds of stuff out of virtual simulations, but nothing can take the place of real life."

He nodded his head, "So true. So true," he agreed, and in his swelling respect for her, he decided to join her in researching the logs.

Standing next to her, he realized that she was short, and only stood a few inches taller than he. This made him smile a little; something that she noticed in the screen's reflection. He sighed and in his deep breath he could smell what seemed like a dozen sweet roses under his nose – a curious perfume that, unlike so many others, had a very soft and natural scent. If Taylor didn't know better, he'd of thought his eyes were rolling to the back of his head with this breath, but then, opening his eyes, he saw before him the rather unattractive sight of a full body scan with clearly visible veins and arteries.

Taking in the image for a moment, he understood fairly quickly what it was that he was looking at and he wanted to point out key aspects of the image to Dr. Reed; feeling a need to instruct her.

Raising their hands, the two simultaneously tracked various circulatory lines in the scan with their fingers, both wanting to point out damage caused by microscopic robots, or nanites, that had been improperly programmed and injected into the bloodstream of a patient. Slowly the two inched closer together, and, as if it were intended, his and her fingertips both ended at the same location – the heart. With this simple touch, a quick glance and a smile persisted between them.

Taylor's stomach leaped into his throat. He quickly realized two things almost simultaneously: that he rarely had any physical contact with another person that didn't involve an operating table or repairing and injury, and that *this* contact was sustained and seemed affectionate.

After a prolonged moment they both jerked their hands from the display and turned to extreme areas of the body, Taylor looking at the feet, while Dr. Reed examined the head. It wasn't but a moment after this that both felt an explanation might be in order. Concurrently each turned to the other to talk and thus created an awkward moment of verbal confusion. The result was that they quieted and stared at each other, and with this she stared hard into his eyes.

"Booooy they weren't kidding..." she said amid a quick yawn.

"Who? Kidding about what?" he retorted, appreciating her deep stare.

"Oh, everybody! They all said that you had the brightest blue eyes ever."

He turned his head in a bashful retreat, only to see the doors of the E.R. open and Dr. Weston walk in, heavy footed, sloppy and seemingly grumpier than ever. Taylor's head filled with a single thought; *Talk about spoiling the mood.*

"Huh." he growled, "Hope I'm not interrupting anything!"

As if actions could speak, Taylor and Dr. Reed confirmed his suspicions by quickly, albeit awkwardly, returning to their respective desks. Dr. Weston immediately picked up on their behaviors, and as if it were a wild animal he needed to break, the man rode his suspicions and thoughts hard for his own entertainment.

"Now don't get any ideas about this kid Dr. Reed." started Dr. Weston. "He's not legal, and I'm certain you'd have to show him everything!"

"I – whaaahht you're talking about!" she said, yawning again, trying her best to look as tired as possible, though she was pretty sure she wasn't about to get any sympathy from him.

"Well, I'm just giving you a heads-up, that's all." he said, shooting Taylor a sideways smirk. "I mean look at him – he's a geek, a freak, and – come on – it'll take years for him to...

Getting up, Taylor quickly walked out of the E.R. entrance and made his way through two other rooms until he reached the Robotic Operating Chamber, all the while he could hear Dr. Weston who, even though he had cut his words short, was laughing inside his head.

Any normal child that age might be frustrated and defensive from such a situation. Taylor, though, was merely irritated by Dr. Weston's gruffness, and only left to avoid being the brunt of more comments or jokes. He was only thirteen, but he had been rated with the maturity of someone well into their thirties. So while he was used to being poked, either physically, or verbally, he had long ago developed a toughness for such situations.

Walking around the Surgical Mezzanine, he looked down at the many operating tables viewable in the lower level. With their white, undisturbed sheets, he thought of how rarely this room, and these tables were ever used. Slowly, his mind slipped to the thought of Dr. Reed and how nice even such a brief moment as what he just had, was for him. He smiled as her high pitched voice filled his head with all sorts of words, some she'd never even spoken.

Slowly he walked by the robotic controls, his hand slipping over each controlling module delicately, his mind deeply consumed in thought. It wasn't until he touched the last one, at the far end of the mezzanine, that his thoughts were uncontrollably pulled out of his head, and at that moment his vision was blocked out by a bright white flash.

When his vision was clear again he could see himself in the operating room below. If anything could clearly tell Taylor he was having a vision, looking down on another version of himself was an obvious sign. Taking in this fact, he stared intently at himself and as his view took in more of the surroundings, he realized quickly that he was operating on what looked like a circle of six children. The image was only there for a moment, then it was gone.

Taylor opened his eyes through the blinding white light he had seen before, only to find that his hand had slipped from the robotic control. With a deep sigh and gritted teeth, he took a stance in front of the control and grabbed it firmly with both hands.

Absorbing himself in the tell tale white flash, he took the vision on fully and could see himself through the observation window working tirelessly on six bloodied and battered children all at the same time. He wasn't letting the computer do the surgeries, though, as is most common. No; instead he was standing in the middle of these six toddlers, cyberly controlling six different sets of robotic operators at the same time. Taylor watched with bated breath as his future self (for it couldn't possibly be the past) whipped his head back and forth staring between the children and the operating screens above them. Turning his head away from the horrific scene below, Taylor then noticed that beside his present self, in the Surgical Mezzanine, there were several scientists watching nervously as his future self continued working tirelessly.

Suddenly, behind him, someone spoke. It was the instantly recognized and welcome voice of Dr. Reed, who was talking to Jay.

"He just told me to come with him up to the landing pad. Said that he knew there was something wrong; that there was going to be a crash."

Jay turned and looked at her, "You know he's a pre-cog right!"

"Sure! That's why I came. I knew that he had to have seen something!" She stared intently at the overly busy future Taylor in admiration. The Taylor in the Mezzanine watched her hands as they slipped delicately over the robotic controls in front of her, and in an instant he knew how he was getting this vision. More than this, with what he had just heard, he knew exactly what was happening and knew he needed to get to the landing pad as soon as possible.

After a bright white flash Taylor's eyes were staring, dry and wide, at his hands, firmly gripping the robotic controls. He released them and rushed out of the Mezzanine and down the stairs.

As he made his way back to the E.R. only one question plagued his brain though. Why would he ask Dr. Reed to accompany him? He could handle just about anything all on his own and he was certainly not so vain that he needed her to watch as he dealt with whatever was going to happen.

Taylor scrunched his face in confusion over this question, and yet quickly enough its answer came the moment he entered the E.R. corridor.

"Get off!" He heard Dr. Reed shout.

She was working desperately to ward off the eager and inappropriate actions *and affections* of Dr. Weston, who, apparently, had taken a liking to her. Why, he was practically on top of her, forcing his face, uncomfortably close to hers, and despite her protests, the man wasn't anywhere near giving up.

Taylor, as if it was instinct more than action, kinetically pulled him from her with an almost violent jerk. His body stumbled over to land roughly on her desk. With a quick rolling and huffing he stood stiffly, attempting to act as though nothing had happened and that no inappropriate action had taken place.

"Dr. Reed, I need you to come with me to the landing pad." the teen said loudly, all the while keeping his burning eyes on Dr. Weston.

"What!" the man said loudly. "Oh, I don't think so! You're staying right here, and that's an order."

Taylor ignored these words and talked sideways to Dr. Reed, who, unbeknownst to him, was staring at the back of his head in awe and confusion.

"There's going to be an emergency, a crash of some sort, and I need you to come with me."

Dr. Weston, with disbelief, turned around to the display screen that was behind him and tapped a few buttons until he gained access to a camera that had its lens perfectly focused on the landing platform.

"There's nothing wrong out there! You're lying!" he said snidely.

Taylor turned away from Dr. Weston and stared at Dr. Reed. Offering her an imploring stare with his bright blue eyes, "There *will* be an accident there, I know it, and I need you to come with me."

She nodded cautiously and her expression shifted to one of panic as she glanced at the screen over his shoulder. It showed that the landing pad had a mass of lab-coated technicians all awaiting the transport's arrival and the children that it carried.

She looked over to Dr. Weston and snapped, "I'm going!"

The thick man quickly, or as quickly as he could, walked to the exit, blocking it with his massive body.

"You two aren't going anywhere. I'm your superior, and I say you're staying right here."

"Listen," started Taylor, "either you move, or I'll move you."

"You're going to have to move me the…"

"Done!" Taylor said quickly, and with a bit of kinetic energy, this thin thirteen year old boy slid the massive man nearly twenty feet from the spot he was standing, all the while simultaneously opening the E.R. entrance door.

Running down the corridor Taylor could hear Dr. Weston's last statement as the doors closed.

"Taylor! You stupid little shit! I don't ever want to see you in the E.R. again! You're fired!"

While he didn't know why, Taylor had to smile at these words. Shaking his head with each running step down the corridor, he listened to Dr. Reed's shaky words.

"Why – did you – want – me to – come – with you?" she huffed with each striding step.

"Well," he answered, "I just – didn't – want to – leave – the two – of – you alone!"

Once in East Tower lift, Taylor cyberly released the safety interlocks and increased the lift's speed by more than triple. Dr. Reed couldn't help but bleed out a nervous stare.

"Don't worry, I've done this before!" Taylor said with a wide smile. Instantly she started to relax, but falsely so, as this was just a calming lie.

SCREEEEEETCH – BANG!

The lift halted harshly at level three hundred, and Taylor and Dr. Reed both fell from the impact, with him landing square on top of her.

He smiled only for a moment over this impromptu awkwardness, but hardly had a chance to enjoy it. When the doors to the lift opened, the two had an instant, gasping audience.

They two stood with a playful difficulty, composed themselves and made their way through the crowd, down the corridor, and to the landing pad entrance. He cyberly opened the door with barely a thought and with a rush of hot air, wind, and loud verbal chaos, was astounded to see so many people waiting for the arrival of the transport.

Slowly weaving their thin bodies through the crowd, Dr. Reed and Taylor found their way to Jay, who had acquired a comfortable place to stand at the edge of the Northwest Curvature.

Jay was looking through a BinocuView; watching the transport on approach. Taylor tugged on his lab-coat, "How far away are they!"

"Oh, 'bout five minutes."

At this moment the man pulled his eyes from the viewer and looked down at Taylor. Immediately doing a double take, he snapped, "What're you doing here?"

"There's a problem!" Taylor said while attempting to put on the most serious face he could manage. "The transport is going to crash!"

Jay looked at him in disbelief, “Dude, you’re kidding. Right.”

Taylor looked at him, tried to force a stern stare into his eyes, and persisted. “I’ve seen it, well – well, I didn’t see it – but, but I know it’s going to crash!”

Listening to the boy’s tone, Jay knew better than to question the testimony he’d been given. He turned back to the speck that could barely be seen off in the distance. In Taylor’s impatience, the teen snatched the BinocuView and stared out at the approaching transport with nervousness, and a growing sense of uncertainty. It seemed fine as far as he could tell. As the seconds passed and the craft drew closer Taylor’s sense of self doubt slowly increased.

17 The Arrival of Six

JAY STARED DOWN AT THE TEEN, who was gazing out over the expanse of the city, and the man's face shifted to a nervous stare of extreme concern. He looked around and could see over a hundred EduCorp staff waiting on the landing pad, and considering what the boy had told him, his worry was building.

Taylor pulled his eyes from the BinocuView. Looking at the crowd around him, his agitation grew by the second as some of the spectators were pressing hard against him as if he wasn't there at all.

"Who are these – people anyway?" he asked amid being pushed by a nearby technician, who was also ogling through his own BinocuView.

Jay stared down at his young compatriot with a smirk. "Oh, come on! Dude, nobody can keep a secret 'round this place. The word's out on these kids and everybody wants a piece. I betcha they've got it in their heads that if they're the first to meet and greet, they'll get the kids for themselves.

"Damn vultures!" Taylor said bitingly, though in his heart he knew that he was really no different, with aims not so far off from his surrounding contemporaries.

Jay, snatching back his viewer, mumbled as he looked out at the transport again. "Less than two minutes 'fore they reach the pad, but – uh – everything looks cool. I don't – see – any sign of a – problem." Jay said amidst being pushed and prodded even further.

Taylor knew this already, and his head was filling with confusion. He knew what he saw in the Mezzanine. He knew this ship was going to crash – or – was that only a possibility. Rubbing his hand on his forehead in uncertainty, a rush of frustration grabbed him as he thought that maybe – just maybe – the vision was only a possibility – and not definite.

Did he overreact *again!*

Thinking fast, Taylor decided to link pathically with the children on the transport. Any normal telepath wouldn't've even tried this, but he knew, as gifted as he was, that he had a good chance of reading the children's thoughts. He could, after all, read telepaths and non-telepaths alike They were too young to be pathic of course from what he had heard from Jay, so on this platform he would definitely be the only one who could delve into their brains and see what was going on inside. Furthermore – he could be the first to, indeed, *meet and greet* long before they ever set foot on or inside The Towers.

One by one he tried to reach into the minds of the children and see if he could detect any kind of consciousness. With a smile, he immediately picked up the shallow sense of their awareness. Keeping his eyes closed in an obvious look of concentration, he spoke so that Jay, who he had pulled to kneeling in front of him, could hear what he was seeing.

"They're all sleeping," the teen whispered. "There's a girl, a boy, another girl, another girl, a boy, and another boy..."

"What – what's he saying?" Dr. Reed asked in confusion.

Jay looked up with a smile at the expectant stare of Dr. Reed. "He's trying to go pathic with the kids in the transport."

"But – but aren't they too young? I mean surely he can't...?" She asked, baffled.

"That doesn't matter to him, he can – uh – he can read the thoughts of non-telepaths too – even kids."

"You must be joking. Nobody can do that!" she said dismissively.

"Come on, babe, this is Taylor we're talking about! He can do anything!"

Dr. Reed rolled her eyes, "I guess so, and *don't* call me *babe!"*

"Ooooh – touchy – touchy!"

Dr. Reed didn't respond. She was staring back and forth, from the approaching craft, to the teen at her side, curious of how the two could possibly be linked.

Inside his head, Taylor moved from one toddler to the next, taking in their appearance, all the while working hard to probe their minds; but he wasn't picking up anything. When he focused on the mind of the last child, who was smaller, and seemingly younger than the rest, the boy woke with a look of instant and extreme fear, seemingly piercing Taylor with a staring set of bright blue eyes.

Taylor was quickly startled by this, and with a look around the transport he could tell that the other children were waking too. Immediately all of them cried and wailed like infants, but spoke no discernable words. Straight away the controls and lights inside the transport flickered with a nervous vibration and it was clear to Taylor that the trip, which had been smooth up to this point, had become compromised.

Jay looked down at Taylor "What's going on? What are you doing?"

"It's not me. There's something wrong with the ship!"

The transport craft was close enough to the platform that no one needed BinocuViews anymore to see it. More notably, no one on the platform needed to be told that the craft was no longer approaching for a safe landing. Gasps filled the hot summer air in lieu of the chaotic conversations all around.

Pulling his consciousness back, Taylor stared at the transport with hard concentration. Working to control it cyberly, he quickly felt his way into the power control system and *tried* to reroute and reprogram the ship hoping force it into a safe landing pattern. *Tried* is the operative word here for Taylor, as it was certainly something he never got the chance to actually do.

As if his brain had been electrically zapped, Taylor felt his mind instantly dejected from the craft and his body shocked with an energy he could not explain. This surge gave him such a jolt that he immediately flew into the air and over the heads of the crowd, hitting the wall of East Tower with a hard thud. He fell to the ground right in front of the doors that he and Dr. Reed had walked through moments ago.

Now badly bruised and aching, he slowly opened his eyes only to see a crowd rushing on him. Snapping his head around, he remembered where he was and what he was doing. He kinetically focused on the crowd to split it down the middle so that he could see what was going on with the transport in the distance.

This happened not a moment too soon for with the parting of a white sea of lab coats, Taylor watched in seeming slow motion as the transport's nose hit the landing pad hard in its approach and, with booming and screeching noises, started to roll head over heels in Taylor's direction. Not for anything but absolute luck, did Taylor avoid being hit by shrapnel and debris that started throwing itself at him.

The crowd of technicians was now running for cover, and through this chaos Taylor's eyes were locked on the transport in instant panic. He realized that if he didn't act fast, he would be crushed by the destructive rolling approach that was perfectly aimed toward him. But his legs were aching as he tried to move, and he realized instantly that he did not have time to get out of the way.

With all the effort he could muster he used his kinesis to block any attacking debris and as such, the boy made a heaving, grunting effort to slow the ship whose advance was so fast that Taylor wasn't sure he could stop it in time.

Closing his eyes to avoid distraction, Taylor took a deep, smooth breath. He could hear the transport crash, roll and *bounce* ever closer as his nerves mounted. He gritted his teeth, and scrunched up his face, fearful of what pain awaited.

All at once the noise stopped. Surprisingly, Taylor heard nothing but the newfound silence that the now muted crowd around him offered and with the pained expression on his face slowly relaxing, the teen opened his eyes. Apparently, just as the transport was about to land on Taylor's legs, literally inches from impact, it had stopped, in mid bounce, so that it was still floating just over the teen's lower body. He could see the backside of the transport right in front of his face, and his legs quivered in pain from the cool release of water from the craft's ruptured storage tanks.

Spectators crowded around in awe. Some even bent over, unable to believe that this huge twisted mass of metal was keeping its position approximately one foot off the ground, levitated by the efforts of a thirteen year old boy.

With an exhale of relief, Taylor saw that he had split enough distance in the crowd so that no one was hurt by the path of the transport, but with the sounds of electrical sparks and mechanical whining of the transport, the teen's attention shifted to his new concern – those inside the craft.

He painfully raised himself up and out from under the floating transport, dropping it with a verbal grunt of release the instant he was clear of it.

In making his way around to the mangled entrance of the wreckage he kinetically forced the protesting crowd of technicians to move out of his way. Looking above the transport, he watched with anxious nerves as a fire billowed and expanded over the A.G. (anti-gravity) drive. Taylor, with extensive knowledge in the mechanics, engineering, physics, of ship design, knew he was out of time. If the fire spread much further, it would cause an explosion large enough to wipe out the entire landing platform and everyone on it!

Trying with all his mental might to kinetically rip the door from its hinges, the teen grunted with mental exhaustion. The exterior alloy of the craft was too strong. With what Taylor was sure was the first of several explosions, he cowered beside the craft, focusing hard on again protecting the crowd around him from injury.

Quickly pulling himself back into focus, Taylor decided that there was absolutely no time left. He took a stance and, holding his hands flat palmed on the warm surface in front of him, he readied his mind to force a telekinetic burst so great that it would launch craft off the platform and away from the crowd. Increasing his focus on the transport in front of him, Taylor listened as the craft slowly ached with the shifting force he was pushing on it. Jay, who had finally made his way beside the teen, realized what was happening and put his hand firmly on the boy's shoulder.

"Come on, kid, are you sure about this?"

Through gritted teeth, Taylor spoke while his eyes remained fixed on the wreckage before him. "Jay, if I don't, it could take all of us out! The blast from the explosion might even bring down the tow – errrs." Taylor's voice slowed as he finished these words. His face glossed over as his mind filled with unexpected images; images of the inside of the transport. Though his eyes were open, Taylor saw as though he were looking through someone else's eyes. He looked around the craft at two rescue workers struggling inside their protective suits. They were trying desperately to remove their safety harnesses. Continuing to scan around he could see that, while badly injured, five of the six children were alive and accounted for.

"Where's the boy?" Taylor said aloud in a half whisper, confusing the whole crowd, including Jay and Dr. Reed, with this question. "There was a boy – light blue eyes, just like me." he added softly.

Vision still obscured by his view inside the transport, Taylor looked at a shiny metal plate in the craft and in seeing his own reflection he realized the truth, that he was looking through the light blue eyes of the boy he had seen earlier when the craft was approaching The Towers. All through him, Taylor was filled with fear, panic and horrific pain; clearly the child's true feelings. But how could he feel this real sense of pain? Only a telepath could...

With a loud booming noise Taylor was pulled back from his view inside the transport by an explosion from the fire above. Keeping his stance, he gasped with a release of emotion, and focused hard on the transport, now with a completely different reason for utilizing his powers. Using both his cyber and kinetic powers, he forced the actuators of the shuttle to try to open the doors while assisting them with kinetic efforts. He heaved as if he had physically forced the door to the transport open with his own hands. The loud screeching of metal and the grinding of gears was almost unbearable, but Taylor persisted with all the effort he could until the twisted metal entrance was actuated enough to enter and exit the craft.

Taylor, momentarily exhausted, looked for anyone to offer a helping hand, but the fearful faces of the idle technicians told the truth instantly. Everyone was paralyzed in fear – everyone, that is, except for himself and Jay.

With an aching in every inch of his body, the teen jumped into the blazing craft and as the spectators watched, Jay followed quickly behind. Within seconds the two exited, carrying a bloodied and battered child each, allowing a sense of grief and horror to consume the crowd. As if like a slow precession, the bodies of four more children floated out from the open door followed by two staggering rescuers, who were undoubtedly very shaken up and barely conscious.

Taylor, fully focused on the children, carefully set them down on the concrete landing pad and turned quickly to the transport. With a loud buzzing alarm he heard the thermal overload warning of the anti-gravity drive. Realizing he had no time to waste, he focused on the transport completely.

Frowning a harsh almost angry stare, and with a reddening, heaving grunt, Taylor pushed a burst of telekinetic energy that threw the transport so hard it flew from the pad and soared high into the air, far distant from The Towers. With hundreds of eyes watching it, the transport finally exploded just as it was about to fall back to the ground and thus the acoustic blast knocked the entire crowd of watchers, Taylor and Jay included, flat on their backs.

Lying there for a moment, stunned by the fall, Taylor shivered from the icy cool wash that had fallen over him. His eyes opening, he watched with a curious giddiness as, over the whole of the landing pad a snowy white cloud descended beautifully over the mass of strewn bodies. Taylor welcomed this feeling for the contrast it offered from the hot July sun, but the coolness and the dim shade didn't last for long. Within seconds the flakes of ice melted and the cool air warmed as the sun burned away any trace of what happens when a large tank of water is exposed to liquid nitrogen in a massive explosion.

Taylor groaned from an aching pain as he felt his body warm in the baking heat. Looking up and seeing the bright blue sky he, at this moment, realized how much he truly missed being outdoors. He smiled and rolled his head to the side. At this, he gasped at the sight of a small girl's bloodied face and one quick look at her neck told him that something had pierced it all the way through.

Half panicked, yet fully determined, the teen got to his feet and immediately cleared any animate or inanimate obstacle out his way of carrying the six children, each horribly injured, down to the E.R. Telekinetically lifting them, he was accompanied by Jay and Dr. Reed, who were the only two he didn't shift out of his way.

Moving with absolute purpose, the three of them walked swiftly into the entrance of East Tower. On his way through the corridor, practically running to the lift, Taylor forced an M-Gen panel to shoot out a Bioelastic Polimizer unit that he immediately used on the six injured children, thus putting them in a single state of rock-hard suspended animation. He had layered them one above the other with only an inch or two between them and, by pressing a button on the small unit, which wasn't much larger than a one inch cube, he enacted the polymer. It quickly engulfed the children in a clear plastic like coating that hardened to a clear and solid state.

The lift ride down to the E.R. would've been fast, simple, and quiet had it not been for the panicked look on Jay's face. Dr. Reed, looking between Jay and Taylor as if she was taking notes, couldn't help but address the man's fretful stare.

"Don't look so worried." She said, and at this Jay turned to glare wide-eyed at her, his face showing an expression of unmistakable terror.

"Hell yeah Why not! We're dropping like a brick!"

"What's the big deal?" she asked in calm contrast and quickly followed this with a calm statement. "He's done this before."

Jay's face shifted. Now, in addition to fear, he turned a stare at Taylor that revealed an unmistakable anger.

"NO HE HASN'T!" the man screamed.

Taylor was a boy who hadn't yet learned to hide the truth amid an accusing stare, and when Dr. Reed caught his shifty, guilty eyes, she had little choice but to share Jay's emotions. Together, the both of them, on either side of Taylor, they watched the numbers decline past the two hundreds and started screaming. Taylor, on the other hand, at having not said a word, only widened a devilish grin.

While still keeping his focus on the interlocks, he re-enabled them just in time to prevent a jolt that he knew the children's battered bodies couldn't handle. Reading the number one hundred sixty-five, Jay and Dr. Reed stopped screaming and it was obvious they shared both a mild sense of embarrassment and a sigh of relief over the fact that they had stopped on the correct floor.

Taylor turned his head up at his current company and with almost a laugh he sneered. "What? Did you really have any doubt?!"

With the lift doors opening Taylor flinched forward. He was face to face with an angry Dr. Weston. This large man's initial response was a grumble followed by a long pause during which he stared at Taylor. The teen was sure the man was trying to search his own empty head for what to say, but Taylor's patience was wearing thin for any kind of parley. He quickly brushed the man, who was thick on so many levels, aside and was followed shortly behind by his two compatriots and the six stiff, floating bodies.

As Taylor continued down the corridor he could hear a distant Dr. Weston yelling that he had been fired and therefore had no business on the Emergency Room floor. While voicing this information, though, Dr. Weston did not advance in any way on the group. Actually, he couldn't, for Taylor was kinetically holding him in place to ensure his noninterference.

Watching the children enter into the R.O.R. or Robotic Operation Room, Jay attempted to follow but was stopped by a telepathic message. Taylor had pathically engaged in a conversation with Jay while simultaneously guiding the children's bodies through the R.O.R. doorway.

"I think it would be best if you stayed with Dr. Reed. I can handle this," the boy said pathically.

"But there are six of them." Jay persisted.

"Aaaaannnnd?" Taylor interjected.

"And you're only one person. You're only a thirteen years-ol..."

Taylor turned his head with a flinch and gave Jay a scolding look. Jay instantly stopped what he was conveying and fluttered his eyes due to the bellowing message that was barraging his brain from the teen before him.

"NEVER, ever use my age as a gage of what I can do! I am not where I am because MY AGE was a factor. I am where I am because MY TALENT and MY TRAINING was a factor. You forget yourself, and you forget everything that I can do. Now isn't the time to start doubting just because things are getting a little rough!"

Jay closed his eyes and took a deep breath. "I'm sorry. I'm sorry." He spoke aloud, and with this, Taylor blinked. The boy realized that the strength of his message may have been too much.

His young face quickly changed to show a soft concern. "I'm sorry too," he continued, shaking his head. "I know that you think you can help, but right now, I'm the only one here who can handle this. Besides, the computer and tissue generators'll do all the work. I'm just going to be in the room in case something goes wrong."

Watching Jay slowly nod, Taylor thought of the vision he had experienced earlier in the Mezzanine before the crash. He wasn't letting the machine do all the work then and if what he saw was true, then there would be no doubt that, at some time, he would have to take over for the computer.

Taylor's thoughts were distracted by a snapping verbal command.

"Go then." said Jay. "Do what you have to! I'll be up in the Mez, watching."

Taylor smiled, still mulling over his own thoughts, and turned to enter the R.O.R. with his head dipped low, eyeing suspiciously the bodies that he guided through the door behind him.

Jay, having run up to the Mezzanine as quickly as possible, watched as Taylor placed the stack of bodies in the middle of the room. The teen then glanced up to see that Jay, with Dr. Reed at his side, were now watching with wide eyes of concern as Taylor kinetically prepared himself for surgery. With an added hustle and bustle, Jay was buffeted by several other scientists and technicians who also took their place in the mezzanine, their eyes nervously scrutinizing either the teenager about to perform multiple medical miracles on six children who were all in mortal danger.

18 Saving the Children

NERVOUS AND ABSOLUTELY UNSURE of how these next crucial moments were meant to unfold, Taylor slowly turned away from Jay and forced the doors of the Operating Room to close behind him. He could feel with his ears that the room was now airtight and, taking his position in the middle of several operating tables, he spoke aloud to the main computer with a voice that preached his insecurity.

"ORC" Taylor started, for that was the verbal call-name of the Operating Room Computer. He then listened as a beep told him that the computer recognized his initiation before he continued.

"Recognize physician authority Taylor, Robert S." he stated, working hard to get a more assured and confident sounding voice from his throat.

Waiting for what seemed an eternity, Taylor knew instantly that something was wrong. The computer was taking longer than expected to recognize his authority, and with a few quick words ORC informed him as to why.

"Taylor, Robert S. is not a recognized authority in the O.R.C. system." said the computer in a soft feminine voice. "Dr. Taylor's authority was revoked from the system at 1435 hours on August 2nd 2452."

Taylor could hear a pathic panic enter his brain from those above him and he turned up to offer a menacing stare at Dr. Weston, who had apparently entered the observation room at the first moment of Taylor's releasing his telekinetic hold. The teen knew that Dr. Weston was the only one who could remove someone from the system; something the man probably did only moments after Taylor left with Dr. Reed.

Wasting no time, he immediately ran to the main computer access station and cyberly reprogrammed the O.R.C.'s security protocols.

While scanning and changing code at an extreme speed he could hear pathic whispers being exchanged between the other scientists and technicians in the observation room. Were they impatient for him to do something? Were they impressed at what was flashing on the screen, or did they doubt his every move? Whatever their thoughts were, he ignored them; resolute in his purpose.

Finishing with the computer console, he returned to his position at the center of the Operating Room. Looking up at those in the Mezzanine, he again commanded for the O.R.C.

"ORC, recognize physician authority Weston, Edward Q." After waiting only a moment the computer offered an immediate response: "Physician authority recognized. Good afternoon Dr. Weston, how may I help you?"

Those in the observation room mumbled between themselves fervently. They were obviously shocked that the child in front of them would use his abilities to such an unauthorized degree. Taylor, on the other hand, was more concerned with the fact that he didn't want to deal with using a false name.

"ORC – *Transfer* current physician authority access, level 9, to Taylor, Robert S.: Passcode 7 – alpha – 2 – 8 – 9."

After hearing several beeping noises, Taylor knew that the computer was re-configuring access to allow for his return into the system.

"Command confirmed. Taylor, Robert S. granted level 9 physician authority."

"ORC," Taylor started again, "Recognize physician authority Taylor, Robert S."

A more timely moment later the computer responded.

"Physician authority recognized. Good afternoon Dr. Taylor. Congratulations on your promotion. How may I help you?"

At the sound of these words a smirk grew wide on Taylor's face and he looked up to see Dr. Weston's massive form rush out of the observation room.

Taylor, now satisfied with his computer access and authority, shifted his attention to getting things started. In this effort, he continued giving commands to the computer. "ORC – Begin biomedical scan of subjects in suspended animation located in place of bed eight."

Taylor said this very quickly, and immediately a bright light lit up in the operating room that moved rapidly over the six children.

"ORC has recognized that there is more than one subject in stasis, please reply."

Taylor responded quickly. "ORC – there are six subjects in suspended animation…" he paused and kinetically turned the bioelastic brick containing the children on its side so that the computer could more easily scan the individual bodies.

"ORC – Rescan."

"Scans complete." Returned the computer, and Taylor walked over to a data panel to read the results of the scan.

"ORC, number the subjects one through six."

Immediately numbers came up on the screen and placed themselves next to each of the six scans. Taylor responded quickly, "ORC, assign these subjects to beds one through six, respectively." He watched the screen as a layout of the 8 O.R. beds came up, and one by one the computer positioned numbers on all but two of the bed positions.

"ORC" Taylor continued, "On my command, begin removal of foreign objects and immediate regeneration of damaged tissue for subjects on beds one through six."

Taylor waited a moment, listening to the computer work hard to configure the calculations and necessary protocols to complete this request.

"Confirmed," spoke the computer's voice, "Awaiting your command Dr. Taylor."

The teen looked at the six bodies in their clear confinement, and offered a short prayer under his breath that everything would go smoothly. He tapped the bioelastic release mechanism, and with a light hissing the clear coating dissolved into a clear sheet that quickly sucked itself back into the tiny unit from where it had originated.

Taylor was very unnerved at how quickly the bodies started bleeding again and he kinetically positioned each child on his or her respective bed with hasty, yet delicate precision. At the exact moment that he finished placing body number six in position and pulling Anesthetizer units over their neck , he looked up to the observation room, catching a direct stare from Jay and Dr. Reed.

"ORC – initiate request for foreign object removal and tissue regeneration."

"Command confirmed." said the soft feminine voice, and instantly six lights came on over the six operating tables. Around each of these lights grew an onslaught of robotic arms with tools of all sorts that started actuating and moving quickly over each of the bodies. Their first task was to use their degenerators to disrobe and exchange the clothes of the children for a bare minimum set of undergarments. Thereafter, the machines started removing debris either physically, or with the same degenerators, while also attempting to repair the severe tissue damage caused during the crash. Fortunately, ORC understood that the most severe of injuries should be addressed first, and thus, the girl that Taylor had once before seen with her neck pierced by a piece of sharp metal, had already had it removed, and her neck being quickly worked on.

Taylor continued to watch, utterly in awe at the numerous and severe injuries these children had received. Feeling he could stare at this no more, he turned his head to instead look up at the far less disturbing data display.

"ORC – Display the vitals of subjects one through six on a two by three grid on this screen."

The computer complied, and Taylor smiled knowing that each of these children, while in some cases half open for surgeries and internal cleaning, had vitals that were improving with each passing second.

Looking down, Taylor suddenly felt a sharp pain inside his head, a pain so great it caused his knees to buckle, making him fall on all fours. As he looked up at the display showing the six vitals, he could see it waver and distort until, with a blasting shock, it cracked down the middle and went blank.

"ORC" Taylor yelled through the pain in his head, "Identify the source – of your electrical – disturbance."

The computer processed for an interminable few seconds, before giving its response: "The source of the disturbance is unknown."

Taylor might have been somewhat satisfied with this response had it not been followed by "Emergency overload, tissue regenerator offline. Emergency overload, matter degenerator offline."

Then, with a sound that he couldn't possibly mistake, he heard the motion of the robotic units all around him slowly come to a stop followed by the computer's voice: "Emergency overload, robotic operators offline."

"No Shit!" he said quickly and, glancing up at the observation room, he noticed that some of the technicians had covered their mouths in obvious surprise at hearing such a young person curse.

The teen snapped his head around at each of the children on the operating tables in a panic for what to do. His hands actually started to shake with nervousness as time was pressing down on him more and more with each fleeting second. He was only one person, and if he had to operate on each of them by hand or cyberly, as he saw in his vision, he scarcely knew where to begin. His eyes moved from one child to the next until he noticed something very peculiar.

One of them, a boy whose body was still open from an internal cleaning operation, was staring at the robotic arm that had rested only inches away from his face.

The boy's awake! And he – he's actually got a smile on his face. Indeed, the child, in staring at the robotic arm and nodding his head from side to side in a varying rhythm, seemed fine, but what caught Taylor's attention so specifically was that the robotic unit was moving to the child's own strange sense of beat. With a rush of blinking realization Taylor put the many events of the day together in understanding.

He looked up at Jay, who was staring down with great concern, trying to keep calm amid several panicked scientists. The teen shouted up to his friend; eyes unchanging through his pain.

"Cyberkinetic! They're cyberkinetic!"

Some in the crowd sneered in skepticism over such a profound statement. Even Jay looked at him in confusion and started shaking his head in disbelief.

"Think about it Jay. They were unconscious in the transport; then they woke up. In a strange ship with strange people, they panicked..." Jay was still shaking his head, eyebrows raised in confusion.

"Come on, Jay, THINK! They panicked and their powers went nuts! That explains the crash." Taylor stared hard at his counterpart, nodding his own head until Jay followed the example. "Right! And now, they're waking up again and shutting down the system." Jay pulled his head back quickly, his eyes widening with understanding.

Taylor was about to speak again when a red-light indicator came on over one of the beds, then another bed... and still another.

Now massaging his temple from the ever pressing pain in his brain, Taylor focused on an emergency kit near the entrance to the Operating Room. It opened at his kinetic request, revealing eight auto injecting hypodermic needles. Six of these shot out from the box and across the room to find their way onto various parts of the children's bodies.

Walking up to the child that was bobbing a dance with the robotic arm in front of him, Taylor watched as the child quickly lost consciousness. Simultaneously the pain in Taylor's head rapidly subsided.

"Sorry kid!" He said looking into the child's closing eyes, "This is exciting and all, but you're just messing things up." Taylor then returned his stare to the main display, and though he couldn't see anything but the massive crack down the screen's middle, he proceeded to talk to the computer.

"ORC – Recommence foreign object removal and tissue replication."

After a moment of different sounding beeps the computer replied, "Unable to comply. All re-generators, degenerators, and robotic operators are still offline."

"Damn it!" he said loudly, and he slumped down, hanging onto the console in front of the non functioning display. He looked to the children, certain that if he did not act quickly they would all die.

"ORC – Are the secondary robotic units still functional."

"Affirmative."

With this one word Taylor felt a ray of hope shine into this oppressive room. His vision was making more sense by the second, and this thought offered him hope that there was still a chance of saving his young patients. He stiffened his body and his resolve.

"ORC – Move operating tables one through six to their secondary positions. Activate overhead operating screens one through six, and bring their secondary robotic units online."

"Command Confirmed."

Instantly the six beds moved inward from their semicircular positions and from the ceiling large displays ejected outward above the beds followed by six long robotic arms.

Taylor looked up and could see a huge commotion working through those in the observation room; and not without good reason. It was a difficult task, indeed, to perform an operation using robotic arms manually, and the moment the computer turned on the new robotic units, a series of controls lit up in the Mezzanine, thus giving a crowd of scientists the idea that Taylor expected some of them to go to work and actually perform the surgeries.

Taylor looked up through the plex windows and shook his head forcefully.

"ORC – Lockout secondary robotic access controls in the observation room."

"Command confirmed, control shutdown in progress."

In the Mezzanine, the control units that would normally be used to manipulate the robotic arms dimmed as the lockout command was completed.

Taylor now stood in the middle of six display screens with six children he had to save, and no one to help him. Closing his eyes for only moment to concentrate, this thirteen-year-old stood amid these extreme circumstances knowing exactly what he had to do next.

With gasps in the observation room the scientists all watched as the functioning robotic arms, sprang to life and immediately went to work on the children, almost seamlessly from where the others had left off.

Taylor was looking wildly back and forth between the many screens and, at times, he would force the ORC system to scan and rescan the children's bodies to make sure that he was successfully removing all the foreign debris they contained. With the tissue generators offline, Taylor had to use old fashioned suture and polyneoplastic techniques to mend the wounds and incisions that were either caused by the accident, or required for surgery.

For Jay, this was all too strange to watch. He, never in his lifetime, thought he would see what was happening before him, yet he absorbed the scene of a teenage child standing in the middle of six battered and unconscious bodies, working hard to bring them into repair, and he, Jay, was filled with wonder. During the next few minutes of operation, he thought that at times, the synchronous movement of the robotic arms was like a strange ballet or symphony with Taylor as the master conductor, and with this he felt a sense of pride that he was, in fact, the boy's best friend.

In the operating room Taylor felt his heart pumping hard in his chest, and felt his brain reaching its limits. He was in full concentrated swing, making every effort to balance his attention between the six children. It wasn't until his first distraction, which came by way of a light tapping noise at the operating room door, that all of the machines powered down with the teen's now idling brain.

Taylor looked to the main entrance and found that Dr. Weston was standing on the other side of the clear door. Behind the man were two large white security robots with their defensive weapons fully activated and directed at the entrance, aimed over the man's shoulders.

Unblinking, Taylor reactivated three of the dead robotic arms and continued his efforts at save the children.

"Taylor," started the falsely kind voice of Dr. Weston through the intercom at the door, "These security robots are here to bring you into custody. So if you stop now, this whole thing can end quietly. Otherwise, they'll have to use force and you and I both know that won't be pretty."

Taylor yelled at Dr. Weston over his shoulder, all the while realizing that his words could be heard by the scientists in the observation room.

"If I leave, who'll finish working on these children?"

Dr. Weston, whose patience was wearing thin, quickly responded, "I will and I'll have help – Dr. Reed. Besides, what does it matter to you?"

Taylor glanced up in the Mezzanine and saw that Dr. Reed had pulled her head back in a look of shock, offered a thick yawn of her tiredness and the following expression told him hundreds of words about how she felt on the matter.

He knew that she had no inclination of working by his side, and that she was ill prepared to handle what Taylor, was doing – even if the workload was divided.

Taylor shook his head, still keeping focus on the six screens around him, "You can't handle six old-school operations at once, and Dr. Reed's been on shift for over 24 hours – she's in no condition. These kids'll die if I leave them to you!"

Dr. Weston, irritated at Taylor's comment, spoke angrily and gruffly into the intercom. "Look at them! Of course - SOME MIGHT!" He then calmed himself and returned to his falsely soft voice, "But that's life. You do your best to save the ones you can, and sometimes it comes at the sacrifice of the ones you can't... you know... for the greater good."

Taylor stopped his activity in the operating room and glared at Dr. Weston, speaking through gritted teeth.

"Your greater good just isn't *good enough*!"

Taylor paused for only a moment after saying this before snapping his attention back to his young patients and instantly all of the robotic arms continued their work.

Dr. Weston now started screaming through the intercom. "Listen you little shit. You get your ass over here right now and open this goddamned door, or I'll have these security dogs do it for me."

Taylor, heaving a sigh of frustration that he had to, once again, stop his work, turned to look at Dr. Weston's robotic sidekicks. They powered down momentarily, and glitched and twitched before turning back on again. Dr. Weston's arrogant face quickly shifted to a pale gaze of fear.

Pointing their defensive weapons at Dr. Weston they stiffly spoke.

"Please step away from the door. This is your first warning. Any further attempts at gaining access through this entrance will result in the use of lethal force."

"You can't do this! The man screamed at the robots while walking backwards. "I activated you. *I* have control over you."

With this Dr. Weston held up a tiny unit over his head between his fingers. It resembled something of a remote and when the robotic security guards noticed it, Taylor had them target and destroy the unit using their degenerator turrets with pinpoint accuracy.

Seeing this through the door, Taylor raised an eyebrow and grinned for only a moment before continuing his work to save the six children around him.

For the many spectators watching over Taylor, tension was ever present as quite frequently the red-light indicators would jump from one child to the next, thus constantly shifting Taylor's attention repeatedly. In fact several times during the operations, the children's oxygen saturation levels dropped below critical, and Taylor had to infuse their bodies with packs of pre-oxygenated synthetic blood just to keep them alive.

In the final stages of the multi-operations, which lasted well over six hours, Jay watched the weary Taylor slowly mend three different children simultaneously. These were the last of the surgery incisions and it was clear that the teenager had pushed himself to the brink for when these three lines were repaired he released his cyber-kinetic link with the robotic operators and collapsed in the middle of the operating room, both sweaty and shaking. The room was now dead silent with the final noises being that of the robotic arms powering down. Taylor closed his eyes feeling his cold body slowly go numb.

Opening his eyes to a bright white light in his face, Taylor seemingly woke with the bleeding color of green grass developing in front of him. This was a great contrast from the cold metal he knew he had collapsed onto only a moment ago and he raised his head to take in his new surroundings.

Blinking his world into focus, he saw in front of him six children, all playing with each other, running and laughing as if without a care in the world. They eventually formed an arc of six, and Taylor watched as one broke away from the group and walked towards him. Lifting himself upright, he now sat quietly, waiting for the approaching toddler, who had a strange expression on his face; a look of great curiosity.

Taylor responded with a smile, and the child squatted and sat in front of him, smiling in return. Taylor cocked his head to one side, asking, "Hey, kid, what's your name?"

Looking at the toddler, Taylor was unable to pull his stare away from the young boy's light blue eyes. The teen felt a clenching in his chest as he realized how strange he himself must have looked at that age, and how everyone else must have felt when they looked at him.

In response to the question, the toddler, with his straight, light brown hair, simply turned around and with a look as though Taylor must have been talking to someone else, turned back with even greater curiosity. The boy then reached down and pulled up a handful of grass, held it out, and opened his hand to let the wind blow the blades away.

Taylor looked at the boy with an uneasy smile, not understanding this gesture, and decided to test the child's boundaries of language.

"Grass." Taylor said softly, nodding to what the boy was holding.

The kindest of bright blue eyes stared back at him. "Gas?"

Taylor wasn't sure what to make of this awkward response. He looked at the other children, then back at the boy again, deciding that formalities might be better taken care of at this point.

He pulled his hand up and put it on his own chest, "Tay – lor" he said before patting his chest and repeating the name. "Tay – lor"

He then held out his hand to the boy, and with his hand close the boys chest, he asked "What's your name?"

The boy looked confused, and Taylor again patted his own chest and spoke his own name.

He reached out again to pat the boy's chest, but the toddler's response to this was quite unexpected. The child reached out and practically jumped on Taylor, holding him tight in an embracing hug.

Taylor, having only a moment to look at the other children, noticed that they all stopped what they were doing instantly and ran over to he and the enthralled boy and started an almost dog-pile of tight holds. Reaching around him and themselves in a web of arms and hands, Taylor, while at first afraid, suddenly filled with a ginger happiness that he could only smile at and he eventually joined in the laughter and soft and gentle warmth that washed over him.

He could sense, as if telepathically, an infinite amount of love emanating from these children, and while he was at a loss to explain why, he somehow could feel himself returning the emotion. The teen, almost overpowered by these strong and unexpected feelings, felt his vision slip away in a wash of white light. Closing his eyes, he smiled with the disappearing sight of young arms and hands all embracing him in love.

Waking *again*, and this time certain of his reality, Taylor felt a sharp pain on his face that was the result of his resting on the metal floor where he had fallen. Trying to lift himself up, his body ached with horrible extreme and his muscles did not obey his wishes in lieu of their own tired weakness. Barely able to turn his head, he stared out at the entrance to the operating room and saw that Jay was moving precariously at the entrance to the operating room, trying to get his attention without offending Taylor's robotic guardian's at the door. With a light blink Taylor shut down the two robots and made the doors to the room open and in a rush there was onslaught of people crowding the room, pushing Jay out of the way.

As if Taylor were nothing more than an object of little interest, all of those who had entered were focused entirely on the children lying in their simple circle around the teen.

"Move – Move – Moooove!" he could hear Jay yell, and as if trying to obey the command himself, the teen realized that his muscles still weren't working. He could barely move at all. All he could feel was that he was physically exhausted, hungry, and fatigued.

"Tay – Taylor, here," Jay said softly, lifting him into an upright position. "Here, drink this. It's Proto-Juice"

Taylor felt a straw enter between his lips, but he had little energy to try and sucking anything out of it. Jay grunted and decided to get things moving by squeezing the bottle in his hands. The teen felt a cold rush of fluid squirt into his mouth, yet most of it actually drained out and washed over his chin, but it was enough to wake his mouth up and start the muscles in his head to work properly, pulling the orange flavored fluid into his body.

"That's better," Jay said softly, still waving his hands to keep other technicians from getting too close. Taylor though, was focused on the few in the room who weren't interested in him at all – he was worried over his circle of patients.

Taylor pulled his head around with wide panicked eyes, "How are they?" he voiced while half coughing up what he had been drinking.

"They're fine!" Jay said dismissively, pushing Taylor to keep from sitting up too quickly.

Eventually Jay helped Taylor to his feet, and as this happened, Taylor looked around in all directions to see the six children. With no red lights, and all stable vitals, they appeared to be sleeping and Taylor sighed wearily with instant relief.

The two started to make their way toward the operating room entrance, but, having only taken a few steps, saw that the door opened on its own. Taylor, still groggy and at times only half aware, barely noticed that Dr. Weston was standing in the doorway accompanied by a small security team.

"Take him into custody!" yelled Dr. Weston.

Taylor would have used some form of telekinetic force to keep the security personnel at bay, but he was too exhausted to try and figured there might be little point as he probably deserved whatever disciplinary action was coming. He looked up at the entrance expecting to see the security rush on him, but instead found that an entire crowd of white lab-coats had pulled their attention from the circle of unconscious children and were pushing their way in front of Taylor.

The teen's ears perked, hearing the voices of different technicians yelling through the crowd.

"That boy's just saved these kids you moron!" said one.

"Yeah" yelled another, followed by, "Who the hell do you think you are – You should be thanking him – not arresting him?!"

Taylor, still very weak, continued to hear commentary in support of his actions. His heart started pounding hard in his chest, forcing his face to grow red with embarrassment. Looking to one side, he could see that Dr. Reed had abandoned the crowd to be at his side, opposite Jay in support. With the great emotion welling inside him from all his defender's comments, he felt exhaustion finally overtake him and without warning to Jay or Dr. Reed, he groaned as his legs gave way and he passed out.

19 Mother Reed

THE FOLLOWING MORNING, having remembered nothing of actually leaving the operating room, Taylor woke in a medical bed with his eyes opening to a digital display of his vital signs. Sitting up with a start, his mind worried over the children that he had worked so on so for such a time, and with such a focus that images of them on the surgical tables were engrained in his tired mind when he first opened his bleary eyes. In searching for these youngsters, Taylor was relieved to see that they were being kept not only in the same area as he, but that he was the seventh in what was a lineup of children. Taylor felt a deeply rooted frustration at this because he realized that the only reason for his being kept so close to them was the fact that his age mandated that he be cared for in the Pediatric Recovery Ward.

Looking back at his vital monitor, he could see that the date showed him to have been out for nearly 16 hours. Feeling a strong urge to get up and move around, Taylor shifted himself around to let his feet fall over the bedside.

He instantly felt a strange coolness about himself and realized that all he was wearing was a standard cloth gown with an open back, and was quickly aware of how little he was wearing in comparison to the last time he was conscious. His blood quickened with the thought that he had been undressed by a stranger while incapacitated.

Shaking this feeling, he stood up. He felt his feet twitch at touching the ice cold floor, and barely taking his first step, he felt a tug on his arm. Looking down, he saw that he had an NVM System or Nano Vital Monitoring System plugged intravenously into his body.

"Why do they still use these stupid things?" he asked aloud, and in his mind he thought that the better choice would always be the WNVM or Wireless Nano Vital Monitor System.

He pulled his free arm around so that he might remove the attachment when he heard a voice yell across the recovery room.

"Don't even think about it!"

Turning his head with a snap, he saw that Jay and, to his surprise, Dr. Reed had come to see him.

"Hey guys! What's up?" Taylor called out while continuing to fiddle with the tube stuck in his arm.

"I said leave it alone!" insisted Jay.

Taylor, eyes wide, stared at Jay with a playfully arrogant grin. "I don't take orders from you. It's the other way around, remember?"

"So you keep reminding me – what a brat." Jay whispered to Dr. Reed, then paused to think for a moment. "Dude, since you're here, in the recovery room, and aren't fit for duty, you actually take orders from..."

"Me!" squeaked Dr. Reed quickly; slapping Taylor's hand to prevent him from interfering with the NVM tube.

"You," he said loudly, "Why you?"

"Because, *sweetie,*" she said in her now familiar high pitched voice, "I've gone home, got some sleep, come back, and I'm just startin' my shift. So you're *all mine!*"

"Well then, Dr. Reed," Taylor said with an insolent tone in his voice, "Tell me – why did you use the wired NVM system instead of the wireless. It would at least let me to be more mobile."

"Honestly, Taylor, like you of all people wouldn't know the answer to that question."

Biting his lip, Taylor hardly had to give this a thought as his eyes passed over the other children in the room, who had the wired version being used on them as well.

"Cyber interference! You don't want anyone to cyberly screw up the readings – good thinking doctor!"

"Thanks." Dr. Reed said this then turned to Jay while reaching out to Taylor's face. "What a *little cutie pie*!" This time her voice was of a higher pitch than usual and with these spoken words she was lightly pinching one of his cheeks, wiggling it quite annoyingly.

Taylor shook his face from her grip, which pained his face to do, and he offered a confused and curious look over to Jay while pointing at Dr. Reed, who had turned to check his readouts from the last twelve hours. In response to this visual inquiry Jay lifted his shoulders as an expression of being just as confused.

Hiding the fact that he was mouthing the words, "she's crazy!" with his hands, Taylor quickly resorted to rubbing his chin when Dr. Reed turned in his direction. She started checking the vitals on the other six children, and when finished, returned to Taylor's bedside.

"Dr. Reed," he asked quickly, trying desperately not to sound annoyed. "Can I have a moment – alone – with Jay for a minute? If you don't mind."

"Of course *pumpkin!"* she said, and Taylor winced as Dr. Reeds voice reached the highest pitch he had heard from her yet. She leaned, over, grabbed his head lightly, and kissed him on the forehead before making her way out of the room.

"What is up with her?" Taylor asked, obviously annoyed to extreme.

"I think you're right," Jay started, "I think she's crazy!"

"Sure thing!" Taylor retorted, "But she wasn't acting like this at all yesterday!"

"I don't know man... I just don't know!" Jay said as if he was trying to both make a statement of how weird Dr. Reed was at the same time as not offering any insight as to why. with the beeping of vital monitors all around there was a moment of rhythmic silence between the two of them. Searching for an explanation of bizarre behavior or trying to find a new topic of conversation, it was the latter that won out and surfaced to break the quiet.

"So!" Taylor said so loudly that it made Jay jump, "Did you put in the application?!"

"Application?" Jay asked, confused for a moment, "Oh, application! For the kids... Yeah, I did that yesterday."

"Annnnd." Taylor questioned insistently.

Jay looked at the time display on Taylor's vital readout. "And the results should be up by now. It's after noon, that's when..."

"So let's see!" Taylor demanded, cutting Jay's words short.

Jay smiled, seeing that Taylor was doing much better than he had been those sixteen hours before – he was energetic, forceful, and at times like this, he reminded Jay of the thirteen year old he was supposed to be; the adolescent child hiding somewhere deep inside. Shaking this thought, the man pulled out a data pad, and turned it on.

After tapping a few screens, putting in a security password, and pressing his thumbprint on the pad, the unit displayed the information Jay was looking for.

The two of them started reading it immediately.

APPLICATIONS FOR EXPERIMENTAL AND ADOPTIVE CUSTODY

The following is a list of applications of the aforementioned order which have come to conclusion for Date August 03, 2452

Subject #	Exp/Adp	Applicant(s)	Department (Exp)	Result
2675A-2680A	Exp	R. Taylor	456UE34	Pending
2675A-2680A	Exp	T. James	475GH26	Pending
2675A-2680A	Exp	F. Wilson	326ER17	Pending
2675A-2680A	Exp	L. Branden	824PE20	Pending
2675A-2680A	Exp	W. Oleson	721BL67	Pending
2675A-2680A	Exp	M. Adams	032CH18	Pending
1275A	Adp	J. Reed	-------	Denied

When his eyes reached the bottom of this short list, Taylor read the most unlikely of subject numbers, and his eyes grew so wide that Jay couldn't help but notice.

"Oh! It's not that bad!" Jay said quickly, so we have some competition. I'm sure that we'll get in because we're the first.

"It's not that," said Taylor quickly, "Did you read the last line!?"

"Yeah," said Jay obliviously, "So what?! Somebody didn't get adopted – big deal!"

Taylor grabbed Jay's head and pulled his face nose to nose with his own. "I'M

SUBJECT 1275A you idiot!"

Taylor released Jay, who immediately grabbed the data-pad again. Looking back at Taylor, the man responded in a lighthearted panic, "Oh, you must be kidding – somebody would actually want to adopt you! Well – well look, whoever applied, at least they were denied. So what's the problem?

"The problem is," started Taylor, "I actually started to like her – I mean really, you know – like her, and now I see this. That explains everything! *Cutie pie... pumpkin – sweetie* – uurrgghh"

Suddenly, as if an explosion went off in his head, Jay's face grew lobster red.

"You mean..." and he pointed toward the exit, and mouthed the word "her!"

"Right!" Taylor said in almost a hoarse growl to compete with Jay's discretion.

"Before all that chaos yesterday, I thought we were hitting it off pretty good. Now I find out that she's trying to adopt me!"

Taylor turned his head, feeling that he could hear strange noises nearby. This attention was quickly distracted by Jay's continuing conversation.

"But honestly – even if you really *liked her* liked her – I mean – you're thirteen – it's not like you could..."

"Yeah I know!" Taylor said loudly. "I'm a freak – I can't have any real relationship – it's practically impossible. Girls my age – well – let's not go there! I mean – maybe not on an age level, but on a personal level – Dr. Reed and I were such a match."

Taylor took a few seconds to think of what he could possibly say to support an argument of him having *any* kind of relationship, and in the process he heard a strange muffling noise that seemed to come from somewhere nearby, but in his searching, the teen couldn't find anything to explain the noise.

"But honestly – we're only seven years different, and if we had a simple five years to let our relationship grow, then would it be so strange – me being eighteen to her twenty-five. Then it couldn't be a *real* relationship."

"Ugh – but not now – now after everything yesterday – she doesn't want anything like that – now all she wants is to be my *mother!"*

"Well," Jay said nonchalantly, "that explains why she's been acting all weird." He paused and, looking at Taylor's depressed face decided to lighten the mood. "Look on the bright side! At least it was denied."

The both of them nearly jumped out of their skin as they heard wailing through the intercom beside Taylor's bed. Apparently, the noises that Taylor and Jay had heard were the intercom system by the bed, and for the past minute or so, Dr. Reed must have been eavesdropping on their conversation. Looking to the side of the recovery room, Taylor and Jay could see through the observation window, that Dr. Reed had quickly gathered her belongings and left.

Taylor looked up at Jay, "Great... Just great! I finally meet a girl I like. She's smart, she's cute, and despite my best efforts at charming her, she wants to be my mother!"

"Well it's not all *that* bad!" Jay said quickly, and with an aggravated stare from Taylor, the man retracted, "Okay – that's really, really bad!"

Taylor, about to turn to Jay to speak, had his attention diverted by changes in the data screen. At the top of the screen the word "UPDATING" flaOne by one the "pending" status on all the other applicants for the six children started changing to "withdrawn."

"Jay," he said excitedly. "Look at the screen. Look at the screen! What's happening?"

"Well," said a somewhat confused Jay, "Best I can guess, everybody's pulling their app for the kids."

"Why would they...?"

"Because!" said Jay, stating as if it were obvious, "Man, they all saw the fight you put up yesterday for them kids – you really kicked some surgical butt out there! They prob'ly just think it's only fair."

Taylor's face grew into a huge grin as one by one all of the other applications changed to "withdrawn". This smile immediately rescinded when Taylor saw that an extra applicant had been added to the bottom of the list.

"Dr. Hathaway!" read Jay, "But she wasn't even there yesterday. Does she even know what happened?"

Taylor, grabbing the data-pad, tapped the department code "007ED07".

"Evolved Mental Development – Advanced Youth Division"

Jay looked at this application and, hoping for the best, thought that their experiment might be able to acquire half of these children under its umbrella.

"Maybe we can take three, and Hathaway can take three." Jay said with an optimistic tone.

"That just wouldn't be right." responded Taylor in a sullen voice.

"Wha..." Jay turned and looked at his teenage counterpart, confused by the response he was just given, "What? Why would you say that?"

Taylor jumped from the bed, ripped the NVM tube from his arm without a thought except to cyberly silence the audio from the monitoring system, which showed that he had instantly gone flat-line, and thereafter pulled a second gown from a nearby shelf. He proceeded to put this on, backwards, to cover his backside, talking as he moved.

"These kids, all six of them, are brothers and sisters." he explained while desperately trying to tie his first robe in the back, eventually giving up and doing it telekinetically.

Jay, looking at him with a face of total disbelief, expressed his feelings with a simple, "You must be joking!"

Taylor shook his head, "I am certain of it. I – I can *feel it!*"

"Perc" Taylor said quickly, commanding the use of the Pediatric Recovery Room Computer, "Recognize Physician Authority Taylor, Robert S."

"Physician Authority Recognized. Good morning Dr. Taylor. Hope you are feeling better. Congratulations again on your promotion."

Taylor blinked at this response. "Oh crap, I forgot to change the security protocols."

"Permff..." Taylor was about to access the computer again when Jay put his hand on the boy's mouth to keep him from doing so.

"No need!" Jay started with a quick, but soft voice. "You *have* been promoted."

Taylor pulled his head from Jay's grip, half irritated, half confused. Jay merely added, "The EduCorp Supervisory board made an executive decision. After so many eye witnesses saw what you did and heard what *he* said, they instigated an inquiry into the E.R. and Medical Management Team. Trust me, there were plenty enough complaints to warrant the decision they made."

"And what was that?" Taylor inquired, though he could sense the words before he heard them.

"They decided to demote Weston and put you in his place."

A wide truly childish grin grew on Taylor's face, but the giddy expression did not last for long. Within a few seconds, with Taylor thinking ever so hard and weighing his options carefully, the elated teenage boy shifted to a glare of seriousness.

"I – I can't take the position." he said soberly.

"What?!" Jay bellowed, standing defensively beside the bed, "Why the hell not?"

Taylor looked up at the ceiling of the recovery room and started to speak. "Perc – run a comparative analysis of the genetic markers for the DNA samples obtained for subjects," he paused and leaned to look at Jay's data-pad, "2675A thru 2680A."

"Command confirmed," declared the computer, it passed the time by beeping and calculating in the background. Jay's patience for this quickly ran very thin, as evidenced by his immediate questioning of Taylor over his ridiculous decision.

"Come on, Dude. What's this all about? You can't just give this up? You're like the youngest super ever in the E.R."

Taylor did not respond to Jay's comments, but carefully listened to the computer's inquiry instead: "What conditions do you wish to use as a filter Dr. Taylor?"

"Perc" Taylor said, stiff lipped and unwavering, "Filter according to familial, hereditary, and common parental markers. Override vital display on this screen and display the requested data."

Taylor's flat-lined vitals disappeared and in a few short seconds it was instantly apparent by the DNA and RNA markers that these children were not only siblings, but that five of them were exactly the same age.

"You see," said Taylor looking up at Jay, "I have to quit the E.R. and work full time with these kids. They *need* me." he said solemnly.

Jay looked down at him with a smile and, as if forgetting the maturity of the teenager he was staring at, he scrubbed the boy's head with his hand.

"Dude, I forget how much of a kid you still are. 'T sounds to me like you need them more than they need you!" he whispered with almost a laugh.

Taylor, swiftly making a futile effort to reform his hair, responded arrogantly, "I am not a child – nor do I need these kids for *friendship.*" And he said this last word with an arrogant laugh.

"I wonder..." Jay said with a curious stare between Taylor and the children. "Have you at all thought about the fact that *you* might be related."

Taylor's mind, as if it had a switch inside his head that had been turned lit up with ears, eyebrows, shoulders and a stare to the computer that was quick and purposeful.

"Oh – wow! No! I – Perc – compare genetic markers and alleles of subjects 2675A through 2680A to those found in myself and filter for possible familial ties."

The computer took a moment to process Taylor's own genetic code, and after the computer had finished its job, it notified Taylor with a simple "comparison complete – no familial ties recognized." Jay's idea and Taylor's excitement quickly faded into nothingness.

There was nearly a minute of awkward silence between the two of them that was only broken when took a deep breath and spoke with a smile.

"It was worth a try. And besides when we get these kids we're all gonna be together a lot more."

"If we get them you mean." Jay replied.

Taylor looked at his friend and so desperately wanted to mention the vision that he had seen in the operating room – a vision that showed him working closely with the children – trying his best to teach them the most basic of words. He wanted to let the man know that he knew it wasn't a question of *'if'*, but *'when'* this would happen. But Taylor was familiar with the limitations of future premonitions and for this reason he kept this information to himself. He hated the thought of this vision, and the fantastic emotions that came with it, being nothing more than a half memory of things that were never meant to be.

Taylor half winced over his thoughts and at that moment he and Jay shared a feeling of uneasiness before turning their heads in different directions. Jay stared over the data-pad, optimistic about their application's "first in" preference. Taylor looked and eventually paced up and down the length of children lined beside his own bed. Biting his lip, running his fingers slowly of the rails at the ends of their beds, he felt a mix of fear, worry, and uncertainty rush through him.

PART TWO

LOSS OF INNOCENCE

20 A Walk in the Park

JAY PEERED OVER HIS DATA-PAD with a nervous set of shifting eyes. He cautiously took in the five young faces staring at him with their full attention hanging on his every word. He always found that when he was alone with the children, the best way to keep their attention, without becoming some sort of telekinetic plaything, was to tell a story. The best stories he knew were always the ones from his real life experiences with Taylor and as such, for these children, their favorite was the one that told of their arrival at The Towers.

To make the stories more interesting Jay would pepper these tales with telepathic images of his memories as he told them. He could gage how good of a job he was doing based on the 'oohs' and 'aahs' he got from their eyes-closed faces. This did, however, cause a considerable drain on him and in looking around at the children's expectant faces he held up his hands.

"That's it kids!"

There were instant moans and Jay could see disappointment build in their ten little eyes. He was about to stand up and brush the grass off his pants, but as he leaned forward to do so his ears were met with several protests.

"That's not it!" insisted Orion with a sour look on his face. "We're all still practically vegetables. Father hasn't even woke us up yet, and no one has any idea about all our powers!"

"Yeah!" Grace and Aspen chimed in together before Aspen continued, "and what about father's fight with that evil lady, what's-her-name," she nudged Grace in the side, forcing her to respond loudly, "Hathaway! But she's boring – I wanna hear about that Zeldin guy."

"Yeaaaaahhh!" the other four bellowed at him.

Jay cringed at hearing this name, horrible memories entering his brain that he immediately tried to clear out lest the children get a hint of this history. Jay then scratched his head. Thinking with half scattered ideas he pointed a shaking finger slowly at each member of his young audience.

"Yoooou – youuuu – ugh!" he grunted. He desperately wanted to offer some harsh sounding form of "that's the end, and that's that!" kind of statement, but when he looked into their curious, hungry little faces the best he could come up with was, "Come on, dudes, I'm tired. I need to get something to eat. Maybe we can go again later.

They all dipped their heads low and, as if sharing the same bad habit, mumbled to themselves in anger.

"Hey, here's a cool idea. Why don't –," Jay said, offering a cautious smile to the small group, "Why don't you go all out and practice using your powers."

With their faces lighting up Jay thought he had hit the perfect idea. Perfect that is, until Grace and David both seemed to show a great interest in wanting to use Jay as their practicing tool. A look of fear fell on his face as he watched them stand up and approach him with a shared malicious grin.

Jay's blood ran a contrasting cold to the hot Metro Park pseudo-sun. He held up his hand, flat palmed and trembling. "Hold it!" he said loudly. "I don't know what the two of you're thinkin' but don't forget about your *father's* rules." This forced the two children to stop for a moment. On every other occasion without fail, Jay would either ignore or correct a reference to Taylor as their father, and he was hoping saying that he *was* their father might have an emotional impact.

The man's efforts to quickly endear himself to the children with this reference seemed not to have worked, for they continued to advance in his direction, and, still terrified of them, he slowly and fearfully stepped away.

It was nearly immediate that Jay remembered his choice to sit the group in the corner of the third level of the Los Angeles Metro Park. As a result, there was nowhere to go but a few feet towards the nearby fences. Grace and David stopped their slow pursuit and stared at each other with what seemed the most devious of smiles before running at their target. Jay, at a complete loss for what to do, screamed and covered his face in fear.

When nothing happened after several seconds he parted his fingers and realized that the focus of the children wasn't him, but rather the backpack he had just dropped. The two must have seen that, in planning for the trip, he'd brought with him several balls, blocks, and electronic devices in case he had to give them a higher degree of stimulation.

He lowered his hands in relief, but felt horribly embarrassed as he was now looking out at five children who were all laughing at him hysterically.

"Hey! Uncle Jay." David called, walking away with three different colored balls floating in front of him, "You know, you scream like a girl!"

Jay, while flattered at the thought of being called uncle, waved a fierce hand for the children to leave him alone after suffering such an insult. He walked away from the laughing children and trudged a slow line to a vending machine. Pressing his thumb on one of its selections, the machine plopped out a chocolate flavored proto-bar.

He continued picking a different flavor over and over until he had eight different bars in his hands. He gripped them tightly in frustration then shoved them in his pockets, all the while shaking his head.

"I don't know why I bother." he said aloud, "Should just let 'em starve!"

With a cropping shadow from behind Jay turned around and his eyes opened wide with surprise as he saw that Caitlin was standing behind him.

"You know," she said softly, still a sore sight with her mismatched outfit, "I wouldn't blame you if you did."

Jay, offering a false look of being confused asked curtly, "Blame me for what?"

She smiled with a look that showed him \that she wasn't fooled by his false ignorance. "You know what I mean – letting them go hungry," she said, and shortly after she added, "That was a really horrible thing they did to you right then. Making you think that they were going to attack you. *I mean really.*"

She and Jay slowly started to walk around the park, now holding hands at her request, and he listened as she put on false tones of concern and emotion.

"*Honestly,* all they had to do was ask what was in the bag, and that would've saved you all the trouble," she paused for a moment, "and the screams."

Jay stopped walking and Caitlin stared up at him. "Sorry," she said, and she offered him a smile that he only barely returned. "Well you do have to admit, your reaction was a *bit* over the top." She said this and used her free hand to pinch a small amount of air at the word "bit."

His smile widened, "I guess I should learn to be a little less dramatic."

"Well," she said softly as they turned one corner of the park, "you could try trusting us."

He looked at her, surprised at this wise request, but had the perfect response planned in his head before she finished the statement.

"Trust," he said looking down at her with a serious expression, "is something that is earned, not just given, my little one."

Caitlin looked up at her tall counterpart, mouth gaping in surprise at what he said. He, however, reveled in the fact that his comment forced such an expression. He stopped again and squatted in front of her.

"I see your look, and come on... What makes you think that any of you *have* earned my trust?" he asked softly. She looked at him with two large brown eyes, and little by little he could feel his heart melt.

"You know we're only having fun Uncle Jay." she said, unblinking. "It's like father said. We're trapped inside these little bodies with these huge gifts, and we want to use them. We want to show the world what we can do!" she grew excited as she continued, and Jay smiled at seeing her glowing energy.

"So what! We have a little harmless fun here and there. Has it ever been anything serious?"

Jay's face shifted from a smile to a face more serious. "Wow, little C. I guess what I said really bothered you, didn't it?"

"Well," she said quietly, "Yeah! You basically said you don't trust us! I mean, don't you think that if it came even close to getting out of hand that we'd back off and make sure you'd be okay." Jay was about to speak, but Caitlin wasn't finished and felt the need to let out all of her feelings. "You're ours, you and Father both. We love you, and you might think you're taking care of us. But the truth is; we're taking care of you too!"

Jay grinned, "You know it!"

The both of them smiled at this and Jay felt a part of his brain suddenly flip over. His face shifted and Caitlin knew that he was about to adopt a more serious note to the conversation.

"I know, I know what you're saying," he said to her softly. "I've been there through it all, I know what you do is all out of fun, and it's always been safe. I also know that with your powers, as great as they are, I can trust that you'd never let anything really bad happen to me."

Jay stopped and, almost laughing, continued, "Funny I should be saying that a group of ten year olds would keep me safe, when it should be the reverse." He pointed his finger at her, reminding her of how close this statement was to what she had just said.

Finally he stood up, grabbed her hand, and continued leading her around the park. "You know, now that I really think about it, I guess you kids have earned my trust – in your own twisted way." He grabbed her hand a little tighter than normal, "I should be willing to take on anything you guys can dish out, and laugh about it right along with you." He looked down at her smiling face and sighed, breathing in the warm summer air. "I've seen and been through so much with *your father*, and now that I think about it. Life would've been so boring without having him or the six of you around to keep me… uh… occupied."

Having said nothing else between them, the two continued around the park, watching the many other visitors, and enjoying the overall happiness around them. They passed by a baseball field being used by one of the local schools, a football field, and a set of seesaws that children were bouncing on playfully – and in seeing all of this Jay and Caitlin's minds were filling with and playing a barrage of memories from the past where they had, time and time again, enjoyed the many outside activities offered by the Metro Park.

As the two made their way almost all the way around the park Jay was consumed in watching Aspen and David play telekinetic games with the balls he had brought to the park. His attention shifted then to Orion and Grace, who were controlling remote operated jets and mini-transports that hummed through the air. The group had already acquired a small audience, that cheered and applauded their talents, and at times Jay was so engrossed in watching this that he was completely ignorant of the girl at his side.

She looked up at him because he stopped walking. As if his brain had fallen out of his head some several steps back, she could see that he was mindlessly gawking at the crowd across the park. Stepping away, she grabbed the nearby fence with both hands and looked out over the city. Seeing its tall buildings and fast moving transports, she suddenly felt a longing for her father and her younger brother; a longing that mounted when she spotted the EduCorp Towers off in the distance.

****

Walking into the darkness that was lab-room L, Taylor willed the lights to come on and found that he was pulled between two points of interest that he knew required his attention equally and immediately. Not sure which to attack first, he weighed each one in his mind. First there was Johnny, who had once again endured an encounter with this strange sphere and who he'd wanted to talk with ever since this ordeal began. Second there was the sphere itself, resting quietly in its container, and, for extra security, was also enclosed in a containment locker. This sphere, whose purpose Taylor scarcely knew, and whose makers he was desperate to discover, baffled him to the highest degree.

Being torn almost equally in this manner, Taylor decided it best to pull his brain out of the mix and let his heart make the decision an easy one.

Walking up to the boy, Taylor saw that the child was still unconscious, and was facing away from him as he approached. With a sigh Taylor tilted his head to one side and noticed that Johnny was holding himself in a simple fetal position. Taylor could only assume that the child's unending tiredness was from whatever drug was in his system. He put his hand on the back of the boy's head, rubbed it gently, then spoke to reassure him, though he was certain no one was listening.

"Don't worry! Everything's going to be fine. I'm here now."

He looked up to the ceiling and called to the laboratory computer, coded to respond to "LAB."

"Recognize personnel authority Taylor, Robert S."

"Authority recognized, good afternoon Dr. Taylor, how may I be of service?"

"LAB – Run a complete scan, including standard and extended biochemical searches, to determine if any foreign substance…"

"Do you have to be so loud!" called a voice from right under Taylor's nose.

Taylor looked down in surprise and saw that Johnny had quickly rolled on his back and looked up at Taylor with squinted eyes.

"The lights I can handle," he said in a soft, yet irritated voice, "but with this headache you're voice just booms."

"You're awake!" Taylor said loudly, and on seeing Johnny grab his own head with both hands repeated this in a whisper, "You're awake!"

"Duh." the boy said softly.

"Well?" Taylor asked eagerly. "How do you feel?"

"You mean other than my headache!"

"Well, what I mean is. Are you okay?"

"Hmmm," the boy thought for a moment "I do have this horrible pain..." Taylor's attention was suddenly peaked as the boy continued, "it's right here on the side of my finger."

Johnny held out his hand and put it beneath Taylor's stare. The teen scanned the finger up and down expecting to find some sort of puncture mark, or sign of distress, but on seeing nothing, he released the finger at a loss to explain the complaint.

At that instant Johnny quickly reached up and pinched Taylor on the nose, offering a short "beep" at the same time.

Taylor quickly grabbed the child's hand and pulled it around and over the boy's head, forcing him to sit up, helpless in accepting a quick hug from behind.

"You're fine," Taylor said laughingly, "you big faker!"

After a few rocks back and forth Johnny's eyes rolled around in his head very strangely, forcing Taylor's immediate concern.

"Woah," Johnny said on being released, "I guess I'm not as okay as we think I am."

Taylor slowly lowered him on the bed, "Lay down, I want to do some scans." he said and looked upward, this time careful to speak more softly.

"LAB – Perform a high resolution neural scan of Johnny Matthews. Display the data here." and at that moment Taylor tapped a nearby display screen.

"Command confirmed. Please wait."

They both watched as a white robotic arm pulled itself out of the wall and circled over the top of Johnny's head several times.

"So, I have to ask. Do you remember who came into your dorm last night? Did you – uh – did you get a good look at 'em," Taylor asked, taking advantage of the time it took for the computer to scan the boy's brain.

"No, there was a bright light behind 'em – I couldn't really see anything. But I got an… impression."

"Impression?" Taylor repeated, half questioning, half understanding. Impressions, as Taylor understood them from visions, was like a feeling that a person gives you when you're around them, and when you see that person again, you feel the same way – it's an impression – something that even Taylor couldn't explain with total clarity, but that he completely understood.

The two exchanged a look of concern, and with the robotic arm making one final scan of the Johnny's head, the boy started blinking his eyes uncontrollably. Taylor watched with panic as the child's eyes were again rolling around in his head without focus or uniform direction.

Taylor punched the emergency stop button on the wall, forcing the robotic arm to return to its original position. The teen now stared at the boy in complete panic, pulled him up and offered a shake, then a hug and a calming voice in his ear. With a sigh he felt the boy cough and flinch as he slowly worked his way out of this strange behavior. Taylor then rested the child back on the bed with a scrutinizing stare.

Putting his hand on the boy's forehead, he watched as, finally, two bright blue eyes returned to what looked like normal. After a few blinks, the eyes looked up at Taylor.

Taylor could feel that Johnny made an effort to sit up, but with his hand in the way the teen was able to prevent this.

"I don't think so!" he said forcefully, "You need to stay down!"

"What! What happened?" asked Johnny, eyes searching about desperately for answers and as Taylor caught sight of them, he knew that they were filled with fear.

"It's okay Johnny, you're fine." Taylor said softly, and after giving the boy a moment to relax he offered a questioning face. "I was hoping I could ask *you* what happened just now. What do you remember?"

"Not much." the boy said, shaking his head with wide confused eyes. "I saw the light from the scanner – then it got real bright and there were a bunch of white flashes, and images – there were images – like pictures. It was like someone was showing me pictures over and over again, but each one was a different one…"

Taylor lit his usual sideways grin at the boy. "And you said you didn't remember much," he said with a laugh.

Johnny looked at him, half confused. "But I can't remember any of the pictures... just that there *were* pictures."

Taylor's smile grew even larger. "That's fine. Anything is better than nothing – always remember that!"

Taylor looked upward purposefully and again addressed the computer.

"LAB, was sufficient data collected from the scan to comprise composite image of Johnny's brain?"

"Affirmative."

"LAB," Taylor continued, "display the data as previously instructed."

With many different colors coded for different parts of the boy's brain, a graphic image came up on the screen. Looking at it passively, Taylor immediately instructed, "LAB, correlate this image with standard biological data and neurological scans. Remove anything from the display that would be considered normal."

Slowly much of the image grew dark and Taylor watched as that which was left resembled something of a web running through the boy's brain. Johnny himself was twisting and squirming in his bed, to his own great discomfort, trying his best to see what was on the screen above him. When he was finally able to comprehend the upside-down image, all he could do was frown.

"What's all that?"

"I don't know, Johnny, that's what I'm trying to find out," Taylor said stiffly. "LAB – Can you identify the remaining image on the screen?"

"Affirmative."

Taylor instantly waved his hands in frustration, causing Johnny to laugh. The teen was irritated at the fact that his question was answered so simply, nothing more and nothing less than what he asked, thus telling him he needed to rephrase the question.

"Lab – *Please* identify the graphic representation on the display screen and its nature." The computer's response was immediate and much more satisfying.

"This graphic represents microscopic metallic fragments, electrically charged, and self propelled; each with different electromagnetic signatures. At their current rate, they will be completely dissolved in their natural environment and flushed out of the subject's body in less than twelve hours." Immediately red circles came up on the screen noting the areas of Johnny's brain where the presence of these anomalies was most dense.

"What does that mean?" asked Johnny, though Taylor thought the boy might have understood some of what the computer said.

"Nanites!" Taylor said purposefully, trying not to pull his eyes away from the screen, but the immediate reaction of the boy prevented this. Taylor could tell that this one word put the boy in an instant state of fear and panic.

Johnny tried to jump out of his seat at hearing that is brain was infested with microscopic robots, but he wasn't fast enough for Taylor, who had kinetically pulled out a tranquilizer gun and used it on the boy's neck.

"Calm down, Johnny, everything's going to be fine – just relax – when you wake up – everything'll be fine!"

In only a few seconds the boy was asleep, holding one hand to his neck, and one on Taylor's own nearby hand. Taylor's heart ached and he sighed as the child's hand fell to a limp hang over the side of the bed. Taylor repositioned him on the bed to be comfortable, but flat and straight.

"Sorry 'bout that kid." he said softly and he gently laid his hand on the boy's forehead.

As he pulled his hand away, looking at the display, he could see that Johnny's neural patterns and heart rate had become quite erratic.

"LAB – What's happening to Johnny?" Taylor shouted to the computer.

Conversely from his last inquiry attempts with the computer, it is superb programming technique that often saved Taylor when he was in a panic, for when some of the simplest questions are asked, the result can be the most complicated response from the computer so that it might supply the needed answer. Thus the following ensued...

Three robotic arms shot out from the wall to scan the child from head to toe, and each with a different colored light. Taylor had to stand back as yet another arm beeped a strange tool around his entire perimeter.

When they were all finished, the arms returned to their resting location and the resulting scans popped up side by side on the same screen where the boy's vitals were displayed. Thereafter the computer retorted and audio explanation.

"A type 3 tranquilizer has been given to subject Johnny Matthews. This tranquilizer is having a negative interaction with the anomalies in his frontal cortex."

"LAB – Can de-replicators be used to safely remove these anomalies from their current positions."

The computer beeped its thoughts away, but Taylor's patience was running extremely thin.

"Come on… hurry up!" he said loudly, and he grabbed Johnny's hand tightly as he waited for the answer, watching as the boy's heart-rate fluctuated and his neural activity would peak off the charts, then drop below normal.

After what seemed an eternity of waiting the computer offered its calm response: "The anomalies can be removed if they are neutralized."

"LAB – how can the anomalies be neutralized?"

The computer's answer to this question was much faster than the first, though the pacifying voice was getting on Taylor's nerves.

"A high voltage, low amperage shock would render the anomalies inactive."

Taylor shook his head quickly at this, and snapped the next question within seconds. "LAB, what are the risks in performing such a procedure."

"There is a thirty percent chance that subject 'Johnny' will suffer memory loss and/or minor brain damage."

"LAB, what are the risks if this procedure is not performed?"

"At the current rate of vital sign declination the subject has no chance of survival."

Taylor's mind felt like it was going to explode. He was uncertain of what he should do, yet was unwilling to risk having the child at his side suffer irreparable brain damage. Scanning the numbers offered by the computer, his eyes lit up with an idea.

"LAB, on my command; administer a neural charge at fifty percent voltage and amperage of previously calculated values for two seconds then immediately scan and remove disabled anomalies."

The computer calculated for a moment, the confirmed the request.

Taylor took a deep breath, releasing the boy's hand, but wishing desperately that he didn't have to. "LAB, initiate the requested procedure."

"Command confirmed."

Nervous and practically shaking, Taylor watched as two robotic arms again pulled out of the wall. One put itself over Johnny's head and with a jerk all over the child's body, forcing even Taylor to jump; he watched the robotic arm zap Johnny's brain.

Seconds later the second robotic arm scanned the boy's brain and, by the noise it was making, Taylor could tell that it was actively de-replicating several nanites.

Both arms retracted themselves into the wall and Taylor saw that Johnny's vitals, while still uncomfortably sporadic, were more stable than before.

The computer offered a report in its usual calm demeanor: "Twenty percent of the anomalies have been removed."

Restlessly listening to the computer, and immediately grabbing a firm hold of the boy's hand, Taylor had only one question left to ask. Not taking his eyes off the child, he opened his mouth, and barely able to get the words out, he exhaled the inquiry fearfully.

"LA – uh – LAB. Are there any signs of neural damage?"

He waited with bated breath as Johnny was once again scanned by the computer.

"Negative."

Taylor slumped down in his chair and exhaled a sigh of relief. Carefully wording his instructions, he commanded that the computer should repeat this same process, including the full neural scan, every two minutes until at a minimum 95% of the nanites had been removed.

The computer complied and Taylor waited and watched as the two robotic arms repeatedly scanned, removed and rescanned the boy's head. Leaning back in his chair, he was finally ready to relax and let the lab computer do all the work. Resting his weary gaze for only a moment, when he opened his eyes again they were drawn away from looking at the boy in front of him by movement in a nearby containment locker.

Getting out of his chair and walking toward the locker, he watched through two layers of plex as the strange chrome colored sphere, arms fully extended, thrashed about uncontrollably in its cylindrical container. Continuing his approach, Taylor's curiosity was peaked over this new activity.

21 Taylor's Old Book

"WHAT'S THE MATTER LITTLE C.?" Jay asked, pulling his attention away from the activities of his other four students and thus *finally* noticing the girl's somber stare over the city skyline.

"Hmmm," she mumbled, turning in his direction, yet eyeing her siblings enviously. "Oh, I was just wondering how father was doing with Johnny?" she said in a voice that was very quiet and reticent, all the while casting a passive stare back out over the city.

"Huh? Bull!" Jay snapped, noticing her far distant stare. "I know you. It's something else." he added accusingly, standing behind her, gently putting his hands on her shoulders, "I think – I *know* what would cheer you up!"

She let go of the fence and looked up at him with half a smile. "What's that?"

He pulled away from her, ran a few paces to his backpack and within moments waved for her to come over. Intrigued, she walked to his side, thereby returning to the same spot where the whole group was sitting nearly an hour before. He stood, holding something behind himself, and her intrigue was mounting.

"You didn't think I brought anything for you," he said with a smile and she looked up at him seemingly puzzled. "You know, for your powers!" he explained.

From behind his back he slowly revealed a book. Caitlin's face lit up. She stared at it with a growing smile as he held it out for her. It was an actual old fashioned book – with paper pages and everything. She was amazed, yet when she reached to touch it, Jay pulled it back, offering quick words of encouragement.

"You know," he said with a grin, "you're a lot like Taylor; wise beyond your years."

He pushed the book out further, and she reached for it. It was turned over so she couldn't read the title, and for the second time Jay pulled the book away just before she could make contact.

"I know the easiest way for cognitive abilities to work is by touch, but soon, I am certain of it, you'll learn, as Taylor did, to pick up visions without an object to channel – like when you go to sleep. This is an old children's book of Taylor's. I borrowed it from him, one of his favorites when he was young. He wanted me to see how far back you could go with it.

"Are you ready?" he asked, and with her impatient nod, he quickly shoved the book hard into her hands, hoping to jolt the vision into her brain.

She only barely had the thought to grip it tightly before her view went completely dark. She kept her eyes closed tight, focusing on pushing her thoughts back into the physical history of the book.

With a whooshing halt of the environment around her, Caitlin whipped her head around quickly to take in her new environment.

Seeing a bed with a little boy sleeping inside, she felt the need to cower away and hide, but quickly accepted this vision for what it was and that she couldn't be seen. She smiled at the boy under her nose. His short, messy, yet clean-cut hair, his cute placid young face, it all made her sigh with a smile. Taking in all the features of his young expression; she knew that he somehow seemed familiar to her. She looked around the tidy room, and quickly realized, seeing a nametag on the nearby nightstand, that it was Taylor – a very young Taylor. She giggled a little at this, thinking how funny it was to see him at such a tender age.

The boy rolled to one side, and with a loud beeping that startled not only him, but her as well, he slapped the alarm clock on the nearby stand.

Caitlin took a closer look at the clock in an effort to see the current date, and gasped when she saw that it was July 16th 2443.

But surely that must be wrong. She found it hard to believe that this was a boy who was, this very day, celebrating his fourth birthday. Thinking hard, she only barely remembered that Taylor had once told her and her siblings of the fact that in his youngest years he looked older than his actual age because of the experiment he was in and the unexpected hormonal side effects that it had on him.

She could swear that by the looks of him he was seven or eight and when she finally shook off the shock of seeing him at this age she giggled even more with secretive delight. With a silencing inhale she saw Taylor pull his legs over to get out of bed, but what's this? They both noticed at the same time that there was a package beside his bed – why, he nearly crushed its brightly colored bow when he tried to drop his feet to the floor.

Caitlin eyed the package with increasing suspicion and curiosity all the while pulling any and all memories of conversations Taylor had offered of his youth. But the truth was that Taylor talked very little of his early years and she was dying to know who could possibly have given him a present on his birthday. In her mind she had good idea that she knew what the gift was, but it was the person giving it that she puzzled over most.

Taylor slipped himself lazily off the bed, wrapping his legs around the present beneath him in a sort of coddling guard and when he'd fully rested on the floor he quickly plucked a small name card from the package and mouthed the words on it slowly. Peering over his shoulder, Caitlin could just barely make out the hand written message from her awkward position over the boy.

Happy Birthday Taylor.
May this bring you
peace of mind my child.
With Love,
Victoria Young

Victoria Young? Caitlin questioned in her mind, and she pondered the name over in her brain while watching the boy savagely rip open his gift.

"Victoria Young, Victoria Young," she repeated out loud, over and over again...

Without warning, as she stared at the smile of a happy boy ready to celebrate his birthday, her vision quickly pulled itself out of focus, as if like being on a rollercoaster that was going backwards, until it finally rushed into focus and stillness.

Caitlin shot her head around in what seemed a hundred directions before she realized she was in an office. A very messy office by the looks of it. Books were scattered everywhere and she appreciated the fact that she was standing in the one part of the room that had a clean space of floor. She was in front of a desk whose tall black chair was turned away from her. This chair seemed to have no one in it, or at least that's what she thought.

With a beeping noise Caitlin turned around, realizing that someone was requesting entrance into the office. She turned back to the chair expectantly and, with a swift and smooth motion the chair behind the desk whirled itself around.

She could see, sitting in the chair, the makings of what was to become her teacher. Now ready to take in fully what she could about this vision, she quickly scoured the office for some indication of a date, and when she found it by means of a clock facing Taylor on the desk; she read that it was November 12, 2450. Taylor was eleven years old and by his attire, she could tell that he was working for EduCorp. She might have had a mind to laugh about this appearance, dressed in a suit with a lab overcoat draped over it, but she could see by the look on his face that this was not a good time for laughs.

Looking back towards the door, she saw a tall, thin, blonde haired woman enter his office and the instant Caitlin saw her face, she put two and two together.

"Victoria Young is Dr. Young. On the council!" she said freely, knowing that no one could hear her.

She had only absorbed this thought for a fraction of a second before it was dejected by Taylor's ranting at the woman.

"How long have you known?" he asked in a hot and acrid voice.

Dr. Young pulled her head back in surprise and responded, "Well good afternoon to you too," she said politely and, after looking around for a few seconds, offered another comment. "Shall I call in the maid?"

He gritted his teeth, something that Caitlin can never, *ever*, remember him doing in her presence, and he repeated, this time somewhat more calmly and desperately. "Just answer my question, how long have you known about my condition. That I'm sterile!?"

"Oh, Taylor." Dr. Young exhaled, realizing his purpose of contention it was clear that she did not expect to have this conversation when she entered his office. Moreover Caitlin was taken aback that she should be privy to these words, this subject, these emotions that she could feel emanating from him. It was all so very raw.

"I now have a job where I am surrounded by children every day of my life." He pleaded harshly, "I've finally decided that I want to stay here and work with them as a career, and now I find out that I can't have any of my own! What the hell kinda crap is that?"

Taylor frowned and persisted, "So I'll ask you one last time. How long have you known?"

"Taylor, honey," she said softly, though he frowned, interpreting her words as condescending. "The council and most of your technicians knew about that a few days after you were born. It's some kind of genetic defect – one that didn't come up in our initial scans. Those came up fine because we were looking for – well – bigger problems. Then, when you were brought into *Prodigy* a much more detailed scan of your genetics was put on record. That's when the company was notified and the defect flagged – but we figured it wasn't something that would affect the program so it was just filed away as some tiny detail..."

Taylor's face grew a bright red, "Yeah, now you tell me; now that I already know. I had my first company physical and this – this was the last thing *I* expected." Taylor continued, becoming more belligerent by the second, yet Dr. Young stood, stiff and firm like an elegant willow weathering a massive storm, "How is it possible that everybody in this friggin' place knows every damn detail about me, and I'm the one who has to find things out by surprise. This is just – it's – it's ridiculous that's what it is."

With a rattling of the objects on Taylor's desk Dr. Young and Caitlin could tell that the boy was losing his kinetic control. Caitlin turned and looked to Dr. Young. She couldn't help but stare at the woman with thick distaste, though she didn't know why. Eventually she turned away, and with welling emotions her heart pounded loudly in her chest she noticed that, near the end of his yelling, Taylor was almost in tears.

Standing amid this argument, Caitlin understood his frustration, for she too was often annoyed at the fact that her trainers knew so much about her, and there seemed to be nothing sacred from their finding out. But at least she felt close to them. Taylor and Jay cared about her – so she knew that this wasn't nearly as horrible as what Taylor had to grow up dealing with. She thought to herself how impossible it would be to live and try to thrive in a place where a group of absolutely passive strangers had your every inch measured, and every ounce weighed, and knew more about you on sight than you knew about yourself, and these details never warranted a care, or concern, or even a moment of personal affection – just simple bits of data stored away – part of a larger project wrapped around a small child. Staring at the young boy before her, Caitlin's heart ached with a silent pity for the life he had to live inside The Towers.

Breaking Caitlin's deeply felt thoughts, she turned as Taylor spoke. His words were soft, yet still unmistakably angered.

"Ever since you walked into my room, those years ago, I thought you were someone I could trust. Someone I could count on to make sure that I stayed on top of this life that's been built around me." He glowered at Dr. Young and could see her face slowly shift to one of sorrow.

"I love kids – I want kids of my own!" he said angrily. "How could this happen. I'm practically perfect," he pleaded, "Oh, except for this one little itty bitty freakin' problem!"

Caitlin quickly welled with embarrassment that she was watching such a personal discussion about Taylor that she was sure she wasn't ever meant to hear and yet, with her love of stories and of personal history, she was consumed by what she was hearing and seeing, and couldn't bear to pull away.

"Taylor," yelled Dr. Young so strongly that it made the two children in the office jump. "When should I have told you? With your *situation*, and at your age, when should I have told you?"

Taylor stood up and took a deep breath to retort, but was cut short by the continuing words of Dr. Young.

"Sit down and shut up for a minute!" She paused paced in front of his desk, "I wasn't sure when would be the right time, or if there would ever be a right time to tell you. I mean think about it. At what age would you actually have a normal, *physical* relationship with someone?"

"You're eleven years old for god's sake!" she continued very nervous to hear any answer to the question she was about to ask. "I mean you're not having these thoughts – you haven't actually..."

"No" he responded quickly, "Like I'd have the time anyways!"

"Well good, and besides, I don't think there's a person out there who's worthy of you as it is. But think about this, Taylor, I don't know if anyone could pick the perfect time to tell you the truth of these things."

She sighed, collected her thoughts, and spoke again with a definitive seriousness that Caitlin understood, for she had heard it in some of Taylor's speeches as well.

"I think it was *best* that you found out on your own. So what if everyone else knows about it. Big deal! You know now and now you have to deal with it. Would've hardly been any different if I had told you, would it?"

"Yeah! Well..." Taylor started, but then stopped, losing the words of what was sure to be more biting rhetoric. Tears welling in his eyes, the emotion seemed too much for him.

"This sucks, this just freakin' sucks!" he said and he sat down in his chair again and whirled himself around to stare at the huge wall with his many books and degrees. Slowly Dr. Young made her way through the office of floor strewn books to Taylor's side.

"Come on, Taylor," she said, putting her hand on his shoulder, "It's not as bad as it sounds. You know you could always ado…"

"Don't you dare say adopt. Don't you dare," Taylor snapped, staring up at her in anger. "I've talked with you enough for you, of all people, to know how I feel about that."

Caitlin, eyeing the two arguers, now stared at Taylor with a look that could almost kill. Did she hear him correctly? He didn't believe in adoption. That just didn't make any sense. Why was he making such strong efforts at trying to adopt her along with her brothers and sisters if he didn't believe in adoption? She stared at him for an answer to these questions, but it might have done her well to look at Dr. Young as it was she that responded with exactly what Caitlin was waiting for.

"I know, I know... you don't want to fix someone else's parenting... bad parents, bad kids, blah, blah, blah." Taylor wheeled around at this, surprised that she could mock his feelings on the matter, but she continued. "You know, you can be such a selfish idiot sometimes. You think that by adopting, you'll inherit someone else's problem. Well here's a newsflash *kid*, you're a great guy, and I have no doubt that you'll be a great parent. So instead of thinking about yourself, think about your kids... whoever they might be. You might inherit a little problem. But they'll be getting a big solution. They'll be getting you!"

Caitlin, fully absorbed in what Dr. Young was saying, moved herself to the woman's side. Her anger at Dr. Young was subsiding and she took in the possibility that this emotion was tied to what Taylor was feeling. Now, as she was closer to the woman's side, she was growing to appreciate, and even like Dr. Young more and more, and at each point that the doctor had made to Taylor she nodded her head forcefully in the boy's direction as if to say "Yeah!"

Taylor's face gradually drained pale as he looked at Dr. Young. He saw in her eyes some kind of affection and love that he had never seen from anyone else in his life. It was there, hiding inside her, and he almost felt guilty for accusing her of any wrongdoing. Caitlin noticed, by seeing and feeling the emotion that came with the vision, this attachment between the two, and it baffled her.

The boy had no choice, at seeing the only set of caring eyes ever to look at him in these towers; he forced his anger down into a spiral of despair. Dr. Young turned to the door of his office swiftly and quietly and as she walked out she spoke soft words to the air, declaring that she would leave Taylor "to think" before adding, "I'll be ready when you want to *talk*."

Caitlin, on the other hand, looked around wildly. She had only just realized that this vision was tied somehow to the book that had been put in her hands, and she wasn't quite sure how it all fit.

As Dr. Young left she could see that Taylor was now wiping away tears that had run down his face earlier. The boy looked at his office, a mess from the books he had thrown to the floor in anger, and started kinetically placing them back on the shelves behind him. He never turned around to see where they went, for he was familiar enough with his surroundings to know where the shelves were, so the books just started picking themselves up and flying over his head to place themselves neatly where they belonged.

With a snap that made Caitlin jump, Taylor reached out his hand and caught one of the books as it was about to fly by on its way to the shelves.

He put the book on the desk, and opened it, offering a smile. With a soft and solemn trudging of words, he spilled his thoughts into the air with a quiet exhale.

"Hhhhhhmm. God, how this book mirrors my life with every page – every metaphor." These words puzzled Caitlin to the point of intrigue. *What did he mean?*

Looking down at the open book all she could see was the brightly colored picture of an old man holding a small piece of wood. The man was painting a face on it with a brush. Caitlin did not understand the significance of this at all. In fact, she was more distracted at the look of the old man, having only ever seen a few pictures of people who had reached that appearance during the last few months of their life.

Taylor slammed the book shut, once again startling Caitlin, and he spoke into the unresponsive air. "With all the kid's I'll be working with, maybe I *won't* need any of my own." He sighed, "Adopt! What was she thinking?" While he was saying these words Caitlin took the time to admire the cover of the book, and to sound out its title for the first time.

"Pin ohk chi oh" she said aloud and confused. She did not understand this word, but it hardly mattered. At hearing Taylor's harsh disdain for adoption she no longer focused on the book, but rather at the *child* holding it. To hear him so strongly dismiss adoption she was angered her to the core. So great was this emotion that she screamed at him, not afraid of any response for she knew he couldn't hear a word she was saying.

"Not adopt! Ha, that's what you think. You will you selfish little brat." It seemed that as she commenced with this vocal venting she experienced a feeling of exhilaration over the fact that she could insult him with impunity. She continued, "She was right, you are an idiot. 'Cause, 'cause guess what – there are six of us: Three boys and three girls. So how 'bout them apples? Man, I'm so glad we were a pain in your butt when we were little – you – you – aeeerhgh!" she grunted.

Taylor stood up, turned around and put the book on the shelf, which he could barely reach at his height, and eventually pushed it onto the shelf fully with his kinesis. He took a breath and with a funny tilt to his head, he whispered, "Three boys, and three girls. That would've been nice."

Caitlin placed her hand over her mouth in absolute shock at what she had heard, and whether from her moment of fear that there was the impossible possibility of him hearing what she had said or that she released of the book in her hands, her vision rushed away from her again and she realized that her post cognition was at its end.

Opening her eyes, she gasped for air, instantly feeling light headed.

"Wooahh... Jay said, holding her at the shoulders as she was about to fall over. "You alright?"

She nodded and steadied herself.

"You were in there a long time, 'bout two minutes. That's pretty good. But you have to remember to breathe little one!"

She only barely smiled at him, trying to catch her breath, and when she realized he was trying to pull the book from her hands she snatched it away and ran with it.

Jay, under normal circumstances might have tried to stop this, but as he fully expected it, he let her be. He had little doubt that she had seen a vision of Taylor's past. It may have been very personal, purposeful even, and as it was revealed to her through this book, the plain object would have a much greater value to her now.

Caitlin stopped running when she looked behind and saw that there was sufficient distance between her and Jay and her siblings. Squatting under a tree so that she could enjoy the cool shade, it was here, finally in a distant and comfortable quietness, that she turned the book over and offered herself a chance to read its cover for the first time in the physical world.

Pinocchio

She had considerable trouble sounding out the name: "Pin ock chee oh."

Offering a very confused face at saying this word, she thought to herself that it made little sense and shook her head dismissively as she opened its large leather binding. To her relief, and irritation, it was a few pages into the book that she saw a phonetic spelling of the title to show her the proper way to say it and revealing that she had done so incorrectly.

"Pin oh key oh" this only cleared things up a little as she still couldn't relate the title to anything she had ever seen or heard.

Intrigued, Caitlin moved slowly, page by page, reading the book, fascinated by the pictures of the older man and ALL the references to things magical and paranormal. Within a few minutes she was completely absorbed in the words of the story, and while this method of reading differed greatly from her usual virtual or digital methods, she turned each page carefully, and admiringly, seeing each word and picture as a priceless piece of art.

Off in the distance Jay had taken to watching the other children, but a commotion all of their attention and with their upward gaze, they could see a transport slip into the side of the third level of the Los Angeles Metro Park and land itself near where they were standing. It wasn't a full size transport, but rather a mini version; ten-passenger instead of the usual twenty. With the EduCorp logo emblazoned on the side and a quick telepathic message from inside, it was clear to both Jay and the children where the transport had come from, and who it contained inside. In an instant the lot of youngsters were bounding full of energy in the direction of where the craft had landed.

The entrance to the transport hissed its way open and as it did Taylor stood at the door, waiting to step out. He exited with a smile, covering his eyes from the pseudo sun beaming overhead, and was rapidly surrounded by his students, all eager to talk with him or rather at him.

"Where's Johnny? Is he okay?" Aspen asked loudly, followed by David, who was practically bouncing off the walls. "Yeah, yeah, where's little J., we need an extra guy."

Taylor squatted down, eye to eye with his students, happy to see their glowing faces, and turned to them one by one not saying a word. He watched as they grew more and more impatient, and his smile gleamed ever wider by the second. When he finally turned to Grace, who forced her own face to be a mere inch away from his own, she spoke loudly at him expectant of answers. "Well, is he alright?"

Taylor blinked for a few seconds and turned. As if playing a recording over in his head, he heard the next sequence of comments both out of memory and with his own ears. The timing was impeccable as the next statements came.

"Is he good to play?" Orion asked blandly, followed by the energetic repetition of David with, "We need a *fifth* person!"

Aspen, who was looking over her sibling's shoulders at Taylor, asked with peaked curiosity, "What happened to him?" This all seemed too strange to have to experience over again, but to push the whole effect over the edge; Taylor caught a glimpse of Caitlin, who had just joined the small crowd.

As she caught the edge of the group she started yelling and commanding in a loud voice, "Make way! Make way! Give him room to breathe why don't you?" Taylor couldn't help but laugh a little at how exactly she matched his memory of what she looked and sounded like.

At this moment Taylor felt a presence standing behind him, and in turning to look he could see that Johnny had stepped off the craft. The boy was rubbing his neck and eyes from waking as he had slept on the trip over. Smiling, Taylor stood, snatching Johnny up with a rousing bit of laughter, and placed the boy on his own shoulders, then, leaning forward, flipped the boy over so as to make him land on his feet. Finally, after standing full upright, Taylor said his first comment since stepping into the park, "I'll just leave him here with you – to play!"

The children rushed on Johnny, who offered a smile to his siblings at the attention he was getting, and as he was escorted away Taylor offered a simple and yet stern pathic message to the boy

"You need to be careful, Johnny, especially considering..."

Taylor didn't finish the pathic message, but he could see that it had put a damper on Johnny's mood and forced a somber look on the boy's face, but just the same he, Johnny, turned and ran with his brothers and sisters, happy to be with them again.

Taylor offered a slight chuckle as he watched the group run rampant, and as he sat on the steps of the transport, which offered its own shade by the raised door, he saw that Jay was on the approach. Worse than this, the man was already barraging him with pathic questions of whether he had learned anything new.

"Slow down! Slow down! What's the rush?" Taylor suppressed, as Jay sat beside him, so that the pair could watch the children together.

"So," Taylor continued, desperate to change the subject, "I saw that Caitlin had my copy of *Pinocchio* in her hands. Eh - did she tell you what she saw."

"No," he said, grumbling at first. "Kid just ran off with the book. Few minutes ago I saw her reading it. I could tell that she was really into the story!"

"Hmmm," Taylor mumbled concernedly as he watched Caitlin take her place under the same tree as before. She immediately pulled the book out again and started reading.

"Maybe I should go talk to her." Taylor said soberly.

"Not so fast buster!" Jay snapped firmly, grabbing Taylor's arm.

Taylor looked at his arm, being held by Jay, and was quite surprised at this action. He looked at the concern on Jay's face and knew the questions inside the man's head even without any kind of pathic link.

"Oh, for heaven's sake – the boy's fine. He might be a little light headed now and again for the next few days. But his scans are fine."

"Dude, the sphere?" asked Jay in an almost accusatory manner.

"Now, that's a different story!" responded Taylor animatedly.

Jay waved his hands furiously as if to say "Come on – out with it!"

Taylor smiled and, after a moment's pause, proceeded to tell Jay of his experiences with Johnny, and the discovery of nanites in the boy's brain. On hearing this Jay worked a stare of anxiousness on his face, to which Taylor informed him that there was nothing to fret about, and that he, Taylor, was able to remove the nanites with no negative side effects.

"*Cheese and rice*! So that thing – that *thing* put them there?"

"Oh absolutely, no doubt about it." Taylor answered unconcerned and matter-of-factly.

"But – I – I don't understand – what's the damned thing good for – what's it want with our kids – what..." Jay spewed, voicing his many and varied thoughts.

"Well," Taylor started, holding up his hand to cut off Jay's words, "after I set L.A.B. up to remove the nanites, I was sidetracked by the sphere itself. The thing was going crazy. I mean at first, when I walked in the room it wasn't doing a thing, then all of a sudden it just started going nuts..."

Taylor continued to tell the story, with a mix of verbal words and pathic images, and Jay listened carefully as the details of what happened in the lab before Taylor's arrival to the park unraveled slowly in his mind. While mentally both carefully watched the Johnny play with his brothers and sisters, off in the distance.

22 Johnny's Plight

APPROACHING THE SPHERE'S CONTAINMENT LOCKER, Taylor sensed that it wouldn't be safe to get too close.

This intuition proved to be right, for the sphere had found a way to use each of its tentacles at a point of equal pressure around its cylindrical confinement, causing this first level of restraint to burst inside the locker and offer the sphere more space to maneuver. It was therefore only a few seconds before it found away to shatter the door of the locker, exploding it in Taylor's direction.

The teen kinetically seized the shards of plex material in mid air and forced them to drop like tinkling bits of solid rain. Behind this the sphere shot itself out from the locker and, surprising to Taylor, it had no interest in him at all. It was making its way across the room, clicking its tentacles with every step, working to move ever closer to its unconscious boy target. Taylor couldn't help but feel a chill run up his spine from the sight of the thing in full action.

At the last moment, before the sphere had a chance to touch Johnny, Taylor kinetically held the sphere at bay, and while his stare was focused on the unit, he addressed the lab computer again; curious to find out what made this strange object tick.

"LAB," he commanded, placing the struggling sphere on an examination bed, totally binding it with his kinesis. "Perform a complete, high resolution scan of the subject on bed five. Identify the subject as 'Sphere'."

The computer responded quickly to this command forcing the three robotic arms to eject from the wall to scan the sphere. With gleaming tentacles it quivered almost fearfully.

After the scan was complete several screens lit up on the nearby display and Taylor became instantly fascinated by what he saw. He studied the internal schematics of the machine and found its mechanical workings to be the most advanced design he had ever laid eyes on. The unit had backup system after backup system to keep it functioning, and, more interestingly, it actually had six independent processors – each one fully capable of running the machine. There were multiple microscopic actuators and electronic units to control the many arms of the sphere; there were ultra fine tubes that ran the full length of the sphere's arms to inject a supply of nanites into the sphere's target.

Taylor hummed and gasped in awe. He leaned in closer to the screen, focusing hard on it, carefully analyzing the nanite administering system. For Taylor, whose fields of study included a PhD in nano-technology, catching and examining an electronic specimen like this was a real treat. He, consequently, couldn't help but give the screen in front of him *his full attention.*

Several quiet minutes passed with Taylor taking many mental notes over what flashed on the screen before him. Pulling his face away from it he saw, for only a fraction of a second, the reflection of a long blunt pipe hovering behind him. The glint of a slithering wiry grip was all that hinted to Taylor who, or what, was behind him. With no time to react and a hard pain on the back of his head, then another in the front from hitting the screen face first, Taylor was given an instant and assaulting headache.

While the hit didn't knock Taylor out, it did knock him to the ground, and as he turned up to look at his robotic assailant, what he saw next left him utterly speechless.

Johnny jumped out of bed and grabbed the sphere, metallic tentacles and all, and threw it across the room. Taylor had a mind to interfere, but just as he was bringing his pained face into kinetic focus he saw Johnny stare at one of the nearby beds. The bed-sheet on it flew into the air and wrapped itself around the sphere. This worked temporarily to keep the robotic unit at bay for a moment, but with the ripping of the sheets, it freed itself with the sharp ends of its pointed arms.

Panicked, Johnny focused on a nearby wall panel. It opened, the panel itself skirting violently across the floor. Instantly thereafter cabling pulled itself out, eventually wrapping around the sphere. The weight and size of the cables was far too much for the robot to contend with. It was trapped and immobile, and on seeing the condition of his metallic adversary, Johnny simply stood beside the thing, patting it on its chrome noggin.

He looked at Taylor and offered a simple, "thanks" to which Taylor gazed at the boy, amazed and confused.

"What the hell was that?" Taylor yelled as Johnny stepped aside to admire the confined robot.

"Huh..." The boy shrugged, looking up at Taylor. "Whaddaya mean" he asked, head cocked.

"You!" Taylor said loudly, "You're kinetic now?"

Johnny held out his arms in innocent exposure, looking over his body ignorantly. "I am?"

"Well that wasn't me that magically wrapped that thing up. So who else was it?"

"But I thought that *was* you?"

The boy now looked over his limbs in excitement as if he could see something different about himself. These lifted emotions seemed to bleed over into Taylor, who quickly snatched up a tool from a nearby table. Looking at the boy, he quickly voiced a, "Catch this, *with no hands!"*

Taylor threw the tool into the air and, just as it was making its way past John-

Johnny's head, it stopped in mid air. The boy's eyes were fixed on it and with a few light motions of his hands he was able to make it move and slide through the air with no problems.

The tool, a neoplastic-gun designed for wound healing, dropped to the ground when Johnny lost his concentration due to the rattling and shaking of the confined sphere.

Taylor immediately looked up to the ceiling, "LAB, locate and remove any sources of power for mechanical subject 'sphere'."

The computer responded and within seconds the sphere offered only a few small twitches as it lost all its power.

Taylor motioned for Johnny to take his place back on the bed, before ordering the computer to run more scans of the boy's brain. Expectedly, the scans didn't cause Johnny to blink and flinch as they had before and Taylor saw that, indeed, there was definitely something worth seeing after the several resulting images came up on the nearby screen. The two graphics that interested him most were those of the geographic activities in his brain and of his neural activity and frequencies. Comparing the two, it became immediately clear to Taylor that new areas in Johnny's brain were being used that had been dormant before. These new areas of activity were the obvious source of Johnny's now displaying high neural peaks of activity in all five areas of evolved mental capability.

"Amazing!" Taylor said aloud, causing some alarm for Johnny, who was quite on edge considering recent events. "I – I can't believe it!"

"What – What's wrong with me – What's going on?!" Johnny snapped fearfully.

"Nothing. You're fine. You're better than fine. According to this scan you're brain's peaking in all new areas. You're now a kinetic and a cyber, and you've got improved precog, postcog, and telepathic abilities."

Johnny's face grew a half-smile, "How's that possible?"

"Well," Taylor said thinking to himself, "I have a theory, but I want to check it with the computer first."

"LAB, theorize possible reasons for the increased activity in Johnny's brain geography considering recent scans in comparison to historical ones."

The response from the computer was almost immediate. Taylor and Johnny both listened carefully as the computer explained.

"LAB has concluded – there is a 96% probability that the before mentioned anomalies activated the inactive areas of the brain of subject 2675A.

"LAB," Taylor started again, "Did you perform a complete structural and electromagnetic save of anomalies that were de-generated from Johnny's brain."

"Affirmative"

"Good!" Taylor said purposefully. "Lab, re-generate one of the anomalies in this container." He said this while holding up a small clear cube he'd retrieved from a cabinet under Johnny's bed. Inside it a very tiny flash of light let Taylor know that the task was done and he immediately ordered the computer to "perform a frequency lock on the nanite and download all programming contained in its memory, saving the data under filename 'Sphere Data 1'."

Taylor patiently watched as the nearby screen scrolled rapidly with code, which he scanned as fast as he could, but even he could not keep up with the computer's download and display speed.

Resting his eyes for a few seconds he looked over at the sphere, tied up and powerless. Despite the pain he was still feeling on the back of his head, and despite all the chaos the sphere had brought him and one of his students since early that morning, Taylor stared at the shiny chrome object and for the first time wondered if its purpose was as bad as he'd previously thought.

* * * * * *

"It took the computer nearly ten minutes to download all the code in that one little nanite." Taylor said in a tone of irritation as he stared restlessly at the grass beneath his feet.

Both he and Jay had taken to walking the perimeter of the park while Taylor had pathically continued his recollection of what had happened in the lab. This seemed to keep their bodies occupied while their minds were both working over-time in either offering or receiving the tale. As usual, Taylor would communicate some of the more detailed parts with full images and emotion filled experiences to make sure that there was no confusion. But, between the two of them, they were simply too tired to recount the entire tale in this manner, and thus Taylor resorted to the spoken word.

"Dude, why so long?" Jay asked, surprised that any download of information would ever take more than just a few seconds.

"The nanites were using an ultra-low-frequency band to communicate with the sphere's main processor, so it was the only frequency LAB could use for the download."

"You know," Jay said, "That'd explain why Johnny was having those flashes near the end of his scans. Usually the last part of any scan involves low frequency electromagnetic pulses to finalize the image resolution."

Taylor pointed his finger at Jay with a wink, "My thoughts too!"

"So, anyways," Taylor continued, "When the download was finished, I thought it best to take a break and come here. I'm really interested to see Johnny *stretch his legs* as it were."

"Do you think it's safe?" Jay asked

"Well even if I didn't what would be the point? The boy's got no nanites in his brain right now, so what you see in front of you is all him!"

Jay smiled, "Amazing, telekinetic and cyber-kinetic all in one go!"

With these words Taylor offered a look of concern.

"I wonder if someone's trying to test out new technology." He looked at Jay for any theoretical answers.

"What? You think someone's trying out experiments on our kids – but that's illegal!"

"I – I'm not sure?" Taylor said nervously. "I am suspicious, but – well, maybe I can get some answers when I look at the code from the nanites. Just the same, if I could think of just one person..." Taylor stopped his words, gave a sudden cough, and nodded in the direction ahead of the two of them. This was an indication to cease the conversation, for they could see that Caitlin was quick on the approach, still carrying Taylor's book.

"Here's your book, father." she said with a smile, and as she turned a smile to Jay, she continued, "I'm not quite finished with it yet, but I took a look at the clock and it's about time for us to get going."

"Well," Taylor said with a smile, "if you're not done with it yet, then you keep it for a while and... Oh wow, would you look at the time, we do need to get going!"

Caitlin pulled the book close to her chest and began rocking side to side, content that she could keep it a little longer. She offered a sideways grin and added, "We don't want to be late now do we?"

He kneeled down in front of her and smiled, "No, Precious, we don't. Why don't you get the others and we'll all meet back at the transport."

She giddily smiled, said "okay" and turned to her siblings. She had only taken two steps in their direction when she stopped dead in her tracks. She could see, off in the distance that Aspen, Grace, Orion, and David, who were flanked by a crowd of bystanders, were all sitting in a circle around Johnny, who was, she couldn't believe it, levitating three colored balls into the air.

She dropped the book in her arms and voiced a quiet question to her now attentive adult audience.

"Wha – What's going on with Johnny? He's" she paused to catch her breath, "Is he kinetic now?"

Taylor walked up behind her. "Oh, uh – yes, dear, I was going to tell you but..." Taylor then offered a menacing stare at Jay that the man should've let Taylor talk to the girl when he had the chance.

He turned back to the girl under his chin. "It has something to do with what happened last night."

"I – I didn't know" she said sadly, "I've been reading that book, I – hadn't even noticed..." As she said these words tears slowly began to fill in her eyes, and Taylor could see that she was undoubtedly upset.

She ran away from Jay and Taylor, but not in the direction of the other children. She, instead, decided to return to the tree whose shade she had enjoyed for much of the early afternoon and that now seemed to be her only comfort.

As Taylor watched her race away he told Jay to gather the others while he talked with her.

With her knees pushed up she rested her forehead on them and as Taylor approached, he could hear her crying beneath her hair.

"Caitlin... Caitlin..."

She shook her head as a signal to be left alone, but Taylor knew better.

"Come on little Cate... we need to talk. What's bothering you so much?"

She grunted a simple "ugghh" and tried to shrug him off when he sat next to her, holding her carefully with one arm.

"I know it has to do with Johnny, but I don't see what the problem is."

She cried a little harder at the mention of her brother's name, but looked up at the finishing of the statement.

"Oh, come on! Is it really that hard to figure out?"

He looked at her with raised eyebrows, looking for her to say more. Often this was all he had to do for Caitlin to spill her emotions – she was such a natural talker. With Grace, who was always too quiet, it was a different story, but not with Caitlin. She poured her thoughts freely when she saw that Taylor was genuinely interested in what she had to say.

"Let me tell it to you like this." She started, pulling her head up and whipping her hair around. "I walked all the way around this park talking with Uncle Jay because I had nothing to do. He brought a bag full of stuff for everybody else, they all got to play, you know, using their powers. Not me! No. I talked with him and talked with him, and I'm not saying it was boring, but it wasn't like what they got to do. They were surrounded by a crowd of people from the park – all amazed at them – they got all the attention."

"All I got to do was talk – eventually all I could think of was you and, well, mostly Johnny. He'd be in the same sitch' I was in. So we'd at least have that much in common and we could do what we always do – just have fun together.

She paused and tears filled her eyes. "But not anymore!"

"There, there little one. It's okay. Not that much has changed. The other's still don't share your gift the way Johnny does. You still have *that* in common.

"Big deal!" she said loudly, "What can he do with that! He's probably going to spend the next month playing with his kinesis more than anything else!"

Taylor tried to smile to keep spirits high, but found this difficult and instead just held her close, hoping that this would make up for it.

With the rustling of grass behind them, Taylor and Caitlin both turned around to see a very sober looking Johnny walking towards them. His head hung low and his hands in his pockets; one might think him the last person to do any cheering, but Taylor smiled and immediately waved for him to come closer.

"Johnny, just the person I wanted to see…"

Johnny talked to his feet as he walked closer, "Actually, I was kind of hoping that I could talk with Caity – alone – for a minute... if that's alright."

Taylor offered a slight look of disappointment, thinking it best if he could stay and help guide the conversation, but something in him, precog or pathic he wasn't sure, but something he couldn't explain made him think better of it.

"Well, uh... okay" He gave Caitlin one last hug before standing up to walk to the transport and as he stepped he pathically told the brother-sister pair that they had five minutes.

Johnny watched Taylor walk across the green grass. When there was enough distance between them, Johnny sat down beside his sister, hoping it would make her more comfortable than for her to have to talk up to someone. This seemed to be effective as she started talking immediately.

"Doesn't it bug you that he always thinks he knows everything!" she said with a voice of arrogance.

"Well," Johnny responded lightheartedly, "I just about think he does."

This made Caitlin frown, and forced Johnny to do some quick clean up. He started looking around for cues to help.

Think... Think... he repeated inside his head. *Ah of course...*

He looked at Caitlin and started speaking aloud.

"Do you remember, the first time we came here – to this park?" he asked.

She turned her head and nodded, "Yeah, what about it!"

Do you remember how crazy Dad was trying to keep all the others from using their kinesis because he was afraid someone would get hurt?"

"So what!"

"So... you and I were the only ones that could do anything with our powers without getting into trouble."

She stared at him with a sideways grin. "That's because no one knew what we were doing."

"*Exactly*! No one knew! We were running all over the place, grabbing everything and anything just to get impressions. We had so much fun it was insane!"

"You had so much fun, you mean!" she spoke to Johnny with a false angry tone. "You kept taking everything I found and stealing it right out of my hands.

Johnny laughed and smiled at this, and the two of them started nudging shoulders on each other to see who would fall over first.

Caitlin, who stiffened immediately, looked at her brother with a strange expression of curiosity.

"What's that look for?"

"Oh, nothing! I was just... well."

"Come on Caitie, spit it out!"

She paused and dipped her head low, "I was wondering what happened to you this morning. I mean what happened to make you have all these new powers?"

He smiled and put his forehead to hers, then spoke in an enigmatic tone. "Why tell you, when I can show you."

In a few short seconds the two of them had their eyes closed, and it took a mere few seconds before they separated with Caitlin sounding winded.

"Woah..." She said aloud. "That was amazing. How did you do that?"

He smiled, "If I could tell you that, *I'd be the teacher*. All I know is, it's just a little bit more about the new and improved me that I've figured out – but don't let that fool you – I'm still your irritating little brother – and when the dust settles – remember – you're my favorite."

She laughed and the two stared at each other with wide grins. Then, with their eyebrows suddenly raised, they were simultaneously messaged by Taylor to get back to the transport..

With her jumping and running, Caitlin was obviously in much better spirits than when Taylor had left, and seeing this made the teen sigh with relief. When the two late comers had returned to the craft Taylor smiled at them, using both his hands to rub their heads gently.

"It's good to see you smile there, Kid-O!" he said looking into Caitlin's eyes. She responded with a quick fake frown, which he mimicked, making her laugh as she jumped into the transport to sit between both Johnny and Grace.

With the transport closing itself up and the craft lifting from the park and shooting off toward The Towers, Taylor stared at the far distant peaks of the building thinking that everything was fine. For the most part this was true, but for someone else in the cabin, there was much to figure out.

Caitlin's brain was working overtime trying to solve a problem. She was scheming, plotting, planning, and fidgeting – all the while working hard to keep her thoughts a secret from everyone, well, almost everyone.

With a devilishly grinning Johnny at her side, a grin that she was unaware of, Caitlin grew tired with her face being warmed over by an onslaught of true sunlight when the craft lifted above city skyline. Eyes closing, she smiled, thinking, hoping for what she imagined would be a new and brighter future.

23 A Splinter

WITH THE SLIGHT HUM and rocking of the transport mixing soothingly with the heat of the July afternoon, it was little wonder to Taylor that the children were all getting tired. He, looking over his shoulder at the group of them, would love nothing more than to just abandon the rest of the day and have a pleasant evening of games and dinner, then take them to the recreation room and watch a few movies until the night was over. He knew, though, that there were still two classes scheduled for the day: Organic Chemistry, and Differential Equations, thus keeping him from his desires.

While Taylor himself was pleased with how things had finally settled down for the day, he hated having to go back to EduCorp with these children. Taking them back engrained in his mind now more than ever that their lives were not normal and that until he could get them under his wings, his roof, and his guardianship they never would be. Inside his head he wished so much that he could just turn the transport around and head it in the direction of his apartment. Why couldn't he just call up his work and let them know that neither he nor the children would be returning... ever!

As always, Taylor only wished this, and in his mind he dreamed of making a decision like the one rolling around in his head, full well knowing the reality of the situation. Actions come with consequences, and the repercussions of an action like that would prevent any happiness he could ever want for himself or for his students.

As these thoughts rationalized themselves in his head, Taylor sighed and glanced at each of the children once more. He watched the slow nodding of their heads to the rhythmic rocking of the transport, their eyes growing heavy with tiredness. Turning to look ahead toward The Towers, he forced a smile. *It won't be much longer.*

Looking up in waking excitement, Johnny felt a sharp jolt in the motion of the transport. Looking out the front and side windows he could see small explosions all around the craft. Not knowing what was going on, he tried moving to the front of the transport, which somehow had a great deal more space than he remembered when he fell asleep. Still shifting hard as he moved, the boy was curious to see how the automated piloting system was doing, but his shoulder was grabbed by a large hand just as he got to the front of the craft.

Johnny turned back to the source of the hand and could see Jay's mouth telling him to stay in the back yet, for some reason, Johnny couldn't hear the words. The boy looked around wildly. He hadn't really taken in much of the detail of his surroundings, and to his shock, he saw that Taylor was on the floor, unconscious, and that Aspen and David were looking out the windows on either side, as if completely unconcerned about their teacher. Then, with a sharp pain that he didn't understand, Johnny looked down and saw a bandage on his forearm, and could feel a very real throbbing pain underneath. Johnny was taken aback. He knew when he had fallen asleep that he had neither pain nor bandage with respect his arm and as he thought of this, he looked around and noticed that all of his other siblings had the same white patch in the same place on their arms too.

"What's going on?" He said loudly, though no sound was coming out of his mouth. In a panic he tried desperately to speak his fears, "Where's Grace, where's Orion and Caitlin? Everything was fine like two seconds ago."

In looking at Jay he could see that the man's face showed a great concern and fear like nothing the boy had ever seen.

An explosion on the port side of the transport caused a sharp jolt of the craft. This unsteadied Jay, and at the same time, forced a voice out from the front of the craft. This seemed to be the only thing that Johnny could actually hear and it came out loud and clear.

"If you two want to make it out of this thing alive you'd better do a better job of keeping those things off our ass!" He recognized the voice instantly as his brother Orion. And Johnny watched as Jay attempted to steady himself from the last blast. At that moment the boy knew that now was his chance to see what was going on up front.

He leaped to the head of the craft and saw that the primary navigation system was completely offline. *But wait,* he thought – *the emergency control door had been unlocked – it's seal – broken.* Johnny opened the door below the display console of the craft. Inside, he eyed both Orion and Grace in the emergency cockpit, a very tiny space that sat in the lower front of the craft, just at the nose.

Between the two of them, Grace and Orion were focused on completely different things. Grace, who was working diligently under the secondary control panels, looked up at Johnny and offered a half pained smile. Her face was dirty and she had a deep cut that ran down the side of it which had obviously bled itself to being clotted. Orion was looking out the front window, which showed that the craft was headed for the edge of the city, the high walls gleaming in the distance. The boy was obviously driving the transport, not using his hands, but using his mind. He was willing it to fly faster than transports were meant to and making it do maneuvers so fast the inertial dampener was having trouble keeping up with the shifts in movement and direction.

Grace suddenly looked up at Orion, she had pulled some small computerized box from underneath the console and called out "Got it!" Again, more words that Johnny heard clearly.

Orion looked at Grace saying loudly, "Good, destroy it!" But at the moment that Orion turned to his sister, he noticed Johnny looking in on them. He mouthed the words, which seemed almost in slow motion, "What are you doing here! Get back there!" and he waved his hand for Johnny to go to the back of the transport. What was most strange is that while he could read the lips of his brother, and understand what was being said, he didn't hear anything. Anything at all!

Johnny pulled his head from the manual cockpit, and closed the door. Turning around the boy decided to look out one of the side windows. In doing this, his face was only inches away from Aspen's. She turned and looked at him for a moment only to acknowledge his presence, then turned to look out the window again.

"Do you think you could give us a hand here?"

She said this loudly, and it was clear that she was directing her words at him, and he heard them.

"With what?" he asked, though his voice was still absent, and in looking out over the massive city his eyes were met with its impressive sunlit skyline.

Aspen pursed her lips and furrowed her brow, giving him an instant look as though he were an idiot, and pointed to the rear of the craft.

Johnny shifted his stare out the window and could see, only barely visible from his position, about fifty or so missiles that were all headed for the transport, and more were rising from the city every second.

He backed his head from the window and put his hand over his mouth. He was now filled with both fear and confusion as to how the lot of them had plunged into such a life threatening situation; a situation where their usual savior, Taylor, was unable to offer any assistance. Continuing to step back, he fell hard into one of the transport's chairs.

With a white flash Johnny raised his head quickly, inhaling a deep breath. He looked around wildly and saw that he was surrounded by his siblings, all sleeping. Looking ahead he could see that Taylor and Jay were sitting in the two forward-most seats, and between them, the emergency manual cockpit still had its tell tale seal intact.

Taylor and Jay were not conversing, just looking ahead at the view of Los Angeles and the fast approaching EduCorp Towers.

The boy quickly realized that everything was back to normal. Everyone was in their place and the ship was only lightly rocking from turbulence. He had experienced a vision in his sleep. Exhaling a breath of relax, he noticed that in front of him David, Aspen, and Orion were also sleeping. Further forward, the bench seat Taylor and Jay were sitting on had enough room for another person between them, and in seeing this, Johnny got an idea.

He quickly stood up, put his foot between David's legs, put his hands on the back of the bench, and flipped himself over to land directly between the two men at the front. Jay was instantly startled by this quick action, while Taylor seemed only mildly impressed.

"I was wondering how long it would take you!" Taylor said, turning his head to look down at the boy with a smile.

"Take me? For what?" he asked with a playfully ignorant sound in his voice. Taylor responded with an obvious, if not expectantly curious stare down at the boy

"Tell me what you saw. Just now – back there."

Johnny shot his eyes down to a weakly placed gaze at his own knees. In his mind he was a little annoyed at the fact that Taylor always knew what was going on, sometimes even inside other's heads. Still, there was no use in delaying the inevitable.

"Well," the boy started, "How much do you know?" he asked quickly.

"Not much. Just that you had a visio..."

"Hold it! Hold it! Wait a minute!" Jay said loudly to break the conversation. "Am I wiggin' out? You're sayin' that *he* just had a vision and *you* picked up on it!"

"Well – Yeah!" Taylor said quickly with a voice that meant something more like "Get with the program!"

Looking back at the boy Taylor persisted, "I know you had a vision, and that near the end of it you got really scared, but that's about it."

"Oh," Johnny said apprehensively, snapping his eyes back down at his tiny bare knees.

"That's all... 'Oh,' That's it? I don't think so! Don't clam up on me now! Just spill it! What did you see?" Taylor was almost playful with his words and it was clear to both Johnny and Jay that he wasn't at all concerned about the boy's uneasiness or his fear.

"Well, if you have to know," Johnny started in an irritated voice. "I saw us all in a transport like this. But the one I saw had a lot more room."

Taylor nodded, conceding to Johnny's details of what he had seen.

"Anyways, Orion and Grace were both in there," he said pointing to the emergency manual control door, "and Aspen and David had their faces glued to the side windows."

"Tell me little dude, were either of us there?" Jay asked curiously.

"Yeah," Johnny responded quickly, "you were there with Aspen and David, but your face – well, you were scared out of your wits."

Taylor started to laugh at this, knowing how skittish Jay can be at times.

"Don't laugh," Johnny snapped, "You were unconscious!"

Johnny heard a noise from behind in the cabin and suddenly whipped his head around to see five curious faces all looking and listening to what he was saying.

"Wha – you guys are awake."

"Sure," said David almost giddy, "it's not like you could just jump over our heads and we wouldn't notice."

Caitlin waved for David to be quiet, "Shhhh... go on Little J, what else – what else did you see?"

"Well, the reason I was so afraid at the end was because the transport was under attack. There were explosions all around us! Orion was flying the transport like a maniac using his cyber, and Grace had her head stuck under some panel in there," he said pointing to the emergency door again, "she pulled out some strange – eh – box thingy..." He offered a small pause for her response.

"Locator beacon." she said in a very bored tone."

"Right! And Orion told you to destroy it." Johnny continued, "But when you looked out from under where you were, I saw a huge cut on your face." He drew a line on his face with his finger to mimic her cut and in response she unconsciously rubbed her cheek with worry while Johnny continued. "And we all had something wrong with us. We all had bandages on our arms – right here" and he anxiously pointed at his arm to show everyone where before continuing his rant. "And, uh, Orion, you screamed at Aspen and David that they needed to do a better job at keeping something off 'our ass.'" When Johnny said this the other children put their hands on their mouths and gasped.

"What?" Johnny posed innocently, "He said it." At this point the boy pointed at Orion, but this did little to move the attention from the fact that he, the youngest child of the group, had used such a word.

"Whatever," the boy continued, "Orion told me to get back to the main part of the transport. I did, and I looked out the window. I didn't see anything interesting at first, but when Aspen pointed to the back I saw what was trailing us and that's when I really, really got scared."

Taylor smiled and put his hand on the boy's shoulder, "And what did you see?"

"We were being chased..." he said, thinking hard of how to put his memories into words, but his thoughts were interrupted by Jay, who was growing more nervous with each of the boy's words.

"Chased? Dude, chased by what?"

"Oh about fifty missiles!" Johnny said excitedly, forcing the other children to exchange their own set of nervous stares.

"Not possible," David said quickly, we'd've been blown out of the sky instantly, there's no way a transport like this could keep up.

"Well," Johnny said with a slight grin, "That might be true, but with Orion at the wheel we were going so fast it was insane. Plus, you and *her,*" he said pointing at Aspen, "were knocking as many missiles out of the sky as you could with your kinesis. That was why you guys had your face stuck to the windows."

Caitlin, who was initially intrigued by the story, soured her face quite abruptly. Johnny, noticing this, reached up and nipped her chin lightly with his fingers. "What's wrong?"

"Well, through the whole story I haven't heard my name at all."

Johnny's eyes slowly widened as he desperately searched for the right words, but his mind filled with the same kind of fear he had the end of this last vision."

"You... you weren't there!" he said with a shaky voice.

He offered a contagiously panicked stare up to Taylor, "She wasn't there. Why wasn't she there? What happened to..."

Johnny was ranting worse than ever, forcing Taylor to put his hand on the boy's mouth with a soft "Shhhh... everything's fine. She's right here. Everything's fine."

As the teen was saying this, the craft offered a slight thud for it had reached the landing pad of The Towers. But it seemed that Johnny's fear had, indeed, bled over to the others for they all jumped when the ship made its relatively smooth landing.

Taylor snapped his eyes to the transport's clock and realized that they only had fifteen minutes to make it to their next class. He cyberly opened the door to the transport and playfully told them all to hurry off. Instantly the whole lot of them seemed to snap out of their fearful gaze and the line of children comically made their way across the concrete pad to the entrance of West Tower.

With the eight of them into West Tower's main lift, Taylor noticed, to his mild irritation, that the children were in no shape to go to class. They were filthy, covered in grass stains and dirt. In response, Taylor quickly forced the lift to accelerate its ascent and told the children that they all were to quickly get changed and report to class in ten minutes.

With a quick smile from Caitlin, Taylor knew what was going through her head. He smiled at her through the reflection on the doors of the lift, "Yes, Caitlin, that means you have to get changed too... And for goodness sakes, put on some matching clothes." The children all laughed at this statement, and Taylor felt he had succeeded in lightening the mood at least a little bit.

When the doors opened six young bodies ran, almost on top of each other, to make it to their respective dorms. But Johnny was held back by Taylor, who made a telekinetic effort to keep the boy for a quick and private conversation.

When the boy turned around to face Taylor, the teen smiled. "Two things." Taylor said pathically, counting on his fingers in a fashion that didn't fit with his wordless conversation, "First; don't tell the others any more about your visions unless I'm there." The boy instantly offered a pouting look as if he'd been accused of something bad and Taylor quickly amended. "You didn't do anything wrong back there – it's fine – I asked and you told, but in the future – I just – well – I don't want any unnecessary panic or worry. It's okay!" Taylor reassured.

"Second," the teen continued. "I'll have a makeup session for this morning's class scheduled for you. Hopefully it'll be sometime early tomorrow."

Johnny nodded and with a smiling head tilt from Taylor and a light rub on the cheek the boy proceeded to catch up with his siblings. Taylor watched the boy's happy carefree scamper and couldn't help but smile with this, a fleeting moment of contentedness.

24 Jay's Lesson

TAYLOR, FEELING VERY PRESSED FOR TIME, ran down the corridor, trying to catch the last class of students before they had a chance to leave. This was, in his mind, the best way for others to see his punctuality. Even if his students weren't there, his presence would be enough to show this side of him.

He skirted past four lines of teenagers; students all leaving from the previous class and, while passing their many faces, he noticed he was receiving a great deal of unwarranted attention. This included waves and high fives from some of the guys and winks from some of the girls, though he couldn't understand why, and despite the positive energy, it made him feel very uneasy. He didn't have to try to pick up any of their pathic thoughts either. They were *all* offering him one message or another and with the barrage of simultaneous thoughts he was getting it was impossible to decipher any single stream of consciousness. He snapped his mind closed instantly, avoiding what would obviously have been an instant headache.

As he made his way to the end of the lines of students he saw that he had only just caught the door as it closed behind Dr. Rayburn. Taylor knew this man was an supervising instructor who none of the other students liked. Taylor had, however, never really experienced any real interaction with the man. Taylor's passing from class to class was mostly spent catering to his nearby students, so he only rarely had a chance to interact with any of his counterparts. Just the same, Taylor knew that the man had only been with the company for three years, yet from what the teen could pick up in student reprimands and harsh overpowering conversations, he knew he didn't like the man very much.

"Hmmm" Dr. Rayburn huffed, slowly jutting out his chin aggressively. "Apparently some of these students were in Dr. Swanson's class this morning. They saw you show off your – uh – *abilities*." He forced upon Taylor a disapproving stare, "Now that's all the whole bunch of 'em can talk about!"

Taylor, irritated at the way Dr. Rayburn, a thin, slick-haired, short man, said the word 'abilities' as though it were a disease, offered his own condescending frown as he slipped past the man, who wasn't making it easy for the teen to enter into the classroom without some kind of an awkward moment. It was clear that Dr. Rayburn was baiting for a conversation, but Taylor felt not the least bit inclined to bite. Instead he simply kept his sour expression with each inch he made weaseling through the door.

While a frown was on his face outside the classroom, when Taylor entered it and the door closed behind him, he immediately shifted his look to an attractive smile, reflecting emotions that were ready to explode. Dr. Rayburn had inadvertently explained the peculiar behavior of the students in the hall, and as Taylor paced the classroom he replayed the faces of the student lineup in his head. His grin widened almost to the point of laughter with each passing second realizing how with a small display of his powers, he'd suddenly elevated himself to some celebrity status; something to be admired in the eyes of those teenage children. Taylor almost laughed – those children were only three years his junior – and now they held him up to such high esteem.

Shaking his head of such prideful thoughts, Taylor eventually took a stance behind the head desk and, using his cyber and kinetic powers again, he forced the auditorium style desks to fold up into the wall while placing a new set of desks in a semi-circle for his own students. Indeed, within a few seconds Taylor had readied the classroom for its small group of occupants.

With the light hiss of the classroom's automatic doors, Jay walked in just as Taylor had taken his seat. Having just followed the children to their dorms in a desperate effort to make sure that they did as they were told, the man was heaving and out of breath.

After a moment's rest the man composed himself and stood at Taylor's side, offering the back of the teen's head a deeply worried and expectant stare. Taylor, who hadn't yet looked Jay in the face and therefore thought everything was fine, was further oblivious to Jay's nervous fidgeting fingers at his side. Calmly staring at the data display in front of him, Taylor was scanning the protocols for the next class and was just at the point of addressing his anxious compatriot when his words were cut short by an attack of instant hostility.

"Aren't you *at all* concerned with what Johnny said – what he saw – what he...?"

"Hmmm," Taylor absently questioned, still staring at the screen in front of him. "Oh, you mean on the transport; his vision? No, not really," he said blandly, refusing to avert his concentrated stare.

"And why not?" Jay pressed curtly in a voice that pushed the edge of anger.

"Because," Taylor whispered, telling of his own growing irritation, "Johnny's vision is based on a 'what if' that would never happen, so it doesn't really matter. In the pre-cog world that's called a splinter – a vision that has no real chance of happening or any basis in reality."

"Huh?"

"Do you remember, this morning, my explanation of how precogs work?" Taylor asked, ready to enter teaching mode before his real students ever entered the classroom.

"Wha – Dude, what does that have to do with anything?"

"Oh, it has everything to do with – eh – everything." Taylor said awkwardly, finally looking up from his desk's data display. "Remember – precogs see all sorts of versions of the future – what they see is like the frayed end of the string I had in class."

Jay's face was unchanging with Taylor's explanation so far, and, as a result, Taylor had no choice but to continue, " Well, what Johnny saw was what pre-cogs like to call a 'splinter' – an offshoot from any real possibility – something that is so unlikely, and yet, by some strange means of horrible decision, still possible – it's like a small bit of string that just sticks out so far from the other lines of the future, which are so much more probable."

Despite his anxiousness and anger, his increased understanding caused Jay's emotions to slowly deflate as he accepted that an explanation that would, in one way or another, get him to relax. This happened to be a talent that Taylor, as the man's best friend, was getting very skilled at. Just the same, since leaving the transport, Taylor had expected having to explain away Jay's impending nervousness, but the teen would rather have done it with his students around to hear.

"Listen," Taylor said placidly. "When we left the park and were coming back to The Towers, I – I wished to myself how great it would be if I could just take the kids away." Slowly Taylor's voice pushed itself into a guilt ridden tone. "In my own mind I thought it would be so great if I could just take them home and not have to worry about all *this!"* Taylor said this and was waving his hands around, motioning at the room they were in.

"Yeah, you probably think that a lot," Jay responded sympathetically – a tone was somewhat unexpected to Taylor.

"Well remember," the teen continued, trying to comfortably regain his teaching mode, "most visions are a reflection of both decisions that people do and don't make. Like what I told you earlier. There are thousands of possibilities for the future – thousands of views – and only a few – a very few – are definite."

Jay nodded his head, now with an even greater degree of understanding.

"Right." Taylor said at seeing this, "So Johnny's vision of the future was probably based on a decision to take the kids away from this place forever, and *without* permission. It is a rash, impulsive, and impossible decision – that makes it practically an impossible vision – that's called a splinter – something so far broken off from reality that there's really no chance of it ever coming true. I mean I know that if I even tried, I'd have the Evol Crew out for me – and because it's me – I'm pretty sure it'd be all of 'em and – well – let's just not think about that..."

"I understand" Jay said nodding. "So you're saying that if you tried to turn that craft around and skip out on takin' the kids back here, Johnny's vision's what would happen."

"Exactly." Taylor said with a happy glow as he leaned back in his chair.

"*Not exactly!"* Jay growled, and his tone again caught Taylor by surprise, almost making him fall out of his seat as he tried to sit up.

"Dude, there's no way the city's defenses'd shoot up a hundred missiles just to knock out one little transport." Jay was now pacing, and Taylor watched his words grow more heated. "Yeah – carrying a bunch of kids – 't's totally bogus! I mean there's the metro police for that kind of thing. There's just no way anyone would attack a transport full of kids using missiles! I could just see the headlines now!"

Jay's ranting was growing harsher by the second and it was clear to Taylor that the man wanted to be interrupted; to hear something to explain this away. The teen was ready rise to this occasion.

"What do you want me to say? If I say you're right – there's no way it could happen – then you can just wash the entire vision out of your head as not possible – that it is impossible for a ship full of kids to be attacked like that. Or you can consider it, and just discount it as something that would still never happen – a decision that would never be made. I – I can't explain everything. Not even *I'm* that good."

Taylor cast his eyes back down to the data pad before him. "Besides, everything is fine! Right now everything is fine! So relax – there's nothing to worry about." There was an obvious dismissive anger in Taylor's voice and Jay had little choice but continue to press.

"Come on Tay, how can you say that?" Jay pleaded, "There's an actual version of the future where one of the kids, one of *your* kids, is missing. Totally AWOL, and you don't even care!"

Taylor snapped his eyes up from the desk in front of him and offered Jay a very angry look. He was about to say something, but was again cut off.

"Er, that sounded harsh. I – I know you love 'em. Hell, I defended it just this morning. I know you love them... probably more than I could ever understand." Taylor shifted his head into nodding at these words, yet Jay persisted, "But dude, love and worry are two different things." He paused for a moment, and Taylor sat, not saying a word. When Jay did continue, it was in his most serious tone of that day, completely absent of any Classic California expressions.

"I worry. That's right, no big surprise there. But I'm used to it, and you should be too. You and those kids, you're so powerful, so gifted, but there are times when they look to me for answers – but they're answers I can't give. I don't understand everything about what it is you all can do – so when it comes to that I've only got *you* to bridge this huge lack of understanding."

At this Taylor shook his head with a smile, yet Jay still persisted, "I worry and I love - I love them - sure. I love them because when I talk, they listen and when they talk I listen. I listen to what they say, and when they're frightened, I see the fear in their eyes. I have to say it, though. I don't have your gifts, so I can't begin to understand what happens to them half the time. And even though I know you *seem* to know everything and have *all* the answers, I don't, and I *know* you don't either. So I'll continue to worry."

Taylor listened with held breath as Jay continued, his emotion showing strongly in his face, "What if that vision could come true - what if it were possible? – Or the one you had last night? – Or the one in the last class? I just don't see how you can let them all just roll off you like that."

"Jay," Taylor interjected, working to ease the man's concerns, "I get visions and impressions all the time. I've had two or three impressions since I entered this classroom. Most of 'em I ignore. I have to! I can't panic every time I get a bad vision. I just can't! I've told you that."

"Yeah, but you've had so many bad ones lately – I mean, doesn't that tell you something?"

Taylor shook his head, "I've had three and four times as many bad visions in one day before and it's turned out to be nothing... Absolutely nothing!" Taylor paused and returned the favor of cutting Jay off in his words just as he had been cut off before.

"I'm starting to think that the only way you'd understand is if you had this gift – this curse – this sight that I have. But that really isn't possible – to live it – to walk in it – swim in it – hell almost drown in it. Then you'd understand. I know I've told you this, but I guess I'll have to tell you again. I can't let my visions, my premonitions – I can't let them rule my life. I've been living with 'em for almost fifteen years, and most of the time ignoring what they make me see and feel is the only way I can ever get by. Only when I'm certain of what I've experienced – and I've got all the facts, can I do anything about what's going on in my head – otherwise I'm just adding to the chaos in my brain – second guessing my actions and pulling myself in a thousand directions."

With Taylor's mouth agape, ready to add more rhetoric, he closed it quickly as the door to the classroom hissed open revealing six children, including an appropriately dressed Caitlin. Taylor offered Jay a stare of commanding silence. This seemed easy enough as, in turning to the children, Jay sighed, fully appreciating that they were safe, were together, and were now where back to a simple routine of being in a classroom and learning lessons.

The children entered politely, completely unaware of the discussion they had just interrupted and without a care they sat at their corresponding desks ready to take on the next set of virtual classes.

25 Table Manners

AT THE CLOSE OF DINNER THAT NIGHT, sitting in a dimly lit dining room at one end of a long mahogany table, Taylor found himself to be completely miserable after having finished a gluttonously large meal. Indeed, with the groans he was hearing around the table, he could tell that his six students had also eaten their limit. He decided today that each of them could have whatever they wanted for dinner, as long as it was an appropriate dinner meal.

This was not usual for their dining habits. Most often Taylor would order a single large meal from the M-Gen panel for everyone to enjoy – hopefully. Unavoidably at least one of the six would always be unhappy with the food he chose to prepare and while the only thing all of them could always agree on was pizza, even this would have a variety of toppings to suit their varied tastes.

By their own decision, each child at the table had dictated their meals to the M-Gen panel in the conference room and Taylor's nose was met with a barrage of conflicting smells that somehow still seemed appetizing.

Tonight, it was cheeseburgers for David, a cheese-only pizza for Johnny, spaghetti for Caitlin, breaded shrimp for Orion, boneless chicken breast for Aspen, and turkey and stuffing for Grace. Taylor decided to have his favorite, filet mignon. It took all but a few minutes to create the meals and over the varied dinners Taylor watched the satisfied faces of his students culminate into a misery of overfilling.

Taylor had, at least three nights a week, always reserved one of the Tower's many private conference rooms so that he could have dinner with what he considered his family. Jay did not attend this evening, though he usually did and, as it happened, the man had a date. In looking out across the long table, he wasn't at all bothered by the empty seat at the other end. He knew, and actually appreciated the fact that Jay made social efforts outside work, even if he, that is to say Taylor, rarely did. So, on this particular evening, Taylor took advantage of Jay's excursion to send the man on a special errand.

The truth was that Taylor loved his dinners with the children. Sometimes, when he couldn't reserve a conference room, he'd still sit in the cafeteria hall and eat with them just the same. He wanted to have as many dinners with this, his pieced together family, as possible.

In Taylor's mind there was never a better time to learn about and to hear the thoughts and concerns of your loved ones than over a good meal. Granted, this theory has backfired a few times when discussions would turn into arguments, then into physical food fights. But these were very rare indeed and Taylor had decided for himself long ago that if those squabbles had never occurred, he might have thought there was something wrong with this batch of siblings, who he knew would and should have built in rivalries.

"So who's ready for dessert?" Taylor asked looking at a table woefully surrounded by tired faces.

A short round of burps and giggles followed by comments of "Not me!" or "I've got to let my stomach settle!" went around the table. Only David seemed to have room for more, and while he wasn't even close to being thick or "healthy" as the polite term is applied, it always baffled Taylor how the boy could eat so much and keep his relatively small size.

"Well, David, I'm with the rest of them, I think we should wait a few minutes. Why don't we all just have a little talk instead?"

Orion and Aspen seemed more than happy with this idea while David and Grace replied with moans. Looking over at Johnny and Caitlin, Taylor saw that the two of them were in their own private discussion already.

"Ahem…" Taylor offered a false cough. "Can the two of you tell me what is so important to discuss that it cannot involve the rest of us?"

Caitlin looked up, "Oh! Uh – well..."

She and Johnny both had innocent looks on their faces as though they had done nothing wrong. "I was asking Johnny a question that maybe you can answer."

Taylor nodded "Go ahead,"

"Well," she started with a concentrated look on her face, "I'm not quite sure how to put this, but – uh – here goes." She took a deep breath and braced herself in her seat. "When I want to have visions, of the past you know, I can grab on to something and force it to happen. And now I've only just barely started picking 'em up naturally. You know, without touching. But when these happen, it's a lot like when I'm asleep, or almost asleep. I can't tell if it's real or not." She paused and glanced at her brother, "Johnny was telling me that he has the same problem: always thinking it's real, but then it turns out to be a vision."

Taylor offered a wide smile. "Interesting... Once in a while I still have the same problem. I'm not quite sure that anything can be done about it. Having uncontrolled visions is a lot like having dreams. You rarely know you're in one, and often times you think it's real, even when it's not. The easiest way to tell the difference, and this is what I always try to do, is to identify the date or time by looking at some clock or calendar. If you can do this, and keep a clear head, then you can at least have a chance of figuring reality from vision. At night – try to control your visions by guiding your tired minds into happier thoughts, like I told you in class. That always helps!"

Caitlin smiled and nodded her head in understanding.

"Now, let's talk about your other classes." Taylor said, forcing an almost inappropriate energetic tone.

"So what did you learn in Organic Chem. today?"

Orion, being the obvious academic overachiever of the group, spoke almost immediately, "We learned over three thousand organic, name, and step reactions and their applications."

Taylor nodded, "Oh, yes, I remember that class when I took it - So absolutely boooooriiiing!" With this comment he heard giggles around the table but noticed a slight frown on Orion's face.

"Well it was. I'm so glad the computer could just plug all that stuff right into my brain. I mean learning the lessons in that class let's me do all kinds of things in my head when it comes to chemicals and the like, but the class itself," he looked around the table with a grin, and five of his students joined in with a chorus of the word, "Boooooriiiing". He laughed with them again and could see that even Orion's spirits were lifting a little.

"Hey, it's okay not to enjoy every class you take. My feelings won't be hurt. I'll completely understand. Just be happy you don't have to learn things the old fashioned way." The table grew quickly silent, and Taylor knew he had stumbled on a tender topic.

"I see I have hit a sore subject here." He looked around curiously through the thick silence and his eyes met Johnny's.

"Well, yeah!" said the boy with a sarcastic tone. "The way we learned about how it used to be sounds more like torture, not education."

"Honestly," Aspen started up, "It must have been horrible to be a child back then. To be judged on how well you learned something the way a teacher taught it. And if the teacher wasn't any good, you suffered. No standards, just grades."

David started to laugh, "Could you imagine, being held back because you got a G!"

Orion looked over at his brother with a smirk, "It's an F you dunderhead, and if you lived back then you probably would have!"

David and Orion both grew quiet with stern looks from Taylor.

"I'm sure you would have all been at the top of your classes if you lived back then. But at least now you don't have to worry about active learning, the passive way is so much easier, and it doesn't have the side effects of degrading and judging a child by wavering and misguided standards." Taylor thought for a few seconds then added, "No. Learning, active or passive, is not important, what is important, and what I hope to see from you is active application – maybe not now, but later in life."

He received a few confused looks from his students, to which he responded in an almost lecturing tone, "I want to know that you can take what you learn and make a difference in your lives and a difference in the world around you. I know that now you are only ten years old –" Taylor paused at hearing a sigh from Johnny, "and nine, so I know that making a difference isn't so easy, or even possible, but there will come a time when all that you have learned will become useful and it will be on those days, and at those times, that I'll be most proud of you."

He looked around at his students, satisfied with what he had just said, and was hoping to see that he had, in some way, offered them a guiding statement that would penetrate their young minds. Instead, all he saw was the confused faces of children. Their lack of comment seemed to resonate in his head like a cricket in the dark.

Taylor quickly thought to himself that it would be best to save this lecture for another time, when they were older perhaps, and more able to understand the deeper meaning of what he was trying to convey. Now was definitely not the time, especially since he could see, looking over at Johnny and Caitlin, that the two were giggling, with their eyes closed, and they were clearly holding something, together, under the table.

Taylor stood up and put his finger to his lips as a sign that the others should be quiet and slowly he crept around the table and positioned himself behind and between the two preoccupied children. With a swift motion of both his hands, he gripped the two of them at the neck. He knew that this would afford him at least a glimpse of what was on their mutual minds.

With a quick drop to darkness Taylor watched as four of the children in front of him, but not the two he was holding on to, dissolved away and the chairs they were in were replaced by empty chairs. In front of him, on the table, appeared a couple who were dressed in lab-coats. The two children that he was still holding onto were still sniggering and apparently hadn't noticed his hands on their necks, or Taylor's presence in their vision. Being curious of what was so interesting and funny, Taylor continued to watch the couple as they kissed each other in ways that he quickly deemed inappropriate for his nine and ten year old students to watch.

He could see from where he was standing that Johnny and Caitlin were getting their vision by simply holding on to the frame of the table, their fingers intertwined so that they could share the vision. Shaking his head he had the full intent of pulling the children back in their chairs so that he might look down at them, straight in their eyes and let them see his disappointment. He slowly firmed his grip on their necks, and, just at the moment when he decided to pull them back, he noticed that the female of the couple, whose face he couldn't see amid the obtrusive kissing noises and close interaction, was someone he recognized at first full sight. It was Dr. Hathaway.

He thought to himself that this was definitely a side to her that he had never seen before. She seemed a far different character than the one he had to deal with earlier that morning. She was still very aggressive though. She forced her male partner onto the table, ripped his shirt off and… Taylor instantly pulled the necks of his students hard, causing them to release their grip on the table, and slowly Taylor's view of this vision started to bleed away into darkness. But at the last second Taylor noticed the man to which Dr. Hathaway was offering her attentions.

Dr. Richardson! Yes. Taylor was only just able to recognize that the man who was on the table was Dr. Richardson. Instantly, just before the vision completely left Taylor, he reached down between Johnny and Grace, who had all but completely dissolved out of view, and grabbed the table's edge. Quickly Taylor's vision reached total clarity, and the children had completely disappeared into nothingness.

Taylor watched Dr. Hathaway and Dr. Richardson writhe on the table and his mind quickly had several thoughts at once, but the greatest of these he worded aloud, knowing that no one could hear him.

"So that's how she got to be his second in command!" And he quickly felt as though he was intruding on some private moment that would be better left unseen, especially considering the fact that he and his students had just had dinner on that very table.

"What's that?" Dr. Richardson asked as Dr. Hathaway pulled something from behind her back. Taylor couldn't help but watch with bated curiosity as Dr. Hathaway had some sort of drink – a small vial in her hand.

"Here," she said softly, "drink this, it'll help you to relax!"

She said this in a sultry voice that Taylor would have never associated with her.

Dr. Richardson grabbed the small bottle, pulled to top off with his mouth, and gulped it down quickly.

As Taylor stood watching, he could feel hands pulling at his arms, though he couldn't see what his appendages were feeling. Then, with his hand slipping off the table, his vision swiftly dissolved into the present, and the last thing Taylor could see from it was Dr. Richardson slowly turning into a faceless, unrecognizable figure.

From a darkness that bled slowly into color Taylor looked out and across the table saw four curious faces staring at either himself, Caitlin, and Johnny.

"Maybe we should have dessert someplace else," Taylor said in a soft and quivering voice. Caitlin and Johnny, knowing what they had seen thus far, agreed to this and quickly rose. Taylor waved his hands for the others to get up and the seven of them left the room with Taylor concentrating hard to put all the leftover food and dishes in the M-Gen for easy clean up.

Later that night, the children made their way back to their dorm rooms completely tired from the day's events. Taylor initially didn't follow them to their rooms, but rather decided to go to his office, which was only straight down the hall. He'd only entered the small room for a fraction of a second before he darted down the hall after he children, calling for them with excitement.

"Hey you guys! Before you call it a night, I've eh – got a gift for you!"

They all turned and gathered around Taylor with eager eyes, expecting some kind of gift. Instead, he kneeled in front of them, and spoke softly, careful to make himself clearly understood.

"I had Jay get a little present for each of you: A ring." On finishing this statement, he could see that there was a bit of disappointment rising in a few of the children's eyes – primarily the boys, and Taylor wasn't at all surprised by this reaction; in fact, he almost expected it.

"Oh," he said quickly, "I know it isn't anything wonderful or fantastic, but after what's been going on I decided I needed something that could help me keep track of you – in case there was a problem like we had last night." He turned and gave Johnny a quick glance.

"You should find them on your pillow, nightstand, or dresser, but when you get yours, put it on. It's the only way I can make sure you guys are alright twenty four hours a day.

He reached his arms out to the six children, and they all huddled in to give him a final group hug for the night.

"I love all you guys..." He felt a quick poke in his side to which he added, "and girls!"

He pulled his arms back and patted them off to bed. They ran the short distance to their dormitories and it was clear to Taylor that while they were disappointed over their presents at first, they were still exited to have something new of their own waiting for them.

On walking into their dorms it was Aspen who so quickly made her way to her bed and noticed the ring on her pillow. She quickly closed her eyes, and started pathically communicating to her siblings that she had found the ring.

One by one, she heard a resounding, "Got it!" in her head from her brothers and sisters who had discovered their own. A few seconds after David, who was the last to send a message that he'd found his own ring, Aspen was startled to hear the ring in her hand make a strange noise. With a flash of light, Aspen dropped hers on her bed and watched with both fearful and yet excited emotions as a holographic recording shot itself out from tiny lights hidden on the inside track of the ring.

The image was quickly recognizable as Jay and Aspen sat delicately on her bed to watch and hear the figure speak.

"Hey there, kids. If you are hearing this, well, then you are *all* hearing this because the message has been coded to play at exactly the same time. Aspen, this is your ring. It is to be worn on your right index finger. Now, I am sure you will notice when you first pick it up that it is too large for you. But that's okay because these rings are self sizing. It's a one-size-fits-all kind of situation."

Aspen leaned over the holographic image, and she quickly confirmed what he had said by placing her finger next to the ring. In fact, this ring was so large it would easily have fit around two of her fingers. But she thought to herself that this was no matter if what he said was true. With a smile, she looked back at the holographic image as it continued.

"But Hey kids enough of this stiff stuff, man these things are soooo cooool. I gave one to Tay, and I've got one too. You kids are gonna love these things – They're all tied together, and you just give 'em a squeeze, you'll activate their external holographic menu. Dude, it's awesome"

From here Jay described how the holographic system had a built in program whereby one could navigate options on determining the location and proximity of any of the other rings, reading the vitals of those who had the rings, and quickly communicate with those who had the rings if necessary.

"Now Taylor wants you to put these babies on tonight, and tomorrow he's going to take some time out to show you how to work 'em. So – uh – until tomorrow then little ones!"

The three dimensional digital image dissolved and Aspen, who was listening closely to what Jay was saying, quickly grabbed the ring, but dropped it on her bed as it startled her once again with the reappearing holographic image of Jay, who offered a quick message before dissolving one last time.

"Oh," he said as if he had forgotten something, "And don't get any ideas about hackin' these things – they've been coded with a gigabit cipher so they can't be screwed around with. Even the best cybers can't begin to understand how they're coded. So Orion, Grace, you can try, but you'll fail in crackin' their security.

"Crap!" and "Geeze" were the quick messages that Aspen received from her brother and sister on hearing this message.

She slowly approached the ring apprehensively, and after waiting almost a minute, decided that there would be no more messages that would scare her into dropping the ring again.

She put it on her right index finger, and slowly it worked though steps to resize itself. She watched with slight amazement as the ring quickly scanned her finger, and with a series of strange mechanical noises, slowly shrunk down to a proper size. Indeed the ring fit so snug that any effort to remove it seemed futile. It was only after several seconds of pulling and tugging that the menu suddenly popped up. Aspen thought quickly and started tapping options with her left hand until she saw one to remove the ring. She quickly tapped this button in the air, and was met with a password inquiry. She sighed with the realization that only Taylor had the authority to force the rings release. Squeezing the sides of the gold metal band once again, the holographic menu disappeared, leaving the girl with almost no light in her room.

It seemed that almost instantly she started receiving messages from her brothers and sisters about this new "gift". David, Johnny, and Caitlin all telepathically agreed that they had been tricked into putting the rings and now they could be tracked wherever they went.

Aspen quickly looked toward the ceiling and started sending her own messages.

"I can't believe you guys. Father did this for a reason. He wants to make sure that we're all safe. I think it's wonderful. It really shows how much he cares about us. And Johnny, of all of us you should realize this most after everything last night."

She finished her telepathic transmission, and listened for a response, to which there was none.

It was clear that either they either had nothing to say, or they were blocking her from hearing their private messages to each other on the matter. Either way, Aspen was satisfied with what she had pathically said and stood up to get herself ready for bed.

But on getting to her feet, she heard a request at the door. It was nearly ten o'clock at night – *who in the world...*

Aspen's mind raced over the thoughts of the intruder entering into her brother's dorm the night before, the fact that he or she had no face, and of the strange sphere that had attached itself to Johnny's head. With a chill running up her spine, she quickly armed herself by levitating a large marble statuette of a horse that she had on her dresser and with her nerves on edge she inched ever closer to the door, with the horse floating just above its entrance.

26 Ordinary and Extraordinary

"YOU CAN PUT THAT DOWN, Aspen, it's only me!" resounded a familiar pathic voice in her head.

It was Taylor, and on realizing this Aspen quickly replaced the marble piece and stepped to the door to allow him entry. He stepped in and took a quick glance around the room, trying to take in anything new she may have put up as decoration – her room was, as he knew, the one that was most constantly changing.

"Can we – uh – have a seat?" Taylor said, trying to make this late night visit more comfortable.

She felt her heart pound quick and loud in her chest. It didn't make any sense that he would be coming here this late at night, and it was this change from the usual, and this special attention that made her exceedingly anxious.

"Of course." She said quickly and she held out a hand in the direction of a desk chair nearby while she sat on the bed facing him.

"Well," she said looking at him with curious eyes, "what's up!"

He picked up the marble piece on the desk and grinned at the idea that she might have been able to subdue some unsuspecting intruder with it. "What's up?" he repeated softly as he finally took the chair she had offered. "I was kind of hoping you could tell me!"

She looked at him in confusion, and with this he quickly added, "This morning, when I asked you how everything was, you said *fine* in a way that clearly meant everything wasn't. Is there..." he paused in his talking as she lowered her head in embarrassment, "Is there anything you want to talk about?"

Aspen, with her head lowered, felt her heart pound still more loudly in her own ears. Is it possible that she was *so obvious* this morning? Thinking back on what she had said, she knew that she certainly didn't mean to be and at the same time, this inquiry into her state of mind brought a whole different set of emotions to the surface that she didn't expect.

Lifting her head, Taylor could see that tears were swelling in her eyes. She opened her mouth to speak, "I'm fi...!"

"No, you're not!" Taylor cut in with his best effort at caring words. "I know you better than that." He then paused to calculate his words carefully. "Now you know that I'll eventually find out what's going on. So why don't you save me the trouble of rooting it out and just tell me what's going on? I'd rather hear it from you anyways."

Aspen looked at Taylor with a stare of despise. She knew that what he said was true. It seemed impossible for her or any of her brothers or sisters to keep a good secret from him, much less a bad one. He always found ways of seeking out and finding stray thoughts, thereby revealing the truth. The frustration she was feeling in her own head seemed to push her emotions over the edge. She covered her now tear spewing eyes and rolled herself face down on the bed, sobbing.

Taylor felt somewhat frustrated and yet heart wrenched at the same time. He wasn't sure if he had said something wrong or not. It bothered him how dealing with his kids could be such a delicate task at times. Just the same, he knew that this was par for the course and that if one of his kids was hurting, he would try find out what the problem was no matter what it was.

Taylor stood and moved to sit on the bed beside her. Slowly he put his hand on her back and rubbed it softly to offer some sense of comfort. This seemed to have the opposite effect, for she cried louder and harder at his simple touch. To make matters worse, without warning her motions started bleeding over into his own, for he started welling tears and he felt a sense of hurt that was unexplainable.

"Shhh... It's going to be okay" he said softly through his misty eyes. "You know, I'm sorry 'bout what I said." He paused and realized that his words seemed to slow her tears. He decided that maybe this would be the best comfort that he could offer, and pursued it further.

"You know, if you don't want to tell me what's wrong, I won't pry. You can tell me in your own way and in your own time. I understand. It's just... well. I hate to see you *so* upset."

Her crying had almost completely stopped and with this Taylor decided that now would be the best time to leave. He pulled his hand from her back, "Well, I'll just go now. You get some sleep. I'll see you in the morni..."

His words were broken by Aspen's sudden reaction to his attempt to leave. She had quickly rolled over and kinetically grabbed Taylor lightly by the neck, keeping him in the room.

Stopping, he turned and sat back on the bed. Aspen looked up at him and finished her heaves from earlier tears, then reached over his shoulders and held him in a firm, yet hanging embrace. He only thought to respond by rubbing her back return.

"Shhh... baby, shhh."

Within a few seconds her tears were gone, and her breathing resumed at a normal pace. She pulled herself away for a moment to look him in the eyes. It was on occasions like this, when she was so close, that she found his light blue eyes to be one of his greatest comforts. She looked down away from them and spoke softly.

"You want to know. Okay, fine I'll tell you. But you have to promise – *prom-*

ise – not to tell the others."

Taylor quickly nodded his head and pulled her close so that he could hold her as she spoke. She heaved a few quick breaths and let the words quickly flow from her mouth, thinking that the faster she got things out, the better everything would be.

"Well, I've been vidpals with this guy named Tommy. He lives in Chicago-M, he's twelve, and uh, lately we've been sending messages back and forth like crazy." Taylor nodded and she continued, "Well, a few days ago I decided to tell him about my..." she paused for a moment and it was clear she was looking for the proper word to finish the statement. "I decided to tell him about my *powers*."

Taylor's stomach turned over – in all the world, early development of telepathy or any of the other powers has only ever been seen in seven people – in telling this *Tommy* boy the truth, she'd singled herself out as one of the most extraordinary people on the planet. Taylor sighed and listened as Aspen continued, yet his mind was imagining what kind of repercussions such a revelation could cause.

"So I told him. I told him about the rest of us too..."

She paused for a moment, and looked up into Taylor's eyes.

"How did he take it?" Taylor asked in what he hoped was a soft paternal voice.

"Well," Aspen started apprehensively, "He was cool about it at first. But as we kept sending messages, all he could talk about was what I could do. And lately, when we do live feeds, all he wants to do is show me off to his friends. I tried not to let it bother me..."

Taylor looked at her with a frown. He never liked it when his children kept the truth or their true feelings bottled up, especially when it really mattered and in this case he certainly felt that it did matter. Aspen looked up at Taylor's frown and seeing the disappointment in the teen's eyes, she instantly rebutted, "but it did bother me – it really did." She paused and took a breath, catching her place, and continued. "So last night I decided to send him a message letting him know how I felt. And that I wished things could be like they were before I told him, when he thought I was normal."

Taylor looked at her with a smile. "Well I bet you felt a lot better once you got that out of the way didn't you?"

Aspen's eyes started to well with tears again. "Yes... and no!" she cried out and Taylor was instantly confused. He sat and listened as she explained. "I felt better about letting my feelings out, but he sent me a message this morning saying that we should just stop being vidpals all together."

"What?!" Taylor said loudly, "Why'd he do that?"

Aspen's eyes continued to well with tears as she handed him a pink data pad waiting to display a brief video file.

Taylor was almost instantly offended at looking at the young boy. He was wearing a black plastic baseball cap, had piercings in his lips, ears, eyelids, nose and both cheeks. He talked at the screen waving his hands and head almost uncontrollably. Taylor focused on the pad and unmuted the speakers. As if the looks of things weren't bad enough, this kid was just wreaking of thick attitude that Taylor could hardly stand to hear or watch.

"...I can't believe you! Girl, you know how embarrasin' that was? I checked my messages wi' my friends, and you all gettin' serious on me. Wha's that about. 'Sides, girl, you can't just take back the truth. It don't work that way. You not normal. You a *abnormal.* Ya know, I thought you was cool when I found out who you really was. But, geez girl, if you gonna be all sensitive 'bout it – well that's it – I'm out. Man, forget this little thing we got goin' on here."

Taylor's mind started to fill with anger. He could hear the words, and seeing this kid, this little *punk* kid, give nothing but attitude over someone's true feelings, it heated him almost to the point of rage.

The image faded out, and Taylor found himself looking into two tear filled eyes, eager to be comforted. This, however, was not the mode in which Taylor found himself. As a parent, or rather a parent to be, he found himself being judgmental, harsh, and overprotective all at once.

"How in the world could you even listen to his messages? He's nothing but little punk boy reeking with bad attitude. He's rude, arrogant, selfish, self-centered, to say nothing of his ability to speak, or lack thereof."

"Well don't worry. I won't be sending him any more messages okay." She instantly wept loudly into her own hands, and rolled herself face down onto her pillow.

Taylor's initial reaction was to stand and distance himself from her and her strong emotions. But after only a second he sat down beside her again and he couldn't help but wonder where all her tearful emotion was coming from. He couldn't understand why all this would make her so upset. Her life, here, was as complete as it could be. She had family, friends, and peace of mind.

Only after thinking on this for a moment and in the stillness of her breathing and slight sobbing, did Taylor realize that there was obviously more emotional attachment to this boy than he or Aspen could ever have realized.

"Aspen," Taylor started, "how do you feel about this boy Tommy."

She looked up, surprised at this question, and instantly became defensive.

"Well, I don't *like him,* like him, if that's what you mean!"

Taylor's face instantly widened to a smile. "Good!" he said quickly, though he didn't believe it for a moment, "then I want you to forget him completely. He wasn't worth your time. Besides, you have plenty of people who care about you right here. You don't need anyone else."

Aspen stiffened her lip and blinked. The last of her tears pushed their way down her face, and she nodded her head, looking firmly into Taylor's eyes. He rubbed her back, and stood, looking at a nearby clock and realized how late it was.

He gave her a kiss on the forehead, stood, and turned to walk out the door. At the last second, before exiting, he turned. Picking up the pink data pad sitting on a table near the doorway, he focused on it and in a few seconds the screen started to flash and change. Setting it back down, he turned and looked at Aspen, who found herself curious at his actions.

"You know, little one," Taylor started, "no one is ever normal."

To this she looked up with almost a frown, and he quickly added, "To be normal is to be ordinary. Everyone in this world finds a way to stand out, that's what makes them special, individual, and different. You, your brothers, and your sisters aren't any different in that respect. *But,* you were all born to stand out, without any special effort, and that makes you more than ordinary. That makes you extraordinary and extraordinary people need extraordinary love."

Aspen smiled at this, stood, and rushed on Taylor to give him a hug. He kneeled to receive this, whispered a quick, "I love you!" and "Goodnight." in her ear, and made his way out into the now dark corridor. Before the door closed Aspen sent him one quick pathic message.

"Don't... don't tell the others about Tommy – I don't think they'd understand."

He stared back, shook his head and responded. "Asp – I don't even understand – but your secret's safe with me." He stepped backward from the entrance to her room and the doors quickly shut mere inches from his face.

Aspen stood near the door for a few seconds, with tears of contentedness now filling her eyes. She, for a simple moment, found that she had truly nothing to be upset over, and that her life was as close to being perfect as possible.

Lying in her bed, she noticed the glow of her upside down data-pad on the table near the door. She telekinetically made it fly through the air and into her hands. Eyeing its bright screen she could see a list of names, E-Addresses, and – powers. Could her eyes be right? She rubbed them quickly and saw in front of her a list of names of people all around the world. They all had highly developed powers beyond telepathy, and, Aspen's heart practically flipped in her chest – most on the list were actually in their teens.

That night Aspen spent nearly an hour scrolling down this list of what seemed like thousands of names, categorizing them by age and abilities, looking up information on each of them through the WSN. She was unable to satisfy her curiosity over these people before falling asleep with the data-pad on her chest and a delighted grin on her face.

* * * * * *

After exiting Aspen's dorm, Taylor walked up the corridor and found his way to lab room W484L. On entering he could see that the room was as he had left it. With the strange sphere back in its container and containment locker, and cables still pulled quite messily from a nearby access panel.

He kinetically replaced the cables and the wall panel while verbally addressing the computer.

"Lab – Lights"

This quickly brought brightness to the room which Taylor's eyes were not ready for. He squinted for a few seconds, but still proceeded.

"Lab, display file 'Sphere Data 1' on this display.

Within seconds the display that Taylor was standing next to lit up and the screen showed a long series of programming code. Taylor sat at the desk, reading and sectioning the code little by little until he had digested most of its contents. He found protocols for nanite control, neural pattern detections, and programs for self defense and proximity scanning. To his immense gratification Taylor also identified the procedural code used to enhance a person's evolved mental abilities.

He scanned this code over carefully and marveled at how detailed the programming needed to be to complete the process. As he finished looking through this large section of the massive program, he found his eyes growing heavy. Looking at the clock, he wasn't at all surprised that several hours had passed and the time was ticking ever closer to three in the morning.

It was this tiredness that made him almost miss the last section of code: a series of markers and definition statements. Here, he was able to read a series of lines that defined the purpose of some of the sections of code, and how the program was intended to function. He was glad that whoever wrote the code for this sphere and the nanites had, as good programmers often do, a good respect for defining code with comments.

Reading it, Taylor opened his eyes wide, waking slightly with the detail it revealed:

```
*//R        DEFINITION "CYCLIC OS CHECKS" COMMENT LINES
*//R        Parent program controls the regular checks of subprograms
    A-K
*//R        DEFINITION SUBPROGRAM A "Pattern Check"
*//R        Subprogram checks neural patterns for recognition (sub-
    jects 2675A-2680A)
*//R        DEFINITION SUBPROGRAM B "Pattern Filter"
*//R        Subprogram filters out neural pattern of subject 2275A
*//R        DEFINITION SUBPROGRAM C "Filter Check"
*//R        Subprogram runs Subprogram-D every 15 minutes if Subpro-
    gram B registers true
*//R        DEFINITION SUBPROGRAM D "Physical Check"
*//R        Subprogram runs a physical check of subject to verify com-
    patibility
*//R        DEFINITION SUBPROGRAM E "Implantation"
*//R        Subprogram initiates nanite implantation if subject is
    compatible
*//R        DEFINITION SUBPROGRAM F "Upload"
*//R        Subprogram initiates upload of neural pathway reprogram-
    ming
*//R        DEFINITION SUBPROGRAM G "Interference Check"
*//R        Subprogram terminates Subprogram-F if neural or physical
    interference detected
*//R        DEFINITION SUBPROGRAM H "Proximity Scan"
*//R        Subprogram performs scans and determines source of inter-
```

```
    ference
*//R        DEFINITION SUBPROGRAM I "Hibernation Shutdown"
*//R        Subprogram forces a 6 hour hibernation if interference is
    due to High neural patterns of subjects 2675A-2680A to prevent ex-
    cessive neural trauma
*//R        DEFINITION SUBPROGRAM J "Defense"
*//R        Subprogram initiates a series of detection and self de-
    fense commands if physical/electrical interference is preventing
    access to subjects 2675A-2680A or implants.
*//R        DEFINITION SUBPROGRAM K "Transmit"
*//R        Subprogram transmits all data to net-address *********
*//R        COMMENT LINES COMPLETE
```

Seeing the reference numbers for his children and himself so easily recognizable, Taylor's curiosity peaked.

"So this thing was *meant* to target the children and avoid *me*." he said aloud and his mind quickly reflected on the fact that when he was in the presence of the sphere it was almost always inactive, and when the children were around, it was more responsive.

This initially spawned the question of why the sphere had attached itself to his foot in the council chamber and to his side in the lift earlier that morning. Taylor quickly answered this question when he read the description for the "Filter Check" subprogram. The sphere would perform a physical check every fifteen minutes if Taylor's neural patterns were detected – probably just to make sure it was him - *This must have been what it was trying to do when it attached itself to me*.

Taylor continued down the lines of reference, hoping that the programmer might have offered something to reveal their identity.

"Nothing." he said in frustration. It was most irritating to him that whoever programmed the code was good enough to block out the transmitting address in the final line of reference text, and as Taylor scoured this part of the program, he realized that the address was cryptically scrambled in an effort to keep it from being identified.

With the late night passing slowly by, Taylor thought of the events of the day, rubbed his eyes, and slowly let his tiredness wash over him. His mind wandered to the council meeting that morning, and the many visions he had experienced through the day. Then, all at once, it hit him.

Quickly Taylor spoke to the computer. "Lab – Download file 'Sphere Data 1" to an M-Gened memory module at this station."

Taylor waited a mere second near a replicator panel until it beeped that it had completed the requested task. He then quickly walked out of the lab willing the lights to turn off, and faced the security access panel.

Here, once again, he adjusted the security code to prevent any entry except his own. He turned and quickly walked down the corridor and entered a lift whose numbers descended rapidly.

* * * * * *

Peering around the corner, Johnny and Caitlin could see the door to the lab room. It was Johnny that noticed a light was still on in the room and held Caitlin back.

"Not yet," he whispered, "The light's still on!"

Caitlin heard the beeping of her watch and this forced her to look at it, noticing that it was close to three in the morning.

"Who could be in there at this hour?" she said impatiently, and with this she noticed her brother hold his nose up and close his eyes.

After a second or two he spoke softly, "It's father."

She shook her head for a second, and then smiled, "I can't wait 'til I can do things like that!"

Johnny turned and looked at her with an expression that almost resembled fear. "You know, we'll be in big trouble if he catches us!"

"Oh, don't be such a worry wart!" she scolded, and the two of them flinched at hearing the door open. Taylor exited and swiftly walked to a security panel where he adjusted the codes and protocols.

Johnny and Caitlin continued to wait and watch until Taylor finally snapped his eyes away from the panel and made his way down the corridor and into the lift. When the numbers above the lift door showed that the Taylor had lowered sufficiently into the hundreds the two children made their way across the hall and stood at the doorway.

Johnny knew immediately that Taylor had adjusted the security protocols so that it would be even more difficult to get in. Moreover, he also knew that a cyber, and a talented one at that, would be the only one who could get into the room. The boy stood back from the console, and with a deep concentrated look, he focused on its display.

After a quick second lights came on around the console, and Johnny knew he had activated it. He forced the security code to display itself, but this revealed very little to Johnny, who was not well versed in programming code.

"We have to go back." he whispered forcefully.

"What!" Caitlin hissed, "Why, what's the matter?"

"I can't understand this gibberish!"

With a quick heart pounding shock the two of them heard a third voice behind them.

"I can!"

Caitlin and Johnny both turned with looks of terror, believing themselves to be caught, only to look into the eyes of Orion, whose voice annoyingly sounded so much more grown up than it actually was.

To complicate matters Orion was being followed by Grace, David, and Aspen, who were making their way around the corner with ridiculous maneuvers, trying to keep on to the walls, while crouching, and sneaking around.

Caitlin quickly hissed, "Oh for heaven's sake, you look like idiots."

"Yeah, what are you doing here?" Johnny asked in frustration.

Orion lifted his right hand to show one of the tracking rings they had received. He quickly squeezed its sides and tapped a few holographic menu options until, with absolute clarity, the ring showed the location of all six of them, now huddled near the door of the lab room.

Orion squeezed the sides of his ring again. "I suppose the real question is - what are *you* doing here?"

"I'm going to show Caitlin how I got my new powers!"

The four others stared at Caitlin, and only Orion seemed to understand what the real purpose to this night venture was all about.

"So you want to do what Johnny can do?"

Caitlin nodded her head, somewhat embarrassed.

"So do we!" Orion said quickly, and the others behind him stiffened a quick nod of the head as if to say "yeah!"

"Good..." Johnny said with almost a full voice that surprised the group and he then whispered more quietly. "Good, then you can help us with the security lock!"

Caitlin and Johnny separated, and Orion stood in front of the console. He cyberly forced it into activation and instantly started changing the code. While Orion was not nearly as fast as Taylor, he was able to do the changes faster than most would be able to follow, and after nearly an eternal minute the doors to the lab shot open.

Filled with a sense of fear, they all stepped into the room, but it was Johnny that rubbed his head in very specific places. Only he seemed to have any idea of what to do or what to expect.

27 3AM Alarm

FEELING THAT HIS OFFICE would probably not be the safest place to send messages, Taylor made his way down to the 132nd floor of the EduCorp Towers – here, well below level 300, all four of The Towers were interconnected, and the level that he had chosen specifically was one of the 5 archive levels at the heart of the EduCorp building. Here, all of the training programs that have ever been used, past, or present, and even those of future training protocols that were being tested, were stored in massive databanks.

But Taylor was not interested in this part of the archive level. No, he knew, because he had been there once before, that at the core of the massive building, hidden deep between the many storage drives and hard computer cores, was a library of old books. More than this, he knew that there were a few offices that had no network access except for a single wired connection to the main computer core. It was here that Taylor had learned he could communicate in a manner most secure, and as he walked through the cool, dark and quiet halls that hummed of the hard drives and super-computers all around, eventually passing dozens of rows of them, he came to a door that certainly didn't fit with the rest of the entire building. In fact it had an actual twisting knob to open it, something that Taylor was sure would baffle nearly everyone in the entire building, but he had read about them long ago – just a simple twist and the door opens – *huh – who knew.*

He opened the door, and on closing it after entering, he could tell that somehow this old fashioned swinging door still made an air tight, and from what he could tell, soundproof seal to the place he had just entered. Not pausing even for a moment, he continued quickly through rows and rows of old books that smelled of aged antiqueness, his mind fluttering with the events of the past twenty-four hours. He was piecing together bits of information in his brain, clarifying what he knew, how it all worked together – *but was it really possible.*

He entered one of the office cubicles at the core of the books. It had a single terminal and as Taylor sat down at it he found that he was unable to keep focus through the many ideas and images that were running through his head. He did, however, have a clear idea of what his next step should be. In the small three walled no ceiling room, he attempted to will a desk light to come on, but quickly realized that it had no wireless abilities and so he resorted to turning the thin knob at the back of the fixture.

He turned on the older model computer on the desk which, fortunate for him, did, in fact, have at least an archaic wireless keyboard for him to cyberly link into. So, sitting at the dusty device, he started writing an urgent request to have a meeting with the Education Council as soon as possible. He also added in this request that he needed a GC representative there. The note was simple and direct, but, being unsure as to whether it would be taken as serious as he would like, he coded the message 'Level 6 Urgent' which, according to GC and EduCorp standards is one level below the highest in terms of urgency.

He had, for only a moment, considered coding the message as level 7 but thought better of it because, had he done this, all of the council members would've been startled in the middle of the night with a request to attend an immediate meeting, and as he saw it, this didn't require *that* immediate of attention.

For courtesy, Taylor also forwarded a copy of this note to Jay so that the man could see it first thing in the morning, and be ready for the unscheduled meeting when he arrived at The Towers. Pressing the send button, Taylor's nerves were edgy.

Taylor felt a knot in the pit of his stomach – and whether it was his gut telling him he was right, or his gut telling him he was completely wrong he could not be sure, but if his suspicions were correct, then he was going to be making some very serious allegations against a certain employee at the company and, as such, he felt it best to make sure that his thoughts and any proof he might have were ready and immediate for the council to see. Filtering his ideas for clarity, he started creating a rough digital timeline of the events over the last day and a half, detailing the start of what he deemed a conspiracy. As he drew out the events slowly from his brain, the facts actually made more sense to him and it wasn't but a few minutes into this task that he noticed a very disturbing read red light blinking under his hand.

But this light wasn't coming from the desk beneath his fingers. No, it was emanating from the ring around his finger, thus immediately sending a wave of panic through his body. This bright red glow was an emergency light inside his ring and it's being active meant, at a minimum, that something was wrong with his kids.

Face aglow in his dark surroundings, Taylor felt his new ring and squeezed its edges to reveal a bright holographic menu. He might have tapped one of the standard buttons, but they were partly obscured by a blinking emergency message. Taylor tapped the message, forcing two holographic images to show. One was the vital signs of all six of his students, and it clearly showed that their neural activity and heart-rates were all elevated. The second image showed a map. On seeing this, Taylor's eyes nearly fell out of his head. The kids had somehow ended up in Lab W484L.

Taylor squeezed for the holographic image to dissolve, and as he did this he could hear a strange rumbling all around the dark office. This rumbling got louder and stronger, so much so that Taylor felt a panic swell in his chest until, quite unexpectedly, the rumbling had stopped. Sitting in perfect stillness, thinking that the shaking must have been some strange tremor or earthquake, Taylor flinched and dumped this theory when the keyboard on the desk slowly lifted into the air. It floated quite stationary for a few seconds until, with a shock, Taylor watched whip across and crash into the cubicle wall.

Unsure of what was happening, Taylor pulled a data pad from his back pocket and uploaded the data from the older computer to it, blessing himself that he could do what he needed without the demolished keyboard. With a turn, he stepped out of the cubicle and into the rows of books surrounding it.

Taylor would've zipped past these rows of archaic antiques and musty pages just as quickly as he had entered, but as he stepped between the shelves he was shocked to see that the warehouse sized room was in total chaos. Books were pulling themselves off the shelves one by one, and falling to the floor. The lights in the high ceiling some forty feet overhead were coming on and off at an annoyingly rapid rate. Taylor was baffled, his nerves were on edge and as he ran between the high shelves of books he had to keep a sharp mind about him to block several books from hitting him in the head, stomach, or chest.

Hoping to find shelter and relief when he made his way to the mainframes of the archive room outside the traditional library, he was met with loud noises and red lights. The mainframe itself had shut down. He walked up to one of the massive drive units and saw on its display that it had, in fact, shut down all external connections. Taylor knew that this could only mean an outside data attack was detected, thus forcing the entire EduCorp network to shut down. This, Taylor knew, meant that a severe and very advanced attempt at breaching the EduCorp data systems was under way. Taylor immediately thought of his kids and what was happening hundreds of floors above his head. He quickly made his way to the main west tower lift. But at looking at it he was met with doors that were opening and closing both violent and fast. What's worse, from what Taylor could see, was that the doors were opening even when no lift was present. He quickly decided that taking the stairs, while tiring would be his best option.

He went to open the manual door, which opened simply enough, but as he started to move through its entrance, the door, all on its own, closed hard on his hand. From the sharp sound and pain, the teen was certain that some of the bones in his wrist hand itself had shattered. The door shot open, then closed again, so hard in fact that the small glass windows in the door cracked down the middle.

Pained and coddling his now injured appendage, Taylor would not be dissuaded from getting to his students. He concentrated very hard on the door, forcing to open and keep stationary. With the chaos around him and the kinetic force he needed to keep hold of the door, using his kinetic ability proved to be the only way he could make it into the stairwell before the door slammed shut behind him, almost crushing his whole person in the process. He pushed himself in the stairwell so quickly that he nearly fell over the stair railing to what would have been an obviously messy end.

Once inside the main stairwell, Taylor looked up and realized, being on the 132nd floor, that he would have to climb over 350 flights to get to his kids. Heaving a sigh of panic he looked wildly around, thinking it impossible that he could get to them in time to keep them from any harm from whatever was happening all around The Towers. He stared downward and only at this point did he smile at seeing the smooth curved railing on the side of the stairwell. All at once Taylor had an idea.

He stood firm on the flat part of the stairwell, amid the noise of the slamming door beside him and the pulsating lights. He concentrated on the railing and without too much trouble he was able to break off a short piece using his kinesis. When this happened, he unavoidably shot the railing across the narrowly confined space so fast that it implanted itself in the nearby wall.

Seeing this, Taylor was quickly reminded of how David had done something similar earlier in the day and with this thought of one of his students, he stiffened in his resolve to get to them. So, with a sigh, he carefully concentrated to now remove the arched railing from the punctured wall.

Kinetically placing it above his head, Taylor held onto it tightly with his functioning hand and forced it to rise higher into the air until his feet were dangling above the floor. He then forced himself and the railing to move to the center of the stairwell, where he would now have a straight shot upward to the level of his choice. He turned his position so that he could clearly see the floor numbers printed on the wall of the well.

At this point Taylor made the mistake of looking down through the center of the stairwell and at seeing the never-ending spiraling staircase a sense of vertigo caused him to lose his concentration. This momentary lapse caused him to fall a good fifteen stories before regaining his thoughts and slowing the railing to a stop.

Taylor now forced himself into a calm state of mind and as he looked up he realized that there wasn't much difference in the appearance of the two directions. Up might have been just as frightening as down if it weren't for gravity's one-way nature.

Casting his eyes back at the number of the current floor, he now forced the railing to rise higher and higher, though he was careful not to accelerate too fast for fear that the increased force would cause him lose his grip. This being the case, it was still only a short while before was able to see several floors passing his view each second. Once he caught himself passing the 400th floor he slowed his ascent until he reached his stop at the 484th floor, where forced the railing to the side of the stairwell so that he was able to stand on firm flooring again, and with this his mind filled with fantastic relief. He had, indeed, climbed over 350 floors using just his kinesis in the matter of just over a minute – and thankfully, he lived to tell the tale.

Still with slamming doors and flashing lights, Taylor found it difficult to make his way into the main corridor and when he did, the absolute chaos he saw was mind boggling. There were trinkets and objects flying through the air and a nearby M-Gen panel had already forced a good pile of food, and computerized parts and equipment into the hall. Taylor slowly made his way to stand front of the main lift so that he could get his bearings. It was here that Taylor noticed a body lying on the ground, unconscious, and bleeding.

He kneeled over, still cradling his injured hand, and turned the body over to reveal the face of Dr. Hathaway. Taylor shook his head and smirked.

"Why am I not surprised?" he said aloud, and was relieved to feel that she still had a pulse. On close inspection, however, he could see a laser burn in her shoulder that ran clean through. Questioning how this could happen, Taylor's eyes met the answer in the form of two large white robotic feet that had planted themselves near Dr. Hathaway's head.

Taylor recognized the awkward heavy white feet as those belonging to the security desk robot. Wrought with uneasiness, he turned his head up only a fraction of a second before his neck was tightly and painfully gripped by a robotic hand. This hand lifted him into the air and with a flash of light in his eyes Taylor could tell that the robot had performed a retinal scan.

Looking the robot dead in its *eyes,* Taylor believed any moment he would be saved by his identity. The robot paused for a few seconds, and Taylor felt his heart fall through his stomach when he noticed by reading the robot's display on its chest that its security code was being randomly edited and changed. His fears quickly confirmed themselves when the robot voiced a stiff, "You are not authorized to access this level. You have thirty seconds to vacate. Failure to comply will result in the use of lethal force."

Taylor was dropped to his feet, which fell beneath him, and he landed hard on his backside. Quickly grabbing Dr. Hathaway by the wrist Taylor pulled her down the hall away from the lift and the robot that was following and still counting down the time.

He found his way to lab room W484L, whose doors seemed to be opening and closing faster than any other he had seen, and he was sure there would be no way he could enter the room without being cut in half.

He started concentrating on the access panel hoping to override the power to the doors. It was in the thick of these coded thoughts that his injured hand was grabbed by the robot quite unexpectedly. Taylor screamed in pain and as he was lifted into the air by this hand, he noticed the robot's silence more than anything. In fact, with all of his focus on the panel and Dr. Hathaway, Taylor hadn't realized that the robot stopped its count somewhere in the teens.

The robot finally spoke, "You cannot interfere. You cannot interfere. The procedure is not complete. You cannot interfere."

"Procedure?" Taylor questioned only half heartedly, for the pain in his hand forced his brain to lose all focus.

"You cannot interfere. The procedure is not complete." the robot repeated once more, and it attempted a quick swipe at Taylor's head with its free arm.

Taylor focused hard and stopped the metallic hand inches away from his face. With absolute firmness and determination the teen smirked, "You wanna bet!"

He cast his eyes up at the robotic arm that was holding him in the air, forcing it to release its grip. Now, being as he was much more prepared to be dropped, he landed square on his feet.

The robot quickly ejected its laser unit and aimed it at Taylor's head. With a quick telekinetic rush, Taylor forced the robot to whirl around backwards, and as the laser went off it cut through several wall panels and M-Gen panels, causing electrical sparks to fly everywhere.

Taylor focused on the laser unit and telekinetically ripped it from the robot's body. The robot stomped its feet loudly and forced some form of anchoring system to plant its legs firmly into the concrete floor.

Fully turning its upper torso around, the robot seemed to stare Taylor down. The teen was half surprised by this action and listened as the robot continued to profess its mantra. "You cannot interfere. You cannot interfere."

Taylor moved from the doorway of the lab and focused on the *head* of the robot. He was attempting to turn it slowly around, keeping its focus away from himself and Dr. Hathaway. With a quick and unexpected jolt the robot forced both of its arms directly at Taylor's chest.

Only with speedy mental reflexes was Taylor able to split these hands a few inches apart, while turning himself sideways to prevent being hit.

The robotic hands completely crushed the panels behind Taylor and the teen felt a rush of fear fill him as he realized that such a blow would have killed him for sure.

The robot started struggling, unable to pull its arms from the panels it had penetrated and Taylor realized that now was his chance. He focused again on the robot's head, where its main processor was located, and did his best to decapitate his metallic nemesis.

After a few short seconds he had successfully turned the robotic cranium full circle and on facing the robot directly again Taylor could feel the arms on either side of him quickly stiffen up and squeeze at his midsection forcing him to grunt in pain from sharp metallic edges cutting into his sides. Still, however, he focused on the head of the robot, continuing to turn it. Once he'd turned it another half it stopped. Its actuators and controllers had reached their extreme, and the teen knew that it was now or never. Forcing himself to ignore the pain in his wrist, and the ever increasing pains in his sides, he winced his eyes in total concentration.

Crack!

The actuators in the robot's neck broke in half and with Taylor's continued focus the robot's head spun over and over again at ease until all of the wires and connections had completely twisted themselves off.

After a few seconds the robot's constricting arms fell limp and Taylor pulled himself over them to safety. He slowly lifted his shirt to examine the cuts and damage inflicted by the robot, all the while spouting verbal bits of anger and pain. Satisfied that he was fine, he dropped his shirt and returned to his true purpose.

He stepped back to the entrance of the lab and telekinetically focused on the doors, keeping them open just long enough to drag Dr. Hathaway through them before they started slamming again, just barely nipping at her shoes.

On standing upright and fully absorbing the room he was in, Taylor's mind seemed to have all thoughts leave him over his shock. The sphere was attaching to and detaching itself from the heads of each of the six children, all of whom were standing at the far end of the laboratory. As he approached, this machine either didn't notice or didn't care about his presence and therefore continued its constant probing and monitoring of the children as if he wasn't there.

All at once Taylor had come to a realization – that all of the chaos inside the EduCorp Towers, all of the disturbances, could be caused by a cyber or a telekinetic. In fact, Taylor reasoned, it was David, Aspen, Grace, and Orion whose powers were totally out of control and were causing all of the chaos abound in the building.

So when the robot said I could not interfere – was it really the sphere acting through Grace or Orion, Taylor wondered.

Looking at the odd activity before him, Taylor was apprehensive about interfering and felt it best to see if there was any real danger to the children. With this in mind he pulled out a scanning rod from a nearby supply closet and in looking back at his students he only barely had time to notice a robotic arm pull itself from the wall and swing in his direction. Taylor was immediately on the defensive, kinetically stopping it. He was suspicious of the sphere trying to cause him more harm, but he quickly realized that the arm was only swinging through a series of random movements, obviously a side effect of random cyberkinetic interference.

With the scanning wand in hand Taylor made his way back to where his students were and found it strange to be standing less than a few feet away from the sphere, which was propped on three of its unused tentacles, and even still, this thing did not consider him a threat. He then walked up to David, whose eyes were moving wildly under closed lids, and started scanning, starting with the boy's feet and slowly moving to his head.

It was here, when Taylor had just reached David's forehead that the scanner picked up something unusual and it was at this time that the boy's behavior under the scanning light started to change. The boy started twitching and blinking uncontrollably, very similar to the way Johnny did when he had been scanned earlier the day before.

Taylor pulled the scanner away, and concentrated on it, pulling the data out of it and just reading it in his mind. As could be expected, Taylor discovered that there were severely high levels of neural activity, especially in the telekinetic patterns. The scanner also picked up a large number of foreign objects inside the boy's brain.

"Nanites." Taylor said aloud, and whether it was that the sphere heard him, or it detected the scanning that had just been performed, something caused one of the tentacles to pierce the scanning tool straight through, and throw it across the room.

With a sinking feeling in his stomach that worked through his entire body, Taylor felt an increasing nervousness over what this unknown machine was doing to his kids, especially since he wasn't certain of any possible side effects to this radical and bizarre procedure.

His uncertainty of what was going on, of the idea of horrible and unknown neural side effects weighed heavily on Taylor's brain and with these thoughts he firmly decided that he should do whatever necessary to stop what the sphere was doing as soon as possible.

Remembering the simplest way to immobilize the unit, Taylor seized a medical M-Gen unit from the supply cabinet and aimed it straight at the center of the sphere. After performing a rapid scan, the portable M-Gen's display showed a layout of the internal workings of the machine. After a few seconds of searching, he located the sphere's different power supplies.

With no resistance, no climax, and no struggle; no, just the simple pull of a trigger, the sphere once again became immobile and clunked to the ground with a loud bang. Immediately the lights in the lab came on and were stable. All around, Taylor's eyes shot in a thousand directions as he took in the fact that things were rapidly getting back to normal... whatever that would be at this point.

Despite his less than positive feelings towards her, Taylor had great concern for the welfare of Dr. Hathaway. All things considered though, he still knew that his most immediate and pressing concern should be for his kids. He telekinetically placed each of them, along with Dr. Hathaway on a different bed in the lab and addressed the computer directly. As he did this, he pulled out a bio-elastic polymer unit to encapsulate Dr. Hathaway until he had a chance to deal with her.

"Lab" he said, but then paused and thought for a few seconds before attempting to obtain security clearance.

"Awa… Awa... Awaiting command." the computer sputtered in a broken stutter.

"I thought so!" Taylor said, and he addressed the computer again.

"Lab, recognize Physician Authority Taylor, Robert S."

"Phys Phys Physician authority-ee-ee recognized. Good *afternoon* Dr. Taylor How ow ow may I help you?" the computer buzzed in broken verbiage.

"Lab, perform a complete memory dump and reload *all* standard protocols from secure ROM location Delta 484-17L."

"Command con con confirmed."

Instantly the lights in the room went dark and, in his air tight surroundings, Taylor sucked his own lip nervously in the long deafening silence that shrouded over a room full of unconscious children. After these impatient seconds he could hear the mechanical workings of the room's computers and see the displays in the room slowly flicker back on and boot to their standard startup screens while the lights came on again. All the robotic arms in the room returned to their retracted and dormant positions and Taylor could hear, as if he knew what it sounded like, the *room* was functioning normally.

Feeling confident that any programming errors were cleared out of the system Taylor again addressed the lab computer.

"Lab – Recognize physician authority Taylor, Robert S."

"Physician authority recognized. Good *morning* Dr. Taylor. How may I help you?"

"Well that's better," Taylor whispered before commanding again, "Lab – recall procedure… oh crap!" Taylor quickly realized that with the memory dump he just performed, the procedure he used on Johnny to remove the nanites earlier in the day would no longer be active in the system.

"I am sorry, Dr. Taylor, the procedure 'Oh, crap' is not recognized."

Taylor found himself both amused and frustrated at hearing this response and quickly programmed in the steps needed in order to remove the nanites from the brains of his students. After offering the several commands needed, a sigh of relief seemed to add bit of humanity to the actuating and robotic noises that now permeated the room. Watching the lab working hard on the six kids, Taylor quickly pulled a curtain around their beds and realized he had nothing left to do but tend to Dr. Hathaway's injuries while he waited for the nanites to be deactivated and removed from the brains of his students.

Walking up to her body he couldn't help but force a wide grin. He pulled a tissue generator from the storage cabinet under her examination bed and readied it for use. It was at this time, trying to use both his hands, that Taylor realized, or rather remembered, that his right wrist, now horribly swollen, was probably broken. He stared down at its black and blue color as though it had somehow just reattached itself to his body.

"First thing's first!" Taylor said wincing, and he turned the generator on his own wrist. Doing this gave his hand and wrist a strange tingling sensation that increased until it caused a slight sense of pain. This pain was the easiest way to tell when the tissue generator had done its job. Replacing the tissue generator with a bone replicator, Taylor finished the repair to his wrist and after turning the unit off, he admired his now properly colored wrist. He flexed it up and down and could feel that though it was still tender, it was certainly well on its way to a full recovery.

Snatching up the tissue generator again, he turned to Dr. Hathaway. Looking over her stiffened body, Taylor sighed at the idea that he had to help her when she had so strongly tried to ruin the life he was trying to build with his students. Thinking of this, he felt a sense of irony wash over him as he tapped the release mechanism for the bioelastic polymer unit.

With Dr. Hathaway no longer in stasis and her body now limp and movable Taylor carefully ripped her shirt open to reveal the partially cauterized wound through her shoulder. He immediately put the tissue generator to use so that in less than a minute her wound was healed. He then used the bone replicator, and scanned her shoulder to discover that, indeed, all the damage had been repaired. Taylor immediately started pacing, having nothing to do but wait, and he couldn't help but gravitate his attention to the activity behind the translucent plastic curtain that separated him from his kids.

Occasionally staring down at Dr. Hathaway from different angles as he walked around her examination table, he could not help but be so frustrated at her. He was frustrated at her involvement, at her unconsciousness, and so very frustrated at how her appearance was so deceiving both in regards to age and personality. If he had judged her age by looks, he would have guessed her to be 23 or so, and if he judged her personality, by the soft attractive face, with a perfectly shaped nose and lips and shiny blonde hair that even though slightly bloodied, still seemed somehow perfect, he would have guessed her to be nothing less than angelic.

Angelic – ha! Taylor knew that nothing could be further from the truth. Having taken an unauthorized look at her personnel file over five years ago he knew that she was well into her seventies and Taylor didn't need the file to tell him that she had the personality of a shark. A chill preceded his shaking head as he sighed over such a deceiving gentle face. With half a grin, it was at times like this that Taylor knew that some time later in his own life he would not look his age and he should be grateful for the long and youthful life that the Methuselah Virus offered everyone on the planet.

Clearing his head, the teen continued his pacing and his looks of uncertainty. His better judgment told him it would be smart to leave her be. His deeply rooted, agitation laced curiosity, on the other hand, said that he needed answers; answers that only she could provide. With a stiffening stance Taylor commanded that the computer place restraints on Dr. Hathaway's arms and legs during which time he kneeled and pulled a stimulator gun from the cabinet under her examination table. Quite to his surprise, on rising he was face to face with Jay who had just entered the lab in a rush of heaving breaths, dressed in quick untidiness and wearing the most terrified expression on his face.

With a deep inhale of ozone that had permeated the air, Taylor looked between the woman slumbering in front of him and the man gawking at him, wondering who he should address first.

28 Interrogation

EXHALING THE TAINTED AIR IN HIS LUNGS, Taylor addressed the only other conscious person in the room.

"What are you doing here?" he spewed in angry surprise.

Jay offered an expression of 'what do you think' on his face as he held up his hand to show his own ring which was still blinking a red silhouette.

"What's going on here, and what the hell happened outside?!" Jay retorted when he saw Dr. Hathaway on the table and the injector gun in Taylor's hand.

"Nothing, well, I mean..." Taylor stumbled in his speech for he could see on Jay's face an accusing stare that was expectant and waiting for an explanation of why Dr. Hathaway was restrained on the table and he, Taylor, was ready to use an injector gun on her.

"Oh, come on! I just saved her life!" Taylor said loudly, responding to the accusatory stare. He then waved his hand towards the exit door, "and that flippin' robot just about ripped my head off a few minutes ago!" Jay's stare shifted to dissatisfaction. "Listen," Taylor continued, "I was just about to... uh... well..." Taylor grumbled and waved his index fingers in front of his face as a signal that he'd rather communicate telepathically to save time.

Jay nodded to this signal and with a concentrated gaze Taylor offered a rapid, yet detailed recounting of what had happened. Gasping, Jay showed a clear face of understanding. In fact, Jay seemed more overwhelmed than anything. He had already had what he considered quite a full day. To have this happen, well it just seemed to put things over the top, something Taylor could see in Jay's eyes when he released their pathic bond.

Looking down at Dr. Hathaway, Jay was now filled with just as much a want to know the truth as Taylor and so the two of them stood over her, utterly consumed with questions as to what she was doing on the 484th floor at this time of the morning. At the least, Taylor was certain in his own mind, she could explain some of what had happened in the previous day.

Jay snatched the stimulator gun from Taylor's hands. "Dude! You've done enough. You look like crap. Get something to eat. I've got this"

Taylor nodded and turned to a nearby M-Gen panel, forced it to make him a simple ham and cheese sandwich, then sat in a chair facing his counterpart, who used the injector on Dr. Hathaway. With a simple hissing noise, both could hear a standard dose of stimulants introduce their way into her system. With this she started groaning, and at the first hint of her eyes opening she panicked and thrashed about on the table.

Jay quickly pressed his hand on her forehead, "Calm down! Calm down! You're alright. You're safe. Come on girl, calm down!"

Dr. Hathaway's grunts finally subsided and Taylor almost smiled at seeing the writhing fear in her eyes and thought that it served her right for messing with his kids.

"What! Where am I?" she asked in a quivering and uncertain voice while continuing to twist her arms and legs uselessly inside their restraints. She looked up at Jay, but as there were several bright lights behind him, so she could not readily see his face amid the overpowering silhouette.

"You don't remember?" Jay questioned calmly, and waited for a response.

On hearing this Dr. Hathaway was filled an immediate memory of the robotic security guard and the laser that had struck her through the shoulder. She jerked her head to look at where there should've been a severe injury, but all could see was that her shirt was torn and bloodied, but there was no damage to her skin except for a slight redness that she could sense was tender to the touch.

She looked back at Jay, still not knowing who he was, and became insistent.

"Who the hell are you?" She looked down at her body, all tightly wrapped in straps, and twisted her wrists even harder, "Get these things off me!"

If she had been more careful, she might have noticed Taylor between her feet, slowly eating his sandwich, but she only focused the restraints and the man beside her, clouding what she could see in her anger, still unaware of who else was in the room. Jay moved from out of the path of the light, thus revealing his face. She realized who he was, but before she could speak Jay quickly responded to her command. "Not just yet doc. We've got a few questions, and we want – no, *we expect* answers."

"You!" she said insultingly as if the sight of Jay disgusted her.

"Yes, princess, me," he responded, smiling down at her.

"You let me go this instant or I'll have you fired by morning you..."

"Chick, you better watch yourself." Jay said quickly and calmly, "You're definitely not in a position to be making threats or insults. Now again, we have some questions that *you will* answer."

"We have questions?" she snapped insistently, "What we?" and with this Taylor pushed himself in his hovering chair so that he was now beside her. Dr. Hathaway heard the hum of the chair's movement and turned her head to now come eye to eye with Taylor. Now he couldn't help but smile for, at the sight of him, her panic increased to violent levels as she struggled to free herself from her confining hold.

"Dr. Hafaway," Taylor started, messily talking with his mouth full of food before swallowing, "don't struggle, there's really no point. Even if you could get free, I could hold you here with less concentration than it takes for you to chew gum..."

Despite his words, Taylor could see that she was still struggling, and that her wrists were now rubbing themselves raw. "Calm down!" he shouted loudly, desperate for silence from her squirming efforts. He concentrated to hold her body firm and unmoving.

Though the process was slow, it took less and less effort for him to keep her still, so he knew that he was finally getting through to her. In less than a minute she was lying calm and appeared relaxed on the table.

"What do you waaaaant?" she asked in a whimpering voice and Taylor and Jay could see that tears were now flowing down the sides of her face.

"What were you doing here this early in the morning doctor?" Jay asked after pathically telling Taylor to let him ask the questions.

Dr. Hathaway didn't hesitate in offering an answer to this question. "I was writing a formal complaint against your friend over there!" she said loudly, though Taylor could distinctly hear quivers of desperation in her voice.

"No. That's not what I meant." Jay persisted, "What were you doing *here?*" he asked waving his hand around to define specifics.

"I didn't want to go to this floor. It was an accident! You don't understand!" she pleaded as she was met with looks of disbelief from both Jay and Taylor. "It was! I was headed down to the ground level," she started again, sounding even more desperate, "I was going down to leave. But just before I hit bottom the lift started going crazy *again*!"

"Again?" Jay asked curiously and he was immediately met with a distracting cough from Taylor who was pointing at himself with a grin.

"Ah, right!" Jay said quickly with bright eyes and he returned his look to the now fierce stare of Dr. Hathaway.

"You! Uhrgh," she grunted, "I should've known!" she said in an angry heave at the realization of what was behind her lift ride the morning before. "Anyways, I got off the lift at the first chance when it stopped solid. The lift didn't even stop level with the floor. I had to climb up just to get to a floor I could reach. When I did it was weird, the hall was dark and the lights were going crazy. I didn't know what the hell was going on. The last I remember there was a loud clanging and a sharp pain in my shoulder!"

"Aaaaaammmmd…?" Taylor persisted, mouth again full of sandwich.

"And what? That's all I remember!" she said, shaking her head fearfully.

Taylor, willing to believe that after the attack her memory may have been somewhat unreliable, decided that the best way to know for sure what happened was to use his post-cog abilities.

Having finally finished his sandwich, Taylor stood up and reached out to grab one of Dr. Hathaway's strapped down hands. This caused her to flinch fearfully, all the while spewing, "Don't you touch me! Don't you dare touch me... you – you – *freak!*"

Taylor, being unphased by this comment, grinned and jetted out a single finger to make contact with her skin and he concentrated hard on rewinding time so as to see what happened earlier.

As if a black veil had been pulled over his eyes, Taylor's vision went dark then, with a lurch, a small room rushed upward from beneath him. Once again he felt as though he were being dropped through a ceiling. He looked around quickly and could see that he was in a lift that was zipping through the thirties on its way downward. He could also see Dr. Hathaway, who was standing quite idly square in front of the door.

Suddenly the lift stopped and Taylor was certain that if he actually had a body, it would have been knocked to the floor as Dr. Hathaway was. Looking down on her he could see a look of fear and panic in her face as she turned up to look at where the lift had stopped. The numbers were now counting upward and at a much faster rate than standard. She kept to the floor as the lift shook with its increased speed. He heard her say the words, "Oh no! Not again!" as the lift moved well into the two-hundreds. This comment made him smile, at least in the vision, and probably in the real world too, but he wasn't sure.

Because he was standing next to her in the laboratory, Taylor was certain that Dr. Hathaway would survive the lift's erratic maneuvers, but as he saw the level indicator passing four hundred, he couldn't help but let her fear spill over into himself, for there was now less than fifty – forty – thirty levels before reaching the shaft's end for West Tower.

Strangely enough the lift did slow its ascent as it neared the peak, and it did this so rapidly that Dr. Hathaway, for a few seconds, appeared as though she were floating in the lift itself. Taylor marveled at this coincidence of physics and, with a clapping of her shoes and an exhaling grunt, Dr. Hathaway landed on her feet. He watched as she pounded the console to force the doors to open, but there was no response. With a hard jerk the lift started its descent back down the shaft, picking up speed slowly until it was passing several floors a second.

This series of ups and downs proceeded for a few minutes until, with some strange combination of passing floors and the lift's doors opening and closing at odd intervals, Dr. Hathaway was preparing to jump off the lift at the next available opportunity.

True to her word, Taylor thought as he watched the 482nd floor slowly pass below foot while the doors slowly closed, then the 483rd when they started to open again. Within moments Taylor could see the 484th floor on approach, and he pushed his consciousness through the doorway just fast enough to watch Dr. Hathaway lift herself out of the lift after it had stopped.

Taylor shifted his gaze in all directions looking for the security robot that he was certain would attack at any moment. With the silence in the halls only being broken by the occasional clump of an object falling out of the M-Gen panel nearby, Taylor didn't have to look for long to see that the robot was, in fact, still dormant in its hibernation slot.

The teen moved his consciousness right up to it, waiting for it to spring to life, and was even disappointed when nothing happened for nearly a minute. He turned, watched Dr. Hathaway wander out of sight and return to the main corridor after a few seconds.

Taylor's consciousness flinched as the laser unit on the security robot sprang to life. His nerves grew uneasy with the realization of what was about to happen, but Dr. Hathaway was busy peering through one of the door windows, completely unaware of the activity nearby.

The robot stepped from its holding slot and smoothly clanked its way in her direction. Dr. Hathaway had just noticed the robot's feet when the laser cannon fired, silently slicing a hole in her shoulder. Taylor winced with a sense of the pain that the shot must have caused, but this was short lived as the teen snapped his attention to a dark figure that moved out from one of the rooms down the hall. Taking a closer look, he could see that the person was exiting Johnny's dorm. Taylor knew now that this person deserved his special interest.

The teen almost laughed because on close inspection of this dark image, it didn't have a nose, mouth, or eyes. Shaking his head, he hissed, "What is it with these people?"

He followed the dark figure, dressed all in black, as it made its way beside a bleeding and kneeling Dr. Hathaway, and with a stare that was aimed directly through Taylor, the figure started manipulating the security robot. With a few rapid steps the robot ran toward Dr. Hathaway and with a quick thud it tapped her on the back of the head, knocking her out.

Instantly Taylor came to a simple realization that it wasn't his children or the sphere that had caused harm to Dr. Hathaway. It was this person, a person that Taylor was almost certain he could identify, that was manipulating the security robot.

Now standing idle, the robot powered down and the dark figure closed his eyes for a moment before making his way to the lab where the children were. The door opened and just as the figure was about to enter Taylor heard something quite surprising.

"You are not authorized to access this level. You have thirty seconds to vacate. Failure to comply will result in the use of lethal force." Taylor and the faceless figure both turned and saw that the robot had re-activated itself. It was making its way towards the lab door, focused on the dark intruder. Taking a closer look at the robot, Taylor saw that its security protocols were being randomly edited as he had seen once before. Turning back to the dark figure, Taylor could see that it was facing the robot in what he could only assume was deep concentration.

"Bad idea!" Taylor thought to himself, and sure enough, the faceless figure was quickly shocked into an involuntary muscle jerk that forced him to jump some thirty feet through the air before he hitting the wall near the lift entrance.

Only barely revived, the figure leaped into the lift shaft, just as the doors were closing on another lift that was shooting by.

Taylor found himself more frustrated than ever at the thought that this perpetrator was a cyber, so to speak. Realizing no new answers would come to him through the rest of this vision, he was just about to release himself from it, but at that moment he could see someone slowly walk up to the body of Dr. Hathaway, unaware of the security robot behind him and about to attack. It was himself...

Taylor pulled his hand back from touching Dr. Hathaway, and with a great sense of dizziness he collapsed into a chair that was quickly put into place by Jay.

"So…" Jay asked quickly.

"So nothing!" Taylor said in a tired voice, "She's telling the truth."

Dr. Hathaway, who was making a futile effort to free her hands from the restraints, suddenly stopped and stared at Taylor in surprise. She would have thought it better for him to tell a lie and say she's guilty of something and certainly didn't expect this kind of honesty.

Taylor continued, casting his eyes at a control panel with concentration, "But what you didn't know, Dr. Hathaway, was that someone was there, in the corridor, when you were knocked out."

"Well I didn't see anyone." she said coldly as though he were trying to accuse her of something.

"I know. The person came out of Johnny's dorm just as you were making your way back to the lift. I have a pretty good idea I know who it was, even though when I looked at their face I saw no eyes, nose or mouth to speak of, so their identity was hidden."

Jay nodded at hearing this and realized that person must have been the same one in Taylor's vision the morning before. Dr. Hathaway, however, looked confused.

"That's not possible! Is it?" she insisted and asked as Taylor pushed a button on the table to force her to slowly sit upright.

"I was ho… ping you'd ask that doctor." Taylor said with a yawn, and he explained.

"You see, when a person is given a powerful mind controller, much like the one you gave Dr. Richardson two nights ago, it has the effect of..."

Taylor saw a great look of surprise on Dr. Hathaway's face.

"What?" he asked with a smirk, "You didn't think I knew about that?"

"I don't know what you're talking about!" Dr. Hathaway spewed, and she turned her head to look away from Taylor.

"Are you sure?" Taylor asked in dramatic tone looking at Jay, who was more confused than ever, but the teen continued to pressure her calmly. "You know, with one touch I could verify that."

At these words Dr. Hathaway flinched to look eye to eye with Taylor, "Fine," she said, her face contorted with anger, "So you know I gave him something, but you don't know what it was for. I didn't even know."

"Yes. We'll get back to that. But for nooooow let me explain." Taylor said, offering yet another yawn. "As I was saying before, when a person is given a powerful mind controller, it has the effect of wiping their identity from the visions post-cogs get when trying to see the past. This is mostly because impressions of them are tainted and untrue by the fact that they are being controlled."

"This evening, at dinner in one of the conference rooms, Caitlin and Johnny caught a vision that I sort of *looked in* on, and I must say that what I saw was, well shall we say inappropriate for them to see..." Taylor then gave Dr. Hathaway a scornful look, "You really should be careful where you decide to do things like that, I mean after all, you're at a school."

Dr. Hathaway turned her head and stared at the plastic curtain across the room, she could see the silhouette of several moving robotic arms and her curiosity was heightened by the activity, but Taylor was still persisting in his explanation and interrogation.

"Let's get to it, shall we, Dr. Hathaway." Taylor pressed on seeing her distraction.

"I know you gave Dr. Richardson some kind of mind control drug. He's the one who put that – that thing – that sphere in Johnny's room the other night, and he did it on your orders, didn't he?"

Taylor paced around her, very careful to scan her every thought and facial expression for anything that might slip out. Dr. Hathaway, on the other hand, didn't move. She simply stared at the plastic curtain, mesmerized by the robotic dancing silhouette.

Taylor's impatience was mounting its peak. "You can ignore me doctor, that's fine! I'll get the truth from you one way or another, you know that." At these words Dr. Hathaway turned to Taylor and, feeling she had no choice, spoke harshly to him.

"Fine! You want the truth. I'll give you the truth." She looked between Jay and Taylor and with a concentrated stare started communicating pathically with the latter.

On slowly having his mind filled with different images, Taylor quickly grabbed a neural recorder from under the table and slapped it on his own neck. With a quick tap and beep he could tell that the unit was functioning normally, thereby recording every image that entered his brain.

When Taylor was able to fully focus on the telepathic images, he worked hard to hold communication with Dr. Hathaway and let the pathic images consume him completely. This was something that could only be done if at least one of the two communicating telepaths is well endowed with pathic powers. Fortunately for Taylor, he always carried this with him at all times. So with a deep breath he blinked his eyes quickly as Dr. Hathaway's thoughts took focus.

Indeed, all around him the lab dissolved out of existence and in its place Taylor could see a smaller room form. It was an office of sorts, with pictures and degrees posted on the walls and a desk in its middle. Lastly he saw a person... Dr. Hathaway, come into form from a fuzzy dissolve. She sitting at the only desk in the office, working hard on some report that Taylor could not read. In fact as he stared at it he was certain that it didn't make any sense at all. He lowered himself over the display for a closer look.

Now only inches away from Dr. Hathaway, she turned and stared straight at him, giving him a quick chill.

"This report isn't for your eyes," she said shakily, "and it isn't important. Just pay attention."

Taylor pulled his head back in surprise. She must be a more gifted telepath than he had previously given her credit for if she was able to interfere in her own pathic memories like that. Now that he thought about it, in fact, she'd have to be gifted just so that she could offer this memory to him in a third person perspective.

Stepping back, he heeded her words and looked around the office for something of interest, still not sure what he was supposed to notice or what was to happen. It was just as he made his way to the small room's entrance that the request light lit up above the door. The Dr. Hathaway of the past quickly responded for the requestor to enter and thus revealed a delivery man.

The gaunt mousy man, wearing a brightly animated ball-cap displaying "UMPS" (United Metro Postal Service), walked straight through Taylor and rapidly made his way across the room to place a small parcel on her desk. She stared down at it for a moment, confused of its small size and nature.

"Do I need to sign for this?" she asked politely, but before she even finished the question the delivery man was already half out of the room walking with ever increasing speed.

Put off by his abrupt departure, she opened the package quickly. It was only a few inches in any direction making her fearless about pouring its minute contents onto her desk. There were only two small items inside: A piece of plexi-paper and a memory module with the word "ONE" printed on it in red.

She opened the plasti-paper and her eyes were met with flashing red letters:

GC PRIORITY

LEVEL 7

Dr. Hathaway's face and color drained to a nauseating expression.

"Oh no!" she whispered in a soft distressed voice before taking a deep breath, snatching up the memory module, and rushing out of the office. Taylor's consciousness glided with her as she sprinted down two different corridors to the main lift. She went straight to one of the conference levels and on exiting the lift, searched for the nearest available room.

Taylor was beside himself over how things can come full circle, for as she made her way into one conference room, he noticed himself and his six students gingerly making their way out of another, having just finished dinner.

Once inside Dr. Hathaway locked the door using a high level security override and made her way to an M-Gen panel across the room. She pulled out the memory module and plugged it into a receptacle on the panel. Immediately the panel powered itself up and offered a beeping noise that it had finished generating something.

Dr. Hathaway opened the panel and pulled out a metallic box with the letters GCSD printed on the side.

"Science Division?" Taylor said with heightened curiosity.

He watched Dr. Hathaway open the box to reveal several items, the largest of which was the infamous sphere he had been dealing with over the last day, then there was another memory module with the number 2 printed on its side, and a small vial, which Taylor had seen before in his vision with Caitlin and Johnny, and lastly, he saw a small receiver unit.

Dr. Hathaway snatched up the new memory module and plugged it into a nearby data panel on the wall. Within a few short seconds the room was filled with a strange voice that was obviously being masked to prevent identification.

"Dr. Hathaway," boomed the deep voice, "You have been activated to begin initiation of Operation Omega Six,"

At hearing the word "activated" Taylor's mind spun in a hundred different directions, not the least of which was why the GC was so interested in his kids, and what the purpose of *Operation Omega Six* was, though the number six gave him some inclination.

He listened as *the voice* ordered her to immediately call Dr. Richardson to the conference room and seduce him into drinking the contents of the vial and give him the *sphere*. She was also ordered to monitor the receiver she had just replicated at all times and conjure a smear campaign against Taylor to the Education Council at the scheduled session on the following morningin the hopes of discrediting the *Prodigy 2* experiment.

"Dr. Hathaway," the voice continued, "You cannot fail. If you do, the Omega 6 candidates will be at risk."

As the voice closed its instructions, Dr. Hathaway stepped away from the data panel and sat at one of the chairs at the conference table. Taylor could distinctly see that she was tearing up. It was with a deep breath then, that she pulled her composure together and instructed the computer to locate Dr. Richardson just as Taylor's bond with Dr. Hathaway lost its hold.

With the same smooth dissolve that he had entered into the reality of Dr. Hathaway's thoughts, he was ejected from them, and dizziness, either from the lost link or from his own myriad of thoughts, made him half fall to the floor. Blinking his eyes quickly, and looking wildly about his surroundings, he caught the panicked stare of Jay, who had grabbed the teen's face and forced an eye to eye glance.

"Are you alright?" he asked in a shaking voice. "Come on Taylor. Talk to me!"

Taylor pulled his stare away from that of his friend, and he started nodding his head, "I'm fine, Jay! I'm fine!"

After a few seconds with his head down and rubbing his temples, Taylor looked from under his long fallen hair and gave Dr. Hathaway a dark piercing angry stare.

"What is *Operation Omega Six* Dr. Hathaway?" Taylor pressed while bracing himself on a counter across from her.

"I can't tell you!" She said with a stiffness and defiant strength in her voice.

"I'll only ask you one more time..." Taylor retorted, returning the same stiff and defiant tone to her as he asked her again, "What is *Operation Omega Six*?"

"I told you, I can't. It's classified Top Secret!" she looked at practically every inch of the room in an effort to avoid looking at Taylor.

Taylor reached out his hand slowly, threateningly, in an effort to touch hers, making it obvious to Dr. Hathaway that her secrets – her inner thoughts – were at risk. She quickly shook her head, then stared straight at the ceiling and shouted in a very loud and monotonous voice, "As an identified GC employee with high level security access, and being in possession of vital security information, I am telling you now, if you perform an illegal read to acquire said information, you will be sentenced to no less than twenty years..."

Taylor's mind washed away the words she was saying. He didn't seem to care of the consequences of forcing an illegal read on her, even if she had identified herself. His hand continued to creep closer to hers. It was now less than an a few inches away. He was almost there.

"All anomalies have been removed from subjects one thru six."

The familiar voice of the lab computer seemed to have distracted the teen, who snatched his hand away in an instant.

"Come on Taylor. Let's see how the kids are doing!" Jay said with an unsteady smile. He had been watching nervously, hoping that Taylor would decide to pull his hand away on his own. To have touched her would have complicated the next several days to a degree that Jay didn't even want to think about, so to be offered such a quick and easy way out that he was eager to lay out such a simple suggestion.

Taylor balled his hand to a fist and stared at it curiously before offering Dr. Hathaway an almost apologetic grin. Turning around, he quickly split the curtain hiding the children, stepped through with Jay, and closed it so that Dr. Hathaway would not be able to see what was happening on the other side.

The woman lay helplessly strapped to the examination table for what seemed an eternity of several minutes before Jay returned from behind the translucent curtains. The woman could clearly see that tears were welling in his eyes, and not a few seconds after seeing the man she heard wails from Taylor.

"What's the matter?" she asked nervously, but she wasn't sure she wanted to hear the answer.

Jay took a seat beside Dr. Hathaway, looked at her with a fierce red-eyed stare, "They're not waking up!" he said stiff lipped and firm.

"Not waking up!" she repeated, "But they have to…"

"What was that?" Jay shouted. "What was that? No! Doctor, they don't have to wake up, and they're not waking up. They're – they're flat!" he said, letting her know that they were, as it seemed, brain-dead.

"Flat!" she offered with a confused expression, "All of them?"

"Yes," Jay affirmed in a harsh, hateful voice. "All of them. They're showing no neural activity. Would you like to explain?"

"Shit!" she said angrily, "Shit – shit – shit!" At this point it was clear that Dr. Hathaway was visibly disturbed by this new information and her lower lip and chin started to quiver with emotion as she forced herself to stare up at the ceiling rather than look at Jay when she spoke. "This wasn't supposed to happen." she said desperately as Taylor made his way through the plastic curtain. "You weren't supposed to interfere," she added, staring at the teen with a look of almost desperate apology.

Hearing this phrase, one that he had heard several times before, Taylor would've burned her alive with his eyes if he could, but he had neither effort, nor words that were strong enough to break through his threadbare emotional state.

He slowly made his way over to the data panel on the nearby wall and through a series of buttons, pulled up the message he had initially sent to the council for an emergency meeting. He recoded the message to be Level 7 urgent, and resent it.

"Jay, I've got another meeting with the council. If you don't mind, I'll take Dr. Hathaway to the chamber myself. You stay here, with them. I want someone close in case there's any change."

Jay nodded his head as Taylor focused on Dr. Hathaway's examination table. It obeyed his cyber commands to release her.

"Am I going to have any resistance from you?" he questioned. She slowly shook her head in response before standing. She took a moment to eye the plastic curtain that separated her from the children. Turning a low gaze, she made her way by Taylor's side and together the two exited the laboratory with Dr. Hathaway in the lead.

Just as the door was about to close Taylor could sense the very dismal emotions of Jay radiating behind him. The man had walked back through the curtains to see to the children, all the while overflowing with trepidation and despair.

29 A Month of Rest

IN THE YEAR 2452, after their arrival to the EduCorp Towers, after their accident, and after their grueling cyber powered surgeries, *the gifted six*, as they would soon be called, did not immediately wake in the recovery room to welcome Taylor into their lives. In fact, they did not welcome anyone into their lives for a full month, for that is how long they lay in a coma like state.

Inside the recovery room these children became a semi-permanent fixture amidst the lights, machines, and their own data displays that showed how healthy; how very healthy, they were. Indeed, most subjects in the recovery room were only there for a few hours as modern medicine seemed to always have a way of getting people back on their feet. But these children were in an enigmatic slumber that Taylor did not understand.

Even for Taylor himself, it only took a few hours from his waking before getting back into the swing of work again. And, being as he was well on the mend, he decided to continue his responsibilities as the new supervisor of EduCorp's Emergency Room and Recovery Ward for at least the time it took the children to get better. While this responsibility did mean tending to the several sick and otherwise injured subjects and employees of the company that filtered through the Emergency Room, Taylor still spent every spare moment he had watching over these, the most peaceful of youngsters. Taylor was, in fact, drawn to them, as strange as it was for any of the other doctors in the ER to understand, and not even the boy himself could offer a reason as to why.

In fact, much to Taylor's irritation, the entire staff of the ER was far too afraid to enter the same room as these unresponsive youngsters for fear of the rumors that were being spread about their gifts and how dangerous they were. Apart from everyone else though, Taylor never gave the rumors a thought, partly because he was a thirteen-year-old boy who could take care of himself, and partly because he had dealt with the children first hand, and knew that they were really – basically – harmless.

As the days passed, to Taylor's relief, the rumors subsided and the affectionate name of "The Gifted Six" finally started to permeate the staff, but still no one signed on for the responsibility of caring for them, and it was for this reason that he had little choice but to keep them under his close and watchful eye.

With his odd attraction to them, and his having to tend to their basic needs until they woke, and since he had worked so hard to save them after such a catastrophic arrival, Taylor was more than hopeful that he would be the person to greet them into the world when they did wake. Sure Jay would come and visit once in a while, but for the most part the only one who was consistent in giving attention to these children was Taylor and so it remained... for a short while.

In the first few days of watching over the children Taylor spent a lot of time referring to the computer, hoping to postulate some explanation of why they weren't waking up. For all accounts the computer reported six perfectly healthy children who, within a few days of their surgeries, showed no signs of trauma from the accident. Taylor even went so far as to find a follicle stimulator which he used to help their hair grow back over the areas of their heads where he had shaved them so as to clearly see the incisions he needed to make to remove debris from deep inside their scalp and skull that had been embedded during the accident.

Yes, despite the large amount of damage that these young bodies took, their neural activity was showing as normal... or at least as normal as they could be. Taylor could clearly identify their biology as the bodies of five five-year-old children, and, of course, one four year old. But their neural patterns resembled more the likeness of infants, not young children.

According to archived files, the latent neural patterns of anyone in a coma should reflect the complexity of their mental maturity at the time of trauma. So these children should've had the brain patterns of toddlers, but what made it very confusing for Taylor when he looked at the daily readouts was that the patterns were far less developed – more reflective of babies, newborns actually... practically blank slates – not toddlers. "To put it simply," Taylor was explaining to Jay one morning, "It's as if they were born just a few days ago."

The only difference between standard infant neural patterns, and that of these children, was the fact that, in different combinations, they displayed marked peaks in the five familiar areas of evolved powers. Taylor, at first, was not sure of these findings except for the fact that he knew one or more of them was a cyber and he recalibrated the bio and neural detectors to ensure their proper function. On retesting, the results were the same; two cybers, two kinetics, a precog-postcog, and a postcog.

After this discovery Taylor was certain that their close age, being genetic siblings, and the existence of their powers was no coincidence. He had a strong feeling that these children were the result of some kind of genetic experiment. While Taylor looked for something in their history, some post cog vision he could pull from holding their hand or putting his hand on their heads, nothing, absolutely nothing could be gleaned from contact with the children.

Without any true details to their history Taylor decided to keep his suspicions about their artificiality a secret, and not without good reason. If word got out that these children were genetically altered or manipulated, an inquiry would be stared and most likely they would be kept from participating in any experiments or projects at EduCorp – including Taylor's.

Standing over one of the children, Taylor spoke aloud with no one to hear, "So you're all spruced up, and nowhere to go." This comment was in strict regard to the fact that with these abilities, and all of their vitals being normal, there was no reason why the children shouldn't wake at that very moment.

Much to Taylor's surprise, and despite the staff's fear of the children, several of them approached Taylor asking what he'd like to name "his kids". The first few times this happened Taylor would blush and, feeling embarrassed, he would say calmly, "Oh… I don't know… I haven't really thought about it..." in a voice that told the others he clearly had. Midway through the second week of his caring for them, however, he abandoned this modest answer and simply told them that the names were a secret.

The fact was Taylor already had a full list of names for the children, though he didn't feel bold enough to ask the council for the right to name them yet, especially in their current state. There would be little point to naming children who were not awake to hear the names they were given, but Taylor had decided their names shortly after being handed the alphabetic dossier for what they could be called. "A, C, D, G, J and O".

Taylor continued to try and piece together what he knew about these children, but their most bizarre quality was not their close ages, nor their abilities, nor even the fact that they had not yet woken. No, to Taylor there was one thing which he could not explain about these children that baffled him far beyond all their other qualities. Still unable to explain it, every time he entered the recovery room Taylor somehow felt compelled to regularly dote on the children. This feeling was so extreme at times that even when he entered the recovery room for other patients, he would instantly go to these six children first, despite the absolute need for his attention to be directed elsewhere. It was as though his thoughts on entering the room were being wiped clean and he was being rewired for another purpose – rewired to focus on them.

The best Taylor could figure is that telepathically these children were attempting to bond with him on an almost subconscious level, and while he actually made efforts to monitor this with all kinds of detectors and readers, nothing was ever recorded to support this theory.

Because of this strange sense of bonding, or so Taylor thought, he was getting frustrated at having to deal with these children by a number, and not the names that were all at the tip of his tongue. He hated that, until they woke, he would have to refer to their number rather than a name, and yet he felt that if he could address them more personally, he might be able to pull them out of their slumber vocally, calling them by anything other than their numbers. All these thoughts running through his head made Taylor even more disposed to the idea that these children needed names – real names and that he should soon approach the council on the subject.

Oh how Taylor wished that the children could at least be treated as humans rather than objects and that if they could hear their names it might make a difference in their waking. Still, he wasn't sure if it would all be worth the effort. The name would certainly be something they didn't recognize and because of this their numbers may as well have been just as good as names as there wasn't any emotional attachment to them either.

Only at the start of their third week of care, after Taylor had reported his findings regarding their evolved neural patterns did he seriously consider changing his mind on approaching the council in regards these children and their names, for it was at this time that another project leader started taking an interest in the children. She was an experimenter from a separate division of EduCorp and with her own team flanking her entries and at her disposal, it was clear that she definitely had goals far different from the ones Taylor had envisioned for the children.

These new visitors seemed harmless enough however, as all they initially wanted to do was take notes. But they kept referring to the children as subjects and numbers over and over again. Indeed, Taylor had never heard anyone else do this over the past two weeks because, so far, he was the only one who offered them his constant attention.

Listening to these new faces in the Recovery Room calling the children by numbers over and over again; it was as though they were talking about things rather than people. Taylor observed that they wouldn't even go so far as to recognize gender. This frustrated the teen, making the him itch to approach the council and give the children names, but still, Taylor was able to overlook his new visitors and their coldness for the sake of having the extra company.

These EduCorp scientists were lead by an attractive blonde by the name of Dr. Hathaway, a name Taylor instantly recognized from the application sheet as his competition for the children being placed in one of only two experiments. When she and Taylor first met he was both polite and accommodating, showing her where to find all the data she needed regarding the children's arrival and their current state.

She seemed to return the disposition, but Taylor instantly felt a cold nature in her words that he could only explain as her inborn competitiveness. From their first words, where each introduced themselves, Taylor knew this woman meant business – and she also meant trouble.

Taylor took the time to look up Dr. Hathaway's records to see what he was up against in his competition for these children. From those records, he saw that she was both aggressive in her technique and aggressive in her projects. Some had described her as reckless, but those that did were usually the ones that criticized her work and lost projects to her or her division.

He found that most of her work, which was in the field of helping develop evolved mental powers, was centered on efforts to advance a person's telepathic talents. Her most ground breaking achievements, to Taylor's surprise, were her contributions to the Prodigy project, and her protocols designed to instigate early evolved abilities. These protocols were summarily scrapped when they were determined to be counterproductive from a social standpoint, but still, Taylor was tickled to see that she had worked on the project which bore him such fantastic advanced development.

With all of this focus on mental powers and these six children displaying such promise in these areas, Taylor had very strong suspicions about what kind of project Dr. Hathaway had in store for the children. Her experiments strictly focused on their abilities and, he could only assume, not on getting them up to the educational and social par that they need be. This, to Taylor, was very troubling.

During the first few days of having Dr. Hathaway and these new scientists as extra company in the recovery room, with their watching and monitoring the children, Taylor felt himself very relieved to have the extra activity. It wasn't until the end of the fourth week after the children's arrival that things suddenly and drastically changed.

"Hey Tay!" Jay greeted with an overzealous tone.

"What's up big guy?" Taylor returned politely, and it was quite clear that he did not share the same enthusiasm as his friend for this early hour in the morning.

"Oh, not much, not much. I just heard some news about our new whities here in the recovery room." Taylor looked intrigued at hearing this and his eyebrow immediately perked. "Turns out they may be removing their bid for your prized subjects here." Taylor quickly looked up in surprise at hearing this and he saw Jay motioning a hand towards the six children who were lying completely quiet and unaware that their future was being discussed.

"What!" Taylor said loudly, and it was this that instantly attracted the attention of the other scientists in the room, each still monitoring one of the many data displays above the children.

Immediately Taylor cleared several papers and data pads from the surface of his desk so that he could see the date and time printed at the corner of main display beneath its clear surface.

"It can't be." the panicked teenager hissed in a whisper to himself and, as he held his breath, he quickly tapped a series of buttons on the display until he reached a screen that gave him the information he was looking for.

"Oh crap!" he deflated and as he read the screen his face quickly changed from a look of surprise to one of anger.

"What's the matter?" Jay asked through a voice of bewilderment.

Taylor stood up from his desk, legs pushing his chair far behind him and he looked over at Jay with an angry redness filling his face. "Someone's been meddling behind our backs!" he hissed and he made his way across the room to Dr. Hathaway. She was standing over the youngest of the six, looking at the child's neural patterns on a data-pad in her hands. He saw that she was shaking her head as if disappointed by something.

Taylor kinetically pulled the pad from her hands and threw it across the room, forcing Jay to duck to avoid being hit square in the face by it.

"I'd like to know just who the hell you think you are to pull a stunt like that on my watch." Taylor said loudly during which time he felt a slight headache coming on. His brain started throbbing from what he knew was such a radical change in mood and as he looked around he could see that several eyes were staring at him in surprise at his strong voice and language considering his apparent age.

"I am quite certain that I don't know what you're talking about!" Dr. Hathaway responded in an arrogant tone as she motioned for one of her team members to get the fallen data-pad.

"Oh," Taylor said in a disbelieving tone, "so it wasn't you that apprised the council of the status of *my patients* without my knowledge."

Jay made his way to Taylor's side, and asked quickly, "What's going on? What are you talking about?"

"Stay out of this Jay. If you don't know, just stay out of it!"

Jay quickly closed his mouth and flinched his head. He was completely distracted by Dr. Hathaway's assistant, who seemed unable to catch her data-pad as it was winding its way across the floor. With this, Jay smirked, realizing that Taylor was playing some sort of joke on the man.

But Taylor's headache was increasing with his anger and he gave himself a small injection of meds to try to ease the pain as he listened to the words pouring out of Dr. Hathaway's mouth. "You know as well as I do that after three weeks, if a comatose patient shows no signs of improvement that it is standard protocol to have them moved out of recovery and into hospice care, and moreover that they should be removed from any experimental custody list."

"That's true," Taylor said softly, now grabbing his forehead from the pain, "but the council would have to receive at least one recommendation for this transfer in order to accept it and it is at the discretion of the supervisor of Recovery and ER."

Dr. Hathaway looked at him confused by his response, "I thought you'd be happy that *I* made the recommendation, and that *you* weren't forced to do it later. You and I both know a project leader of special interest can make the same recommendation"

"Listen, these kids could wake up at any minute, there is no reason to believe otherwise."

"You mean there's no reason to believe that they might wake up at all."

"No!" Taylor insisted, "That is not what I mean, and you know it. I'm warning you doctor. You and your team are very close to wearing out your welcome."

Dr. Hathaway grinned through the side of her mouth as she walked over to another of the children's beds. "These subjects are not under your experimental care yet, so there is nothing that you can do to keep us from…"

Taylor was about to spew out a verbal defense on Dr. Hathaway with yet another argument, but both were immediately distracted by Jay.

"Come on Taylor, enough with the data-pad," the man said sympathetically after watching the technician hit his head on a desk in attempting to chase the pad across the floor. "I think you've proved your point."

"Huh," Taylor said in surprise as he noticed the data-pad skimming across the floor, shortly followed by a technician, rubbing his forehead, in a white lab coat.

"That's not…" he started, and as he finished his statement he made direct eye contact with Dr. Hathaway, "meeee…!"

They both immediately started running from one child to the next, looking at their neural patterns with hungry eyes and it was Taylor that noticed the first sign of a change on the display screen above one of the girls.

He clearly saw that the telekinetic peak in this child's neural patterns was spiked high enough to actually manipulate something in the real world. "She's telekinetic alright!" Taylor said with a smirk looking down at the small girl in front of him and he felt immensely relieved to see some active change, especially on today of all days.

Dr. Hathaway rushed by Taylor's side as he initiated a neural recorder to monitor the girl's brain activity.

"You know," Taylor sneered at Dr. Hathaway with a smile, "I *am* so glad it was *you* that recommended their transfer to hospice and not *me!*"

She gave Taylor a snarling look and turned back to the display. After a few seconds of watching the screen, tapping her fingers on her lips with a curious impatience, Taylor eyed her hands as she reached into her lab-coat and pulled out an injector gun. While Taylor was immediately curious over what he was seeing he was not prepared for what happened next. Dr. Hathaway reached out and gripped the girl's arm and used the gun so fast Taylor barely had a moment to register what happened.

With a quick concentrated look Taylor kinetically forced Dr. Hathaway's hand to release the girl and immediately both of the woman's arms went straight into the air at his willing them to.

"What the hell do you think you're doing!" he said almost at a yell.

"Starting phase one of the Titan project on subject 2679A." She said this in a matter of fact way while rubbing her wrists from the pain Taylor had inflicted on her.

Taylor shook his head at the mention of this girl as a number rather than a person and persisted with his anger filled questions. "Titan project… what the hell is that?" With the question he could see that he had attracted the attention of everyone in the room. Most were staring due to the fact that it wasn't every day that you saw a thirteen-year-old go toe to toe with an experienced project leader.

"It's my project, Dr. Taylor. I'll be entering these children into it when they are well enough…"

Taylor cut her off mid sentence. "Oh I don't think so!" he said firmly. "Not on my watch!" and as he said this he and everyone else in the room was distracted, if not terrified by tools and equipment that started rattling around the room. Then, one by one the beds in the recovery room levitated a few inches off the ground.

"Taylor!" Jay said in surprise, to which the teenager turned his head and said loudly, "It's not me…"

Looking at Dr. Hathaway with a fierce stare he decided to kinetically seize her arms again in hopes of getting an answer to his next question, "What did you give her?"

"I can't tell you!" Dr. Hathaway said with almost a squeal as her arms quickly stiffened at her sides. "It's classified" she said coldly, "'need to know' for Titan project members only."

"That's it!" Taylor said loudly so that all the room could hear, "That's it! Everyone that's part of this – this – Titan project – OUT! NOW!"

"Oh, come on Dr. Taylor, don't you think you're overreacting!" Dr. Hathaway said as she squirmed inside Taylor's firm kinetic grip.

"No!" he said while concentrating on the other members of her team, "I don't". And with additional kinetic focus he forced each of the members to slide on the smooth floor in the direction of the exit door, which he additionally opened before pushing them through it.

When he was finished there were only three people left standing in recovery; Jay, Taylor, and Dr. Hathaway.

"Let me be very clear about this doctor." Taylor said both firm and loud, forcing Dr. Hathaway to stand and face him, though he could tell that she'd rather not look him in the eye. "These children are under MY care. They are in MY recovery room, and they are MY responsibility."

He took a deep breath and steadied himself from the anger that was welling through his veins. "I had no problem with you observing these children. You could record all the data you needed for your project and I couldn't give a damn. But you first overstepped your bounds by recommending that these patients be transferred without consulting me first, then you flat out *assaulted* one of my patients in front of me by giving them an unknown drug."

"Assaulted!" Dr. Hathaway screamed, "Now I know you're overreacting!"

"Overreacting…" Taylor said waving his hands around the room, watching the tools still vibrating, and the beds still levitated, "You should've done this in a controlled environment!"

"Well," Dr. Hathaway started in a falsely innocent voice, "How could we know what this new drug would do to a telekinetic mi…"

"Sloppy!" Taylor yelled, "Disgusting sloppy science… You should know better!"

"I will not be lectured to by a – a – a child!" Dr. Hathaway said firmly, hoping that she might instill some degree of fear in Taylor because of his age.

"You will!" Taylor persisted, "Because you need it! You'll be lucky if you have a job after this!"

"You can't be serious," Dr. Hathaway said with almost a laugh, and before Taylor could respond she cut his words short. "You just want me out of the way so you can have these children in your own project!"

If it were possible, Taylor felt himself fill with even more anger than before. "I," he started softly in opposition to his emotions, "would be reluctant to concede custody of these children to your care, I admit. After all, you lack any personal emotion that's needed for this kind of work." With this Dr. Hathaway's face turned sour while Taylor continued, "You're horribly irresponsible, and your ideas and methods are dangerous, and while I have made every effort to help these children get better, what you have done is – well it's... it's..."

"Counterproductive" Jay chimed in at which point Taylor nodded his head.

"To say the least!"

"You don't know what you're talking about!" Dr. Hathaway hissed and Taylor immediately snapped at attention.

He quickly forced her body to the entrance of the recovery room as he continued to address her. "You and your team are no longer welcome in this recovery room as long as these children are here! Is that understood?" he asked in a firm parental voice.

"You can't order me around!" She said as Taylor pushed her through the doorway with his kinesis and she finally stopped moving when she settled into the center of her idle group of technicians.

"You can't tell *me* what to do!" she yelled firmly, "You're just a..."

"Say it!" Taylor snapped, cutting her off. "Say I'm just a child. I've already read the thought rolling around inside your brain. I just want to hear the words with my own ears!"

Dr. Hathaway stopped the phrase as if she had been suddenly turned to stone, her mouth still gaping wide with the word 'child' at the tip of her tongue. She quickly grunted, screamed and wailed her way down the corridor in frustration. She was, to Taylor's euphoric pleasure, leading her team of confused experimenters back to West Tower's main lift and finally they all left the Emergency Medical Level.

With a deep breath, Taylor turned back to his room of children, all of whom were levitating, but were all lying peacefully before him. His mind was spinning over all the different tasks he now had to do: he wanted to know what happened to trigger the child's kinesis, he had to figure out what Dr. Hathaway had given the girl, and make sure that it didn't have any side effects, and lastly he needed to write a long report detailing how an EduCorp staff member broke protocol, assaulted a patient, and initiated an experiment on an unregistered subject.

With focus on three different data displays Taylor cyberly went to work while Jay, who was still standing and beside the teen, had eyes that snapped in all directions. The man was nervous from the rattling equipment on the walls, but Taylor's three way focus was unchanging and he was filled with a purpose and a fervor that he hadn't felt in nearly a month.

30 Fighting for the Little Ones

WITH RELATIVE EASE Taylor found that Dr. Hathaway had only given the little girl, who was still unconscious under his nose, a high level neural stimulant or a derivative of sorts. The drug's purpose was simple; to temporarily increase a subject's pathic, kinetic, cyber or cognitive abilities.

Knowing that this drug did what it was supposed to do, Taylor couldn't help but be curious over the nature of the Titan project and what it might be able to do for the children. But as these thoughts passed through his mind, Taylor reminded himself of the fact that these children, in Dr. Hathaway's care, would be miserable. Even if she could somehow incorporate an accelerated maturation program into their training, she would do little to help these children feel less like numbers and more like the curious, attention starved, human miracles that they really were.

When all was said and done, Taylor scheduled an immediate meeting with the Education Council the following morning and while this was not his first time entering into the council chambers, it was his first time ever having a less than positive reason for being there.

He slept well that night, having had a full day's work behind him, and while the cool quietness of his well seasoned dorm room surrounded him in the familiarity of where he grew up, his mind kept gravitating to thoughts of the children he had dealt with that day. While they still didn't wake, there was activity and change in their status, and his brain was buzzing with this thought, this change and what it could mean. His mind tired itself of these deep thoughts right up to the moment he fell asleep.

While, in falling asleep, Taylor had little worries of what the following morning would hold in the council chambers, when he woke his brain was absolutely panicked with the myriad of thoughts he was muddling through just to get a clear idea of what he was going to say to the nine leaders. It was most typical that Taylor entered the large glass room to report on either the progress he was making with the Prodigy II protocols, or to report his own progress in his higher levels of development and education. But this time, and for the first time, he was walking through the chamber doors at his own request and not theirs. He was to report the wrongdoings of an EduCorp employee and still he hadn't decided if he would recommend for her dismissal from the company.

Dressed in a simple suit that was partly covered by an unbuttoned white lab coat, Taylor inhaled a deep breathing sigh as he exited the lift to enter the chambers once again. Taking echoing steps on the large, empty marble floor, Taylor saw that Dr. Hathaway was already in the room, addressing the council and with each step closer her words grew in volume and ferocity. She was accusing him of negligent behavior in his treatment of the children while they were in recovery.

"... and when they showed signs of waking, he did nothing, absolutely nothing to help stimulate higher neural function. *I* took the first step in administering..."

"An illegal medication." Taylor added quickly, cutting off her sentence. "One not approved by the supervising physician, one which you admitted yourself, was the first drug to be used in your own *Titan* experiment – thus starting it illegally."

The council immediately began muttering between themselves, and Taylor could see the familiar face of Dr. Young staring back at him across the long wooden table. She looked concerned at first, but then relieved to see him enter and immediately defend himself. Turning her stare, Dr. Young immediately changed her focus.

"Is this true, Dr. Hathaway?" she leaned over and asked of the thin attractive blonde and Taylor at once couldn't help but compare the similarities between the two women – not that they looked exactly alike, but that they looked similar – and Taylor had such contrasting emotions for each of them.

"I'm waiting for an answer," Dr. Young said quietly, looking at Dr. Hathaway with eager eyes. Dr. Hathaway was looking around at the council, unsure of what was the best way to work out an avenue of escape from Taylor's quick accusations.

"Haven't you heard a word I've said?" She asked indignantly of the council, attempting to divert from the topic at hand.

Immediately Dr. Herrington, of the neural development chair leaned forward, "Do not answer a question with a question... simply answer the question you are asked. Is what Dr. Taylor has presented to us true?"

"Well," she started softly, "Yes... but you don't understand, he was just standing there, he wasn't doing anything!"

Dr. Young leaned forward with a lopsided smile on hearing this, "and before you decided to administer any medication, did you defer to his authority to do so?"

Dr. Hathaway quickly lowered her head, and she knew that her downhill slide was not going to change anytime soon. "No." she said with a quiet demure tone as if asking the council to forgive her without speaking the words. "I do apologize, but I had to do something!"

"Go on." Dr. Young said with her hands folded beneath her chin, and on hearing this, Taylor's jaw nearly dropped to the floor. *Go on! – You're giving her a chance to explain her actions*?

Dr. Hathaway looked up at the council and slowly a grin worked out of the side of her mouth. She too could not believe that the council was giving her a chance to vindicate herself.

"Well," she started, "Dr. Taylor and I both noticed strange telekinetic activity going on in the recovery room and it was clear that one of the subjects was responsible for its occurrence."

"And how did you know that it wasn't Dr. Taylor?" Dr, Herrington asked, and immediately the other council members nodded to the question.

"Well, he said so," she responded in a matter of fact way, "Dr. Wess asked him to stop throwing a data pad around on the floor and he was surprised by the question because it wasn't his doing."

"And what happened next," Dr. Young inquired.

"Well, we both got very excited – we were sure that it was one of the subjects in the recovery room – possibly dream associated kinetic activity. We started running from one child to the next, checking their neural output to see if they showed any sign of change."

"And?" questioned a council member who even Taylor did not recognize, for he must have only taken the chair in the past month or so.

"And we found that subject 2679A's neural peak in the range of telekinesis was well into the active range. I thought that something should be done to help instigate this to a higher degree, but Dr. Taylor only seemed to want to take a recording. I – I had no choice. I started the first stage of the Titan project on the subject by giving *it* Evadol 22.

"First stage and last!" Taylor murmured so the whole council could hear.

Dr. Hathaway turned her head to Taylor, who was standing at the opposite podium, facing the council, "To put it clearly," she said loudly, as if to drown out any of his future comments. "He wasn't doing anything!"

Dr. Young now changed her focus to Taylor and, for the first time, Taylor thought his head might explode with everything he wanted to say and the multitude of ways to say it. But the teen deflated anticlimactically, instead, deciding it best to take a deep breath, and keep calm.

"Everything that you've heard is almost entirely accurate." Taylor said softly, baiting for the question that he quickly received.

"Almost?" Dr. Herrington responded testily.

"Well," Taylor started, "What you have to understand is that everything she said happened in a period of about 30 seconds. It's not like I had a whole lot of time."

At this the council started leaning towards each other, whispering. Taylor took this as a positive and continued, "That's right, and when you think about it, my inaction at the child's bedside was really only about 10 to 15 seconds. She rushed to make the decision to override my authority based on this extremely short time that she considered 'negligence'"

"That's not true!" Dr. Hathaway yelled across the room and Taylor quickly responded, "Oh really! Then what would you call it? Taking your time? "

"Fine," Dr. Hathaway grunted in anger, "15 seconds, so what!"

The council was not at all pleased with this response and it was clear to both presenters that the table's interpretation of this new information was that Dr.

Hathaway was attempting to mislead them.

"I have no choice," Dr. Young started after conferring telepathically with the other council members, "but to recommend an investigation into your actions Dr. Hathaway."

Dr. Hathaway's mouth hung wide open. As such Dr. Young's motion met with unanimous approval from the rest of the council. The councilwoman, looking at Dr. Hathaway's emotion filled expression, offered a cold retort. "Don't worry doctor, we will keep you informed as to our findings, it should only be a few days… And for our next order of business..." she continued, and it was just at this point that Taylor realized Dr. Ellington was not present to hold charge over the council for this session. He had been head of the council for the past two years, and Taylor had already become quite used to this man running the show. Apparently Dr. Young was acting head of council in his absence and, if Taylor were not late in his arrival, he might've noticed this from the moment he entered the room. He quickly reasoned that his emotions had apparently blocked the truth of his surroundings.

"Ah, we see that Dr. Taylor has placed two requests on the council this morning for immediate attention." Dr. Young read from the display in front of her. "He is requesting a decision in the matter of adoptive experimental custody for subjects 2675A-2680A, and he's also asking that we apply proper naming procedures to these subjects."

Taylor took a deep breath and he was thrilled not only to have both his inquiries addressed immediately, but also that Dr. Young would be head of council for these proceedings. Knowing what he did of the differences between the Prodigy II and Titan projects, he was certain that she would side with him without question.

"To address the first," she started in a soft voice, "We will allow for a brief debate between the only two competing parties for their care. To the presenters; please note that this decision will be made exclusive of the investigation into Dr. Young's actions. Now, as I understand it," she continued, now looking between Dr. Hathaway and Taylor, "you two are the only one's applying for their care."

"That is correct," the two said in unison and Dr. Young looked over her display further, still addressing the two of them, "and I understand that you are both the heads of your projects."

"That is correct," they said in unison again, and at this they gave each other an unpleasant stare.

"Well then," Dr. Young said resting her head on her interwoven hands again, "Debate away…" She paused and watched as both Taylor and Dr. Hathaway stared at each other fiercely, attempting to figure who is to go first.

"Dr. Hathaway," started Dr. Young, offering a small grin to Taylor, though Taylor didn't notice and he felt his face burn with a sense of panic. Dr. Young continued, "…let's keep this simple. The most basic question to ask is this… Why do you feel that these children would be more suited to your program, the ahhhh…" Dr. Young now looked over her data display quickly, "Titan, yes, yes, The Titan Project?"

Dr. Hathaway smiled, and as she composed herself Taylor, for the first time, noticed how beautiful she was in the morning sun of the council chambers. Indeed, if it weren't for the fact that the two of them were arguing against each other, Taylor had the flash of an idea that she would be worth pursuing.

With a rapid lurch in his spine, Taylor found his perspective of Dr. Hathaway instantly changed as she addressed the council.

"It should be obvious that the Titan Project is better suited for these children." She spoke with an arrogant tone that made it easy for Taylor to forget the slight and extremely brief attraction he felt for her.

"The goal of the Titan project is to advance a person's evolved mental abilities as far as they could possibly go. The project itself has been on hold, waiting for suitable subjects. Finally, with the arrival of subjects 2675A-2680A we not only have viable subjects that are displaying a disposition for advanced development – but they're so much younger than our target age group. With their abilities our project won't be on hold anymore and the many man-hours of development won't go to waste"

"Why was the project on hold?" voiced a council member that Taylor did not readily recognize, and as the man stood at his podium the teen quickly researched who the man was.

"Simple." Dr. Hathaway said with a smile. "We have been waiting for the perfect subjects; those who actually display evolved powers beyond standard telepathy. These children fit the bill perfectly. They've got early developed telepathy and each shows the potential of having at least one other power."

The council members all frantically tapped at their data displays to see the information Dr. Hathaway was talking about and as they all recognized how gifted these children were, they chatted amongst themselves feverishly. This low level of verbal noise continued until Dr. Young once again broke the din with her request to continue the debate by listening to the other project leader's argument.

"Dr. Taylor – your rebuttal?" she said coldly, and Taylor saw what he almost thought was a smile on her face.

Could it be, he thought inside his own head, *that she's playing the council like an audience...*

While his head spun with this idea, he thought it best to simply do what he could with what he had to try to save these children from what would clearly be a miserable fate under the *wrong* project or at a minimum – under the wrong project leader.

"While I cannot disagree with my client that these children are the most gifted group that have ever entered the doors of EduCorp, I cannot help but wonder if the Titan project is more about doing something because it *can be done,* and not because it *should be done.*"

With these words the council members instantly began whispering with each other, this time more loudly than before, and again the same council member addressed a question to the debater. Taylor now recognized this council member as Dr. Evans of the linguistics department, and before he spoke, he hushed for the rest of the council to be quiet.

"Dr. Taylor, while I am certain that I along with the rest of the council understand what it is that you are saying, can you please explain further – for the record?"

"Certainly!" Taylor said offering a slightly arrogant tone in an attempt to match Dr. Hathaway.

"As described by Dr. Hathaway, the Titan Project has a strict focus on developing a child's evolved abilities as far as they can go, but not with respect to their maturity. Some of you may have noted in the reports I sent you this morning that these children are not displaying neural signals that are in line with their physical age."

Taylor could now see that several of the council members were murmuring again as he continued. "While I know nothing about what their life was like before their arrival to EduCorp…" on saying this, Taylor saw that several of the council members looked at him with confusion and expectation. With this he quickly added, "Believe me, *I've tried*, but I can't *see* anything before the crash. All I know that every bit of hard data points to the fact that these children have the mental age of newborns."

Murmurs at the council table increased in response to what Taylor had said, but he persisted with his rebuttal.

"They aren't ready to have their abilities tampered with. They're too young, and too immature. It would not only be careless to put these children in the *Titan Project*, but it would be dangerous and heartless..."

"These kids need to be cared for by someone who never forgets that they are children first, and experiments last. They have needs. Needs for development that the Titan Project ignores…"

"You just don't want them to be like you!" Dr. Hathaway said loudly across the chamber and with these words the council's light chatters instantly went silent. All, especially Taylor, were surprised by this outburst, and it was clear by the look on her face that Dr. Hathaway was angered by much of what Taylor was saying. He opened his mouth to respond but could see that Dr. Young stood to interject and decided better of it. Dr. Hathaway, on the other hand, ignored Dr. Young and continued stammering without regard for any of the council's actions or words for several of them were waving at her to stop speaking. She did nothing of the sort.

"Are you so afraid that there could be someone out there more evolved than you? Are you afraid that you're not the *only one* whose *soooo* gifted?" Dr. Hathaway bellowed at Taylor. "Are you afraid that these children could be more powerful than you?"

Two other council members stood in protest to Dr. Hathaway's outbursts and just as she was about to continue one word penetrated the room louder than anything else causing her and the council to take notice.

"Yes!" Taylor's teenaged voice shouted, and with this, Dr. Hathaway grew a large smile while the council all showed a great face of shock.

"If that's what you want to hear doctor, then there it is. Yes, I am afraid they'll be more powerful – that they'll be powerful at all."

Taylor waited, and let the council take a moment to absorb his statement before he continued. "These children need to be developed and matured Dr. Hathaway. They are already behind in their learning, and while I hope that in the next 48 hours they will awaken, with like newborns, fresh, and completely unaware of the delicate world around them, it scares me out of my mind."

Taylor could see that Dr. Hathaway was looking to get a few comments in, but she was offered no opportunity through Taylor's continuing statements.

"Yes, I say that the world is delicate to these children because I have seen what they can do. I have experienced it firsthand. Many of the scientists here at Edu-Corp were there on the rooftop when the cyber-kinesis of at least one of these children caused that transport to crash those weeks ago."

These children need to be matured. They need to be taught. This was the one advantage that I had when my *abilities* came about. I was fully aware, and well matured to the world around me. I understood action and consequence. These children understand nothing and it scares me to think that in the matter of a few short hours they could wake up and be in control of powers that few can understand or manage."

Taylor could now feel a great sense of emotion welling inside him as he continued to address the council, and as he looked over at Dr. Hathaway, he could tell that she was finding herself at a loss for words to compete with what he was saying, so he continued.

"There are two paramount reasons why the *Prodigy II* experiment is best suited for these children. The first is the fact that it is the only project designed specifically for the developmental states of these children. It would focus on accelerating their education and maturity so that they would eventually lead normal lives. The second reason is... well... *me!*"

Taylor heard a huff of disapproval from Dr. Hathaway, but he did not let this bother him as he persisted in his explanation.

"Let's put ourselves a few weeks into the future." Taylor started, and he now turned his podium to face Dr. Hathaway directly. If these children are under the Titan project and they decide to throw a temper tantrum, who will be able to control their cyber-kinetic or telekinetic abilities? You?" He asked now looking rhetorically at Dr. Hathaway."

"These children can take a simple lab room and turn it upside down and inside out... total chaos without the right kind of control." He paused and could see that Dr. Hathaway had something at the tip of her tongue to say to him.

"Ah," Taylor continued, "I am sure that the Titan project has *certain* methods of control. Let's see... Drugs, confinement, and restraints? I'm sure those are fine. But let me see if I get this straight... We're going to help these children develop their abilities, and then when they use them in a fashion not suited to our liking, we restrict and punish them."

Taylor hit his hand firm on his podium and yelled "THEYR'E CHILDREN! They need to live like children. They are gifted, and they shouldn't be punished or drugged because of it."

"And how can these children be controlled if it becomes necessary?" inquired the soft voice of Dr. Young.

Taylor returned his podium to face towards the council, "How?" Taylor asked rhetorically as he looked quickly at the faces of each of the council members, "This thirteen year old body in front of you has all the control you'll need."

Dr. Young looked at him with a grin, "I thought that's what you were going to say!"

What happened next Taylor couldn't possibly explain, but as he saw a flash of it coming, he was prepared nonetheless.

As Dr. Young stood from the council table, having finished her last statement, she raised her hands and quickly revealed two hand tranquilizers which she immediately shot at both Taylor and Dr. Hathaway. Taylor used his kinesis to prevent the darts from making contact with either of them, and after a brief moment of shock from the council, two of them lifting themselves from beneath the massive metal table where they hid to protect themselves, Dr. Young spoke with a high degree of gaiety.

"Sorry about that."

She sat down quietly and Taylor instantly knew what she was doing, even if the rest of the council, and Dr. Hathaway were totally confused and somewhat terrified of her actions. He stood there, with the background thought of holding the tranquilizer darts in their current positions, and walked around the one pointed at his own chest.

"These children will have abilities far greater than anything you could possibly imagine." He started, offering a grin to Dr. Young. "You have to be prepared, and capable of handling just about anything." With this he turned to Dr. Hathaway and focused on the dart in front of her. He made it shoot across the chamber towards himself. With a quick reach into the air he caught the dart and again started to speak. "If you cannot handle something as simple as this," he said waving the dart, "then I believe you quite incapable of handling what could be *thrown* at you by these children.

The council continued chattering, and it was with several nods that Dr. Young again stood to address Taylor and Dr. Hathaway.

Dr. Young spoke at the council table softly, reiterating what Taylor had brought to their attention. "I, for one, am certain that it would be in the best interest of these children that they be entered into the modified Prodigy project, thus named *Prodigy II*, by Dr. Taylor, both for reasons of development, and that it be in the best interest of their safety that they be in the company of someone that can handle their," Dr. Young paused for a moment, "their – gifts. It is for this reason that I put forth a motion to the council as such, but not without a stipulation to Dr. Taylor."

Taylor could see an almost instant look of firmness in Dr. Young's face and with this his heart sank into his stomach and his hands went both cold and numb.

"As I understand it Dr. Taylor, you have discovered that all of these children are siblings, and yet their genetic differences are so erratic that the only explanation for their existence and the presence of their abilities is that they are the product of genetic manipulation and experimentation."

Taylor's stomachache quickly turned to nausea and he opened his mouth to offer an explanation.

"I can explain…"

"There's no need to explain, Dr. Taylor, the information is all in your report and besides, I am only offering a warning. When I initially read your findings in this regard, I had one decision to make, to keep these children from care at EduCorp or to keep them in the care of EduCorp."

Taylor listened to her words with bated breath – she paused and he felt it impossible to wait for her to declare what her decision had been. He almost wanted to order it out of her, but just stood there, nervous and awkward in front of the council.

"I chose the latter," she finally breathed. "I chose it because, like you, I believe that these children, and their abilities, need a close and watchful eye. I'll even go so far as to say that we can extend our five student to one parental mentor limit to be six, just for these children, and just for this case."

Taylor's stomach quickly returned to a sense of normalcy and he continued to listen to Dr. Young as she spoke to him. "My stipulation to you is this. If, at any time, you believe your experiment to be harmful to these children because of their genetic *artificiality,* or that this said artificiality may result in *any* other complications, I demand that you report it immediately and allow the council to conduct a proper investigation to determine the best course of action. If you are to acquire custody of these children, this is the stipulation that I place on you as their caregiver."

Dr. Young's stiffness did not lighten as she finished her rhetoric and, as Taylor thought she was finished, he waited for her to put the custody motion to the council.

She did not, but instead continued by addressing Taylor's female counterpart, "In addition, Dr. Hathaway, I am certain that there will be another opportunity for you to implement your Titan Project on other children, but I am going to keep this project on hold and ask that you submit a complete account of its safety protocols for the council's review. That being said…"

At this point Dr. Hathaway grew an angry shade of red, and with a great venting of anger she stormed out of the council chamber having nothing else to say to anyone in the room.

"Huh," Dr. Young scoffed as she watched Dr. Hathaway turn to face the council while pulling the doors to the council open. "Well, all those in favor of this motion," Dr. Young said loudly.

To Taylor's relief, there was only one dissenting vote to this action, and that was by the hand of Dr. Richardson. As such Taylor was planted to the spot and waited the final task of council to address on his behalf.

"And finally," Dr. Young said with a sense of relief, "As to the naming of these children, while I am a proponent of the idea, I have only one question to ask." As Dr. Young spoke, he could tell that the question she was about to put into words was going to be one that Taylor could answer easily. As such, he almost grinned as she started to speak again.

"Do you think it wise to re-name these children at such an old age? Or, uh – let me put it this way. How do you know that these children don't already have names?"

Taylor looked toward the council and only took a moment to think of his answer, "Well," he started with a sound of confidence. "As the council knows, these children were born off the grid and can't be identified by any means. In addition, I will remind the council that their neural patterns suggest that they all have the minds of infants that are only a few weeks old. If they were to wake tomorrow I don't think they would have neither the memories nor the comprehension to understand the difference between their new names or their old ones."

The council almost unanimously nodded their head at this statement, and with Taylor's confidence building from this, he continued, "I expect that these children will wake soon, and unless I am mistaken, it will be as if they were born on that day, not some date four or five years ago. I just think it right that when they open their eyes, that they be greeted by properly given names." The council nodded, and it was with a strange sense of pride that they stared at this young teenager before them, so matured and unnaturally wise – in their minds it was a curious question if he was ready for the task they were about to hand him – but the answer, they knew, would only be offered as time passed and history would write itself out.

31 Revived

"AND THAT WAS THAT! Today is their thirtieth day at EduCorp and I can finally call these kids by name." Taylor said, beaming at Jay, who was himself positively bouncing with euphoria.

"So what'd ya name 'em?" Jay asked, and in response Taylor pulled out a data-pad from his lab-coat and handed it over with an even brighter glowing smile.

After a few seconds Jay nodded his head as he looked down the list. Then, jumping up, he offered a quick retort. "I've got to see 'em. See if these names fit…" and with that Jay quickly ran out of Taylor's office with the teenager following only inches behind.

Together the two made their way to the recovery room and to their surprise; they could see that the neural patterns of the children were changing. The computer was displaying each child's patterns increasing and decreasing in frequency as if the children were…

"Dreaming!" Taylor said loudly on inspecting the patterns closer. "They're dreaming." He repeated and he ran between them in a rush of excitement and panic.

"Well it shouldn't be long now!" Jay said as he continued to walk from one child to the next, looking at them with the thought in mind to continue comparing their newly given names to their appearances.

"Hmmm," Jay said as he stood beside one of the children, a girl that Taylor knew possessed cyber-kinesis. "I'm not sure about the name Grace. I just look at her and I see trouble…"

Taylor walked around the girl. In looking at her closely, she was squirming and seemed to be having a restless sleep now that her brain had kicked into a higher gear. He continued to move his eyes between the child and the display of her vitals and as he did he offered a wide smile.

"Yeah, so the name might not fit. Trouble – huh?" he said with a laugh, "If that's true let's hope the name'll help keep her *out* of trouble."

Jay peered from under his forward tilted brow, "I hope you're right!" he said with a slight smile, and as Taylor took in the words and the look on his counterparts face, he noticed that man's face quickly changed from one of happiness to one of shock.

With a snapping turn behind him, Taylor could see that each child's vitals had drastically changed. They were peaking at extreme highs and to make matters worse – their bodies were convulsing on their beds

"What the hell's going on?" Jay asked in a panic.

"I – I don't know!" Taylor shouted over the strange vocal noises being made by the children.

"Perc, lock out all your wireless com and input lines and, initiate restraints on recovery beds one thru six." Taylor said this firmly, and the computer quickly responded by pulling restraints tightly over the six young bodies.

Taylor then rushed around the children to get a closer look at their vitals. He could see that their heart-rate and their body temperatures were going through the roof, and that their neural activity was peaking in a way that Taylor had never seen. His head started pounding with fear and the unexpected pain from the many telepathic wails of the children. Their pathic outbursts kept getting louder and louder, almost making it impossible for Taylor to think. The only idea he had was to give them some kind of sedative to force their bodies to calm down, but he was afraid that this would force a setback.

In his moment of indecision, when he looked to Jay for some hopeless sign of what he might do, the room suddenly fell silent. Taylor looked around the recovery room and could see that the children all had stopped their noises, and their movement. On once again looking at their vitals, Taylor noticed that their heart-rates were normal, but that their neural activity had gone flat.

"Go to the emergency room!" Taylor screamed, "Get some help!"

With this command Jay quickly left the room and at the closing of the door behind him Taylor was filled with a sudden sense of being all alone. This feeling, indeed, caught him by surprise, which was apparent by the tears that quickly filled his eyes. He had been alone with these children before, but this was the first time he was in the recovery room with them and he was not filled with the urge to dote on them like in the past. He was with the children, but he did not feel in their company. His senses told him that they were gone and that he was utterly alone.

In fact, as he stood there, between the six beds, in the newly silent and pristinely white recovery room, Taylor had returned to a feeling of loneliness he had experienced nearly ten years before when he first read the details about his mother's death. This was a feeling that Taylor all at once could not bear. The teen sat in a chair next to one of the children; the one that he knew to be the youngest, whom he had just named Johnny, and he could see that the boy's limp body lay before him with no sign of life other than the steady heartbeat offered by the digital and audio readout of the overhead computer. Neurologically, however, the boy was a flatline.

Taking a deep, aching breath, he softly grabbed the boy's head, slipping his fingers beneath the child's thin light brown hair, forming a firm, but still gentle grip around the temples as he concentrated. He was trying to force himself into the boy's brain using his pathic abilities. With furrowed brow Taylor shook his head and opened his eyes.

"Aaaargh!" he whispered in a low grunt as he dropped his head in a sense of despair. He could sense nothing, absolutely nothing going on inside the child's head.

He took his hand off Johnny's head in frustration and he, either out of anger and frustration or complete hopelessness, slumped out of his chair and onto the floor, tears now free flowing down his face.

As Taylor sat there, with only the light sound of the monitors to keep him company, he looked up at Johnny's hand, just at the edge of the recovery bed. He wasn't really focusing on the hand itself, and it was for this reason that he almost missed the fact that the fingers of the hand actually moved. He had to wait a few seconds, watching the hands even closer before he again witnessed their obvious movement; slight, but obvious.

He looked at the monitor, which he could only just barely see past the child's bed and, waiting for some sign of activity, Taylor was convinced that there was something going on with this child. With almost a jump Taylor saw the movement of Johnny's fingers coincide with a strange peak in the neural display above the boy's head.

"Huh!" Taylor breathed with a tear-filled smirk of hope. He then grabbed the boy's hand with one of his own, and wiped the tears from his face with his other. Patiently, he waited for what he was sure to be a repeat of the same occurrence and he hoped to feel the muscles in the child's hand convulse.

Sure enough, after only a few seconds, Taylor felt a slight flinch in the boy's fingers. What he didn't expect was his own almost seizure like feeling that accompanied it, for it was at the moment he felt the tiny fingers jerk inside his own that the teen's entire body went stiff and all of what he was seeing went immediately to a bright white.

With a quick resolve of color Taylor saw that he was looking down at his own hand eclipsing a child's hand. Both were wrapped around a piece of black coloring chalk. He quickly pulled his hand away, forcing the child's hand to slip and a streak of grey to quickly slide itself across the paper where the two limbs had clearly had been drawing.

"What did you do that for father?" a child's voice asked of Taylor as he was taking a few seconds to absorb his surroundings.

At first he pulled is stare from the two hands and looked into a pair of bright blue eyes – almost a reflection of his own and it was as if his heart could explode with an emotion of uncontrolled love. He quickly snatched his eyes away and looked around. He could see that he was in a bright room, which he identified as the EduCorp Atrium, located at the top of West Tower. His eyes moving to the voices his ears could hear, he saw before him five young children all dressed in what seemed to be their *Sunday's finest*.

Oh my god – It's them! It's really them.

"Yes… Yes!" He said to himself as he pointed out in his own brain the features and similarities that he could attach to each child.

"But wha…?" he said aloud as he quickly turned back to the child who was now under his towering stance. Indeed he was much taller than he might have ever imagined himself as a fully grown individual. "What did you call me?"

"Don't be silly, Dad!" the child said with a grin looking up at him, and those eyes – this was the young child he had been watching so closely only just a minute before.

"But... but I'm not! I've already tested… we're not related…" he said with an almost shaking voice.

"Oh come on, don't give up yet," said Johnny firmly and it was at this time that Taylor identified the boy as being probably twelve or thirteen.

"You were doing so well," the child added "it almost looks just like them," he said light heartedly.

Taylor took a step back for a moment and looked at the picture more closely. "Huh!" he whispered, realizing that that he didn't know how to draw or sketch very well and, *of course* – Johnny's hand was over his – the boy was trying to teach *him* how to draw.

Did he just call me Dad? – The teen recanted in his brain as he stared at the group of children all properly posed in front of him. He could hear their giggles and see their smiles. There they were, fine and well, and calling him their father…

"Come on, father, hurry up – we don't have all day."

This was certainly a view of the future – *but how could any of this fit?* He asked himself as he glanced down at Johnny again.

"Come on, father!" insisted a female voice looking out from the five children across the bright sunlit room. "You can't give up on us that easily!"

Taylor looked up to see the girl he had just named Grace. As he took in her older face his hand was jerked down so hard it was as though his arm was about to be ripped off.

Dropping down from the extreme force, he turned to the child just at his side. Nose to nose with Johnny with no choice but to stare at the boy's bright blue eyes, and he listened as the child spoke in a voice that was unnatural and strange.

"She's right. You can't give up on us that easily!"

Taylor, as was very rare in his life, felt fear and worry consume him as everything around dissolved, leaving him to lastly see Johnny's piercing gaze. These shiny emotion filled eyes were the final objects Taylor would see of what he figured was a very strange and almost nonsensical view of the distant future.

The flash of white that washed away his vision quickly blended into an onslaught of color, and Taylor instantly saw in his view the neural activity of Johnny in front of him, and he could see by counting on the screen, that there had only been three pulses of activity in the boy's brain. He quickly determined that the entire vision he'd just experienced took place in a mere fraction of a second, but still Johnny's final words resounded in his head – *You can't give up on us that easily!*

With a quick jump, both physically and telekinetically, Taylor got to his feet again. Standing over the child beside him he instantly noticed how much shorter he was compared to his recent vision. This was of little consequence to him as he purposefully commanded the computer to remove the restraints from Johnny.

His face stiffened to a serious expression as the only thing that ran through his mind was the fact that these children had referred to him as their father. Just the word – the calling – it made his heart ache – and he could still hear each of their individual and perfect voices resounding in his brain.

With a determination rarely present in any thirteen-year-old, Taylor forcefully grabbed the small boy and pulled him close, forcing their heads side by side in a very tight, almost uncomfortable embrace. As Taylor closed his eyes and forced his brain into extreme focus, he could hear equipment rattling all through the recovery room and the last thing he could see was Jay entering the room with a small team of emergency room technicians.

When Taylor did close his eyes, he was met with only blackness and as he concentrated on entering the mind of the child in his arms, he could hear the sounds of the machines around him and of those entering the room slowly fall into silence. He slowly exhaled a breath with the final words of "Don't move!" words that Jay and his company of technicians were only barely able to make out.

Taylor now saw before him a bright flash that narrowed itself to a single bright dot in the distance, like a single shining star, and as he approached it, by what means he wasn't sure, Taylor could hear the voices of several laughing children. He thought that because of the size of this very small shining dot that it must have been quite far off in the distance, but he realized his error in perception when he had to stop himself quite abruptly only inches away from where the sparkling speck was, floating in this dark space.

Being so close to it, Taylor could see that it lit up his entire body, which was wearing the same clothes he had been wearing in the recovery room. The teen then reached out to touch it, and the moment he did, he felt a sharp sting at his index finger – also in that instant he could see that his finger, his hand, his arm – his whole body was quickly contorting and sucking into the shining speck – he could feel a sharp pulling in his arm to match what he was seeing. This strange sensation overtook him so quickly that he didn't have time to pull his hand away before being completely consumed by this glowing little phenomenon.

As his body rushed inward Taylor was once again surrounded by a bright blinding light. *But what's this – there's something different here…*

It was clear by his shifting motion that Taylor was now rushing through some strange bright conduit unlike anything he'd ever seen or could explain. He looked about and at times could catch images that lined the outside of this conduit every now and again. Unsure of what it was that he was seeing, Taylor concentrated hard enough to slow himself down and get a better look at one of these images.

He eyed the curved image that lined the side of this large misty translucent tube and saw the moving bodies of his six patients and very unexpectedly saw himself move in the way of his own view.

"Visions! Visions of the future!" he said aloud, and as he did this he watched the image on which he was focusing slowly fade away into a bright white color. He continued to keep his position in this strange conduit, carefully digesting what he was experiencing. It was only after a few seconds that he noticed the bright white conduit fade into a dull grey color. Then, it started to dissolve completely and Taylor realized that he was now floating amid some dark and strange unending empty space and he watched as the conduit continued to dissolve and pull itself further and further away.

Focusing on the empty space around him and letting his non-existent eyes take in this strange environment, he absorbed an image into his brain that he was sure he'd never forget. Before him, emanating from a bright source in the far distance, there were thousands, no, no hundreds of thousands if not millions of other conduits all around. They branched off each other and interwove, at times reconnecting and separating. Looking around Taylor realized that he was floating amid a fluid flow of infinite glowing strands.

"What in the world…" Taylor started to speak aloud, but he was cut off by a voice he couldn't identify.

"We're losing him…" a male voice said. "He's resisting…" said another, a female.

Taylor quickly realized that his efforts to understand his surroundings were working against some higher plan and he changed his focus so as to quickly catch up with the dissolving conduit that had left him behind a few moments ago. Wanting to help this unknown plan that, it seemed, was his only hope of saving his children, Taylor forced his brain to move quickly through the conduit to the bright unknown source in the distance.

Now moving faster than ever, with hundreds of images whirling past, he moved towards his unknown destination, the bright core of all the conduits, both fearless and hopeful to find a solution there.

Taylor slipped in and out of many twists and turns through this quick journey until, much to his panic, it ended, and he was quickly shot into absolute darkness. He forced his body to turn, and when he did he watched the end of the conduit – the bright misty tube, disappear into nothingness as he shot out of it at high speed.

Only after what seemed several uncomfortable seconds did Taylor feel a sense of gravity – a sense that he was slowly descending onto some strange platform that was being lit by an unknown source. As he approached this platform from above he got the strange feeling that he was being placed there – for he had finally rested his feet in the middle of a strange circle of individuals. He stared at them, six of them, and while his brain was having trouble wrapping itself around the idea, it was after a great deal of concentration that he identified each of them as his six precious patients.

He opened his mouth to say something, but this was quickly averted one of them speaking first. It was the tallest, and thinnest of the six, Orion by the looks of him, who spoke clearly in a voice that was not of the age he appeared.

"We know why you are here. We've been waiting for you!" The adult said calmly using a child's voice.

"But how?"

"Don't worry, father!" said another adult voice, and Taylor quickly whirled himself around to see a young, attractive adult sitting behind him who he was sure hadn't been there before. She was very beautiful and as Taylor looked at her in confusion he noticed that her features were growing less and less mature.

"It's me… Aspen," she said, and in the span of a few seconds this individual took on the form of her younger and more recognizable self. Taylor watched this with a very bewildered expression that slowly – very slowly – turned to a face of understanding.

"Aspen! – Riiiiiiight!" he said as her maturity finally reach that of a toddler. He had an incredulous tone in his voice that caused another to call for his attention.

"Johnny!" called a female voice and when Taylor turned around he quickly recognized the girl he had named Caitlin. "Johnny, you got us here, now what!"

Taylor rapidly turned his head again and as he did he had the quick thought of how dizzy he was getting in trying to keep up with everything. With this new turn though, his eyes met those of the child easiest to identity. It was Johnny. Despite the fact that he looked much older, the boy's eyes were unmistakable.

"Listen," Johnny started in a soft voice, "I know this must all be so confusing… seeing as we're all different ages and everything, but it's really easy to explain."

Johnny paused and Taylor, following the lead of the other six, slowly sat down on the strange platform that Taylor only just now realized didn't have anything on it at all – it was simply a large flat surface. This detail, however, was quickly washed away when the teen looked around at the individuals in front of him. He was amazed at watching them quickly get older and younger at the same time, spanning several years within just a few seconds.

Placing himself in the middle of a circle of aging and youthing individuals that he marveled at watching, Taylor found himself very expectant of answers and explanations

"Well, go on then!" Taylor said with nervous and impatient trepidation.

"Okay, so here it is. We've all just hooked into this machine that allows our – uh"

"Our consciousness" Orion chimed in quickly.

"Right, the machine allows *our consciousness* to exist over great distances of space and time."

"Riiiight!" Taylor said with a disbelieving tone.

"It's no joke!" Johnny retorted quickly, and as Taylor looked into the adult's blue eyes he could see that the individual in front of him was getting younger by several years, thus causing him, Taylor, to have a strange sense of discomfort. As Taylor watched closely the size and maturity of the adult slowly digressed to that of a young teen.

"We can control our appearances based on our feelings and emotions. As you can see, we get older and younger here by mere thought."

"Yeah, no kidding," Taylor said with a stare of amazement. "So who built this – this – machine?"

"You did!" chimed the voice of a barely recognizable Grace, "With the help of me of course!" she said with a widening smile.

"So what's the point of this thing?" Taylor asked, trying to satisfy his curiosity.

"I'll get to that in a second," Johnny said with a very calm adult voice that certainly did not match with his physical appearance.

"You have to know only a few things about this machine. First is the fact that our consciousness is not linear here. Our consciousness is now spread over sixteen years, from *our* beginning to the time we hooked into the machine, so you can do the math to see how far we have come, and what we have seen."

"Not linear?" Taylor asked with a very puzzled voice, though he actually had some idea of what this might mean.

In return his question was answered and his suspicions were confirmed by Orion, who spoke with what seemed to be the wisest of voices. "We exist now at all times in this place – from our beginning, where you are now – to the time when we hooked into the machine – sixteen years later," Orion continued, waving his hands around his head. "But in all this time you are spending here, know that only a fraction of a second is truly passing in your time."

Johnny then chimed in. "But more importantly, this machine does, in fact, allow our consciousness to travel back through time all the way to *our* beginning, and that is why you are here."

"Your beginning?" Taylor asked after hearing this expression for the third time, and he did so with an almost laughing curiosity.

"That's right, our beginning… The here and now – *this is our beginning*." Orion said slowly and softly.

"Now?"

"That's right," sounded the soft voice of Aspen, "We're here so you can take us back to our bodies – to start our lives."

"But you're – you're older, and smart, and aware, and how…"

"Don't worry" chimed in David, "You'll only be bringing back our 'essence' in a manner of speaking. We won't remember anything of the lives we have lived, and ehhh unfortunately, we'll still have all the negatives that go along with that!"

"So – uh, what do I do?" Taylor asked with uncertainty

"Oh, that's easy," replied Grace, "Guys on the left; girls on the right!" She said, and with that they all stood up and started walking, or rather weaving in and out from their current positions to take their places around Taylor in what seemed to be very specific locations. As they did this Taylor watched closely as those around him who were still children actually matured to adulthood in just a few seconds. Try as he might, Taylor still couldn't shake the strange feeling he got from watching this. Just the same, he felt a little better knowing that at least now they were all the same age, an age that Taylor had to equate as being older, but not necessarily wiser, than he was.

When they all stopped moving, each one turned to Taylor and looked down on him. He quickly took this as his cue to also stand and as he did he could see that Johnny, fully aged, broke from the circular formation to stand right in front of him. Taylor's eyes were constantly gravitating to Johnny's with their light blue color keeping his attention in the most irksome of ways.

"Now everybody has to touch you!" Grace said this softly and as she did Taylor could feel that five hands, two on his left and three on his right were taking their grip on his shoulder, being sure to actually touch some part of his skin either on his upper arm, or just inside his collar. Taylor, still however, was staring into the Johnny's light blue eyes, and after a moment the *man* in front of him spoke.

"When I touch you," Johnny started, "we'll all be connected, and you'll wake up. But you won't remember any of this."

"Wait!" Taylor said in almost a panic. "I won't remember any…"

"It's just the way the machine works," Johnny cut in, "and as far as we can tell, we're the only ones that the machine will work on."

"But how will I know to build the machine? How will you know?" Taylor pleaded desperately while his brain cogs spun so many concerns and questions.

Johnny grew a small smile on his face, one that seemed to remind Taylor of his own, "There's nothing we can do about the memory loss… you're just going to have to trust fate. I'm sorry." Johnny spoke in a very sympathetic tone shaking his head and at this time Taylor could feel these adult *children* massaging his shoulders for comfort.

Nothing left to be said, Taylor stood still as Johnny raised his hands. Taylor's eyes were now moving side to side, watching these hands glide to positions on either side of his head, uncertain and almost afraid of what was going to happen next. The teen looked deep into Johnny's eyes and he, Taylor, only in the last second, realized that there was something strange about Johnny's expression and the movement of his hands. Taylor sensed that the man in front of him was hesitant to make contact. There was something wrong. Taylor could almost feel a deep sense of despair, a sadness that was deeply rooted somewhere inside. *Was there something wrong with the future?*

"Wait!" Taylor said just as he felt the hands touch his temples.

Instantly everything pulled away from Taylor with such speed that he could only see a small speck of light rushing away until it had disappeared completely and Taylor was floating in the dark. Then, with a rush of emotion and a physical sense that his surroundings had completely changed, he felt an exhale of his own breath and the resonating words "Don't move" filling his head.

Then, with the quick sound of children's wails and the beeps of machines around him Taylor felt a pounding in his head that he couldn't explain. He was filled with a feeling that he had somehow experienced a great deal in a short time, but all he could remember was closing his eyes and telling Jay to not move.

But wait, *he could hear the children!* They were awake and this sound filled him with such a great sense of joy he lost all control and his just barely opened eyes immediately welled with tears.

As Taylor pulled Johnny, whom he had been holding so tightly to, away from himself, he realized that this child was the only one not crying. He was simply showing a face of grogginess.

Taylor, quickly gaining his senses, rapidly looked around at the children in the room. With a deep sighing breath Taylor saw that the emergency staff was still standing at bay, held in place by an awestruck Jay. They all had expressions that spoke volumes about how they had no understanding of what had just happened and why now the children now seemed perfectly fine.

In his confusion Taylor himself tried to concentrate on what had happened, but his mind couldn't pull anything out of what he'd just experienced. He couldn't remember, nor did he know what he had done to wake the children around him.

Standing carefully, Taylor delicately laid Johnny back on the bed. The teen was filled with such relief, and so wet with tears on his face and overjoyed at the activity in the room that he only just noticed the fact that his lower body was completely covered in urine from the child in his arms having no control over his bladder.

Listening to the cries, feeling and pointing out this dampness, he looked at Jay and spoke the first thing that came to his mind.

"Like I said, '*just like newborns!*'"

32 The Conduit

JAY FELT VERY UNEASY watching Taylor and Dr. Hathaway leave the lab room, and as the doors closed he looked around at the inactive children in his company and realized that the sounds of the machines about him would be his only comfort.

He stood from his seat beside Aspen's bed and slowly paced between each of the students. "They seem fine enough, just their brains aren't working" he thought.

He had made his way back in front of the chair he had been sitting in before and was again standing beside Aspen's bed. He leaned forward to get a closer look and when he did, he could have sworn that out of the corner of his eye he could see movement coming from Johnny's bed.

He walked over to the boy and leaned forward yet again to see if a closer look might reveal something that could help these children. Sure enough, he saw the boy's face twitch and his muscles clench ever so slightly that, had he not been so close, he wouldn't have noticed.

"Of course!" were the words that were screamed across the lab as the doors to it opened and Taylor re-entered, shocking Jay who was so close to Johnny that this frightened him to stiffening straight up before practically falling over.

"Of course!" Taylor repeated as he walked toward the translucent curtain, "Arrrrgh, how could I be so stupid?" He rhetorically asked as Dr. Hathaway followed shortly behind and, by the look on her face, Jay was sure that she might have an answer to the last question.

After pulling back the curtains, Taylor looked over each of the students very closely for some sign of activity, practically ignoring the fact that Jay was trying to pick himself up off the floor.

"Let me save you some time there…" Jay said, holding on to a robotic arm that had not yet returned itself to its dormant position since removing the nanites from the children's brains.

"He's the one you want to watch!' Jay said, pointing his finger at Johnny.

Taylor took a stance above the boy, "I know!" he said, with Dr. Hathaway moving around to the other side. He witnessed the boy twitch his face again, and with a smile, he inquired, "You again, huh? Just like before."

Neither Jay nor Dr. Hathaway was sure what sense to make of Taylor had said, but both were relieved to see that there was improved activity on the part of at least one of the children.

Taylor grabbed the boy, and propped him to sit in an upright position. "Well," Taylor said looking over at Jay, "Here goes nothing!"

He pulled the boy close and closed his eyes while at the same time, fully concentrating on the child in his arms, trying desperately to work his way into the child's mind. For a few seconds nothing happened, then, all at once, as if timed to the twitching of the boy's body, a bright flash appeared in Taylor's dark view.

Taylor gasped with an apparent rush of thought. It was as if a small book of memories had opened in his brain, he suddenly remembered seeing this same glowing speck not just once, but twice before. Once, five years ago, and again just yesterday; when Caitlin needed his help most desperately.

He approached and touched the glowing speck, for the third time, and after passing through what seemed like an endless conduit of strange and seemingly darker visions, he once again sat amidst his six students.

"Back so soon?" Caitlin said with a smile, "Well, my apologies for that."

Taylor looked confused at the girl who was keeping her age the same as she was in the current time, though he could distinctly remember that in this *place* all of the children could change their age and appearance as they saw fit.

"Why are you apologizing?" Taylor asked of Caitlin, and he started feeling a bit more comfortable with this scenario; as if after his third visit he should be dubbed a veteran.

"Oh, silly me…" she said light heartedly, "It was my idea to go to the lab and see how Johnny got his new powers..." She then cast her eyes over to her brother, "remember that."

"Of course I do," Johnny said with a smile, "but it was our fate…" Johnny then paused and spoke again, "if we *didn't* do that then – well…"

Johnny's voice was interrupted by a coughing from behind Taylor. It was Orion, who was shaking his head.

"Right, right," Johnny repeated quickly, stiffening up and offering a serious, albeit out of place, expression on his face.

"Okay." Caitlin ordered. "Places everyone…"

The six stood up around Taylor and as he watched each take a position to grab him once again, he suddenly waived his hands in the air… "Wait, wait, wait…" he said aloud, causing the others to stop their actions.

"I know this must be all commonplace to you but I'm getting confused here… I've got questions – questions that I want answered."

Orion shook his head looking at Taylor with a glare of disapproval. Taylor did not give in to this attempt at visual degradation.

"Don't you give me that look Orion Phillip Quentin Matthews, I said I want answers and I want them NOW!"

The six adults around him quickly digressed in age to that of young children, and Taylor quickly realized that while enough years may have passed for their six faces and bodies to have changed in the future, Taylor would ultimately look eleven years in the future the same as he did right now. Thus it was no surprise that his forcefulness would instantly remind them that he is, and probably always would be, their superior.

Now faced with six youngsters and their puppy-dog eyes, Taylor continued to address them softly. "Okay, alright, I've got three questions," he said calmly. "First: If all of you are hooked into the machine, why aren't I?"

Before Orion, who Taylor was still looking at, could offer an explanation, Grace barked the instant answer. "You are hooked in!"

"Huh…" Taylor replied in confusion. "Well, then where the hell am I?"

At this point Orion took over. "You're right here…" he said pointing directly at Taylor.

There was a long pause and Taylor's face didn't show any sign that he understood what was being said. "Look at it this way," Orion said quickly, "Your future mind, right now, is being overridden by your present mind... every time you come here – the future you gets knocked out – and you – the one I'm talking to right now, takes over."

All of the others around him started nodding their heads. "Yeah that's a good way to say it!" Johnny said to this effect, and even Taylor slowly nodded his head with the realization that his present consciousness was overriding his future consciousness.

"Weird!" Taylor said with a shaking of his head, to which Orion responded, "Very. But this whole thing was your idea to begin with."

"Huh!" Taylor responded, but quickly discarded the half question and quickly moved on to his second inquiry. "Okay so, why is it that Johnny's the only one that seems to pick up on this stream of consciousness?"

The other's around Taylor looked a bit confused, but Johnny understood the question and answered it easily enough for Taylor to understand.

"All of us pick up on the signal – we do. I'm the only one that actually has a physical reaction to its energy."

"It's because he's a *natural* precog" Aspen added sassily.

"Hmmm," Taylor responded, "Well that was an easy one and it explained why I could pull you out the *last time*," Taylor said with understanding as he nodded to Caitlin, who smiled.

"So my last question, why did I build this machine?"

Orion shook his head. "Can't tell you that one."

"What do you mean you can't tell me – I'm going to forget all this crap when I get out of here anyways, so who cares? Just tell me what I want to know and we can be done with it." Taylor was insistent and his face looked as though it had been peppered by irritation while his voice grew louder with each spoken word.

Whereas Taylor was hoping he could force his superiority over his students, as he had done before, to get the answers he was looking for, this time was different.

Orion responded by forcing himself to grow to adulthood. "We can not tell you." The boy bellowed, "This is something that even here you cannot know the truth!" he repeated using a far more powerful and mature voice.

For the first time, seeing Orion, who had always been the most responsible of his children, taking a controlling roll, Taylor felt somewhat inadequate to stand against him, and he watched with a strange sense of surprise as his own body started to grow younger and younger until he, himself had returned to being a young boy.

"But I'll forget…" Taylor pleaded, and he was shocked to hear that his voice was still that of an adult though his body was not.

"Taylor," Orion said, and for the first time hearing his name spoken by one of his students actually caused him a sense of discomfort.

Must be my size. Taylor thought as he stared around from this new, shorter perspective, and he watched Grace nudge Orion in the ribs.

"Sorry. Father…" Orion voiced apologetically and he spoke more softly in his continuing explanation. "Knowing the answer to the first two questions might help you to understand what is going on in here and we have no problem helping things move more smoothly, but knowing the answer to the last question could be counterproductive, and inside this realm, as harsh as it sounds – we are all here for only one purpose – so do as you are told – and know that it is for the greater good."

Taylor's questioning stare only changed slightly as he listened, yet he stared at Orion as though he was expecting more.

Orion simply persisted. "Just know that this is the way it has to be. That you have come here for one purpose and one purpose only – to bring us back – *again!*"

Taylor reluctantly nodded his head as the six around him started approaching him to, again, make contact.

"So let's finish this!" Orion commanded, and with that, Taylor suddenly felt himself grow over three feet in the matter of a few seconds.

Johnny took his place in front of Taylor and, just as before, Taylor got the feeling by the look on Johnny's face that something had to be terribly wrong with the future or the state of things in the future – but he knew, with everything he had just heard, and that he knew he could take none of his learned information back with him, that he would do well to not ask.

Johnny made final contact and once again Taylor felt a rush through both his head and body that quickly brought him back to the reality of the present with a white flash.

Very quickly Taylor could hear the rush of clanging and zapping noises that eventually became the noise of the room around him from his loss of his cyber and kinetic abilities, but this all quickly abated and once the teen's ears registered the silence he tried to remember what it was that had just happened.

Just as before though, he had no memory of what he had done, where he had been, or what, if anything, he had seen. He opened his eyes, abandoning his futile mnemonic efforts, and saw that his students – his kids – were slowly coming around.

"How did you…" Dr. Hathaway started to ask, but she was cut off by Taylor raising his hand for her to be silent and he quickly lowered his head between his knees and massaged his now throbbing temples.

"I'm not even going to ask." Jay said as he slowly walked around each of the children who, with their questioning eyes, started asking a great many questions of Taylor and Jay on a telepathic level. They might have asked the same questions verbally, but decided better of it when seeing someone in the room that they instantly recognized as untrustworthy.

As he got up to leave, Taylor quickly made eye contact with each of the children and pathically offered two simple statements.

"Hold your questions, I'll answer them later." And after a pause of telepathic silence, "I love you – more than you could possibly imagine."

Despite his instruction, there was one final question, from Aspen. She asked why Dr. Hathaway as in the room with them.

"Yet another long and fantastic story which I will gladly tell you later." was his pathic response. He replied in this manner to avoid wasting any more time, though he had an expression on his face, half nervous, half serious, that put all the children on edge, and their faces showed it.

"They aren't very talkative are they?" Dr. Hathaway asked as she left the labroom with Taylor by her side. On hearing this several of the students offered high pitched giggles.

Taylor turned his head and smiled, "Should they be?" he asked with a wink, and instantly Dr. Hathaway knew that the whole lot of them had been communicating telepathically, though she still found it interesting that they were so young and possessed such powers.

Just before the closing of the lab doors, Taylor offered a quick look to Jay as a way of letting him know that he was now leaving the children under his care, and he expected nothing out of the ordinary to happen while he was away.

"Wh – where are you taking me?" Dr. Hathaway asked as Taylor guided her both physically and telekinetically to the main lift of West Tower.

"We are going to the council chambers where you and I will be doing some explaining of what has happened this evening. I'd say enough time has passed." Taylor added gruffly, "the council should be convening right about now."

"But the children are fine – you can't..." Dr. Hathaway squeezed a look of absolute terror on her face at the idea of having to tell the council everything that had happened.

"'Can't – can't what? There are no 'can'ts' This entire building was in total chaos because of something you started, something you did – not for EduCorp, not for the betterment of its children, but for something outside company. You've been working two different sides!" Taylor said firmly as the lift doors closed. "You've got a lot of explaining to do."

On the way up the lift Dr. Hathaway tried to calm her nerves and collect her thoughts, but there was little use. She was panicked, and decided it best to break the silence with a question that had been pressing on her brain for a while.

"How did you – you know – revive them?" she inquired softly.

"I don't really know what I did. I can't remember. It was only that I remembered that I'd done it before. I remembered having the same situation happen years ago. I guess being in the same predicament reminded me of what happened then and I thought there was a chance I could do it again."

Dr. Hathaway shook her head as though Taylor were making no sense. She decided it best to return to silence and when the doors opened to reveal the dark council chambers she felt her stomach fall through her waist, past her knees, and settle somewhere at her heels. She was terrified, and when she looked at Taylor, she thought she had never seen a man that looked more confident.

33 Conspirator Revealed

AS THE TWO ENTERED INTO THE CHAMBERS Taylor quickly looked down at the locator ring, which was now free of any emergency signals, and he squeezed its sides twice in rapid succession. This, he learned, was an easy way for the ring to display the current time.

"5:38AM" the ring blinked in tiny red lettering that hovered just above his hand.

On seeing this, and the dissatisfied looks on the council members' faces, Taylor knew that he had woken them out of what he was surely a good night's sleep.

Only Dr. Ellington and Dr. Young seemed to have looks on their faces that didn't match the other council members, who, in Taylor's opinion, had expressions as though there were some horrible smell in the air. These looks, while not pleasant, quickly changed when it finally struck the council that Dr. Hathaway was not approaching the council table and they realized that she was not going to take her seat as acting chair for her department.

As the council sat in their seats with one swift motion, Taylor noticed the deep violet shades of the sky behind Dr. Ellington who remained standing. "Why, Dr. Hathaway, are you not here, with the council?"

Taylor looked at her with the thought that she might take this opportunity to start some kind of smear campaign against him. Instead, his brain absorbed words falling from her mouth that, for a moment, increased his respect for her.

"Part of the reason for this emergency meeting has a lot to do with me. I..." she paused and took a deep breath. "I would think it a conflict of interest to be subject, witness, and council in the matters of this meeting."

"Very well." Dr. Ellington accepted amid a whirl of murmurs passed around the council table before to Taylor and nodding his head as though he were making a command of "speak."

Taylor tilted his head toward the microphone, which was projecting from his podium at a lower angle than he would like, and just as the teen was about to speak, mouth open wide for the first words, he was interrupted by a rushing figure through the council chambers.

Taylor instantly recognized this figure, with his hooded face unseen, ss the same member of the Evol Crew that was in this very room the morning before. There was no mistaking the attire that was practically the trademark of the Evol Crew. Taylor grinned. While he didn't fully understand the purpose of this individual in the chamber then, he now fully understood that the person was there on his request for a member of the GC, and it was greatly appreciated.

"This is an emergency calling of the council." Dr. Ellington barked, addressing the swift moving figure, who quickly, angrily, and albeit clumsily took his place in the same chair he had sat in before, just to the left of the council table against the large glass window.

"That means," Dr. Ellington continued more heatedly, "that it is closed to everyone except necessary EduCorp staff."

The man ignored Dr. Ellington, whose young looking face was now contorting with extreme anger. He took one step in the direction of the hooded figure, ready to spout a verbal attack when his actions were met with a much unexpected interruption.

"Actually," Taylor chimed in, "I requested the presence of a GC representative. I think it best, considering the nature of this meeting, that he is allowed to stay – if you please."

Dr. Ellington, with his head turned to Taylor, quickly shot an evil stare to the mass of red cloth before returning to his position at the center of the council table. He looked from side to side at the council members and, seeing several consenting nods, Dr. Ellington quickly sat and continued addressing the council. "It is decided then!" He said angrily, still clearly upset at being ignored. He paused for a few uncomfortable seconds to reach a better level of calm and eventually realized that all eyes were on him. "Oh – Right then! Dr. Taylor – You were about to say something…"

Taylor leaned forward, yet again, to speak into the microphone. "I would first like to offer thanks to the council for seeing me on such short notice. I would also like to say that what is about to be revealed to the council is very disturbing and very, very serious." Taylor spoke in a calm but stern voice, and as he continued he turned his head to Dr. Hathaway. "I am going to offer Dr. Hathaway an opportunity to explain herself and her actions to the council, but this comes with a warning that should she alter the truth, or omit certain truths about events that have occurred in the past several days, I will intervene."

Dr. Hathaway dropped her head in acknowledgement of what Taylor said before she spoke and when she did, her voice was cracking with awkward and shaky nerves. Taylor could see, with nearly every word she uttered, that she spent most of her time looking at the person cloaked in red.

"I have a confession to make," Dr. Hathaway opened, "I haven't been completely honest with the council, and unfortunately, I haven't been completely loyal to EduCorp or to its purpose." With these words the response from the council was a good deal of inter-chatter and, in some cases, stern stares between members who were obviously communicating telepathically.

"While I have been working for EduCorp these past few months I have also doubled as an employee of the GC."

While this was astonishing to some of the council, neither Dr. Young, nor Dr. Ellington showed a face of surprise. Taylor, all the while, focused his attention on the reaction of the Evol Crew member.

There was nothing, not even a nod at the mention of her working for the GC.

Dr. Hathaway continued, not offering a chance for the Council to ask any questions in response to this last statement. "As a GC employee, I have upper level responsibilities and clearance. It is because of this that I cannot reveal all of the details of my assignment, not even to you, the council, but I will offer as much information as possible so that you understand what has been going on here these past few days."

The council members started looking between each other with stares of dissatisfaction at this response, but Dr. Hathaway quickly interrupted this with words spoken in an entirely new and almost insolent tone.

"My re-employment here at EduCorp was under the cooperation of the EduCorp Company itself. CEO Isaacs signed me on with a whole list of conditions, not the least of which was the understanding that EduCorp could get specific concessions from the GC and CESPA in trade for its cooperation.

This information was the first that Taylor himself didn't know, and on hearing Isaacs' name the teen was shocked.

Dr. Gerald Isaacs, while an adopted and raised child of EduCorp, found his way into getting a job with EduCorp through the financial side of the company. He had since worked his way through to the top, carefully earning favor with the right people in the right positions, to the point where he now sat in the company's highest position. This isn't to say that the man didn't have talent - it had been said that no one ever knew more about the business and management of EduCorp than Dr. Isaacs. The volumes of data on the subject that he had both read and written have been incorporated into many of the courses taught virtually to EduCorp's experimental students and subsequently to the world.

Dr. Hathaway did not offer much time for the council to absorb this new information before she continued revealing more of the underlying *conspiracy;* a term Taylor was now comfortable in using to describe the events of the past few days.

She recanted how Dr. Richardson was asked, by the company, to make sure Dr. Hathaway was his right hand. He eagerly accepted, and part of her responsibilities was to keep a close eye on the progress Dr. Taylor had made with "subjects 2675, 6, 7, 8, 9, and 80A."

Taylor cringed at these number references, but did not interfere as Dr. Hathaway continued. "But you have to understand, the GC's always been interested in them - always!"

After a brief pause, Dr. Hathaway detailed how she was "activated" through special orders from the GC and how she knew that this meant she would be starting a project not approved by the company, and that while she knew what she had to do

– she also knew that it meant trying to separate the children from Dr. Taylor. This mean that even she would be unable to use them as experimental subjects because eventually they wouldn't be in the care of EduCorp. Instead they would be taken by the GC.

There were instant efforts by the council to inquire, but Dr. Hathaway was adamant that this secret project was one that she couldn't detail because even she did not know all the facts surrounding what its purpose was. She did, however, offer the truth of her seducing Dr. Richardson into consuming some form of mind controlling substance which would force him to act against his will. She said that this explained why he wasn't at the council the morning before, and why he wasn't there now – he's simply sleeping in one of the empty dorms – waiting for a time when he'd be needed.

Taylor, listening to every word Dr. Hathaway spoke, still focused on the man cloaked in red. He was waiting for some sign that the man either approved or disapproved of the information being given, but there was nothing. Other than the occasional turn of his darkly hidden face, Taylor could see no indication of acceptance, denial, anger, concurrence, or discordance – nothing.

There was a long pause when Dr. Hathaway finished her testimony, and Taylor took this as a sign that he should continue. This, as it turned out, wasn't difficult for him, sure there was an angry side of him that wanted to lose control and just bash Dr. Hathaway with every ounce of energy he had left in him that morning. But in front of the council, and for much better reasons than just raw emotion, he decided better of it. Taking a deep breath, he found it best that he proceed with what he knew to be fact.

"Thank you Dr. Hathaway," the teen said in a loud and forceful voice and, with a quick look into her eyes, she knew that he meant for her silence from this point onward. Indeed, she scrunched her face in anger at the idea of him telling her what to do, but she still complied.

"So," Taylor started as he addressed the council, "I think it best to first of all state that I wasn't fully being truthful yesterday when I described that sphere as a neural recorder. In fact, while I knew it *was* a recorder, I wasn't sure what it was truly designed for at all – but I had the full intention of finding out and determining who forced it on Johnny the night before – because it wasn't – either Jay or myself."

"Excuse me, Dr. Taylor" interrupted Dr. Ellington, in a loud voice which now meant for *his* immediate silence. "Let's get to the point, shall we. Why we are all here..."

While Taylor had been so involved in creating his own conspiracy theory and taking in the actual events of the past day, he had forgotten that all of the council had woken themselves in the middle of the night for an emergency meeting that, at this point, seemed to have very deep roots into both the GC and EduCorp, but no real direction.

"Right," Taylor responded quickly. "Well, first let me get to the obvious. In the past few hours it should be noted that this entire building, and who knows how much of the surrounding area, went completely haywire because of the use of that... that sphere I showed you yesterday."

"I don't understan…" Dr. Harrington's voiced, but Taylor interrupted in response.

"Let's put it this way…" Taylor said while firmly gripping his podium, "I've analyzed the sphere, and it has one purpose; to rapidly develop all signs of evolved powers by using nanites. These nanites connect different parts of the brain by modifying unused and dormant pathways in the brain. As far as I can tell the procedure is completely harmless, but it does have side effects."

"Side effects?" Dr. Young inquired, though she was certain that the answer was coming fast enough.

"Indeed." Taylor said with raised eyebrows, "When this sphere is activated and attached to any of my students – who, I might add, are the only ones it's targeted for – it seems that a side effect of what it does is actually boost the children's already developed natural abilities. More than this, those boosted existing powers are completely uncontrolled..."

"That can't be good." breathed a different council member.

"Exactly!" Taylor said pointing his finger at the woman excitedly. "Their inborn powers went haywire. David and Aspen's kinetics forced objects to fly around all over this building – it was like nothing I've ever seen from these children. Orion and Grace were forcing electronic madness all over – the doors and lifts, computers and security systems were all going crazy."

"And what of Caitlin and Johnny?" asked Dr. Ellington.

Taylor, looking directly at the council leader, quickly realized that the man wasn't looking at any kind of data display and again it struck the teen as interesting that the man would know his subjects by name, without having to look them up amidst a list of thousands of children's names – ahhhh, but he should've known better after the previous morning when Dr. Ellington had inquired about Grace. He shook off this mild prideful realization and, with a deep breath, he continued.

"I haven't had a chance to talk with the two of them since they've come around, but I am certain that their post and precog powers were going crazy. More to the point for you, the council, I am certain that this entire building is going to need a complete overhaul with physical and data housekeeping throughout."

"They couldn't have done that much damage!?" Dr. Harrington half asked with disbelief.

With the touch of a few buttons on his podium, Taylor activated the holographic display in the council chambers and was able to access the security system. It only took of a few images flashing through the air for the council, with an overwhelming gasp, to recognize the severity of what had happened during the night.

Taylor quickly glanced down at the console and tapped more buttons to display security logs and data logs from different divisions and departments throughout The Towers. All showed erratic data entries made between the hours of 3:15 and 3:30 that morning, which included gaps and missing entries.

"As you can all see," Taylor voiced with confidence, "there is an absolute need for all EduCorp staff to not only perform a physical clean-up of The Towers, but a data cleaning as well. Now I know the main data core for worldwide virtual distribution was safe from corruption, but the internal network was, obviously compromised."

"Indeed!" Dr. Ellington responded and he turned to the rest of the council. "I guess that should be the first motion of the morning."

The motion was passed unanimously, with the decision that all EduCorp staff was to spend a minimum of 2 hours with either physical or data housekeeping and, feeling satisfied, Dr. Ellington moved on to the next order of business without hesitation.

"I suppose - ," he started, looking at Taylor with a strange, almost accusing look with a single eyebrow raised. "I suppose you would like to recommend some kind of disciplinary action of Dr. Hathaway, possibly even her complete removal from EduCorp all together."

Taylor worked hard to hide a grin after hearing this.

"While the idea does tickle my brain," he started with almost a laugh, "I'm not interested in any discipline on the part of Dr. Hathaway..." These words were hard to say, and Taylor was sure that if it weren't for his forced maturation, he would've spoken a completely different set of phrases. He took a deep breath and would've continued, but he was interrupted by a resounding "What!" that screamed its way across the chamber. He turned a forceful stare in the direction of Dr. Hathaway. She was the source of the outburst and he couldn't help but think that it made little sense for her to object to this statement. Nonetheless he continued.

"Seriously, I am not interested in any disciplinary action. She was acting under orders from a higher source... the GC, and it was under agreement with the highest levels of our own company. I will leave it to the council to decide what kind discipline to take, *if any*."

Taylor paused for the council to absorb this statement for a few seconds before continuing. "What I would like is for the council to intervene in the matter of how the GC has been able to place an employee in our ranks and use that employee for their own gains. It is these actions that I believe require investigation. Additionally, I am worried about my own experiment – my data – my beloved students, they're tainted now – and I think it most responsible to request that the council do whatever is necessary to find out exactly what the GC's interest is with my students."

At these words Dr. Ellington cleared his throat to throw another motion for the council's decision - but this was quickly stopped by Taylor.

Taylor saw that the man in red was now shifting uneasily in his chair, and he, Taylor, decided to continue speaking to see how far he could push this person – this unknown celebrity. Maybe he could push the man far enough to have *unsecured thoughts*. This man was, after all, a member of the GC and might actually be privy to information Taylor was looking for. With this in mind, the teen continued speaking, baiting, and concentrating hard on the thoughts of this mysterious member of the Evol Crew.

"Under the orders of the GC six children, not to mention countless others in the walls of these towers were put in mortal danger. It only makes sense that we should find out the purpose of this unsanctioned experiment. It is clear that we do not know how far this conspiracy goes. We have heard testimony of how it reaches the top of the company, but who knows how many others are plotting, scheming, and manipulating their positions for the benefit of the GC and not for EduCorp, or more importantly – not for the children.

All through his own words, Taylor was continuously staring at the dark gaping faceless hood that wrapped itself around the head of the Evol Crew member, and despite the teen's best efforts, he sensed no stray thoughts emanating from the person. In his focus he had inadvertently paused long enough for Dr. Ellington to begin speaking.

"Well," he said with an almost exacerbated voice, "I guess the council has a tall order in front of them today and as I see it, this is one we cannot ignore. Before I put this to the council, however, I want to ask you, Dr. Hathaway, what additional information you can provide about the motives of the GC for these experiments, and what purpose these experiments serve, if you at all know."

Dr. Hathaway lowered her head and offered a long silence, obviously deep in thought over what to say. She returned her stare back to the council. "I can tell you what I know but…" she started, and quickly her eyes shifted to the red Evol Crew member.

"I ha…" she stopped in mid word and it was during this long pause that Taylor turned to see where she was staring. In that instant, as if it had lasted much longer, he all but lost every ounce of breath in his chest. He could see that the red hood of the Evol Crew member had been pulled back to reveal, in full view, the man's identity.

If Taylor's reaction wasn't sufficient to fill the room with shock, several members of the council, including Dr. Young and Dr. Ellington, helped to overflow the room with awe.

"You!" Taylor shouted as he stared at the Evol Crew member's thin gaunt face. While still youthful in appearance, like nearly all the rest of the world, the man's eyes and older hairstyle reflected years long past – dating him in an instant.

"I have - nothing more to say…" Dr. Hathaway said with her eyes wide and her face quickly lowering to stare back at the podium in front of her.

It was clear that Taylor was the only one to see what a negative impact this dark stare had on Dr. Hathaway, yet he and all the rest of the council, were filled with immediate hatred from the moment it was revealed who was hidden beneath the now pulled-back crimson hood.

Dr. Young and Dr. Ellington both stood and, between the two of them, they filled the air of the Council Chambers with acrid anger. Dr. Young's face twisted so horribly with ferocity that she, indeed, looked as unattractive as Taylor had ever seen. Finally, with some sanity coming to the half comments and sounds emanating from the two senior council members, Taylor was able to make sense of what they were saying.

Dr. Young gripped the table in front of her, leaning over from what seemed the weight of horrible and heavy emotion.

"Dr. Zeldin – H – h - how dare you come back into these chambers again – how dare you come back to The Towers – your history – I, I can't believe it." She said these words with a desperate turn to Dr. Ellington.

This man, who was all too angry for words himself, opened his mouth to spew something harsh, but the words seemingly got caught in his throat. So he'd close his mouth – then opened it again only to stop his words short. He did this repeatedly three or four times while Dr. Young continued to verbalize her own disbelief.

This man, Dr. Zeldin – someone who Taylor had a long and tumultuous history with, waited patiently and calmly like a stone statue weathering the ages. And when enough time had passed, and the last of Dr. Young's harsh comments finished resonating through the chambers, Dr. Zeldin inflated his chest with a deep and arrogant breath.

"Are you all finished?" he asked calmly and indignantly. Taylor spied him angrily, unable to believe that this man – a man that he despised more than any other – ANY OTHER that he had ever met in his life – was actually a member of the Evol Crew; a group that, until this moment, he'd held in such high regard.

Taylor's memories of the man were now flashing – throbbing in his brain. He remembered how the man earned his trust – remembered how he used that trust – then betrayed it – putting Taylor himself and even Jay in mortal danger.

"I know what you all think of me." Dr. Zeldin continued in his irritatingly calm voice. "But that makes little difference here. I'm on orders from the GC. I've always been on orders from the GC – ALWAYS!"

Dr. Young grunted a harsh noise, but Dr. Zeldin persisted.

"Oh aye – it's true – I've always acted under orders from the GC – even back then, I was doing as I was told."

In the pit of his stomach Taylor felt that things were going to suddenly get much worse. His head started pounding and feelings of both anger and despair quickly filled his brain. Was he feeling emotions that were fast on approach? He could sense despair in his throat, but didn't know why. Snapping his attention back to the council, Taylor wanted to keep control of the situation, despite what had just been revealed. To this end he stared at the man now revealed to be Dr. Zeldin and focused hard to keep the man's mouth closed while he, Taylor, spoke to the council.

"Dr. Ellington. I think it best that the council proceed – if you want to continue questioning Dr. Hathaway, or if you just want to start an all out investigation, I don't care – but I think it's pretty clear – we all want answers."

Dr. Ellington nodded his head at this request, his jaw flexing in anger, and with a glance up and down the council table, he was able to receive telepathic messages from everyone present except, of course, from Dr. Harrington, who nodded his head in the affirmative.

It is settled then. Without any delay," he started, in a somewhat somber tone,

"The council has unanimously decided to proceed with a red level investigation concerning the events of the last 48 hours. Named in this investigation are Dr. Hathaway, Dr. Richardson, Dr. Zeldin," Dr. Ellington then almost choked on his next words as he repeated, "Dr. Zeldin, a noted GC representative. Additionally, Dr. Taylor and Dr. Wess, your names will be on the report as experimental leaders, but not named as perpetrators."

At this point Dr. Ellington turned to Dr. Zeldin in expectation of some kind of verbal response, but judging by the harshly flexing muscles in Dr. Zeldin's face, Dr. Ellington knew that Taylor was keeping a firm grip on the man to keep him under control. Smiling – the council leader continued, happy that he wouldn't be interrupted by any protests or further disturbances from this initially unwanted guest.

"It is also the decision of this council," Dr. Ellington added with a direct stare at Taylor, "that the application for adoptive custody of these children is to be pushed through as quickly as possible, in the interest of the children's safety; and that until such time as this investigation and custody is decided, I put forth that Dr. Robert Stanley Taylor be granted immediate temporary custody at his already approved home..."

There were more words to follow, but Taylor's ears started pounding inside his head. His heart and his mind were elated with the words he had just heard, but for some reason his emotions didn't seem to match – *there was something wrong... something wasn't right.*

As much as Taylor wanted to heed his intuition's warnings, his mind washed away all of this in lieu of what Dr. Ellington had said and done – handed the children over to Taylor, so that finally all of his wishes for his students, his kids, could come true. The council had truly just given the green light for everything he'd been hoping for over the last year and even long before. His adoption was just a formal statement away from being final.

"With that being said," Dr. Ellington added at a point when Taylor was now able to fully concentrate on his words. "I think it best that you get some rest Dr. Taylor. We will have some of the EduCorp staff prepare for the children's departure…"

Taylor looked down at the podium, standing firm in front of him, and he held on to the frame tightly just to keep himself still from the excitement. In doing this, though, he seemed to have completely forgotten about Dr. Zeldin. The man, who stood nearly as tall as Taylor, walked smoothly to the front of the council table, as if he was floating instead of walking.

"Before you finalize your decision on this matter," the man started in a chilling voice that gave Taylor a lurch in his stomach, "I would like to ask for a private meeting with the council… to discuss – the *details* that you seek – to help you find the answers you are looking for."

Taylor watched as Dr. Ellington's lip twitched. He could see in the council member's face a degree of anger welling up over the fact that this man, Dr. Zeldin, who so arrogantly and rudely ignored him, was now asking permission to address the council privately.

"And how exactly do you fit into all of this?" the councilman asked with an almost rude air.

The red-cloaked Dr. Zeldin turned his head and offered almost a grin to both Taylor and Dr. Hathaway. "I am one of those who've been watching these children very closely over the past few years. I am the one who has been giving instruction to your lovely doctor here…" he waved in Dr. Hathaway's direction. "But the most appropriate question you should be asking isn't 'who am I', but rather, 'what do I know'." He paused for a moment before pacing from one end of the council table to the other.

"I know why the GC has such a vested interest not only in these children, but more specifically in helping them to develop their... gifts."

"I would tell you now," the man said quickly raising a thin finger into the air." But there is someone here who shouldn't... no, no – who can't hear what I have to say on the matter." With this, Dr. Zeldin's raised finger lowered to point directly at Taylor.

Taylor's stomach began to ache, both with anger and with fear. "What the hell are you babbling about?" the teen questioned without really thinking of the words before he spoke them.

The man instantly curled his finger and shoved it in his cloak, thus folding both his arms so that only his head could be seen protruding from the mass of cloth covering his entire body.

"I will say no more unless he is ordered to leave..."

"You cannot dictate…" Dr. Ellington spoke loudly in anger, but he was immediately cut off by the bellowing voice of Dr. Zeldin across the table.

"I can and I will! You have no way of learning the information that I hold unless you heed to my demands. I need no introduction – I am a GC employee with top level clearance, which means that you can, in no manner, hold me or attempt to extract information from me by any means, without of course committing a crime..." The man paused to offer a quick smile to the council before he again spoke, this time in a soft singsong voice. "All I ask is that one individual be kept out of the know – so that you can be brought in. That's it. Just one little request."

The man held up his finger again, and when he pointed in the direction of Taylor this time, Taylor could tell that there was something different about this man than most other men. He had an arrogance like nothing Taylor had ever seen. It must stem from Dr. Zeldin's being a member of the Evol Crew.

With the clarity of these thoughts Taylor realized something he hadn't thought of before. If all of the Evol Crew had a developed power – that would mean that Dr. Zeldin had a power of some sort, but, as long as he had ever known the man, the teen had never seen any display of this. Moreover, considering what had been happening over the past day, Taylor felt he had a pretty good idea which power Dr. Zeldin possessed. This was confirmed when the finger that Dr. Zeldin pointed at

Taylor raised itself slightly.

With a loud crack Taylor could hear the large retractable doors to the chamber open behind him, and it was at that exact moment that Dr. Zeldin proved himself a cyber-kinetic.

This had the immediate effect of getting the undivided attention of the council, whose eight sets of wide eyes quickly turned to Taylor with expectation. They clearly believed that the teen was controlling the doors.

Taylor inhaled a deep weary breath. It wasn't that he wanted to, in fact there was nothing less that he would want to do at that very moment than to concede to Dr. Zeldin's wishes. But Taylor's mind was teeming with ideas about what he was seeing, and what he had been able to figure out so far about what was going on. If he wanted answers – then maybe he could get them if Dr. Zeldin told his many hidden secrets to the council. There was always one truth – like a law of life – that Taylor understood. *Two people can keep a secret – but only if one of them is dead.* Surely if the council could learn the truth, it would be only a matter of time before Taylor could too.

With this quick thought inside his head, he nodded, turned, and left, not speaking a word, but slowly succumbing to the dark feeling that had been washing over him for the past several minutes. For some reason, he felt that leaving the chambers was the last thing he should do at this moment, and that everything was in jeopardy. But he didn't know why, or how. He needed answers – answers on one evil man could seemingly provide.

With Taylor's head low, and his keeping from making eye contact with anyone else in the room, each step he made came slow and heavy, and before he knew it, he was stepping through the threshold of the chamber and out into cold corridor to the lifts.

34 Denied

AS TAYLOR WALKED OUT of the Council Chambers his mind kept thinking the same thing over and over again. *Better that the council knows than no one knows...* And he played this thought repeatedly through his brain, peppered with the occasional addition - *two people can keep a secret, but only if one of them is dead – I will learn the truth – eventually.*

These ideas offered him confidence, and a bit of relax. Maybe he could get a read from Dr. Harrington – who he hoped, as a non-telepath, hadn't fully perfected the art of blocking Taylor's efforts to read his thoughts.

Just as Taylor turned and sat in one of the waiting chairs outside the room, he received a quick telepathic thought from inside the chambers. It was in the voice of Dr. Young.

"Don't worry Taylor. If you need to know, I'll tell..."

This message was quickly drowned out in mid sentence, "You will do nothing of the kind. You are required to keep all information in these chambers confidential... if you..."

At this point the chamber doors finally finished closing and Taylor was only kept company by the competing messages in his brain. But try as he might to listen to Dr. Young's pathic transmissions, the interference of Dr. Zeldin's pathic thoughts kept ringing in his brain, completely drowning out everything else. As an Evol Crew member, he was, indeed, well trained as a pathic blocker, so Taylor had little choice but to shut down his efforts to listen just to keep from getting a headache. It was for this reason that, only moments after the doors had closed, Taylor could not hear, pathically or otherwise, anything that was going on in the Chambers. So, for the moment, he had little choice but to wait, quiet and alone.

While a timepiece on the wall outside the chambers dictated that only a mere ten minutes had passed since the doors had closed, Taylor felt as though it were an eternity. And just as he got up to start a nervous pace back and forth in front of the chamber's entrance, his standing was met with the lift doors opening behind him.

Brining an instant smile to his face, he saw that the lift was filled with his six beautiful, yet groggy-eyed students, who were chaperoned by an equally tired Jay. But it only took Taylor a moment's thought on this and his smile faded into a quick dark frown. Despite this look, and their exhaustion from the morning's ordeal, the children all perked up at the sight of the impatiently waiting Taylor. In their minds it was as if he had been expecting them.

The teen, expressing a look of concern, offered a quick pathic message inquiring of Jay why the children had been brought to the Council Chambers.

"I was ordered." was the quick and obviously clueless response Jay returned. Taylor looked down, spending every free effort to pat and rub the heads of the children around him while offering comments, compliments and smiles, but his concern for them grew ever more present. His brain was quickly making a connection between what was going on here with the children, and there in the chambers, and the foreboding he had been feeling since Dr. Zeldin's identity had been revealed.

With a fast and sharp cracking sound the chamber doors opened, joining the stares of the eight member pseudo family in the waiting room with nine who were looking out curiously from the chamber itself.

"Oh, good, they're all together," Dr. Zeldin said pompously, but what was most obvious to Taylor the fact that the man's face was, again, hidden under the familiar crimson hood.

Taylor made every effort to ignore these spoken words. Instead, the teen was looking for Dr. Harrington, eager to read the thoughts he'd so desperately hoped for. But Dr. Harrington wasn't there. Taylor scanned the room quickly and saw that, in fact, the man was nowhere to be found. Taylor's eyes fell on Dr. Ellington who stood and waved for the group of them to come in.

At this they walked in with the children 'oohing' and 'ahhing' over the chambers as they were always impressed with its appearance, and when they all had taken various awkward positions between the two podiums in front of the council table Dr. Zeldin started to speak.

"You will notice, Robert..." at this the teen cringed, "that Dr. Harrington has been asked to leave the chambers – he has taken the service exit and is on his way down to the lobby as we speak. So now for the bad news – ahhhh - well, here goes... Dr. Taylor it is my duty to inform you…"

"I don't think so!" Dr. Ellington shouted in a voice so loud it reverberated off the walls and offered a ringing echo in everyone's ears,

"The decision has been made…" he continued, "But this – *this* is my duty!"

"Indeed." retorted the empty cloaked orifice of a hood before stepping aside to allow the council leader to continue.

"There is no easy way to say this, Dr. Taylor..." but your experiment, Prodigy II, has been forced to come to an end."

Taylor and Jay's ears perked to hear each word the council member spoke with total clarity, though Taylor's heart flooded with a sense of deep anguish – *he knew what was coming next.*

"With these children's care now up for adoptive custody, it is my sad duty to inform you, Dr. Taylor, that despite the ruling of the council just a moment ago, your application for custody has been denied."

Taylor's ears pounded with the loud noise of blood pumping hard through his head. So much was this that he could only barely hear the words of denial from the children around him. They all quickly huddled around him, as if offering protection from some unknown force. Johnny was the last, not fully understanding – yet able to comprehend from his siblings actions – that what was going on wasn't good.

"You can't do this!" Jay screamed at the council and he turned to Taylor. The teen's eyes were swelling with tears as he looked down at the children that he had hoped to one day he could call his own.

Dr. Ellington ignored the emotional displays from those in the chamber, and quickly spouted more words above the din. "In a vote of five to four, the council has decided to remand custody of these children to a top level department within the GC.

Taylor's ears perked. *Five to four?*

Quickly the thought occurred to him that a vote like that could only happen if Dr. Hathaway was asked to act as a council member. He turned to her with words coming into his brain that he knew he couldn't say in the company of his students. Instead only one word came out...

"You!" he said in a venomously accusing and gruff voice.

Dr. Hathaway, now sitting at the end of the council table, offered a quick, "it wasn't me!" before a deep booming voice broke in, instantly quieting the mass of crying and angry voices in the chamber.

"Everyone calm down," sounded the voice again, and this time Taylor, Jay, and the children realized that it was coming from the intercom speakers in the chambers.

Taylor didn't recognize this voice, but he, along with the heads of the children around him, started flinching in all directions to spy who or where the voice could be coming from. Who was speaking these words at them from above?

"Please – everyone – quiet!" the voice bellowed again, and after a few seconds the children, the council, and anyone making any kind of sound came to an absolute silence.

With a quick blinking on the side of the council chamber, the holographic image of a black haired man appeared. Taylor quickly recognized Dr. Gerald Isaacs the CEO of EduCorp. The holographic image was now staring down on the council chamber as if he could one by one glare at each of the members in the room with a look of parental control.

"Dr. Robert Taylor," the CEO said slowly and softly through the speakers in the chamber while his large digital face looked down at the teen. With the mentioning of his name Taylor felt his heart grow heavier and heavier with the approach of what he was certain would be the end of his time with his closely watched, and much beloved students.

"It is unfortunate that we meet under such extreme circumstances," the large face spoke, and with every word Taylor heard, he felt a stronger dislike for the image in front of him. It irritated him how this man could speak in a fashion so detached from the situation he was witnessing and that he had caused. Taylor wanted to scream at this man, who, as powerful as he was, had agreed to a conspiracy that had ultimately put Taylor here, with his heart broken and no learned reason as to why. Taylor wanted to scream at him that he wouldn't allow this.

Yes, he wanted to tell this Dr. Isaacs how he felt, and had the thought in mind to use everything in his power to keep these children at his side and as his own. Still, however, he held his tongue and listened silently to the man who spoke from the only office on the top floor of the building's North and tallest tower. Even this fact, though, instilled in Taylor's mind how distant Dr. Isaacs was from the situation, and how the CEO didn't realize exactly how much each of Taylor's pieced together family loved each other.

"I have watched you these past several years with such a great interest," Dr. Isaacs continued, "You first impressed me with your ability to learn so much so very fast; then, again, with your powers, and I was so very amazed with your ability to so maturely, so capably handle these beautiful children."

Taylor thought, for just a moment, that maybe the CEO might change his mind and back out his deal with the GC. Maybe he would allow Taylor to still have custody over the children, to protect them from the plans the Governor's Council had for them. Just maybe..,

As Taylor's mind filled with the hope that someone higher on the bureaucratic food chain would heed to his desires and show him emotional mercy, Dr. Isaacs continued.

"We at EduCorp, and undoubtedly those at the GC should be ever grateful for your services," the man continued as he offered a scowling stare to Dr. Zeldin. "But these children are needed for a greater purpose. One which, it is unfortunate, you do not have the clearance to learn about."

"It is the hope of the GC that I allow these children to be taken from you now, right this very second, and that you might never see them again."

At this point the children all began to whimper and cry at Taylor's side, holding on to whatever part of lab coat, clothing, or limb they could to keep themselves as close as possible to him. Taylor, himself, was holding a stiff face to keep from offering emotion, but his hands were caressing each of his student's heads in turn, in an effort to keep them calm.

"I, in fact, agreed that this could be done if things got out of hand." At this point Dr. Isaacs paused and looked somberly at the children surrounding Taylor. "However, in light of recent events, namely you saving these children only a few hours ago from what seemed to be a neural flat-line, I believe we owe you at least a few more hours alone with them so that you might offer them a proper departure."

Taylor could hear the angry mutterings of Dr. Zeldin as Dr. Isaacs continued, "Transport of the children will commence at 8PM this evening, and I order that they, along with Dr. Taylor get at least a few hours rest before they are granted complete, undisturbed access to the EduCorp arboretum starting at noon. I will meet you all there at seven, where you can say your final goodbyes."

Taylor, heart thumping in his ears and his eyes filled with tears, offered a small "Thank you," before looking down at the children and slowly shrugging them off and directing them towards Jay. While this was happening Johnny, who seemed to be the most upset by the news of having to leave the only father he'd ever known, turned to the hooded Dr. Zeldin, and out of both anger and curiosity, kinetically forced the man's hood backwards.

At this happening the man quickly turned to the children, of which Johnny was the only one looking in his direction. "You!" the child said aloud pointing in the direction of the man.

Taylor, on hearing this outburst, spun on his heel to look at Johnny, who now had his stare transfixed on the tall thin-faced man.

Taylor walked up to Johnny, put his hand on the boy's shoulder, and quickly asked, "Do you recognize him?"

The boy turned and looked with his light blue stare directly into Taylor's. "He's – he's the one that came in my room the other night – he brought that silver ball into my room!" The boy hissed wispishly as if he were out of breath. "I couldn't remember his face until I saw it again... That's him, but it's – it's not him."

Taylor could sense and see a swelling confusion in the boy's face. Johnny was obviously not making the connection that Taylor was. Indeed, with a quick surge of conjoined thoughts the Taylor was able to make some sense of what the boy had remembered of that night, Taylor's vision of that night. He came to the immediate conclusion that this man, Dr. Zeldin, somehow found a way to control Dr. Richardson, and Johnny was probably seeing both of them occupy the same facial palette, Dr. Richardson in the real world, and Dr. Zeldin in some kind of mental override.

Taylor reasoned that Dr. Zeldin controlled Dr. Richards through the light green substance Dr. Hathaway had given the man in the conference room two nights ago.

Indeed, when Taylor couldn't make out the man's face during the vision he experienced while holding the sphere, it was only because Dr. Richardson was under the control of Dr. Zeldin. More than this, Dr. Zeldin had somehow found a way to use his cyber-kinetic powers through Dr. Richardson. That's how Johnny's dorm was able to be opened without security access.

Dr. Zeldin snatched his hood back over his head when he realized that Johnny had somehow recognized him on an unpredicted telepathic level, and the man practically ran to the lifts outside the chambers with a rush of red cloth billowing behind.

Taylor reacted quickly, controlling the lift to not respond to his approach. In an instant Dr. Zeldin took a step back, and Taylor was certain the man was about to try using cyber-kinesis to force the lift to open.

"I wouldn't do that if I were you!" Taylor offered with a wide grin for all to see, especially Dr. Zeldin, who turned around in an instant.

Quickly this red cloaked figure pulled his hood back to once again reveal his face. "And why is that?" he asked smugly, looking around at the chamber entrance and the mahogany corridor that surrounded the two of them rather than at Taylor.

"Well," Taylor started, "Apparently I know something you don't, so let me teach you something I have learned in being around other cyber-kinetics." he said moving his hand in the direction of the children, who were all still very upset at what had just transpired and had exited the chambers to be by Taylor's side.

"I'm certain there's nothing you could teach me!" Dr. Zeldin said arrogantly, and in an instant he flipped up his hood and turned back to the lift door.

Taylor once again offered a strong concentration on the lift, forcing its doors to stay closed, and after a mere second of watching Dr. Zeldin concentrate on them himself, what Taylor had warned would happen actually transpired for several to see.

Taylor had to duck as Dr. Zeldin offered a severe muscular jolt that forced his body to jump some sixty backward.

This caught the attention of the council, and while not all of them sided with Taylor in regards to keeping the children, they all had a great distaste for Dr. Zeldin and were, therefore quite entertained by seeing the man jerked back from the lift so far that he actually collided with the doorframe to the council chamber itself.

Taylor had, years ago, shown the council what happens if more than one cyber-kinetic attempted to control the same device. Then, it was at Orion's peril, and it had landed him in the emergency room for an entire afternoon at the age of 7. As such the council was not entirely surprised to see the cloaked man fly through the air so abruptly. In fact all of them either offered a smile or a laugh at seeing this. Taylor on the other hand felt it a perfect time to gloat.

Now, with his arms folded behind his back, the teen paced toward the mass of cloth, and strewn arms and legs. When he reached Dr. Zeldin's head, which had rolled himself over in confusion along with the rest of the man's body, Taylor leaned over and offered a high pitched, "hmmm" before walking away and forcing a quick telepathic thought into the man's head.

"I'd be willing to bet the GC hasn't ever pitted you, a cyber, against another cyber in all of your romps around the world. 'D'ya ever wonder why?"

Dr. Zeldin was aching, doing his best to get back to his feet, but Taylor managed, with small bits of telekinetic trickery, to keep the man struggling for some time. All the while Taylor continued to pathically lecture the man. "Never try to control a machine that is already in the hands of another cyber… if you do, the results can be… well…" and at this point Taylor replayed the image of the cloaked man flying backward in the chamber, so that he might see it from a different perspective. Taylor then walked back to the lift and waited calmly for what he knew would be harsh words from Dr. Zeldin as he again tried to depart.

"How dare you!" the man spoke loudly. Taylor could only widen the smile that was already on his face.

"I warned you, and you ignored me!" Taylor said with a fading smile that made his face turn serious in a matter of seconds. "Now let me offer you another warning. You will stay away from my students, you will not lay a hand, or a thought in their direction EVER again!" he said stiffly as he cast his eyes in the direction of Johnny who had made his way to the teen's side.

"Hah!" the man said as he stood with gripping fists facing the direction of the lift.

"I've warned you, as I did before… should you not heed my warning, well, you might find yourself a little more than just head over heels when I'm finished with you!"

At this point the now disheveled cloaked man whirled around and quickly threw a punch, a laughable physical punch, in the direction of Taylor's jaw, which was instantly met with a kinetic blocking. Taylor then forced the lift doors to open, then telekinetically threw the man into the lift before offering a final word of parting.

"I am warning you... don't even think about coming near *my children*!"

With this, he forced the doors to close slowly as he offered a little finger wave to the man as he then forced the lift to drop quickly to the bottom floor, and he forced it to stay there as a message that the man was no longer welcome at the EduCorp Towers.

Taylor turned around and leaned against the lift doors. His emotions held back for far too long, he offered a screaming wail of hard emotional pain for the entire chamber to hear, and with his voice came the unexpected cracking of the marble floor beneath his feet. Indeed anger, fear, and hatred as he'd never in his life experienced fully overwhelmed him now. He turned to his students who were all being comforted by Jay. At this point all Taylor could do is let the sadness of having to say goodbye wash over him. His eyes filled with tears as he approached the group, but in the last few steps he wiped his face dry with his lab coat and kneeled in front of the children.

It would be nothing for Taylor to try and steal these children away – to take them as his own, by force, using his powers – all of them – and try to create a life with them. But he knew that this life would be hidden, it would be unsafe what with the Evol Crew in pursuit, and it would not be a life that he wished for his kids. The best he could do is try to appease the GC, to learn of what was going on, and find out as much information as possible. Until he knew more, however, he still had to face his children – he had to answer their heartbreaking questions, and look into their tear ridden faces.

Taylor shuffled them all back into the council chambers, where he felt he had the room and the company with which he should want address his children. He felt it was fitting that they see the fruits of their decision to separate him from his students, and so, with half gazes to his students, and half stares to the council he tried to talk to them.

"I..." Taylor started, but found that he barely had the effort or the breath to speak, and now more than ever he felt the long hours of the last two days mix with his high emotions so as to catch up with him and fill him with tiredness. "I am going to resign this afternoon, first thing." He said loudly for all to hear.

The children all turned with their sad shiny faces and they quickly dried their own tears.

"We won't let them take us…" Caitlin said in an angry tone, and in an instant she added, "I won't go!"

Taylor smiled at this sentiment, but simply responded, "There's nothing you can do my little one."

"Sure there is!" she retorted and with a concentrated look she one by one forced the chairs from the opposite side of the council table to fly upward into the air toward them and crash into the wall above the chamber entrance before they quickly came crashing down...

"That – that wasn't supposed to happen, I was just going to move the chairs over for us to sit in so I could show you... I'm kinetic now." she said with wide eyed surprise and an apologetic voice,

Taylor pulled her close and lightly scrubbed her head, turned to the other children, and one by one he patted them on the head, rubbed their cheek, or gently gripped their shoulder. He worked hard to keep his emotions in check as he spoke to his students, but did so in a loud enough voice for those in the council to hear, though he knew that the decision had been made, and there was little he could do about it.

"I am sure you all have new and even improved powers with the help of that – that thing." Taylor said half irritated and half somber.

A few seconds later Dr. Hathaway ran over from where she had been standing as part of a circle of talking council members and she offered a gasp of surprise, "Who did that? Was that you, David, or you, Aspen?" It was clear that she knew this action wasn't performed by Taylor, and she was intently interested in finding out which of the children had used their kinesis, but more impressive to Taylor was the fact that this woman, as ever he had known her, used their names to address the children. *She actually used their names!*

"It was me!" Caitlin said aloud before Taylor stood in front of her as a wall of protection. He quickly added, "If you're wondering, that sphere did add to their abilities. Now if you don't mind, I would like the last few hours with my children to be ALONE!"

Dr. Hathaway nodded with almost a smile then lowered her head as she turned and walked swiftly back to the council members. Taylor then turned back to his children and asked curiously, "Do you all have more abilities than before?" Taylor asked curiously, and to this Orion offered a response. "Yes – yes we have..." the boy said softly, and he added, "I had my first vision today... I saw us in the future, in the – in the," tears started to fill the boy's eyes as he slowly breathed the last words, "in the arboretum – saying goodbye!"

Taylor slowly scruffed the boy's hair with a smile, and looking down at the children he offered a wide yawn. "I think it's time we take the advice of Dr. Isaacs and get some rest... It's six-thirty now," Taylor said as he turned and noticed a brighter shade to the outside city, and he continued, "Let's all meet in the arboretum at noon so we can get some alone time before Dr. Isaacs shows up."

The children all nodded and, together with Jay, they all entered the lift to return to the dorm level of West Tower.

As Taylor pushed the "Go" button to take them to the desired level, but on doing this his vision was filled with a white flash. In a mere instant he saw himself unconscious on the lift floor, surrounded by his six students and Jay. It seemed as though he were dead. With a great sense of fear Taylor pulled his finger away from the button and just as quick as the image entered his brain, it dissolved into nothingness.

Confused by what he had just seen, the teen quickly looked down as though nothing had happened. His emotions were peaked and he wanted nothing more than to stop time and keep these children as close to him as possible – close, protected, and loved. But the button had been pushed, the eight of them were descending, and Taylor evenly massaged and comforted all of his students with a heavy heart that only weighted down his soul more and more with the lift's rapid descent through each level.

35 Sharing Another Vision

TAYLOR, ON TRYING TO REST in an empty dorm room located one floor below that of his students, found it exceedingly easy to fall asleep amid his high emotions, tears, frustrations, and absolute exhaustion. After having found the few hours rest he needed however, he spent the rest of the time in the late morning tossing and turning with his mind full of ideas and dreams of escaping from The Towers with his students. Maybe it would be worth it. He didn't really know what the GC's plan for his student's was after all, and knowing that Dr. Zeldin was involved, a man with whom Taylor had an aggravated history with that was far worse than Dr. Hathaway – he was overly consumed with worry over their safety.

Still it was quite apparent that stealing the children was not a feasible option for him, and his mind rolled over one thought which, pressing on his brain more and more as he lay in bed, forced him to rise and sit at the room's desk – whose main surface was also a data access panel.

He focused on the screen, forcing it to turn on, and thereafter cyberly navigated to a page on the EduCorp intranet. It was the administrative mail page, whereby Taylor could send messages to several departments within the company by typing in the department name. As such, Taylor sat at the desk for several minutes trying to decide the best way to put the words in his head onto the screen. But there were quite more than just words running through Taylor's mind. He was going through the events that took place in the chamber that morning. He was reliving the whole scene all over again, hearing each spoken word, trying to see in his mind if there was ever the possibility that he could have forced things to go differently.

After he'd exhausted this in his brain, Taylor tossed another idea over in his head for several minutes. Putting his thought to action he wrote a long passion filled resignation letter, speaking of his disappointment in EduCorp, and how he felt that the emotional well being and needs of the employees and students of the company came second to some unspoken agenda. He spewed the words out of his brain so quickly – continuing on about how the company's ethics were compromised because of its participation in some conspiracy whose purpose seemed to put the children, whose responsibility it was the company's first priority to care for, in harm's way. Taylor's thoughts were mixing almost nonsensically, but his brain continued.

Biting his lip, he quickly thought of how the council members themselves were not immune from being manipulated by the GC for the goals of some enigmatic experiment that was seemingly untested, but still recklessly applied to children.

With all of these things going on, Taylor added that he knew that it was time to resign, because in his mind the system he'd grown up with, the system which had in the past had tried to protect himself and the children he cared for had now failed.

Yes Taylor, with all of these words emanating from his brain, decided that it was time to leave the company for good. He felt, after all, that he could not walk the halls of this place without the heart wrenching feeling of knowing that his students – his kids – who he'd spent so much time with over the past five years, and who had known him as their father – had been taken from him by the company in which he had placed such a great amount of trust.

With pages and pages of thoughts of reasons to leave now spanning across the data screen several times over, Taylor blinked and wiped it all clean. With a quick sigh he mentally penned another letter. This was still a letter of resignation, however, it was short, simple and to the point. No one would confuse it, everyone would understand it, and while people might ask why, they would not attempt to change his mind on the matter.

DEPARTMENT TO: **Human Resources/EEC (EduCorp Education Council)**
INDIVIDUAL TO: **Jaylen Edward Wess (Employee Number E9263Q)**
FROM: **Robert Stanley Taylor (Employee Number E1275A)**
DATE: **JULY 18, 2457**
SUBJECT: **RESIGNATION**

Without option for negotiation, this letter is to inform required departments of my resignation, effective immediately, from employment at EduCorp, Inc.

Questions concerning this matter, or any issues / inquiries into the Prodigy II project should be directed to either Dr. Jaylen Wess or the EEC.

Best Regards for the Future

R S Taylor

Dr. Robert Stanley Taylor

After carefully scripting his name at the bottom of the letter, Taylor quickly tapped the send button. He did these last two tasks physically to put a real signature to the letter and allow the data screen to perform a thumbprint read on the send so that there would be no confusion that it was Taylor who actually sent the letter.

Instantly Taylor thought how ironically funny it was that he'd rarely had to worry about these many negative thoughts in his time at EduCorp, and only within the last 48 hours had his concerns and opinions on the company changed so drastically so as to now doubt the motives of the highest levels of its management and supervision.

The teen stood and turned to look at the dorm that wrapped itself around where he was sitting. It was cool, but empty, with the only sound being that of the ventilation. He felt a chill that seemed to emanate from the room itself, which had no personal effects due to its lack of an inhabitant. Instantly Taylor was reminded of his apartment, of the thought of its empty rooms and of how all his hopes of having his kids move in with him were now dashed.

His heart hit bottom when he thought of the idea of returning to this apartment, empty, and without the possibility of it being filled with the children he loved so much. So frustrating was this depressing notion that Taylor felt a need to sit on the bed beside him. This seemed a physical representation of giving his emotions a rest. He inhaled a deep sigh. All at once the teen angrily gripped his bed-sheets on both sides. He was filled with the realized anger and panic that his life was going to be changing in just a few hours.

If only I had more time – he thought to himself, and as the excitement in his brain forced his heart rate to rise and pound in his ears he mumbled to himself. "I can't just let them leave so – so – suddenly."

He thought of the senselessness of it. "It's like cutting the head off an animal. They're bound to retaliate... They won't cooperate" he muttered, and with these words Taylor's fear for his children mounted even higher.

As Taylor sat, concerned for how his students would be treated, and how they would react in their new surroundings, whatever those surroundings would soon be, Taylor glared at the only clock in the room, which was sitting on the night stand beside the bed, and he watched the bright green minutes move slowly by – an image that seemed mildly familiar to him.

11:38 – 11:39...

At the moment this minute ticked over to 11:40, much to Taylor's expectation, the clock's alarm went off. Taylor instinctively reached out to silence it, but when his fingers touched the slightly warm surface of the top button that gleamed in the sunlight his view grew slowly misty white until he could see nothing. Then his view filled with color and as he looked over at the clock beneath his fingertips he was taken aback to see the time it displayed. 10:24, and rather than seeing the green colored digits as he had noted before, now the numbers were illuminated in bright red.

Confused only for a moment by this change, Taylor immediately recognized that he was now in a view of the future. In fact, remembering the clock he saw in the room before his view had faded out, he was certain he recognized the clock as the same one he had seen in his vision two nights prior – brightly lighting up his apartment through the PlexView screen – a clock that he had seen from across the city and across time itself.

He turned away from the current red-numbered clock, only to nearly jump out of his skin. He was sitting next to a child, a boy who, he was certain, could not see him sitting there, but was actually staring straight through him.

This child, obviously a student of EduCorp's, was sitting on the bed, and with eyes snatching away from the window, the child started playing a game on a tiny data-pad in his young, yet rapidly moving hands.

Taylor, for a moment, smiled at seeing this because it reminded him of the many times he'd watched his own students do the same. He looked around the room, which was markedly different from how he'd seen it before. It was now cluttered with a child's messiness, and the walls were covered with pictures and drawings of all sorts.

Being lit by the sunny day outside, Taylor became instantly aware of when the sunlight quickly vanished, darkening the whole of this tiny scene. A rumbling noise accompanied this darkness and both Taylor and this boy were filled with a great interest over what was going on outside the window. To satisfy their curiosity both made their way to look outside and see, with such a fantastic view of the city skyline, what was going on outside The Towers.

It took a moment for Taylor to absorb this breathtaking view, and when he glanced at the child by his side, the boy was showing a face full of awe over what he was seeing. Taylor snapped his eyes back to the window, and instantly a clenching lurched in his stomach.

Outside the window the bottom end of what was clearly a cyclone had shot its way down and past their view, and, having so fresh in his mind the detailed and repeated vision from two nights before, Taylor knew exactly where and when he was. The teen stood in awe as he reconciled the strangeness of seeing this vision from a completely different location. From this perspective Taylor was much closer to the cyclone, and as he accepted the vision for what it was, he readied himself to get a closer, more detailed look at what exactly was happening both in the skies above and on the ground below.

Flashes of light lit up the dorm room in a daunting fashion that caused Taylor to force his eyes into an upward stare. He pressed his face against the glass expecting that his nose and cheek would actually flatten. Instead, his heart leapt into his throat as, at that instant, his head was pushed outside the window so that he was unexpectedly half outside the building and was able to look straight up into the sky. He had all but forgotten that this was a vision and not a true physical reality.

After pulling himself in and out several times to fully appreciate his non-corporeal form, Taylor took a deep breath and pushed his head and most of his body outside The Towers so that he might get a clear and unobstructed view of what was going on overhead.

In Taylor's mind words could do little to explain the awe he experienced from the view he had. The swirling clouds above, while thick, were not completely opaque to what was beyond them, and for this reason Taylor could see that the darkness that overtook the city was not entirely due to the strange weather pattern, but instead that hovering above those clouds he could see the lights and solid surfaces of a massive craft of sorts. Taylor could also identify several protrusions and he continued to stare, not wanting to miss a single detail.

There were more bright flashes and Taylor saw, barely visible through the clouds, that there were several other crafts zipping around the larger one that Taylor had been eyeing. They were, Taylor just realized, attacking the larger craft. The teen watched as these smaller craft buzzed around the large ship, firing at it. Judging by the size of the smaller ships in perspective, though, Taylor knew that the larger must be absolutely massive, miles wide in fact. In staring, though, he still couldn't identify any letters or symbols to tell him what Metroship the larger or the smaller had come from, or who the manufacturer was.

Taylor could not help but continue to stare in awe and attempt to take in the view above him until a bright flash forced him to close his eyes. At this moment Taylor thought that the vision might have finished itself, but with the return of his sight he realized that this was a mistake. On opening them again, he caught what would be his last glimpse of the strange and massive craft as it quickly made its way directly upward with an instant velocity. Then trailing in its wake, the smaller craft followed in pursuit, but Taylor understood, with a descending pulsating light, that the damage had been done.

H watched, with a growing sense of inevitability, as the bright object slowly made its way down the spiraling cyclone until it ejected itself from the bottom of the brownish grey swirling funnel, displacing the moving clouds with a curling twist as it did so. Taylor recognized this bright pinpoint instantly from his memory and, as such, he took extra care to see if he could make out any details regarding what it was, or at least what it looked like.

This effort was useless, for as Taylor stared, he could only see that this bright light was – exactly that – and nothing more, just a bright light that accelerated as it fell toward the ground.

Taylor, half his body still protruding from the side of West Tower; fell backward with the blasting bright flash that emanated from the ground. This light, accompanied shortly after by an increasing rumble, caused a look of terror to wash over the face of the child who had been standing near Taylor through the whole ordeal, unwavering in his curiosity of the goings on outside. They boy had not seen as much as Taylor, and therefore really had no idea what was going on. But with his fear overtaking him, the boy bolted back to his bed where he pulled himself under his covers. Within seconds Taylor felt a shift in his sense of gravity such that he knew he was being pulled downward at an odd angle.

"It's starting," he said in a silent whisper.

Then, much to his shock, his thin body and his perspective had sucked downward from the level he was on to the one below. Here he could see another dorm room, and another child – a girl. She, however, was still braving the thought to look out the window.

Then – swoosh – Taylor plopped downward again to the next level where he could see yet another child... then – swoosh – another – then – another and another.

One by one Taylor kept moving downward until, by his own forced concentration he was able to keep himself or rather, his consciousness in one location. This last shift, placing him in an empty dorm, did not stay still for long. Covering his ears uselessly against an ear-piercing crash, he could hear and feel that the entire building had buckled on itself several floors below, and with a slow rotation he realized that the upper portion of West Tower was now falling into the pull of what Taylor was now ready to call a weapon.

Taylor worried over all of the children he'd just seen and his heart imploded with emotional despair. As if his feelings had burst into the physical world, Taylor felt great bodily pain as his ears deciphered the screams of hundreds of children. These screams were all out of fear for, with a strange sense of vertigo, he watched the room around him slowly rotate to be completely upside-down. Sensing the great many emotions from those in the future, he was sure that his fear was actually the terror of the many children experiencing this full and horrific destruction of the world around them.

With a jolt, Taylor, who was now standing on the ceiling of the dorm he was in, realized that the highest floors of West Tower had made impact with the ground. His terrified heart then listened as children's voices all around him continued to scream horribly, this time out of pain rather than fear. He quickly gripped his head focusing hard to pull himself out of this vision for he knew that within seconds it would reach its horrific end.

The screams around him did their worst to distract Taylor's concentration, keeping him there much longer than he wanted. He was ready to give up and accept the pain of what was to come until, with an ever familiar pull to his shoulder, Taylor felt a child's hand grab him painfully and snatch him from this catastrophic false reality.

36 Children Under Guard

WITH A BRIGHT FLASH Taylor opened his eyes to reveal the dorm room he had never actually left, but with one small difference. He could feel a very sharp, very real pain in his shoulder.

With a quick glance, he looked back at the clock that was now tightly gripped in his hand.

11:45AM

His mind then fully absorbed the reality of the world around him. The Towers were fine. He was fine, and his children, he was sure, were fine.

The same vision – again! He thought to himself and yet he still wasn't sure what this vision was trying to show him. He wasn't sure of a lot of things. He wasn't sure what was going to happen to his children now that they were about to leave The Towers or how they worked at all into what he had seen. One thing he was certain of was that he knew who the hand belonged to that had pulled him ever so painfully out of the vision he'd just experienced.

Taylor quickly stood up, and bolted to the door, then down the corridor to the lift. Both of course opened at his willing them to, and he made his way to the level just above.

As the doors opened, Taylor was greeted by several EduCorp Security Personnel who instantly blocked his path. These Security Personnel, or ESP as they had been called – a name that was a point of great amusement to Taylor – were each wielding high voltage shock sticks that Taylor knew they were only marginally trained in manipulating.

"What the -!" Taylor said with a huff, not expecting, yet instantly rationalizing their presence in the corridor. He was certainly not told that he would be kept from seeing his students, and so it was odd that, on their seeing him, they all seemed ready to pounce. Taylor's ears perked with the muffled voices the ESPs talking as though he wasn't able to hear them.

"It's him!"

"It's him?"

"It's him!!"

"How can you tell?"

"The eyes!"

"Oh wow! It's him!"

"It's who?" Taylor asked with false ignorance, almost amused at how he had become the enigmatic center of their attention.

Instantly one of the ESP's spoke up, "We're sorry, but – but you – you are no longer authorized to ac – access this level," the voice spoke very nervously, from behind his protective face mask.

Indeed Taylor was hoping not to have to use force to reach Johnny's dorm, but he needed to make sure that the child was okay, and seeing what he had moments ago, he felt he didn't have time to talk his way to the room.

Still, Taylor smiled at the ESPs, looking several of them in the eye, and he slowly turned around to face the lift doors from where he had come and as he did this he spoke only two words. "I understand!" Taylor then cast his eyes downward at the tile floor beneath his feet.

It was obvious that the ESP's were expecting Taylor to enter the lift when he had cyberly forced the doors to open. What they weren't expecting, however, was what Taylor took advantage of.

He raised his head, snapping a wide smirk of a smile, and with a meager kinetic effort, he forced all of the ESP's to rapidly and smoothly skate straight down the corridor behind him with one simple but firm push. They met their end crashing hard against the wall at the far end and Taylor was certain that at that moment the entire mass of them had been sufficiently zapped and re-zapped by their own shock sticks so as to render each of them quite unconscious.

Taylor, still grinning, turned around and took a moment to observe his mindy-work (not to be confused with handy-work). Seeing that he had cleared himself an easy unobstructed path down the dorm hall, he swiftly made his way to Johnny's room, all the while his face morphing from that of being almost playful, to being very serious.

With a quick scan of the security protocols at the door, Taylor realized that all of the changes he'd made the morning before had been reversed and he saw to his mild surprise that he also no longer had proper access anywhere in the building due to his resignation.

Indeed, Taylor knew that the EduCorp human resources department was exceedingly efficient. So much was this that he recalled one employee who resigned – on good terms no less, and still had to be escorted out of The Towers due to the fact that his clearance wouldn't allow him proper passage through certain corridors. The man's clearance had been modified before he could even leave.

With this in mind Taylor avoided offering a scan at the dorm door and simply forced it open cyberly. On entering he expected to find Johnny in the same state as he had two nights ago – unconscious, drugged, and trapped in the same horrible vision, but this wasn't what he walked in on at all. The boy was sitting up; looking frantically over a data-pad which he put away the instant Taylor entered the room.

"'S everything alright?" Taylor asked curiously, looking around the room as if determined to find something out of the ordinary.

"Fine!" the boy said, with a somewhat beguiling smile and a hint of guilt on his face.

Taylor was horribly confused by the overall wellbeing of the boy. The child was practically happy, which didn't make sense considering he would be saying goodbye to both Taylor and the only home he'd ever known in just a few hours.

"What's going on?" Taylor asked curiously as he looked with raised eyebrows over Johnny's shoulder at the data-pad which was now covered by the bed's blankets.

"Nothing... nothing, just chattin' with 'Rion."

"Uh huhhhh..." Taylor responded with what was an unmistakable tone of disbelief. Taylor quickly forced the data-pad high into the air where he caught it in his hands. Johnny looked upward to track the object and as he watched, with a growing look of concern, that his father figure caught it. Taylor could not help but notice this immediately.

"What do we have here?" Taylor asked as if he were about to discover something incriminating.

"You were chatting with Orion...?" Taylor repeated, mocking Johnny's earlier answer. "I see – what you were really doing was..." Taylor quickly scanned over the page, "chatting. – Chatting – with – Orion."

Johnny's face showed a marked look of relief as he exclaimed, "See! I told you!"

"But what... What...? I just had a... huh?" Taylor spoke random words in absolute confusion. This state of mind, however, did not spread to Johnny, who calmly retorted.

"Oh, you're here because of the vision!" he said excitedly.

"Well yeah!" Taylor said almost accusingly at the boy.

"Yeah," Johnny responded blandly, "You were sucked into that one pretty deep. I almost thought I couldn't get you out of it."

"But how did you...?"

"I think that metal ball had something to do with it. It must have er – enhanced what I could already do, *and* gave me all the *'extras'*" Johnny said almost giggling as he stared with a smile at his data pad, tapping it in a few places, then putting it down.

Taylor could see that the pad was blank but still lit up. The teen barely paid this any attention because he was far more relieved that Johnny was far better off than he had expected.

"What's with the clock?" Johnny asked curiously.

Taylor snapped his eyes down at his own hands and saw that one of them was still holding the clock in the room he'd been in before. He'd somehow forgotten to let it go, his grip being so tight from the vision, and the pain in his shoulder being so great.

"Oh, uhmmm, this is for you..." he said awkwardly as he set it on the counter.

"Well, we've got our rings now, remember?" I don't need a clock." The boy said with a smile.

"Right! Right!" Taylor said quickly as his eyes scanned the room awkwardly. Johnny quickly frowned at where Taylor had set the clock and immediately picked it up and put it over on the window shelf, looking inward to the room.

"That's better!" the boy said, and as he stepped away Taylor realized he only had a few minutes before noon, and the others should soon be ready to go to the arboretum.

"Come on, let's go or we'll be late!" Taylor said half excitedly as he forced the dorm door to reopen.

With this, Johnny quickly pulled off the simple white, long sleeve shirt he was wearing and threw it across the room as he made his way to the dorm's exit. On seeing this action Taylor got an eerie ominous feeling in the pit of his stomach as he watched the shirt slowly slip off the clock in the window. The clock, which was clearly facing the inside of the dorm before, was now turned around. The thrown shirt had caused the clock to spin around and now face the outside of the building. Taylor had a feeling he knew exactly what the window and the clock would look like from the outside.

Johnny stopped at the doorway to his dorm, offered a grin to Taylor, and snapped his tiny fingers. At that instant the data pad on the boy's bed turned itself off. Taylor raised one eyebrow in surprise over this slight display of Johnny's new cyber-kinetic ability.

"Seem to be getting better at that every time," the boy said as he shirtlessly bounded down the hall to an M-Gen panel where, with the push of a few buttons he activated the machine. Waiting for it to complete its task, he turned and leaned against the corridor wall.

With a few groans catching his attention, Johnny looked to the far end of the corridor and noticed the ESPs were all still struggling, and barely aware.

"What happened to them?" the boy asked with a sarcastic note of concern.

"*I* happened to them!" Taylor responded with a wink.

"Oh," Johnny said, looking at the status of the M-Gen panel. It was still working hard with lights blinking for the task it had been given. Johnny looked up quickly and with a smile to Taylor he lightly tapped the front of the panel. "I'll figure these out soon enough." he said confidently.

Taylor initially widened his smile, but that soon faded to almost a frown as he thought of how each of his student must all be going through very different changes with their powers, and how, over the next few days, he wouldn't be there to experience and help them with all their new talents.

The teen lowered his head as Johnny opened the panel to reveal new shirt and it was only after putting it on that the boy noticed the change in Taylor's attitude.

"Father," the boy said stepping under Taylor's nose, forcing the both of them to stare eye to eye. Taylor put his large hand over the boy's face, practically covering it completely, and moved the child from his view.

"Don't," Taylor said soberly, "Don't call me that. Please don't call me that."

Johnny knew immediately what was going through Taylor's mind and quickly offered support by offering a simple telepathic message.

"Don't worry, *father,* everything is going to be fine... I'm sure of it."

Taylor quickly raised his head, turned to look at Johnny, and lit a temporary grin. Taylor should at least be happy for the moment and bask the boy's naivety for whatever time they had left together.

"Sure! You're right, I guess." he said and in response Johnny quickly asked "Hey, can I get a ride on your shoulders just one last time?"

Taylor rubbed the shoulder that pained him and shook his head, "Sorry Little Johnny, when you pulled me out of that vision you really gave my shoulder a sharp jolt. I don't think so. Not this time."

Johnny lowered his head in almost a pouting fashion, and looked up at Taylor with his own set of light blue eyes and a begging expression of "please!" that was accompanied by a lower lip that jutted out just enough to melt Taylor's heart.

A moment of awkwardness stood between the two of them, and just as Johnny had turned his head, giving up the shoulder ride, Taylor quickly voiced the words "What the hell!" and one handedly picked the child up and put him around his neck and shoulders.

"Woaaahh" Johnny said with surprise and the boy could tell that Taylor struggled a little with the pain in his shoulder.

"Geeze," Taylor said with a grunt, "what have you been eating? Lead bricks!"

Johnny offered a quick laugh and reached around Taylor's chin. "Perfect," the boy whispered, and when Taylor heard this his head almost flinched.

"What?" Taylor asked, but Johnny quickly responded.

"Oh, eh, the way you got me on your shoulders – and this," he said gripping Taylor's head, it's perfect!

"Right!" Taylor said softly and once the boy had a full and steady grip, Taylor squeezed the sides of the ring on his finger rapidly to reveal the holographic display of the time. "Hmmm..." Taylor sounded with a curious tone.

"Where is everybody...? They're all late!"

"I'm sure they'll be out in a minute... relax!" the boy said from overhead.

Sure enough, in less than a minute each of the children came out of their dorms. They were empty handed at first, but within minutes they each had generated heavy bags loaded with what Taylor was sure were necessities for their departure.

"Where's your stuff little J.?" Caitlin asked with a smile, and at that the boy turned quickly to his dorm – "Oh I forgot, I've got my stuff all ready in my room!"

"Don't worry, I got it!" Orion said, shaking his head and with no scan or push of buttons, the boy entered Johnny's dorm and exited a few seconds later with a backpack that he tossed up to his brother.

Johnny almost fell over to catch it, but caught it just the same, and while he steadied himself Taylor grabbed the boy's ankles for improved balance.

"Well," Taylor said with as light-hearted a voice as he could muster, "Is everyone ready?"

"I think so." Johnny said, and he jerked his heels, making Taylor feel like a horse, and thereby forcing the teen to inch toward the main lift. Turning, and bobbing, Johnny turned to his brothers and sisters adding, "How 'bout it? Dave, Asp, are you ready?"

The kinetic brother and sister pair, standing shoulder to shoulder, nodded their heads with mischievously wide smiles. Taylor was oblivious to this and just as the lift doors opened the teen felt a piercing pain rush through his head and body before completely blacking out.

37 Back Up – The Plan

JOHNNY READ THE MESSAGES as they quickly popped up on the screen. It always irritated him how Grace and Orion were able to instantaneously force messages on the chat screens while everyone else had to slowly type out theirs. It wasn't too bad though, he and his other siblings were quite affluent typists. But even then, Aspen was the best at over a hundred words a minute.

ORIONPQM: NO, NO, NO. EVERYONE SHOULD STICK TO THEIR ORIGINAL POWERS. T'S THE BEST WAY WE CAN MAKE SURE THERE ARE NO MISTAKES - BUT COME ON, WE HAVE TO GET MOVING HERE. WE'VE GOT ABOUT FIFTEEN MINUTES BEFORE WE'RE SUPPOSED TO BE READY GUYS SO COME ON - LETS FOCUS HERE!!!

GRACEHIM: RION'S RIGHT - WE NEED TO MAKE A LIST OF WHAT WE NEED FIRST!

JONNYKLM: WELL WE BETTER HURRY UP. I JUST GOT HIM OUT OF ONE OF THOSE AWFUL VISIONS AGAIN - HE'LL BE HERE SOON I'M SURE!

CAITYDEM: ARGH! FINE - SO LET'S GET GOING!

GRACEHIM: RIGHT SO FIRST THERE'S THE ESCAPE.

ASPENBCM: WHAT ABOUT THE ESP'S

JONNYKLM: FATHER'LL TAKE CARE OF THEM.

DAVIDEFM: HOW DO YOU KNOW?

JONNYKLM: I'VE SEEN IT, HE'S COMIN' TO CHECK ON ME. BUT THEY WON'T LET HIM GET A FOOT OUT OF THE LIFT.

ORIONPQM: PERFECT! THEY'LL TRY TO STOP HIM, AND HE WON'T STAND FOR THAT!

JONNYKLM: EXACTLY!

ASPENBCM: SO HOW DO WE TAKE CARE OF FATHER?

JONNYKLM: GOT IT COVERED! I SNEAKED A SHOCK STICK FROM ONE OF THE ESP'S WHEN I WENT FOR A SNACK - REPLACED IT WITH ONE OF THE TOY VERSIONS I GOT FOR CHRISTMAS LAST YEAR.

GRACEHIM: GOOD! SEE IF YOU CAN GET HIM TO PUT YOU ON HIS SHOULDERS WHEN HE SEES YOU - HE ALWAYS LIKES TO DO THAT!

JONNYKLM: THEN WHEN THE TIME'S RIGHT - ZAP!

GRACEHIM: EXACTLY!

CAITYDEM: OK - SO THEN WHAT - WE NEED A PATH OF ESCAPE.

ORIONPQM: RIGHT - I'LL DOWNLOAD BUILDING SCHEMATICS AND CHANGE THE SECURITY CODES TO ALLOW US ACCESS WHERE WE NEED IT.
DAVIDEFM: WAIT A SECOND! WHERE ARE WE GONNA GO ONCE WE FIND A WAY OUT?
JONNYKLM: THAT'S IT! THAT'S IT! THAT'S IT!
CAITYDEM: WHAT!
JONNYKLM: MY VISION, THE ONE I HAD IN THE TRANSPORT. MUST'VE BEEN CAUSE OF OUR ESCAPE - SO THAT MEAN#$%&(^
ORIONPQM: THAT MEANS WE NEED TO USE A TRANSPORT TO ESCAPE - BUT WHERE WERE WE HEADED?

Johnny almost didn't even want to answer. He hated it when his brother cut off his transmitted with his own cyber-driven messages. Still, to speed things along, his hesitation was minimal.

JONNYKLM: BEST I CAN GUESS WE WERE LEAVING THE CITY.
DAVIDEFM: OF COURSE! THE FOREST OUTSIDE THE CITY WOULD BE THE PERFECT PLACE TO HIDE
ASPENBCM: WHAT ABOUT SURVIVAL - YOU KNOW - FOOD, SHELTER - THEN THERE'S STAYING HIDDEN - YOU KNOW FROM SATELLITES.
GRACEHIM: WE NEED AN M-GEN. WE CAN DO ALL THAT IF WE GOT ONE OF THOSE.
DAVIDEFM: I'LL DOWNLOAD ALL THE REPLICAION PATTERNS.
GRACEHIM: NO! I'LL DOWNLOAD THE PATTERNS. DAVID, YOU GOTTA PULL OUT THE M-GEN AFTER WE'VE TAKEN CARE OF FATHER.
DAVIDEFM: RIGHT. HEY ASP - YOULL PROBLY GOTTA KEEP LITTLE J AND FATHER FROM FALLING AFTER THE SHOCK.
ASPENBCM: GOT IT! NEXT QUESTION - TRAINING? JUST 'CAUSE WE'RE LEAVING DOESN'T MEAN WE SHOULD STUPID. GRACE, DOWNLOAD ALL FATHER'S FILES - AND SEE IF YOU CAN FIND ANYTHING ON THAT METAL SPHERE THING.
GRACEHIM: NO PROB!
CAITYDEM: ALL THOSE PATTERNS - WE'RE TALKING ABOUT A LOT OF DATA. WE SHOULD PUT THE FILES INTO A BULK FOLDER THEN SPLIT THEM BETWEEN A BUNCH OF DATA PAD#$%
JONNYKLM: FATHERS HERE FATHERS HERE FATHERS HERE FATHERS HERE.
ORIONPQM: I'LL TAKE CARE OF IT - PUT THE PAD AWAY!

Johnny read the last message and quickly put the pad under his blanket just as his dorm room opened and Taylor entered. In the back of the boy's mind he was almost giddy over the fact that, somehow, he had figured out how to cut off his sister's typing with his first ever cyber message.

Even this couldn't keep him from covering the guilty look on his face, and this is what most certainly gave away that something was going on.

Johnny felt his heart stop when Taylor forced the data pad from the bed, though, and was nervous that the entire plot to escape would be discovered when Taylor looked the unit over carefully. Much to his relief, however, when Taylor handed the pad back to Johnny, it showed nothing more than an extensive two way conversation between Johnny and Orion that Johnny himself did not remember having. It was at this point that Johnny was grateful over his brother's cyber talents. He imagined that Orion had quickly penned up some simple conversation between the two of them to distract from the masterful plan they were all hatching. Moreover, Johnny felt a bit of relief in knowing that he hadn't actually lied to Taylor for, in fact, he was chatting with Orion.

The two quickly exchanged a few nervous words to clear up what Taylor thought was eminent trouble for Johnny by way of the boy's having another horrible vision and, all at once, Johnny's eyes were distracted by Taylor holding a clock in his hand, and while the boy asked about it without thinking, Taylor's answer was instant and obviously insufficient. Johnny sometimes thought it interesting how his father figure would cover up obvious errors by making it seem as though he meant to do something incorrect. The boy knew he had seen the clock before, but couldn't remember from where, and simply decided it best to humor Taylor, knowing that he'd brought it by mistake from the other dorm, possibly because of the teen's deep precognitive vision.

Once ready to leave Johnny almost offered a sigh as he glanced down at the thick long sleeved shirt he was wearing and realized that he was dressed much too warm for the July weather outside. He quickly removed it and made his way out of the dorm to keep Taylor from noticing anything else that might be construed as suspicious.

It was at this time that the boy looked down the hall and realized how predictable his father was. With a believable sound of ignorance the boy asked, "What happened to them?"

Taylor offered a quick response and inside his head Johnny realized that the plan was already in play – even if it was only a few minutes old and, now that he was being honest with himself, not very well thought out.

Now, do I just come out and ask him to give me a ride on his shoulders? Johnny wondered.

Hmm, no! The boy answered himself, and as he waited for his shirt to replicate he could see that Taylor was falling deeper and deeper into a mood of despair.

Johnny attempted bits of conversation trying to work in a way that he could ask Taylor for a ride, but more-so he tried to just make the man feel better and keep the mood light.

I'll just ask – Johnny decided, and as he finished mouthing the request he could see the negative response come faster than he'd expected.

Desperate for what to do next, he instantly moved to his last resort – *the face.*

Several times in the past few years Johnny had worked on and perfected the face which Taylor could never deny. No matter what the request, it seemed the man couldn't say no. Lowering his head, Johnny started the stare from beneath his brow, puckering his lower lip ever so practiced in an effort to win over what he wanted.

It – It – It wasn't working! Johnny thought, and as he slowly worked his face back to normal he felt a quick pull on his arm. Much faster than he could respond, Johnny realized he was exactly where he needed to be, riding atop Taylor's shoulders.

"Perfect" he whispered without thinking. *Everything was going as planned.* Johnny thought to himself. *I've got the shock stick... The shock stick, oh no! I've forgotten it! Wait, wait! Calm down.* The boy rolled around solutions in his head, and he realized that surely all he would have to do now is ask one of his brothers or sisters to get it and put it in his own backpack.

Though running a little late, Johnny was much relieved to see that his siblings were ready with the plan in full swing. They exited their dorms and generated bags that the boy knew were full of data-pads, all loaded with information from food patterns to education protocols, and no doubt some games and other things.

With the exchange of a few words and a quick telepathic message, Johnny watched as his brother Orion retrieved the shock stick and backpack that Johnny had forgotten, and when it was thrown in his direction, he felt a quick surge in his stomach, for he was almost unable to catch it with his free hand. Though Taylor didn't see it Johnny offered a fierce look to Orion for offering such a poor throw. He also offered a few poor looks to his siblings as a reminder that they weren't supposed to be so happy.

Everyone had trouble with this and as Taylor glanced at each of them, asking if they were ready, they all replied in the affirmative. Taylor turned to the lift, heavy hearted as the children could see, but Johnny turned himself quite uncomfortably to keep an almost giddy stare at his siblings as he was the only one Taylor couldn't see.

Smiling, Johnny worked hard to stiffen his resolve as he would make the one and final "no turning back now" move of the escape plan. "How 'bout it? Dave, Asp, are you ready?"

The two nodded their heads, and as the lift doors opened Johnny pulled the shock stick from his bag, charged it quickly and tapped Taylor's temple.

Unexpectedly, Johnny himself got a slight twinge in his thighs from the high voltage and, much to the credit of Aspen, he was carefully pulled from Taylor's shoulders and placed on the ground while Taylor himself was forced to stand still, unconscious, and motionless.

All at once the children seemed to get to work like a well rehearsed team.

Orion, focusing on the lift doors, kept them open while David concentrated hard on the M-Gen panel just opposite Aspen's dorm door.

"Be ready!" David said to Grace as she and Caitlin pulled pillows and the mattress out from Aspen's dorm and put them against the wall opposite the M-Gen. All the while he had generated a small scalpel and packet of omni-bandages, six to be exact, and, when the machine was finished and emptied; the boy took a firm position beside it, lowering his head and focusing hard inside his own mind.

With the sound of a few buckling braces they all knew the time was right and that the impact noise would attract a great deal of attention.

David furrowed his brow in strong concentration and, as could be expected, a huge booming crash resonated through the corridor as the M-Gen panel pulled itself from the wall and landed hard, albeit safely in the protection of the mattresses and pillows that had been put in place.

With a quick processional movement the six children, an unconscious Taylor, and the M-Gen all loaded into the lift.

Aspen, the last to enter, screamed as she turned to see that her ankle was being grabbed by an ESP who had freed himself from the mass of bodies at the far end of the corridor.

She looked down at the man who hoarsely voiced, "You aren't going anywhere!" and he pulled out his shock stick and tapped her leg repeatedly. Aspen squealed from the expectation of pain, but when nothing happened, she looked down at the man with a devilishly beautiful smile, realizing he must be the ESP in possession Johnny's toy version of a real shock stick.

"Really!" She said arrogantly, and with a sassy flick of her hair she returned a low browed stare to the ESP and watched as his eyes grew wide. With a thrusting jolt at the man's middle, his waist lead his entire body as it was pulled kinetically back into the pile of bodies at the end of the corridor.

All of the children laughed as they could hear his screams echoing through the halls. Not wanting to waste time, though, Grace pulled out a data-pad with the schematics Orion had downloaded and she forced the lift straight down while Orion kept a very close eye on the security scripts. He could see that someone was aware their escape efforts and attempted to force all lifts that had come from their floor to stop.

"Hah! Nice try!" he said aloud, and he started editing code faster than any security personnel could type. In his head he could only imagine the frustration he was causing the security protocol managers hiding in some low and unseen office in The Towers. The boy laughed with a devilish grin.

David, all the while, focused hard on Aspen's bare forearm, using the scalpel he had generated to cut a very small slice in it with the scalpel he had generated. Her grimacing pained stare was all he could bare as he worked carefully to hold her arm still while he worked. When he was finished she did the same to his, and with a nervous awkward flinch they each watched as a small pellet kinetically shot itself out of each of their arms. Then, with quick action, David wrapped Aspen's arm and Aspen David's with the omni-bandages David had replicated. They worked perfectly to stop the bleeding from these small new injuries, and once the two were satisfied that all was well with each other, david didthe same with their siblings, who had already rolled up their sleeves in expectation of what needed to be done.

Stopping at a random floor, Orion forced the doors open and David threw out the handful of small metal pellets he had been collecting. These pellets were, in fact, tracking devices usually implanted in all EduCorp students. They are only utilized by EduCorp security, if necessary.

Once they were thrown, David lit a smile. "That should keep 'em busy for a while! Now, where to – the landing pad?"

Orion nodded and the lift shifted in movement, but this didn't last for long.

"Wait, wait, wait!" Grace yelled in the lift, and she forced it to stop.

"What about Jay?" she asked in a panic.

"What about him?" David responded.

"Shouldn't we make him come too? They'll ask him all kinds of questions."

"She's right!" Caitlin piped up quickly,

"What?" Orion said turning his head from the control panel to stare at his sister as though the girl didn't know what she was talking about.

"Sure... think about it. Heck, they'll think this was all Father's idea, and they probably won't believe Jay when he says he doesn't know anything. They'll probably put him in jail for conspiracy or aiding or something like that..."

"Hmmm Right! Let's - gouhhh." Orion said, and with a jolt the lift started to work its way sideways – a direction that neither Grace nor Orion had anticipated – but that actually worked in their favor.

"What's happening?" Caitlin asked in a panic.

"Security overrides," Orion huffed as he watched the access panel he'd been using go blank.

"Damn!" he uttered, and with a gasp the other children stared at him in surprise.

"What!?" Orion said looking around at the shocked faces of his siblings, "Oh, whatever – Caity get me my bag!"

She quickly threw the boy's backpack at him, and as he unzipped it Aspen started muttering, "Is this as far as we're going to get?"

"Ah hah!" Orion said loudly, "Not yet! I've got more tricks up my sleeve than that! And he pulled out a unit that only Grace seemed to recognize.

"Orion Phillip Quinton Matthews," Grace said with surprise, "Those are illegal!"

It was a Wireless Net-Cracker or WNC, designed by hackers, and used to break into the most secure networks. It's most notable features were its gigabit coding cipher, its 7 transceivers, all operating at a constantly oscillating frequency. Orion was beside himself that he decided to replicate one of these. He held it firmly in his hands and looked almost laughingly at Grace.

"Illegal, huh, well I won't tell if you don't." The boy said, offering his sister a quick wink, and he stared at the unit forcing it to break into the EduCorp security mainframe whereby he continued editing the same security protocols he'd been working on before.

With a jolt the entire lift stopped... With stares in Orion's direction he answered their unspoken questions with irritation. "They've stopped all crossover traffic – There's no way I can hack it. Some kind of safety override. "Go ahead," Orion said looking at Grace, "Keep us going down I'm a little busy here!"

Once again Grace focused her mind on the lift and forced it down again as Aspen quickly asked, "Where is Jay anyways?"

Johnny looked down at his ring and offered it a squeeze. Within seconds the boy had navigated to show that Jay was sitting stationary in the arboretum.

"Level 490, but that's in South Tower!" Johnny said in a panic.

"Fine," Grace said looking over at David, "I'm taking us to 298 – that's the main crossover level just under the landing pad We can't ride the lift for cross-over," she confirmed this with a shaking head from Orion, "so we're going to have to make a run for it. D, when these doors open you need to clear a path so we can make it to the other tower. Asp," she said looking purposefully at her sister, "You're going to have to move Father fast, and I mean fast..."

Everyone stared up at the lift numbers as they fast approached the 298th floor. As such Grace stopped the lift quite abruptly and once everyone regained steadiness she looked at her brother and sister again, "Ready?"

They both nodded their heads, and Grace forced the doors open.

Zap – Smack

In a fraction of a second the door slipped open and a streak of laser shot through the lift from the lower part of the door, where none of them had expected to see anything. The shot skimmed Grace on the cheek forcing her to instantly close the doors.

She offered a hand to her face before pulling it back in anger, showing that she was bleeding and, with deep breaths, she worked hard to hold back tears.

"Aaargh," she spewed angrily. "Those shots are lethal! They're trying to kill us!"

All of the children looked at each other, first with expressions of fear, then, looking down at Taylor, who'd been lying on the floor since they'd all settled into the lift, they stiffened slowly to a more resolute determination. Looking at the man, who seemed to be resting almost peacefully, they re-realized their purpose.

"Let's try that again." Grace said with a firm, angry tone, and she grabbed David by the wrist, forcing him in front of the lift doors. This boy, furious at his sister's injury, almost screamed with the telekinetic force he'd mustered, and in his mind he wanted to make sure that everything was out their way. In this effort, he kinetically forced everything to move outward from the main crossover corridor. During this time, everyone in the lift heard a loud crash and instantly Caitlin moved to catch David who nearly collapsed from the effort.

The boy came around after a few seconds, and pulled from his pocket a proto bar which he kinetically unwrapped and started eating.

"Good shfuff," David said with a smile, and Caitlin practically dropped him when she saw that he was fine.

"Boys!" she growled, and she turned to the doors of the lift with apprehension as Grace slowly forced them open.

"Move!" Grace said once she saw that the doors had an opening large enough for everyone, and everything to make it through.

As the children bounded out of the lift, all carrying backpacks, and Aspen gliding Taylor, and David the M-Gen down the corridor, they realized how great a job David did of taking care of anything that might have been in their way.

They ran past several ESP's who had been forced outward so hard that their helmets and body armor were melded into the corridor walls, keeping them from making any movements despite their best efforts.

"Great job David!" Orion said as he sprinted down the corridor and noticed that, for the distance of about a thousand feet from one tower to the other, every inch of the corridor walls was flexed outward, buckled and damaged from the child's efforts.

"Thanks!" the boy replied, impressed with his own efforts.

With a crash behind them, though, they could hear that a lift beneath the one they were riding had smashed into and forced it out of the way. Once this new lift was in position, ESP's poured out of it. A few shots were fired that barely missed the lot of them, and it was clear that things were getting very, *very* dangerous.

Orion turned to Johnny and Caitlin, "You two, do something."

"But you said..." Caitlin started but she was immediately cut off.

"I don't care what I said, just get back there and wreak some havoc."

The two looked at each other first with looks of concern before showing matching wide grins of pleasure.

They fell back from the rest of the group and turned to face the onslaught of ESP's. One by one they knocked each one of them to the side of the corridor. They couldn't really control exactly what they were doing, but it was easy to just knock them around, and keep them rattled.

Still, even with their best efforts, the two children eventually realized that there were just too many of them. Having yet another lift pour out more ESP's into the corridor, and seeing in the distance that some of them were prying others form the wall to help join in the ranks, it was clear that the two of them were no match for so many.

Caitlin looked at her brother, "The ceiling! Bring it down, bring it down!" she screamed, and at this the two looked upward and with only a few seconds concentration they worked together to force panels, electronics, and tons of structure and support to fall downward into the corridor. Once they'd completely obscured the path so that it would take quite some time for the ESP's to break through, the two let up, turned to each other with a nodding smile, and started running to catch up with their brothers and sisters.

Once everyone had made their way to the lift, Grace was relieved to see that there was no one inside when she opened the doors. They all crowded inside and Orion put his WNC unit away, opting to use the onboard panel to once again keep track of and rapidly edit EduCorp's security protocols.

Grace turned to the full lift of passengers and offered a fierce stare that was only hardened with the sight of her bleeding cheek. "This will be quick, and it'll be rough, so get ready!"

True to her word, she climbed nearly 200 floors in less than a minute, causing a huge degree of discomfort for everyone in the lift as the stop caused each to lift a few inches from the lift floor before landing again.

David stood in front of the door, but hesitated in taking any kinetic action as he realized that just on the other side Jay was probably standing unaware of what was going on. Still he wanted to be prepared for anything.

"Everyone, move to the sides of the lift!" He said loudly, and, heeding his warning, each in the lift carefully positioned themselves against its walls. Aspen even forced Taylor's body to hold itself to the edge of the lift as well.

All at once, with tensions high, a nod from David, told Grace to force the doors of the lift wide open.

Swoosh!

The doors opened, and save for the sounds of the bird calls from the arboretum there was nothing else to be heard. Everyone made their way out of the lift cautiously. Step by step these children felt prepared for anything that might try to catch them off guard and Orion pulled out his WNC again in an attempt to tap into the ESP communication infrastructure making sure that, even on an electronic level, they were prepared for anything.

It was this on-edge nature that forced Grace, whose face was still stinging badly from her earlier encounter with the ESP's, to kinetically throw Jay from where he'd been standing.

"There you aaaaaaaaahhhh!" Jay screamed as he was lifted from the ground and thrown hard against a palm standing nearly twenty feet away. Sure all of the children jumped when they heard this outburst, which came from between several bushes on the side of the main path that ran through the arboretum, but it was Grace that reacted with instant, and accidental force.

The children all approached Jay in a rush, and as he struggled to stand and defend himself from the children, they all worked hard to calm him – to let him know that everything was – well – *almost fine!*

Jay wasn't necessarily the bravest of men, but he had a great memory, and it was for this reason that he recognized what he could only call "the future on fast approach!" This was what he called it when he could recognize what he'd been told of the future as actually happening.

Looking at Taylor's unconscious body, Grace's bleeding face, the bandages on the children's arms, and taking into account the events of the morning, he knew what was going on. The future was, indeed, on fast approach.

"It's happening isn't it?" he asked of the children as he lowered a branch which he'd broken off of a rather young oak standing nearby as a mode of self defense.

Johnny nodded his head staring unblinkingly at Jay with his light blue eyes, hoping to offer some sort of comfort.

"It's time!" the boy then said and he reached out to grab Jay's hand.

Jay, who was staring at the stick he held lightly in both hands, thought hard of what he'd heard and experienced over the last two days. He looked at the faces of the children, noticing that Caitlin was still a member of the group, where she was predicted missing before, and it only took him a moment to realize what he needed to do.

Dropping the branch, he forced his face of seriousness to change into that of an almost playful smile.

"Well, somebody's gotta keep you kids in line! I guess that's me!" Jay said in an almost arrogant tone as he grabbed Johnny's hand and walked with the others back to the lift.

On entering the space inside, and each person taking their place in what was now becoming a very confined area, Orion and Grace made sure of their safe passage to the landing pad between The Towers. The others prepared for what they were certain would be an uneasy path to freedom.

"You know," Caitlin said softly to Jay, slowly working her hand inside his own, "I expected it would take a little more convincing than that!"

He looked down at her face, with its widening smile, and offered almost a laugh. "You know, you're the only reason I decided to come." he replied, and she looked up at him in confusion. Her face then turned pink from a sense of embarrassment and he continued with a smile. "Come on girl, knowing what I know, I gotta make sure *all* you kids get outta here safe and sound! No matter what!"

"So you think we're all going to make it?"

"I know so!"

"But you – you're not going to try and stop us – talk some sense into us, or whatever?"

"Caity," Jay said softly, though his nerves tried to demand a more severe tone, "Sometimes right and wrong aren't black and white, and sometimes they only seem so. This is the right thing to do, even if it doesn't seem so."

She smiled kindly before exchanging an uneasy glance with him when the lift came to a stop at level 300. They knew this was where the landing platform of The Towers was located and with the stopping of the lift, they all felt an increasing nervousness build inside them. Orion forced a security camera to display the landing platform and reveal that outside the door dozens of ESP's were waiting for them. With angry grunts, David and Aspen instantly took their places in front of the doors with Grace ready to force their opening when, with a soft "Wait," Jay decided to intervene.

"Wait! You want us to wait?" Orion asked indignantly as he pulled his eyes away from the security panel.

"Well, yeah!" Jay said squatting down between the children, "I have an idea!"

38 Cornered

JAY LEANED IN TO HUDDLE with the children so that they could hear his plan, but his efforts were interrupted as the cabin slowly resonated with the groans of Taylor who was finally coming around from his earlier shock.

"Whhaaaarrreeemmmaaaay"

Jay shook his head and once the verbal noise had ceased he started to divulge his plan to the children. Twice in the middle of his explanation Taylor continued his groans, and such was Jay's irritation at this that he quickly snatched the shock stick out of one of the backpacks and tapped Taylor on the head with it.

"Huh – out like a light! Amazing."

The children, who were initially surprised by this display, giggled once it had been done. They realized that it was for the best that Taylor still be unaware of what was going on until they were all safely away from The Towers and out of the city.

Outside the lift, members of the ESP crowded around its entrance. The mass of black uniforms with armor, face shields, handheld laser cannons and shock sticks were all twitching with nervousness as they waited for the lift doors to open. None were willing to force them open over the fear of what the children would do. Instead they all simply waited for what could be called "the first move," not really knowing who was going to make it. Amid their ranks whispers and rumors started moving rapidly through the crowd.

"I heard they completely destroyed 298."

"Yeah, I heard the same - also heard they killed their teacher just so they could escape."

"No – really."

"Yeah, and did you hear what they did once they finished him off?"

"No – what?"

"They folded him up and put him in one of their bags – Jones told me – said he could hear the man's bones breaking when they did it!"

"Disgusting! – But – did you say it was their teacher?"

"Yeah, Dr. Taylor, most evolved man on the planet, just barely eighteen, and murdered by his own students."

"But he's so – so – powerful – isn't he."

"Listen – they're his students; prob'ly caught him off guard. Besides there are six of them and only one of him, there's no way he'd stand a chance."

"Hmmm – we'd better be ready for anything."

"Shhhh – I hear something."

With a few blips and buzzes of the speakers outside the lift, the ESP's listened closely as a young voice boomed out of the intercom.

"EduCorp Security Personnel, this is Orion Phillip Quinton Matthews, one of six children here in the lift. I'm giving all of you a warning. Put down your weapons and let us leave The Towers in peace or there will be consequences."

For many on the platform, it was very strange to hear such an arrogant tone come from a voice that sounded so young, but after a moment the camera above the lift panned across the crowd of ESP's who all took a moment to brace themselves and hold their laser cannons at the ready.

"I see you're not going to make this easy," Orion said through the intercom. "You have one last warning. We are more powerful than you can possibly imagine – we don't have to open these doors to take action, so you have one last chance to drop your weapons before it's too late!"

Stepping forward, the captain of the ESP squad separated from the group. "There's only one way you're leaving this rooftop and that's in our custody!"

The man then turned and fired his handheld laser cannon on the three transports behind the mass of security. One by one each exploded, revealing nothing but debris in the wake of their flames, all the while the camera moved swiftly to catch this new activity.

"You leave us no choice!" Orion said through the speaker, and with one final look at the ESP captain, the boy watched the man aim at the camera itself.

Having this watchful eye removed, the man then turned to look at his crew giving them a signal to be ready to fire, but before he could finish laser fire spewed rapidly past him at the opening doors of the lift.

The children quickly made their way through the doors, walking through the barrage of red streaks seemingly unscathed. They ran as fast as they could to one of the other lifts on the other side of the landing platform, through the crowd of ESP's, kinetically throwing them out of the way as they approached.

Those ESP's who were still on their feet, however, flanked around the children, following them to the lift while the captain struggled to stay in the lead.

Once in the lift, the children went straight down as fast as they could. The ESP's, on the other hand, entered several other lifts located around the platform, ready to follow and meet them where they landed.

Within seconds the entire platform sat quiet with only the occasional crackle and sizzle from the transport fires and laser shots that happened to hit other equipment.

"That was so cool!" Johnny screamed from behind a supply crate near the lift where they had waited inside so patiently.

"How did you know we could do that?" Caitlin asked tugging on Jay's lab-coat as she and the rest of her siblings slowly pulled themselves from behind other crates.

"I didn't – but I figured since you've all been hooked up to that sphere thingy – well... it was worth a shot."

"But..." Caitlin tried to inquire further, but her words were cut off by an answer before the question. "Oh, well Taylor used to do that to me all the time when I first started working here." Jay answered rubbing his head and head free of sweat from the mid-July heat. "False imaging he called it."

"Well," Orion said with a smile, "The title fits. Force people to see things that aren't there... Good job you two!" he said looking at Caitlin and Johnny who had telepathically tricked thirty or so individuals into believing the whole group of them had made their way safely from one transport to another.

"And nice touch with the kinesis." Grace added giving a quick nudge to both Aspen and David who'd forced several of the ESP's off their feet to give the illusion of self defense.

"OK guys were going to have to be quick about this!" Jay shouted as they all ran to the maintenance hangar housed within North Tower.

"Right." Orion said putting his hand on the hangar door. "Unless I'm mistaken, there should at least be one or two company owned transports in here for repair. Once I get this door open – Grace – you need to do a complete diagnostic on all of them – simultaneously – see which one is most flight worthy, then prep it. Everyone else needs to get strapped in, and make sure those two," the boy added pointing at Taylor and the M-Gen, "are in good and tight. We won't have much time – once the door is open the hard wired alarm'll go off and it won't take long for the ESP's to realize they've been tricked."

Jay offered a laugh at hearing all of this and in his own head he was so amazed at the discipline and downright organized misbehavior of the children, "You guys are... are just so darn impressive!" he said looking down at the group who were all crowded at the hangar door.

All at once Orion opened hangar doors at a much faster speed than normal while Grace practically rolled into the dark space and focused one by one on each of the transports inside to initiate their diagnostic mode. There were four in the hangar, and once she finished activating each one she moved her focus back to the first.

"Nope!" then to the second, "Maybe,", then to the third, "This one's pretty good," then to the last, "Definitely not!" and her eyes moved back to the third where she quickly forced its loading door to open.

They all quickly boarded and as Grace and Orion cyberly opened the emergency manual cockpit to the transport the latter asked half interestedly, "What was wrong with this one?"

"Seat strap sensors are malfunctioning?" Grace responded flicking several switches inside the small space, preparing the craft for flight readiness.

"If this things going to take off at all I'm going to have to take the sensors offline completely."

Orion responded to this by turning to his brothers and sisters in the main cabin. "Make sure you do a good job strapping in, the belt sensors are offline." He said loudly with his voice competing with the revving and anti-G engines.

After several seconds of clicks and zips and with the loading door closed, it appeared that everything and everyone was strapped down tight. Then, offering a nod to her brother, Grace pressed her finger lightly on the button to release the docking clamps, but quite to her surprise, her brother pulled her arm down away from the control panel.

"Everyone down!" He yelled to the back of the transport as he pointed only for a moment so that Grace could see that another transport was on approach. She reached up, not even looking, and pushed the master power switch so as to quickly shut down the entire craft.

On landing, this new transport already had its loading door open, and not a moment from when it had touched the platform did a red hooded figure bound out to survey the damage from the transports that had been destroyed earlier. The man continued to walk the platform, occasionally reaching up to stroke his fingers slowly down the sides of his hood.

"We don't have time for this!" Grace hissed at Orion.

"Shhhhh! He's leaving." The boy said as he observed the hooded man walking to one of the lifts.

The lift doors opened, and the commotion that followed terrified both Orion and Grace, who were the only ones that could see what was going on.

"It's too late!" Orion whispered softly and he looked over at his sister whose bleeding face suddenly lit up with wide eyed panic.

She sat upright, looking at the crowd of ESP's that had poured from the lift onto the landing pad, but who hadn't yet seen her.

"Not if I can help it!" she bellowed, and with what telekinetic abilities she had gained in the past several hours, she forced several black uniforms to be strewn across the platform while she simultaneously hit the main power and docking release switches with her fist.

Pulling hard on the manual controls, she forced the transport to launch itself across the platform and into the air in the matter of a few seconds.

Thinking they were free and clear of The Towers, it took the increasing intensity of laser fire and the unresponsive nature of the transport for Grace to realize that somehow she did not have full control of the craft and that it was returning to the platform.

"What the!" she said pulling the controls in a number of different directions. "You don't want to work, fine, I'll make you work."

"WAIT!" Orion said just as the transport turned its nose back towards The Towers.

"Grace, he's controlling it cyberly," the boy said in a loud whisper, pointing at the hooded figure standing in the middle of a circle of firing ESP's. The man was pointing one finger at the ship, and with the shaking of his hand it was clear that he was doing everything he could to compete with Grace's maneuvers.

As far as the ESP's were concerned, it was everything they could do just to keep track of the transport, which was now moving back and forth, weaving in and out, and thus making it a very hard target to hit.

Inside the cabin, much greater concerns were arising. With the inertial dampener offline by way of the hooded figure cyberly disengaging them, the passengers inside the transport were shifting in their seats quite mercilessly.

"I can't – can't break free!" Grace said moving the controls faster and faster trying desperately to keep ahead of the cyber commands of the crimson figure on the platform. Then, all were caught off guard by the unthinkable.

"Ahhhhhhh! Help!" Resonated through the transport. Caitlin's belt had come loose and she started shifting out of her seat, knocking her head and bouncing hard around the cabin.

Swoooooooshhhhhhhhhhh!

All at once the cabin was filled with the earsplitting sound of fast moving air. The loading door had opened itself.

Had it not been for the attention and fast moves of Jay, who rapidly unbuckled himself and jolted for the door, Caitlin, who he'd caught by the wrist, would have fallen perilously over 300 stories to her death. Instead, it took everything Jay had to use one arm to hold on to the door's safety strap, and the other to hold on to the girl, who was now completely outside the transport.

"One of you! Do something!" Jay yelled at the other three children, who were all sitting terrified in the cabin of the transport.

"Grace," David screamed to the front of the cabin, "Stop fighting him for a second, so I can get a clear view!"

She looked at Orion with a sideways and yet pained grin as she released the controls. With instant smoothness the transport stopped its wavering. This offered enough time for Jay to pull Caitlin into the transport. He turned around and set her safely on the cabin floor when a sudden look of pain overtook his face.

Caitlin screamed as she could see blood slowly soak his lab-coat at the shoulder, and while Jay started to stumble backwards toward the loading door, she jumped to push the emergency override at the door's side so as to close it and keep him from falling out. Safe from falling, Jay was, but well he was not. He hit his head square on the door as it closed, knocking him out.

David, on the other hand, had released his strap and weaved his way quickly to the front of the transport where he was able to get a clear view of the red hooded figure, who had, once he gained total control of the transport, waved for the ESP's to cease fire.

With one raised eyebrow, David forced a telekinetic punch at the man forcing him to fall backward, hitting his head on the ground. This knocked him out, and, for a fraction of a second, showed his face to the children in the cabin. To no-one's surprise, this was the face of the GC representative they'd seen in the council chambers earlier that day – the one that Taylor called "Dr. Zeldin," a man which they had heard many horrible stories of, but had never had the occasion to ever see, for Taylor never felt the need to show the children what this man looked like.

Once freed from the hold of Dr. Zeldin, Grace immediately grabbed the transport controls, and forced the craft in a straight line directly north of The Towers. All at once there were cheers from everyone as they were all filled with a newfound sense of absolute freedom. Cheers were coming from everyone that is, except for Caitlin.

She was frantically looking through a first aid kit located on the other side of the loading door of the transport. She saw all kinds of tools and trinkets, but didn't know how to use any of them. Tears filling her eyes, she continued to watch Jay's body offer blood to the cabin floor. She was so scared from her close call with death, and so terrified of losing one of her mentors that her hands were shaking uncontrollably.

All at once the warm fingers of her brother, Johnny, had slowly worked around hers. "Calm down!" he said softly to her, "Everything's going to be fine, you've got it right here!"

"But I don't – know – how..." she said weeping every word, still shaking inside Johnny's hold.

"It's okay – I do!" the boy replied softly, and he slowly removed the tiny unit Caitlin had been holding and, placing it in front of Jay's nose, he tapped a short series of buttons.

Slowly the bioelastic polymer engulfed their teacher, and hardened around him, keeping him in stasis for the remainder of what everyone hoped would be a safe trip.

The two children then used straps from either side of the loading door to literally attach Jay to the craft, making sure that he would be held firmly into place.

Wiping away her tears, Caitlin knotted the last tie on her side of the door, and in looking out the window she admired the fantastic view of the city as could be seen from their altitude. Not even able to breathe a sigh of relief, her eyes grew wide as her face changed to a transfixed gaze of fear.

39 Freedom Flight

"WHAT'S WRONG WITH YOU?" Johnny asked, looking at the fearful face of his sister and not understanding why she'd be so frightened now that they were finally free of a life they had barely been living in for the past five years.

Caitlin hardly moved a muscle but to reach beside herself and grab her brother's chin. Slowly, she rotated his head to look out the window. When he finally saw what she did, it didn't take long for his face to resemble a look much like hers.

"We've got company!" the boy shouted in response to seeing some twenty or thirty police transports all headed toward them.

In the emergency cockpit of a commuter transport there's never a need for offensive detection of hostile craft or weapons, and for this reason Grace was ill aware of what was going on behind her. She looked downward and cyberly activated a viewing screen that was linked to a camera on the back end of the transport.

Both she and Orion's eyes nearly fell out of their respective sockets. Some thirty or forty of these police transports were now headed directly for them, and more were adding to their ranks every second. To Grace's dismay, these police transports were designed for much greater speed, and were catching up very fast.

"What the hell man?" she growled loudly at her brother. "We're just a bunch of kids!"

"Actually," Orion said in a serious tone looking at his sister who had returned her stare to the city skyline, "I think we've proved that we're a lot more than just a bunch of kids."

With a purposeful stare Grace cyberly released the speed safety interlocks of the transport, increasing the velocity of the transport to nearly triple what it was before. This had the simultaneous effect of causing the police transports to quickly shrink out of view, and cause a rush of laughter and wails to roll through the cabin of the transport. The inertial dampeners were working well, to a point, but severe jolts were still be felt by the passengers, and this gave the whole cabin a strange sense of inertial euphoria.

"Woahhhh!" was heard bellowing through the cabin as offered by David, who was thrilled by the shifting gravity as caused by the increased speed.

"Get back there, make sure everybody and everything is strapped down tight" Grace commanded Orion, who bolted from the emergency cockpit.

After a minute or two of flying at high speeds and feeling that she had sufficiently lost her followers, Grace realized how misled she was when a flock of new police transports elevated from the city directly in front of her. She needed to change directions, and while she was sufficient in her maneuvers and her speed to keep them at a safe distance; what happened next no-one in the transport could have expected.

As Grace was forced to make her way seemingly back towards The Towers, she looked in her rearward facing viewer to see, surprisingly, that all of the police transports were breaking formation and heading back toward the lower city levels.

"What! What are they doing – They're not following...? What the heck's goin' on?" Grace's eyes shot down to the consoles at her sides. While she had no intention of communicating with the police transports, she activated an on-board communicator in an attempt to eavesdrop on their frequencies. Cyberly she forced the communicator to hone in on the signal.

"zzzzt Repeat zzzzt Repeat zzzz all units fall back – SMX's have been initiated under GC order 2671B."

"Oh crap!" Grace grunted offering a quick, albeit worried look to Orion who had just returned from the main cabin. She glanced at the rear view screen again and could see that the police transports, while still in view, were keeping their distance.

"Everybody hold on!"

With the sounds of clicks ad the zips of straps being tightened Grace knew the cabin had heard her request, and she quickly turned to her brother.

"Orion," she said with a serious and commanding voice, "You need to take control of the transport. Fly fast, and fly crazy! I've got work to do!"

She immediately released the controls to the craft and crawled down below the control panel in front of her, and hardly offered Orion a moment to catch the controls of the craft. "I don't know how to fly this thing!" Orion said fretfully, grabbing those secondary controls in front of where she had been sitting.

She quickly pulled her head from beneath the control panel, "You're a cyber – idiot! Duh!" She then stopped and realized the harshness of her words, and decided to soften the blow a little. "You just – just – do what *we* do best – and hurry, the smart missiles could be here any second."

Orion, while feeling somewhat insulted at her initial comments, focused more on what he'd heard than how it was said. "Smart – did you, did you just say smart missiles?"

"Yeah, they learn the patterns of their targets, so you're going to have to go a little crazy if you want to keep them off us long enough for me to finish!"

"What are you doing?" Orion asked as he focused hard on the instruments in front of him, getting a feel for how they operated, and what each one's purpose was.

"I've got an idea, I just hope it works" she said both firmly and enigmatically.

Orion looked down at her and she gave him a quick wink that he noticed caused her to use of the bloodied side of her face. He realized quite instantly that this was no time to be timid or squeamish. He looked ahead forceful and concentrating while Grace once again pulled herself back under the control panel.

Sure enough, it was only a few seconds before Orion could see, and feel by way of nearby explosions, these "Smart missiles". They were extremely fast, and it took Orion's total concentration to simultaneously crack all the transport's speed safety interlocks so as to go as fast as possible while also steering it at the same time.

"Brace yourself. It's gonna get a little bumpy..."

With this being said, Orion turned the craft straight downward into the city. With his heart sufficiently in his throat, the boy pulled out of this dive only to add to the tension by weaving in and out of the other transport traffic and buildings at reckless speeds.

He managed to keep the missiles from what would obviously have been a disastrous impact, but unfortunately he wasn't able to lose them. They were tricky and found ways of cutting him off and sometimes used shortcuts to keep within a nervously close range.

"Can – Can you please – please – try to fly – straight!" Grace shouted in an annoyed voice as she was working hard to steady herself with the many turns and shifts her brother forced the transport to perform.

"I can't fly straight! They'll catch up and – and..." Orion paused and offered a smile while he slowly exhaled, "wait a minute..."

Grace could see this grin despite the fact that the boy was concentrating deeply on the view ahead and she was curious of what could be rolling through his head that would force him to smile so widely.

"What – What are you thinking?" she asked wanting to be let in on what he was thinking. He didn't give a response to her directly, but quickly turned his head to look to the back of the cabin.

"Aspen, David!" He yelled, "Get up and pick a side!" He waited a few seconds but saw that the two only offered confused expressions.

"Let's try that again!" He yelled, having to now look back and forth between the front of the craft and the cabin. "Get out of your seats... NOW! Aspen, you take that window! David, you take that one!" Orion was nodding to the windows on either side of the craft, and this time, with his loud commands, his siblings listened.

David and Aspen stood, and as they made their way, cautiously, to the windows at either side of the transport they looked out with equally fearful expressions. Just as they had gotten close enough to see the missiles they flinched at hearing their brother's voice again. "You've got some work to do!" Orion said spryly as he elevated the craft higher above the city to avoid impact with an oncoming missile. Their entire transport was now illuminated by the afternoon sunlight and the glare seemed to light up the inside of the craft so that even Johnny and Caitlin took an interest in seeing a new and fantastic view of the city skyline.

"See if you two can knock those puppies out of the sky!"

With a leaning, David and Aspen were forced to hold onto hand rails as Orion forced the craft to make a sudden and sharp turn. This was followed by an immediate jolt and a bright flash in the window.

"What the hell! Come on guys – snap out of it! Get busy back there!"

David and Aspen gave each other fast looks of fierce, devilish, deviousness before they returned purposeful gazes back out their respective windows.

From this point it only took a few seconds for the results of Orion's request to show itself on the view screen as one by one the missiles either ran into each other, or began spiraling wildly through the sky, losing their target and redirecting elsewhere.

"No!" Orion shouted at seeing this. "Make them run into each other in the air, but don't let them get back to the ground, they'll kill innocent people.

"What about innocent children!" Caitlin screamed to the front, amazed that she had just heard the total disregard Orion had for himself and his siblings.

"Listen!" The boy snapped as he turned his stare to the back of the cabin. "There are only eight of us, but millions down there. We can't risk a greater attack than we're already facing by making ourselves *real* criminals!"

I think it's a little too late for that!" Aspen said loudly staring to the rear of the craft. For Orion, the view-screen clearly showed what she was talking about. Digitally the screen was too small to make out an exact number, but it was clear that there were hundreds of missiles now seeking out the transport with more joining their ranks each second, and two by two Aspen and David continued to work them out of the sky by making them run into each other.

All at once Orion had to quickly force a sharp left turn as he noticed there were more missiles taking position directly in front of him and thus the journey through the city had become far more difficult than he had expected even with the aid of his brother and sister.

"How's it going down there?" Orion asked Grace quite insistently.

"Fine." She said blandly and offered no other response, thus heightening Orion's curiosity.

"What are you doing anyways?" he finally asked, giving in to his *need to know*.

She shouted loudly from beneath the console, "I'm trying to pull out the universal beacon." And with that, she quickly pulled herself out from under the console, and left the emergency cockpit for nearly a minute before returning with one of the bags she had packed before leaving The Towers.

"What's in the bag?" Orion asked even more curiously than before.

"Some – necessities!" She said with a precarious pause in mid sentence.

Orion, who had forced another fierce turn to avoid more missiles, had quickly realized that he was now headed back in the direction they'd started – that is, headed back to The Towers.

"He's desperate to get us to come back!" Orion said quickly looking up at the new direction they were now headed.

"Who?" Grace asked, even though he realized the answer to his question the moment he asked it.

"Mr. Red Hooded Man – That's who! I wouldn't doubt he's got some control over these smart missiles 'cause each time I turn it just takes me closer to The Towers"

A few rumbles of the craft caused Orion to become quickly unnerved as he turned back to yell at his siblings. "If you two want to make it out of this thing alive you'd better do a better job of keeping those things off our ass!"

Orion then turned the craft straight down, rolled it, and turned it back to their original heading out of the city. This forced most of the missiles to reconfigure their path, and successfully put some distance between the transport and the surviving missiles that were still chasing them. In his mind, Orion digested the thought that he had, indeed, said what Johnny had once quoted of him, and that with the downward turn, this would offer the boy the chance he needed to poke his head into the emergency cockpit. But first he'd expect to hear...

"Got it!" Grace shouted holding up a strange black box with a mangle of wires still hanging from it.

In an instant Orion showed a sign of relief, but still had little idea of what his sister's plan was for this unit. While looking at her, he noticed, as if he could have expected it, Johnny standing at the cockpit entrance, curiously staring between the two of them before changing his gaze to watch the edge of the city as it came nearer and nearer.

"Get back there!" he said to Johnny waving his hand for the boy to return to the main cabin.

Johnny, who was again distracted by the familiar look of Grace's damaged face, snapped at attention and did as he was ordered. He immediately made his way to a window, standing beside Aspen. The boy's own sense of déjà vu seemed almost complete at this point, but it solidified itself when he heard his sister clearly state, "Do you think you could give us a hand here?"

This was as far as he'd seen in his vision, but it was obvious to him that there were some distinct differences between the reality of now, and the vision he'd had before. The most apparent of the differences was the fact that Jay, who was fully mobile in Johnny's vision, was now perfectly stiff in bioelastic stasis. Additionally, while Caitlin was missing in his vision before, she now seemed fine and well, less, of course, a little emotional distress.

The best Johnny could guess; his prediction of what had happened may have helped to change things for the better.

Yes – yes, he thought. *I told Jay about my vision, and he watched Caitlin like a hawk. He saved her from falling out of the transport!*

With this in mind, Johnny felt a surge of energy. His vision had helped to save his sister, and it gave him hope, and will to escape from the peril that seemed ever so close. He turned to Caitlin and offered a quick order, but it wasn't so much an order as it was a request.

"You help David, I'll help Aspen. If we're good we might have a chance at beating these things.

In less than a second Caitlin unbuckled herself from her seat and glued her face to the side of the transport. She watched carefully the missiles that were headed in their direction, wanting so much to use her new abilities; to develop them and to show that she could make a real difference in their efforts to escape.

"Got two!" she said loudly as she'd surprised herself by forcing one missile into another and causing both to explode.

"We've already done dozens and dozens my dear," David said turning to his sister in arrogance.

"That doesn't count!" she huffed, "You have to start counting now; now that all four of us are doing it."

"Got two!" Aspen said behind her, offering a wink to Johnny who had just crashed two as well. From this point it only took a few seconds for the competition to catch on and soon numbers were flying across the cabin.

"I've got ten!"

"I've got twenty"

"I've got twenty-five!"

You can't have an odd number," David shouted at Johnny in disgust as he assumed his younger brother was trying to cheat.

"Yeah, but I got three in one! So there!" Johnny said in a manner quite full of himself. Aspen immediately supported this claim with a quick, "He's not fibbing, I saw it!"

All at once, the four heads were instantly staring back through their windows, but after a while the whole lot of them became both tired and fatigued from the efforts they'd put into what they affectionately called *Missile Destruction.*

Despite their exhaustion, the missiles kept coming and coming and Orion had little choice but to continue changing his direction even if, as it often did, the new direction led the transport further from their goal.

All the while, in the cockpit, Grace continued to disassemble the tracking device she had pulled from the cockpit. She started by pulling out a strange tool that fit on her index fingertip, and, with a squeeze of it on her thumb, it emitted a thin bright red line that she pointed in the direction of the box. Slowly she cut it open, and once she'd done this, she used it quite randomly on the inside to begin cutting at the inner workings.

After a few seconds of this she turned the box over in the cabin to allow several parts to fall quite messily to the floor. Automatically she set the box down and sorted through the mess until she found what she was looking for. She raised it up, and pulled more tools from her bag.

Orion caught sight of this and inquired lightly "What's next?"

Grace responded simply while continuing to work. "This little thing right here," she said holding up a walnut sized object that had several bright flashing lights, "this is what defines this tin bucket as a transport; not just any transport through. It defines us as this specific serialized transport.

Orion, while continuing to steer and avoid missiles that were relentless in their pursuit of the transport, sustained his inquiry about Grace's plan. "So why don't you just destroy it?" he asked almost irritatingly."

"Well, if I destroy it, the smart missiles will figure out what's happened and find something else to track, like our heat signature instead. If I throw it out, the missiles might be confused for a moment about the split between heat and radio signal, but this confusion won't last for long. – No, no. I have a much better idea."

Orion started waving his hand in frustration that she should reveal her plan, and do so quickly.

"Arrrgh. I'm going to copy the signal!" She said in irritation as she pulled a large item out of her tool-bag.

Orion glanced over and his eyes widened in panic. "What! No. What are you doing with that?" he asked in awe as he noticed she was holding his Wireless NetCracker unit.

"Sorry O. I need the parts!" she said calmly as she started cutting away at its back panel using the same laser tool as before."

"What! Nooooooo!" he said whiningly.

"Hey!" She shouted trying to break his taxing high pitched ranting. "Don't you have a pattern of this thing saved somewhere?"

"Well, yeah!" he said, as he continued to focus on the view ahead.

"Good! You can make another one, but right now" Grace said fiercely, "I need the parts!"

She immediately started pulling parts and wires out of the small book-sized until and she lined them up on the floor beside her chair. One by one she started reworking them, using a barrage of other tools. She repeatedly kept grabbing the part she had pulled from the tracking device. After a few more minutes she gathered up seven little objects, all larger but seemingly the same as the tiny device she had pulled from out of the box she had retrieved from behind the control panel.

"Well, it's now or never!" Grace said excitedly, holding these objects in her hands as she stood and finally took a seat beside Orion.

"What do you mean 'it's now or never'?" he asked, still nervously unsure of what she had up her sleeve.

40 Grace's Decoys

"DIVE!" GRACE SHOUTED, her eyes staring forward, but her brother only responded with a questioning 'I don't get it' stare.

"Dive?"

"Dive – into the city!" she said, eyebrows raised and hands pointed forward.

He turned his head and with a quick shift of his own body he forced the transport to swerve and miss two smart missiles which that were headed directly for the transport. He wasn't quite sure what idea she had knocking around in that head of hers, but somehow thought better than to ask.

"Here goes nothing!" he said loudly, then shouted to the cabin filled with his other siblings, "Hold on to something!"

"What's going on?" they all yelled almost simultaneously.

"Oh, not much, just a little something I call the 'spiraling dive of death!"

In an instant all of the children's eyes grew wide with – not fear – excitement!

They all moved quickly to their respective seats and strapped themselves in, with Caitlin taking extra care to make sure she was definitely, doubly, and absolutely tied in tight, with no chance of her strap coming loose as it had before.

"Everybody good back there?" Orion asked as he looked at Grace, who nodded having already strapped herself tight to her seat with her strange creations all blinking curiously in her hands.

One by one those in the main cabin yelled the word "Go!" and once the forth one had sounded clearly from Caitlin, the craft moved into a quick plunge, only just missing one missile that, as a result, crashed into another just above where he had changed directions. The resulting explosion caused quite a rumble and bright flash that made all those in the cabin suddenly nervous over what was happening.

True to his word, Orion forced the ship into a spiraling dive which Grace called a 'useless display of childish showmanship' considering that a normal dive would have done just as well. All the while the four *conscious* passengers in the cab were screaming fits of elation over the maneuver and once Orion pulled out of it at Grace's request they were all screaming "Again – Again," while laughing in hysterics.

Even Grace found herself smiling, but her smile faded quickly as both purpose and focus forced her to regain mental composure. She had initially assumed that they would have a certain degree of safety by keeping themselves low within the city's infrastructure for a few seconds, but with their transport now standing still amid the tall buildings, the smart missiles which had them targeted didn't hesitate to drop to these inter-building altitudes for the sake of attempting to destroy their target once again.

"Move!" Grace commanded, and, had Orion been a fraction of a second slower, their transport would have been blown to tiny bits raining down on the crowds below. Grace then ordered that Orion join the ranks of the regular transports, which were moving along standard flight patterns and, obviously, at much slower speeds.

"Are you crazy?" he said as he reluctantly approached one of the bustling paths of transports.

If one could equate the Los Angeles Metroship as a living entity, it would be these paths that could best be described as the city's veins and arteries. With its high speed circulation of people from one place to another the description seemed to fit. Now, however, it was clear that Grace wanted to preempt that flow by traveling much faster than any of the other transports.

"Listen," Grace said without looking at her brother, "these missiles are designed to avoid civilian casualties – I'm sure you can get through this city much faster than they can, and eventually they'll just have to rise above the city skyline just to avoid hitting buildings."

"Yeah, then what?" Orion asked as he was carefully weaving in and out of the other transports.

"Then we lose them..." Grace said with a smile.

"And how do you propose we do that?" Orion asked with snide disbelief.

"Hello!" she said waving one of the tiny blinking objects in her hands, "We send out decoys!"

"Oh – wait a minute..." Orion added with a serious tone, "what about civilian casualties – we can't trick a rocket into firing at a transport filled with innocent people."

"Not a problem!" Grace said with a smile, "if the missile gets close enough, it will see that the signal from the real transport and the fake one I'm going to attach are so close together, and it'll abandon its efforts because it, like you, will not risk innocent lives just to hit its target."

"The missiles will wait and wait, expecting that eventually the signals will separate. By the time any of the missiles've figured out what's going on, we'll be gone!"

"OK, so how long before you're ready..." Orion asked impatiently, as he too was feeling the wear and tear, but unlike his sibling's kinetic efforts, his was from having such a long running cyber link with the craft around him.

"Well," Grace grunted as she pulled hard on the release for her straps and she practically fell to the floor due to a shift of the transport. "Sorry," she said rolling over almost in laughter, "I think I'm ready now," and she pulled herself up to a kneeling position.

She looked out to the flow of traffic and pointed her finger at several of the other transports, "You're going to have to follow the other crafts to get close enough for me to attach these transmitters."

Orion, who wasn't looking at his sister for the sake of rapidly navigating the transport between both building and traffic, tilted his head forward and communicated telepathically, "Just let me know when you're ready. Let me know what you need. I'll deliver!"

She nodded her head as she left the emergency cockpit, and, stumbling through the cabin, she could feel and see that her other brothers' and sisters' eyes were on her. They curiously watched her every move as she made her way to the loading door, where she offered almost a grin at looking over Jay's rigid body.

"What's going on?" Johnny asked curiously, and with a quick turn of her head, Grace offered a sly wink to the entire cabin.

She returned her stare to the door. "I'm ready!" she sent to her brother telepathically, and in a few moments the door opened itself at Orion's willing it to. This would not have been an amazing thing on the ground, but traveling at high speeds alongside other transports, and with a polymerized person strapped to the door and a young girl ready to reach herself over an empty, freefalling gap – it made for very entertaining viewing for the spectators in the cabin.

Orion, who had targeted an unsuspecting transport, worked his way directly beside it. When he was just a few feet away from it Grace leaned out with one of the eight transmitters in her hand. She grabbed a handle cut in the frame of her own transport and braced herself, stretching her arm as far as it could go. But it seemed she still couldn't reach the other transport to attach the transmitter. She forced her arm out further and further –feeling the muscles in her arm pull all through to her fingertips, but still her reach was short of where it needed to be.

"Closer... closer..." she kept sending to Orion and as she did this she could see passengers from the other transport mouthing words to each other. Indeed, had she seen what she was doing from their perspective, she was quite certain she'd have something to say just as well, but she tried to ignore the many onlookers as their faces came closer and closer until –

Boy – did that woman just call me a boy! And – that – that man just called me a boy too! And – they're all pointing. Boy – boy – boy!

Grace turned her face angrily and with a quick punch of her hand she hit the other transport in anger. Fortunately the transmitter was wedged between her fingers and, aside from relieving a little frustration; she completed the task of sticking the transmitter to the first transport.

Looking up she could see that all of the missiles were now following closely above the skyline of the city, and as she pulled herself back inside her own transport, she could see several of the missiles veer off from the pack as the decoy transport had changed directions while they had not.

"It's working!" she relayed to her brother in an almost telepathic scream, and this was followed shortly by "Okay – Next!"

Orion continued to target transports as he weaved his way in and out of traffic making sure to proceed in a direction that brought him closer and closer to the edge of the city. Meanwhile, one by one Grace tagged different transports, each heading in a different direction, causing more *smart missiles* to fall victim to the simple misdirection she had created.

Once she was rid of the last transmitter Grace looked skyward to see if she had distracted all of the missiles.

"Urrrgh!"

Frustrated, she could see that nearly a dozen were still tracking them, no doubt by the heat of their engines rather than the transmitted signature beacon of the craft.

Damn! Grace thought pulling her head back in the transport, and the entire cabin seemed to pick up on this pathic thought as her siblings quickly jerked their heads.

"What's wrong?" Aspen asked curiously, and as Grace turned her head, everyone could see that she was deep in thought, biting her lip as she made her way back to the emergency cockpit at the front of the transport.

She pathically told Orion that they were still being followed by more missiles and that they had to find a way of getting out of the city without a heat signature.

It was as these words fell out of her head that her eyes quickly lit up. She offered a grin to Orion and a few seconds later she hurried out to her siblings.

"You and you!" she commanded pointing at David and Aspen, "Get ready – we need you to levitate the ship when I tell you!"

"What!" Aspen retorted with panicked surprise.

"We've got to shut it down! The missiles are still tracking our heat!" Grace grunted in an obviously irritated tone.

"Shutting down the ship won't get rid of our heat – the engines will still be hot afterward!" David retorted in confusion over a plan he felt had no chance of success.

"Ugh," Grace sighed as she was tiring of having to explain herself repeatedly. "We're going to shut down the engines and let the craft freefall with the vents open – the airflow should cool down the engines pretty quick. You two will keep us from crashing, and guide the craft to safety.

Aspen shook her head vigorously, "Are you crazy?"

"It's our only chance to make it out of the city. These missiles won't let up until they've hit their target, and we need to hurry before the others get smart and catch on to the decoys."

"But..." David started to argue before Grace quickly waved her hand in his face. "This discussion is over – you need to be ready, I'm going back up front – listen for our signal."

She proceeded to the emergency cockpit, and thought it best to completely ignore David and Aspen who were still making efforts to change her mind showing both expressions of fear and doubt.

"What's going on?" Orion asked, quite curious over his sister's actions.

"Well – here's the deal..." she said with a deep breath and she proceeded to offer the details of her plan yet again.

"But" Orion started, "there are only a few of those things left, why don't we let Aspen and David just take care of them?"

"Smart missiles – remember? You don't think they'll know something's up when other missiles are just exploding for no reason?"

"Ahhhh!" Orion said with a nod, and he gripped the controls, "well, I'll keep hold of the controls to try to keep from hitting anything..."

"Sorry," Grace said putting her hand over his, "The hydraulic system is electrically managed, they'll be shut down too – all that'll be operating are the digital thermometers on the engines.

"Hmmm," Orion said with uncertainty, "We'll have to time this just right then."

"Of course," Grace said with a sideways grin, "Would you expect anything less than perfection?"

The girl then strapped herself in as Orion asked seriously, "Are they ready?" nodding to the back of the transport.

"Of course they are!" she lied as she pointed a direction for him to guide the transport, and as he did so, he also made sure to slowly force the craft to fly just under the existing traffic. This served the purpose of temporarily hiding their heat signature as well as giving them a clear shot to freefall without impacting other transports.

"Well, here goes nothing!" she said, and she offered her brother a quick glance and a nod.

Orion forced the engine intake vents fully open just before shutting down the engines and releasing control of the vessel. Grace was manic in her efforts to switch off every piece of equipment required to run the craft. Bit by bit lights were turning off until all that was left in the cockpit was a digital readout on a tiny display in the center of the controls. All the while the cabin was filled with the dual sounds of screams of elation and horror.

As Grace watched the digital closely for the temperature drop, she kept mumbling the number 10 degrees over and over.

This was, as she had known from her prior research of the SMX design, the thermal differential threshold. Outside, she knew the temperature was somewhere near 38 C. This meant that the engines would have to drop to 48 or less in order to be undetectable to the missiles.

The entire craft was shaking with the fall, and in a panic Grace watched as another transport took off from a nearby building and headed straight for their own craft. Very unexpectedly the freefalling transport shifted its direction quite rapidly and thereby avoiding the oncoming craft.

She turned her head to Orion who was focusing with a very concentrated look out the front window.

"Good work!" she breathed stiffly as she was talking shortly from excitement. He turned to shift his stare repeatedly between his sister and the digital temperature gauge.

She looked at the gauge herself and noticed the temperature of the engines was reading near 50 degrees. In a panic she yelled at the cabin for Aspen and David. "Now!" she screamed, noticing that there was less than 300 feet between the transport and the hard, unforgiving pavement.

While the craft was slowing down considerably, the approach was still fast. Both Orion and Grace looked meaningfully with furrowed brows, out the front window of the transport in an effort to help in kinetically keeping it from impact.

With a lurching force that caused her shoulders to ache against the straps that held her body in place, Grace squinted and grunted in pain, but when she opened her eyes again, she was met with the panicked stares of several pedestrians who were walking at ground level. Those who were not staring at the craft and those who were either covering their heads or running for cover, were completely unaware of the fact that the craft had stopped some thirty or so feet from the ground, and that they, those on the ground, were safe.

"We've got to get moving. Now!" Grace said insistently. She was certain that with enough notification from those on the ground who witnessed the almost fatal crash, the missiles would probably divert from their eight other targets.

Johnny, who had unbuckled himself from his seat, poked his head through the emergency cockpit door, "You two had better get a look at this!" he said as he waved for both Orion and Grace to come back to the main cabin.

They complied in a rush, bumping into each other as they made their way. What they saw when they did get out of the cockpit was quite amazing.

Aspen and David, who were sitting next to each other during the fall, were now holding hands and gritting their teeth with their eyes closed in hard concentration.

"I've tried talking to them, but they won't say anything." Johnny professed.

Grace reached her hand out to tap David on the shoulder, but this was intervened by Orion, who grabbed her hand while shaking his head. "I wouldn't recommend that." He said softly before adding. "I think it's all they can do just to keep this thing in the air – it's got to weigh several tons."

"But..." Grace started, but Orion wasn't finished and interrupted her question.

"They're just keeping this thing in the air – *We* have to get it out of the city."

Grace turned her head to the emergency cockpit. "Well, if it's up to us, I guess we'd better get busy!"

Orion nodded his head saying "Right!" before the two once again entered the transport's emergency cockpit.

With relative ease both Orion and Grace used their newfound kinesis to guide the craft to the edge of the city. All the while keeping their eyes peeled for any approaching smart missiles or police transports.

But there seemed to be nothing keeping the children from crossing the city's edge. This edge, this dividing line between freedom and capture, was only a few hundred feet away. Annoyingly close for all of them to have to go through so much just to cross it undetected. Just the same, they looked out of the transport's forward windows in euphoria and expectation as the massive north wall approached. Indeed, around all of the metroships stood massive 2000 foot walls which were a minimum of 100 feet thick. These walls were designed for the dual purpose of keeping the unwanted out, and keeping the wanted, or hunted in.

Slowly pointing the craft upward, Orion and Grace spotted a standard inter-metro traveling route, which they approached from the underside and used as camouflage in order to physically cross the border unseen, though there was little else that could give them away by standard detection.

"Woah!" Orion said softly as the transport made its way over the wall, for his eyes met with bountiful shades of green that skirted around high mountain tops all contrasted against the bright blue sky. Nowhere inside the cities borders could a person see such natural beauty, and it was for this reason that everyone who was able in the transport looked out and slowly filled with the same sense of wonder over what they saw.

Once over and beyond the high dividing border, the transport craft lowered very closely down the side of the wall and as the children looked out the windows, they could see that the green all around them was developing slowly into tall trees of all sorts standing a hundred feet tall or more and offering shade when Orion had found a place where he could slip the transport under the foliage.

This being done, he and Grace worked tirelessly to navigate between the trees in an effort to finally put some distance between them and the city that they once called their home.

With the darkness from the trees overtaking the transport, all inside felt a sense of change - change from the lives they had lived, and while each child reflected differently on the past they were leaving behind, all of their minds couldn't help but gravitate on the same immediate thought; short term memories of the past several hours, memories of the council telling them that they were to be separated from the only father that they'd ever known... and for Johnny, memories of a vision that kept coming back into his and Taylor's mind, a vision that the young boy linked directly to the city and hoped he would never see again.

The transport took the children into a new and unknown life, and into this unknown they went willingly, but not unprepared. They had the tools needed for survival, and they all knew that Taylor was the most important tool they had brought with them. Those who were able stared at either their unconscious teacher, their solidified mentor, or at each other. Abating their nervousness and doubt, was their love for each other. This was their sole reason for escape, and right now, this singular driving force was enough of a reason to leave everything else behind without a moment of regret.

PART THREE

OLD WORLD NEW WORLD

41 Into the Forest

TO LEAVE ONE WORLD BEHIND and enter another would've been difficult for the children, especially Johnny, but they had Taylor and with any luck this man would be able to bring Jay into repair. And even though there was a foreboding darkness that shrouded over the transport carrying the six children, their tools, and their mentors, they were all still filled with hope and what love they needed to build a home outside the world where they had been raised. So weaving in and out of trees, with glints of light flashing over their half sober, half excited faces, it was Orion who was focused hard on finding an adequate place to settle down and hopefully call home.

After a good twenty minutes the boy motioned for Grace to help direct the craft in a direction just to the left of where they were headed. Slowly the transport turned and made its way to a very dark, very dreary looking corner of the massive forest around them.

"Here!" He said as he pointed downward; a signal that they should land.

"Are you freakin' crazy? Why here? It's the darkest..." Grace started, sounding very confused not to mention disgusted at her brother's location choice.

"Exactly! Dark means lots of cover – it'll be harder for them to see us." Orion said blandly pointing his finger straight up.

Grace took this as he had meant – a reference to satellites that were always scouring the planet's surface keeping track of the "unregistered" population in an effort to make sure the off-grid communities didn't get out of control. With this understanding the two slowly lowered the craft and as they did so it settled rather unevenly.

Unstrapping herself quickly, Grace moved to the back of the transport and checked on both David and Aspen. They, with their heads hanging low – almost between their knees, were rubbing their temples quite purposefully.

With Orion following Grace out of the cockpit, both Johnny and Caitlin joined in surrounding the two kinetics to see that they were okay.

"Are you alright?" Caitlin asked both curious and concerned.

"Fine!" Aspen said forcefully, "just have a headache,"

"And we're hungry as heck!" David added and with that it seemed that the whole half-dozen of them now realized how consumed with hunger they were.

"I've gotta get some air." Orion said shaking his own head slowly and after untying the encapsulated body of Jay from the loading door, he opened it with a quick stare. This let a rush of warm, thick, and strange smelling air into the craft. The boy waved his hand in front of his nose for a moment, and just as he attempted to take his first step off the craft, he fell hard on the ground outside.

Both leaping from the ship, Grace and Caitlin made their way around their brother and pulled him back into the transport.

David, knowing instantly what was wrong, pulled out one of the bags he had brought for the trip, opened it, and started tossing proto-bars to each of his brothers and sisters. "Here," he said with a smile, "I was saving these for later, but I think we could all use one now."

Grace, who had worked tirelessly by Orion's side during their flight from The Towers, didn't even consider the drain it would take on him to control the ship for so long. She unwrapped the chocolate flavored nutrition bar and started feeding it to him slowly.

After only a few seconds Orion opened his eyes, grabbed the bar, and started eating it ravenously and it was after a few seconds of this, with only the sounds of chewing working into the quiet of the transport, that David broke the verbal silence.

"So – wha' a' we gomma do mow?" David asked, his mouth overflowing with bits of food. He had been eating, as it seemed, more greedily than even Orion, and thus completely abandoned all care for manners.

"Best thing we can do is to wait for Father to wake up." Aspen said shaking her head at her brother's lack of etiquette. All eyes turned at this point to Taylor, whose head was showing signs of reddening from the use of the shock stick. Patient and quiescent, the children all sat around Taylor for nearly a half hour before he finally started to rouse. He started to groan and move slightly, then, with all the children staring at him, Johnny was the first to speak the obvious.

"Look!" he said excitedly, "the last zap's wearing off!"

"Last zap?" Orion and Grace both asked in a surprised tone.

"Well, yeah! I had to keep zapping him like every ten minutes or so just to keep him under." Johnny said this in a matter of fact way as though he had done nothing wrong, but Grace was concerned, and quickly rushed to Taylor's side. She lightly slapped his face a few times and propped his weight under her tiny frame while the others helped and in a few seconds the teen was sitting quite comfortably on one of the bench seats in the transport.

Rubbing his forehead Taylor started to look around. With a snap in his neck, and instantly large eyes, he realized he wasn't where he last remembered being, and he stared quickly and purposefully around the transport, checking all the faces that were staring at him, trying to gain his bearings for the situation in which he now found himself and make sure the children were okay.

His eyes stopped on Jay, whose rock hard form was sitting on the transport floor near the loading door.

"What happened?" Taylor asked looking again to his students for answers.

"Well," Johnny started almost with a grin, though his voice was trembling with nervousness. "We kind of – escaped," he said lowly, leading into what he was certain would be shock on the part of Taylor.

"Escaped!" Taylor said angrily, "What do you mean '*escaped*'?" The teen stood but nearly passed out from still being very light headed after the many shocks he'd been given by the youngest over the course of the trip. "You're – you're – I'm – we're..." Taylor was almost in a panic over what he'd heard and it took Johnny, who pulled Taylor's face to stare eye to eye with his own to calm him down.

"Father – It's okay we're fine!" Johnny said softly.

"It's not that!" Taylor said firmly, but at least more calmly than before. "We're all wanted now – and I'm not sure if they think I'm a criminal or not!"

Taylor put his hand on his head, stood up quickly, and once again, with his eyes rolling backward, he sat with a slump with his legs collapsing beneath him.

"Dad! You need to relax!" This time the voice came from three different directions; Johnny, Aspen and Caitlin, all showing faces of unease.

"Relax! – How are we supposed to live? – What are we supposed to do now – *Run* for the rest of our lives?! You kids – you just don't – don't think! Whose idea was this anyways?" Taylor was now talking both loud and angry. He was visibly upset over what was happening, and he could see that his mood was spreading to his children, but this was none more present than in Orion.

"You knew this was coming – and you didn't do anything... you'd let them just take us!" Orion shouted across the transport. "We all knew this was coming!" he repeated as he made his way to the loading door, and on jumping out onto the soft brown forest floor he offered one last statement, though he didn't turn back to see the effect it had.

"Look around you, *Taylor*. Tell me if what you see makes sense. Tell me *this* wasn't meant to be?"

Taylor, who felt a pain in his heart on hearing Orion refer to his name so sarcastically, did as he was told, even if the order came from a child, and started glancing around the transport half trying to understand what Orion was talking about, and when his eyes landed on Grace's face, still partly covered in dried blood, yet clearly showing the cut that had pained her several hours before, he knew.

"Your vision!" Taylor said whirling his head around to Johnny, "It – it came true?!"

Johnny, along with the other children nodded their heads. "Everything!" The boy said in an excited half whisper.

Orion, however, was so upset that he had started pacing, his face growing both red, and tear filled from anger.

Looking from the transport, Taylor called out, "Orion, you get back here right now!" but this didn't seem to have an effect on the boy, who had continued to walk away. "Orion, I'm talking to you!" Taylor persisted, but Orion continued walking, taking more steps, and with each one the child's face grew angrier still, especially at hearing Taylor's stern tone. Taylor, on the other hand, was growing desperate to keep Orion close to the transport, unsure of where they had landed or how safe it was.

"I'm sorry!" Taylor yelled, and he repeated the apology, this time replacing his desperation with sincerity. This had the immediate effect of forcing Orion to stop dead in his tracks. The boy turned his head slowly around and looked over his shoulder back at Taylor, who was still sitting quite uselessly on the bench seat inside the transport.

"Was it your idea to bring the M-Gen?" Taylor asked more calmly as he waved for the boy to return to the transport. The teen had only just noticed the M-Gen sitting in the back of the transport, and, in his own mind, the tiny idea that this escape might work started to grow in his mind. Maybe they could somehow live out normal lives far away from the city.

"No, it was Grace!" Orion said as he stood perfectly still and perfectly without want to return to the transport.

"Hmmmm." Taylor hummed as he continued to look about – "and obviously you've stolen this transport – no doubt you've been chased all the way to the edge of the city – I would ask how you managed to elude the police transports, but I think I've got a pretty good idea." He said this loudly and almost at a laugh in an attempt to show Orion that his anger had all but completely left. While this wasn't entirely true, Taylor did have one thought in the back of his mind – *What's done is done. Now we can only make the best of it!*

"Police transports!" David spewed, his face still half covered in chocolate. "They were the least of our problems! Try smart missiles – they were on our tail right 'til the end!"

"Smart missiles – what model?" Taylor pressed with his eyes and his voice growing in severity.

"X" Grace said matter-of-factly, and she bounded out of the transport to tend to Orion. This, as it turned out, was a failed attempt to get him to return to the craft.

At this point, it wasn't that Orion wanted to stay outside because he was still upset over Taylor's anger. Orion, rather, decided to stay outside because he now found himself a very comfortable log on which to sit, and it happened to be in a relatively cool place outside the transport. This being made clear to Grace, Orion felt little reason, or effort to want to move at all.

"He's not mad anymore. He's just resting." Grace told the group quite plainly on her return, and as they all sat looking about the transport with what seemed an interminably uncomfortable silence, Taylor caused them to snap at quick attention when he addressed them quite purposefully.

"So what's first?" He asked of the group looking between their faces.

"Well," said Aspen, who had been quite the wallflower since Taylor had become conscious, "As I see it there are two things we have to address."

Her brothers and sisters were looking at her as though whatever she might say would be nonsensical. "There's him!" she said pointing at Jay, who was still safely stored in the hardened polymer, "and there's that!" she said pointing at the M-Gen sitting at the back of the transport.

"Good! At least we're headed in the right direction," Taylor said and he made his way over to the M-Gen to inspect it closely. "Ripped it clear from the wall did ya?" he asked rhetorically, and all at once the children in the transport felt their stomachs lurch with the terrifying thought that doing what they had to free the unit might have caused it to become unusable. Slowly their faces drew to obvious expressions of concern and doubt. Taylor saw this and quickly decided to lighten the mood.

"No worries! No worries! It can be fixed, and it can be used. It will just take some time to get everything figured out." Taylor then stood, braced himself firmly, now expecting the possibility that he might be just as lightheaded as before, and carefully readied himself to step out of the transport.

He was able to get outside, all the while being closely watched by the children around him, and he walked over to Orion, who was facing away from the transport. He put his hand on the boy's shoulder, then pulled his arm fully around the child's neck and chest in a calming hug. For Orion, this offered the quick effect of him lightly flinching for he hadn't expected it, but this dissolved into feeling of comfort and relief that the boy was all too ready to receive.

Orion looked up at Taylor and offered an almost apologetic smile. "I'm sorry I walked out like that!" he said as he stood and turned to return to Taylor an equally unexpected hug. Orion was never much on showing emotion, but it seemed that with so many changes going on in his life, and for that matter, everyone else's lives, Taylor could expect to see some shifts in the behavior he'd grown accustomed to from each of them.

"It's Okay, I understand." Taylor said, all the while looking wildly about at the dark, dank surroundings. He was quite impressed with how complete and thick the coverage was from overhead with nary a ray of light making its way through the trees.

Taking a few deep breaths of the humid, somewhat musty air from the forest, Taylor turned and made his way back into the transport, stepping slowly with Orion at his side.

The children were intrigued and fully ready to explore their new surroundings, especially now that they felt safe with Taylor being awake and aware. So, with hardly a thought, they quietly made their way in different directions, each looking for something to catch their own interest.

"Don't go too far," Taylor shouted pathically after them as they headed off, "and stay under tree cover at all times!" he added. With this, he watched the children distance themselves from the transport while he, himself, started rummaging through the tool bag Grace and brought. Looking for schematics, for tools, and in some cases, hoping for a miracle, Taylor was happy to find that it most cases this brilliant little girl had brought exactly what he needed.

Realizing that the versatility of an M-Gen would solve nearly every problem they could encounter away from the city, Taylor's hands and his kinesis were all working hard with the tools he had in an effort to not only modify this stolen unit to work on its own, but he also needed to find a way to link it to the transport's power supply at least long enough to perform a standard boot and some basic pattern downloads.

He smiled almost to the point of laughter several times during the process of his repairs, noting how well prepared Grace was when it came to what he needed. In particular her toolkit was a priceless commodity for the repairs he had to perform. She had nearly every tool imaginable, so during the several hours it took him in working diligently on the absconded M-Gen he had little need or requirement that wasn't met inside the kit, or inside arms reach.

In the quiet of the forest, however, Taylor jumped at one point when Johnny popped his head in the transport quite unexpectedly. "How much longer, I'm starving!" the child said with his hand rubbing his stomach quite obviously.

"Indeed!" Taylor replied offering a look that meant something more like "So what! Can't you see I'm busy!" but without actually saying the words. Taylor did, though, take a moment to check the time on his locator ring: 7:30PM.

Taylor then watched Johnny slowly make his way back outside, then between several trees before disappearing. Looking down at the M-Gen panel before him, he took a deep sigh, returning again to his previous task. Lifting wire and several tools kinetically, Taylor lowered his head to slowly begin his work again, but his eyes and his thoughts shot back up in a flinch.

"The rings!" Taylor hissed, and he darted out of the transport, looking wildly around to see if any of the students were still close by. At first glance he couldn't see any of them, but after a few seconds, the sounds of nearby steps revealed that Johnny and David were already making their way back to the transport. Taylor rushed to them with an almost panicked expression on his face.

"Those rings I gave you, where are they?"

Without a moment's thought, both boys raised their right hands to reveal the gold bands resting on their middle fingers.

Taylor, watching and forcing at the same time, cyberly activated the rings and entered the password for their removal before causing the rights to lift off the boys' hands and fly overhead. He caught them in mid air and took them inside the transport. When he returned where the boys were standing he had in his hand a small metal box rattling with the rings inside.

"Do you need to find the other rings?" Johnny asked curiously as he gazed on Taylor's wildly shifting head.

"Yes!" Taylor said without looking at the boy, "Where are the others?"

"Sure!" Johnny said, and he turned quickly, pointing his fingers in two opposed directions, narrating the locations of his siblings.

"Caitlin's that way with Aspen – they found a really cool stream. Grace went that way, she's with Orion. I think they were going to try practicing their kinesis on rocks and stuff."

Taylor made his way back into the transport and with the loud sounds of clanging objects falling to the transport's metal floor the two boys looked at each other quite puzzled. Seconds later Taylor came out from the transport holding a second small metal box. He reached out and handed this new one to David.

"Here!" he said forcefully, "you two, find Orion and Grace, get their rings and put them in this! The password is T O L K I E N"

The boy's stared at Taylor, confused by the odd password, but did as they were told. In snatching the metal box from Taylor, David recognized it as one of Grace's all purpose parts holder. He looked at his brother and, with a jerk of his head toward the forest, the two ran off into the tall trees disappearing from view in seconds.

Taylor made his way in the direction Johnny had pointed for Aspen and Caitlin, hoping that the stream the boy spoke of wasn't too far. At first Taylor thought it would be a good idea to call out their names to get their attention, but decided against this rationalizing that he didn't want to attract any attention – *any attention.*

As Taylor made his way through the trees, sometimes using his kinesis to push branches out of the way, he kept thinking of how stupid it was for him not to think of the danger of having those rings, or worse, that he actually used his own without thinking of the consequences. With the occasional leaf or branch wiping across his face Taylor was determined not to slow down until he'd reached the girls and put their rings in the tiny container he'd pulled from Grace's toolkit.

In his mind, he could connect the dots as such: his life, now that he'd escaped from the city and from The Towers, was certainly under great scrutiny. With this, it would take little time for the authorities to come across the purchase of these rings, and with how many he had purchased it would be pretty obvious what their purpose was. It would therefore only be a matter of time before those authorities, no doubt lead by Dr. Zeldin, would then track the signals used by those rings to help locate he and the children.

Taylor continued to rush through the trees, his legs seeming to move faster and faster as the fear of their capture washed over him. So much was this fear that in front of him, Taylor's kinesis was now wedging an obvious path straight ahead. He was now flexing large and small trees alike out of his way so as to provide the most direct path to where he hoped the girls would be.

All at once Taylor slowed his pace when he heard a voice seemingly in the distance, and yet nearby at the same time – "There he is... There he is – d'you see him?"

Taylor's heart dropped as he thought to himself – *Am I too late?*

42 The River

SPLASH – SPLASH – SPLASH – Without seeing it, Taylor had stumbled into a small stream that weaved its way through the floor of the forest. He stopped, knowing he was close to his destination, before walking again. Looking around as he went, he made his way to the center of the stream where it was deepest, but also where he could get the best view of its banks with the hope of spotting Aspen and Caitlin.

"Someone's coming!" Taylor heard a voice say, and his head jerked around almost in a panic. He only just noticed the rustling of trees on the side of the stream, and despite the darkness due to the thick coverage, Taylor could make out Aspen's brightly colored dress.

Taylor trudged to the edge of the water and made his way up its edge, hoping to catch up with the girls on dry ground.

"He's running!" Taylor heard the voice, a female voice, say, but this time he wasn't certain that what he was hearing was an actual voice.

"Who is that?" asked the same voice, and it was clear now to Taylor that the voice was inside his head. This voice quickly overlapped itself answering the questions it asked almost immediately.

"I don't know." the voice said, with the addition of "I can't see his face – come on – turn around – turn around!"

Taylor was panicked as he made his way to both Caitlin and Aspen. He thought that maybe they had spotted someone – maybe one of them was conversing telepathically and he was picking up on it. Maybe the girls were trying to approach someone they saw in the forest – someone they wanted to *turn around.* Taylor knew this was a bad idea and he made way down the stream as fast as he could manage.

Not wanting to get the girls' attention until he was close enough to protect them, Taylor quickly ran into the trees and made his way along the stream's edge, yet far enough in the woods so as to not be easily spotted.

"What's he running for?" He heard the voice in his head speak again.

"He's afraid of something!" the voice quickly responded to itself.

Running faster and faster, Taylor finally caught up to the girls, but to his bewilderment he could see that neither of them were talking, nor were they focused on anyone they could see. Rather, the two of them were simply walking along the stream tossing rocks into it just for fun.

"Ooohhh! There are girls with him!" Taylor heard inside his head, and for the first time he realized this second telepathic voice was that of a male. He had been wrong about where the messages had been coming from.

"Father what's wrong?" Caitlin asked as Taylor rushed down to get their attention. Not so far distracted by the voices in his head that he couldn't remember his purpose for finding them, Taylor quickly grabbed both Caitlin and Aspen's hands, cybered their rings into action, entered the password, and pulled their rings off. With two clunks, he dropped the rings in the tiny metal tool container he'd brought with him. Taylor felt a small sense of relief at doing this, but as soon as he closed the container his eyes and head quickly turned, looking sharply into the trees.

"Oh – he's cute!" the female voice said with a quick question to follow. "What's he looking for?"

Taylor continued to listen inside his own head as several comments came streaming from their unknown source. But Taylor had his own questions – *Where were these voices coming from? Who's watching us?*

These questions seemed to be met with more unwanted telepathic inquiries coming from some unidentifiable source.

"Is he dangerous?"

"He's from the city, of course he's dangerous." the voice responded to itself sternly. "But he has children with him!" the voice quickly retorted on itself, and at this Taylor realized that the voice, wherever it was coming from, was more afraid of him than the reverse.

Must be an outsider – someone off the grid! – Taylor thought, yet he still looked around, uneasy about the fact that he was being watched by someone he couldn't see.

Snapping his head around in odd directions, Taylor's concern slowly bled to the children at his side. Caitlin and Aspen were both showing confused looks to Taylor for his actions before they too started looking into the trees trying to spy what it was that worried him so much. Reaching up and grabbing his hands, Caitlin at his left and Aspen his right, it was Caitlin who spoke first.

"Maybe we should get back to the transport." She said this with a nervous, almost quivering tone. She had quickly adopted Taylor's paranoid behavior by looking at all directions into the trees whereas her sister was staring focused in a single direction, though neither knew what they were looking for. Caitlin's immediate thought, however, was that if Taylor had reason to be concerned then there was definitely something to be worried about.

"The girls must be his!" The voice chimed in Taylor's head and he quickly looked down at Caitlin, squeezed her hand firmly and thereafter did the same with Aspen's.

"Can you hear that?" Taylor asked of the two girls. But their response was two sets of confused eyes staring back at him housed in shaking heads.

"Hear what?" Aspen asked as she turned to stare into the trees where she had been looking before.

"Er – I don't know – I keep hearing eh..." Taylor paused, looked down at the faces of the girls, and decided it was better not to tell the truth. "Never mind! Let's get back to the transport..." With that the three of them made their way back into the woods at a rapid pace.

"Let's see where they're headed." Taylor heard the male voice say very slyly. With these words, the teen was compelled to stop instantly some fifty feet into the rough. He told the girls to stay put near a large pine while he made his way back to the stream.

With a few slow steps into the water, the chill of it causing his toes to curl, Taylor turned to face where he believed his unseen watcher was. He waited for a few minutes standing quite exposed to the high trees around him when he heard, again, a female voice resonate inside his brain.

"Why did he turn around? – What does he want? Why is he here?" were three simultaneous comments he heard and could just barely decipher them from each other. Another voice, a different one, also entered into his brain.

"This isn't good. – We're not safe. – Why now?" This voice was different, it was the same male voice he'd heard before and as such, it was clear that there were only two watching him from the trees, one female and one male.

Well, it's now or never – Taylor thought, and with that he took a deep breath.

"I don't want anything – And you are safe!" Taylor shouted into the trees. "I'm here – we're here because we've – *escaped* from the city!" Taylor paused at saying this and he waited to hear the voice again.

"Who's he talking to?" sounded the male voice, followed by the female, "What's he mean 'escaped from the city'"

"Oh for heaven's sake" – Taylor pleaded in a whisper and he once again began yelling into nothingness, yet watching the trees very closely for activity.

"I'm talking to whoever it is that's watching me from the trees! I can hear your thoughts! Now why don't you just make nice and show yourself." Just as soon as the words left his mouth he saw a rustling of the high branches on the other side of the stream nearly a hundred feet away.

"Not possible! – Not possible! – have to tell the others!"

Taylor heard these words over and over in both the male and female voice as he trudged his way across the stream. When he made it to the other side he ran toward the trees that had shaken.

"He's made us!" the male voice said and this was followed by a strange sequence of words.

"Set – pull – aim – lead – release..."

With a quick whistle through the air, Taylor knew what was coming and he raised his hand in time to both kinetically slow and physically catch an arrow whizzing through the air. He was amazed at how accurate the aim was, for he knew that had he not caught it, the arrow would have shot straight through the center of his chest.

Dropping the weapon, Taylor looked long and hard at the trees in front of him, but he could see no activity. In his head, however, he could hear the words "not possible – 't's not possible" and other ways of saying this same phrase over and over again.

Taylor could only imagine that shortly after shooting the arrow, whoever it was had darted off, escaping through the trees. The teen thought of running through the thick woods on the other side of the stream, but felt there was little purpose. Whoever was there was long gone, and headed in a direction nowhere near their transport.

Disappointed that he couldn't make a friendly first contact with the outsiders living in the forest, Taylor made his way back to the girls and decided it best to find the others and remain close to the transport.

On trying to get back to where he left the girls, he saw that they were standing at the stream's edge, unable, as most children aren't, to actually listen to what they were told. Taylor could see the fear on their faces from the fact that their guardian had just been attacked. But he just grabbed their hands lightly offering them a simple statement to help keep them calm.

"Don't worry girls – I think they're more frightened of us than we are of them."

"I wouldn't be so sure of that!" Caitlin said, her face showing a dreadful look of terror as she eyed the arrow Taylor was still holding.

Taylor looked down at the girls with a smile, "Come on. Let's get back to the transport. I think it will at least be safer if we're all together until we can get things settled."

With a swift walk, the three made their way back to the transport, where they saw Grace, David, Johnny, and Orion huddled around the replicator with Grace actually holding tools and apparently *repairing the M-Gen!*

"Don't..." Taylor yelled as he watched Grace reach for a splicing tool. "Don't even think about it!"

43 Voices Only Two Can Hear

GRACE, ALONG WITH THE OTHER CHILDREN, stood with a jolt. The girl, tool in hand, offered Taylor a happy look of surprise before handing Taylor the tool she was about to use.

"*We're* practically finished – just gotta splice the transport's power supply to it."

Grace said this with both confidence and an expression of eager anticipation over Taylor's approval. Taylor, however, only offered a glance of skepticism with words to match. "Yeah right!" He said as he put his hand on the girl's shoulder, walking around her to inspect the M-Gen more closely.

With several nods of his head and an occasional "hmmmm," Taylor started laughing, forcing Grace's face to instantly turn sour. Taylor immediately reversed this with a quick... "Oh – it's fine – fine – fine indeed. I'm just so – impressed!"

Grace's face twisted into a now pained but smirked expression, something Taylor hadn't seen on the girl in some time. He liked what he saw and noticed that she was happier amid the attention she received from her brothers and sisters, especially with David patting her painfully hard on the back, which she returned by punching him hard on the shoulder. But what made her most happy and made her eyes light up was when Taylor put the splicing tool back in her hand.

"Would you like to do the honors?" He asked with a beguiling grin.

She didn't need asking twice before snatching the tool from Taylor's hand. She then approached the transport's auxiliary power panel located just forward of the loading door. She pulled up the bulky supply cable from the M-Gen and readied the tool for splicing.

It would have been easy to just plug the cable into the panel directly, but as the M-Gen was ripped from its housing, there wasn't a proper plug at the end of the power cables. Splicing was the only option. To make matters more difficult for Grace, these power supply cables were heavy and extremely difficult to hold and splice at the same time. Having dropped them three different times, Orion finally jumped into assist his sister in completing her task.

"There's one – two – three – four!" Grace said as she carefully and clumsily spliced each large cable directly into the panel. She stood back to inspect what she had done, but was quickly shifted aside by Taylor, who felt it best to look over such an important part of this happenstance repair for himself.

"Hmmmm – good – okay. Now let's get some power..." Taylor said as he turned to look at his students with a wink.

Taylor focused on the transport, causing it to power up slowly, making sure to keep the anti-gravity engines offline. He then quickly shifted his stare to the M-Gen, and with a great pounding of hope in his chest, he watched the tiny diagnostic readout light up and after a few seconds it showed lines of hard written code flashing rapidly on the screen before finally resting on the word "READY:_"

Taylor, who was immediately excited over the idea that there were no errors detected in the startup diagnostics, focused on the unit's screen. Watching as he forced lines of code to come into view before being edited at high speed, Taylor at least, knew that things were moving in the right direction. And after the flash of several of these pages of this code, which he modified, the protocols of the M-Gen were hopefully reconfigured to handle a new and stand alone nature. Orion and Grace were probably the only ones who knew that, in fact, had Taylor not done this, the unit would have believed itself to be part of a larger network where it would expect to find its replication patterns online.

On finishing editing the code Taylor quickly stepped inside the transport for a few seconds, and came back out carrying two of the backpacks the children had brought.

"Let's see if we can find something to replicate" Taylor said as he opened one of the bags. "Wha – what the... there's nothing but data-pads in here!"

At this the children started giggling around him, and his eyes grew wide with a presumed understanding. "Do these have – eh – do these all have patterns in them." All around the children nodded their heads, and Taylor almost laughed as he stuck his hand in one of the bags to pull out one of the pads. "You guys really did plan ahead..." he said with a smile.

Holding the pad in his hands, Taylor focused on it for a moment, forcing it to turn on with a bright flash. This was immediately subdued with a dark screen and a flashing red message reading:

"Warning – Memory full – please delete files/programs to increase available space."

Taylor quickly tapped away the message and began scrolling down a long list of M-Gen ready patterns – he saw that this one was completely filled with different patterns for boy's clothes – more specifically he saw that these patterns were of only boy's shirts.

Taylor was confused at first to see such a finite list of items in this data pad, but then his brain wrapped around the real scope of what all these data pads had loaded in them. Each pad, from what Taylor could see, held at least 1000 patterns in it, and as Taylor counted the bags the children had brought, he estimated that they must have generated and some 500 or more pads – that is, of course as Taylor assumed, if all of the bags were all filled with the same thing.

As Taylor's realized the children's ingenious plan, he couldn't help but ask, "If all these bags have data pads, and all the pads are loaded with patterns – you must have loaded – eh – How many patterns did you load?" He asked this in a tone filled with wonder and was met with a quick response.

"Oh, not all the bags have patterns" Orion said almost in a laugh as if somewhere between defending their actions, and yet being amused at the same time.

"This bag," He said walking up to Taylor and grabbing one that had not opened yet, "is full of extra data, programs, all of your virtual training classes, and your lab data covering every stage of our experiment and let's not forget – courses for our finished education."

Taylor nodded his head with a smirk. He was now even more impressed than before, "As far as how many patterns we've loaded," Orion continued offering a sly grin to his siblings, "somewhere just under half a million. If you're interested, the bag you're holding is full of guy's clothes and accessories. That bag over there," Orion said pointing randomly inside the transport, "is filled with girls clothes – Those two have food – that one has other equipment – and well – we tried to think of just about everything."

"I can see that," Taylor said as he approached the M-Gen, with the pad in hand. "But most of these are brand-name patterns that have to be paid for – you can't have bought all of these eh..." Taylor looked at Orion, who only offered a devilish grin, and with this he thought it better not to ask. "Uhhhh, never mind!"

Taylor shook his head and though on this, trying to figure if he should hold his children at all accountable for what they had done. They did, after all, live in a time where anything could be generated and the material needs of the world's population were always satisfied completely – with no waste. But the only way businesses can attract and attain profit is to charge for the download of a brand name pattern for use. He shook his head further, knowing that each pattern had a price, and while certain government patterns can be found at no cost. Basic food and simple clothing included, brand-name items, equipment, and specialty foods had to be purchased before they were downloaded. As such Taylor could only imagine the hundreds of thousands, if not millions of credits that Orion had technically bypassed spending in order to get the hoards of patterns contained in these many, many pads. So, with only a split second's thought, Taylor questioned if he should hold his students accountable for this grand thievery.

Taylor slowly returned a smirk to Orion, accepting that he and these children were wanted criminals just for their escape and what that entailed, and he decided that the theft of these patterns for the purpose of survival was necessary. Additionally Taylor rationalized that since there was little to no chance that these many patterns would be shared or pirated out to a larger public, he equated it as only a minor offense.

Emptying his head of this rush of thoughts, Taylor made his way back to the transport, and after a few minutes inside he came out carrying a different data pad from the one he had before. With a look of concentration he focused between it and the M-Gen, forcing one of the patterns in the pad to be transmitted into the generator's buffer. Once this was finished. he reached to the ground, picked up and put a small rock carefully inside the M-Gen's replication window.

"There that should do it! Now – everybody pick a tree!" he said satisfied with what he had done, but on turning around he could see that his comment regarding the tree was met with looks of baffled confusion.

"Come on kids! I may be good, but with this kind of repair I don't even trust my own work! – remember, this is matter generation – which means huge energy – so pick a tree and hide behind it!"

On saying this, with his hands wildly waving around in demonstration, Taylor saw that the looks of confusion slowly shifted to looks of concern and doubt. "Go – now!" Taylor said pointing at the children to go each to a different tree.

They did so, Johnny being the last to clumsily trip and find a place to hide, and Taylor even kinetically moved Jay's plasticized body behind a tree before finding his own to use as protection just in case anything went wrong.

Taylor peered around his tree at the M-Gen, and as he focused on it he saw that David was curiously working himself around his own tree to get a look. "I don't think so!" the teen said looking at the boy with a frown, and with a telekinetic hold, he forced David to stand firm and stiff behind his tree.

"All of you - stay still!" He shouted as he purposefully pointed at each one of the children with his finger landing lastly on the encapsulated body of Jay. "Especially you!" Taylor said with a smile and a wink, hearing sniggers from the children as he turned to face the M-Gen once again.

He looked with a fixated stare at the machine and as he pulled himself back around his tree he forced the unit to generate the pattern he had uploaded. After a few seconds Taylor and the children heard a simple sound that was music to their ears. It was the familiar light beeping noise that had meant the M-Gen had finished its task.

Taylor focused hard kinetically to keep all of the children hidden behind the trees as he came from behind his own and walked toward the generator.

As he did this he could hear complaints from the children for their being restrained, but he didn't care. He tapped a button on the M-Gen and with a quick wisp of air the unit opened itself to reveal a tool of sorts that Taylor recognized immediately. It was small, round, and flat, about two inches in diameter, and had two loops on one side.

Taylor pulled the object out and inspected it – he had to hold it in different positions in an effort to get the best use of what little light he had so that he could see every detail. Just as he had determined for himself that there were no flaws, his thoughts were interrupted by an outside voice.

"Oh, they've brought a Generator with them," Taylor heard, and in an instant he felt his heart jump into his throat. Turning around quickly he started scanning the trees, his head moving in all directions. So much was his concern that he lost his hold on the children, each of them pulling from behind their own tree.

David was the first to reach Taylor and the boy quickly snatched the tool from the teen's hands. But Taylor was too full of worry to care about this tiny device, and while the children busied themselves with looking at the newly created object, passing it around and inspecting it to make sure it had no flaws, Taylor walked between and separated them as he started pacing, looking up into the trees intently. He was concentrating hard on trying to pick up stray thoughts that might be running through the forest from any unseen observers.

"I told you! He can hear our thoughts!" Taylor heard a voice declare, and this was quickly overlapped with another. "Idiot!"

Taylor's ears perked as if he were listening to the words being spoken and not transmitted. Quickly his mind was filled with more words.

"How is that possible!? We're not telepathic! He can't – how can he? – We have to tell the others!"

Standing for a minute to listen, Taylor could hear nothing, but the mumbles of the children and the silence inside his own head. Caught quite off guard, his hand was grabbed by Johnny who, when he looked down at the boy, showed a worried expression framing the boy's light blue eyes.

"I heard them too!" the child said calmly, and together Taylor and he stared into the trees expecting to find something or nothing, but not sure which.

After nearly a minute Taylor pulled his eyes down from their upward stare, and returned to the children. *Back to work* – he thought, and with that he grabbed the new tool from Aspen, who was examining it curiously.

"In order for me to determine if the M-Gen is functioning properly I'll have to use this tool!" Taylor said quite matter-of-factly, and he pulled Grace in front of himself. With a quick drop Taylor squatted to stare at the girl eye to eye. He then slipped the strange new object over his index and middle fingers and used his thumb to give it a squeeze on the side. With a bright light the unit lit up.

Lifting the tool to the girl's face, he slowly moved it up and down over where the girl's long cut was clearly visible. Slowly the tissue under the tool fused and healed together. This offered Grace a slight tickling sensation which made her smile almost to the point of laughter. But this look quickly lessened itself when her smile caused a feeling of pain that ran through all of that side of her face. Taylor knew what had happened and gave the girl a raised eyebrow – "stay still!" he said as he worked the tool up to where her eye was – "Now softly close your eye, but don't squint or it will hurt even more.

Grace did so, and with the disappearance of light from the other side of her lids, she could tell he was finished. She opened her eyes to stare into the light blue eyed gaze of Taylor. He quickly wiped her face with his sleeve and smiled at her.

"There, now you're all beautiful again," he said, and she responded by quickly rubbing her face. She could feel that it was smooth, with no blemishes, and no scar. Whirling around to her siblings, they each inspected her face and were all quite impressed that there was no evidence of her face ever having suffered any damage. He then handed the tool to Orion and showed the boy how to use it so that all of the small wounds on each of the children's arms could be quickly mended.

With a deep sigh, Taylor was satisfied that the M-Gen was functioning fine, but realized quickly, in looking around, that he now needed to address the most important and most pressing issue at hand. Taylor knew that while the M-Gen had been reprogrammed to de-replicate matter into energy, and thereafter take that energy and convert it into a newly requested pattern of matter, there was still one simple problem. Where could he find a constant source of matter that could be used to replicate anything on request?

Taylor only had to ponder this for a moment before the solution came to him. Knowing what he had to do he turned to the children around him, and addressed them quite purposefully. "We have to change our campsite, everyone, back in the transport!"

Both Jay and the M-Gen were levitated by Taylor and inserted into the transport after the children had entered. The children then looked out the loading door curiously while Taylor lowered it as much as possible, but without damaging the cables running from the M-Gen to the outside access panel.

At last Taylor slowly levitated the transport a few feet off the ground and forced it to follow shortly behind him, he made his way through the forest on foot. Indeed, walking as slow as he was, it took Taylor much longer to reach the stream where, as nervous as it made him considering recent events there, he decided to relocate their new campsite – or rather to create their new home.

Setting the transport several feet away from the water's edge, with the loading door facing the smooth running waters, Taylor opened the transport, allowing the children to exit, and while they were climbing over each other to stretch their legs and take in their new surroundings, Taylor stood amid the trees, looking about for activity, listening hard inside his own head to make sure there was no one watching them, or at least making sure that he couldn't *hear* any threat.

Feeling satisfied that he and the children were alone in the forest; Taylor went to work at setting the stage for creating a new and comfortable home for himself and his students. As such, he worked feverishly at changing the M-Gen to suit the construction requirements for creating this new residence.

It only took Taylor a few minutes to replicate a water pump and other tools and equipment that he used thereafter to modify the M-Gen so that it could utilize the stream water as its newfound source of bulk material. He also modified the unit to generate objects and materials outside the standard generation compartment by adding design concepts borrowed from the specs of the ReConstructor 7500; the same unit he had used to repair the classroom in The Towers just the day before.

After having allowed the pump to flow freely for several minutes Taylor was satisfied with its function and felt that it was time to plan out their new home.

Taking input from each of the children's requests and demands, Taylor designed a floor-plan which utilized the space between the forest's many trees, leaving empty circles for them to grow. The resulting layout for their home, an intricate honeycomb pattern, wove through the forest covering some ten thousand square feet according to the computer model. At this size, it allowed for 5 bathrooms, 8 bedrooms, an infirmary, two kitchens, four independent living areas, and two separate dining rooms.

Taylor, at one point, thought that the design was growing unnecessarily elaborate, but this didn't change his approach, and he encouraged the children to add whatever they felt would make their lives more comfortable.

During this design process, Orion had, unbeknownst to everyone except Taylor, cyberly forced each of the many data-pads to download their contents into the M-Gen, whose newly added memory module was vastly superior to the standard memory of the M-Gen alone. This being done, construction of the home could be easily started first thing in the morning using the many preloaded patterns.

And so after a few short hours, with generated food as dinner in between, Taylor and the children finished what he considered a rough design for the space in which they would live. It had, in his mind, room for improvements that he would address on construction, but it was, indeed, a good plan.

The actual construction, which would proceed the following morning, was being planned step by step in Taylor's head as he lay in the large environmentally controlled tent he had generated for himself and the children to sleep in that night. In his thoughts he was assigning chores and responsibilities to each of the children, setting out a time schedule, and it was nearly immediate that he decided the construction of their home could be done in one day with the almost unending use of the M-Gen panel and each of the children's powers, including Johnny and Caitlin's new ones.

On finishing his plans in his own head Taylor lay exhausted from the events of the day, and while his life as he knew it had been irrevocably altered, he was content. Rolling on his side, he could see all six youngsters sleeping soundly with only a battery powered night light offering a soft glow to give each child the feeling of safety amid this new and strange place of rest.

Closing his eyes, Taylor's thoughts slowly swirled into images of his new home, his new life, and the voices of the children. *This is our new home and these children are finally mine* – he thought, and his heart joyously ached with each word.

And so it was here that his dreams began. He saw himself chasing the children through halls and corridors. This was in play, with each child running to stay away as he weaved through a veritable maze of twists and turns trying only half heartedly to keep up with them. Indeed, this was a good dream for Taylor in the midst of everything he had experienced in the last two days, and he was happy to receive it... for a while.

Smiling in his sleep, Taylor quickly stiffened as the children in his dream all stopped and repositioned themselves in what seemed a straight line in front of him. They then turned around to face him one by one and as they did this, they spoke the same line in a dark voice that was not their own.

"They can't stay here – they have to go!"

One after the other, the children said this and each time louder than the one before. This caused an immediate fear to rush through Taylor's body, and even though there was no reality to what he was seeing and hearing, in his stomach he could feel an uneasiness wrenching inside. In his dream the halls and rooms which had been brightly lit before, slowly dimmed to darkness, and, in the matter of a few seconds, the dream had turned from pleasant and wanted to bleak, ominous and feared.

At the last child, Orion, finishing the same repeated declaration as the others, they all reached out and lunged at Taylor. He felt a single hand grab his arm and instantly he woke with a start.

Taylor sat upright, amid the dim glow inside the tent, and in doing so he bumped heads with Johnny who was grabbing him by the arm trying to shake him awake.

With a seizing deep breath Taylor found his senses heightened, and he looked wildly around the tent only to see that Johnny had fallen to the floor, rubbing his forehead in pain. Taylor waited, staring at the child. The boy looked up with almost a grin. "I tried to wake you – I – I guess you heard the voices too?"

Taylor perked his ears uselessly again trying *hear* anything. But unlike his last efforts to listen to the unknown, which yielded no results, now Taylor could hear everything. He heard voices of men women and children, all around. The voices were all pathic, and some of them, like in his dream, were saying "*they* can't stay," while others were simply questioning "Who are *they?*"

With a barrage of this and other queries and statements penetrating his skull and just as many questions of his own complicate the thoughts in his brain, Taylor decided it was time to leave the tent and address the obvious mass that was waiting outside.

He unzipped the exit, stepped outside, and with this, he heard a swarm of new thoughts come into his brain so fast he could barely see straight much less stand proper with what seemed a painful mass of confusion in his head.

"Come one people," Taylor yelled out into the trees, "I'm trying to get some sleep here!"

While this did not quiet the thoughts of those unseen watchers in the trees, it did have the effect of consolidating many of their thoughts into several chorus phrases. The largest of these, "He *can* read our thoughts!" along with "It can't be!" were those he recognized immediately.

"Listen!" Taylor said loudly, and as he did this he turned and could see that all six of his students were poking their heads through the unzipped entrance like a strange vertical line of peas in a pod.

"Listen," Taylor said again, this time with less force, "we aren't here to harm you." He paused and he could hear that, strangely enough, the voices inside his head were subsiding, at least in volume, and, with this internal relief Taylor looked at the six concerned faces staring out from the tent. Filling with a newfound determination, the teen continued to address those he could not see.

"My name is Taylor, Doctor Robert Taylor, I am – or – uh – I was a teacher in Los Angeles. These six children..." Taylor paused, thought for a moment while staring again at the young faces that were now looking all about trying to figure his audience, and with a deep pained sigh he continued. "These six *orphans* inside this tent are my students, and, as I have spent nearly every waking moment with them over the past five years, they are all but my children by blood, and in the same respect, I, their father. I love them very much." Taylor spoke these words of endearment for both his unseen audience and the children to hear.

"They, like me, are gifted with powerful minds, and it is because of this that we have escaped from the city. There are those inside the city that want to take them away from me; they want to take them from the only parent they've ever really known, just because of their powers." Taylor paused for another breath, and continued what he hoped to be his last statement before retiring to bed for the night. "You should know, by the way, that it was the children's idea to leave the city, and they worked hard to escape its high walls and even higher security, despite their young age. We haven't come this far only to leave because of a few off-the-grid outsiders. We are staying. Now if any of you have anything to add – well – our tent is open."

As the moments passed Taylor could hear the voices subside lower and lower until they were nothing but a whisper – telling Taylor that they were all leaving, offering him the peace he had been looking for.

Taylor, after waiting these several minutes, turned and waved for the children to return to their makeshift beds and go back to sleep as he too re-entered the tent. He left the zipper to the tent lifted and one flap raised as a show that he welcomed anyone brave enough to enter, and as he lay down to sleep he perked his ears trying to listen to voices, either real, or inside his head, but found that other that the soft whisper of the children beside him, there was total silence and all the uncontrolled thoughts from those outside had ceased.

"Peace at last!" Taylor whispered, and with that he closed his eyes to sleep, a little more restless and completely unable to have the same pleasant dream he'd had before. Still, however, it was sleep nonetheless.

Waking the next morning, it was clear to Taylor that his message to whoever was listening outside the tent, while effective for short term rest, did not invite nor permanently fend off the unknown visitors. It was both he and Johnny that roused to the sounds of persistent and numerous pathic voices, whose source was clearly the same as the night before. The two could hear that these pathic thoughts were much less curious, and much more threatening than before, and it was Johnny who walked to his teacher, stepping over the sleeping bodies of his siblings as he went.

"Dad, - are you hearing what I'm hearing?" the boy asked nervously.

"I am." Taylor relied, and with these words the teen focused hard on separating the many thoughts. He could instantly discern the phrases of "attack," "drive them off," and several others that did not bode well for the immediate future of himself or his students.

Taylor stood up quickly, exited the tent, and looked in the trees around him. Here, for the first time, he could finally see those who had been unwillingly interjecting their thoughts into his and Johnny's brains.

44 A Morning Fight

LIKE MONKEYS IN THE TREES, there were dozens of onlookers that had come from somewhere, or maybe nowhere, in the forest. And when Taylor looked up, he was frustrated that a first meeting with those outside the city was on such an unpleasant note, especially when in his mind he had done nothing wrong – he offered no words or actions of hostility. Even so, when he stared into the trees he wasn't able to see a single set of eyes, not one face, not a single expression to offer him an idea of who he was up against. Indeed, everyone in the trees was wearing a strange uniform that covered every inch of their bodies, including their faces.

But not being able to see any faces was the least of Taylor's focus as he gazed into the trees. In fact it was the head-to-toe uniforms of these individuals that caught his eye the most. This attracted his attention so quickly and yet made him wince at the same time because the uniforms of these many men and women were lined with strange curving paths that glowed in bright bluish white strips up and down their full length, even over their heads and their feet.

Taylor was immediately confused by what he saw. He had assumed that these outsiders, being away from the city and off the grid, had little to no technology available to them. Yet it was clear that this assumption was wrong as, with his continuing to take in the detail of those in the trees, he realized that they were wearing something manufactured from what seemed to be very advanced technology.

So concentrated was Taylor's stare that he barely noticed the two approaching images walking towards him through the trees. But it should really be no surprise that he didn't notice them though, for with a strange distortion of light it was as though they appeared out of nowhere!

"Cloaking suits!" Taylor murmured half in shock as the two approached, and he took in every detail of these suits, now understanding their purpose, and yet still confused as to how this group had perfected a technology that even the government had been working on for so long, but hadn't yet been able to figure out. Taylor's eyes moved from the uniforms' brightly lit shoes all the way up to the strange stocking like hoods that covered the faces of those who were now only a few feet away. He clenched his hands unsure of what was going to happen next. Hoping for the best, but preparing for the worst.

He continued to stare with peaked nerves as one of the pair reached up and fiddled with their glowing hood. With the pulling of two bright strips at the neck line this person disconnected their hood from the rest of the uniform and slowly the hood's bright glow dimmed. Taylor stood, with bated breath as this person revealed their identity.

The teen immediately acknowledged gender – male, and as the man spoke both to him and to those in the trees, Taylor took in the details of the man's face.

"So – Robert Taylor – you want to live here?" the man said with an arrogant tone. He was thin, muscular, had a tiny gold rod piercing his lobe, bright red hair and green eyes. He was, by most standards, attractive, except for a large scar that ran down his face, ironically enough, it was near the same place Grace would have had a scar if her cut was left unattended.

Taylor took in the words that this man had said, but before an answer could be uttered, the man continued. "We are warriors, we protect our own, and we don't allow outsiders into *our* forest – so if you want to stay here, you'll have to fight for your own piece of land. For the land on which you stand has already been claimed."

Taylor could hear loud calls of those in the trees. His eyes shot up quickly and in his mind, he was considering knocking several of them to the ground.

"*Fight!*" Taylor said loudly almost at a laugh, "for *my* piece of land – you *must* be kidding!"

On saying this Taylor's head instantly filled with what seemed a thousand screaming thoughts that were not his own and his legs almost buckled from the weight of these uncontrolled non-pathic messages.

"I, Rowna, am leader of this clan of warriors and I enforce our laws." The red headed man said haughtily. "And the owner of this land has agreed. They do not want to share it with you. You will have to fight to keep the property or concede and leave." This man, who called himself Rowna, spoke firmly, and Taylor, try as he might, could pick up no stray thoughts from him, which was odd as he could hear stray thoughts from just about everyone else. The teen did notice, however, that as Rowna spoke he motioned toward the individual standing at his side and could only assume that this person was the one who had claim to the land on which Taylor stood.

Taylor's mind was working hard to filter out the thoughts coming from his many spectators, and as he absorbed what Rowna said he felt a bit of shock over what he deemed a barbaric ritual that made little sense in the modern age.

As Rowna turned his back on Taylor he spoke one final blow which made Taylor wish just that much more that he hadn't woken up that morning.

"You will fight! Unless you wish to leave, but I'd have to wonder where you'd go – all the land here, for miles in any direction, is claimed by one or another of our clan. And should you choose to stay, the person on this land has agreed to fight to the *death* to keep steadfast on their own land." Rowna shouted these words, and

Taylor could hear more jeers coming from those in the trees.

"Now, what would that prove?" Taylor shouted offering several sour looks to those he could hear expressing the worst of thoughts. "That I can kill someone – that – I can defeat one of yours – how useless!" He turned at this point and could see that Johnny had woken his brothers and sisters who were all, like the night before, peering out at him from the tent entrance.

"I doubt you could stand a chance..." the man named Rowna shouted with a grin before he quickly added, "especially against someone *you can't see*!" The man tilted his head to the figure at his side, who, with an initially brightening of their suit that made blink, disappeared into nothingness.

What happened next, Taylor felt he could scarcely forget. Not knowing where this person went, Taylor realized the danger he was in when he felt a sharp pain at his side followed by a hard push at the back of his calves causing him to fall backwards.

All around him Taylor could hear the laughs of those in the trees, but he himself was not amused, and on turning his head Taylor could see that the children were showing faces of fear. Rolling over and lying flat on his back, Taylor could feel, with a sense of humiliation, his student's eyes watching him as he buckled in the middle from what was unmistakably a foot stomped in his gut.

Quickly rolling over again, Taylor tried as best he could to clear his head of the barrage of thoughts that were constantly penetrating it from his high-sitting observers. He wanted to listen to the footfalls of his unseen enemy, hoping to gain a bearing on where the person was, but it was useless with all the noise going on in his head.

He stood, only for a moment, before he felt a sharp pain crush his nose and force him to fall hard on his backside. He had been punched in the face, and it was obvious from the sound and feel that his nose had been broken.

The next few minutes were filled with one painful hit after another with Taylor unable to see who, or where the next blow would be coming from. With his body aching, and his kneeling on the moist ground, he felt an arm reach around his head and he could tell that whoever was fighting him was now trying to break his neck.

Taylor desperately looked to his side and could see, through his own glistening sweat and blood that the kids were looking out of the tent with hands over their mouths and tears on their faces in absolute terror at what they were watching.

With what effort Taylor had left he reached above himself and could feel the head of the person who was holding him so firmly. With a roll of his body, and a pull of his hand he forced the person above him to flip hard over and he could tell by the rustling of *the leaves* in front of him that his opponent had fallen hard on the ground.

"The leaves!" Taylor heard David yell, and in an instant the child darted out from the tent and blocked an unseen hit which was meant for Taylor's head. Taylor was at first amazed by this, but when he noticed bits of dirt and debris floating in mid air, he quickly identified that a foot was well on its way to making an impact with his own forehead before David intervened.

Slowly rolling over, Taylor, weak with the pain of his many injuries, could do little at this point but watch David dart to and fro, with seeming perfection, blocking partially seen hits one after another, and to his amazement David was actually landing some hits of his own on his invisible opponent. All the while Taylor noticed that the boy's eyes were focusing hard on the ground, kinetically throwing leaves into the air to help get an idea of where his opponent was and what he was doing.

Taylor slowly raised himself to an aching stance and at gaining his footing he filled with so many emotions all at once. He was consumed with such a sense of pride as he watched, so very impressed, that this young child could do so well against an unseen adult opponent, especially considering all the child had to rely on was the movement leaves on the ground and those being thrown in the air. He, secondly, felt like an idiot in not noticing this himself; the one clue that could be used to understand the movements and positions of this opponent.

Taylor's glowing pride and self realizing ignorance was cut short by the voices in his head all converging to a familiar phrase that was now being thought by those in the trees. "Set – pull – aim – lead – focus – release..."

Looking at those who were resting on the high branches, Taylor could see that many were now aiming arrows at David and ready to release. All at once Taylor leaped for David and curled him up in a ball of protection using his own body as a shield while at the same time focusing hard on sensing and kinetically stopping all activity around them both.

Total silence was all Taylor heard when David and he finished rolling, and when he opened his eyes he could see, as if he and David were an oversized pin-cushion, that the they were surrounded by an array of shiny metallic arrows that had stopped only inches from impact.

With a wave of kinetic energy Taylor forced the arrows to fall to the ground, and this, he could see, was followed by a movement in the leaves which he quickly and easily read.

Raising his arm, Taylor blocked what unmistakably was a foot that was trying to kick him hard in the head – again. He quickly reached with his other hand and grabbed the foot. In holding it, he was able to get a kinetic grasp of it, and as such he used his kinesis to manipulate this limb and throw his unseen enemy hard against a nearby tree.

This impact was very near the man who called himself Rowna, and as such the man looked down at the ground – "Get up – Now!" he barked.

Meanwhile Taylor rushed David inside the tent.

"Thanks! – I've got it from here!" Taylor said rubbing the boy on the cheek only to realize the child's shirt was being bloodied-up from the inside. Turning the boy around, Taylor could see that a single arrow had penetrated the child's shoulder straight through from the back.

David smiled not showing a single tear, "It hurts, but it's okay."

Taylor was enraged. He contorted his face in anger and tore off his own shirt which he tied around David to hold the child's arm still and close to the body.

He rubbed David quickly on the head and could see he child's face finally filling with tears from the pain. Taylor started losing his own emotional control through his great empathy for the boy, and on leaving the tent and standing full height, the teen glowered around in the trees at the many faces he couldn't see.

"What's wrong with you people?" Taylor screamed both loud and full of emotion. "He's just a child! You would kill a child over something so – so – petty!"

Taylor took a deep breath and as he watched the slow movement of leaves near Rowna, his anger was only increased by the many thoughts that were now emanating from those in the trees.

"Any interference – we attack – our orders."

"So it was a child – he could obviously take care of himself."

"So it was a child – who cares – this is *our* land!"

These, along with other thoughts too numerous to detail were all entering into Taylor's brain so fast and they were so thick he could barely focus on the ground in front of him so he might have a fighting chance against the invisible fighter. The only thing he could think to do was silence the thoughts – silence them from interfering in his concentration. Raising his hands to his temples, Taylor closed his eyes and worked hard to focus.

THUD! One of the hooded figures in the trees fell to the ground – then – THUD – another then – THUD – THUD – THUD – THUD...

One by one all those in the trees started raining down as Taylor looked at each hooded figure, focusing hard on silencing them in his mind. This was something Taylor had only done once before in his entire life and as his anger was near its peak, he knew that now was no time to hold back. He watched, almost happy, as the bodies continued to fall to the ground.

Finally Taylor offered a darkened stare to Rowna, who still had no detectible thoughts. The man's face, however, showed a total look of shock as he, Rowna, had no choice but to notice his many fallen *warriors*. At this moment, for the first time, there was fear in the man standing before Taylor.

Taylor stood quite still now staring at the leaf crushed footprints of the unseen beside Rowna. He watched closely, unmoving, and with a quick lift of those leaves and the earth beneath, Taylor realized that the fighter was making a dash at him. Taylor, focused on the ground, threw a wash of leaves into the air. From the forming silhouette of a body Taylor could tell exactly what his opponent was doing – lunging for him. He quickly dodged this, spun himself around, and struck hard on the back of his now easy to spot opponent.

With a mass of leaves crushing themselves to the ground Taylor could tell that he had forced the person to fall flat on their face and stomach.

With a rustle of the ground debris Taylor could see that the fighter had lifted themselves up quickly and that the impression made by their hand had lifted so fast it could only mean an attempt at hitting him from a low position. He used his foot to block the hit, and kicked where he assumed the head of his opponent to be. This approximation was correct, and as such he felt the impact hard on his bare feet.

Still this fighter persisted, eventually standing at full height, and with another rush of footprints and leaves, Taylor could tell that the fighter was again trying to make another dash for him. But all at once the impressions on the ground stopped and the leaves lifted higher into the air.

A jump – Taylor thought, and with this he rolled backward – his body feeling the aches of his earlier blows – but this did not distract him so much that he didn't act. Indeed, as Taylor rolled, he kicked his feet high into the air and made impact with what he presumed was be the middle of his opponent's body. This forced an unexpected flip in the middle of his enemy's jump, and as such, Taylor's opponent slid far on the leaves of the forest.

Taylor's eyes now filled with a split second of nervousness as he saw two long swords appear form nowhere.

He must have pulled them from some hidden spot in the cloaking suit – Taylor rationalized, and with this, the teen kinetically forced the swords high into the air not knowing if his opponent's grip was good enough to keep hold, or if it was just the swords he had snatched up. This was of no matter, for Taylor turned the swords back to the ground and forced them downward so hard that they stabbed deep into the earth, penetrating straight to the hilt so that there was no chance of them to be removed.

"Try again!" Taylor shouted at his invisible enemy and as he did this he, Taylor, took a firm stance, and waited for *the leaves* to make the first move.

He didn't have to wait long. He could see that they had once again decided to rush for him. This time more cautious than the first, Taylor could tell that a short roundhouse was being kicked in his direction by way of the leaves being lifted into the air. As such he blocked it and could feel his opponent's body move quite predictably into a series of punches and kicks all of which he physically prevented with blocking moves for each one.

Taking only a moment to glance toward the tent, Taylor could see that the children no longer had worried faces, but were now actually cheering, almost giddy expressions of victory – That is – except for David and Caitlin. These two were deep inside the tent and Taylor, along with the rest of the forest, could hear the loud cry of David who wailed at having the arrow snatched through his shoulder by his sister. Looking ever more focused, Taylor could see that David had a harsh look of pain on his very pale – and growing ever paler – face.

With a surge of anger Taylor gave a quick blow to the abdomen forcing his enemy to bellow over in pain. He then followed this hit with a sharp elbow to the back of the neck forcing the fighter to fall flat to the ground.

"It's time to finish this!" Taylor growled. With anger growing inside him, and knowing the position of his nemesis, Taylor kinetically forced the unseen body high into the air then crushed it hard to the ground. He could hear a groan of pain when he did this, and it almost pleased him to do it again – and again. Having thrown this body to the ground several times more, Taylor only stopped when he felt a small hand grab his own. Not that he wanted to stop, but at looking into the eyes of David, staring up at him with such a sincere expression that was washed with a pale pallet of color and framed with his long blonde hair, Taylor realized that his attention was required elsewhere.

The teen kneeled in front of the boy, gave him a hug that seemed bloodied from both sides, and while the teen thought he could walk the boy to the M-Gen, this was preempted by David collapsing in his arms. Taylor's heart fell to the moist earth beneath him. This boy, bloodied and unconscious, had saved his life. Now it was time for Taylor to return the favor.

45 New Enemy, New Friends

WITH A FIERCE STARE OVER HIS SHOULDER, Taylor kinetically focused on Rowna and the unseen fighter in an effort to keep both of them perfectly still. Then, with a second set of thoughts, Taylor concentrated on the M-Gen, readying the machine for use.

Moving the boy to the machine, Taylor used a small sample of the child's blood as a template to create more of the same in an I.V. bag that he then used to transfuse into the child. Then, reaching into his own pocket, he pulled out the handheld tissue replicator to mend the wound on both the front and back of David's shoulder. On finishing this Taylor tightly held the bloodied body of David and with each passing second the teen filled with more intense emotions. So much was this that he lost control of his hold over both the invisible fighter and of Rowna.

Being completely unaware of this, Taylor's distressed face looked up when he heard the rustling of leaves by his side. To his surprise he watched as his unseen fighter revealed himself by remove his cloaking hood. Practically holding his breath, Taylor saw that his opponent, who at one point had come so close to killing him, was a – a woman; a beautiful, red haired, green-eyed woman.

Taylor stared in shock. "She's your - she's your sister?"

"Hardly," Rowna said turning a disappointed look to the woman, "She's my great-great-granddaughter. Isn't that right Delissa?" The man spoke with an arrogant condescension to the woman at Taylor's side and at hearing this Taylor's lip curled with almost a snarl as once again his judgment of age was so far off the mark it was, in his mind, ridiculous.

The woman, looking down in shame, turned and rushed to the aid of one those who had fallen hard from the trees at Taylor's will.

Pulling off the hood of this person, she looked at Taylor, her eyes welling with tears to match his, "What have you done!" she screamed, and Taylor, only at that moment, took in the fact that she was holding a teenage boy. The child looked to be some thirteen or fourteen years in age, had a pierced ear much like Rowna, and Taylor could only assume that this young man was a close relative – possibly Delissa's son. But before Taylor had even taken a breath to respond to the dark accusing eyes of Delissa, she ran toward him to attack. Taylor, seeing her coming this time, barely had to concentrate to use his kinesis and keep her frozen in mid air.

She had jumped at him with an arrow gripped firmly in her hand, which he made her drop before manipulating her to take a stable standing position. Her mouth offered words only slightly less foul than that which Taylor could read from her mind.

He walked past her, admiring her tenaciousness, and when he looked to Rowna he had a sense that this man knew better than to attack someone with abilities the likes of what Taylor possessed.

"Let me first tell you, *Delissa,* that your son is fine." Taylor said on pathically picking up the truth that he had already suspected. "In fact, everyone here is fine. I'm sure in an hour or so they'll all wake up with only a bad headache, and maybe a broken bone or two from their fall." Taylor spoke with his eyes focused on Rowna whose face muscles were now flexing to offer an angry gaze back at the teen.

Taylor shrugged this look off and turned to Delissa. "As a doctor, I'd be happy to mend any injuries they suffered, but then again," Taylor paused and offered a smirk, "maybe I'll let their pain remind them of their lethal efforts against young David here."

"The boy interfered..." Delissa grunted angrily and with barely a flinch Taylor forced the woman's mouth to remain closed against her will.

"That boy," Taylor said, but then corrected himself. "Those children obviously have a higher respect for life than you or any of your so called warriors – death for land – it's ridiculous – and you weep for yours but think nothing of mine who could have been filled with arrows – what an image to show as a reflection of what you are all about." Taylor paused and sighed, "and what a set of two sided standards we have here?" His mouth being sick with the taste of blood, and not for wanting to show disrespect, Taylor spit on the ground near the feet of Delissa, who shunned his actions in her mind.

Taylor walked around her and approached Rowna again. The man's face stiffened, half in anger, half due to his own arrogance. Taylor was sure this was all because the man could hardly believe that he had experienced such a decisive defeat at the hands of one man and one child. With Taylor standing so close to him, the two stared at each other, hard focused and completely unable to determine each other's thoughts, despite the fact that Taylor had the upper hand in this regard.

After a few moments of uncomfortable silence, Taylor decided to release Delissa from her kinetic hold. His ears perked as he could sense that the woman ran not toward himself, but toward the teenager she had so dotingly tended to before.

Taylor, matching her concern for hers, went to David, whose head was resting against the side of the M-Gen, and from what Taylor could see, the child's face was showing a great deal more color than before.

Putting his hand on the boy's forehead, he watched as David opened his eyes and smiled, "Did you win?" he asked softly. Taylor smiled in return and pulled the boy close, "of course *we* did!"

After a few moments Taylor lifted himself and helped David to do the same and, although the boy was unsteady and weak, he did not complain. Taylor stretched his arms, looked about and could see the many bodies lying around this place that he so desperately wanted to call his new home. "It's time to set things right!" Taylor said looking across at Delissa.

Taylor shifted his gaze to the M-Gen nearby and focused on it for a moment. When it had finished obeying his request, Taylor pulled out two different pieces of equipment. One; a scanner, the other; a bone mender, which he used in sequence to repair David's punctured shoulder blade.

"I'm fine!" the boy said softly when Taylor had finished the repair, and before Taylor had a chance to make sure the boy was properly healed he was pushed away, and the child said quite firmly, "Go! – See to the others." The child then whispered, "We need to make friends here – not enemies!"

Taylor was quite impressed with what the boy had said and, though these orders were coming from a ten-year-old, he thought it best that he do as he was told.

He picked up the tools he had used on David and walked to the side of Delissa, who was now trying to pull straight what was obviously her child's shattered arm. She scowled at him, to which he offered a fierce stare forcing her to check herself.

"Listen, either you let me help this boy, or I'll knock you out too!"

Delissa frowned, and held the boy close in her arms.

"You steady him – I'll pull!" he said gruffly. She responded as instructed, and he offered only one small statement to give this woman solace over her child's injuries. "Best to do this while he's unconscious so he can't feel it anyways." And just as Taylor finished this statement he pulled the boy's arm straight and into position all the while using his scanner to ensure the bones were in proper position. He could tell that while the child showed no signs of pain Delissa's sympathetic reaction was quite present in the flinching of her face.

"This will only take a second." Taylor said as he used the bone mender to fuse the bones in the boy's arm back together.

Once this was finished Delissa's face, and that of the boy in her arms, were suddenly and unexpectedly covered with dirt. This dirt and a mass of leaves and earth had been kicked up by Rowna.

"This isn't over, your fight was supposed to be to the death. If he's going to take a parcel of land, blood has to spill for it."

At this moment Taylor didn't know whether his mind was more filled with anger, or with confusion at this man's stupidity, and as he stared with raised eyebrow up at Rowna, it didn't much matter which made him act first.

With a seizing around his neck, Rowna was instantly lifted a good foot off the ground and was slowly pushed back to one of the forest's trees that he eventually hit quite hard.

"Are you insane?" Taylor asked while Rowna made attempts to talk in gurgles. His neck being kinetically gripped so hard, Rowna had little choice but to listen as Taylor continued to lecture a man that was assumedly five times his own age.

"I could snap your neck right here and now." The teen said, and at this he kinetically lifted an old fallen piece of log some six inches in diameter, and with barely a blink he forced the log to crack in half with a loud bang.

"As you can see, I could do it with hardly a thought! So don't tempt me... if you really want someone to die, why not let it be you."

On saying this Taylor could hear the thoughts of Delissa entering into his brain.

"Please – do it – do it now!" and while Taylor would have loved nothing more than to reveal these thoughts to Rowna, the teen merely allowed the man to drop to his unprepared feet. Dropping to his knees, Rowna gasped and coughed, gripping his own throat as Taylor spoke.

"If death is what you want, I can give it to you – but make no mistake – I'll give it to *you* and no one else."

With a terrified upward gaze into Taylor's fierce bright blue eyes, Rowna crawled away and eventually ran into the forest, afraid for his life and leaving those he had once led behind. Taylor watched almost in laughter as this self proclaimed warrior and leader scurried into the forest like a skittish animal.

Some moments later Taylor stepped to Delissa's side, towering over her as she sat, coddling her son.

"I heard what you were thinking – about Rowna, when I threatened him..." Taylor whispered softly, and as he scanned Delissa's son's arm a second time to see how it was doing he could hear the leaves rustle behind him. Turning, he realized that he was being flanked by the other children, who had left the tent to come and see those who had been watching them in the forest up close.

"He's just a kid – like us," Aspen said on seeing the boy in Delissa's arms.

"Yes he is, Aspen." Taylor said, smiling, "and his name is," Taylor paused and looked at Delissa for a fraction of a second before the answer came to him, "Tristan."

Hearing her son's name, Delissa sighed with a gentle smile and stared down at the boy. Watching this, Taylor slowly filled with a bit of hope that things might be turning for the better.

Taylor looked between the heads of the children and stared off in the distance to the M-Gen. With a look of concentration he activated the device, and on its beeping readiness he ordered Orion to get what the machine had produced. The boy returned with two syringe guns, and as such Taylor was about to use one of these on Tristan's neck when Delissa interfered.

"What are you doing?" She questioned excitedly, holding her hand over the boy's neck.

"This will help him come around. It's perfectly harmless."

After saying this Taylor put his hand over Delissa's and slowly pushed it out of the way while his other hand used the injection gun. Taylor could sense nervousness in Delissa's fingers as she slowly moved her hand away from Tristan's neck and Taylor took this opportunity to stare into Delissa's eyes, really noticing them for the first time. Delissa returned this gaze, and found herself mesmerized by Taylor's bright blue eyes.

As the next few moments passed what Taylor least expected seemed to slowly happen. Her face of fear and dislike seemed to shift to one of – respect? Or admiration? Or was it attraction?

Taylor looked downward at sensing this, but it wasn't quick enough, for with blue clashing against green, his eyes met that of Tristan's. The boy neither wanted, nor needed ant explanation for what he was seeing before acting on what he did not understand.

The boy quickly flailed about for a moment until he was able to get to his feet and once there, he reached behind himself and pulled an arrow that he readied to shoot directly at Taylor. To Tristan's surprise though, his aim was quickly interfered with by, of all people, his mother who selflessly stepped in his way.

"Stop, Tristan! You don't know what you're doing!"

"Yes, I do mother. Now get out of the way!" he said quite furiously, but his words were met with a stare and a tone of voice that Taylor could never emulate – that is to say, Tristan received the commanding stare and powerful tone which only a mother could offer.

"I don't think so You do not tell *me* what to do here!" and with this, Tristan pulled his bow ever tighter. Delissa's stare hardened. "Tristan Riley..."

She would've finished his full name but he grunted horribly, relaxing the force on his bow, "MOM!" She pursed her lips, shook her head, and continued her orders.

"Now you put that bow down and get your butt over here and apologize."

"Mother No!" Tristan pleaded desperately.

"Yes!" Delissa said with a growl as she stared her son down with harsh eyes. Taylor almost had to laugh in watching such a strong-willed young man break down and do as he was told.

After the comical apology from Tristan, Taylor decided to introduce his six students, and while the boy was cordial, it was quite obvious that this boy wanted little to do with the other children.

Taylor, shaking his head with a grin, handed Tristan one of the syringe guns. "Here, help your mother revive the others." With these words, Orion handed the second gun to Delissa.

"When they wake, I'll just them to go home. I'm not in the mood to answer any of their questions – especially Janet – oh – she's gonna ask all kinds of questions – ugh she's so nosey!" Delissa rambled on with with a nod to Taylor, who responded to only the first part of the comment.

"Good, I and mine will stay in the tent until you've all gone," and at these words Taylor couldn't keep himself from asking, "Is it really a problem, my being here on *your* land?"

She shook her head with almost a smile, "Not as far as I'm concerned – but I know some are going to want explanation. God I can hear her asking already," Taylor instantly saw distraction in Delissa's face and didn't understand this lat comment, but listened as the woman called out to her son. "Tris – get Janice up and see if you can't shew her off first – see if you can't scare her off with all these bodies lying around!"

Tristan mumbled in response "Sure thing mom – whatever you say!" but Delissa turned back to Taylor, continuing to speak as he was just about to enter the tent.

"You see, for any piece of land that is claimed, our – uh – laws say that there can only be one man and one woman who are of age. That's the way it is."

Taylor nodded his head. "Hmmm, then I have two questions." He said nervously, "First – where is Tristan's father, and second – what's considered 'of age' around here?" Delissa's answers came quick and were somewhat unexpected.

"Tristan's father is gone. He left 'bout five years ago and never came back – and all I can say is good riddance." Taylor could sense from her leaking emotions that she was, even now, struggling with the disappearance of this man, that she missed him, and that she loved him, but that she was trying to convince herself that she was better off.

Delissa readied her first unconscious person, who had landed a few feet from the entrance to the tent, before she looked up at Taylor again. She could see in continued questioning stare, and realized that she had not answered his second question. "Oh – eh – as far as age, it's twenty years – one tenth of a full life."

Taylor's mind started buzzing. He had, for the past several minutes, felt an instant to this woman, and he knew that while he was not of age, Jay was. So if he was going to make this situation work – and make it where he had a fighting chance with her and not against her, certain truths needed to be switched up a bit. Thinking fast, Taylor, for the first time *really* appreciating how youthful the Methuselah Virus kept his Jay's appearance, solved this problem in his head and spoke with arrogant confidence to set the woman's mind at ease.

"Hmm, well, then I guess it's just you, me, and the kids, and, if nothing else, I guess that makes us partners on this here homestead. Two people – one man, one woman, both of age." Taylor spoke with a false cheeriness in his voice, hoping to help Delissa's slowly shifting mood. He knew was lying about his age and that eventually he would have to lie about Jay's age as well, but she certainly didn't need to know, and it wouldn't be so farfetched to let her think what he wanted for the sake of avoiding any arguments or other, more physical conflicts.

Johnny, who was standing close by and had heard the conversation thus far, tried desperately to object. "Twenty, but you're only..."

Taylor quickly put his hand over the boy's face... "I was only *thinking of staying here, I know*. But after all this... well let's just say I'm committed."

He looked down at the boy, offering a smile and a quick pathic message to explain, before declaring in an unmistakable voice, " we're staying, and that's that!" With complete understanding Johnny nodded and thus Taylor's lie regarding his own age was allowed to persist.

Delissa smiled, tranquilizer gun in her hand and, with a sense of purpose, she waved for Taylor and the children to get into the tent.

For nearly an hour of patient waiting while Delissa revived the others, Taylor and the children all readied themselves with clothes that had replicated the night before, and Taylor showed Caitlin how to use the tissue replicator to heal his own wounds. Having done this, and thus hidden all signs of the morning fight, Taylor and the children had only the recounting of what they had seen, or in David's case what he had done that morning, to stay occupied.

Finally, interrupting David's very spirited account of the morning's fight, Tristan opened the entrance to the tent. Strangely enough, Taylor noticed that the boy's attitude had totally changed and it was with an immediate smile at the children that he told them it was okay to leave and walk about the forest.

"Mother, don't you think it would be best if we showed them around?" he added when he pulled his head out of the tent. She nodded, "Sure!" and waved for them to follow as she made her way into the trees.

In walking through the forest, Taylor stayed close behind Delissa at first, but she realized how distracted he was by her form-fitted cloaking suit and so it was she who decided, almost giddily, that it would be best if they walked side by side. Tristan, on the other hand, found himself very well occupied by the company of the children, and became completely impressed and at times a little overwhelmed at how gifted they all were in possessing such powers.

Taylor, looking back occasionally, noticed this good attention, and turned to Delissa with a glance of absolute curiosity. "You know," he said softly so the others couldn't hear, "It seems that both you and your son have had a change of heart, and in such a short time, and not that I'm complaining,"

"But you can't understand it." Delissa said finishing Taylor's question for him.

"Well – yeah!"

"It's Rowna." Delissa said looking down at the ground as if embarrassed.

"Rowna!"

"Yes. He's the only one of us who actually has some kind of weak form of telepathy. He is the oldest of us and he spent his youngest years in the city, but his parents, my great-great-great grandparents left the city and moved out here when he was only twelve. He, well, I think he's only half telepathic – and I think he found a way to tap into our emotions – he forces us all to be more aggressive. I know he's used this to his advantage before, but for the most part he – uh – well let's just say he's helped us survive this long."

"Sounds like he was brainwashing you!" Taylor said softly to her, trying hard not to offend or back tread on what seemed a positive direction in their relationship.

"One might say it was for our own good though!" she added, but in an instant she retorted, "Don't get me wrong, I was glad to see him run off like that, and I can't help but hope he's gone for good!"

"I know!" Taylor said, and with a simple look he reminded her that he had read her thoughts earlier and knew that a more aggressive side of her actually wished him dead.

As they all walked through the forest it was on several occasions that they would stop and Delissa would point in what seemed several random directions to define who lived where, and what property barriers existed between different clan members. This would be peppered with bits of gossip about different clan members and disagreements, family feuds and arguments – but all through the conversations Taylor noticed one aspect that seemed to be missing.

"Are there other children out here?" He asked, and in his mind he thought he might be able to do some good by teaching and training any of the wayward youths of the forest.

"No – not really – Tristan is the youngest – he was – eh – a *mistake,* next in line after him there's Janice – but she's twenty-five and has already taken a husband."

Delissa could see Taylor's inquisitive stare in response to these words, and she knew that, next to Janice, he would be filled with so many questions about what was going on out here in the forest.

"Once they're of age, it's easy enough to keep the males in our clan sterile, and we just don't have enough land to keep expanding. If we pushed our borders or our numbers any larger – we'd be noticed. It's happened once before and, from what Rowna has told us – we'd do anything to keep it from happening again."

Taylor wanted to press this issue further, but thought better of it, instead listening to other gossip about other clan members and the trivial goings on in a world that he never knew existed outside the walls of the city he once called his home.

After about an hour Taylor, the children, Tristan and Delissa all made their way back to the tent and on the children entering it, Delissa quickly spoke. "I can't help but ask – Tristan says he saw a body in your tent, all stiff and shiny – is he just pulling my leg or what?"

In a panic Taylor had somehow forgotten about Jay, and he still didn't have the heart to tell Delissa the half truth of the matter – she had *another* grown male on her land, so he recalled his plan and pulled out the simplest of lies.

"Oh, that's Jay – he's my assistant. He was injured during the escape so we had to put him in suspended animation 'til I had a chance to – eh – fix him." This was all true but as Taylor expected, Delissa was offering a concerned look over having two grown men roaming about her piece of land for others to see.

"Oh, but don't worry though," Taylor interjected on hearing these thoughts, "his being here won't break your one man one woman rule – he's only just turned eighteen." In his lie, Taylor couldn't help but project a little of himself onto his friend, and so, with the truth concealed, Delissa lit a small smile of relief with these words.

"Good! Now, not to be rude, but Tristan and I have to find food for dinner tonight. Since have to hunt for more than just two, this is going to take a while."

"Oh – I have a better idea!" Taylor said smiling as he and Delissa stood ever closer in front of the tent entrance. "Why don't you come by our home for dinner tonight?"

"What, that piece of fabric, you call that a home?" she said laughingly.

"Just come back at seven. I guarantee you'll be impressed."

She smiled and nodded before stepping over to stand under her son, who had occupied himself by climbing up into one of the trees.

"Okay, if you say so – but if we stay hungry – we'll be very – very cranky – you know – we haven't had to be cannibals in like twenty years or so." Taylor's mouth dropped fully wide, and with a wink, Delissa revealed her simple joke, thus reminding Taylor that he still had a great deal to learn about the new people that he was living with and amongst.

With a light thud Tristan jumped down from the tree and, with his mother by his side, the two slowly made their way into the forest and as they did Taylor shouted one last comment. "Remember – at seven – and come empty handed!"

Having carefully watched them move off into the darkness of the forest, it was a light tug at Taylor's tan colored slacks that forced his attention downward.

"What?" He said, not in an angry voice, but more in a voice of curiosity.

"So they're all gone now?" he heard Grace ask as she was looking up from the entrance, "So what do we do now?"

Feeling as though he'd just made two wonderful friends, Taylor felt that now was the best time to impress them with his feats of architectural genius.

"Now, my child, - now, we build!" And with this being said Taylor entered the tent and squatted between six curious and glowing faces. A quick glance at the clock that had been placed in the corner of the tent told him that there was less than nine hours before Delissa and Tristan would return. With a deep breath he realized that they all had their work cut out for them.

46 Making a Home

NOW THAT TAYLOR AND THE CHILDREN were free from the watchful eyes of those in the trees, he felt that building their new home should be the first priority. Actually, he had to be honest with himself – as well as things had turned around between he and Delissa, he knew he had a great deal of work to do so he could have a home ready, and maybe – just maybe have Jay ready by the time she arrived at seven. He wanted to impress her, and as it was already past 10 in the morning. He knew he had to tell the children what his plans were soon and, with this thought, he could already hear the objections in his head.

"Eight hours! Are you crazy?!" Johnny said in an annoyingly high pitched voice as he sat fidgeting quite restlessly between his siblings, who all had looks that, if looks could be translated into words, would have sounded just the same.

"Come on guys." Taylor pleaded with the youngsters, "We can do this – but it has to be a '*we*' thing, not an '*I*' thing, because I know I can't get this all done on my own." Taylor said while waving the rough data-pad sketch of their new home in front of the children.

"But where do we start?" Orion asked with a look of absolute bewilderment.

"Oh, well, uh – I've already kind of planned it out in my head." Taylor could now hear groans from his young audience, which he ignored, and continued, "but it's going to take work, absolute concentration, and the use of a lot of proto-bars."

When Taylor finished these words the children's faces all lit up. They had assumed that Taylor would be the only one using his powers to complete construction of their new home and that the rest of them would do – of all things – manual labor. David and Johnny gave each other a quick high-five when they realized the truth; that Taylor was really going to let them loose.

Taylor lit a smile, "Now calm down, calm down!" As these words came out of his mouth he shifted his stare from one of almost giddiness to a now serious and stern lecturing expression. "Now if this is going to work, I'm going to need everyone here to cooperate with me. If I ask for something to be done, I need it to be done quickly, efficiently, without question, and most importantly, I need it to be done safely. I want each one of you to use the eh – the eh" Taylor was now stumbling for the right words, "the – ah – the powers you were born with."

In an instant Johnny and Caitlin, who were sitting side by side, now lowered their heads in what looked like expressions of shame. Would Taylor, again, shut them out of actually enjoying the talents they had acquired by forcing them to sit and watch the others?

"You two," Taylor said as he knelt in front of them. "I want the two of you to team up with David and Aspen. I think we can work with your telekinesis and have better results. I don't quite trust your working with the intricacies of cyber-kinetic control just yet."

After saying this, Taylor was afraid the two might react negatively to the idea that he didn't trust them for some task, but in seeing their faces of absolute elation, he realized that he couldn't have been more wrong.

Before leaving the tent, Taylor handed each of the children what looked like clear smocks to put over their regular clothes. Not understanding what these were, the children showed displeased and questioning stares, but Taylor quickly explained that these were thermal suppressive covers that eventually molded to the existing clothing, making itself hidden to the naked eye while at the same time making it so that all their heat signatures, could not be read. Indeed, while Taylor wasn't sure if their heat signatures might be confused with the many other off-gridders in the forest, he was much more comfortable just knowing they weren't being watched at all. And so, in exiting the tent under the guise of being hidden from thermal satellites, this transplanted family began its marvelous construction project.

With Taylor and the children all exiting the tent, they carried with them different items, or in the case of the kinetics, who carrying several things. This included the still polymer encased body of Jay, the clock, the sleeping bags, sheets and other small items. And when the tent had finally been emptied, Taylor, with nary a concentrated thought, disassembled it and turned to face the group.

Aspen was the first to have a question even before they got started, "Father, what about Jay – when are you going to – you know – fix him up?"

He smiled at her, "when we get our home built, sweetie, then I'll take care of him. I want to make sure I've got the right tools, and that I'm prepared – don't worry – he's got a shelf life of at least another day!"

"Oh!" she said with a voice of relief and those around her started to giggle.

With that, Taylor looked at the M-Gen and, giving it an eye of concentration, forced it to create the first set of panels needed to construct their home. Taylor focused on these and moved them into position on the forest floor. As he did this he lit a bright smile on his face, for he felt that finally – after such a long time together, he and the children were actually building their new and final home.

Using the M-Gen at its full capacity, Taylor was able to create more panels, sheets of metal, walls, and surfaces that had been downloaded from the data pads the children had brought, and while all the parts had been designed to be interconnecting, Taylor had them bolted and welded into place for extra security. Here, he could think of nothing better than to have Orion and Grace cyberly use tools he had generated for that purpose. For an extra precaution, Taylor had the entire top surface of the home lined with thermal suppressor panels made of the same material as the smocks he had given the children. With any luck these would help the building hide any internal heat signatures from being detected. It was with this thought that he truly had to congratulate Orion for the thought to download such a material, to which the boy humbly said he merely grabbed as many patterns as he could in the few minutes he had.

As the day quickly passed, Taylor and the children were able to rapidly see their new home take form. It was, interesting for each of them to watch as this physical reality grew from the rough ideas in their heads and into the solid metal and composite existence that sprouted before them. They all watched and continued to use their cyber or kinetic powers to assist in the construction efforts of this home, but even still, there were some areas of the home, particularly those where the trees were protruding through the floor-plan, that the children didn't fully understand.

With extra pieces placed much like sturdy spikes that worked their way into the center of each open area, most of the children felt that the parts didn't make much sense in these locations. In fact, only Orion seemed to grasp what Taylor's master plan was. He smiled at Taylor, and near the end of the home's construction the boy seemed uncontrollably happy. He was, without a doubt, a child who knew a secret and was ready to burst.

"This is gonna be so coooooool!" he said excitedly as he welded one of the last few thermal suppressive panels to the top of the structure they had built.

From David and Caitlin the simple question of "where's the front door?" seemed to cause Orion's smile to grow ever wider. Taylor, seeing this, and wanting the final result to be a secret until it was ready, offered a sharp look to the boy, "shhhhh – pipe down – it's almost ready!"

Orion quickly stiffened up and with Taylor having placed the final panel on top of their new strangely shaped residence and Grace welding the last few interlocks solid, the boy smiled at the nearly finished product.

"Now everyone stand back!" Taylor said firmly, and with this Orion faced his siblings, held out his arms and slowly worked them into a slow backward pace, offering a wink to both Johnny and Grace as he did this.

The children, however, had hardly moved back but a few feet when, quite to their surprise, the entire home they'd just worked so hard to build started rattling and shaking. Then, with "ooohs" and "aaahs" the children watched as the structure slowly lifted itself upward.

Taylor was kinetically raising this new artificial structure, which weighed several hundred tons, and while his kinesis was much stronger than that of his students and fully developed, he was still struggling with the effort. With hard concentration he was extra careful to keep the home level while the children, looking high into the trees where their new home was being relocated, watched it ascend higher and higher; only slightly nervous when they saw the straining look on Taylor's face.

It was near the top of the trees that the youngsters noticed, and not without comment, that the strange spikes they had placed around the tree-trunks were hanging quite uselessly from their hinges perpendicular to their residential base, and as gravity took its hold on these metal protrusions, they both elongated and became sharper. As this happened, one by one, the children realized the purpose of these strange parts which they couldn't rationalize before.

Taylor turned for a moment to offer his watchers an awkward smile. Looking back he stopped the home's ascension having levitated it some thirty or more feet into the air, just reaching the peak of where the trees began to branch and produce thick foliage. Slowly he allowed the home to lower but not before focusing hard on the many spikes, forcing them inward toward the trees at their center. This had the effect of an eerie creaking noise which only ceased when the structure had completely rested with its spikes pushing hard into the sides of the trees.

Quite uneventfully, Taylor sighed, walked up to the M-Gen, and caught a proto bar that he forced the unit to practically throw in his direction. He ate it quickly, feeling his body replenish itself as he did so, and when he turned to the children he realized that all of them, Orion included, were quite confused about how they were supposed to lift themselves some thirty feet into the air so as to enter into their new home.

Taylor smiled, and with a wink of his eye he cyberly caused the start of a strange motorized sound that almost made the children jump. Still staring upward, they watched as a simple makeshift lift, lowered itself. The panel that made up the floor to the platform was quite unnoticed from the underside of the massive structure, and when it finally reached the forest floor Taylor tapped a few buttons on a small console that the lift had on its side. What he was doing, he informed the children, was calibrating the lift so it knew exactly how far down the ground was. With the nodding of their heads, Taylor waved for the children to board the lift. Not needing to be asked twice, the six of them quickly crowded onto it and Taylor tapped the button for it to rise into the overhead residence. He stayed behind, and kinetically placed Jay and the now disconnected M-Gen on the lift when it had returned.

It took Taylor less than a half hour to completely configure the separate M-Gen nodes throughout their new home so they could replicate food, clothes, and plumbing, and with the main M-Gen unit at its center, the home was fully powered, plumbed, and accommodating in every way possible.

When he had finished this task, Taylor walked up and down the corridors of his new home, and he could sense a definite feeling of déjà vu from the dream he had experienced the night before. He looked in on each of the rooms of his children and saw that they were now working feverishly in front of their own wall installed M-Gens, generating different object in an effort to make their rooms, in some way, reflect their own personality.

Taylor smiled at this and ran through each child in his mind. He tried to predict the décor of each room. The two whose rooms came easiest was that of Aspen and Grace. Polar opposites, he could see Grace's room darkening with black, sparing bits of white, and shades of grey. In contrast, he could see Aspen covering her walls with bright colors, flowers, pastels, and the like.

He then thought of David, whose fascination with the orient always reflected in a very Zen look. He could see browns, and reds with gold accents. His mind then moved to that of Orion's room, and he could see a mismatch of all kinds of colors and patterns, but not as an effort of decoration. Instead, as Orion fashioned himself the brightest and the best learned of his siblings, he would cover his walls with charts of the known parts of the galaxy and planets in the solar system, the milky way, elements from the periodic table, and he would clutter his room with all sorts of tools and trinkets that would reflect his varied interests.

Taylor shook his head at this thought. He, himself, was not as messy as Orion, but between Taylor and no one else, Orion *was* the brightest of his siblings; the brightest, but unfortunately, the least fun.

Caitlin, who was often so star struck with the many actors, actresses, and performers of the day, would cover her walls with an ever changing barrage of posters that she had undoubtedly already downloaded for herself. She, who was more closely aligned with Aspen, would keep the colors in her room bright, but not *too* bright.

Johnny, who so often reminded Taylor of himself at that age, would decorate his room with as little as possible. Not really sure what interested him most, and not sure if he could commit to any specific theme or idea of decoration, he would keep things as simple and clean as possible, easy to tidy, easy to care for, with very little on the walls, very little to distract, or give away about what his real personality was.

Taylor instantly flinched. His thoughts had moved to the final resident of the new home, Jay, and the fact that this man was still sitting in the quiet, and somewhat incomplete, ill equipped infirmary.

Walking quickly through the halls, Taylor's mind moved through a series of tools he would have to replicate before he could even begin working on the man, and as the teen entered the infirmary he sighed at the sight of his best friend being so badly injured. Taylor had, in fact, paid so little attention to the injuries this man had endured, that he now felt bad for the jokes, and the ever increasing time Jay had spent encapsulated in this polymer stasis.

Turning around, Taylor offered a loud, "I'll be in the infirmary for a while. I'll let you know when I'm finished." To which he heard a few 'okay's and 'alright's in response. He then turned around, the door closed, and with it, Taylor could hear the nothingness that was the longest silence he and his best friend had ever experienced while in a room together. With a deep sigh Taylor washed away these thoughts and reminded himself there was little that technology of the day and his knowledge of medicine couldn't repair.

Turning to one of the M-Gen nodes in the infirmary, Taylor cyberly forced it to close and after a few seconds it beeped an ever familiar sound. This was only the first request he made of the unit, and after nearly ten minutes, Taylor had finally replicated everything he needed, not just for dealing with Jay, but for the possibility of dealing with whatever these children might need in their time outside the city. From an *Expando*-bed to lay on, an *Expando*-sink which he immediately plumbed into the water system, and an entire list of scanners, tissue replicators, data consoles and displays, all which he neatly placed on an *Expando*-table.

Taylor was, indeed, grateful that Orion specifically downloaded the entire line of *Expando* products, whose portability and small design were all compact enough to be created inside any M-Gen console when requested.

Taylor looked around the room and, at realizing he had every piece of equipment, tool, device, and sensor he could imagine he would ever need, he turned to the rigid, shiny body of his friend. Walking up to Jay with a scanner in hand, he whispered softly, "I think it's about time we let you out of here!"

Despite their apparent lack of interest, outside the infirmary door six young faces were hard pressed against its cool surface in an effort to hear what was going on inside. They could discern the quick assembly and placement of the furniture, they could hear the M-Gen's many beeps, and as the room grew quiet for an uncomfortably long period, it was Caitlin who decided to chime in quickly and offer a solution to the unknown of what was going on.

She turned to her siblings, "This is crap! If we wanna know what's going on in there, why don't we just look." She said this and for a moment her brothers and sisters offered a series of confused expression, but with Caitlin tapping her own temple, they all nodded in understanding.

She and Johnny both had the ability to see inside rooms using their pre or post cog abilities – looking into the very immediate future or past to see what was going on, and so, combining their efforts, they stood side by side in front of the door. "Best if we do this together," the boy said, and as he and Caitlin held hands, between them four other hands grabbed theirs, and with their free arms, each placed a hand on the door.

Closing their eyes, the six children saw blackness at first, but this quickly changed to a swirl of color and slowly clouded images came into view. Before long they could make out the image of Taylor who was approaching Jay with a scanning tool.

"Hmmm, punctured the heart, both lungs, partially severed the left arm right through the humerus. And you've lost some blood, my friend." Taylor said shaking his head as he noticed the scanner's readout stating that Jay's blood volume was somewhere near 2 liters low.

He walked the scanner over to the M-Gen, and with a bit of concentration he forced the unit to activate and produce an equivalent amount of oxygenated blood, identical to Jay's as if it was from the man's own body. Taylor then returned to Jay's bedside and propped the scanner on the bed by clipping it to the frame, setting it to "constant mode" so it would keep an uninterrupted watch over the man's vitals.

It was at this point that the children all became quite curious over Taylor's actions and, as if they were a single consciousness, the whole of their view moved to Jay's bedside to watch as Taylor tapped the small polymer node box located just above Jay's nose. At deactivating the controller, the shiny coating covering Jay's body slowly softened and pulled itself upward into the node until all of it had been consumed by the tiny object.

Jay's body slowly flattened to the contour of the bed on which he was placed and in an instant the scanner at the end of the bed offered a long beep which Taylor recognized as a flat-line – that is to say, Jay's heart wasn't beating.

Taylor didn't waste any time. Using tissue replicators in both hands; one for Jay's arm, the other for his chest area, after thirty seconds he could see by the green glow emanating from under his fingers that both areas had become completely healed. He then quickly set up the transfusion to replace Jay's lost blood supply, while simultaneously grabbing the defibrillator and respirator units, both of which the children recognized immediately, having seen them used in many of their online entertainment programs.

The defibrillator was shaped like a large wide arch with several needles pointing inward, and a digital display at its top. Taylor kinetically removed Jay's shirt and put the unit above Jay's blood covered chest, and with a tap on the unit's display, it lit up in several places. The most notable feature it had was the glowing needle tips that were all pointed towards the center of Jay's now bare chest. Taylor focused on the display and could see that it showed how each needle was pointed at a different part of the man's heart. As, however, most bodies are not exactly the same, the needles needed their aim adjusted. The unit took only a few seconds to do this on its own and Taylor knew the device was ready when a green button lit up on its side.

Taylor placed the respirator on Jay's mouth and, all on its own, the unit reached up with two tiny plastic rods and closed Jay's nose while also forming an air tight seal around his mouth.

Taylor saw a green light illuminate on the respirator when this was done and he activated it and the defibrillator at the same time. All at once the several glowing needles brightened at their ends and, with many glowing shocks, each one shot a dart of electricity into Jay's body in sequence. Meanwhile his chest was slowly rising and falling with breath from the forced air of the respirator. Taylor watched as the defibrillator needles slowly and properly adjusted to the breathing motion.

While the shocks of the defibrillator had the effect of causing Jay's heart to pump one complete cycle, it wasn't enough to force it to restart completely. Taylor tapped the unit's green light again, but still – only one cycle.

This continued twice more before Taylor pressed the green button while also flipping another switch nearby labeled "constant cycle," whose purpose it was to keep the shocking sequence constant. This had the effect, on the outside, of offering some strange light show to the children who were still pathically watching from their own unseen perspective. They, however, were too concerned about Jay to appreciate the light being cast all around the room. No, these children knew that if Taylor had to switch the unit to this "constant" mode, things were more serious than previously thought and as the time continued to pass the children felt their hearts sink do a deepening sense of misery.

After watching and waiting for nearly five minutes the children's view suddenly became clouded and in the matter of a few seconds, all focus was lost. All around the children slowly opened their eyes.

"What the heck man, why'd you let go?" Grace said to Johnny as she jerked her hand from the others that were all entangled between he and Caitlin. She watched his hand slowly slipping from the door's surface and just as the words came out of her mouth she looked over and saw that Caitlin too had pulled her hand from the door. Indeed, both cognitive siblings were offering very somber expressions on their faces. With a whirl of telepathic continuity the other four children heard the same thoughts emanating from both of them, "If I'd only got to him sooner!"

Grace lowered her head, "sorry," she said softly as she rubbed Caitlin on the shoulder before doing the same for Johnny.

Caitlin's eyes were slowly welling with tears and, as it started to sink in that Jay was beyond repair, all six children jumped at hearing something that caused a shivering chill to rush up their spine. A man's voice, screaming in absolute pain, resounded through the infirmary.

All at once the children offered each other looks of bright eyed confusion and they joined hands to quickly reenter the room with swift telepathic focus.

As the image came in, clearer and clearer, the children could see Jay sitting upright, he was rubbing his head with one hand, and his chest with the other. They could see that he had several small puncture marks in his chest, and it was all too clear what had happened.

"How could you forget to strap me down?" Jay grunted as he rubbed his head from the massive headache he was experiencing. Taylor, now using the handheld tissue replicator on Jay's chest *again,* was shaking his head, "I'm sorry – I – so – sorry. If I had others here I might have had time – hell – you're lucky you're alive."

"How bad was it?" Jay asked turning his head to Taylor, who was now scanning vitals.

"Let's see," Taylor started, staring at the scanner's display, "through the arm, and the bone in the arm, through the lung, and two chambers of the heart."

"Yeah, nothing a little zip zap couldn't take care of right?!" Jay said smugly and as he watched Taylor's face look from the pad and turn somewhat sour the man realized it wasn't quite that simple. "Oh – eh – well. If it was *that* bad then I guess I should say thanks or something..."

Taylor's face quickly shifted to that of a smile. "That'll do fine." Taylor said, scrubbing the man's head lightly.

"Now – let me fill you in on things since we've arrived."

"Arrived?" Jay asked with almost a panicked curiosity, "speaking of which, where are we – and how long have I been out?"

Taylor offered a defined stare that Jay recognized immediately, and with a streaming of pathic thought, Jay learned of everything that had happened, including some of the thoughts the children had passed to Taylor, so that he, Jay, learned much of what had happened as if he was actually there.

"Wow!" Jay said loudly on blinking his way out of the shared telepathic vision, "What a hottie, that Delissa. I'd let her kick my butt any day, and those cloaking suits! Dude, how cool is that?!"

"Just remember – you're only supposed to be eighteen – and I'm over twenty, so I'm older than you... *Okay*!" Taylor said with a smile forcing Jay into the lie he had concocted.

"Whatever – it's not going to matter much anyways." Jay said in a shifty tone and as he did this Taylor offered a look of confusion, "What do you mean it's not going to matter?"

"I'm – not – staying," Jay said slow and soft while lowering his head. "It's nice that you planned a room for me in this amazing place you've built, and from what I can see I am impressed, but I - I'm not staying."

"But – but why?" Taylor questioned both softly, yet a bit forcefully.

"Taylor – your life is with your kids, – mine – it's in the city. I have friends out there too – I have a – a fiancée."

"Fiancée? But..."

"No buts – I've got my life to live – and you have yours. – Now I know what you're thinking – that they'll have all kinds of questions for me when I get back to Los Angeles – and that I might tell them where you are – but – right now," Jay said looking around, "I barely know where *here* is."

"Well – why did you bother coming with the children then – they'd of done fine without you – and – no offense, you've been nothing but dead weight since we got here!"

"Why do you think?" Jay asked shaking his head all the while realizing his friend's frustration. "I came because of Caitlin."

"Caitlin? She has nothing to do with..."

"She has everything to do with my being here, and you know, for someone who's supposed to be so smart, you sure can be pretty stupid sometimes." At this Taylor flinched and Jay continued, "Duh – after Johnny's vision I was worried about Caitlin and when I knew the vision was coming to life I just – I couldn't let that girl leave my sight. I had to make sure she'd be alright. If I hadn't been on that transport she'd've fallen out - DIED before we ever really left The Towers! That's why Johnny didn't see her in his vision – she was DEAD."

Taylor closed his eyes and recounted the thoughts which the children had passed to him the day before. He could see David's memory of Jay catching Caitlin's hand at the last second, and he could see the boy knocking over Dr. Zeldin.

With a sigh, Taylor sat on the bed beside Jay. "I see it, I see – I'm sorry, I had no idea." Taylor whispered almost apologetically and with this Jay added, "For once, I was right, and I was there when I needed to be – but you're all safe now, and I have my life to live – so I will be taking my life – back into the city – and live miserably ever after – without my best friend, and more than likely, without a job – but that's just the way it has to be."

"Well if that's what you want then you can leave in the morning, but the least you could do is have one last dinner with us."

Taylor jumped from the bed, making his way to the infirmary exit.

Slowly the image before the children clouded as whispers of the word "Go!" permeated the air between them.

All at once the children opened their eyes, staring at the infirmary door again, and it was only a fraction of a second before the door opened to reveal Taylor staring down at them, shaking his head.

"Come one in guys, I know you've been watching," he said as they made their way past him and through the door where, all at once, they crowded around Jay's bed, each in their own way begging him not to go.

"Okay, kids. I get the picture. You don't want me to leave. But you're just going to have to deal with the fact that I'm not staying here! I can't. I have a life back in the city. I – I want the city – I need it."

Aspen grabbed Jay by the hand, "But we need you..." she said staring at him with the most adoring eyes she could muster, and while this gave Jay an almost laughing smile, he just put his hand on her cheek and rubbed it softly with his thumb.

"You don't really need me. You only think you need me. You have Taylor here." Jay looked over at his friend. "He's all you *really* need."

The children shook their heads with denial, and for the first time Jay, looking into each of their young round faces, felt that they really – really liked him... no, that they loved him – each in their own way.

47 Last Dinner

LEAVING JAY WITH THE CHILDREN in their new treebased home, Taylor paced under it watching the time closely, and as the seven o'clock hour came and went he felt his heart rise to almost a panic, then fall to despair. He continued to trudge through the twilight of the evening hour, surrounded by tall trees and for the first time appreciating the sound of the stream nearby. As the minutes passed he hoped against hope that Delissa and Tristan would actually come by for dinner as he had asked – even if they were late.

The teen kicked up leaves to help his mind pass the time easier, but as his nervousness and expectation both increased, he felt a sick feeling in the pit of his stomach. His mind mulled over the possibility that they wouldn't show, and for some reason just the thought pained him more than he expected. He decided to fend off his uneasiness by focusing on the mass of leaves in front of him. He kicked the mound into the air and caught it kinetically, forcing it to spiral around himself, moving in an assortment of directions, and while he didn't need his hands for this task, he often thought it interesting to wave them around with his kinetic efforts.

Taylor once, when watching Jay conduct an orchestra through a pair of headphones, explained this pseudo-kinetic action as being the same. The music would continue whether Jay conducted or not, but sometimes the conducting was fun – and thus it was often the same with Taylor's kinetic efforts, especially when they were more recreational than work. And so Taylor continued, for several minutes, to swirl the leaves in front of him, up and down, through loops he had created with his arms, high overhead, then quickly dipping low to pass swiftly between his own legs. It was no wonder that he lost track of time. He was so involved with the fun he was having with the leaves that he could so easily manipulate, but as he forced them to rush across the open space in front of him, they stopped quite unexpectedly some distance away. It was as if they had stuck to something he couldn't see.

"There you are!" Taylor said loudly, and at saying this, two bodies, one full height and one a little shorter, revealed themselves. Taylor felt his heart sink when he realized that he had forced the mass of dirt and leaves right into Delissa's face. He immediately approached, apologizing with every step, and as she disconnected and pulled her mask off he could see that she wasn't upset, but rather confused. She looked around quickly with a purposeful, perplexed, and finally, an almost amused look on her face.

"So uh – where's this home I was supposed to meet you at?" she said smiling at him.

"It's a secret – I can't tell you." Taylor responded, and at this Tristan pulled off his own mask. "I told you he couldn't do it!" the boy said snidely to his mother.

In front of himself, Taylor forced the leaves to begin swirling, low at first, then higher, and eventually he forced them to spiral between Tristan and Delissa as well. Taylor, smiling the whole time, quickly retorted on Tristan's prior comment. "I have built a home – here!" he said with a small pause, raising his eyebrows, "but it's a secret, and I can't tell you where it is."

At this point the leaves swirled quickly behind Taylor and formed what became an obvious arrow that pointed itself straight upward and thereafter bobbed up and down repeatedly.

"I just can't tell you – I told my kids this would be our little secret." Taylor persisted with a playful grin, but after a pause, and with the laughing of Delissa and the awe of Tristan at looking upward, Taylor offered a false look of shock. "The leaves are giving me away aren't they?" He shook his head, shifting his stare back to a smile, and as he turned his head he quickly whirled his hand around forcing the leaves to once again make a quick lap around about the three of them before quickly forming a small mound in the middle of the forest.

Taylor winked his eye at Delissa and with a smile he said "You're late by the way..." and as he said this the overhead home slowly lowered its lift, causing Tristan to almost laugh with giddiness as he became more and more impressed with what Taylor and his small band of youngsters could do in just a few hours. Delissa on the other hand, merely responed, "Sorry. We got a little tied up at home."

"She couldn't figure out 'what to wear'" Tristan said mockingly in a high pitched voice, to which Delissa lightly kicked the boy in the calf from behind.

"Owwww."

Taylor smiled, "so – I see you're wearing your cloaking suit again."

With a quick wink to return the one he had given her earlier, she turned around, "Do you think you could help me with that by the way?"

He could see when she turned, that on the suit there was a long zipper up the back that was interfered with by several interlocks of the bright strips which, no doubt, were part of the intricate cloaking technology.

"Uh – sure." Taylor said, and as he reached out to grab the zipper he could see that Tristan was watching him with a great eye of scrutiny. Taylor pulled his hand away and opted, instead, to kinetically unzip and detach the interlocks of the outfit. Delissa turned, expecting Taylor to be using his own hands for the job, and felt herself quite disappointed when she saw that he wasn't.

She quickly squirmed out of, and rolled up her cloaking suit just as the lift raised itself into the bright white lights of the new residence. She was in obvious contrast with her surroundings as she was wearing a different body suit underneath, this one completely black with only a stripe of white at the ankles, wrists, and neckline. To complete her look she pulled some small metal piece out of her hair and instantly her mane of hair fell in a swirl of red color causing Taylor's bright blue eyes to stare in awe. He was amazed at the beauty that she hid so well in such a small space. In staring, his eyes met hers and, at this point if he wasn't before, he was quite smitten with her now.

"Woah!" he said in exclamation at this change of appearance and he turned to see that Tristan was also working his way out of his own suit. He was wearing a similar body suit as his mother's, but his had a more masculine design to it, with its zipper up the front, and no white at the wrists, ankles or neck.

Just as Tristan had gathered up both his and his mother's cloaking suits, all three were met by Jay who decided it best to shake Tristan's hand first out of politeness and respect, "So you must be Tristan!" he said smiling at the boy, hoping desperately for a warm reception.

"And you must be that human popsicle I saw earlier!" Tristan said arrogantly, and while the back of his head was quickly smacked by Delissa, all could hear the giggles of the children who were peeking around a nearby corner. Jay showed a brief face of displeasure then quickly washed it away and greeted Delissa with a simple hand gripping and a slight bow. "Delissa, it is a pleasure!"

She could see that Jay was taking in her full form, but she did not seem to mind and again the children offered their giggles over the whole affair.

"Well, you've met the children." Taylor said waving for them to show themselves fully. "And Jay, my assistant, I am happy to report is all healed up from his injuries and practically good as new."

Jay kept eye contact with Delissa, and found himself quite taken by her beauty. Not wanting, however, to tread on his friend's territory, he opted to turn all attention elsewhere, and as she walked by he whispered loudly to her, "My dear, you are beautiful and I think Taylor's in love"

Taylor was barely able to make out this comment and after a noticing cough, he forced everyone's attention to the two doorways before them. "I think it's time to show you our new home." he added, eyeing Jay with a scolding expression.

Delissa, looking about the area they had been lifted into, saw white walls lit up by tracks of soft pin-lights which glowed bright enough to illuminate the entire room, but were somehow softened so as to not pain the eyes. The two doors which exited this room were placed at strangely odd angles and as the group took one of these into a corridor, Taylor proudly explained the details of the new home.

It took less than ten minutes to work their way up and down the weaving corridors, which Delissa and Tristan had commented on several times, and as Taylor stopped near the end of the tour he turned and looked at his two guests before speaking. "Here is the rooming circle. It has twelve sides, and thereby twelve rooms, like a clock. You are standing in one of them."

Tristan and Delissa looked down at the floor for a moment then each one peered down a different hall. They could clearly see the curved walls, and as they looked around the curvature, they could see multiple doors leading to other rooms.

Taylor continued to speak to the group, detailing the home. "Each room down this hall is either a bathroom, or a bedroom for one of the children, for myself, or for Jay."

At this point Jay sighed, and Taylor quickly added, "But as I have just learned, Jay will not be staying with us. He has decided to return to the city tomorrow."

"Deilssa, who had smiled through the entire tour and was seemingly having a great time, quickly soured her face and she turned to Taylor.

"What! He can't leave – If he goes back to the city they'll know where you..."

"Relax!" Taylor said slowly reaching up to hold one of Delissa's shoulders. "I'm going to give him a sedative in the morning to keep him resting, and when he wakes, he will be at the city's edge with a beacon in his pocket that he can activate when he's up and about. The city can pick him up at the wall, and despite their no-doubt numerous questions and post-cog probing, he won't be able to tell anyone where we, you, or any of this is because he'll've never been aware of the trip out or the trip back. So it's Okay – you can relax!"

"Yeah mom, 'relax'" Tristan said as he was stepping into the rooming hall, being lead by David who wanted to show off his room first.

Delissa sighed, "Fine, Okay fine. I'll try not to worry, but..."

"No buts" Taylor said looking Delissa straight in the eye, "Everything will be fine, and YOU TWO," Taylor shouted down the hall, "dinner first – fun later!"

All at once the children, Taylor, Delissa and Jay made their way to the dining room, which had been decorated by the children and was filled with all kinds of plants from the surrounding area, and in the center of the room was a large dark cherry-wood dining table, large enough to conveniently seat ten.

Taylor took one end and Delissa the other of the long table, and after a moment's wait Aspen and Orion, who had gone to the kitchen, came into the room with several large silver domed trays between them.

"Ah dinner is served." Taylor said loudly, and after Aspen and Orion took their seats, Aspen slowly raised the trays overhead and placed them in the center of the table before removing the silver lids and floating them out of the room. Taylor offered a slight look of concern at seeing the trays move out of sight, but his mind was met with a telepathic whisper from Aspen who happened to see his expression.

"Don't worry," she said, "I'm just setting the lids on the floor in the kitchen. We'll clean them up later."

He nodded his head to her and thereafter addressed the group, "Delissa, Tristan, our guests. I have let Orion decide our menu for the night, and as the preparer of our meal, I feel it only fitting that he offer introduction to the food we are about to eat." With a nod Taylor forced all attention to Orion who quickly blushed, but still stood and started to speak, shaky and nervous as he went.

"Well – eh, first we have a dish of chicken piccata, capers and all," at this Taylor found himself already impressed for the children knew that this was one of his most favorite of meals, but a few around the table offered sour scrunching of their faces. Orion noticed these bitter expressions and he continued with a sigh. "Next, we have a plate of prime rib, ready to be cut, another of ripe vegetables, a tray of turkey, dressing, and mashed potatoes, one of Pizza and Cheeseburgers, just for you

David, and finally several loaves of hot fine bread and butter."

It seemed that on finishing the menu Orion had mentioned a few things he knew his brothers and sisters would appreciate, but the most impressive reaction came from Delissa, who spoke loudly across the table.

"How in the world could you? I don't understand how... This is all so amazing, and to think you built this, and prepared all of this – in just one day... but – but how?"

"Delissa," Taylor responded at seeing her delighted bewilderment, "my students here are very intelligent, and while I've worked hard to make them so, they have exceeded my expectations at nearly every turn. So it should be no surprise that when they decided to escape from the city, they had a plan to give *me* – or rather – *us* everything we would need to make our lives as comfortable as possible. – So enjoy it. It's here, you're here and, as I believe, nothing in this world ever happens without there being a reason for it!"

Delissa closed her eyes, took a deep breath and, at offering an odd smile and to her son, the two began eating slowly, trying much of the food as if reserved, cautious, or nervous about the content.

"Is there – something – wrong?" Orion asked nudging Tristan, in the side.

"Hmmm," the teenager murmured with a mouth half-full of food, and, on swallowing, he added, "well, we have to work for what we have. It's our way – to – well – struggle. That is why we live off the grid."

"You wouldn't understand..." Delissa added quickly and as she put her hand on her son's knee, she gave a quick look that told the boy to say no more. Orion, however, was not satisfied at ending the conversation this way.

"Sure I do!" the child voiced quickly, "In the city there is no struggle. People work all kinds of odd jobs, but there really isn't any struggle – or conflict or hunger – there's *no need for anything like that*."

"I think, Orion," Taylor interjected, "that Delissa and Tristan believe a struggle, or a conflict, a fight for what you want or need in life is what gives your life and the things you have value."

"I wouldn't mind talking to her more on the subject, but not here, at our first dinner. It's just not – appropriate." Taylor said softly looking for an adequate word to finish his statement, and in so doing he looked down the table and saw a mouth filled young face look up at him.

"Who cares? This food is great!" Tristan said as he found himself more comfortable eating what was in front of him and with this outburst Delissa looked with a scolding stare at her son. "Tristan – mind yourself. *His* beliefs aren't ours!"

"Well," Taylor said loudly and in an obvious effort to change the subject he looked down the long table to Delissa's other side, "Jay, this is your last dinner with us. So is there anything you would like to say to – you know – to be official like and all."

The children all stared at Jay tapping their glasses, and several of them shouted "speech – speech!" before Jay stood up and waved his hands to settle the group.

"Come on, dude, you know I hate it when you do this kind of crap!" he said, shaking his head, standing, and looking down the table at Taylor. "I don't really know what to say. As I look around this table at the six young faces I have watched growing up for the past five years, I just – I hold each one of you so dear to my heart, and I know I'll miss you more than you could possibly imagine. You know, it is hard for me to do this – to leave you all like this, and for the first time I mean it when I say, it hurts me more than it hurts you."

"I'm giving up seven people out of my life, while each of you is only giving up one. And as I look around this table I see such a strange set of diverse personalities and I can't imagine what life is going to be like without you – but I'll find out – and no matter what I'll always keep you in my heart."

Jay then focused his stare at the end of the table.

"And to you – Taylor, who has truly been a father to these children when all others were afraid to enter same room with them. You are my friend, and I respect you – I admire you – you're like a brother to me. You should know – just know that I envy you." To this Taylor offered a perplexed expression. Jay smiled and offered a simple answer. "You have found your purpose, your place, so young in life, while I am still trying to find mine. I am going to miss your wit, your charm and your energy, but most of all I am going to miss watching you live your life to its fullest with and through these children. You are all my friends. You, Taylor, are my best friend. I love you, and I will miss you."

While Taylor was only barely able to keep his composure at these words, it was the children who seemed to slowly break down, tears flowing down their faces, a reflection of memories of the past, and when Jay finished, they struggled to smile as the man took his seat.

Taylor looked across the table at Delissa, who wasn't smiling, or frowning, but rather had a beguiling expression on her face. With a raised eyebrow she stared at Taylor and shook her head with disapproval.

While Taylor wasn't able to decipher this expression, he thanked Jay for the kind words and the table finished its meal with the children retiring to their rooms, each wanting to pull Tristan's attention in their own direction, and the young teenager loving the interaction and the attention from other children that, at his age, he didn't get enough of.

"I think I'm going to get some sleep too – I'm just so tiiirrrreeeed." Jay said ending in a yawn. Taylor nodded, realizing that the man's body might require some resting time after healing itself so fast.

Taylor, not able to keep himself from doing it, put his hand on the man's shoulder and pulled him in for a quick hug before letting him to bed. He, Taylor, felt a wrenching in his heart. Something close to a panic, and he knew that he would miss this friend of his, someone that he had known for more than half his life, and was his one and only true friend.

48 One Final Vision

SITTING IN THE DEN of his new home, finally alone with Delissa, Taylor felt nervous to the core, something that he wasn't used to, and something that had been building she and her son had arrived. In finding rest on the yet unfurnished floor of this large room, Taylor looked over at her without any thought of what to say. This was quite an intimate setting for the two of them and was, by far, the closest thing he had ever experienced to a date. His loss of words persisted, and it showed in the long, almost uncomfortable silence that lingered between them.

"Soooooo," Taylor said slowly to break the discomfort, but his clumsy rhetoric was quickly cut off by Delissa.

"Sooo – why did you lie to me?" She asked bluntly, now with a smile on her face.

"I didn't – huh – what are you talking about?" Taylor asked with confused, heart-fluttering, stomach-sinking panic.

"Listen – It's a good thing Jay *is* leaving – I mean he's a nice guy and all, but he's not eighteen, and you and I both know it! And he can't work a story to keep a secret either..."

Taylor slowly rubbed his own forehead, "that speech – five years with the kids – that's it isn't it."

"Well," Delissa said with a smile and a slight squint of her light green eyes, "it's a little more than that – actually, it's a lot more than that. I've been watching the two of you and, I have a feeling – just a hunch – you're not as old as you say you are..."

"I never said how old I was!" Taylor retorted in almost a panic, watching her sprawl out to a comfortable position of lying on her side. "No – that's true – but you did want me to believe that you were..."

"Old enough!" Taylor said firmly trying to cut Delissa off.

"Are you?"

"Listen, I've been with these kids five years too you know..."

Delissa turned her head to one side and squinted to almost a wink... "That's true, but," she sighed, "there's just something – I can't put my finger on it..."

"It's nothing!" Taylor interjected and he quickly decided to change the subject.

His mind immediately gravitated to thoughts of his birth and his geriatric mother. She was found in the forest, just north of Los Angeles. *Why, she would've probably been from around these parts.* Instantly his mind seared with how he could ask questions without drawing suspicion to his own age. If he was clumsy about it, she would figure out in a heartbeat that he was only eighteen, and any romantic thoughts he was having, and for the first time in a long time *he was actually having them,* would be thwarted.

"Hmmm, my students were found out here in the forest you know," Taylor started, hoping for a completely different approach. Delissa looked surprised, and he continued. "Sure, at the age of five, out here in the forest, with no memory of who they were, or how they got out here." She looked interested and yet a little taken by his hungry stare at her. But still he continued. "I was wondering – in the past twenty years or so – have you ever had anybody go missing, you know, from your *clan?"*

Delissa turned her head to one side and slowly started to nod before opening her mouth with an unexpected response. "Nope! Not except for Kyle."

Taylor stared at her with curiosity and she quickly responded with a bland retort. "My no good husband – left 5 years ago – everybody else out here's been fine. Or have left on their own – we've even taken in a few from the city over the past year or two."

Taylor was intrigued. He had retreived at least something of an answer out of her, and avoided the truth of his age, at least for now. And in so doing, he and Delissa spent the rest of the evening talking about the difference between life on and off the grid. Taylor often had to keep Delissa's emotions in check as she became quite heated over how the two of them had lived their lives so differently. Even here Taylor was careful to skirt certain details about his life so as to not reveal his age, and a few times he was afraid Delissa might have picked up on this, but if she did, she certainly didn't press the issue.

With a quick look to a clock on the wall that was showing it was somewhere past one in the morning, Delissa decided it best to end the night. She walked to the rooming corridor and was concerned that there was no noise coming from the rooms. Taylor, following behind, pointed that the two should take opposite routes of the rounded corridor.

All rooms showed to be empty except for Taylor's, which was at the opposite end of where they had entered the corridor. His large bed showed seven children all resting quietly in front of a large blank plex screen.

Delissa was about to enter the room when Taylor grabbed her by the shoulder.

"No – wait..." he whispered, and as she turned her face to his, he could see the confusion. "Watch this!" he whispered.

Taylor raised his nose to the air and, closing his eyes, he focused on all seven of the slumbering children. One by one each of them woke and slowly shuffled past Taylor and Delissa, offering a "g'night Dad," as they made their way to their rooms.

Tristan, being the last to wake, rested his head on his mother's side and while she rubbed his face gently he looked up at Taylor. "Hmmm - did you even say anything just then?" he asked, and Taylor responded by shaking his head and tapping the side of his temple.

"Cool," The boy whispered wearily and with that he and Delissa slowly made their way to the home's exit.

As the two readied themselves to be lowered to the ground below, slipping on their cloaking suits in the process, Tristan turned to his mother.

"Can we come back tomorrow?"

She gave the boy a quick disapproving look, and he knew better than to ask twice. Upset, he turned his head downward and listened to his mother's words.

"We can't get used to this. It's – it's not right. Tomorrow you stay home and stay to your lessons – and I will hunt. That's the way it has to be!"

The look on Tristan's face turned even more sour and as the lift lowered the two of them to ground level Taylor only shook his head.

"It doesn't have to be this way." he said, but he was unsure if she heard. In his mind he'd love for nothing more than to help teach and train Tristan with what he was sure would be the boy's first experience with virtual classes. But this, he knew, would be massive breach of one of the fundamental differences between Taylor's life and Delissa's.

Stepping away from the hole in the floor, Taylor made a mental note of needing improved safety around the home's entrance, and with weary eyes he slowly shuffled his way to bed.

After entering his room, throwing clothes in his empty closet, and readying for sleep, he finally slipped into his bed. But despite the comfort of where he lay, Taylor's mind was far too busy to do anything but think itself to tiredness. He would have thought, in having a home of his own and his children dreaming safe and sound nearby, that sleeping would have been easy for him. Instead, his mind twisted so many thoughts in and out of his brain. He couldn't believe how frustrated he had become over Delissa. How could she get under his skin so easily? Not even Dr. Hathaway had bothered him this much.

He couldn't put his finger on exactly how he felt about this new woman in his life. He knew it wasn't heated anger – it wasn't annoyance – well, maybe it was – but it was so different!

He wanted Delissa's approval, but at the same time he didn't want to be or become something he wasn't. Sure there was the lie about his age, but that was minor. No – Taylor was a scientist – he lived by technology – he was raised by technology – and so were his kids. He wasn't going to change any of that just because her ideology or homology frowned on it.

Taylor's mind shifted to his students. They still had a chance. They could still grow up and live in the city, so there wasn't a real need for them to adopt a lifestyle like Delissa and Tristan's – No. They could still live in the comforts of modern day and when the time came, Taylor and the children would make their way back into the city. Yes – this was how it would be.

Taylor decided these thoughts in his brain, but still found it difficult to absorb the idea of leaving Delissa, and even Tristan behind. Yes – he could – he could convince them to come with him into the city. Shaking his head and rubbing his eyes Taylor rolled over and realized that his tiredness must be affecting his judgment – "There's no way they would ever come with me to the city." he said aloud, and with those being his last words to fall into the night, Taylor closed his eyes.

With a warm face and squinting eyes, Taylor welcomed the sun of the next morning unable to remember his dreams from the night before. He sat up and could already hear the laughing voices of the children outside his door. He quickly grabbed a robe from his closet as he exited his room. He followed the laughter of the children all the way into the kitchen where he was met with an array of strange odors to match the curious faces all staring at him quite expectantly.

"It's about time, sleepy-head!" Aspen said as she grabbed his hand and walked him past the kitchen and into the dining room where he, again, was met with more strange smells.

He stood beside table and saw several dishes all prepared, it seemed, for him. Looking out at the varied, and sometimes chard appearances of the food, Taylor wouldn't presume all of it to be edible and he was certainly reconsidering adding a good lesson or two on cooking into the children's virtual training programs.

He sat at the chair which was kinetically forced into his legs by Aspen and, as he was pushed up to the table by her, he couldn't help but wonder and ask, "What's going on here?"

"Breakfast... duh!" Grace said as she entered the dining room carrying more food, and for the first time – was she? – She was! – she was wearing – pink!

Taylor shook his head in confusion, but this was answered quite ambiguously by David who entered the dining room with his mouth already filled with bits of what looked like chocolate. "Do we need a good reason to have a feast around here?"

"A feast – come on guys – now there's no need for all this."

"Sure there isn't." Orion said with a smile as he joined the group in the dining room, his face messy with a face full of food. "But then again – why not?"

Taylor unnecessarily rubbed his eyes and couldn't believe that Orion, the neatest cleanest of the boys, had his face covered in – was it – mashed potatoes.

Taylor quickly stood from the table almost in a panic. He walked up to the boy and wiped his face clean, but, as if out of nowhere, the child pulled out a spoon full of more of the same, and started eating it – or rather – inhaling it as if he hadn't had a meal in days. It only took a moment for Orion's face to look exactly as it did just a moment before – messy with food.

Taylor turned his head and saw that Caitlin was ready to bring out yet another tray of mismatched food items offering more color and smells to the table at which he was forced to sit at again by the shifting chair that Aspen was manipulating.

But this was all too much for Taylor to bear. He stood up, walked back to his room and as he slowly passed the children's own rooms down the arched corridor, he was shocked to see each one was filled with trinkets, toys, electronics, tools, and all sorts of other things. To make matters worse Taylor could see that the children's M-Gen nodes were all working hard to make more of the same, slowly regurgitating an electronic mess of stored patterns.

He made his way to his own room and saw that even his M-Gen was producing massive amounts of – of – stuff, and making more by the second. He didn't know what to think. As he made his way around the corridor he noticed that one room, and only one room, wasn't a cluttered mess.

"Johnny – what's going on here?"

The boy turned around with almost a smile, "Hey, this is your dream – not mine!"

Taylor wasn't quite relieved to hear these words, but as he looked around at everything he saw, he realized that these words were more literal than figurative. He *was* having a dream, and it seemed that the events and his conversations with Delissa from the night before had somehow worked their way into his brain to create some kind of strange – horribly warped dream.

Taylor sighed – why was it always Johnny who was his foundation back to the world of the real. This thought consumed Taylor for a few moments before he walked into the boy's immaculate room. Now that Taylor really looked, however, immaculate wasn't the word – it was empty, and the M-Gen was emptying it further, item by item, each second, eventually taking away the child's bed, leaving nothing but the child sitting quietly in the middle of the room.

"So – the others are wasteful – and I am just – well – plain – empty and boring... is that it?" Johnny questioned harshly, and as the child turned Taylor could see that the boy's light blue eyes were reddened with anger.

"Is that what you think of me?" Johnny repeated.

Taylor put his hand on the boy's shoulder and in the instant that he made contact both their views quickly changed. It was as if a flash fire had consumed the two of them and the entire room all at once, and as it did this it changed their entire appearance and their surroundings. Taylor's eyes glanced around quickly and saw that Johnny's room had returned to some degree of normalcy, and that, while they stood to gaze out the window of his room, he, Johnny, spoke very somberly.

"Why can't I get this out of my head?"

Taylor took his place beside the child and in looking out the window he could see streaks of clouds between the branches of the trees overhead. They both watched the clouds billowing thicker and thicker. They were moving fast though, and as Taylor moved his head to the side to look in the direction the clouds were headed, Johnny looked up at him and spoke.

"Do you really have to see to know where the clouds are headed?"

Taylor felt a chill run down his spine. He realized immediately that this was, again, the same vision which the two had been sharing for the past two days.

"But why... why come back here?" Taylor asked firmly of the boy.

"That's not the question you should ask yourself father..." Johnny murmured with a false smile, "The question you should be asking is – why are they here too?"

The child tilted his head backward twice and with that Taylor turned around to see five young faces all looking at him with expressions of fear and confusion.

"Father – what's happening?" Aspen asked nervously as they all collected at Taylor's side.

"I – I don't know..." Taylor said and while this may not have been the truth, he thought it best to keep what he knew to himself. Even with this protective thought, Taylor's mind was spinning and his head was filled with Johnny's quiet voice.

"We all have the gift now – to see – and this is what we see. My gift may be strong – like yours..." At this point, even miles from the cities edge, a familiar bright flash made its way through the trees of the forest. Johnny's gaze, however, did not waver from the window as he pathically spoke, "their gift is weak now – and even still, this is what they see. So ask yourself – just ask, 'why is *this* what they see?'" Johnny pathically instructed softly, and at finishing these words Taylor could feel a shift in his own sense of gravity.

Was it possible that, whatever it was that had attacked the city in his visions before, it was strong enough to destroy things even way out here? Taylor's mind was answering this question with disbelief in his brain as he turned his stare out the window and realized that the view was changing. The trees that supported their home were slowly bending and flexing in the direction of the city.

Taylor and the children, Johnny included, were all pressed hard against the wall of Johnny's room and all Taylor could do was think about waking up the children. He wanted to wake them up from this nightmarish vision more than anything and when he woke too he would find that they were all safe in their beds. He closed his eyes and focused hard on this thought, telling all the children to do the same.

With a great pounding noise he could hear and feel that the home which they had, in reality, just built the day before was now dragging itself along the forest floor, crashing into trees as it made its way toward the city's edge.

Taylor focused hard on trying to keep the children safe, still not sure if any telekinetic effort would be useful in this seemingly indelible view of the future. With a great crash Taylor's ears seemed to almost burst and when he opened his eyes he saw that the room they were in was now cracked in half, and they were fully exposed to the outside air.

Taylor closed his eyes wishing with all his heart to wake these children up from their horrible nightmare and, with a rushing face full of earth and tree limbs it seemed that his desires had painfully come true in an instant.

Taylor sat up as usual, sweat covered – heart pounding, and was filled with the sense that all around him the room was shaking – vibrating, but he was too distracted by the screams and yells from the children to focus on this for long.

One by one he quickly ran through the round corridor, turning each child's bedroom light on to make sure they were all okay. He passed Jay, who was making the same effort, and while Jay didn't know what was going on, the man was still just as concerned for the children. Jay had, after all, worked so hard to ensure their safety.

Taylor continued to make his round, now having to listen to Jay scream at him,

"What the hell's going on?"

"Shared vision," Taylor said quickly.

"Not another one!" Jay replied quickly to which Taylor retorted, "Same vision as before; ended the same as before..."

"Well of course it did – if it's the same one...!" Jay spewed and he decided it best to just wait and let Taylor run in and check on each of the children in his own way. With this, the teen moved quickly past him and continued entering, leaving and re-entering the different rooms.

At the last one – David's, Taylor was filled with relief to find each child in their bed, each having woke up with a shock much the same way as Taylor did just a few moments ago.

With a sigh, Taylor made his way out of the last room with a lowered head and waved for Jay to go back to bed before he, Taylor, slowly made his way back to his own bedroom. The teen felt a chill in the air as the door to his room opened and the coolness of the metallic floor certainly didn't help matters. For this reason Taylor made his way to his closet to grab his robe.

On looking inside, though, he quickly realized that the closet was basically empty and he had yet to M-Gen himself anything else to wear. He had nothing for clothes other than those he had tossed in the closet a few short hours ago and the T-shirt and boxers he was wearing at that moment.

He felt the need to laugh at this and he thought to himself – if he had really been paying attention he would have recognized his previous reality as a dream from the moment he grabbed and put on his nonexistent robe.

49 Taylor and Jay Meet

A SEVEN-YEAR-OLD TAYLOR WOKE with a start from a dream he instantly couldn't remember and while he knew it was one he'd rather forget, he found himself troubled at his inability to recall it.

Turning his feet over the side of his bed, he jumped down from it and moved to sit at his desk where he cyberly forced a light, his data display, and virtual helmet all to activate at once. He turned to look at the clock and could see that it was only six in the morning and that his first VR-class wouldn't start for another hour. He then decided to surf the WSN for a while and see what interested him. First though, as always, he checked his correspondence to see if any messages had come in through the EduCorp network.

Staring at the screen with a focused look, he made the computer log into his mail account in record time. Scanning the screen he immediately forced it to check and delete the unnecessary items – junk mail. Of those that were left, Taylor instantly filtered his acceptance letters to his virtual degrees into different folders. Today there were three.

"Well, I guess today's the engineer's day," Taylor said with a smile reading the subject lines of these messages quickly. On this day, October 6th, 2446, Taylor found he was accepted into baccalaureate programs in Chemical, Mechanical, and Electrical Engineering. He would, of course, accept all of them, knowing that EduCorp would pay the meager fees for the training, and while the government's education system might prevent this kind of workload for any *normal* student, Taylor would merely send courtesy copies of these letters to the Education Council so they could override the restriction.

Taylor felt his heart immediately sink as he was now left with only four other letters each coming from one of his instructors or caregivers. These letters were standard, kicked out by the EduCorp network after the first few sessions of classes, and as Taylor was soon to complete these courses, which he had just started, he immediately responded with his own standard letter of – "Thanks for your comments – your class was great – and have a nice life," or something like that.

What Taylor was hoping to see more than anything as he filed these last electronic letters away, was something, anything from outside EduCorp. He was hoping somebody on the outside was looking to become friends with him.

Now obviously it would be foolish for someone to sit in front of their computer or mailbox and expect mail to come from friends if they had none to speak of and hadn't done anything to find or get new ones. With Taylor, however, this was not the case. He had applied to an outreach program whereby teenage students inside EduCorp could make friends with those on the outside via being vid-mail pals. In the application process a student is only able to list their basics – age, gender, interests, and first name only (with no last name Taylor entered his as "Taylor" and not "Robert")

Taylor had heard wind a few days ago from his S.I.'s that several of the other students who applied had received responses. He was, however, nearly seven years younger than all the other applicants, and therefore stood out horribly from the rest

"That should stand for something." Taylor thought in his head, but then he countered this with a quick retort – "what self-respecting teenager – nearly adult – would waste their time writing letters to a seven year old?"

These thoughts, passing through Taylor's mind, only made him that much more upset. He didn't feel self pity, but more a sense of anger that no one would give him a chance, and felt he had so much to offer by way of friendship.

Taylor closed out his mailing program and noticed that a mere five minutes had passed. *What to do – what to do*? He started surfing the WSN and, as was most common, found that his best place to waste time was in the tech forums.

Here Taylor uselessly passed all kinds of time answering questions and posting comments about software, hardware, and all sorts of other tech topics. He had tried several times to correspond with those he had helped, but, as it seemed, no one was interested in chit-chat – no, they just wanted their program fixed, or their question answered, so they could move on about their day to day.

This didn't bother Taylor though, for he took advantage of the forums to check out software glitches, and, for his own entertainment, Taylor was particularly interested in games; be it game design, game engines, game characters – anything game related. As such, today, he navigated his way into a forum of postings from game programmers having coding issues.

Often Taylor would receive grief from his instructors and overseers, especially Dr. Young, in regards to his fascination with games, but Taylor would only comment, "You can put everything it takes to be a man into a boy – but in the end he's still a boy – and only time can change that." These happened to be words he uttered to her just two days ago, and in thinking of this comment he smiled at his own quick wittedness.

In focusing on the data-pad before him, Taylor passed the simpler games and moved straight to the VR type. It was here that he noticed a user who posted questions about a game that was in-work. He, Taylor, was immediately intrigued that this person would be so generous as to offer the entire game online for anyone who wanted to present their input. Viewing the game requirements, Taylor noted that the game mandated the installation of the G-E^3 Pack – that is to say – the Gamers Equilibrium – Endocrine – Express Pack.

Taylor's ears and eyebrows both perked at seeing this – "Ah, now here's a challenge."

With this kind of coding technology a game would be as real as possible by manipulating a player's equilibrium and endocrine system – faking the brain into believing the reality of the game – of course within certain safety protocols. More interestingly about the G-E^3 Pack upgrade, however, was the final E – for Express. With express coding a virtual game could be accelerated up to twenty times the speed of reality – or rather – If the user was playing a game for what they believed to be 5 hours – they were actually only playing for 15 minutes in the real world.

Indeed this express technology was the backbone of most of the virtual training sessions under the Prodigy program – and only just recently had consumer computers become fast enough to handle the breakneck speeds of game-play at this accelerated pace.

Taylor rubbed his hands together with the giddiness of a child at Christmas as he opened the game packet and started reading the descriptions and questions from the forum user:

> "In testing the game on DISPLAY MODE the timing is fine - but in the VR-E^3 MODE the game is exceedingly slow - I must have done something wrong with the code but I can't figure out where? If you can fix this problem please ensure proper E^1 and E^2 coding as well."

Taylor saw that these comments were followed by messages from other forum users – mostly consisting of "Good luck!", "Yeah right!" and one user who suggested programming changes that had nothing to do with E^3 timing, and Taylor knew that what this person recommended wouldn't help the game at all. Taylor frowned. *If they can't add something to help they shouldn't waste the forum's time with their needless comments,* he thought with a frown.

The boy continued scanning the screen, skim-reading about the game, its size, and description. He was actually looking to see if there was any data about the programmer and it was at the bottom of a long-scrolling list of details that this search came to light.

```
PROGRAMMER DATA
NAME:       JAYLEN WESS
AGE:        17
CONTACT:    JEWCRAZY2429@NYC.SEDU.ORG
```

Taylor was floored. Most of the users he helped in coding were at least in their thirties and some up to the hundred-and-thirties – this was just a – a kid. Teenagers rarely have the patience for the detail required create a VR world – *most of them anyways*. Now, knowing this little fact, Taylor was chomping at the bit to down-

download and play this game and see how good this kid really was.

With barely a blink Taylor forced the download of the game and when it was complete he put on his VR helmet and initiated it in programming mode to allow play with programming interrupts.

Opening his eyes Taylor could see an empty street unlike anything he had ever viewed before. The buildings were all short, standing at ten stories or less, and as the teen scanned the open space in front of him he could see – were those – cars? Yes – cars lined much of the street's edge.

Taylor was fascinated at what he was looking at – he could see at the corner where he was standing, a sign that stated "5th Street" in one direction, and "Main," in another.

I think that's the game's title – yes. "5th and Main" Taylor reflected, and while he wanted to take in more of the scene with its added feeling of a brisk cool morning and the smell of cut grass, he quickly remembered that he was there to test the game itself. Turning quickly, he thought to look down at his own body. He saw that he was wearing some strange long coat – tan in color, and, now that he thought about it, he was wearing a – a hat – a grey hat with a brim that curled at the edges... "Clothing and body positions are correct," Taylor thought, looking down at his limbs, and he noticed that under his long coat that he was wearing a light gray suit with shiny black shoes.

Taylor made his way to a building nearby. Looking into the glass window he could see his adult character's reflection. "Why does this look seem so familiar?" the Taylor whispered to himself.

Pulling his arms to his sides he noticed a metal object sticking out from his waist. It was a gun! With a quick cathartic realization Taylor identified the image before him – he was playing a 1960's detective – or – was it 1940's?

Taylor wasn't sure of the date, but he now knew the general idea of the game, a mystery. He had somehow missed this detail, which he had undoubtedly skipped in his reading of the game's description. Being satisfied of his understanding of the game, and of his virtual appearance, Taylor made his way back to the *"5th and Main"* sign hoping to reveal the next part of the game. He waited – and waited – and waited – until finally he noticed a person off in the distance walking in his direction.

This man was – old – why by any estimation this man was practically ancient. Taylor, however, digested this character's appearance and considered that, at the time, the Methuselah Virus hadn't been released to keep everyone looking young and pristine.

Why, this person looked the exact opposite of pristine. He was older, gruff, overweight, and aside from the suit he was wearing, there was hardly an appealing attribute to his appearance. Taylor walked right up to the man and started speaking.

"Are you here to meet me?" Taylor asked, and he watched as the man gave no response. Walking around the large, gruff individual, Taylor eyed him as, slowly, his mouth opened, and a low dull groaning noise came out.

"Ahhhhh" Taylor said aloud, and he raised his hand.

With a snap of his fingers the game paused itself and showed before him a series of semitransparent floating rectangles. This was the main programming menu which Taylor was all too familiar with, and he cyberly navigated through a series of options, scanned lines of code, and checked different input values until he found exactly what he was looking for: the timing index. To his expectation there was no value set for it. "There's your problem Mr. Wess!" Taylor whispered.

He forced a value of twenty for this blank number and the instant that the the menu closed the large man in front of Taylor started speaking normally.

"Of course I'm here to meet you – but we were supposed to meet *at the sign.*" The man was insistent about this and pulled at Taylor's adult arm.

Taylor nodded and slowly the two made their way back to the *"5th and Main"* sign. "So what seems to be the trouble sir?" Taylor asked, now feeling ever more ignorant of the game, and wishing he had read the description in more detail.

"My daughter's gone missing and I don't know what to do. I – I need you to find her!" the large man said, and quickly he pulled a picture from his pocket to show to Taylor.

The boy, who was playing in the image of a man, grabbed the photo and in looking at it saw a young, beautiful blonde woman with a striking smile and stare who, in Taylor's estimation, must have inherited her looks from her mother. He smiled at the large man and just as he was about to say something his eyes were distracted by a fast moving object – it was a car – actually running. The vehicle drove down 5th Street and in his fascination with it Taylor didn't notice that one of the windows of this car had opened itself.

All at once a metallic tube stuck out from the open window and Taylor was caught quite by surprise when it flashed with several loud bangs. All at once the large man in front of him fell to the ground – thankfully away from where Taylor himself was standing. It was immediately clear to Taylor that the man had been shot, in primitive fashion, by an old fashioned projectile gun. Indeed Taylor might have assumed there was a chance to save the life of this large man with the nauseating thought of CPR, but the flashing see-thru word DEAD above the body told the boy otherwise.

Taylor brought his eyes up from the large man and noticed the vehicle turn the corner, but just before it went out of sight the series of numbers on the back of the car popped up in large print over Taylor's view, seemingly recording itself onto the game. These numbers then quickly hid themselves from view.

"Hmmm – Those number must be important!"

Taylor stood, now amid a crowd of people that were coming out of the surrounding buildings to stare and gawk at the large man whose body was encircled in its own blood.

"Well isn't this quite morbid!" Taylor said loudly.

All at once the voices of those around the body, the noises of those walking toward the ever growing mass, and the motion of everyone except Taylor stopped.

"Morbid – of course it's morbid – it's supposed to be morbid – it's the 1900's"

Taylor whipped his head around to see a tall thin blonde-haired teen-aged boy staring at him.

"You're – you're Jaylen aren't you?" Taylor asked, taking in the teenage image for a few seconds.

"Yes," the teenager said with a smile, "I am. I was notified when you started the game, and well – here I am – and you are...?"

"Taylor – Robert Taylor."

Jaylen turned his head feeling that he, somehow, knew that name, but in looking at the corpse of the large man before him, his mind shifted its focus to the game.

"Hey well – uh – thanks for fixing my game!" Jaylen said looking up at Taylor who, with this false image, stood a few inches taller than the teenager.

"No problem! – And don't mind that morbid comment. This is a pretty cool environment – very different – and very retro. I'm impressed." Taylor offered a smile and with that the boy named Jaylen inquired, "So are you good with game programming? 'Cause I could use a little help with some of my other – *more involved* projects!"

Taylor was surprised to hear that this teenager was actually engaged in more complex games than the current one. He looked over at Jaylen and with a smile just responded, "I'm one of the best – if you've visited the tech forums enough I'm sure you've seen my name."

Jaylen's mind snapped into focus with half memories of Taylor's name at the bottom of several fixes that had been logged all through the tech forum site.

"It's you! – I've – I've seen your name at the bottom of more fixes than any other programmer..." Jaylen bellowed excitedly, "man you're good!"

"You have no idea!" Taylor said as he paced the intersection, and with just the thought of doing so and a wink to Jaylen, he forced the game back into action.

Jaylen was immediately surprised and impressed – "How – How did you?"

Taylor tapped his temple and Jaylen realized quickly the full, albeit cyberkinetic, nature of the individual standing in front of him.

Taylor walked from one corner to another and as he did so he noticed his footfalls as well as his perspective slowly change with each step. Was it his imagination or was he getting shorter – and did the concrete now feel, oddly, as if it was directly underneath his feet with no protection?

When Taylor reached the opposite corner he turned to look at Jaylen from a distance. Jaylen had made his way out and away from the crowd of people that were still mindlessly talking over the large man's dead carcass, and Taylor could see that the teen had just closed an access screen from the main coding program. He, Jaylen, was now shaking his head with his hand over his mouth staring at Taylor in awe.

Taylor quickly felt exposed and looked down and around at himself knowing something to be wrong. He absorbed the fact that somehow the teenager had removed the game's adult façade for his character. Now, standing in nothing more than his pajamas, Taylor was seen by Jaylen as little more than what he really was, a child of what appeared to be nine years old (Taylor's growth, while slowed, was still more progressed than his actual age).

"You're just a – a –" Jaylen shouted confused, and Taylor immediately retorted, "I'm just a what?" almost laughing, though inside he did feel slightly embarrassed at being so underdressed for the outdoors.

"You're just – a kid!"

Taylor offered a quick frown, "D'you got a problem with that?"

"Well, no it's just – I expected someone – eh – older. That's all!"

Taylor responded bitingly, "listen, if you want my help, you're going to have to accept what you see, and like it! I may be a kid, but I'm a busy *kid...*" Taylor would have finished but he was cut off by Jaylen who quickly asked, "Busy with what?"

Taylor snapped his head away from Jaylen to look at one of the nearby buildings and after a slight pause he answered, "Classes, lots and lots of classes if you have to know!"

"Oh crap! You're that – that – Prodigy kid from EduCorp aren't you!"

Taylor's frown increased, he was about to say something along the lines of – "You say that like it's a bad thing," but just as he took a breath for the words he watched Jaylen's face widen with a huge glowing smile, "This is so cool!"

"What! – whaddaya mean 'cool'?" Taylor asked with his face twitching, not certain of the direction of the conversation.

"Well, I read an article on you. It didn't mention your name, something about protection or whatever, but it talked all about your advanced education, training, and the early development of your – eh – powers."

Inside, Taylor felt himself become even more embarrassed over the fact that so much information had been made public about him and the experiment he was in. But he had no idea that people would actually read something so boring.

"Well, that's great! You know all about me, but I know nothing about you!" Taylor said miserably, but trying hard to speak loud over the distance of the intersection, and with a growing irritation he heaved. Then, with barely the thought of doing so, he forced himself to blink out of existence for a split second before reappearing at Jaylen's side.

The teenager fell over, practically jumping out of his own skin with fear, forcing Taylor to laugh as he helped Jaylen to his *virtual feet.*

"A little skittish aren't you!" Taylor said, and with this Jaylen stood firm upright, brushed himself off, and held out his hand.

"My name is Jaylen Wess, 'm from New York – but everybody calls me Jay."

"Robert Taylor – and if you call me Robert, Rob, Robbie, Bob, Bobby, or anything of the sort, I'll put you in a pink dress, high heels, and put a ribbon in your hair just for spite."

The two shook hands before Jay inquired, "Well, then, what should I call you?"

"Taylor – Just Taylor – In two years it will be Dr. Taylor – but for now Taylor will do."

Jay shook his head and the boy's hand with a smile. "I – I can't believe I'm actually shaking your hand!"

Taylor half smiled from the side of his mouth – "You're not!"

50 Jay Comes to The Towers

THE CORRESPONDENCE between Taylor and Jay had persisted for well over six months, and it was on a bright morning in May that Jay had surprised his young friend with a video message waiting in his mailbox. Taylor's bright blue eyes lit up when he saw the message blinking on his screen, and on bringing it up, the boy found he was even more pleasantly surprised by its content.

The flashing image of a smiling, now eighteen year old Jaylen Wess came up on the screen. "Hey Tay, how's your day – just wanted to let you know – I'm coming to California. Gonna be in LA on the 26th. I've got family I'm visiting and I've already scheduled a tour of your towers. Anyways – gotta go – I'll send you more info later."

Taylor's heart leaped with excitement – his friend was coming to visit – and in less than a week. In his mind he was quickly planning different things the two of them could do around the city – places to eat and visit. The child's mind rolled over the thought that when people visit a new place *it's all about the food.* Needless to say, the excited boy swiftly moved through his week charged with the idea of having a new face to see and a visitor to entertain.

Seemingly quicker than he had expected it, May 26th came upon Taylor quite suddenly one morning as he rolled out of bed, and he was already greeted with several v-mails from Jay detailing his transport trip from New York, and how, in less than an hour, he would be entering LA airspace. Taylor readied himself with newly replicated clothes and overjoyed that, in the last transmission, Jay said that had re-scheduled the transport to drop him off right at The Towers.

Taylor made his way up to the landing pad between the four towers and on exiting the lift he felt that the view here, while always impressive to him, today seemed even more striking. Looking out across the Los Angeles skyline while enjoying the impressive shade that East Tower afforded him, Taylor's eyes scoured the many moving dots in an attempt to pick out any one that might be on approach. Slowly his head turned and it was this change in his view that forced him to notice movement in his peripheral vision.

"Dr. Young – what are you doing here?" he asked on pathically identifying the personal impression of his only company on the landing pad.

"Oh, you don't think I'd miss the chance to meet your only *real* friend, do you?"

Taylor would have responded to this comment but was distracted by a fast approaching transport that, in mere seconds, took its place in front of the both of them. The door opened and Taylor saw what he could only assume was his friend, but, with an odd assortment of accessories adorned, it was hard to tell.

"Is – is that you!" Taylor asked with almost a laugh looking at a tall thin blond haired young man wearing green tinted sunglasses, an orange patterned shirt, white shorts, and – was that – yellow socks. This variety of bizarre colors was enough to make Taylor nauseous. However, as the boy looked his friend over, what was most peculiar about Jay was the number of different gadgets he had strapped all over his body. Taylor could clearly see, a thin rod-looking object strapped to Jay's leg; two flat data-pad looking units strapped to either hip; another strange unit strapped to his forearm, elbow, wrist, and hand in sequence.

Taylor shook his head only slightly – "Good to see you Jay!" he said as they both quickly shook hands, "but what is – all this," Taylor waved his hand pointing out both the equipment and the attire of his friend.

"Oh, eh – I picked these clothing patterns up online – pretty cool huh."

Taylor raised an eyebrow and lit only half a grin, "Yeah – I guess cool might be the word. But what's with all this stuff?" Taylor asked fondling one of the data-pads resting, or rather protruding from Jay's hip.

"Oh all this? Well – let's just say I like to use technology to make my life a little easier."

"And would you like to explain this thing?" Taylor asked pointing at the strange black arm unit that ran its course from Jay's shoulder down to his fingertips.

"Oh, this is the latest in interactive holographic technology – check it out!" Jay then lifted his hand and with a pointing of his finger it seemed as though he cut straight through the air before him and brought up a holographic menu.

Taylor could see from a soft pin-sized light on Jay's shoulder that this was where the image's source projector was. Looking at what Jay had revealed, Taylor was quickly reminded of this data system looked almost exactly the same as most VR interactive menus and while the boy was impressed, he still shook his head, unable or unwilling to understand the need for such a unit.

As much as he wanted to comment on Jay's hardware covered exterior, Taylor realized that the proper time for introductions was growing inappropriately long. Turning to Dr. Young, he held out his hand, "Jay, this is Dr. Young, she is head of the Social Development Department at EduCorp, but don't let that scare you – she's really very nice."

Dr. Young shook her head, then shook Jay's hand and, as if Taylor could expect nothing less, it was she who made a comment regarding the teen's technologically superior wardrobe.

"No offense, Jay is it; but wouldn't those things be better off left at home?" Taylor offered a cough of embarrassment for Dr. Young's bluntness, but he had to admit, he wanted to hear his friend's answer just as much, if not more than she did.

"You can't tell me you don't have some bit of technology on you to help yourself keep in touch."

"Hmmm – let me put it this way," Dr. Young started with a smile as she reached into her pocket, "I have this *bit* of technology."

She pulled out a MicroCom unit, no more than an inch in any direction; this was an earpiece that Taylor often saw her wear as a means of communicating to others. It was a communicator, micro-recorder, and audio player all in one. She slipped the tiny device into her ear, "There, two seconds, and my *bit* of technology is all done."

She said this quite arrogantly and if Jay wasn't at all embarrassed Taylor was certainly embarrassed for him.

Jay smiled, and with the passing of a few seconds he glanced over his own body. With his arm unit, his waist strapped data-pads, and his mysterious leg piece, he was, admittedly loaded down with *bits* of technology, and he was apparently starting to feel conscious of how he may have taken things a bit too far. After this pause lengthened to a seemingly uncomfortable degree, he spoke. "I suppose, then, that you think this must look ridiculous, don't you."

"Not yet!" Taylor said grinning, and with first offering a devilish stare to Dr. Young, he snapped his eyes back to Jay. It only took a fraction of a second for the teen's holographic unit to display a myriad of bizarre images that made no sense at all. This was quickly accompanied by a series of strange beeping and buzzing noises from the data-pads at his hips, and best of all, the long thin rod strapped to Jay's leg popped open from the bottom and out fell a strange mechanical object that expanded quickly to reveal its true form. It was a HandiJax Robot; a unit used to help its owner perform menial tasks or simply carry heavy objects.

At revealing this latest piece of technology Taylor knew he could have some instant fun. He forced the robot to move in a series of dance steps which, to Dr. Young's amusement, were both smooth and rhythmic. Jay, however, was panicked. Too busy trying to check his equipment for errors or malfunctions; he didn't realize exactly what was going on until he looked up at Taylor who was, ever so familiarly, tapping his temple again with a playfully evil grin cast in Jay's direction.

"You don't have to impress me with *toys*, Jay – I'm just happy enough to have a real friend here to actually see *me*!" the boy said softly.

"I guess I should have known better than to cover myself with all this equipment for you to – uhhh – play with."

Taylor quickly stopped his assault on Jay's electronic ensemble, except for the HandiJax – He could see that Dr. Young was still getting a kick out of how he, Taylor, could manipulate the robot so easily and make it so lifelike.

With a pacifying of the activity attached to Jay, the teen acted quickly to remove the equipment, and on finishing, he held everything at arm's length and dropped the items on the HandiJax, which Taylor quickly forced to raise its hands and catch the accessories as they fell.

"There, is that better?" Jay asked with a smile.

"It's better," Taylor started, walking up to the teen and offering a waist high hug, "but these clothes – what were you thinking?"

"Oh, so now you don't even like the clothes?"

"Not really!" Taylor said shaking his head, laughing.

"Damn and these were non-refundable patterns too!"

"That's okay." Taylor said gingerly, "Well get you some new clothes later. On the house!"

With that the three made their way inside West Tower, followed by the Handi-Jax, and on the way down Taylor started listing the barrage of places he planned for the two of them to visit. He spoke very rapidly and Dr. Young enjoyed seeing how excited Taylor had become in having someone to socialize with so comfortably, even if the age ratio was so extreme.

The next several hours were, indeed, quite fun for both Taylor and Jay who saw much of the city, but not before Jay changed his attire to something less "embarrassing" as Taylor put it.

Having dinner that night at a local restaurant, *L.A. House* it was Jay who turned the otherwise casual conversation into one of a more serious tone.

"So, Taylor, not to pressure you or anything – but how much – er – clout – that's the word – clout do you have at EduCorp."

Taylor could see by the look on Jay's face that, indeed, the conversation had turned serious. Shifting in his seat, the boy searched for the best response.

"If I were just any student, I would have very little, but as I am who I am – I have a little more – why do you ask?" he inquired, drinking his lemonade, trying to pretend that others at tables around didn't hear the question and wonder why an adult was asking this question of a child. Indeed, nearly everyone had eyed both Taylor and Jay when the two had sat down, and were curious why an eighteen-year-old would have anything to do with someone half his age. Or maybe the looks were of a different nature – being as age was so hard to tell, maybe they were being watched like a father-son pair – with Jay looking the same as he would for the expectant century, it might be presumed that the two were, in fact, father and son, and they were trying to see how much Taylor and Jay looked like each other.

Taylor washed these frivolous thoughts from his mind as his friend tried to explain away the question that had been asked.

"Well, I've been giving it some serious thought and I wouldn't mind working there – you know – at The Towers."

There was a long pause, at which point Jay broke the silence. "So what are you thinking?" he asked noticing Taylor's eyes slowly wander around the room in thought.

"Well. I don't think it would be a problem for me to drop your name, but you're going to have to finish some kind of formal education first." Taylor was firm, looking at Jay with expectation and concern.

"Oh, that won't be a problem," Jay said as he pulled from his pocket a small data-pad, which he placed on the table, sliding it to Taylor with a wink.

The boy scrolled down a list of courses and degrees that Jay was already in the process of taking, and he was impressed that, with letters to the New York GC, Jay was able to get some of the course-load restrictions removed.

"Hmmm, with a class schedule like this I don't think getting a job at EduCorp will be a problem. But I have to ask – are you sure this is what you want."

Jay's face turned a little sour, "I don't know what I want – but I know what I don't want – I don't want to work my butt off getting tons of education, and at the end of it I still don't have a job or any kind of direction. I want some kind of guarantee that it's not all going to be a waste – I've already heard so much about what's going on out there. It makes me sick that people work so hard to get educated and still can't find work."

Taylor, trying to balance wisdom with his genius, felt himself slowly shift into lecturing mode. "It should never make you sick that people want to get educated – and *you* should want to be educated – as much as possible! And you have to understand, Jay, the world is changing – always changing and evolving – It isn't enough to just simply be educated – you've got to be able to show yourself as more impressive and better than the run of the mill. The bar is being raised every day."

"My point exactly – all I want is a guarantee – that's it – just a guarantee that *something* will be waiting for me when I finish."

There was a long, noticeably uncomfortable pause that Taylor broke with a simple phrase, "That's something I can't provide." Taylor felt his mind shift to a deeper frustration over his friend's request. A guarantee like that might keep Jay from reaching his full potential. Laziness would replace competitive spirit and a drive to work harder for what is desired and needed if a guarantee preempted his efforts. Shaking his head he simply mouthed the words again. "Jay – I just can't."

Taylor could see that, with these words, Jay was not pleased, but between the two of them, it was Taylor who became more upset over the fact that their surroundings had suddenly and unexpectedly changed.

The restaurant around them had all at once filled with very loud music. Looking to the source of this new set of sounds, Taylor realized that the center of the restaurant, which had been roped off earlier to prevent customer seating, had lifted itself some twenty feet into the high ceiling revealing two sets of stairs and a lower level – a dance floor, and a MusicMaster.

Jay's face lit up at seeing this. He stood immediately to get a better look at the area below. "Did you know this place turned into a club at night?" he asked.

Taylor, who had only been there for lunch before and always accompanied by Dr. Young, did not, and he only shrugged his shoulders. He could care less if there was a club in the restaurant; he was in the middle of a serious conversation with his friend.

"We'll have to finish this talk later!" Jay yelled as he slowly made his way to the stairs with many of the other restaurant patrons doing the same.

Taylor shook his head. He didn't want to be a stick in the mud, but all at once he felt as though his quiet evening with a good friend was over. He would have enjoyed nothing more than to go out and dance with Jay or any of the others, but he probably didn't meet with some age or height restriction and, to say the least, he'd probably be trampled if he did somehow manage to work his way into the crowd. No, Taylor decided it would be best if he just repositioned himself to a table right at the edge of the club area and watch his friend and others dance to a very pounding assortment of music.

After a few minutes of watching Jay, Taylor couldn't help but laugh out loud. *He can't dance worth beans* – Taylor thought as he watched what he could only assume was Jay trying to impress some girl with an odd combination of off-beat moves.

Rejected! Taylor witnessed, and even whispered from his chair.

Rejected again!

And Again!

After nearly a half hour of watching his friend work around the dance floor, Taylor no longer saw the humor in his friend's failed attempts at finding a dance partner. Luckily, Jay finally decided to join Taylor at the new table. He was in desperate need of a rest.

"Oh wow" he said, out of breath, and, sadly enough, still bobbing out of rhythm. "Man, are the girls here tough! They'll hardly gimmie the time a day."

"That's because you can't dance!" Taylor said blandly.

"Can too!" he said smiling, not offended but more surprised to hear the comment at all.

"No! No. You can't. I've been watching!" Taylor said with a calm arrogance, continuing to sip his lemonade, which he had to steal away from Jay, who had taken it to help his own dehydrated exhaustion.

"Oh – so you think you can do better!"

"A bowlegged cow in a rodeo could dance better than you. Now sit down and relax – watch how it's done."

Jay stood, pulled his chair around so the back was in front of him, and he straddled it.

"Come on then – let's see what you've got!"

"Are you relaxed then?" Taylor asked.

With a look and a nod, Jay gave the affirmative, but before the teen could say or do anything else, Taylor kinetically forced him to stand upright, pulling the chair he had been sitting on and setting it proper at the table.

"What the!" Jay said with a feeling that he was no longer in control of any of his own limbs.

"Relax – this will be fun – and who knows – maybe you'll learn a little about rhythm and how to *really* dance.

Feeling the beat of the music Taylor forced Jay's body to bounce and move accordingly. Slowly he made Jay dance down the stairs and, with total concentration, he coerced his friend to move both elegantly and forcefully on the dance floor.

It only took a few seconds of being under this control for Jay to actually enjoy his before unseen talents. Occasionally Taylor noticed that, as he forced Jay to maneuver closer to different girls that he, Jay, would offer some cheesy smile. With barely a flinch Taylor forced Jay's face into a more relaxed, more enigmatic expression.

On approaching an attractive brunette, one that had before turned Jay down, Taylor could see that she changed her attitude when she noticed how well the teen could really, *really* dance.

The room quickly fell silent as the song ended, and Taylor knew it was now or never.

"Now let's move in for the kill!" Taylor whispered as he forced Jay to assume a standing position, and thereafter bow and formally ask for her hand in dance.

She offered a beguiling smile, curtseyed – she actually curtseyed – and offered her hand in his. The timing of this couldn't have been more perfect as the club had shifted its musical repertoire to a waltz – but one that still had a strong chest vibrating beat.

Jay and the brunette were making their way around the dance-floor very gracefully and it only took a few seconds for the club to make a space for the two of them. Taylor was actually helping his friend waltz in a club. This was definitely not on his to-do list – but he was certainly having more fun than when the music first pounded through the air.

Still concentrating, but getting used to manipulating his friend, Taylor was giddy with excitement. With the extra rhythm hidden in the 3/4ths beat, both the brunette and Jay, with Taylor's help of course, showed off moves that would normally not exist in a standard waltz and the middle of all his fun, Taylor took a mere second to look around and notice that the entire club was impressed with Jay and this brunette, many even cheering them on.

When the song was finished Taylor released his control over Jay, and hoped against hope that he had shown his friend enough about the difference between cool and cheesy that Jay could introduce himself and converse stylishly with his dance partner. This was unrealized, however, as Jay stood before her, completely silent and unable to think of what to say. Taylor watched this with bated breath, and while there was a distance between he and Jay, he felt as though he was beside his friend, and was so desperate to help in this awkward moment.

"Say something!" Taylor forced into Jay's brain telepathically.

"I – I – she's – she's so beautiful!" were the immediate thoughts Taylor picked up from Jay's mind.

"Tell her," Taylor transmitted in a panic – "Tell her the dance was fun."

"Well that was fun." Jay said smiling, and she responded with a devilish grin and her own blunt reply.

"Man – before I didn't know what to think of you – well I did know – I thought you were just some skeezeball – but now – you're, I don't know, you're different."

Taylor would not have heard these words from where he was sitting, but Jay was good enough to pathically broadcast what she was saying to him. Taylor realized how good of a thing this was because, again, Jay allowed an uncomfortable pause to exist between her words and his own.

"Tell her you just weren't into the other music!" Taylor instructed.

"Oh – well, I just couldn't get into that other music." Jay said roughly.

She nodded her head rhythmically to the current sounds of the club and leaned against a nearby wall. Taylor could see that she was staring at Jay unblinking, but, as it seemed, the teen either didn't notice, or was too frightened to do anything about it!

"Oh geeze, go on – step into her space – get close. She wants you to – can't you see it?!"

He hesitated, but, at Taylor's aggression, Jay was forced to move ever closer, eventually leaning in for might be a scandalous first kiss.

Might is the word, for while Taylor was focused so heavily on Jay and the attractive brunette, he didn't even notice a muscular man who had forced his way onto the dance-floor and through the heavy crowd of people.

Taylor didn't have time to react to the oaf pulling Jay around and hitting him hard with an uppercut to the chin. This hit seemed to offer pain even to Taylor some fifty feet away, and while those around the trio on the dance-floor were offering 'ooohs' and 'ohs' for the hit, Taylor recomposed himself to now try to save his friend from utter annihilation in what was obviously an unfair matching of brute strength.

Taylor could feel that Jay was mentally and physically weak, struggling to stay on his feet after the first hit, and it was now that Taylor decided to take full control over Jay's body, even his words, something that usually is done when the other party is either not completely conscious, or is willing to let it happen.

All at once Jay stiffened and stood upright. "Who the hell are you?" Taylor forced Jay to shout, and with the tapping on his shoulder that even Taylor could feel, Jay's body turned to hear the brunette say quite arrogantly, "That's my – uh – boyfriend!"

Taylor screwed up his own face in confusion – he didn't see that coming. This look was immediately translated down to Jay and while the current situation was a complete surprise, the hit that was on approach from behind was not.

Taylor forced Jay to block this hit, and with a combination of telekinetic and physical impact, Taylor, and now Jay both made efforts to return the uppercut that had been so rudely given before.

Flying some four or five feet in the air, this large man landed and slid backward on the dance floor. He was out cold. The 'oohs and 'ohs' for this hit were much louder, and much more resonant than the first, probably because it was unexpected from someone of Jay's size, and it was because of this outburst that both Taylor and Jay both had a shiver of giddy pride run through them.

Jay turned around to stare harshly at the brunette, who was miserably eyeing her boyfriend with disappointment.

"You California girls are just too crazy for me!" he said, and with these words the teen quickly made his way up the stairs and, walking swiftly by Taylor, offered a silent yet pathic message. "Time to go – meet me outside – I've got the bill!"

During most of the transport ride home a swollen jawed Jay was either recounting how well he danced, or how hard he hit – but in either case these words were always ended with gratitude to Taylor. The boy, on the other hand, felt sour for having helped his friend both into and out of a fight on his first night in Los Angeles. On hearing the ensuing apology Jay only smiled.

"It was worth it, man. It was worth it."

The two made their tired way back to EduCorp and it was easy for Taylor to convince Jay to save his money, cancel his reservation at one of the local hotels, and take up an empty dorm at The Towers.

Taylor placed him in the dorm directly below his own, which was not being used that night, and while Jay slept soundly Taylor decided to stay up. The boy felt the need to work on some kind of proposal letter in an effort to see what he could do about helping his friend get a job at his home. In his mind he still doubted this decision, and was wondering if he was only doing it out of a sense of guilt over the night's events. Even the thought of this seemed a little strange and awkward, but eventually Taylor contended with the balancing idea that there could be some fun in having Jay around when he actually started working at The Towers. So, with a deep breath he started putting words on the data display in front of him – putting his name, and a fiber of his reputation on the line for his friend.

Now Taylor was excellent with words, and usually penning eloquent requests and statements came easy, but no matter how hard he tried, what poured onto the digital page in front of him sounded like nothing more than a pathetic effort to abuse what little influence he had just to offer his friend something that most people don't get in life – a guarantee for their efforts. No, after sitting in front of the display for nearly a half hour with nothing to show for it, Taylor gave up and decided that a request like this wasn't the way to go and slowly a new idea of what to do and how to handle this situation slipped into his mind.

51 Tower Tour

THE NEXT MORNING, despite his late hour of getting to bed, Taylor still rose before Jay, readied before him, and sat anxiously in the corridor outside his dorm. It was only after offering three requests that Taylor lost his patience, stood, walked up to the door and without even a pause in his step he forced the door open, hearing a screech of terror from Jay who had quickly pulled a towel around himself.

"Oh, big deal – I'm getting tired of waiting – I've already been up for over two hours!"

Jay shook his head in disapproval, making his way back into the bathroom while Taylor continued.

"Listen – I've arranged for an extended tour with Dr. Young after the regular one you have scheduled for this morning. – So we're going to see things even the public doesn't get to."

Taylor looked about the dorm, with its small size, trying to imagine how his many belongings somehow fit in his own. His focus on this was so strong he barely heard Jay who spoke while getting ready in the bathroom. "So, have you given any thought to our talk last night?"

Taylor obviously had, and it was his conclusion that this extended tour would either convince Jay to abandon the idea of working at EduCorp, or to focus on it entirely, and that the risk would be worth the reward. Nonetheless, Taylor left the question unrequited and continued his stare about the dorm room noticing its every basic quality and appearance. Taylor felt a hand on his shoulder and, all at once, his vision became very bright and, with a flash of white, his view returned to normal.

Normal, that is, except for the fact that he wasn't where he was sitting just a few moments ago. He was standing over a data display and as he looked into it he could make out a face which was clearly his own, but it was an older version.

Instantly Taylor identified what he was seeing as a vision of the future, and in looking about he took in all the detail it contained. He noticed that he was a little taller; that he was wearing a white lab-coat with his name on it, and that the lab-coat had the EduCorp logo on it too.

Was he – he was! He was working for EduCorp. Staring down at the display before him he could see pages of code. Most students of the company wouldn't recognize this programming, but as Taylor had hacked into so many of his training protocols before, he recognized the program in front of him as one of the same almost instantly.

He also recognized the use of code normally utilized in games – *that's different*, he thought, and his brain started buzzing over the possibilities of combining gaming technique and training protocols. It was this concentration that caused him surprise when another face appeared in the reflection beside his own.

"If you stare any harder I just know the code will up and fix itself."

Taylor instantly recognized Jay's familiar voice and on looking up, he saw that not only was it really him, but that he too was wearing a lab-coat with a nametag and the company logo as well.

"So, *partner*, what do you make of the testing glitches – are they something to worry about – or will they smooth themselves out naturally.

Taylor's mind was spinning – he looked back at the data display in confusion. *Were the two of them working together at EduCorp on the same project? How – how – cool!*

"Taylor – Taylor! Are you okay?" Jay asked and as the boy looked up at his friend, he felt that it was odd that Jay was still uselessly saying his name.

"Taylor, Taylor..."

With a white flash Taylor's vision ended and the wash of color that was the reality in front of him slowly started to come into focus. He was staring at Jay, who was chanting his name, trying to get his attention.

"Wow – you were really out of it there – what happened?"

Taylor shook his head for a split second, "Oh nothing – just – a vision.

"Oh, cool – was it past – or future."

"Definitely future, but I don't want to get into it." Taylor said feeling embarrassed and certainly not wanting to lead Jay into any half-possible versions of their future together.

Jay, who was sitting beside Taylor on the bed with his hand on the boy's shoulder, quickly raised it to mess up the boy's hair before using him as a harsh form of support to stand up.

Taylor shook his head with a playful growl and looked up with a grin. He noticed that Jay had absorbed some of the advice he had offered on fashion and was wearing blue jeans and a white t-shirt with a red Plexivest – the latest in current fashion.

"So the regular tour isn't for nearly an hour what do we do 'til then?" Jay asked in a voice eager to see and do something – anything.

"Well, I think we should at least get something to eat. How 'bout some breakfast?" Taylor said as he stepped to the dorm's exit, cyberly forcing it open.

Jay agreed and the two made their way to a simple eating area just down the hall where Taylor had already M-Gened two plates of of bacon and eggs to be waiting for them when they arrived.

At breakfast Taylor spent a good deal of his time in front of his food forcing several forks and knives to dance across the table kinetically. Jay was laughing quite hysterically, clapping his hands as he watched the pieces of silverware battle it out over a strip of bacon, of course, not without Taylor's commentary to add humor to the tabletop scene.

Quite unexpectedly, though, the utensils dropped. Jay stiffened with surprise as he watched Taylor's face stare almost angrily over his own head.

"What do *you* want?" Taylor asked with a voice to match his fierce face, and with this Jay looked over his shoulder to see a thin man with a pointed chin and sunken cheeks.

"Now, Taylor. We haven't seen each other in months – why so hostile?"

"Tell me one truth that has ever come out of your mouth!?" Taylor spewed, and it was clear to Jay that the boy was more than angry, he was furious.

"I said I would come back – didn't I – and here I am." The man spoke softly in a sing song fashion that made Jay's skin crawl and only seemed to mount Taylor's anger with each syllable.

"Now is *not* a good time – I have a visitor." Taylor said stiffly, doing his best to avoid any eye contact.

"I know I've heard – I don't believe I've had the pleasure."

Jay stood, it seemed, in an effort to intimidate this unwelcome guest for he, Jay, stood nearly six inches taller and it was clear to Taylor that Jay was intentionally keeping an imposing posture. "'Mornin'. Name's Jay – you gadda problem here. We was just havin' some breakfast – I s'pose you could say – yer interruptin'. So while it's been a pleasure n'all – beat it!"

Taylor couldn't help but pull his head back in confusion – *was Jay adopting some kind of bizarre New York accent?*

"Indeed." The man replied both low and cool and, after a long pause during which he stared Jay up and down, he turned his head to the boy still sitting at the table. "Right then. Robert – I will see you later."

"Doubt it! And don't call me that!" Taylor grunted through gritted teeth as the man slowly made his way out of the dining area and down the main corridor. Taylor's comment only caused him to pause for a moment before smiling and finally leaving.

On peering around the corner Jay watched and wanted to be sure that the man had made his way fully down the corridor and into the lift on the other side before he sat back down.

"Who the hell was that guy?" Jay said almost laughing, and Taylor couldn't help but smile back.

"I was about to ask that of you..."

"Oh, well, that's the way lots of people *used* to talk back in New York City – I looked it up."

"Used to aye? Sounded pretty convincing to me!"

Jay returned the grin, but still persisted, "So, again! Who was that guy?"

Taylor's face had turned to show displeasure once again, "That," he said before taking a bite of eggs much too large for his own mouth, "That – waf dogtor Sheldon"

"Doctor Sheldon huh," Jay responded but Taylor shook his head and struggled to swallow what was left in his mouth, "No – not Sheldon – Zeldin, It's Doctor Zeldin."

"Oh, sorry, Dr. Zeldin – what's he do anyways."

Taylor shook his head, "He's with the government – doesn't really work for EduCorp – well he used to, but now he's with the GC – assigned to my project."

Jay's inquisitive mind and mouth asked "why?" before he'd really thought if it was appropriate to pry.

"Well," Taylor started, "I'm sure you could guess a dozen reasons why the government is interested in someone like me, but I couldn't say that I knew for certain which reason it was that *he's* here."

"So why do you hate him so much." Jay asked looking soberly at the boy, who, at the word hate, he snapped his head backward, "I don't *hate* him. Quite frankly, over the last year I haven't given him a thought – but seeing him again – it's something else."

"Huh – If I could guess by the looks you were giving him, hate would be the word to describe it."

"No, no, not hate – More like loathe – despise – detest – but not hate."

"Oh, as if there was a big difference." Jay said standing up, taking both their trays that were now empty of food.

"So – fine – why do you loathe him?" Jay asked on sitting down after checking the clock and realizing they still had time before the start of their tour.

Taylor sat quiet for a minute thinking about this question. He was trying to remember back to the first time he knew he didn't like this man.

While the exact moment came to him in a flash, and the myriad of emotions that came with it stirred in Taylor's chest, stomach, and brain, the reason for this negativity was simple and it was this that he told to Jay.

"He lied to me," the boy said softly.

"So what, big deal, my parents have lied to me before, I don't hold a grudge." With these words Jay almost laughed.

"No, no – It's not that simple – You don't understand. It's complicated." Taylor said staring at the table rather than at his friend. The boy's brain was begging his mouth to tell Jay the truth of this awkward relationship with Dr. Zeldin. For some reason, though, the child's mouth didn't want to listen, and instead, only a deep breathed sigh was the result.

At this time Jay would not learn the truth, but that truth would eventually come out later that day, and it would be through a turn of events that neither could have expected, even if one of them was a pre-cog.

Taylor, having spent his entire life at EduCorp, knew most of the corridors and departments by heart. He had, however, never actually taken the *official* historical tour of the company. So, standing beside his friend Jay, Taylor listened to the information provided by the tour guide for the first time and paid attention intently, despite the fact that much of what was being said he already knew.

As the boy absorbed the first hour of the tour in its basic form, he realized quickly that something between the words was sticking in his mind like a melody that just won't go away. He felt, for the first time, a sense of pride in the company that had raised him, and for the first time he wondered how it would be to actually work for that company.

In listening to the words of the tour guide, Taylor walked the halls and learned how EduCorp had, over a nearly 400 year history, cared for and raised nearly a million students, many of whom were found abandoned throughout the world's cities as mere infants. Taylor's feeling of pride for his guardian company grew ever greater with the idea that, in a manner of speaking, his *parent* was one of the most philanthropic in the world.

Now Taylor had felt pride before – many times in fact. He had pride in his accomplishments; in his classes taken; in his programs and games written; and even in something as simple as keeping his dorm clean, but, for the first time, he felt proud of the fact that he was raised by a company; a company that had, for centuries, taken the world's unclaimed children, and offered many of them their only chance at a normal life.

This was in such a great contrast to Taylor's prior feelings about his own existence, and those he considered his guardians. Taylor often felt like a misfit when he surfed the WSN. Reading about other children and young adults – their normal life – their parents, it often made him ache with a feeling of despair that his life would never be like theirs. He sometimes felt so *abnormal* being who he was, where he was, that he actually thought of doing whatever it took to leave the company and hide away from the world. These thoughts never came to fruition though, and now, at this moment, Taylor's brain had unexpectedly flipped. He vowed inside his own brain, that he would have these negative feelings no more.

After the basic tour had finished, Taylor met up with Dr. Young, who had agreed to augment the standard tour at Taylor's request and for Jay's benefit. She met them at the lobby lift, where the basic tour had ended and the three of them immediately ascended to the 450th floor of East Tower. Walking out onto the marble floor Taylor knew instantly what he was going to see, but his interest piqued at watching Jay whose eyes filled with great wonder at taking in, for the first time, EduCorp's Council Chambers.

"Call me egocentric," Dr. Young started as they walked into the great room, each step echoing on the floor, "but I just had to show you where *I* work first."

Jay, mouth gaping, only offered a slow "woaaaaaaow" and Taylor beamed. The boy remembered hearing somewhere that you can see something differently when looking at it through another person's eyes. He never really appreciated this statement until he saw Jay's awe filled expression. Walking all the way to the back window behind the council table, Jay seemingly exploded with emotion at the amazing view offered from this high floor. He pulled out and sat in a chair from behind the council table, which was not being used because on Saturdays the council usually wasn't in session.

Sitting here, Jay simultaneously took in a deep breath and the fantastic view of the Los Angeles skyline. The transports zipping around, some over The Towers, but many of them below, bouncing from point to point, it all was so amazing to Jay, who had, in living in New York, never experienced such a *real* fantastic view like this one. No, where Jay lived, his view was of the large side of – what else – another large building, and he had never taken advantage of the tall buildings in that city, which had views that were most certainly just as impressive.

Keeping the formality of the tour, Dr. Young started to narrate. "In this room, the many projects, experiments, and programs of EduCorp are subjected to a great eye of scrutiny, *always* with the well being of the children and that of the children of the world as our primary concern. To date I have approved over six hundred experiments, yet denied over two thousand due to inadequate planning, protocol, insufficient educational advancement, or efforts to push too far."

With this Taylor offered an attention getting cough causing Dr. Young to pause only for a moment, ignore it and press on. "Anyways – a little bit more on the structure of the building then. As you can see, at the very top, this room is covered with a simple grid of plex panels. All four towers are like that, but the tallest one is on a solar clock so that at sunset it is covered by a huge metallic shell. Then, inside, computer digitized murals are displayed so that even in the evening, there is still something interesting to see bay way of the sky for CEO Dr. Isaacs to see. The massive roof acts as a sort of dish that transmits and receives uploads, upgrades student statistical data and all sorts of other information via the EduCorp satellite network. The ceiling stays closed until just a few minutes before sunrise – as calculated by the solar clock, so that no matter what, Dr. Isaacs can see the best sunrise especially from up there, and trust me it is beautifu..."

"Good morning – Dr. Young! I didn't expect to see you here at this hour!"

Taylor flinched with this new voice echoing through the room. It was Dr. Ellington – the council leader, who Dr. Young promptly introduced.

Jay was more than pleased to make his acquaintance and while the teen was struggling with the words, he wasted no time in letting Dr. Ellington know of his aspirations to work at EduCorp, "now more than ever," as he put it.

"Oh, I'm pleased to hear that the tour didn't scare you off." Dr. Ellington replied, offering a wink to Taylor that Jay didn't notice and, with this, Dr. Ellington directed his attention back to the aspiring teen. "So – how old are you my boy – I always mean to ask this question when I meet someone new – you never can tell a person's age the way you could long ago – back then it was rude to ask – now, I feel it should be mandatory."

"Oh don't feel bad. I agree," Jay said with a cheerful smile, "I'm eighteen!"

"Finally!" Dr. Ellington said quite loudly and unexpectedly, "someone who's as old as they look. Take me for instance – how old do you think I look...?"

Jay shook his head, "Oh I couldn't..."

"Go ahead. Don't be modest – throw out a number."

Jay furrowed his brow in looking at Dr. Ellington – I don't know – taking your position into consideration I would guess maybe seventy-five." Inside Jay's mind though he was thinking that without this information he would have guessed said twenty-five.

"Hah! Dr. Young is older than that!" Dr. Ellington said with a smile, followed by a yelping "Ouch!" from the hit he received from her at his revealing this detail.

"Honestly though. I'm a hundred and sixty-seven, just turned it this last winter." There was a short pause at which point Dr. Ellington decided it best that he continue the conversation by getting some obviousness out of the way. "So, you're eighteen and you want to work for EduCorp. You are registered for higher education *aren't you*?"

Jay quickly nodded his head and pulled out the same data-pad he had shown Taylor the night before. Reading the information on the tiny screen, Dr. Ellington nodded his head, offering hmms and grumbles. Slowly Taylor felt a slight uneasiness take him over as he heard these noises come from the old man. The word old was used by Taylor only to describe the combination of calendar years and the behavior of Dr. Ellington, even if he did only look as though he were twenty-five.

"Would you vouch for this boy's talents?" Dr. Ellington asked looking over at Taylor.

Taylor paused for several seconds, looking for the right words to eloquently say what a simple *yes* could have done so easily. But before he could take his breath Dr. Ellington quickly added, "Oh for Pete's sake, I'm not asking if you think he's a hard worker – are you crazy – he's eighteen – 'f course he's not – I just want to know if the boy has talent."

Taylor decided, finally, to be brief and simple, "Yes, of course he's got talent. I wouldn't even talk to him otherwise!"

Jay and Dr. Ellington both lit a smile, and with a deep, seemingly pained breath the doctor grabbed Jay firmly by the shoulder. "I want you to visit this office on the 53rd floor – there, you might find a little something worth your while," he said handing back the data-pad after typing in his own bit of information on the screen.

Jay became instantly elated and with Dr. Ellington declaring that he had only come up to retrieve some papers and then parting, the other three all focused on continuing the tour, eventually leaving the Council Chamber several minutes later.

Jay and Taylor both made their way back to the dorm section of EduCorp, and it was clear to one that the other had far too much on his mind to do anything until he visited this mysterious office per Dr. Ellington's request.

When he had a chance to read it, Taylor instantly recognized the room on the data-pad as being in EduCorp's finance department and, with his interest piqued nearly as much as Jay's, he decided to go with his friend to see what this was all about.

They exited the lift on the proper floor and saw that many of the lights were out in this section of the building. Not surprising, Taylor thought. It was a Saturday and there should be no reason for the finance department to be open today. Just the same, the two made their way to the office mentioned on Jay's data-pad – room 53-F27N to be exact.

It was hard to miss for in the darkness of the halls, both Jay and Taylor spotted a blinking light in the distance which happened to be a different data-pad that had been attached to the door with a bit of semi-permanent adhesive.

Jay grabbed the pad and tapped the only button visible on the screen.

A series of words started writing themselves across the screen and as Jay read them his face grew a wide happy smile:

To: Jaylen Wess
From: EduCorp Finance Department
Subject: Scholarship Contract & Commitment Forms

As per the conversation between Mr. Jaylen Wess and Dr. James Ellington, head of the EduCorp Education Council, EduCorp is prepared, through its finance department, to submit this contract by which EduCorp agrees to pay for Mr. Wess' higher education to a level of no less than 3 doctorates as per his current curriculum and he MUST achieve at least the top twenty percentile of his class. In exchange Mr. Wess agrees to obligate no less than the first 7 years immediately following his acquisition of those doctorates in the employ of EduCorp or one of its subsidiaries.

<DETAILS>

Jay tapped the details button that appeared at the bottom of the screen, and in so doing he read through a long, detailed contract that seemed to have no end. He shook his head and put the data-pad away.

"Well, it looks like I won't really need your help after all." he said looking down at Taylor, who had been making every effort to see the data-pad, but with no success. "I've just been given a contract – I guess I made a good impression with Dr. Ellington because according to what I just read, EduCorp is willing to pay for my schooling – if I give them seven years of work and I can be in the top of my class."

Taylor nodded his head, "Wow, not bad – glad I scheduled that extended bit of the tour then." He looked up at Jay and gave the teen a wink hoping for a little gratitude." Instead, the boy got another head scrubbing in return.

In making their way back to the dorm section of The Towers, Taylor had to use his kinesis several times along the way to keep Jay from either running into other people, or into objects in his way. He, Jay, was entirely too occupied reading the contract Dr. Ellington had drawn up, and seemed content just to walk right into

Taylor's dorm, which he was actually entering at that moment for the first time. Even still Jay's eyes did not waver from looking at the data-pad in his hand.

He mindlessly sat on Taylor's bed and made himself at home continuing to read while Taylor, who said nothing of the many times he had to help his friend avoid injury, waited to see how long it would take for Jay to snap out of this reading hypnosis.

As it turned out, Jay did not look up from the contract until he had finished taking in its entire detail, and in so doing, he finally turned to Taylor, "Where are we?"

"This," Taylor said with a grin and a wave of his hand, "is my dorm. I'm surprised you didn't recognize it from what you'd seen on all our v-mails to each other."

"Oh, well – hmmm – I thought it would've been – um – bigger." Jay said as he eyed the room from where he sat.

"Whatever!" Taylor said with a false irritation and, after a short pause, he sat at his desk activating the data display before him. "Make yourself at home, I'm just going to check my mail real quick, then we can head out and see some sights."

Jay turned his head about the room, noticing its overly neat appearance, and he found that the most interesting thing in it to catch his attention was the boy sitting at the desk.

He watched Taylor who, in merely concentrating on the screen in front of him, was navigating through his mail, sorting it, and even creating new folders without having to put his hands on the pseudo keys in front of him, or tap the screen to hit any buttons. So it was in his watching that Jay unknowingly moved ever closer to Taylor, inching towards him in a mesmerized stare.

"Jay – You're scaring me." Taylor said calmly before lifting his hand, putting it on his friends face, and slowly pushing it away from his own without ever taking his eyes off the display in front of him.

"Oh you've got to be kidding me!" Taylor shouted at the screen as he shot up from his chair. "It's Saturday! This isn't – ahhrgh."

Jay moved around to Taylor's other side. "What is it? What's the matter?" he asked, trying hard to read the screen though he was too far away to really take in the words.

"I can't believe he'd try to do this when he knows I've got someone visiting, and he knows it's a friggin' Saturday."

Jay, who was tiring of having to understand Taylor's talking around the problem, quickly pushed the boy out of the chair and sat himself into it to get a better look at the message on the screen. Luckily, Taylor caught himself kinetically, and stood beside the teen, and while he, Taylor, was still angry from the contents of the message, he was unscathed from being so rudely repositioned.

Eyes moving rapidly, Jay read the message and found that even he was irritated by its contents.

GC CORRESPONDENCE
From: Dr. Zachariah Zeldin (GC SE Divisions)
To: Robert Taylor (Subject 2275A)
CC: Dr. V. Young, Dr. J. Ellington,
Subject: Mandatory Testing of Prodigy Subject 2275A

This message is to inform Subject 2275A of his mandatory testing which is to take place at 2:45PM on Saturday, May 26th, 2447 in Conference Room CR287W. This will be a closed session test. Results will be available within 72 hours of the test's completion.

Again, this test is MANDATORY and failure to comply will result in an investigation into the Prodigy Experiment and possible suspension of the project from EduCorp's current experiment structure.

Thank you for your cooperation,
Dr. Z. Zeldin
Head of GC Special Evolution Divisions.

"Hey, don't feel so bad, I'll be here for a week, we'll have plenty of time to see the sights and stuff. It's okay."

As Jay spoke these words he reached up and gripped Taylor's neck firmly. This was something he hoped would reassure the child at his side, but, unfortunately, the person at his side was less of a child than he thought.

"It's not alright – this isn't acceptable. It doesn't happen to any other student. Just me! It's ridiculous."

Taylor pulled himself away from Jay's grip in anger.

Jay only sighed, "Boy – If I had to trade a few inconvenient meetings and tests for the gifts that you have – well – I'd do it in a heartbeat. You have no idea how lucky you really are!"

"Whatever!" Taylor said dismissively.

In looking at the boy, Jay could tell that there was more to his anger than just the scheduling of this impromptu test. No – as Jay had felt before, there was a great deal more emotion tied to the relationship between Taylor and Dr. Zeldin, and Taylor wasn't very forthcoming in the details.

So, with a deep displeased sigh, Taylor came to the realization that there was no way he could back out of the scheduled tests, and thus he settled for *letting* Jay visit his family, which was the teen's whole reason for traveling Los Angeles in the first place. Taylor, on the other hand, would just have to deal with staying at The Towers, taking the tests, whatever they were, and deal with Dr. Zeldin.

52 Jay Saves Taylor

WALKING INTO THE TOWERS late that same evening, Jay was still glowing with cheeriness over the time he was able to spend with his aunt and uncle that afternoon. His stomach was full, and his mind was spinning over how much his cousin had grown. He felt a draft at the tower's lobby door opening, and he was instantly grateful that his aunt, who loved making things by hand rather than M-Gen, had knitted him a dark blue sweater that she insisted he wear.

The thoughts of Jay's family, and his unspoken gratitude buzzed around in his brain consuming him so much that he forgot to offer a retinal scan to the security detector at the door. Taylor made sure he would be able to enter and leave the building easily with this access, but now, as the security guard at the entrance noticed his failure to be scanned, Jay was in for a rude, if not humorous, awakening.

With a firm grip on his shoulder he was stopped by a large muscular man who, in contrast to his size, had a very high pitched squeaky voice.

"Where do you think you're going?" The voice said, and as Jay looked over to see where this question had come from, he almost let out a laugh at associating this voice to the person offering it.

"Oh, sorry, I forgot!" He responded on gathering his thoughts, and he tried to make his way back to the scanners at the door to obtain his clearance. The large man, however, was not letting him go.

With a firm grip that nearly wrapped completely around Jay's upper arm, the man stated firmly, if not effeminately, "Nope – you missed that scanner, now you have to go through me."

Jay's left eyebrow twitched and he complained of his aching arm as he was forced to walk over to security desk. Here he offered his retinal scan, a thumb print, signature, and on getting the green light from the security screen, he had to write a formal reason for his visit to The Towers. As he quickly wrote, "To get some sleep" on the page, he asked the security guard, "Is all this really necessary. My scan's fine."

The guard shook his head with a smile. "Mostly this is to train you! I'm certain you won't forget about this when you pass through these doors tomorrow. It's really simple – just look up into the light and offer your scan – is that so hard?"

"Okay, fine whatever," Jay said as he picked up his knapsack from the security desk and made his way to the lifts on the other side of the lobby.

On his way up to the dorm levels the lift reverberated his cursing of the guard, and yet he still couldn't help but smile and laugh over the man's voice. Waiting and watching the counter progress, Jay felt his head slowly nod into tiredness.

All at once his half conscious mind seized at full attention. With a shock that stiffened his whole body, he felt a pain that he could barely comprehend. As he looked around the lift to see where it came from, he quickly realized that there was nothing in the lift but himself and his bag. Relaxing, he dismissed the shock as a jolt out of his tiredness.

Looking up at lift's digital floor display, Jay became instantly confused at noticing that, for some strange reason, the numbers had stopped. He stared at the floor number "287! But I wanted 370!"

Moving to the keypad, he entered the floor number again and pushed the "Go" button at the bottom of the keypad. Nothing happened. Grunting in frustration he pushed the "Go" button several more times while staring at the display above.

With a heart pounding fear, Jay watched as the lights in the lift flickered, and the digital display offered a word that only increased his panic.

HELP

This was immediately followed by the word

Jay was confused. He kept pushing the button over and over hoping that the lift would stop asking for help and just take him to the floor he wanted.

With a seizing stiffness, he felt another shock run though his body that he was still unable to explain. The pain was practically unbearable, and had it not been for the railing on the side of the lift, he was sure to have fallen to the floor. Shaking his head Jay looked ahead of him and tried using his fingers to pry open the doors to the lift. They didn't open.

He reached down into his bag trying to find something to use to get the doors open, but when he looked back up at the door, much to his amazement, it and the rest of the lift slowly dissolved away. Jay realized quickly enough that he was in a much larger room now. He stood and turned around with a dizzying spin, hearing voices from behind.

The teen instantly recognized Dr. Zeldin, who was staring up at a large display screen showing what he, Jay, knew were vital signs. The teen slowly approached the man, listening to him speak as he moved ever closer.

"You can stop this whenever you want. All you have to do is try!" he said.

Jay was unclear who the man was talking to but he knew where this person was for he saw that Dr. Zeldin had directed his attention to a set of semitransparent plastic curtains. Jay could see a small bit of motion through these, but just as he was about to come close enough to touch the cool plastic sheets his body seized.

With a rush of pain that again struck his body, this time to the ground, Jay's mind was filled with images he couldn't explain, and while it was unclear how the images were entering into his brain, he knew that what he was seeing was projections of was on the other side of the plastic curtain.

From the flashing views Jay could see the plastic curtains high above. He felt his muscles quickly ache from the jerking convulsions that, in frustration, he still couldn't explain.

It was at coming out of this shocked state that Jay heard a screaming voice that, only at its end, he could recognize.

"Taylor!" the teen shouted, but he realized that he had no voice. Getting to his feet he tried to open the plastic curtain, but instead his hand simply passed through it. With surprise the teen pulled his hand back. Not sure what was going on, he washed this out of his mind, quickly filling with concern for his friend. With a firm determination he closed his eyes stepped through the plastic barrier not sure what he would see on the other side.

When he opened his eyes again, Jay's stare was met with Taylor's. They showed him a misery and pain that even their light blue color could not cover. Tayor was lying, or rather tied down to, a bed and it was clear that he had been sweating profusely, soaking the white medical gown he was wearing. His eyes were closed as he was now clearly tired, and Jay moved fast to try and undo the straps keeping hold of the boy's hands.

He should have known. His hands passed right through Taylor's and through the bed. *What was going on?*

"I'll say it again. You can stop this any time. All you have to do is try. You know you have the power to do it." Dr. Zeldin said calmly.

Taylor slowly rolled his head back and forth on the bed as if to shake his head and say "no." But his words said much more. "Why are you doing this? You promised me you'd never – *ever* hurt..."

Taylor would have finished this statement but Dr. Zeldin quickly retorted, "I'm not doing anything. It's all the machine... And you can stop it whenever you want."

At this moment a robotic arm came out from a wall inside the curtained area where Jay was standing. It moved with a strange set of mechanical sounds and as Jay watched it he listened to Dr. Zeldin who persisted in addressing Taylor.

"You could reprogram it if you want. Make it stop. You could use your kinesis and break it at its hinge. Can you see it – what it's going to do? Can you see your future – stopping it – or letting it shock you again? It'll be just like the last time. Remember it – can you feel it."

Jay listened to Dr. Zeldin speak and it was clear the man was saying each word with a purposeful determination. It wasn't to evoke horrible images or tortuous memories, but a desperate attempt to get Taylor to use his powers – his gifts. But as the teen looked down at the boy on the bed his heart ached. Taylor had closed his eyes, and with pained tears running down his face he turned his head in Jay's direction. "I'm not going to do anything! NO cyber – NO kinesis – NO cognitive. Just leave me alone! You can stop this too!"

The plastic curtain opened with a tearing rush and Dr. Zeldin stomped to Taylor's bedside. "No – *boy* – YOU can stop this. Just give me something – anything."

Jay looked at Dr. Zeldin's face and he could see that behind the man's eyes was a stare of saturated pain. He then looked up at the robotic arm, panicked. He could read, quite clearly, the display underneath it. It was counting down, showing some thirty seconds or so left before – as Jay could only assume, another barrage of shocks would come to torture Taylor again.

"I know you don't want to do this – so stop it – stop it – STOP IT!" Taylor said rolling his head back and forth on the bed. "I can see it in your eyes – you don't have it in you to keep this up much longer."

With a quick stiffened look Dr. Zeldin offered a snarled lip and shot his eyes up at the robotic arm. Jay noticed the counter, still with twenty seconds to go, instantly drop to zero. The arm shot downward and two probes made their way to come within an inch of Taylor's chest. With a bright flash the robotic arm shocked the boy and as if the two were tied together somehow, Jay felt as though he were also being shocked.

The pain was unbearable, and again Jay could hear Taylor's cries of pain. When the bulk of the shocking pain had subsided, though twinges were still running through his body, Jay looked at the young boy before him with great sympathy and he himself started to tear up from the heart wrenching feeling he had gnawing in the pit of his stomach. The boy, though, was simply repeating the same words over and over again. "You can stop this! You can stop this! You can stop this! You can stop this!" And, as if he could see Jay standing above him, he looked at the teenagers face, "Jay, help me, you *can* stop this!"

Not expecting to hear his name, Jay stumbled backwards. He would have tripped over cables running along the floor if his feet were solid, but instead his back seemed to hit hard against the wall of the lift that now quickly wrapped itself around him and closed him into its tiny confines. With rapid blinking eyes Jay saw the proper counting numbers of the digital display overhead.

Pounding his fist on the lift's keypad, Jay was frantically trying to make the lift stop its ascent to the upper floors. On doing this he felt a jerk that nearly made him fall over. Then, when the doors opened he ran out only a few feet and approached the nearest wall, whose paneling had a data display embedded in it. Panicked, Jay didn't know what to do – He couldn't even remember where conference room was that Taylor had to go to for his *testing,* and besides, the boy wasn't even in a conference room, he was in a laboratory.

Not so agitated that he had forgotten his wits, he tapped the panel and began searching the EduCorp internal network. Bit by bit he used what computer and programming talents he had to hack into and out of various sub-networks until he had found and cracked Taylor's internally stored mail. Reading the mail, he quickly noted the room, and after a quick sequence of taps on the screen he walked away, leaving the screen still active with the text "Message Sent" blinking brightly.

Jay moved fast in an effort to get to the room where Taylor was being *tested*, or was it tortured. Getting back into the lift, he punched the buttons on the panel hard hoping that somehow it would get him down to the proper floor faster. The teen was shaking in fear, in anger, and consumed by the high emotion from what he had experienced earlier. He wasn't sure what to expect, or what he could do when he got to the testing lab, but he did know that whatever it took to keep his friend from spending another minute on that bed – that's what he would do.

While the lift's display counted upward, one thought kept running through Jay's mind – Taylor could stop what was happening with barely a thought – so why didn't he? Why wasn't he using any of his powers? – If it was part of the test that he should use them, then why wouldn't he?

The doors to the lift opened, and as if he had no time to think about the possibilities of what he could do, Jay stepped out into the corridor hearing Taylor scream once again. He wasn't sure if this was just in his head, or if it was aloud, and as the corridor was dark and closed down for the weekend, he was certain that, either way, he was the only one who heard it.

Feeling his heart pound in his chest, neck, and even ears, Jay was very much on edge, and as he sprinted down the corridor, watching the conference room placards count in the right direction, he trembled ever more with fear. Two more doors to go...

It was at his final step to the entrance to the conference room that Jay was met with a dropping bomb of fear in his mind. *Taylor wasn't in a conference room in the vision.* So this couldn't be the right room. Then, with a high pitched pathic scream that seemed to come from behind him, Jay whirled around and stared at the door just opposite the conference room. It was labeled a lab room, and with the heart wrenching outcry he had just heard, he knew that this was where Taylor was being held. Looking at the door, he didn't want to request entry for fear of what would transpire, no – he needed to get in undetected. But how was he going to open the door?

His brain filled with a rush of technical schematics of doors and locks he had looked up in the past. He voraciously attacked the access panel beside the door, opening it with his fingertips at all sides before pulling out the attached cables nearly a foot and separating the fiber optic chords from the wires. Jay then pulled the panel close to his face, and, with the glow of the optic fibers, he was able to trace the electric pathways of the circuit board.

Separating the wires slowly, looking carefully at each one, he segregated one wire that he started pulling tightly so as to break it from its connection.

"Stop!" He heard down the hall and, much to his relief, he discerned the figure of Dr. Young who was walking swiftly down the corridor in his direction.

His stare instantly went back down to the access panel, but with Dr. Young putting her hands over his, he looked at her and the frustration in his eyes became quite apparent.

"I have access – don't worry." She said softly, and on saying these words, she gently pulled the panel from his hands, lifted it to push it firm back into place on the wall beside the door. She then offered a stern look to the teen at her side and spoke with a voice to match her look. "I got your message just a few minutes ago. What're you doing here and what's this all about?"

"This test isn't a test, this test is..."

"This test is closed to everyone except Dr. Zeldin and Taylor – I'd figure you already knew that."

"Test! What a load a crap! This isn't a test – It's a torture session!" Jay shouted, and Dr. Young looked around the corridors, feeling a small sense of nervousness followed by relief that the department they were in was closed for the day, and that the door beside them was airtight and soundproof.

"What's this nonsense? Explain yourself!" Dr. Young said confused by the teen's words.

"Dr. Zeldin isn't here to test anything – well, he might be," Jay said as he replayed what he had seen back in his own head, "but he's forcing Taylor to endure all kinds of pain, just to get him to use his cognitive and kinetic abilities. He's literally torturing him!" Jay's voice grew louder as he continued his words, and it was clear to Dr. Young that while she couldn't verify what was being said, it was obvious Jay believed his own words, and this offered worry to Dr. Young who now felt that even she would truly like to know what was going on beyond the door at their side.

She raised her hand to the keypad at the door to code in her council override, but found herself still hesitant to enter the room. This hesitation gave way when both Dr. Young and Jay heard, telepathically, another set of Taylor's screams of pain inside their heads. Dr. Young looked at Jay with an apologetic gaze. She quickly turned to the keypad and tapped frantically at the keys.

The door wouldn't open. "Come on! What's wrong with this thing!" she huffed, and she turned her angry stare from the keypad to Jay. He shook his head, "I hadn't done anything yet – you stopped me before I had the chance!"

"That's not possible. My override should work on this door – no matter what!"

She said this with an increased anxiety and, again, Taylor's scream resonated in their brain.

"He's getting desperate!" Jay said as he now realized that the gap between Taylor's screams was becoming more and more narrow. He watched with bated breath as Dr. Young entered her passcode repeatedly, but to no avail, her eyes now welled with tears. "Come on damn it – open!"

Jay nudged her to the side before snapping at her, "My turn!" and he once again pulled the panel off the wall, found the wire he was ready to pull earlier, and, with a firm grip, he removed wire from the panel with a snap. This caused an odd beeping noise to emanate from the door.

"Quick, "we have about thirty seconds before the emergency power comes back on! Help me!" Jay said this as he grabbed one side of the split door, and Dr. Young did the same on the other side.

The two managed to separate the doors a few inches, and, with the increased speed of the beeping, Jay knew they were running out of time. He slipped his body in most of the way, and only just managed to get his leg through the door, before it slammed shut in Dr. Young's face.

Jay looked around the room and could see that he was where Taylor had showed him. More than this, however, Taylor's ears could hear a shouting match between Dr. Zeldin and Taylor, which, Jay was thankful, had distracted the doctor long enough for someone to get into the room undetected.

The teen slowly made his way around the curtained bed. He could make out the shape of Dr. Zeldin through the plastic sheet, and, not really thinking of what would be best to do, he decided on a blunt attack.

Reaching his arms out, he jumped at Dr. Zeldin through the plastic curtain. This pulled the sheet from its rings and wrapped it around the doctor completely. All at once the teenager began punching at the man's sides with all his strength. He could hear the doctor's protests, but he couldn't really make out what was being said, and with the struggle ensuing, the curtain itself had started to slip off, revealing the doctor's head.

The man snapped at attention realizing his view was no longer obscured. Jay only just noticed this before his hands were immediately grabbed by two robotic arms that shot themselves out from the overhead ceiling.

With a flash of movement Jay could hardly keep up with, he found himself hanging from his arms high in the air in no time at all. He heard an awful laugh that resonated though the mostly empty lab-room.

"You!" Dr. Zeldin spewed, "The New Yorker with that horrible fake accent." Jay's face turned sour at hearing this, but he said nothing in return. Instead, Dr. Zeldin filled in the silent gap, "How is it that an idiot like you could get past my security lock."

Jay only stiffened his angry face and turned his head to look away from Dr. Zeldin.

"He's smarter than you think!" Taylor said from his strapped position, "and he's obviously more loyal!"

"Hmmm" Dr. Zeldin hummed loudly turning to the boy on the table, "Maybe *you* can handle pain, but what about your friend here?"

"Leave him out of this!" Taylor shouted, "He's got nothing to do..."

"I don't care!" Dr. Zeldin shouted in a whine and, to Jay's terror, two more robotic arms came down from the ceiling. One grabbed Jay's legs firm around his thighs, pressing hard into his muscles. He would have struggled, but he knew this would only increase the pain. The second arm came down and, lining up with his nose, lowered itself below his chin to begin cutting away at his new sweater and undershirt.

Jay's anger turned quickly to the hatred and loathing that he had criticized Taylor of earlier. He could see that Dr. Zeldin was staring in concentration at the robotic arms. He was holding a control pad, and clearly had those robotic arms and who knew what else available at his disposal. This was something Jay hadn't counted on when he entered the room. Now this simple foe had become much more complicated. He continued to look at Dr. Zeldin, concentrating, hoping to pick up on thoughts, try to see what was going on inside the man's brain.

This focus was broken by a sharp pain in his back for, without his noticing it, the arm that had cut away at his shirt was now stabbing him in the back with something sharp and painful.

Jay only let out a small squeal of pain before trying his best, biting his lip, not to cry out. He looked down at Taylor and could see the boy struggling with his emotions, looking around the room, then back at Jay. But Jay was shaking his head forcefully as he stared down in return. The teen did not want the boy to use any of his abilities to help him, despite the ever increasing pain that was pushing even harder into his back.

Jay could feel the wet warm blood now running down his back, soaking his jeans. His mind was thinking hard of what to do for if something was going to happen it would have to happen soon.

An angry Taylor, though, only shouted at Dr. Zeldin. He started cursing the man as if he could pain him with the foulest of words, to which Dr. Zeldin only turned, walked up to the boy's bedside, and grabbed hold of its edges. Offering an angry look, the doctor made the sharp scalpel at the end of the robotic arm slowly twist and turn. As if it took everything in him, Jay finally let out a wailing howl of pain.

Dr. Zeldin smiled, as if satisfied that he had finally broken Jay's will, and spoke in almost a whisper to Taylor once Jay's screams had subsided. "Now – why don't you save your friend? Just push your mind into the robots and let him go. It's easy..."

He watched as Taylor rolled his head, tears streaming down his eyes, to look anywhere but at Dr. Zeldin or at Jay. This seemed to have the dual effect of making Dr. Zeldin even angrier than before, and at that moment it was Jay, with his body wrenching in pain, who started to feel that he was being abandoned by his friend in this, his time of need.

With a growl the doctor whirled around and walked up to Jay's suspended body. Looking up at the teen he lit an evil grin before he spoke.

"He doesn't even care – I could torture you to death, and he wouldn't do a damn thing!"

"You know – I'm beginning to think he's not holding out at all – hmmmm maybe he *has* lost his grip on his powers." Dr. Zeldin said tapping his lips with his finger in concentration. "Oh well," he said with a sigh, "Can't have any loose ends, now can I?" he asked rhetorically, and with a seizing pain Jay felt the scalpel ended robotic arm press ever harder, and now sideways into his back.

Jay barely listened to these words as he was growing weary from loss of blood.

His attention however, peaked when he noticed on the large display showing an image of Taylor's brain activity, that there was an instant and dramatic change. All at once two different peaks shot up in the neural activity. Something was definitely happening.

Jay threw his head back in pain and offered a horrific yell. He would have thought it was all over but – He turned his head up again when he noticed there was another voice now screaming to match his. He watched, and not without a huge amount of satisfaction, as the robotic arm that was in charge of shocking and torturing Taylor was now simultaneously lifting and shocking Dr. Zeldin, eventually throwing him across the lab.

When the man got to his feet, the arm proceeded to chase him around the room with electronic blasts until, with one final zap; it caught him at the back of the head. He was out cold.

Jay felt the robotic arms release his hands almost instantly and, as if with precision timing, Taylor had pulled the scalpel arm out from his back and kinetically caught him before he hit the floor.

The teen immediately tried walking to Taylor's bedside, but the boy had released his own straps so quick and ran in Jay's direction just in time to physically catch the teen before he fell. With a jerk of his head, Taylor then focused on the entrance to the lab, but without reading the display, he was unable to determine what security code changes would be needed to get the door open.

Taylor let out a scream. At that moment, with a loud bang that filled the room, Jay looked up to see what would be his last view of the night. The door, or rather, the door and its entire frame had split in two opening wide, crumpling the lab walls to either side like an accordion, and with the wrenching of metal and the sparks and cringing noises accompanying the creation of this wide entry, Dr. Young, Dr. Ellington, and the lobby security guard were instantly revealed. They were all standing back in fear.

Jay rolled his head back to look back at Taylor. The boy was focusing hard on the entry, face full of tears and blood from wiping his face with his hands. "Man – you're the coolest!" Jay said with barely a whisper, and while he tried to hold consciousness, his eyes blinked away and he passed out.

The three at the lab entrance all rushed in and crowded around Taylor who was rocking back and forth holding Jay's head, screaming for help.

53 Testing Talents

THE NEXT MORNING Jay woke in the infirmary with a pounding headache, and a strange sawing noise in his ears. When his eyes came into focus he looked to the sound of the noise and observed at the side of his bed that the high pitched voice of the large security guard he met the night before actually lowered itself to a deep grumble when snoring and asleep.

He lit a grin and turned the other direction. Here, he saw Taylor, who was sound asleep in what was clearly an uncomfortable position in an uncomfortable chair beside his bed. The teen pulled his body to sit more upright, feeling pains inside his body from the injuries of the day before. Just beside him in a cabinet he could just reach, he pulled out a clean gown much like the one he was wearing. He balled it up and with a light toss he threw it on Taylor's head. The boy woke instantly with a smile.

"Hey what's the big deal?"

"I should ask you that question." Jay retorted. "I wasn't wearing these things last I remember,"

Taylor offered a little laugh and jumped out of his chair to sit on the bed beside his friend. The ensuing squeak the mattress woke the security guard, though both were confused as to how this was possible when this noise produces was so much fainter than the constant thundering roar of the man's snoring.

"What's that!" the security guard yelled as a knee-jerk reaction.

Jay and Taylor both giggled at this, but quieted when the man stood over them with a menacing stare. The guard then turned around slowly and walked over to another bed. Jay could see that this one had Dr. Zeldin's resting body in it.

"Woah!" Jay bellowed and he turned to offer Taylor a sly grin.

The two started whispering comments to each other about the security guard and, with quite chortles, their topic of conversation became so obvious that the guard picked up on the fact that he was the brunt of their amusement.

"Don't think I don't know what you're saying!" he said in his high pitched tone, but this only seemed to add to the friends' elated laughter. All at once he became flustered and frustrated. He started to approach them again and, with a change in attitude, they offered looks that said something like "uh-oh!" before the recovery room doors opened to reveal a small cluster of people.

As these new arrivals walked in Taylor and Jay took in their appearance and attire; two dressed in grey suits, very stiff looking and too business like; two were dressed in security detail like the one Taylor and Jay had just been laughing at; and one was dressed in a lab-coat and had the thin, pale look of a man who hadn't eaten anything for a week.

They rushed in and, without paying any attention to Jay or Taylor, they surrounded Dr. Zeldin's bedside.

Jay started to whisper in Taylor's ear, "what's this all abou..." but his words were cut off with Taylor hissing, "shhhhh!" The boy perked his ears, as he knew how to do even then, and focused hard on listening to any stray telepathic conversation. There was none to speak of, but at one point one of the grey-suited men turned to look over his shoulder at Taylor. This man then nodded at the lab-coated man, the security guards, and the other grey-suited man.

These two broke from formation around Dr. Zeldin's bed to approach Jay's bedside. "We need you to answer some question's boy," this grey-suited man said with an insistent voice and matching imposing eyes that were staring the teen down.

Jay was unphased. "The name's Jaylen, Jaylen Wess, and you are?"

"That is not important. What's important is finding out what happened to Dr. Zeldin."

"Not sure I can remember anything about that!" Jay lied and he turned to Taylor with a quick stare that told the boy to stick to this story. "What's the big deal anyway?"

"Well, Mr. Wess, from what we can tell, the doctor was attacked – and if that's true, then someone has to be held accountable – I'm sure you know it's a crime to attack anyone who works for the GC."

"Even if it's in self defense?" Taylor asked forcefully.

"That," The man in the lab-coat started as he turned to look at Taylor, "would require a Postcog investigation for definitive proof."

"Well he attacked both of us, if you must know, and I've got evidence enough to prove it, with my injuries and his." Jay said firmly as he pointed to Taylor.

The men kept their attention focused on Jay, and the lab-coated man spoke up. "Well, we know the extent of your injuries Mr. Wess, what we can't understand is how, with the extent of those injuries, you bested Dr. Zeldin, who, right now, has no injuries to speak of and has certainly been trained to take care of himself."

Then the other of the gray-suited men left Dr. Zeldin's bedside and joined the other's with Jay. "If you lie, Mr. Wess, your answers can be used as evidence in an obstruction investigation."

"It wasn't him you idiot's it was me!" Taylor shouted across the room.

"Right!" the man in the lab-coat said slowly, his eyes still trained on Jay. "I refuse to believe that a child took down a GC employee who has been well trained to defend himself."

"Believe it!" Jay shouted. "That boy's got more going on up here than you could possibly imagine!" Jay said vehemently, tapping his temple in an ever familiar way. His blood was boiling and, in frustration, he wished Taylor could do something to just get these idiots out of his face.

The expression of the man in the lab-coat quickly changed. He offered a light "Uh-huh." before casting a stare at the security guard by his side. Then, quicker than either Jay or Taylor could have reacted, the security guard pulled out his shock stick and tapped it at Taylor's temple. The boy was unconscious immediately and Jay shouted for the other security guard.

This large guard, with the high pitched voice, only shrugged his shoulders. He had just been told not to interfere by the third security guard. Now, fully informed of their purposeful visit to the recovery room, the guard with the high pitched voice was ordered to do nothing but stand by and watch.

The man in the lab-coat rolled up one of Taylor's sleeves and quickly wrapped it with a long piece of elastic rubber before using a syringe gun on it. Instead of injecting something, however, the man used the gun to take some of Taylor's blood; actually, a lot of Taylor's blood.

Jay would have done something to stop this, but the tip of his nose was quickly met with the end of a buzzing shock stick that he knew better than to contend with. Jay unwillingly sat and watched as the man in the lab coat filled two large containers with Taylor's blood – each measured 500 ml and, judging by the boy's color they'd nearly bled him dry. With all this going on and his not being able to take action, Jay felt himself getting sick to his stomach, and he started squirming in his bed. It was this movement that caused him to feel the call switch that had buried itself somewhere between the bed's sheets. He pulled it out and pushed it several times quickly without anyone noticing.

After a few seconds one of the emergency room doctors walked in, and was immediately irritated at seeing so many people in the recovery room.

"What's going on here?!"

"This is none of your concern!" one of the grey-suited men said firmly but Jay had immediately rolled over from his bed and onto the floor. Now that he was away from the shock stick he started shouting.

"They just shocked Taylor, they're bleeding him dry! You've got to do something!"

The doctor looked about and saw the boy's pale color and the two containers of blood and realized that this, in fact, was the truth. Moreover, Jay's shouting attracted immediate attention from outside the recovery room. Dr. Young, and Dr. Ellington, both of whom had resumed their normal duties, were just outside the entrance, wanting to see how Jay was doing. They rushed in at the teen's words, watching an ensuing argument between the ER doctor and the grey-suited men.

The EduCorp doctor looked around. He could see the last of the syringe gun's second load being taken by the man in the lab-coat, causing him to almost growl.

"I don't know what's going on here, but I know I don't like it. So let me put this simply. If you're not on EduCorp payroll – leave NOW, or I'll have you removed!"

One of the grey-suited men quickly responded with an arrogant authoritative sound. "I said this doesn't concern you – and if you don't stop interfering, you'll be the one who's removed."

The doctor cast a requesting stare in the direction of both Dr. Young and Dr. Ellington, who quickly intervened.

"I'm afraid I don't understand." Dr. Young said poignantly. "This is EduCorp property, an EduCorp Emergency Room, with EduCorp security!" With these last words she stared at all three of the security personnel, who were now at odds with the different orders they had been given. "And I don't see," she said turning to the grey suited men, "how you are in any position to be making demands or giving orders. So, let's try this again – You will leave, now, or we'll have you thrown in one of our detention facilities until you superiors come to have you removed."

The three security guards started whispering between themselves, and after a few head nods, they all came to an agreement. They stood firm behind and between the two men in the grey suits, whose faces now had become very smug.

All at once, however, this look changed when the guards grabbed them firmly by their arms and slowly forced them to walk towards the recovery room exit; not without protest of course.

The man in the lab-coat, followed behind, but only after walking to Dr. Zeldin's bed, prepping it for removal, and slowly pushing out of the recovery room with Taylor's two large blood vials resting on the man's stomach.

"Where do you think you're going?" the ER doctor questioned, standing in the doorway to block the bed from any further movement.

"I have government orders to transfer Dr. Zeldin into our care, and to get a sample of subject 2275A's blood for testing." With these words, the lab-coated man tossed a data pad on the bed in front of him, landing between Dr. Zeldin's feet. It only took a second for the ER doctor to respond.

"Fine, I don't want this garbage in my ward any longer than it has to be!"

Jay watched, mouth gaping, from under his bed. He was completely at awe over the fact that this man, who had assaulted two people on EduCorp property, was being allowed to go free. He felt his heart pound inside his chest with a frustrating rhythm. As if his mouth couldn't be controlled by his brain, he shouted, "Nooooo!" and tried to follow behind the group, but was quickly held back by an unknown force.

Turning his head, he could see that Taylor was awake, and that, with a bit of kinesis, the boy was being pulling Jay back to his bed. Jay shook his head in anger. Still, even in his weakened state, Taylor was stronger kinetically than Jay was physically, and the teen knew he couldn't counter the boy's efforts. Giving up, Jay hopped back up on the bed and stared down at Taylor in confusion.

"Don't worry about it. He's not worth it." The boy said softly.

Tending to the patients he now had, it was clear to the E.R. doctor, that while one patient had been removed from his care, he was undoubtedly about to have another admitted into it. He quickly pulled another bed to a position nearby Jay's and with a hand of support the doctor helped Taylor make his way to the new bed.

After replicating and IV'ing the boy with an M-Gened transfusion of the child's own blood, the doctor left to assist Dr. Young and Dr. Ellington in dealing with the departing and unwanted guests. This left the room around Taylor and Jay now instantly quiet, even from the sawing noises of a snoring security guard, and it was quite apparent that things had finally settled down. But it was Jay that felt a gnawing in his stomach. He was hungry; hungry for food and hungry for answers. He felt, and rightly so even in Taylor's mind, that an explanation of the details surrounding Taylor's relationship with the evil Dr. Zeldin was owed.

"Tay, I've got to ask..." Jay said, but in usual telepathic fashion, Taylor had preempted the teen's words.

"You forget yourself, and your thoughts. I know. And, I know – you're right. I owe you an explanation," the boy said softly as he turned to watch a new blood supply slowly drip into his own veins.

"So, instead of a long, detailed story of words that could have confused meanings and a confused purpose, I'm just going to ask that you simply stare into my eyes, and focus hard on my thoughts."

Jay was a little confused by this request but did as he was told and, for the first of many times to come, Taylor filled his friend's mind with a barrage of still and moving images, sounds, and emotions. Taylor literally compressed several hours of life experiences into a few seconds of telepathic linking.

The boy had once described this to Dr. Young as the biological equivalent of E^3 – or Express Mode, in telepathy.

Outwardly Jay's face was screwing itself up in a series of strange faces as the thoughts from his friend had rapidly pushed their way into his brain.

In the minute or so it took for Jay to absorb Taylor's projected memories, it was learned that Dr. Zeldin, for a time, had become one of Taylor's best friends. From the time Dr. Young had initiated something called Article 897 back when Taylor had developed his full set of evolved abilities, Dr. Zeldin was under orders from the GC to in on how Taylor was handling his EduCorp instructors and overseers and to make sure that the company was doing everything possible to assist the boy in his *new* developments. So contrasting was this attention that Taylor felt it rude not to appreciate this acquaintance and even strike up a friendly relationship with the man.

Everything, seemingly, was fine for over a year. The EduCorp scientists were working hard to create protocols on how to swiftly develop Taylor's abilities, and Dr. Zeldin was enjoying the boy's conversations and displays of what he could do with his powers.

According to Dr. Zeldin, the government had been making requests to test Taylor's abilities, and that he, Taylor, was now *required* to meet a specified standard for how much he could lift, how many devices he could control, or how far in the future or past he could see. Taylor was more than happy to oblige and exceeded Dr. Zeldin's every expectation. In response, the man seemed to grow closer to Taylor with every success. This was what Jay could see, and the teen could not mistake the emotion that was projected by Taylor. The boy, it could not be denied, felt a growing fondness and respect for this man. Taylor enjoyed the time they spent together, and appreciated having someone in his life who actually cared about how he was doing on the inside; not just how his body or his brain was doing, but him, as a boy, as a person, and as a son. Indeed, Dr. Zeldin had made promises to Taylor of removing him from EduCorp, even adopting him if all the tests went well.

"I've already put the papers in, and you wouldn't believe what the GC can do to get you out of this place, if it's in their best interest." Jay heard these words spoken by Dr. Zeldin to Taylor over a private dinner and the boy, overly excited at the prospect of leaving The Towers for good, was happy beyond words.

Suddenly the images Jay was seeing in his mind quickened. Then, all at once, the speed and broken nature of those images slowed again. Jay looked about and could see Taylor walking swiftly down a corridor. This view was purposefully pushed to a date and time clock on the side of the corridor.

July 16th, 2444, Taylor's fifth birthday. Taylor still looked a few years older than he should, but most notably the boy was visibly excited and happy. He walked down the hall, unescorted, as only he could do at that age, and turning to a large grey door labeled "Lab-room N127L" at the end of one of the halls, he focused on it to open.

At this age, Taylor using his powers seemed even more impressive to Jay, who watched as the boy happily entered this room. It was clear that this was another testing room, and Jay saw by the look on Taylor's face that the boy was instantly confused. Instead of a barrage of old objects, or electronic equipment, or weights, for him to use his cognitive, cyber, or kinetic abilities on, the room was completely empty, piquing Taylor's bewilderment. The boy paced the room slowly and, with a sense of nervousness, his heart lifted when he watched Dr. Zeldin enter.

"I was wondering where you were?" The boy said light heartedly, and he walked to the doctor, arms open for a wide inviting a hug. Dr. Zeldin, however, did not return this gesture. He simply shook his head down at the boy and waved his finger at the center of the room. Taylor took this motion as a way of being told to stand in the room's center, which he did.

"I want you to concentrate. I need your mind clear." the doctor shouted with a resonating echo through the room.

"What's this all about?" Taylor questioned of the man, and he could see that Dr. Zeldin's eyes kept shifting about the room as if something was going to happen, something surprising. It was his birthday – maybe Dr. Zeldin had actually scheduled a surprise party. Taylor wondered if he should pre-cog into the future and spoil any surprises.

Deciding against it, he looked at the man with a questioning gaze. "What's going on?" he pressed, still holding on to his happy and playful tone.

"I need your complete attention." Dr. Zeldin commanded, and the boy turned to face the doctor head on, and stare at him. He focused hard on the man's thoughts, as if his light blue eyes could pierce into Dr. Zeldin's brain and tell him what was going on inside the man's head.

It was this concentration that distracted Taylor so well that he didn't notice the chair that had pulled itself up behind him and with an unexpected collapse, the boy fell into it, his wrists and ankles instantly bound. He struggled for a moment in confusion, looking down at the metallic clasps covering his limbs before shooting up a panicked stare to Dr. Zeldin, hoping for an explanation.

"What's going on here?" the boy said more angrily as he struggled.

"This is just another test," the doctor responded, "but it will be different than any of the others you've had."

Taylor felt his heart sink inside his chest as the chair slowly pulled itself backward against the far wall. He, in just the few short moments since he had walked into the lab-room, had hoped there was going to be some sort of party, surprise, or something, anything to celebrate his birthday, and realized ever so quickly that this was not the case.

"This test is going to be different," the doctor continued, "because you are going to have to defend yourself." The doctor turned his back on Taylor and faced the wall, away from the boy. "In a few seconds several deadly robotic units are going to enter this room through different doors. Some will be wireless enabled, others will not, and one, the RX-9000, is the most deadly device ever devised by man, and deemed illegal to use for any purpose by the GC. Will he survive?" The doctor turned to look over his shoulder, "I guess that's all up to you!"

Taylor looked down at the floor. His heart started pounding harder and faster than he had ever felt. He watched as Dr. Zeldin left the room, and he, Taylor, was hoping to see the man at least turn to look over his shoulder, to say something as a vote of confidence.

The door closed behind Dr Zeldin with no looks, no words, just the pressure-shifting push on Taylor's eardrums as he now knew the room was airtight and soundproof. Taylor was panicked. He didn't know what to expect and as he looked about the room he felt a rush of emotions fill him, not the least of which was anger.

A sound caused Taylor's head to flinch. He watched as two different doors opened at the far end of the room.

With a light tapping noise two robotic units slowly made their way into the room. One was on two legs, looking much like a full formed human once it stood at full height. The other was on four and walked awkwardly and spider like.

Taylor looked down at his wrists and ankles. "Any second now," the boy whispered and, inside his head, he was waiting for these to release so that he wouldn't be permanently confined to the chair. "Any second now," he repeated as he watched the human like robot lift its right hand.

It was with a focused curiosity that Taylor watched the robot's hand extend itself and rotated to reveal, concealed inside what was its arm, a small nozzle. This retracted into a firm position where the robot's hand was and, with a quick spark, a small flame the size of a large candle lit up at the nozzle's tip.

Looking down, Taylor could see that the four legged spider robot had its own weapon of choice, an electronic zapper. Taylor's eyes quickly moved back and forth between the two robots unsure of what was going to happen next.

"Any second now." The boy whispered with gritted teeth as he continued to struggle with his confined wrists and legs. He was still clinging to the hope that he would be freed from these confines.

With a rush of bright flame, Taylor realized that this was not the case, and kinetically he focused hard on the air in front of him. He forced it, like an artificial wind, to move as quickly as possible away from him. This had a shielding effect preventing the blow torch used by the human sized robot any ability to get a flame close enough to burn Taylor.

With a continued focus on the air, and flame in front of him, the boy forced the fire to move in an assortment of directions.

Indeed the boy was entertained by this ability to *play with fire* as it was something he had never done before.

Not losing focus, the boy's view was distracted by the sparking glow of the four legged spider that drew ever closer to his feet. All at once Taylor forced the flame to whirl around and direct itself on the tiny robot. Despite the fact that the human sized robot wasn't aiming to destroy his robotic counterpart, Taylor was successful in redirecting the flame in that direction. Indeed, it only took a few seconds of this for the spider to become nothing more than a smoldering lump. Thereafter Taylor concentrated on the human robot, hoping to *feel* for any wireless abilities, but there were none to speak of. His ears heard, on both sides, that two doors opened on either side of the chair.

Rolling out from these doors Taylor could see two domed tank-like robots, each with a gun turret at its end. Focusing extra hard on his kinetic abilities, he made the flame from the human robot split in two directions for each tank while he additionally focused on his restraints, releasing them all simultaneously.

Taylor stood quickly and realized that directing the flames at the tanks was ineffective as they were both impervious to fire and, before long, they had trained their turrets on him.

Taylor kinetically turned each of the tanks so that the turrets would face each other, and with a loud bang, the two had fired simultaneously on one another.

Taylor had closed his eyes and tried his best to protect himself kinetically from any shrapnel, and when he opened his eyes again he could see that, while the tanks were destroyed, the human robot had stopped its flaming onslaught and had approached him with a few clunking steps. With a quick and firm grip the robot grabbed the boy around the neck and lifted him off the ground.

Taylor was terrified to see out of the corner of his eye that the robot was putting its flaming nozzle only inches away from Taylor's temple.

Keeping his wits about him, Taylor offered an angry look of concentration forcing the robot's hand to quickly whip around and eventually end up with the nozzle wedged directly under its own chin. The boy then focused on the robot's shoulder, eventually ripping it from its socket. This had the immediate effect of forcing whatever flammable fuel the robot used for its flame to leak onto the floor.

Taylor then focused on the other arm, forcing it to release its hold on his neck and thereby dropping him to the floor. He stepped back quickly. All at once the arc of fuel that was streaming onto the floor had shifted its path to flow upward and onto the robot's head.

Taylor's hope that the small flame at the nozzle's tip would cause the fluid to ignite was realized when the robot's head was quickly consumed in flames. Within seconds, and a series of zaps and shocks, the robot twitched and fell over, being completely incapacitated.

Jay's view of this memory slowly accelerated to show Taylor defeating, one by one, every robot that revealed itself to him, including a knock down drag out battle between the boy and the RX9000 – a very advanced robot that moved with agility and dexterity unlike anything Taylor or Jay had ever seen. This machine, while wireless, was so advanced that it tested Taylor's every talent, reflex, and strength.

It was at the conclusion of this paced battle that the projected images slowed down for Jay and he was, again, able to view Taylor's memories at regular speed.

Jay saw a tattered Taylor holding the strange claw like hand of the RX9000 at the inside entrance to the *testing room*. He dropped it to the ground with a loud crash and focused on the door. It had been recoded by Dr. Zeldin and it was for this reason that Taylor had to focus a little longer to get it to open. It was in the middle of this that Taylor had, unintentionally, picked up stray thoughts from someone on the other side of the door.

"Test was successful – schedule a demo in front of the council in a week, then we can press on with Project Handshake. Finally I can be rid of the brat and get back to some real work again." Taylor heard these thoughts in the voice of Dr. Zeldin and instantly his heart plummeted to the floor, resting somewhere beside the claw of the RX9000 he was sure.

Taylor took a step back from the door. He focused with hard determination on its opening. When it did he saw Dr. Zeldin, and only Dr. Zeldin standing at the entrance.

"Well done my boy! I knew you could do it! Man, I'm so proud of you!" Taylor didn't say a word. If the thoughts that he had picked up were coming from Dr. Zeldin, and all evidence was pointing in that direction, then he wasn't sure if a single word out of that man's mouth could be trusted.

Dr. Zeldin reached around and started massaging Taylor's shoulders. "C'mon – let's go get something to eat."

"I'm not that hungry." This was a lie that even Dr. Zeldin should have picked up on, but he didn't, and Taylor, being both confused and angry, walked wearily away from Dr. Zeldin with a miserable false grin and made his way to the elevator.

"What's the matter?" Dr. Zeldin asked, and at this question Taylor immediately guarded his thoughts from being read. The lift doors opened and Taylor stepped inside, but it didn't go anywhere due to the fact that Dr. Zeldin was keeping it in place by holding the request button. "Geeze, I just thought we could celebrate. I mean you did so well and all," Dr. Zeldin said happily.

Taylor shook his head. "I could think of another reason to celebrate and it has nothing to do with any tests," the boy replied with a snide arrogance that caught Dr. Zeldin off guard.

"What's wrong with you?" the man snapped.

"Let's put it this way," Taylor said stepping out of the lift, "I never, in the two hundred years of what life I'm going to have, would ever have expected multiple life threatening attacks from all directions – on my birthday!"

Dr. Zeldin's jaw dropped. Taylor could tell that the man was surprised to hear this news and, with what deceiving thoughts the boy had picked up earlier, he supposed it shouldn't be such a surprise that the man forgot, or maybe Dr. Zeldin never even thought to look up this important tidbit of information.

"I'll be going now." Taylor said as he kinetically forced Dr. Zeldin's fingers away from the request button. With the doors closing and Taylor on his way up to his dorm, Jay's perspective of the telepathic images sped up again to reveal Taylor standing in the middle of a small office with Dr. Zeldin and two other GC representatives who, now that Taylor was remembering, and Jay was seeing them, were instantly recognizable as the two grey-suited men who were, in reality, just escorted out of the recovery room.

"Come on Taylor, show these men what you've got!" Dr. Zeldin said, and it was clear that there was a good deal of frustration in the man's voice. This was clearly not the first time Dr. Zeldin had made the request, yet Taylor merely stood there, staring at the floor, shaking his head in the negative.

"I can't!"

He wasn't looking at the items in front of him, which were of the basic sort; a few electronic devices, a few weights, and a few old garments of clothes. Dr. Zeldin noticed this and the man's patience grew more thin while, with each of his requests becoming more stern, Taylor's tenacity solidified to become absolute.

"Doctor, I hope you haven't lured us here under false pretences," one of the GC representatives said coolly.

"The boy is lying," Dr. Zeldin said hastily and he turned back to Taylor with a look of anger. "What's wrong with you," he growled.

Taylor stared at the doctor, nose to nose, and only offered a purse lipped grin. He decided to offer a single directed telepathic comment to the man.

"I know the truth!"

This short comment was seemingly enough for Dr. Zeldin's face to quickly change to one of concern. He stood and turned to the two men in the room. With an increased trepidation in his voice he spoke to the men at his side. "He's just shy, and that's okay. This was only a small physical demonstration. What you really want to see is right here."

Dr. Zeldin held up a data-pad and without knowing what was on it, Taylor made the dangerous move of simply, and cyber-kinetically, erasing everything.

Dr. Zeldin tapped the data-pad. It instantly displayed a "no data available" message on the screen.

Taylor was certain that Dr. Zeldin was ready to panic, and has he carefully navigated through the pad's basic core memory it was quite apparent that Taylor had done a very thorough job of eliminating whatever files it contained.

"Hmmm, he said confused, that's funny. I thought I had that video right here."

Video – Taylor thought – *if he had a video of my performance for the last test, then there's no way I can lie into making these men believe me if he's got videos.*

Taylor focused hard on the data pad and, without Dr. Zeldin knowing, Taylor had inserted background lines of code into the pad. Dr. Zeldin, however, was mindlessly using it to navigate through the WSN to his personal stockpile of files on Taylor and the kinetic and cognitive test results. He made the request to download the video of Taylor's last test. This, as a result of Taylor's code changes, caused a small sequence of Taylor's own programmed commands to run. To the man's panic at realizing it, this completely erased his entire set of secured online data files.

Dr. Zeldin growled almost to a scream in anger. "You! You did this, didn't you? You reprogrammed the pad. You, uugh." The doctor's hands started shaking. "Over a year's worth of data – lost!"

Dr. Zeldin stood and pulled his hand back in anger. Taylor knew he would have to take it, and here it came. Dr. Zeldin swung an angry smack at Taylor. The pain was extreme, and Taylor could've easily blocked it, but didn't and he could've held in any show of the pain, but he cried, if for nothing more than to draw out remorse from his GC audience.

The men, however, were unsympathetic to the strange orphan boy in front of them, and simply stood, looking at each other – "I think we've seen enough here!"

Dr. Zeldin turned to look at the men and started catering to their every whim, desperate to keep their attention and their approval.

Taylor thought he was finished with Dr. Zeldin, but only a second after the man left the office he popped his head back in through the door, "This isn't over – I'll be back to finish with you – this isn't over by a long shot!"

Taylor only smiled, "Uh, Yeah, I think it is," and he kinetically pushed Dr. Zeldin's head out of the office so hard that he practically threw the man across the hall, and thereafter he forced the door to the office to close again. He could hear the doctor's screams to the GC reps over this. "See – did you see that – did you see – I told you!"

In Jay's mind the voice of Dr. Zeldin slowly faded away, as did the color of what the teen was seeing. Slowly everything went dark, and in a flash he found himself staring at Taylor. Indeed, only a few short minutes had passed and Jay's mind was aching with the many new memories, thoughts, and emotions he had just experienced. So much was this that the teen nearly fell backward onto his bed. His brain had never taken in that much information so quickly, and he felt the need to sit for a few moments and absorb it all.

Jay, since developing his own telepathy, had enjoyed having wordless conversations and, with practice, had learned how to project still images into the minds of his targets, but to do what Taylor had just done, well – "That was amazing!" was all that he could say to let Taylor know that he was both alright, and impressed with how well trained Taylor was at such a young age.

After a long pause Taylor decided to break the silence. "So – are you sure you still want to work here?" the boy asked half serious, half joking.

Jay turned his head and smiled. "Well that all depends – I've been picking up some stray thoughts from *you* on the matter – wha'd'you think? You've been here for a few years. Would you work here?"

"Taking some of what you've seen over the last two days *out* of my judgment – Sure."

"Good! Cuz I think you'd keep things interesting around here, and I don't think I could handle it if it was boring.

Taylor laughed, and while the two spent the rest of the afternoon talking on all sorts of topics and absolutely leaving all negative memories and thoughts of recent and long passed memories out of the conversation, the one subject that kept getting hit on was what it would be like if the two actually worked together; building their friendships together, building their lives together – half heartedly thinking of the possibilities, yet not fully realizing the irony of their conversation.

54 Discarding Jay

WHEN TAYLOR WOKE THE FOLLOWING MORNING his mind was full of many things, not the least of which was how he could reassure himself that what he was seeing was real and that he wasn't having another vision like the night before. He sat upright, pulled his legs over the side of the bed and offered one of them a pinch – it hurt alright. He then turned to the clock in his room and, with a bit of cyber effort, he forced the clock to show the date: July 19, 2457.

"Well that looks about right." Taylor whispered to himself, and he rubbed his leg, wishing he hadn't pinched it so hard.

Walking over to his room's M-Gen, he, for the first time, forced it produce the robe that was missing from his closet the night before. He then exited the room, wrapping himself with the robe and happy to have it, for he could feel a chill in the air that made his toes curl on the cold floor.

Making his way around the rooming corridor, Taylor opened each door and, walking in the rooms one by one, he checked on all of the children. They were each sleeping soundly and, as Taylor exited the last room, he could hear a rustling coming from a different part of his large elevated home.

On making his way through different sections of the twisted floor-plan, the noises became louder. Eventually he found his way to the kitchen and it was here that he saw Jay sitting quietly at a counter. Apparently the man had prepared himself some breakfast and, with a stiff "Good Morning," he offered Taylor a nod to start the day.

"So, how soon 'til we get going then?" Jay asked after a long pause; his mind still firm on the idea of getting back to the city.

"Are you in that much of a hurry to go?" Taylor asked with a frown. The teen had hoped that a night of distress, or maybe – just maybe, a night of memories and thoughts of leaving such a rich history behind, might cause Jay to change his mind.

"Not that I'm in a hurry, but I know Shannon's probably worried sick by now!"

"Oh yes, Shannon!" Taylor said, belittling the name. "How come you've never introduced us? I mean I've always wondered what, or who occupied your time away from work.

"Would it help if I said that you already knew her?" Jay replied with a smile, and at these words Taylor's interest peaked.

"I know her? – Who is she? What does she look like?"

"Take your mind back about oh – ten years or so – when I first visited you and you were still a student of The Towers."

"Yes."

"That first evening, in *L.A. House*... the girl I finally danced with, hmmm with your help, that's Shannon!"

"Her! You're dating her – you're engaged to *her*!" Taylor shrieked, and he almost felt himself sicken from the thought. "Have you danced for her again?" he asked after a long pause and he waited for an answer holding a wide grin.

"Oh, I told her the truth about that a long time ago. She's fine with it! And don't come down on her so hard. She's grown up a lot since that night."

"Well, I'm glad to hear that." Taylor said incredulously while generating himself a cup of coffee and some eggs. When he turned away from the M-Gen he noticed that two of the children, Aspen and Orion, were standing in the entrance to the kitchen. They were laughing about something and, with each one having their arm hooked over the other's shoulder they seemed quite the likely pair to have done something mischievous.

Taylor spied them with an auspicious grin. "You two seem in a good mood. How did you sleep last night?" Both their faces immediately soured.

"Can we just not talk about that?" Orion requested as he pulled up a chair for himself. Aspen merely pulled hers out kinetically.

Taylor sipped his coffee, "Fine by me – but we will discuss it later."

Orion groaned.

Jay turned to the children at the table. "Would you two like something to eat?"

They nodded their heads and Jay immediately generated and gave them plates of French toast with sausage. He *knew* that, as with all of the children, French toast was their favorite breakfast food.

The two looked down at the plate with sour faces – "French toast – blah." Aspen said. "Belgian waffles – can we get Belgian waffles?" she quickly added.

Jay shook his head – "I thought you liked French toast!"

"Not any more – Belgian waffles are better – fruit and whipped cream." Orion said offering a "mmm-mmm" sound to show his desire for the same as his sister.

While it is never a problem to change what food is requested on a plate, it did bother Jay that his assumption of their favorite food was incorrect. This was agitated by Taylor's next immediate comment – "They haven't eaten French toast in several months now – I thought you knew that."

Jay grumbled, regenerated the new plates of food before walking down the hall to the rooming corridor.

"Where ya going?" Orion asked with a smile.

"I'm just going to get some decent clothes on, if that's okay with you." Jay responded in a clearly irritated voice.

Orion mouthed his words behind his back, mocking him, and as Jay moved out of sight, the boy and his sister quickly started giggling.

"I can hear his scream, and I can see the room," Taylor said to the chuckling children before adding, "but I have to ask, did you actually attach each piece of furniture to the ceiling, or did you just use a gravity pad."

Orion and Aspen's eyes grew wide; they hated it when Taylor's precognitions ruined a good surprise.

"Attached." Orion said miserably.

Taking a sip of his coffee and looking up at the ceiling, Taylor counted down, "Three – two – one."

"What the hell!" could be heard resonating through the halls, and with a quick series of stomps that vibrated ever louder in the levitated home, Jay made his way back into the kitchen.

"You evil little children!" he said gruffly and with clenched hands and a reddening face, it was clear that Jay wasn't taking this final prank very well.

"Oh come on, Jay," Taylor said both calm and relaxed. "You can't blame them for one last effort to give you a bit of creative misery; and very creative at that!"

Jay growled, and within a few seconds four other children slowly popped up behind him. They were each giggling until Johnny voiced a playful, yet rhetorical question. "Hey, Jay, how'd you get your furniture up there like that? Pretty cool!" The others, including Taylor, started cracking up.

"You knew. You all knew. You plot against me. I see how it is." He stormed down the corridor and made his way back into his room. He looked up at his inverted bedroom and gritted his teeth. This lasted only a few seconds before, with a flood of his own memories taking over his thoughts, he started to laugh. He was filled with the many happy thoughts of the children laughing, at him most of the time, after a prank they had played.

David, who had been only a few steps behind and was peering out of one of the bedrooms to watch Jay, walked up to the man and grabbed his hand.

"Allow me!" the boy said, and with a look of concentration he pulled each item off the ceiling. With several resonating pops and the pinging of dozens of attaching nails and screws, the boy had the room back to its upright order in no time, even catching and collecting the scattering hardware to keep from making a mess.

Jay scrubbed the boy's head before squatting in front of him, "I'm really gonna miss you guys!"

"We know – and we'll miss you too!" David said somberly and with these words Jay could see the boy's eyes misting up. Jay quickly reached out and pulled the boy close in a warm hug.

In the infirmary later that morning Taylor administered a sedative that would keep Jay unconscious for nearly six hours. This, Taylor believed, would be more than enough time for Jay to be dropped off someplace completely unrelated to where their home was located.

To this end Taylor, the children, and once again the inanimate body of Jay, all entered the transport and under the power of Taylor's kinesis, the craft made its way some 300 miles around the Los Angeles Metroship to the city's opposite side. As the craft's controller, Taylor navigated quickly and sometimes dangerously through the thick trees and hills and on dropping Jay off Taylor put an emergency transmitter in the man's pocket for use when he woke.

One by one each of the children said their goodbyes to someone one that they considered their best friend. Taylor watched this small procession and was filled with the eerie reminder of a wake or funeral. He tended to each of the children as they, with tear filled eyes, needed much consoling.

Caitlin, the last to say her goodbyes and, unbeknown to anyone, slipped a picture of the eight of them, taken several months before from a visit to the LA Metro Park, into his pocket. As she did this her eyes welled even greater with tears.

Taylor grabbed her shoulder. "Come on – we need to get going. He can't wake up while we're around – we need to hurry."

The children loaded into the lift and with another long trip they made their way back home. The journey was a quiet one, except for when the children recounted some memory they had of Jay; a prank they played, or the fun he had with them, though the occasions of this were rare.

Taylor even offered anecdotes of his own and, with all of these, by the time they approached the site of their home, the children's mood was a little lighter than it had been. In addition, a beeping on the transport's sensors made all the children feel a light bit of relief. Jay *had* activated his emergency beacon only a few seconds before they returned their tree-based residence destination.

The children all exited the transport and were happy to know that Taylor's plan, as far as they could tell, was working. But between the six of them, the children were not nearly as active, nor as vocal as Taylor was used to. He tried, on numerous occasions that day, to lighten their spirits, but he resigned to the fact that there was little he could do to settle their emotions.

But Taylor understood this somber attitude as a simple byproduct of the loss they were all feeing. In fact, Taylor mentally prepared himself for the possibility of personality changes in each of the children due to the drastic changes in their life. With a deep sigh as he ascended into their home, Taylor's heart and brain were both heavily weighted with worries thoughts of what lay before him; a new life with one less friend, two new ones, and six children that he had to care for all on his own.

55 Ear Piercing

CLEARLY LIFE WITHOUT JAY WAS DIFFERENT, and quite often in those first few weeks amid the forest, Taylor had to contend with the difficulties of disciplining and training the children on his own. To make matters more interesting, the children had insisted, and he had grown accustomed to, having Delissa and Tristan as guests in their new home. This was rarely at first, then occasionally, then, to Taylor's delight, the two member family started visiting nearly every night.

All things considered, Taylor felt that life was going well out in the forest. He listened and could hear little of the voices that had plagued his first night's sleep there. And as the days wore on he felt that there was less and less a chance of their being found. After all, if the GC had even the slightest clue where they were, Taylor was certain that the children would've been snatched up a long time ago – or at least there would be the effort to try!

No, these worries were slowly working their way to the back of Taylor's brain, and he was overjoyed that the children could find someone like Tristan to bridge the gap between the life they left behind in the city and the new surroundings they had about them. Indeed, for the most part, Taylor was happy with the children's interactions with Tristan – *for the most part.*

"What the hell is that?" Taylor shouted as he followed shortly behind Johnny, who was trying, quite obviously to sneak his way into his own room. The whole lot of the children had just returned from a free afternoon with Tristan and Delissa, a free afternoon they would never have had while living at The Towers. So it was on the children's return that Taylor noticed something odd about Johnny's ear. Despite the boy's efforts to be unnoticed, Taylor wasn't to be deterred. He saw what he saw, and his curiosity was peaked.

"Jonathan Kristopher Lewis Matthews – I am talking to you!"

Now he'd done it. Taylor spoke the child's full name, and he knew that at the mention of any of his student's *full* names they were certain to be in trouble. Because of this Johnny stopped dead in his tracks, inches from his room, a place where he wrongly assumed he'd be safe from any questions.

Taylor walked up behind him, kneeled, and whirled the boy around. Reaching for the child's left ear, he pulled at it and massaged it. With Johnny's "ouch" and pulling away Taylor knew exactly what he was looking at. The boy's earlobe had been pierced – straight through – by some small, sharp, thin, and very crude piece of metal.

Taylor's face scrunched in anger. He worked hard at corking his feelings and thus showed a reddish color in his expression to match his emotions. Standing up, he grabbed the boy's hand and practically dragged him to the infirmary – and not without protests.

"What! What's the big deal! Tristan said it's fine. He – he – he's got one. You've seen it! Awwww – ooowwwch come on!"

Taylor had kinetically pulled the new bit of metal from Johnny's ear, very roughly in fact, and while the ear did bleed, Taylor immediately tended to it with a tissue generator, healing not only the wound, but completely closing up the new piercing.

Taylor had to work to keep his anger at bay. He wanted to blame Tristan for this. He wanted to blame someone for this – his youngest, so to speak, had just maimed his body – and did it without his guardian's knowledge or approval. But Tristan comes from a different background, so would it be right to blame the boy? *Of course it would!*

"This was Tristan's idea wasn't it!?"

The boy was still tending delicately to his ear, even if it had been completely healed and was now pain free. "No – it wasn't – it was my idea – all mine. I wanted it!"

Taylor had a hard time digesting these words and after calming himself he opened his mouth for words that he hoped would question reason into the boy.

Johnny – I'm sorry – but, uh – don't you think you should've asked me about this before just – just – doing it!

"I – I," Taylor could see Johnny's guilt ridden face try to work out a submissive answer – but in the middle of the thoughts brewing in the child's brain the boy's face completely changed. Shifting from this calm guilty expression to one of anger and irritation, Johnny stared Taylor down, ready to pull out words before he thought better of speaking them.

"I don't see what the big deal is? I think it's cool – and I – I..." The child paused then, he laid out those words that Taylor hated hearing the most. "You're not my father. You – you – what do you care?"

Taylor's ears and mind could pick up both the actual and telepathic gasps from the boy's eavesdropping brothers and sisters nearby – namely Caitlin and Aspen. He turned his head sideways for a moment as if to recognize this, then looked back at the boy in front of him. The child had said something just to hurt him, and while this wasn't the first time Taylor had heard that phrase fall from the mouths of each and every one of his students before, his heart never got used to the aching that he always felt when it happened. Still, he had what he felt was the best way to handle this purposefully hurtful phrase.

He smiled, causing his light blue eyes to squint, and moved in to offer Johnny a warm and somewhat unexpected hug. Johnny didn't return this, and after a few seconds Taylor simply whispered in the boy's ear.

"I know I'm not your father, but trust me when I say this. No one you will ever – ever meet will love you more than I do – and don't think there's anything in this world I wouldn't do for you! I love you – I LOVE ALL OF YOU!" He said the last phrase loudly so that the other children could hear, and with all his other words spoken in a definitive and sober manner, Johnny was forced to apologize using a low eyed expression of guilt.

Now as it just so happened, this was not one of the nights when Delissa and Tristan were expected for dinner, and with the day's events so raw in his mind, Taylor was actually happy about this, for he didn't know how he would react to seeing the teen. To make things more difficult, Johnny spent the rest of the evening skulking around the home as if he were an injured animal.

Taylor, on the other hand, tried his best to avoid all of his students. He wasn't sure if he was angry at them as well, or if he was just angry period. He knew he was in a bad mood – and as his children usually supplied him with a wealth of positive energy, he was rarely in a bad mood. But nothing like this had ever happened to his children before, and he had to take a little time to *appreciate* and absorb how his kids were starting to push their boundaries in this new environment.

Later that night, over a hearty dinner, Taylor worked to weasel out the truth, both telepathically and verbally, from each of his students on how it was that any of them let Tristan pierce Johnny's ear, and moreover how it was that Tristan convinced Johnny to let him do it in the first place.

"Listen, kids. I know you look out for each other, and I know that you *all* look out for Johnny, so I have to ask. What happened today that you'd just let this whole ear maiming fiasco go on?"

All the children stared at Taylor as if they didn't understand the question, and in frustration Taylor gripped a firm fist on the table, that he slowly spanned out to a stiff flat palm. "Oh, come on guys. Were you all just sleeping when it happened? Were you even there? I wanna know what went on. And I will find out one way or another – you all know that!"

Taylor stared around the dark brown table, brightly lit by overhead lights. Above it were the faces of his students, staring at him and at each other as if trying to convince all that silence would be the best way out of the whole thing. And the truth came, in fact, from the unlikely source of David, who, amid a mouth full of food, saw Taylor's stare as though the teen was trying to pry into his soul.

Now David knew, as did all the children, that if Taylor wanted to find something out, he could easily do it using his post-cog powers, but they also knew that Taylor would rather have it offered up by a willing participant if at all possible. So when Taylor calmed himself and questioned again, "Would any of you like to explain to me how it is that you let Johnny do that to himself?" and later added

"You're all older than he is, so why didn't any of you stop him?"

After a short pause he then started calling to his students, "Orion – Aspen – Caitlin – David," it was here that Taylor stopped, sensing the boy's weakness, "Daaaviiid."

The child lowered his head and stared at Taylor across the dining table under a heavy brow and the two focused on each other. Within seconds David transmitted pathic thoughts and memories at an accelerated rate from what Taylor was normally used to from his students, but this had been one of many changes that Taylor had been dealing with since the children's last encounter with the mysterious sphere.

And so, with a dulling of what he was seeing around him, Taylor's world changed from that of the dining room to a warm, moist, dark area of forest where he could see all six of his students running through thick foliage being led by Tristan.

"Come on guys – you have to see this! It's just a bit further!"

Tristan was working to take the group ever deeper into the forest, but he was stopped by protests from nearly all six of his followers.

"I'm getting tired – Come on. This is a good spot, why don't we just stop here?" Caitlin pleaded both whining, and tired.

"Whatever!" Grace countered. She was the only one who really wanted to go on, but it was Aspen who convinced all that this was a good place to stop and relax.

"Ooooh wow – look at this guys!" she said, pulling everyone's attention through the trees to a small clearing that allowed light to pass through the tops of what would otherwise be thick cover. As the others ran to the opening Orion was the only one responsible enough to mention, "Just make sure you guys don't come out from under the trees!"

David shot through the trees after this was said and, crawling under some low limbs, the boy couldn't help but express his absolute elation over this newly discovered area. "This is wicked cool!" the child said loudly as he swung himself up one limb to another, and then another and he quickly found himself over twenty feet above the ground, resting perfectly atop a high branch.

Johnny quickly followed and, while he eventually made his way to a branch that was equally as high, the boy was nowhere near as graceful, and Taylor could see through David's memories that the child was struggling with his new telekinetic abilities.

Orion, on the other hand, was baffled by the tree itself. All around he could see different kinds of pine, and fir, but here in front of him stood a massive oak. A detail that neither boy seemed to absorb before climbing its limbs, yet Taylor, like Orion, quickly appreciated how far removed this tree was from its surroundings.

"Awwww, come on, what ya waitin' for?" Johnny shouted down, and at this Orion decided it was his turn to work his way up to their level inside the tree. He did, however, take a much simpler approach.

He kinetically pulled one branch at a time down to his level, where he either grabbed onto it or conveniently stepped onto it, so that it could bring him to a higher level. So, without anything close to the effort that either of the other boys put into their ascent, Orion was able to get just as high as his brothers.

Tristan, who was still sour about stopping short his trek through the forest, huffed a hard working climb up the tree, and when all was said and done the four boys found themselves perched in the tree like large bits of heavy ripe fruit – fruit that Taylor was terrified would fall from their branches.

It was clear that Taylor knew nothing like that had happened, for all the children were fine at the dinner table, but for some reason this did not help his nerves, which were more on edge when the boys started playing and swinging between the branches.

Down below, while all the boys were still one-by-one making their way up the tree, the girls found either a large rock or a log from a long ago fallen tree on which to sit. They talked, and admired the beauty of the world around them.

"I just love how alive everything is out here. It's so different from the city!" Aspen said as she patted the fallen log where she delicately sat.

"I know it's just great – everything is so beautiful. I don't know why they don't let people live out here anymore – it just doesn't make any sense," Caitlin added. She was sitting behind Aspen, braiding her hair, and she turned up with a stare of curiosity at Grace.

"What do you think Gracie?"

"Urrrrgh, what are you idiots doing?" the girl shouted up into the trees. She just had a wad of leaves fall onto her head, and it was clear that she wasn't pleased. "Come on! Don't make me come up there. You know I'll kick all your butts – even you two," she said, looking at David and Tristan as she finished.

She was about to turn her stare back down to her sisters to answer their question, but in the trees she noticed that Johnny, who had been struggling with his kinesis all morning, had fallen and was headed straight for the ground, screaming as he went.

With a focused, almost harsh stare, the girl concentrated on her brother, and slowed his fall to a delicate pat on the ground below the tree. Aspen and Caitlin both ran to the boy's side helping brush himself off as he was half covered in dirt and leaves.

"What happened?" Caitlin questioned with concern.

"I – I don't know – I was trying to jump from one limb to another – and when I tried to balance myself with my kinesis, I just – well I lost it... Get off, I'm fine. I'm fine I said," Johnny finally protested as he was tired of the attention the girls were giving him.

The boy then jumped up, scaled his way back up the tree in the matter of a few seconds and Taylor watched this with bated breath, fearful for what was happening with the boy's powers. Yet still the child hadn't approached Tristan at all to inquire about having his ear pierced.

Taylor impatiently watched the boys roughhouse with each other in the trees, trying to knock each other around, both physically and kinetically now that they all could, and he had to laugh at how chaotic and interesting things were getting. But he noted, clearly, that both Johnny and Orion's kinesis were at times erratic. It was as if they were losing grip on the new powers that the sphere had granted them several weeks earlier.

After a short while it was clear that Tristan was feeling a little left out what with all the use of this extra power that he did not possess. He tried using his cloaking suit to give himself an advantage at play, but no matter how hard he tried, he couldn't compete with the use of kinesis to both find him out and manipulate him. So, climbing out of the tree and sitting on the same rock as Aspen, he was more than happy just watching the other boys while listening to the girls.

Taylor watched Tristan's stare, his wide, almost laughable smile, and in an instant he knew how happy the boy was enjoying time with children near his own age. Shaking his head, he reminded himself of the reason for this dive into David's memories, and his anger put him in check. *How could that – that boy do that to one of my kids!*

Tristan flinched in watching the boy's at play. His ear had been grabbed by; Aspen, who had, for the most part, been leaning back-to-back against the teen. But she grew curious and started asking questions over his one and only piercing.

"How could you do that to yourself?" she asked, half interested, half with a tone that she judged the action.

"Uh, I don't know. I just did it. Well, I didn't do it. Actually my mom did. She did it when I turned ten."

As he said these words Aspen was massaging his ear and Taylor eyed this so closely that he didn't notice Johnny forcefully drop from the tree.

"Hey!" the boy said loudly, standing so close to Tristan he made the teen wince, "What – what does it – take to get one – one of those?"

Johnny was clearly out of breath, and while Aspen offered a look that said she'd rather not be bothered while talking to Tristan, the boy didn't pay her any mind and listened curiously as Tristan talked about the piercing process.

"It's really simple. You just take something very sharp; something like – this," he said pulling a small object from his pocket.

"And you just push it straight through the ear." It'll hurt for a minute or so, but once it's done, it's done."

"What is that thing?" Johnny asked, looking with a face full of apprehension at what Tristan had pulled out.

"Oh, this – it's just an air dart. It's great for hunting, but if you don't put the poison on it, well, then it's pretty harmless."

Tristan dropped the small thin piece of metal into Johnny's hand and while the boy stared at it he massaged his earlobe with his free hand. Taylor's stomach turned as he could see the boy's thoughts slowly developing into what was obviously a decision that he made all on his own.

"Hey. I want one! Do me!" was the simple phrase that fell out of the boy's mouth as he gave the dart back to Tristan and pulled his slightly overgrown hair back to reveal his ear.

Tristan's face lit up, but it wasn't with a happy expression. It was, instead, more reserved. "Ahh – I don't know. Don't you think Taylor'll mind?"

"Naaaah. He won't care! Come on. I've been eyeing yours for a while. It'll be cool." Johnny said quickly, and Taylor was amazed at how easily the boy either assumed what he, that is to say Taylor, would think, or simply dismissed it and lied.

All three of the girls, and now even Orion and David, had crowded around. Though they said nothing, it was clear that with their stares at each other that they were all pathically conversing – conversing amongst each other, but not with Johnny.

"I don't know... shouldn't we do something." Caitlin said.

"Well, I don't see what the big deal is." Grace added.

"I don't like this." Aspen said.

"It's his decision, and if anybody can do it and not get in trouble – well..." David reasoned, and with this Orion chimed in.

"Oh, for heaven's sake – let him do it. If he gets into trouble – well, it's about time – he never gets in trouble. And if he doesn't get in trouble, well then you can all get it done!"

Taylor shook his head at hearing these thoughts. Was his preference for Johnny, the youngest; was it that obvious? Watching as Tristan held the dart in his hand, he could tell that the teen was still uneasy.

"I – I just don't know about all this!"

In response, it was David that pushed the teen into action.

"Oh, just do it. It'll be fine – don't worry 'bout it!"

Tristan, giving in to the many urging voices around him, slowly reached out and grabbed Johnny's ear before firmly holding the dart between his fingers and pressing it against the boy's flesh.

"Now you know this *is* going to hurt."

"I'm fine! Just do it!" Johnny said sharply.

"Well, I just think you're a little young and it... well... I just don't want you crying or anything."

"Cry! Cry! Who do you think you're talking to a big babyyyyyouuuuuu."

Tristan took advantage of Johnny's distracted protests to pierce the lobe. There was no blood, and immediately afterward both Orion and David patted and massaged their brother's back.

"Good job"

"Way ta go!" they said in turn.

Within moments Taylor's view shifted back to the dining room, and with everyone around him except for David still eating quietly, it was obvious that only a few seconds had passed. Indeed the high speed pathic transmission David offered worked quite well and Taylor's face instantly shifted to one of disappointment – a look that he shared with everyone at the table.

Sometimes just an expression is enough to let someone know how you feel.

And it was for this reason that Taylor felt one statement was all he needed after what he had seen.

He looked up from heavy eyes, and smiled. "I love you all so very much, and none more than the other." He repeated this purposefully, "no *one* more than the other. I hope you all know that." His eyes were now looking intently at both Orion and David. He had a feeling that the two might doubt this. That they might feel he favors Johnny a little and for more than just because he was the youngest. Between the two boys, David wasn't even returning the stare, and Orion only frowned, staring sourly with a lazy mouth full of food.

When they all did get the chance to see his light blue eyed stare and the expression on his face, the children, even the girls, all knew of Taylor's disappointment. They knew how he felt, and in their own minds, they could hear what he might say to either lecture, teach, or console them. So, without another word, Taylor felt he had done enough to let the children know his thoughts.

At the end of dinner, after Taylor had bid the children to leave the table, he was deep in thought over what he had seen of them through David's memories. It was after finishing his nightly chore of cleaning up, just as he was about to join the children in the den when his face lit a smile. "That is a funny thing." He whispered, and, while no one was around to decipher this cryptic phrase, Taylor had in his mind a simple thought; that there is a funny thing about children. Sometimes, even when it is known what the right decision is, or what well minded rules and boundaries have been put in place, a child must make those wrong decisions or push those boundaries to and beyond the limit. And Taylor found it funny that despite his best efforts, to guide and teach these children; in this regard they were no different than any other.

*****

"It's my decision. And it's what *I* want!" Johnny said loudly so that not only Taylor, but even his brothers and sisters could hear.

"I knew it. I just knew it – I could see it this morning when I first woke up. And how could you, after what I told you yesterday."

"But this is my body, I can..." Johnny protested, but Taylor interrupted.

"I don't care!" Taylor said, and he took a deep breath at hearing these words. If there was ever a phrase that Taylor couldn't appreciate in so many ways – it was the words "I don't care." Long ago he told himself he would use this phrase as little as possible with his children.

Inside Johnny's room the two were basically alone, and with Taylor closing the door behind him, he sat on the bed next to Johnny, barely able to stand the sight of the boy's *once again* pierced ear. This time, however, it was with a ring that had been conveniently and, Taylor was sure, painfully welded closed. He pulled the boy close to his side, half wanting to inspect the ear, half just wanting to give him a hug at seeing the painful redness of the lobe.

"I'm sorry. I do care. I care about what you want and what you *think* you need. But this – it's just – I don't understand why! Just – just tell me why."

"I – I don't know!" the boy said somberly.

Taylor had heard this tell tale expression from his kids before. Usually it didn't mean that the children didn't know – it's that they had a half a dozen crazy reasons why, but none that they felt were worthy to mention – *ahhhhh the power of telepathy.*

"Well that just isn't good enough, Johnny." Taylor said as he heard ideas and thoughts started churning in the child's head head. "But, I will say this. If you *can* think of a good reason why you've done this to yourself; just one, well, then I might just consider letting you keep the damned thing – after I've healed up your ear and done it properly."

The boy sat, thinking and biting his lip, as he always did, and with his typical angelic stare, a stare that was now tainted and changed with a horrible metallic ornament, Johnny offered the only thing he could think.

"This is *my* decision. And that's the only reason I have. It's my decision; not something Orion, or David, or my sisters wanted. It's me – I did it first – and it's mine. No one can claim that they were older and so they did it – It's all me. That's why I wanted to do it in the first place, that's the truth, and that's my reason."

Taylor was taken aback at hearing this. He'd never heard words like this come from Johnny, and he had to at least admire the boy for laying it on the line so simply.

"I don't like it! I'll tell you right now – I just don't like it. But I can see that you're determined – so I'll say this... As long as I can see good behavior from you – good progress in your classes, well, let's just say you'll earn the right to keep that thing. It'll be day by day – but still – you defied me and went behind my back – so now – I'm going to ask you – what kind of discipline you should receive for that?"

"Hmmm a day of..." the boy started – but he could see Taylor shaking his head. There was instant disapproval that a day was nowhere near long enough of a discipline for this kind of misbehavior.

"A week of..." the boy started, and when Taylor nodded his head, the child knew that this was an acceptable minimum for both parties. Knowing this, Johnny continued. "A week of no games, and I have to stay in the house the whole time."

Taylor nodded his head, and he informed the boy that certain circuits would be deactivated in his own bedroom to make sure the boy had, in fact, nothing but a data-pad loaded with school materials and reading to use for entertainment.

"And I'll know if anyone alleviates any of these restrictions for you – so don't even think about asking."

Taylor stood and walked to the door and just as he was about to exit the room a small smirk came over the teen's face.

"And what makes you think that putting a ring on your ear would do anything to keep that thing there anyways?

And with barely a thought Taylor cracked the ring and kinetically flexed it open so that it could be easily slipped off the boy's ear at any time. It didn't hurt Johnny, but the look of surprise on the child's face was enough to force a light laugh out of Taylor as the boy jumped off his own bed and ran up to give Taylor a hug.

He separated from Johnny, feeling instantly better, but as he stepped away from the boy's room his mind shifted to heavier thoughts. Now the teen had to contend with trying to explain to his other students why he was allowing Johnny to keep the earring, but at the same time he didn't want the others to follow suit. He wanted to let the boy keep some kind of individuality out of what he had done. It was, after all, the boy's own decision – and Taylor was sure that in letting him make it, the others would see this as another form of preferential treatment.

Moreover, Taylor had one other task he felt he had to do if the kids were going to be spending any more time with Tristan. He had to let this boy know that his students are new to their freedoms, and that he shouldn't give in to their requests of change.

Taylor knew these were not going to be easy conversations, but they had to happen soon. With a deep breath Taylor realized that Delissa and Tristan were scheduled to attend dinner, and he would have to deal with all of this; from his kids to her kid so much sooner than he wished he had to.

56 Budding Romance

"JUST – JUST, COME ON KIDS, can't I trust you guys not to go poking holes in your body only 'cause Johnny did! I mean really!" Taylor pleaded, and though he was met with frowns from the other five students. They all eventually consented to his request, albeit their words were latent with harsh attitude.

"He always gets what he wants."

"This is just ridiculous!"

"What – ever!"

"Fine!"

Taylor felt he could've definitely done without their biting words, but he was willing to accept what he could. He tried to bring levity to the situation by scrubbing both David and Orion's head and rubbing Caitlin and Aspen's cheek softly. But this did little to change their lack of appreciation for his request.

Taylor hung his head low and walked out of the large family room that, like the rest of their new home, was now fully furnished. He had gathered the children there to talk to them as a group and in making his way back to the rooming corridor he left them all to think about what he had asked. Passing by Johnny's door, he shook his head. He wished there was something he could've done to avoid this whole situation, but hindsight was useless to him in this instance, and he'd been doing his best to avoid acting on any new premonitions – a habit he was beginning to reconsider. Eventually Taylor entered his own room and, sitting on his bed, he was hoping to clear his thoughts and prepare for a pleasant evening with company.

Having passed nearly an hour with head hung low, it was the chiming sound of a request to enter their home that forced Taylor's weary stare to rise. Indeed by the time he made his way to the lift, he could see that Delissa and Tristan were already ascending the last few inches into the entrance area.

Much unexpected to Taylor, Tristan rushed off the platform and hugged him.

"Hey, Taylor, how's it goin'" the boy said, and at this the boy's embrace forced a low grunt from the both of them.

"Hey," Taylor said with a chuckle. "Well this is unexpected."

Delissa laughed at the two of them and, when Tristan broke his hold so that he could run off to see the other children, Taylor was much more satisfied to offer a similar embrace to her instead. She smiled at him, her angelic stare melting his heart in an instant and he breathed a sigh of content to be relieved of her absence.

"Delissa, how have you been, it's been almost a week."

She whirled her hair flirtatiously over her shoulder and walked with him to the living room. "I know, and sorry about that, but I had a lot to deal with from the clan. They've wanted to elect a new leader for quite some time, and my name's been thrown in."

"Oh – uhhhh wow. I had no idea." Taylor said, and he was surprised that this whole clan leader topic had never come up.

"Well how are things going with that?" The teen asked as Delissa threw her head into his lap and played as though she had just been through an exhausting day.

"Well, the voting is tomorrow so ask me then."

"Ahhh. Well, what are you hoping for?"

"To be honest, I really don't care."

She said this while facing forward and avoiding eye contact – a sure sign that this is what she was trying to convince herself of, but not sure of the decision.

"Well, just so long as they don't elect another Rowna," Taylor replied, staring down at her long silky red hair.

"Oh, don't worry about that... there's no one out here like him! And thank God for that!"

"Hmmm, well. I don't want to put any more pressure on you, but I need to talk with you about your son."

"Tristan," Delissa questioned, sitting up slowly. "What about him?"

"Well, first let me say, he's a really great kid, and I don't want to turn this evening into a sour one, but... oh, how do I say this."

"Come on, out with it!" Delissa pressed, and at this Taylor smiled.

"Oh, fine, I'll just say it. I think he needs to watch what he says and does around my kids."

Delissa stared up at Taylor with a face of confusion. "What are you talking about?"

"Let me lay it out this way," Taylor started, "Johnny came home yesterday with his ear pierced. I took it out and..."

"You took it out? What for!?" She asked.

"Well it doesn't really matter – even after healing up his ear, he just came back today with another one. And even though I don't like it – I let him keep it."

"So what does that have to do with Tristan?" she questioned.

"Well, he was the one that did it – both times. And – well, I have to admit – it got me pretty mad."

"Taylor, honey, I don't see what the big deal is." She said, reaching over to run her fingers through his hair that was now long enough to just start working its way down his back.

"I – eh, oh I wouldn't expect you to understand."

"And what's that supposed to mean?" she asked defensively.

"Oh, don't take it like that – it's just, well. My kids have kind of grown up in a cage, and this is the first real taste of freedom they've had."

"Ahhh, and you're afraid they're going to do everything they can to exercise that freedom." Delissa said with a smile, proving to Taylor that she was more capable of understanding what he was thinking and feeling than he had previously assumed.

"Exactly!" he said in agreement, "And I know this *one thing* isn't the end of the world. But this is my belief, and I see it all the time. Life, all of life, is one giant pendulum. It swings out of balance constantly, and usually the time it does spend in balance is so short it's hardly even noticed. I guess what I'm trying to say is this. Now that we're out; now that we're free, I don't want my kids to go crazy and swing so far out of balance that they forget about rules, about boundaries. At the same time though, I don't want to keep them so far on the other side that they don't get to truly experience some of the freedom's they'd been missing."

"I – I - understand, I get it..." Delissa said, working hard for his silence. "I'll have a word with Tristan. I'll tell him not to, hmmmm, no – I'll tell him to consult with you first on decisions like that..."

"Thanks – I appreciate..."

"Don't mention it. You know, I haven't told you this – but I think it's wonderful how much you love these kids. It's amazing in fact. I mean you don't have any children of your own, and yet you've bonded with these little ones so well."

"You have no idea!" Taylor whispered, full well appreciating her words.

"Well speak of the devil!" Delissa said while looking into the light eyed stare of Johnny. The boy was still rubbing his ear from pain and in making his way into the living room, plopped into a seat right beside Taylor.

"When's dinner. I'm starving!"

"Oh geeze, I told you dinner's at seven." Taylor said playfully, jabbing his finger in the boy's side as a quick way of tickling him.

Delissa snatched her eyes to a clock on the wall. "But it's 6:55 now."

"Yeah – and?" Taylor questioned, and he could see a perplexed expression on her face.

In her mind, he knew that she was rolling around the idea that if preparations for dinner hadn't been started, there was surely no way it could be done in the next five minutes.

"Oh, fine!" Taylor said, and closing his eyes and, lifting his nose into the air, he concentrated for a moment then returned a smile to Delissa.

"What was that all about?" She asked, but before he could respond, a beeping emanated from the kitchen.

"Dinner's ready!" Taylor shouted loud enough so that the entire house resonated with his voice, and with these words he gave his female counterpart a beguiling wink.

With her mouth hung wide she stood, holding Johnny's hand and the two walked into the dining room while Taylor detoured through the kitchen to pick up the food he had requested from the M-Gens.

Within minutes all nine of those in the house sat at the dinner table. Most notably, Taylor and Delissa made a habit of sitting on opposite ends of the long table, and for this particular setting Tristan happened to be sitting just at Taylor's left.

So with everyone settled, it was an instant irritation to Taylor when he listened to Delissa address her son.

"Tristan. Before you go poking holes in any of the other kids at this table, or, well, do anything that you think you shouldn't with them – please ask Taylor to see if he approves."

Taylor stared across the table with a fierce pair of fiery blue eyes. He certainly hadn't expected her to lecture the boy right at the dinner table, right when they sat down, right in front of him, right now, and right in front of the other children!

"I, what, but..." Taylor sputtered, and turning to his left, his eyes met the apologetic stare of Tristan, who, without saying a word, let him know that this whole issue wouldn't be a problem anymore.

The rest of dinner seemed calm and, after a few minutes, conversations struck between the children, Delissa, and Taylor. Words and food were exchanged in multiple directions at the same time, and Taylor, at one point, filled with a euphoric sense of being in the perfect place at the perfect time.

With the evening moving on, everyone worked their weary overfilled bodies into the living room, and as a last-second request, Taylor asked if Aspen could play and sing for the group.

Of all the students, Aspen was, by far, the most gifted when it came to music. She had taken several virtual courses on how to play several instruments and, in Taylor's opinion, there was no voice more pure than hers when she sang. So, with everyone ready for an evening of quiet and relax, Taylor could think of nothing better than to show her off.

"Oh, come on Aspie, just a little something... you know how much I love to hear you sing!" Taylor pressured.

"I – I – oh alright!" she said, and with head lowered and eyes that glanced nervously in Tristan's direction, she offered a hint of a grin before she walked to the M-Gen panel in the living room. "Something short then, if I *have to!*" she said with the tap of a few buttons, and a step to the side of the M-Gen.

Everyone watched with bated breath as the unit slowly replicated a full sized grand piano. First, the M-Gen drew a strange electrostatic outline of the piano and bench, then, slowly, it filled in the transparent outline with the actual matter of the piano – as if it was filling up a glass of water – but instead of clear fluid, the deep glossy black color of the piano filled in the electrostatic containment until, finally, the M-Gen had completed its task.

Walking back to the M-Gen, Aspen pushed a few more buttons and within seconds she pulled out two small items that no one in the room could recognize. But with her back to the expectant group of watchers, she raised her hands to her head, and carefully pinned her hair back with the pieces she had just generated. If it were possible, when she turned around Taylor thought that she looked even more beautiful and as she took her place at the new piano in their living room, Taylor beamed with pride.

Setting her hands on the keys, Aspen played a light series of notes before her voice chimed in, lightly at first, then stronger as the song continued.

Life goes so quickly by,
And we forget to take the time to love,
Concerned with our dreams and with tomorrow,
Or with all the worries of yesterday's sorrow,
All we need is just to try,
To look around and see the sky above,
And open up our hearts so we can love.

When we feel it, we can't ignore
This gift from God called love.
It's not just where you look, but where you find it,
And when you can no longer hide it,
That's when you know it's right
Inside you feel the light so good.
You feel the love you always knew you would.

A warm embrace, a smiling face, a feeling deep inside
You don't know why, you feel the way you do.
You can't explain anything, and you've tried
So give in to loving someone, and they may love you.

This song was short indeed, for when she raised her hands from the piano, Taylor was expectant of more and it took him a moment to realize that as she finished. Her eyes had shifted from a stare at himself and while his heart was still appreciating what he was able to take in of this short piece, he did look up at her to notice that, in dropping her eyes and raising them again, there was an interesting connection – a gaze between her and Tristan. He could see it in an instant. There was something there – something he couldn't quite put his finger on, but he knew enough to realize that he should be at least a little nervous over it.

Aspen lowered her head. In her own mind she felt quite exposed sitting in front of everyone, especially in staring at Tristan in such an obvious way. Then, without announcing it to anyone she decided to play again. Her demeanor instantly changed and she started hammering at the keys to the piano. Taylor recognized what she was playing as a piece from Tchaikovsky, and while he couldn't put his finger on its name, he was overly impressed with her ability to play it from memory. Turning his head, he could see that both Delissa and Tristan were in awe of the girl. She actually possessed a *real* talent that made them speechless.

In finishing this last piece of music, Aspen was satisfied that she had done her duty to entertain the others and distract from her previous and obvious eyes at Tristan. Thus, she quietly rose from the piano, walked to the M-Gen, and with the push of a few buttons, the massive instrumental work of art slowly dissolved into nothingness, completely absorbed into the wall.

In an instant idle chitchat ensued between the children. This mostly consisted of Tristan asking questions of Taylor's students about the city and the reverse with his students asking Tristan to offer details of life in the forest. Taylor was certain that, despite the boy having numerous conversations between the children, Tristan could never get enough about hearing about the city, and likewise with the children hearing about life in the forest. But Taylor had other interests. So, as impatient as any teenager might be despite his forced maturation, Taylor hurried the whole group of children back to the rooming corridor in the hopes of spending some time alone with Delissa.

The second he had this time alone with her, his mind spun quickly to a myriad of different thoughts. Some of these where physical and juvenile, others, if voiced, would've made him sound like his own students, questioning her over every detail he hadn't yet gleaned over her life and history in the forest. But on the surface, he just wanted to be near her and learn more about her. To figure out what made her tick; her virtues and vices, her passions and pains, and on a more intimate level, her loves and her losses.

"You know," Taylor started in a nervous voice after enough conversation had passed that he felt comfortable on hitting this next and delicate topic. "I haven't really gotten any detail on why or how your husband left you. I've wanted to ask for weeks, but I've been a little afraid."

"Huh. You – afraid – that's funny!" she said with an almost laughing smirk before answering his question. "I haven't said anything because I don't think it's anybody's business but mine."

"Oh! Sorry, I didn't mean to pry..." Taylor recoiled, but then with a quick thought, he interjected. "What about Tristan. Doesn't he have a right to know?"

Delissa didn't offer a response by words, but her less than pleasant stare gave Taylor the impression that he was walking on thin ice. Taylor hated getting looks like that. He always preferred to think of Delissa as a beautiful woman. And even though their first meeting was under less than pleasant circumstances, he'd rather have forgotten the many distasteful ways she had stared at him on that day in lieu of remembering her many smiles.

"So, did you like the dinner tonight?" Taylor asked, now reverting to boring, and otherwise useless conversation.

"Oh, it was fine... I guess."

"You guess?"

"Well, I still don't like the whole 'push a button and get whatever you want' bit."

At this Taylor felt a debate coming on, but he'd rather not get into it with her and he quickly changed the subject again, this time spiraling to something even far less pleasant.

"Has anyone from the clan heard from Rowna at all?"

She shook her head in the negative, and instantly the two started talking of clan politics, and how some land possessors were always vying for expansion into new areas of the forest, and even beyond as an excuse for them to increase their families.

"But we can't overpopulate. One of the reasons that the city leaves us alone is that we are few, and we are sparse. There's talk of trying to expand further north and stretch as far as the SacraMetroship. But I think it's too risky. A move like that would definitely raise some flags to the GC."

Taylor agreed, and slowly the two had a politically and ideologically charged conversation about life in the city versus life in the forest, and it seemed that no matter how hard he tried, even on previous occasions, their being together always circulated around this subject.

Indeed, throughout the conversation, Taylor couldn't help but make stabs at Delissa's way of life and the life that Rowna had been forcing on so many people. In his mind he was passively working to wear her down and hoping to break her negative stigma regarding M-Gens and a life that she considered *too easy.*

With hours passing, Taylor and Delissa went to gather up the children from the rooming corridor. It was in this effort that both noticed Aspen and Tristan's absence from the other five children who were, again in Taylor's room.

Making their way around the corridor, Delissa and Taylor found that the boy-girl pair was sitting quietly in Aspen's room. Not wanting to disturb them, Taylor pulled Delissa back and motioned that they should just wait by the open door and listen to their conversation, hidden, but able to see in the entrance via a reflection in the window across the corridor.

"Almost two months ago – he sent me that message – can you believe it – How annoying!" they heard Aspen say, and instantly Taylor remembered the obnoxious boy that had broken her heart by video message.

"I – I can't believe he did that. I mean you're like the coolest girl I've ever met – way cooler than all the *clan* girls and they're so much older!"

"Cooler huh?" Aspen questioned, and Taylor already knew what she was thinking – *cool – and telekinetic.*

"Oh, not like that! I mean you're beautiful – you're sweet – I – I've never met any girl I wanted to really get to know."

Taylor watched with a lurch in his stomach as Tristan, who had been sitting idly beside Aspen on her bed, reached out and grabbed her hand. This wasn't forceful or harsh, but delicate, and considerate. Taylor saw this, and instantly he realized for himself that it didn't matter how the boy could've grabbed her hand, he wouldn't ever have liked it..

"Ahem." Taylor falsely coughed to get their attention, and instantly Tristan pulled his hand away from her and scooted himself a good foot away from her on the bed; a look of guilt washing over his face.

"And just what are you two doing in here?" Delissa questioned with a smile.

"Oh uh – Aspen was showing me her room." Tristan replied.

"I see. Well – the next time you want to show him your room, Aspen, make sure you're not alone... I don't like this whole thing..." and he pointed between the two children quite accusingly.

Delissa smiled, dismissing Taylor's suspicions. "Tristan, it's time to get going."

"Aww, come on!"

"Tristan, don't pout. I was about to extend an invitation to Taylor and the kids to come over for dinner at *our place* in a few days, and besides – you'll see them tomorrow – you're over here practically every day. So no arguments – just go!" she said, patting the boy on the butt as he walked out of Aspen's room.

"Dinner, oh I couldn't possibly." Taylor started, trying to refuse the invitation.

"Nonsense – I'll see you and yours the day after tomorrow – we can make a day of it. I'll show you a little more of the forest – maybe some of the other families if you can handle walking that far – and we'll have dinner."

"But – but" Taylor stymied, yet it was no use.

"I'll not accept 'no' for an answer" she said as the two stood on the exit platform. As it lowered she continued, "so we'll get going now – and I'll see you then."

Putting the children to bed shortly after Delissa had gone, Taylor was unsure of what had just happened. *Was she trying to wear down his ideologies? But he was doing so well in working her into his own lifestyle.* Despite how good of a job he felt he was doing at this, there was still the occasion when she would backlash and refuse an invitation to dinner, as she had done just a few days before, but this could've been due to clan meetings which he had only just learned about.

Clearing his mind of these thoughts, Taylor readied himself for bed and, in putting head to pillow, a completely different thought had entered his brain, one that hadn't come to him in quite a while. He realized, and was relieved to note, that the children were free of the terrifying dream that had plagued them during the first night in their new home. In fact, that was the last time that vision had been seen by Johnny, Taylor or any of the other children.

Smiling at this, his mind felt comfort in noting that his only real worries were two – Tristan's growing relationship with Aspen, and how in the world he could get through a real dinner at Delissa's place – something he had been carefully avoiding these past several weeks since she had started pressuring him to come over.

57 Hide and Seek

TAYLOR WAS TAPPING HIS TEETH with his fingers as he patiently watched the six children who were all sitting quietly around him in a cozy classroom that had been wisely worked into their massive tree-based home. Each had their own virtual helmet, and each helmet was decorated in colors and shapes to suit the child who wore it.

It was during their first classes in the forest that the children showed appreciation and gratitude over the fact that their helmets wouldn't be used by anyone else but them. Taylor, on the other hand, merely noted the efficiency of not having to wait for the children to adjust the sizes of the helmets to fit their heads.

Taylor looked about the room and with a deep sigh he felt a sense of contentedness wash over him. He could spend the next several years with these youngsters in the privacy of the home they had built and the surroundings of the forest, and in thinking of this future he truly enjoyed the freedom that he and the children had away from the city.

With several blinks, these thoughts were broken by a light beeping and the eventual waking of each of the children. Their virtual training was finished for the day, and Taylor, smiling at each one as they pulled off their helmets, was eager to see how things were going.

He, of course, had the option to be freer about the classes and workload he put upon the children, but he most certainly knew how important it was for them to still be properly educated. It would be this education that would give them the capacity and capability to return to the city with all the knowledge and talents needed so they could live a fuller, richer life if they did decide to return.

In addition, Taylor had kept to some of the procedures he always performed at EduCorp. It was for this reason that he had the children line up and, one by one, he scanned them with a handheld unit to make sure there were no adverse effects from the training. There were, however, a few times that even he questioned the need for this. Still, though, who was he to fly in the face of what had worked for the company for nearly four hundred years?

"So – What are we gonna do now? Our classes are all done." Grace asked tugging on Taylor's white t-shirt. He looked down at her, pleased with the fact that she was growing her hair out, even if many of her mannerisms and behaviors were still quite boyish.

"It's 1:30, I think it's time we go say hi to Tristan and Delissa. We should have just enough time to make it over to their place for our little meet."

He could see that all three boys in particular, perked up with this thought. Additionally, what he hoped was just a plutonic bonding between Aspen and Tristan, forced the girl to be just as excited. But he couldn't be sure of the extent of her feelings for him or the reverse and so he had it in his mind to keep close eye on the two of them.

Taylor had, for the past several weeks, been very careful to remind and make sure that the children generated clothing for themselves that was either lined with thermal suppressors, or that they used the thermal smocks he had given to them when they first arrived in the forest. This, it was Taylor's hope, would keep their heat signatures from being read by thermal satellites. Indeed, he was overly cautious about this, telling his students to keep under tree cover, and to keep from looking upward as much as possible so as to not be identified by any unmanned orbiting observers. So, with each of them lined up by the home's exit, he checked them carefully, with a simple pair of thermal goggles before allowing them to board the lift and leave the home.

Once this was done, and everyone was at the level of the forest floor, Taylor turned and looked at Aspen once everyone was off the lift. "Your turn – give it a try."

The girl turned to the platform, focused on it for a mere second, and with a slow buzzing noise it raised itself back into their home.

Taylor always looked for a way to help his students improve their newfound abilities, but over the past several weeks he had documented that, other than those gifts they had possessed from the beginning, their new talents were fading, and becoming more unreliable. In fact, without taking the time to focus, the use of the new powers often resulted in mild to catastrophic mistakes.

Taylor quickly reminded himself of an instance less than a week ago.

The whole group of them was on a picnic and Johnny was trying his best to pick a large magnolia flower from a tree, but was unable to reach it. To help, Caitlin tried to use her telekinesis to slowly lift the boy up to grab it. She ended up throwing him nearly thirty feet into the air where, luckily, he grabbed a branch to keep himself from falling back down. The two instantly started yelling for Taylor, Aspen, or David to assist, and with David being the first on the scene, Johnny was finally lowered to safety. This was when Taylor mandated that the children were not allowed to use their "new" gifts unless an experienced person was there to help.

Taylor and the children found their way to Delissa and Tristan's home with little trouble as they had visited there quite often, and in looking at it, Taylor couldn't help but smile over its simplicity. It was hidden inside a large California Redwood standing over two hundred feet tall. That is to say, their home was carved right out of the tree itself.

As Taylor and his youngsters approached the home of Delissa and Tristan, which was a giant redwood, he could see that all of the openings, including the front entrance, were sealed and therefore it looked like little more than just a massive tree. They knew, however, that several years ago, when Delissa and her now missing husband had decided to use this tree as their home, they had created a perfectly form fitted front entrance and several other openings to act as windows so that, indeed, the lower portion of the redwood was actually a three story home.

Taylor tapped on the entrance, as he knew where it was, but there was no answer. He tapped again – still no answer. Turning to the children, he was about to tell them all to circle back and that they would all return later when the mother-son pair were home, but something caught the teen's eye. He noticed a rustling of some nearby tree branches. The movement was high at first, but then quickly migrated downward.

Taylor realized what was going on just in time, and with a reflex reaction his hand shot out. With the rustling of the trees and leaves stopping only feet from the ground, Taylor ran in the direction of where the movement came from. His suspicions were quickly confirmed when Tristan's body revealed itself from behind the guise of the cloaking suit. Taylor had, in fact, saved the boy from a thirty foot drop and, on seeing the boy's face when his mask was removed, Taylor could tell that he was more than grateful, but terrified at the same time.

Once Taylor set Tristan down and the boy realized he was safe he quickly got to his feet, grabbed Taylor by the arm and practically dragged him in the direction of the children. Taylor was having trouble reading his leader's thoughts, but the word "hide", was clear enough that he, Taylor, knew what to do. With a focus on the bark of the redwood in front of him, Taylor opened the tree at its base.

"Go on – get inside!" Taylor yelled, and in an instant the children, Tristan, and he ran inside.

In the almost pitch black den inside the tree Taylor's six students started chattering amongst themselves instantly as they were confused over what was going on, but Taylor swiftly stared them down with a telepathic message of "quiet!" and thus the ensuing silence was only broken by Tristan and Taylor running up the stairs of the home eventually reaching the third floor.

This level had only two rooms, a bedroom for Tristan, and one for Delissa, but in the ceiling between the two doors of these rooms, just at the top of the stairs, there was a handle that Tristan was just able to jump up and reach. He pulled it down to reveal what, in old fashioned terms, Taylor would have called an attic; a hidden fourth level.

The boy climbed the ladder that led up to another dark room and Taylor followed behind, appreciating the fact that Tristan's cloaking suit still had a glow about it, for this was the only light to be found.

Taylor looked about the circular room, which was indeed quite large, and noticed about a dozen or so wooden handles on the walls. Tristan moved quickly running all around the room pulling these out from where they rested. Much like large corks, these handles pulled out in a diagonally upward direction to reveal pairs of hollow tubes that offered views of the outside forest floor. Taylor tried to visualize what the large Redwood would look like with these holes in it, but the truth was, considering how high up they were, and how small the holes were in relation to the tree, these viewports, barely the size of a grapefruit each, would be nearly impossible to perceive from the outside.

While Tristan was making efforts to open all of these sets of holes Taylor was frantically and pathically questioning him in every direction. "Are you alright? What's going on? Where's your mother? Why are we hiding?"

Tristan started looking in these viewports one by one and as he did so he calmly whispered the answers to Taylor's numerous questions.

"I am fine, I don't know where she is, and what's going on is that there are others in the forest – from the city. I don't know who they are, but my guess is that they're looking for you and *that*, my friend, is why we are hiding – and please! *Get out of my head*!"

The two waited for several minutes, with Taylor eventually calling the children up so that they all were now in this dark circular room. It was decided that each child should be in charge of looking out of two different sets of viewports while Taylor and Tristan either relieved them, or looked in the sets of holes that they weren't. While the group kept this formation for nearly an hour, Taylor was growing quite restless and squatted next to Tristan who was busy looking out of one of the viewports.

"I think it's about time you and I find your mother." He said sounding calm but also concerned.

Tristan all at once started squirming quite purposefully, "No need – he said quickly as he moved to the viewport at his right, nearly knocking Grace out of the way, "she's already here!"

Taylor's face lit up, he pushed the boy's face down to look through the lower viewport while he looked in the upper.

Indeed, Delissa was there, outside the tree, but she was not alone. She was being pushed by two GC security personnel, and in front of her stood one familiar figure, and one that he only recognized by reputation.

The familiar figure, that of the crimson cloaked Dr. Zeldin, was walking beside a black cloaked figure. They were walking right in view of the ports, and the children, all eager to see, took views at either side of Tristan and Taylor.

The small group below stopped their walk through the forest and with a slow smooth pace the person in the black cloak stepped to where Delissa was standing. Delissa struggled hard as this figure reached its hand out to touch her and, to Tristan's ultimate anger, one of the security members hit his mother hard on the back with a charged shock stick.

Taylor himself gritted his teeth at this for he could only imagine the thorough pain from both the hit and the shock at the same time. Delissa, however, being the one who felt it, cried out only for a moment, and when she finished, the black cloaked figure reached out again and put a hand on the woman's shoulder.

"A cog – a post-cog! I should have known!" Taylor hissed. "We have to do something or your mother'll lead 'em right to us."

"She wouldn't!"

"It isn't her choice. There's a post-cog down there!"

Tristan shook his head at Taylor in confusion and Johnny, seeing this, quickly grabbed the teen's head and turned it to look into his own light blue eyes. "Who-ever that is – they're like me – or Caitlin, just the touch of someone – that's all they need to figure out where they've been."

Tristan moved to look out the viewport again and pulling one of the arrows strapped to his back, he quickly took aim at the black cloaked figure below. Taylor, on noticing this kinetically pulled the boy away from the hole.

"I don't think so – you do that and they'll know where we are in a heartbeat. No, I've got a better idea."

Taylor then stared at those down below and noticed that the black cloaked figure still had a hand on Delissa's shoulder. Beside him, Tristan took position, and with this Taylor turned and offered a quick wink to calm the boy's nerves. Then, looking outside again, Taylor focused hard on the forest floor.

The leaves started swirling around Delissa, quite to her surprise, and as she watched this strange movement of the forest debris, she knew exactly what was happening, and even had a good idea who was doing it, but those around her only offered faces of confusion that shifted to fear. As such the GC security personnel along with Dr. Zeldin started stepping away from Delissa and her cloaked counterpart.

It was clear to Taylor that this person, draped in black, obviously had his or her eyes closed and did not notice what was going on around the two of them. When the commotion was finally realized however, *she* let out a yell. Indeed, Taylor was intrigued by the idea that this post-cog, donned in pitch black, was a female. He instantly flirted with the idea of comparing this darkly dressed woman with Grace.

Not wanting to be deterred from his efforts, he lifted more leaves into the air and thus the ensuing tornado like swirl grew larger and larger. With added focus he lifted the cloaked woman high into the air, screaming of course, and, closing his eyes, Taylor did his best to remember the trees of the forest, picking a nice, safe, yet faraway place to set the woman down.

He then focused on Dr. Zeldin and the GC security detail. All at once Taylor forced several swirls of leaves to spawn around each of them, and as he did so, he forced each person inside their own cyclone of leaves to spin as well. They all screamed and yelled in dizzy fear, but Taylor meant no harm to come to them; a good deal of disorientation of course, but no harm.

Delissa looked about herself with a smile. She could barely make out who was inside the center of each swirl of leaves and, knowing that their vision was much more impaired by the fact that they were being spun at an ever increasing speed, she felt it safe to finally make her getaway.

She started running across the forest floor, but found that her feet were all at once stuck to the ground. She tried her hardest to lift them, but, with their firmly planted nature, realized that there was little point. It was as if each foot weighed a ton, and thus both were seemingly unmovable.

Noticing a shift in the trees at her side, Delissa saw a man, this one wearing a green cloak, but his hood was lowered and she could easily make out his face. He was thin, attractive, with long blonde hair, and she could tell that he was focusing on her, concentrating on keeping her in place. The most she could do now was point her finger in his direction.

Taylor, noticing her standstill position, was immediately distressed over the fact that she was still in view of Dr. Zeldin and his security. When he saw her raise her hand and point, he struggled to, but couldn't see what she was pointing at and knew that whatever it was, it required immediate attention.

"Aspen, Go – over there – tell me – what's she pointing at?" Taylor hissed in a whisper.

The girl made her way from one set of viewports, where she could see nothing, on to the next. Here, from this angle, she could make out the man wearing the green cloak. Aspen certainly didn't recognize the man she was seeing, but she did recognize what he was doing. He was – a telekinetic.

"Father – It's a telekinetic – in a *green* cloak, this one!" Aspen whispered.

"Well what are you waiting for – knock him out – do something!" Taylor bellowed; his mind still hard focused on those he was spinning and enveloping in leaves.

Aspen furrowed her brow, squinted her nose, and with a focused telekinetic push she knocked the man hard into a nearby tree. "Oh – that's gotta hurt! – He's out cold!" Grace said looking from the viewport beneath Aspen's.

Taylor was already aware of this as he watched Delissa freely run across the forest floor. He was pleased about this, but knowing that his view of the forest was so limited, he didn't want her to run into anyone else that he didn't know about.

All at once Taylor started panting. His mind was working exceedingly hard and, with a rush of absolute chaos, every leaf that was on the forest floor picked itself up, causing an impermeable fog of brown, orange and yellow color.

Delissa, terrified at the commotion around her, didn't know what to think. She covered her eyes with her arms for protection and decided it best to just stand and wait. For Taylor, this was perfect. He opened the redwood's entrance and quickly forced her into it without her knowing.

When all the leaves had fallen, no one outside the Redwood, either in cloaks, or security uniforms – indeed, no one outside the tree knew what had happened to Delissa, and while several were suspicious that she, and her helpers, whoever they were, were still watching, it was Dr. Zeldin who acted on this assumption.

"I know you're out there *Robert*!" the man shouted gruffly, shaking leaves off his cloak, and he waited several minutes pacing the grounds near different trees not knowing where his supposed watchers were.

"Only you could've done this!" The man shouted before laughing. "I can feel your presence. Don't worry, *boy,* your time is almost up... and soon the children will be ours, it's just a matter of time."

Following these words Dr. Zeldin continued to shout in an attempt to get Taylor's attention, hoping that he might be able to pick up any stray thoughts. But Taylor and the children knew how to keep their thoughts hidden, at least long enough for someone like Dr. Zeldin to lose interest.

The woman in the now dingy black cloak appeared out of the brush having followed the shouts of Dr. Zeldin. She made her way to the doctor's side and, at the same time, the man in the green cloak who had finally lifted himself back to his feet only a few moments before, also approached the doctor. So here, mere feet away from their target, were three of the five member the Evol Crew.

Taylor knew that two of them were operating on government orders, but Dr. Zeldin was clearly still bearing a personal grudge, and he could hear it with every spoken word. Three out of five – that's more than half – and still they didn't get their guy. Taylor offered a smirk that only Tristan was close enough to see.

In Taylor's mind he replayed the newscaster from weeks past, who thought all the world of the Evol Crew. *Well, they definitely screwed this one up!*

"That's a lot of powerful people in one small place." Tristan whispered, but with a quick nudge in the side by Aspen, the boy was immediately reminded that he was sitting in the middle of the largest and undeniably the most talented concentration of mentally gifted individuals on the planet.

"Oh right!" the boy retorted quickly.

"Can they do – you know – what you do?" the boy asked Taylor nervously tapping his own temple

"What? – You mean read the thoughts of non-telepaths? As far as I know, Johnny and I are the only ones in the world who can do that, but if I were you – I'd clear my head – just in case."

Taylor didn't sound fearful, but he did sound concerned. He and the children were all on their guard in case anything out of the ordinary was to happen. So much was the case of this that Caitlin jumped when she heard the door in the floor open. Delissa had realized the familiarity of her surroundings quick enough and decided to join the rest of the group.

"Are you alright?" Taylor asked of her, but she turned her head sharply at his wanting to examine the damage she had sustained from several hits to both the face and body.

"I'm fine – you can fix me up in no time I'm sure. What's going on out there?" she said eyeing the portals around the tree.

Taylor responded with uneasiness. "Not sure – the three of them are just standing there." He said as he stared down at the three cloaked figures that were all still attempting to concentrate on stray thoughts – or at least this is what Taylor thought they were doing.

He watched as the woman cloaked in black reached inside the long garments draping over her body. She closed her eyes in deep concentration, then, opening her eyes moments later, the other two cloaked members turned their heads to her. With nods to each other, they each made their way back from where they had originally brought Delissa. Slowly the GC security detail followed behind, one of them throwing up from the nauseating spin he had endured. Within a few short minutes there was no sight of them at all. Even still, Taylor knew that his life in the forest had just irrevocably changed for the worst. He now had to find a way to get what he needed from their relatively new home, and somehow relocate and build a new one.

58 Tracking Dreams

TAYLOR, WHO WAS QUITE ON EDGE over how close the whole of his family had come to being once again ripped apart that day, hardly had to ask Delissa's permission to stay the night.

He pulled out a tissue generator from his pocket, something he knew, as the guardian of six youngsters, he always needed on hand, and used it on Tristan and Delissa's injuries from the day. Looking up into Delissa's green eyes he offered his usual effort of an adorable smile.

"Sorry I haven't brought anything to eat!" he said apologetically.

"Having no food isn't what *you* should be apologizing for!" She responded stiffly and, after offering a beguiling smile, she turned her stare away from his.

Taylor's mind worked hard at trying to figure out what she meant by this enigmatic statement. Try as he might, though, he couldn't read what she was thinking. He knew that she had been learning, slowly, how to hide her thoughts from him, and apparently she was getting pretty good at it.

He knew he had never given Delissa or Tristan lessons on how to do this, so he could only assume that the children had offered up some of the technique they used to do the same when he was in their presence. He made a mental note to ask them about this later – but it seemed trivial at the moment. He was far too busy staring at the back of her head, taking in her long red hair, fully wondering what confusing thoughts were swirling underneath.

After over an hour from when the intruders in the forest had left, the seven children, Taylor, and Delissa were fully startled by a loud booming noise that could be heard somewhere deep in the forest. This caused them such distress that they frantically looked all about through the viewports, but when they couldn't see anything they all slowly made their way to the lower parts of the home. The children wanted to leave the hidden home to investigate, but Taylor knew better, and after several minutes decided to open only those windows and panels that were absolutely necessary for light, hoping that the distant noise meant that those from the city were still looking for them in some far off and incorrect location.

Feeling a bit cramped, this tattered group of nine had little to do at this point but make the best of what was a home built for three.

Taylor's kids had visited this home before, and while they were always courteous about its meager amenities. The truth was – they would always rather have Delissa and Tristan come to visit, and not the reverse. The home was humid and dank. Taylor himself was confused at how such a simple home could be constructed by those who had, somewhere in their history, mastered an advanced cloaking technology that actually surpassed the rest of the civilized world.

He had pressured Delissa on this point several times, and when he did this Rowna's name always popped into her head and he felt it best not to press any further when this happened. Still, though, this was a great puzzle; one that he hoped to figure out some day.

Taylor spent the late afternoon resting in an old rocking chair on the first level of the home, a chair that Delissa admittedly did not know who it was built by as it was found in the middle of the forest. In sitting in it, Taylor could feel impressions of the chair's past from several hundred years ago, and as he rested with his eyes closed, he could see from images through the darkness of his closed eyelids that this chair had offered many a weary person a calm relax.

Turning to Delissa he smiled, "this chair definitely has some history."

He couldn't help but notice, that each time he tried to talk to her she offered a strange stare. This, to Taylor, was a constant reminder of her odd comment regarding his apology and that there was something else he should be apologizing for.

Taylor shrugged off this feeling several times, eventually looking about his surroundings in an attempt to find distraction. In this effort his eyes went to the short table by his side. It was a permanent fixture in the home as it was carved right out of the redwood tree and was attached to it via one large leg in the center. He had to marvel at the genius of a built-in table.

Moving his eyes to the strange rug in the middle of the room, Taylor perplexed himself by staring at the strange assortment of colors on it and he could tell that under the dust and dirt that covered it, there was a large picture. Strangely enough, his eyes caught the gleaming of several metal rings attached to it at one side. Taylor hadn't noticed these on any of his visits before, and now that he had, he realized that this wasn't a rug at all – why with its large pictorial design – it was a tapestry – yes a tapestry.

"You know – I didn't notice it until now – but this rug on your floor – it's not a rug at all. It should be hanging on a wall."

He said this to Delissa, who had finally sat down after tending to chores which Taylor was too thoughtless to notice and it seemed that this conversation was like honey and the children were bees. They slowly stepped down to the lower level of the home, buzzing around as if they could smell something interesting in the air. Coming down the stairs first was Tristan, who sat next to his mother, resting his head on her shoulder. Thereafter, the boy was quickly followed by Taylor's kids all sitting down around the teen's chair.

"Why would you hang a dirty old thing like that on your wall?" Tristan asked half with curiosity, half accusing Taylor of saying something that wasn't true.

Taylor looked all around the edges of the tapestry, making certain that none of his students were sitting on it, then, with a quick rising motion, the faux rug was lifted into the air by the incomplete row of brass rings that lined its top. Taylor then gave it a quick shake. This had the effect of kicking a lot of dust and dirt into the air.

The children, Delissa, and Tristan all coughed uncontrollably. To their relief though, Aspen waved her hand as a show of telekinetic effort, much in the same habit as Taylor, and forced the dust in the air to swirl about and eventually collect into a small pile in the center of the room.

Delissa giggled, "Man that could really come in handy!"

Taylor nodded to the woman at his side, "ahem – as I was saying. This should be hung on the wall. It is, after all, not even a rug. It is, now that you can *really* see it – more like a large painting – a painting built of thread."

Taylor paused, "So children – who can tell me what this is *really* called?"

They all sat in silence and, after this pause had lasted quite long enough, Taylor decided to offer the answer – "This, my dears, is called a Tapestry."

Taylor then rotated the cloth around and from its newly revealed side everyone in the room could see beautiful colors in the image of a large dragon blowing a harsh breath of fire onto a very small, metal-clad knight.

When all the "oohs" and "ahhs" had stopped Taylor offered what he knew on the topic of tapestries, but Delissa only shrugged, "I say you're making it all up."

"Oh – this is the truth, I swear it!" Taylor retorted in a snap.

Delissa, in a cool unemotional voice responded, "And what would you know about the truth?"

The children were all confused by this statement, including Tristan, and when Taylor had finally absorbed what his ears had heard, the first words that came to his head were also the first to flow out of his mouth.

"What's with you?" He asked almost rudely.

"Oh nothing. Just that I had to learn from total strangers that you – my dear – are not as old as you say you are."

Taylor's heart sank. He was instantly so distracted by his internal worries that the tapestry he was holding up had fallen to the ground quite unexpectedly.

"They told you?"

"Yeah – they could tell that I'd become quite fond of you – I guess you don't even have to be a mind reader to figure that out. Anyways – they used some device to figure my age – then they spilled it. Told me that I was nearly twice your age. I was confused, so I had to ask. Anyways – the point is, I know you're only eighteen – and judging by the unsurprised looks on *your* faces," she said looking down at Taylor's kids, "I can see that you've always known."

Taylor felt himself being washed over in awkwardness.

"Children, why don't you go upstairs for a minute?" He said nervously.

Delissa started laughing, "Don't bother – it's not like I care! I just wish you'd've told me the truth a long time ago. No – I had to hear it from a stranger."

Taylor still showed a look of concern but Delissa did her best to relax his mind.

"Don't worry about it. It's fine. Besides, our families have grown pretty close. There's no point in screwing things up now."

Tristan looked up at Delissa, "But, but," he started in a half confused tone, "but that means he's only five years older than me!?"

She nodded her head and, at this point, Taylor decided it best to come clean about who he and these children were – their history, a history that he had been so guarded about revealing. He told her about his birth, about the *Prodigy* experiment – about the children's arrival to The Towers, and lastly about the series of events that eventually led to his and the children's escape. In the midst of his words, Taylor reassured Delissa that, as he was making an effort to be truthful, he was doing this fully and from the heart – and that no more lies and no more secrets would be kept between them. He felt he had to do this repeatedly as, at different points in his narration of recent events, she offered stares of disbelief and would often either laugh out loud at what she thought too bizarre a tale to listen to, or counter Taylor's words as "impossible." But Taylor continued to reassure, and his students continued to reaffirm, and eventually the whole tale of Taylor and his kids at The Towers was offered up. And as difficult as it was to do, it was eventually believed by both Tristan and Delissa.

That night Taylor and his students had to dine on what was available in the home of their unexpected hosts.

Indeed this mother and son pair had little problem devouring the cooked meat of the dead forest animal they had hunted and killed the day before. Taylor, in good form, followed this example and found that he was quite surprised at how accurate M-Gen panels were in imitating the texture of meat. The taste, however, had a bitterness that he couldn't explain. He tried to pick out what this was, but had little success.

He instead found himself quite distracted at how his students were all picking at their food rather than eating it. He coughed as a way of getting their attention. This did little to change their behavior and, finally, Johnny took the first bite.

The boy's face lit up with a smile and an instant nod, "Not bad!"

His siblings quickly looked up with an expression of fear – "You actually took a bite?" Caitlin hissed.

"Sure did, and it's fine. I mean really good." He said taking more bites as he turned a smile to Delissa.

Taylor watched the boy's face, and while he could tell that the child didn't mind what he was eating, he could also tell that the boy was exaggerating how much he appreciated the food. Delissa, on the other hand, was oblivious to this and, with a widening grin, she beamed over the compliment.

Eventually the others joined in the meal and, while there wasn't a bountiful amount on the table, it was at least enough to satisfy the surrounding appetites for the night.

With the food finished, and being faced with little by way of technical entertainment, the children all decided to rush up to bed, Tristan following as the last to go up the stairs behind Aspen.

"How are we gonna do the sleeping thing anyway?" Delissa asked of Taylor.

With barely a thought the teen instantly shouted. "Boy's in Tristan's room – Girls in Delissa's!"

Taylor could hear groans from both genders and with the sound of stomping feet he could track the movement of the children over his head. He turned his stare to Delissa and could see wide gleaming smile on her face as she shook her head.

"That's not what I meant." She said with a deep stare into his eyes. He noticed this and the fact that she had just pulled two small picks from her hair, letting the locks fall red, shiny, and long over her shoulders. Taylor always liked to see her bright red hair when it was down and free flowing. More relaxed in his opinion.

"I meant the two of us – where are we going to sleep?" she said flipping her hair as she looked around the large second floor room.

Taylor felt his spine shiver – "Eh – well – you can sleep up here – I'll sleep downstairs – It'll be safer that way." He looked around the room, seeing that there was only a small cushioned bench against the wall for her – but he then quickly realized that there was even less for him to sleep on downstairs. In fact, all there was that seemed even remotely comfortable was the rocking chair he had enjoyed earlier.

Making his way down the first few steps to the first floor, Taylor stopped and turned to Delissa. He expected her to be standing at the top of the stairs but, as she was following close behind, this effort to say 'goodnight' immediately turned into an awkward, albeit not completely unwelcome kiss.

A kiss – a real kiss! Taylor's first and it was completely unexpected. He did his best to relax, use the muscles in his lips a little, but nothing could prepare him for the closeness of her face to his. So he closed his eyes, and with her taking most of the control, he felt his mind slowly melt away.

She eventually pulled herself from him and, with a smile, she offered a few words of encouragement. "Not bad – not bad at all for an eighteen year old."

Taylor took a deep breathing sigh and made his way down the stairs, not saying a single word, but instead, just replaying the last few seconds over and over again in his mind. He didn't take his eyes away from hers until he had actually passed under the level of the floor.

Stepping in front of the old rocking chair, he looked at it with distaste. His mind and body were not ready for a night of rest in an uncomfortable chair, and as he looked at it further, he muttered, "Just my luck!" in voice irritation and anger.

Once he had made himself comfortable, or at least as comfortable as he could get, Taylor found that sleep came easily enough, and he welcomed it with the hopes of pleasant dreams.

"Taylor, wake up! – Taylor – Taylor wake – up!"

Taylor kept hearing his name and when his eyes opened they were staring at a frightened Tristan whose expression gave way to Taylor's questions.

"What is it – what's going on? Where are the children?" He said standing upright, nearly knocking Tristan over. The boy responded with a look upward, "There's something wrong – I don't know what's going on – One minute I was asleep, the next I get hit in the head by Johnny. He's shaking – I don't know – just going nuts!"

Taylor ran up two flights of stairs and as he made his way to the entrance of both bedrooms he met up with Delissa who told him even more.

"It's not just Johnny – Caitlin's acting weird too. What do I do?" She asked in a frail and timid voice on the brink of tears.

Taylor ignored this question and rushed in to see Johnny. The boy was held firm down on the bed by David's kinesis who, along with Orion, was standing near the wall of the room.

Seeing that things were, for the most part, under control, he went to the other room where, as if it were a mirror image of the first, he saw at the side of the room that Aspen, in the company of Grace, was holding Caitlin down kinetically as well.

Taylor walked into the room and sat beside Caitlin. He could see that she wasn't truly being violent on purpose. Instead, he determined that she must be in some sort of strange and violent vision. He put his hand delicately on her forehead and with the closing of his eyes he was quickly met with a bright onslaught of color.

"You! You're not supposed to be here!" Taylor heard a female voice say as he took in the fact that he was inside some strange grey metallic cube of a room. He turned around to see where the voice was coming from. As he predicted, he saw the woman in the black cloak. She was standing between the bodies of both Caitlin and Johnny, who were tied down and struggling to break free from being strapped to two examination beds. But now he could see her face. It was a little thick, telling Taylor that she hid more weight than he had realized under her dark shrouding attire. But somewhere behind her eyes, he could see that there was depth, a kindness that he hadn't expected. She was, aside from her slight thickness, a very attractive woman with sandy blonde hair, and as she stared at him with those deep brown eyes, he felt, somehow, calmed for a moment.

Snapping his eyes away from hers, he took in his surroundings quickly. In an instant he was certain that this was some sort of vision or artificial virtual or pathic creation. Either way, he made his way to the children's bedside noticing, to his amusement, that the woman in the black cloak purposefully kept her distance; it seemed, out of fear.

"Johnny – Caitlin, stop struggling. This isn't where you really are. Calm down. It's okay. – Everything's going to be fine." Taylor said softly and as he watched their looks of fear slowly dissolve into relax, he himself calmed down. But with a scowling face, he turned to the woman in the black cloak. What are you doing to them? Why have you brought them here? Why can't you just leave us alone?"

The woman looked at Taylor with a smile and slowly started walking toward him, "Your children still have their part to play in this war – The government knows it – we know it,"

"And you know it!" A voice from behind Taylor spoke loudly. He turned around and could see, with this one in white, yet another differently cloaked figure who, he was certain, hadn't been standing there before.

"Man what is it with you people and your cloaks, I don't get it. Do normal clothes just not do it for you?"

The man standing in front of Taylor, still had his hood up. Even still, Taylor managed to make out a set of shiny bright blue eyes hiding in the dark under the hood. These eyes were fully revealed when the man reached up, pulled back his hooded cover, and spoke to Taylor.

"You know of the war we speak – you've seen it; several times in fact," the man said calmly.

"I don't know what you're talking about!" Taylor said both firm and aggravated, and as the next few seconds passed Taylor felt a slight rush of fear run through his body as he realized that behind him and in front of him, the woman in black and the man in white were drawing ever closer.

"Well, maybe we should refresh your memory!" the woman in black breathed softly.

Before Taylor could react, both had raised their hands to the teen's temples. Once again, what the teen was seeing had changed. It was as if he was suddenly dropped from the sky and the place where he landed looked ever so familiar. He looked to his right and could see, again, the tattered sign of the Los Angeles Metro Park, and now the smell of fish rotting in the sun was so strong it nearly gagged him.

All across the horizon the once tall, bright, and beautiful Metroship of Los Angeles was now a steaming, clouded mound of rubble; the remains of what was to be left after an attack that Taylor had seen so many times.

The wind, blowing billowing clouds of smoke through the air, suddenly stopped. A voice penetrated straight into Taylor's now mourning heart.

"You've been here before, haven't you?" asked the man in the white cloak.

"Ye – yes I have." Taylor said, uncertain if he should admit the truth.

"Well this, young Taylor, is the work of your prized little angels. It is because of them that this has happened – or rather – this will happen. Their escape from the city is the catalyst that causes this surrounding disaster. And if the GC can't have them – then we can't trust them in the hands of anyone else. They are powerful, and can be made more powerful than even you could imagine. But we need them under our control – it's the only way we can stop this *worldwide* catastrophe."

"Worldwide?" Taylor questioned, and as he stared out over the horizon, taking in the loss of life and the horrible devastation, he could feel his mind weakening its resolve against their demands. *If they're the cause of all of this – then maybe it would be for the greater good if...*

"Fine!" Taylor said stiffly before even finishing his own thought. "If they go – I go!" Taylor said stiffly.

The woman in black opened her mouth to speak. She was expecting some kind of denial, and the words of conditioned compliance took her aback.

"I – wh – what?" she questioned half confused. "I – I'm sorry" she said, thinking for a moment. "That's just not possible. That would only complicate matters."

Taylor shook his head in anger, "No! I won't accept that – you can offer that cryptic bull to somebody else – but not me. I need more! They're just kids. My kids! You've got gifts of your own – why don't you figure all this out – you're the great and mighty Evol Crew..." Taylor paused, anger slowly subsiding. *Truly they couldn't be responsible for all this,* he questioned. "They're just children – just children!"

"So you've said!" spoke the woman in black who now stood beside Taylor, looking out over the city. "But you and I both know that they are much more than *just children.*"

All at once the man in white nodded his head. "It's time!"

For Taylor, his vision changed quickly to that of the grey room again and he saw both the man and the woman's hands slowly lower.

"We are sorry, Taylor, but we need those children – and one way or another we will find them," said the woman in black with a sobering voice.

"What if I keep the children from you – or what if they refuse to help with – with whatever your *plans* are?" Taylor asked in anger. He was waiting for a response from her, but instead it came from behind.

"You would put your personal feelings before the welfare of the world."

"No!" Taylor shouted, "I put my feelings before your ridiculous visions and stories of the end of the world. They're insane! There has to be more – there has to be something else. There has to be another way. What military has the power to do all that... can't you figure it out – can't *you* stop it!"

"We can't risk it!" The man in white said as he turned to face a large electronic panel. Holding its frame with his hands, he continued, "Not for probability or possibility. We must be certain, and this is the only way!"

"They'll never go for it!" Taylor said stiffly, and at this both Johnny and Caitlin, who had been all but silent blurted out, "Yeaaahhh – we won't go for it!"

Heaving a deep breath and gripping the panel in front of him even tighter, the man in white turned a dark stare up to Taylor. "If the GC doesn't get what it wants there are other, more *final* options on how to deal with the children!"

At this the man turned this shifty eyed gaze to the two children at Taylor's sides. If Taylor's face could have, it would have turned as white as the cloak he was looking at. He felt desperation overtake him, and he welled with anger and understanding. He knew that this was meant as a threat against the lives of his children, a threat of terminating them if it became necessary.

He focused hard on releasing himself from whatever vision it was that he was seeing. Looking down at Caitlin and Johnny he offered a quick, "Sit tight," before what he was seeing quickly dissolved away. Just as the colors slipped out of view he could hear a few last words penetrate his brain.

"Start the tracking procedure now." The man in the white cloak said, and with this, he heard the voice of the woman in black.

"It won't be long now..."

Taylor opened his eyes, staring down at Caitlin's resting body, and he was at least relieved to see that her once struggling limbs were now silent and calm. Taylor knew that she and Johnny were simply waiting for him to do what he could to revive them from this strange locked vision, but, looking around, he had no tools or devices with which to work.

He looked around at Delissa, Tristan, and those of his students who were still awake. "I have to go – there's nothing I can do here. I need – tools."

The children's faces all showed concern – "What's going on?" Tristan asked.

"They're using Johnny and Caitlin to try and figure our position. If we're going to stay hidden something has to be done, and fast." Taylor spoke both hastily and loud as he made his way down the stairs to the first floor of the wooden home. "I have to leave – now!"

Taylor then turned around and signaled to Aspen and David, "I leave you to keep the others safe, if they find you before I get back, do *whatever* it takes to protect yourself. Don't hesitate – just act – if you have to – use everything you've got!"

Grace and Orion practically took offense to this request, "We're telekinetic too you know," Grace said loudly, and Orion added, "Father, we may not have very good control – but if we have to defend ourselves – then we will do what we must."

Taylor nodded, "I know, I know. I'm sorry."

He then kneeled down in front of all four of his students. Looking at them he could see little in their eyes that might explain how they could be responsible for such a cataclysmic end to the world. They were still so innocent – filled with great life, energy, and a good bit of mischief that at that moment made him smile.

"I'll be back soon."

He was nearly out the door when Delissa grabbed him by the shoulder and pulled him around. "I want to give you something."

The first thought in Taylor's mind was, "Now isn't the time for another kiss – I have to go!"

Luckily, though, these were not the words that came out of his mouth. He just stood in impatient waiting as she stepped away from the door for a moment then moved to a storage closet and pulled out a box that she put in his hands when she returned.

"This was my husband's – it was his spare. I was going to give it to you later – once I could figure out your size and have it altered – but I can see there isn't time. I hope it fits."

Taylor opened the box and instantly he recognized its contents as that of a folded up cloaking suit.

She then put a little box on top of the suit – you'll need this – it's a battery pack. I'm sure the one in the box is drained cuz' the suit's been in the dark all this time."

Taylor immediately pulled the suit out of the box and slipped it on over what he was wearing. He then put on the gloves and shoe fittings. He could feel that the suit itself was stouter than he was, but fortunately, it was semi-elastic and what Taylor lacked in width, the suit offered him in height.

Taylor plugged in the battery pack on his thigh. This had the immediate effect of causing the suit, with its freshly powered veins, to light up. Taylor now knew he was ready to go and with a group hug with his four able bodied children, he gave each of them a kiss on the forehead followed by quick 'I love you's before making his way out the front door.

Taylor slipped the hood over his head and attached the two connecting neck pieces, thereby completing the suit. He looked down at the power unit at his thigh – he could see that there was really only one button to push, and when he did, his eyes, which were looking clearly out of the goggles of the hood, suddenly went black.

Taylor knew better than to panic, and almost instantly a black and white display offered him a rough view of what was in front of him. As he stepped out and walked quickly through the forest he realized that his vision was quite limited. He could see a few hundred feet ahead, but the resolution beyond that became very fuzzy.

Taylor shook his head with an unseen smile, "Sonar." That is to say, Taylor realized the suit used sound to determine its immediate surroundings, much the way a bat would do the same in the dark. His mind was curious as to whether the sonar was UHF or ULF; that is, Ultra High Frequency or Ultra Low Frequency. He assumed it was probably the latter, which would be much harder for other machines to detect – thus preserving the suit's stealth qualities.

Taylor shook his head of these pointless thoughts and started sprinting through the forest. He did, as he was running, feel a bit strange with the thought that he couldn't be seen at all in his movements through the forest. To make matters more awkward, as he ran he nearly stumbled a few times, being unable to see his feet, and, at one point, he could have sworn he heard a noise that wasn't made by him; a noise that was made by something else, or someone else. Either way, Taylor felt compelled to check it out.

He stopped and turned but could only see many tall trees behind him. He walked forward toward the where he thought the noise was coming from and heart nearly leapt out of his chest when he saw, to his relief, a rabbit scurry across the forest floor.

Turning back, he ran as fast as he could to finish the journey to his home. He passed through trees, jumped over fallen logs and rocks until finally he reached the stream near the site where he built the new home. Stopping in the middle of the water his mouth gaped in horror at what he saw.

59 Taken

TAYLOR PULLED OFF THE STOCKING LIKE HOOD of his cloaking suit so that he could see what was in front of him with his own eyes. With billowing smoke, fallen trees, and the smell of ozone in the air, his senses surveyed what was left of the home he and the children had built only a few months ago. While the darkness of the forest was still prevalent and dawn had not yet occurred, it was what little he could see that was before him that filled his heart with anger, frustration, and worst of all, desperation.

Used to calculating a solution for every situation, he was now looking at the residential remains absolutely certain that he had no clue how he could simply walk away from this one. He and his kids were being hunted down by the government using what powerful cognitives and kinetics they had at their disposal and it was clear that these hunters would do whatever it took to get what they wanted.

Surveying the damage, Taylor could see that the core M-Gen system for the home was completely destroyed, that the transport had been damaged beyond repair, and that all his data files had apparently been confiscated. With all of this, it seemed hopeless that Taylor was even capable of getting back to Johnny or Caitlin with anything to keep them from being tracked through their dreams. Taylor's plan to save the day bordered hopeless.

This isn't to say that Taylor hadn't planned for a situation like the one in front of him though. Indeed, Taylor was the smartest person on the planet and, not that he was paranoid, but that he *knew* something like this might be possible.

Turning around, Taylor had to put his second plan into action. He walked to the middle of the stream that ran beside the wreckage of his demolished home. Looking down, he had the intention of focusing on the gravel beneath the stream. Instead, though, his eyes were met with two strange formations in the water, it was displaced by a pair of unseen objects – feet, Taylor figured.

Thinking fast, he spoke into the air. "Who's there?! I can see your feet in the water so I know your there! Show yourself!"

The stiffness in his body and voice instantly relaxed when, to his relief, the cloaked individual slowly swirled into glowing reality, and in taking off his hood, Taylor could see that it was Tristan.

"What happened?" Tristan asked, his eyes now taking in the full color chaos of the ruined home for the first time.

"They were here." Taylor said, his voice sounding sad and almost desperate. "Now if you don't mind..."

Tristan offered a confused look, one that Taylor didn't have time to explain away, and thus he looked toward the boy's feet and, following a focused stare, a small almost indiscernible light started beeping under where the boy was standing. All at once Tristan started growing taller, or at least, that's what he thought, for beneath his feet, the ground was rising, lifting him at the same time.

The truth of it was that Taylor had, in his first few days in the forest, planted his *backup plan* in the bed of the stream. Now that he had activated it, it was lifting itself out of the water.

Tristan eventually lost his balance in standing on top of this newly revealed smooth surface, and to keep from falling, he jumped off the ever rising unit that, at its final height, stood some seven feet tall.

Tristan stood in front of this metallic unit confused at its purpose, but Taylor knew exactly what he had designed it for. The tall, bullet shaped dome had a line running down one side that eventually opened to reveal several tools, containers and devices that Tristan tried to reach out and grab. Taylor, however, slapped the boy's hand with a quick pop, "Don't touch!"

Tristan, who had pulled his hand away instantly, walked out of the stream and toward the smoky debris. Taylor grabbed several of the items in front of him, and after less than a minute, he told the boy that he was ready to return to the redwood to tend to Johnny and Caitlin.

"Come on – we don't have time to doddle." Taylor said looking over at Tristan, and he saw that the boy was holding something in his hand. "What's that you've got there?"

Tristan walked up to Taylor and showed him a small wooden figurine. "I made this for Aspen just after you guys showed up."

The boy held it out for Taylor, who looked at it with a mild grin. He could see that it was a piece of wood, roughly carved to the likeness of a horse. This spawned a question in Taylor's mind that he uttered without even thinking about it.

"What is it with the two of you anyway? I mean honestly, it seems like every chance you get, the two of you are spending one on one time with each other. I have to say, it makes me a little worried." Taylor then grabbed the wood carving and Tristan looked up at him and started to speak. Taylor, however, didn't hear one word of this, for the instant that he touched the wooden carving his mind fell deep into a vision.

Recognizing that any vision bleeding from a sense of blacking out was one of the past, Taylor looked down over a diligent working Tristan. Obviously he was in the boy's bedroom in the redwood, and he could see that the child was working hard with a simple knife over a block of wood. The boy was toiling away at it and bit by bit, and over the next few moments Taylor's view of this shifted to show the boy popping up in different parts of the room as he progressed to finally finish this handmade gift.

Taylor then watched different broken scenes of Tristan walking the gift to his and the children's elevated home and, recalling the day that the boy had, indeed, made a strange and uninvited visit, he relived the moment that the teen shyly gave Aspen the small cloth wrapped parcel. Taylor himself was filled with the overwhelming nervousness that Tristan had experienced as he, the boy, handed the over the object of his hard work. Taylor also relived the feeling of delight when Aspen accepted the gift, looked Tristan in the eyes, to his ultimate thrill, touched him, actually touched him, on the hands softly and delicately as she pulled the package out of his hands.

Taylor looked down at the carved figure freshly opened in Aspen's hands. While he hadn't truly noticed its detail before, Taylor actually admired the effort the boy had put into such a small, relatively simple gift. Yes, it was rough, but in each carved line there was a history that no M-Gen could ever offer. Taylor stared at it, realizing that these thoughts may not have been his own, but, rather, that they might have been Aspen's. Either way, he agreed with them and he stared at this carved craft with admiration.

His view of this quickly changed to show the wooden horse sitting on a shelf in Aspen's room. Aspen, however, was nowhere to be found. Instead, Taylor could hear another voice, a very familiar voice, inside his head.

"This has to be a surprise attack!"

All at once his view of the shelf, and the crafted horse, pulled back to show Aspen's doorway – even further, his view pulled back from the rooming corridor, and even further back to eventually reveal the outside of the home.

Looking over the shoulder of three very familiar individuals, Taylor could hear words emanating from the three raised, colored hoods: red, green, and black.

"What if they're actually in there?" Dr. Zeldin asked, and at this the woman in black, quickly retorted from under her hood, "They're not in there – but it's where they've been living, and besides, it doesn't matter. If they're in there – then we get them out quickly, and without a chance for them to retaliate. If they're not in there, then there's got to be something that can help us find out where they're hiding. Either way we gotta get in there, and fast."

"I've got it!" The man in green said, offering a wink to Dr. Zeldin. He, the man in the green cloak, then turned to the elevated home and with a hard focused look he went to work on it kinetically.

After several passing seconds, little could be seen at first by way of any effort or change, and Dr. Zeldin was showing growing impatience. That is, until the home and the trees around it started to creak and ache.

Dr. Zeldin and the woman in the white cloak looked at each other with raised eyebrows. With a flinch, they each covered their eyes as, in front of them, the metallic beams used to hold the large home in the air buckled. This started a chain reaction of gravity doing its worst continuing to bring the home down and within seconds the whole of it was all smoke and rubble.

Taylor was horrified. He watched as the three members of the Evol Crew, along with their supplied security, rummaged through the home. It seemed that anything of interest was immediately handed to the woman in black. She would hold what she was given and, if it proved useless, she would throw it aside. It didn't take much for Taylor to figure out what she was doing – trying to get impressions or visions of the past from these many items – and as Taylor's eyes scoured the debris he noticed Tristan's wood horse being picked up by one of the GC security.

It was placed in the woman's bare hands, and just by the touch of it, she knew she had something of value. She closed her eyes and gripped it tightly. Taylor waited, bated breath, hoping her vision didn't start the same as his.

This was an unrealized wish however, for it only took a few seconds for her to drop the figure to the ground, turn to Dr. Zeldin and grunt in total frustration, "We were so close. So close!"

With a snap of his fingers Dr. Zeldin caught the attention of everyone within earshot, and it took them all only a moment to gather themselves into formation and move in a direction that was, strangely enough, not toward Delissa's home.

Taylor watched as the woman in black tried to point Dr. Zeldin in the right direction, but the doctor grabbed her firmly over the shoulder and said, quite plainly, "I've got a plan!"

Taylor's heart sank on the spot and, as he looked down in instant despair at the crafted horse on the ground, his vision slowly dissolved.

Blinking feverishly, Taylor looked up from the wood figurine in his hands, and in staring at Tristan, he only caught the last part of what the boy said regarding his relationship with Aspen.

"So really, it's nothing for you to worry about."

"Are we too late?" Taylor whispered rhetorically, and Tristan blinked at this response, not understanding the point of the phrase.

With a loud resonating boom that could be heard all through the forest, both their heads jerked in the same direction. Taylor was certain he knew what was happening, but Tristan was confused, and it was apparent that if Taylor was hoping he could keep the children's location a secret, he was, in fact, too late.

With a stare in the direction of Delissa's home, Taylor focused hard with his kinesis, and his efforts were immediately felt by a rumbling in the forest floor. The stream and rocks in front of him started to cleave themselves apart, and the trees on the other side flexed and bowed until, with huge cracking noises, they broke like twigs against his kinetic efforts. In his heart and in his mind he was panicked – he knew he had to move quickly.

Beside him though, Tristan was shocked at the sight before him and in plugging his ears and kneeling to the ground Taylor could see that the boy was scared out of his wits. He grabbed the boy by the arm, and while Tristan couldn't hear him yell the word "run," reading Taylor's lips to understand what was being said was easy enough.

Moving fast, the two headed straight for the redwood home and with trees, shrubs, rocks, and other debris clearing from their path as they went, the two made excellent time. But this proved little by way of purpose, for when Tristan and Taylor arrived it was clear that they were still too late. They could see that the large redwood was cracked and fallen over, and the home inside exposed. Tristan knew instantly that Taylor hadn't done this; no, it was something else, and it was this massive tree falling that they had heard several minutes earlier.

The two walked up to the large fallen tree, which had an odd series of strange large metal cables and hooks attached to it, and Taylor heaved in anger at what he saw – another home – destroyed. Tristan, who was fearful of the whereabouts of those that he had left in the now ripped open redwood, quickly jumped on the gaping hollow trunk. He rummaged through the remains, but it was clear, especially to the Taylor, who telepathically determined it, that there was no one in the area save the two of them.

Taylor slumped wearily across the grass, walked up to the tree, and, knowing what he had to do, he slowly took a deep sighing breath and put his hand on what was left of the hidden home as he closed his eyes.

Taylor's pitch black vision filled with the deep hues of the colorful leaves around him, and he could see that he was still standing beside the large redwood stump; the tree still fallen over.

With a strange disoriented feeling, Taylor looked around and saw himself and Tristan nearby. In a blink, these two images from the past started running backwards with the separated trees pulling in to wrap around them in a chaotic caress. Shortly after this Taylor – that is, the Taylor of the present – noticed a rush of dust and leaves move inward toward tree stump. The noises around him were quickly drowned out and in all directions he could hear the build of thundering noise. He turned around to look at the tree, and saw that it, as huge and massive as it was, actually lifted itself from the ground and firmly planted itself on the stump.

Taylor was in awe with his reversed vision. This was something that so rarely happened in his post-cog efforts, and it always tickled him with a strange sense of elated curiosity to see, even if now was not the time for those feelings.

He turned back to the tree, and with all the activity and sounds around him now subsided, he realized that his perspective was in the right place at the right time and now, was actually moving in the right direction. He looked about the tree, into the sky, and around the forest, but could find no evidence of anyone on approach. The forest was, in fact, completely quiet, and with Taylor not knowing where an attack would be coming from, he did his best to keep his eyes looking in all directions.

Then, causing Taylor to snap his stare straight up, the sound of rustling trees was overshadowed by the shrill sounds of large metal hooks whizzing through the air. These hooks hit their target, the giant redwood, in several locations, and with silent movements Taylor watched as several small crafts flew overhead. These hooks were attached to the crafts via large metal cables, and as these vehicles flew to the full extent that their cables would allow, the large redwood ached with the force of the pulling.

Taylor thought in his head that these crafts weren't large enough to pull down a full grown redwood, no matter how hard they tried. One thing, however that Taylor hadn't considered in that instant, was the structural compromise of the tree's trunk, which had most of its wood removed so that Tristan and Delissa had a place to live.

The tree did finally crack at its base, allowing the crafts overhead to pull it over completely. They, of course, detached the cables just in time to prevent themselves from being pulled down by the collapsing tree, and once this had happened, Taylor flinched when he noticed that, right at his side, the man in the green cloak was kneeling, and taking aim. His hand was lined with six tranquilizer darts and while he had no gun or pistol to fire these, Taylor knew immediately that the man would be using his own kinetic abilities to fire the shots.

Taylor and the man in green watched as the children and Delissa slowly made their way out from the now upturned stairwell entrance to the third floor. Waiting until all seven were in view, with Delissa moving frantically about shouting for Tristan, the man in green made his move. He used the six darts on the children, who had no time to react. They were knocked out in mere seconds.

Delissa turned to where the darts had come from. With a scowling stare and a harsh stance she practically growled at the green Evol member.

Looking down at her feet, Delissa noticed a small overturned cabinet at her feet from the debris of the now broken home. She kicked open the cabinet and with her foot she threw an object into the air. This was a weapon; a weapon that Taylor instantly recognized. It was the sword she tried to fight Taylor with several months before.

Taylor knew that she didn't have a chance against the telekinetic, but he had to admire her tenacity. So he watched with a prideful heart as she took position between the unconscious children and the telekinetic in front of her and waved for him approach her.

He did so, slowly, and offered words as he walked.

"I'm a telekinetic, little girl. There's no way you could even hope to defeat me – Just drop your sword and move out of the way before *I* move you, and trust me – I won't be polite."

Delissa, shifting her stance back and forth, blinked for a moment before she slowly lowered her sword. She even stared at her own hands with a look of doubt and fear that Taylor had never seen. Taylor was shocked – he didn't expect her to give up so easily. The teen then watched as the man at his side slowly approached the children.

Taylor kept his eyes on Delissa, and he lit a smile when he saw her shifting stare. *She has something up her sleeve.* Taylor then watched as his suspicions took form in reality for when Delissa saw that the time was right she flicked her wrist upward, and with a smooth rounded motion she threw her sword at the man in green.

Taylor could tell that her aim was true and, had it not been for the fast reflexes of the telekinetic, she would have been successful in piercing him straight through the chest. He, Taylor, practically shouted at seeing this, and while it was clear to him that the course of events had already been written and he should've known what was going to happen, he just had to make known his feelings on the matter, even if the only person listening was himself.

So, as the sword flew through the air, the man in green was able to move himself a few inches, and slightly deflect it with his kinesis so that the blade just sliced through a bit of his cloak before completing its path and stabbing the side of a distant tree.

The telekinetic then used his power to throw Delissa against what tall standing portion of the trunk was still there and, holding her still, he laughed. This gaiety subsided when, all around him, the man could hear a strange rattling. This eventually grew to a rumbling noise that caused the trees to sway and slowly part while bits of debris did the same on the forest floor.

The laughter that once came from the man in green had completely shifted. It was now coming from Delissa, and when all the air had left her lungs, she heaved a deep sigh.

"He's coming!" she called and she continued to laugh as she spoke, "He's coming. Taylor! Taylor!" she shouted his name; then stared hard at the man in front of her. "If I were you I'd get out of here now – or there'll be hell to pay!"

"You know, "I can see why he likes you," the man in green said. "Lots of spunk – and you *are* a pretty one aren't you?" The man then turned his head skyward, and with a focus of telepathy, he called to the pilots flying overhead. The crafts started circling ever closer to the site of the fallen tree.

Reaching up, he then kinetically grabbed one of these craft and held it in place. Slowly, just overhead, the cargo hold of the craft opened and the man in green forced the children's bodies to raise high into the air until they were completely consumed by the craft and the cargo doors had closed. He had to release his hold on Delissa to do this, and as she watched she had the immediate thought to intervene. Taylor could tell by the look on her face, though, that she was frustrated in realizing that any action on her part might cause him to drop the children, who were already at such a dangerous height.

Once she saw that the children were safe inside the craft overhead, she decided to run for the man in the green cloak in an effort to catch him off guard. This proved absolutely useless for with a mere wink in her direction he forced her to stay planted where she stood.

She stood, perfectly still, but continued to scream for Taylor, though with the increasing noise of falling trees, there was little she could do to call attention to herself by way of using her voice. Her heart wrenched with pain as she saw the craft holding the six children quickly dart off, and Taylor himself, in watching this view of the past, not only felt her pain, but his own as well. He so much wanted to take part in what he was seeing, but there was nothing he could do to effect any change. To make matters worse, the teen watched as a second craft took position above the man cloaked in green, and with a final telekinetic effort, Delissa and the telekinetic were elevated high into the air.

With the craft sealed up and taking off with these two inside Taylor had mixed feelings on seeing her depart. He knew that this was one less ally he had in the present, but that it might mean one more ally for his children.

With the ever increasing noise, Taylor turned and watched as the trees behind him bowed and separated to reveal an image of himself from the past followed quickly by Tristan and, with the union of Taylor's past image with that of the present, his vision quickly went black.

Opening his eyes, Taylor's mind was spinning with thoughts of where his children might have been taken, how he could find them, what he could do to get them back, and even more pressing for the moment, how he was going to tell Tristan that Delissa had been taken along with the children.

Turning to the boy at his side, who was searching for any clue as to what transpired moments before, Taylor searched for the right words to come into his brain to explain the vision he had just seen. It was useless though, for there seemed only a void in his head that was eventually filled with high and mixed emotions.

Taylor glanced around the forest and he caught sight of the sword that Delissa had thrown. Walking up to it, he tried pulling it out of the tree it was embedded in, but found that, quite to his own awe, the sword was stuck at least a good three inches into the bark.

Taylor had no choice but to pull it out kinetically, all the while amazed at the woman's strength to have pierced it in so far.

Taylor grabbed the sword as it flung itself from the tree and, walking up to Tristan he put it in the boy's hands.

"She did what she could – put up a good fight!" he said, and the boy, looking at the sword, started welling tears at the sight of it.

"Is she – is she dead?" the boy asked, looking up at Taylor with his shiny face.

"No, no! No – she's been taken, like the children!" Taylor said calmly, and he put his hand on the boy's shoulder to comfort him.

Tristan pursed his lips and screwed up his face in anger and, holding the sword firmly in his hands, he actually tried swinging it at Taylor.

While Taylor hadn't expected this, his reflexes were fast enough to avoid any damage, and, looking at the teenager, he decided against kinetically holding him. He didn't say anything while Tristan vented his heated emotions.

"This is all your fault! We were fine! – Fine; until you showed up!"

Taylor only shook his head at hearing these words – as true as they were.

He wasn't quite sure the best action to take, or the best words to say to offer the boy comfort, but, with Tristan running at him making another effort to lash out in anger, Taylor quickly used his kinesis to spin the boy around at the last second. Putting his arm around Tristan's neck, he used a telekinetic hold to keep the boy still as he held him firm – his best effort of a parental embrace.

"It's okay Tristan – we'll find them – we'll find yours and mine – it'll just take time."

It was clear that Tristan, overflowing with frustration, was finally, slowly relaxing, and with an agitated heave, he looked into Taylor's eyes. "How are we going to find them – they're gone and we've got nothing – absolutely nothing to go on to find them."

Taylor's mind accepted these words with a realization of their truth, and in his own despair he looked down at Tristan's glowing suit, his eyes following the bright veins, and he questioned how he could track down someone if he had nothing for use in tracking. His eyes moved to the boy's hand, still firmly gripping the sword and, though he hadn't seen it there before, Taylor's eyes caught a green color that was of a very familiar hue.

Reaching down he snatched the sword from the boy's hand and, in looking at it closer, he saw that the sword, when Delissa had thrown it, had torn off a bit of cloth, only a few square inches, from the man's green cloak.

Taylor's eyes grew wide with expectation, and as he held the cloth tightly in his hand Tristan's look of surprise turned to one of almost relief.

"Is that – Is that what I think it is?" The boy asked.

"It is," Taylor said as he filled with quick very shallow impressions and thoughts from the man in the green cloak.

Taylor focused hard on trying to see either the past or the future through this piece of cloth. His thought was to either see where the man in green had come from, or where he was going. Either way, he had a definite chance of getting answers that were impossible to achieve before.

He held the cloth, rubbing it between his fingers, focusing on the man in green. Tristan watched this eagerly, hoping that there would be a quick answer revealing the whereabouts of his friends and his mother.

Taylor's eyes scrunched up and, with a strange series of flinches, he started to stiffen. This forced Tristan even more on edge than he was before and, after a few seconds, Taylor's face relaxed. When he opened his eyes Tristan could no longer stand the wait.

"Well!" the boy pressured immediately.

"I – I don't know!" Taylor said, and after a short pause to catch his breath, he continued, "I tried looking into the past and the future, but all I could see when I tried were flashes eh – like walls of black and white – it was very strange. I've never had anything like that happen before! I pushed and I pushed – I know there's something there – I can feel it, I can sense it, but I can't get past something – there's something I just... argh – I don't know"

"White and black – what's that?" Tristan asked rhetorically and while Taylor might have disregarded these words, they struck a chord with him as soon as they hit his ears. He too was asking the same question and after only a second of thinking, an answer, or at least a theory, came to him.

"I think I'm being blocked!" Taylor said aloud, and with these words Tristan looked confused. Still, though, the boy knew the right questions to ask, though he was frantic in doing so. "Blocked – but how – by who? Can you get past it? What do we do now?"

"I – I don't know how they did it, but somehow they did. It's like the paths to past and future visions are tied up with a knot!" Taylor explained cryptically, though Tristan still didn't seem to understand. "I just can't seem to get anywhere?"

"Aaand," Tristan pressed annoyingly.

"*And,* they're too powerful. I can't seem to get past anywhere past the wall."

"Well, can it be done?" Tristan pressed curiously, and it was clear to Taylor that the boy was hoping Taylor had more ideas rolling around in his head to fix this problem. Taylor picked up on these thoughts, and answered the boy's question with less than pleasing words.

"It would be near impossible to break a block like that." Taylor ranted, and with that Tristan looked down at the ground in despair. "But," Taylor added and the boy's eyes lit up, "it *can* be done, if someone is focused enough, and powerful enough."

Tristan looked Taylor in the eyes with a concentrated stare and the thoughts of the child seemed to flow directly into the brain of the adult almost instantly.

"The sphere, sphere – use the sphere, that'll make you strong enough!"

"Are you crazy," Taylor shouted, though the boy hadn't said a word. "God only knows what something like that could do to me!"

"Would it work?" The boy asked persistently, ignoring the fact that his thoughts had just been invaded, "Would the sphere make you strong enough to see past the block.

"I'd have little doubt, but it's not programmed for me. It might just end up frying my brain if it's not reprogrammed!" Taylor said loudly.

"Let me get this straight." Tristan said arrogantly. "We're all alone out here, my mother's gone, my friends are gone – wait – no – your sole purpose for *existence* is gone, and the *only* possible way to find them is in your hands right now. If you're being blocked – then you find a way to get past it – *any way you can*!"

Tristan's was insistent and commanding. His eyes started misting again and Taylor's face showed both a look of shock and a look of amazement. Though he had only known Tristan for these few short months, he never thought he would see the boy make such perfect sense – dangerous sense – but perfect sense.

"Fine," Taylor said firmly, "but I don't have the sphere here, I don't have an M-Gen, and even if I did, all the data I brought with me from The Towers was taken from that wreck of a home they left behind.

Tristan shook his head with a frown of anger, "Well, who made the damn thing in the first place?"

Taylor blinked his eyes at hearing this question and as Tristan watched this strange behavior the boy realized he had hit a nerve. Slowly, though, Taylor's expression changed. Taylor held the green cloth between his fingers and his brain seemed to pick up on something and with only a few images entering his brain Tatkir quickly put the cloth away in one of the many pockets of his cloaking suit. All at once he stared down at Tristan with a grin. The boy didn't recognize this look, but if anyone who knew him had seen even a glimpse of this stare, they'd know that Taylor was planning something. His eyes were staring out, for no reason, into the deep gaping chasm that had been created in the trees, and in his head, as he so often had done in the past, Taylor was planning something – something big.

60 Hidden Lair

"HOW LONG to reach the city's edge on foot?" Taylor asked, staring at the boy.

"About three days – on foot." Tristan replied with a short pause in his phrasing.

Taylor instantly heaved a breath of despair. He knew he needed to get back to the city, and the quicker the better, before any cognitive trails ran cold.

"Buuut..." The boy paused, and with a perceptible tone in the teen's voice, Taylor quickly realized that Tristan had something up his sleeve.

"What – what do you mean 'but'?"

Tristan turned to the forest and started walking, "Follow me!"

"But that's the wrong way!" Taylor said, noting that the Los Angeles Metroship was in the opposite direction.

"Trust me!" Tristan said, and with these words Taylor got the flash of an image from the boy's brain. He could see what looked like a hangar – and ships – strange looking ships that he'd never seen before. But quicker than he could take in any real detail the image was gone.

Taylor knew that the boy had, in fact, seen something – or been someplace that might offer some real benefit to their trek back to the city. So, although he didn't like it, he put his faith in the teenager before him and the two made off through the trees.

While it was still as dark as ever amid the forest, dawn had broken nearly an hour before, and the bits of daylight were welcome as the two made their way through the thick trees. The journey was slow, and Taylor was growing impatient over the fact that they were, indeed, walking away from the direction of the city and not toward it.

After over an hour of climbing, walking, hiking, and at times sliding down hillsides, Taylor was growing weary from emotion and from the journey. He was becoming increasingly desperate to find out where this teenager was leading him. Taylor, in fact, was continuously looking over his shoulder with a nervous anxiousness that the two of them were walking further away from the city's edge, not closer to it. He tried to pick up stray thoughts from the boy but couldn't, and in response to this he only whispered, "Fine time to start that now." He said in reference to the fact that the boy was now actually blocking Taylor from reading his thoughts.

Taylor did, at one point, recognize where they were when he saw a familiar clearing in the trees. *Yes, yes – there was the stump that Tristan was sitting on next to Aspen when Johnny asked about getting his ear pierced.* So – what? Was this where Tristan was hoping to take his students that day when they all had tired so early? He would've asked this question, but Tristan was moving far too fast, and Taylor didn't want to slow down for idling conversation. Still, realizing where he was – he was sure that they were getting very close to their destination.

"Here we are." Tristan said as he approached a large sequoia.

Taylor looked at the tree and, knowing that the people of this forest are renowned for hollowing out the trees as a way of storage or residence, he knew there had to be more to this wooden giant than just bark and branches.

Confirming his suspicions, Tristan opened a section of the tree that lay between two large protruding roots to reveal a small hidden door. Inside there was total blackness and Taylor felt a cool rising draft as he followed Tristan into the trunk and down a spiral metal staircase. As the moments passed, Taylor felt nervous about what was hiding below, but at the same time eager to see it all the same.

"Wait here!" Tristan said just as they reached the bottom of the stairs, and as the boy made his way so far into the darkness that Taylor couldn't make out his image any more, the older called out in a loud whisper.

"No wait – where are you going?"

Taylor heard the boy offer an eerie echoing giggle in the darkness, and, at this, Taylor decided to use a sense of telepathic radar to "feel" his environment.

He could tell that he was in a large room, and that, in front of him, there were several large strangely shaped objects. Walking forward to see if he could touch one, he was shocked and nearly knocked over by the onslaught of light that beamed straight into his face.

"What the hell?" Taylor shouted, and as he said this his eyes slowly adjusted to his newly lit surroundings. All around him, Taylor could see what looked like a hangar; the same as he had seen before in his flash from Tristan's thoughts. There were four crafts, all unlike anything Taylor had ever seen. In fact, these craft appeared almost organic compared to the boxy, hard edge craft used for either government or civilian purposes.

Taylor walked up to the one that was shining its light directly at him. He stopped when Tristan jumped out from it and landed directly in front of him.

"What is this place? And what are those things? How did you – find – this – pla..." Taylor stopped his words as he turned his head to examine and take in more of the hangar's details. He stopped talking because he could see several cloaking suits hanging on the walls and in open lockers nearby.

Seeing these cloaking suits, Taylor was overwhelmed with thoughts, assumptions, theories, and questions of what this place was, or what it was meant for.

Tristan only muddled these theories in a simple matter-of-fact way by answering Taylor's questions without them ever being asked. Taylor actually appreciated the boy's lack of energy or embellishment so he could simply hear the facts.

"I followed Rowna one day. He's always been the one to give members of our clan the suits. But I always wondered where they came from. So I followed him. I guess he stumbled on this place a long time ago. I know this place has an M-Gen, but I've never used it cuz' I don't know how. And it has these ships, the suits, and a few empty rooms. For the most part, though, it's pretty boring."

Tristan looked across the room in confusion, though.

"Funny, I thought there were five ships – not four."

"Could Rowna have taken one when he left?" Taylor asked smugly, but Tristan shook his head.

"Rowna never left. I came down here last month. I got nervous when I heard noises, so I used my suit, moved slow, still hiding, and that's when I saw him. He was eating food from the M-Gen. My guess is he's been down here the whole time.

Taylor, while surprised to hear this, did not feel it had any bearing on their current and more dire situation. Wherever Rowna was, Taylor didn't care. If he, Taylor, was standing next to a ship, he had a way of putting his plan into action at full speed. As he thought the plan through even further, his mind shifted to thoughts of his kids. These were now his greatest worry.

They had been missing for a few hours now and Taylor feared for how they would be treated if they woke up and were unwilling to cooperate. Would they use their kinesis to escape? Would they be harmed, or punished for doing so? Taylor gritted his teeth at the thought of this and immediately climbed up onto the craft at his side. "Come on – we don't have that much time!"

In jumping inside the ship, Taylor was surprised to see that, aside from having an area for passengers, the cockpit was actually quite roomy.

Inside the cockpit itself, the bulk of the instruments and displays were in front, with little on the sides or overhead, and with two seats, one in front of the other, Taylor sat in the forward seat and took in all the controls as Tristan took the seat behind him.

Taylor saw that there were only a few buttons and levers – one main control stick, and, to his relief, a simple main power switch that he pressed immediately when he saw it.

Once the craft had been engaged, Taylor focused hard on the screen in front of him to force plans, schematics, and programs to come up so that he might understand the mechanics, programming, and electronics of the machine he was about to fly. To his ultimate confusion, however, Taylor realized that the programming was unlike any structure he'd ever encountered; the mechanics were, seemingly, backwards; and the wiring itself didn't make any sense.

"Why would they... That can't be right... Is that the... or the..." Taylor whispered in half finished sentences. He would have continued, but he heard Tristan scream from the seat behind him. This made Taylor flinch. He turned to look at Tristan's seat. It was empty. He then turned forward to watch in horror as the boy fell off the front of the craft and down to the cement floor. He tried to focus on the boy, but he wasn't in time to prevent a very hard impact.

Standing up and looking out the cockpit window, Taylor watched as the boy rolled himself over in excruciating pain. It was clear that the child's arm, with one too many joint-like bends, was broken. Still, though, Tristan had enough of his wits about him to look up and point at the top of the craft.

Taylor turned his head quickly and could see a moving shadow from the hatch entrance. Slowly he made his way to it, and, climbing the exiting ladder, he raised himself up, keeping his mind in constant focus at all times.

Once his chin was above the line of the hatch he saw a hand come over his head quite rapidly, and with this hand holding a sharp blade, Taylor immediately forced it, and its owner, to remain still with his kinesis.

Turning around, there was little surprise to Taylor that Rowna was, in fact, trying to cut his throat.

With a furrowed brow, Taylor threw the man across the hanger and pinned him against a far wall. Rowna grunted and tried to speak, but Taylor was focusing hard even on the man's jaw to keep him silent. While climbing out of the craft, the teen watched the man on the wall with a dark stare and only offered one stiff, angry command.

"If you want to see the light of day again, you'll keep your damn mouth shut."

With each passing second Taylor's face offered a strong reddening look of disgust as he made his way to Tristan's side. Helping the boy to his feet, Taylor hobbled him over to a bench, offering only a few words of comfort.

"I know it hurts, Tristan. If you have to, just let it out, cry if you have to – I don't mind." These calm words were immediately followed by a low, quivering wail of pain from the boy at his side. Taylor's heart ached with these sounds and he reminded himself of how he often gave his kids the same advice. He always believed that if there was a good reason to cry, and a great deal of pain is a good reason, then it shouldn't be held in. Tristan, who wasn't raised in this manner, wasn't used to this, so while he did allow himself to cry, Taylor could tell that the boy was working hard to choke back and quickly hide his expressions of pain.

Just at the last steps to the bench Taylor heard more groaning from where he had pinned Rowna to the hangar wall. Looking up at him, Taylor could see that he was trying to speak. He, Taylor, took a good look at the man, really absorbing his appearance and how much change had taken place since he fleed into the forest those months before.

He was considerably fatter and, unlike before, he was unshaven and dirty. It was hard for Taylor to believe that this was, at one time, the clan leader that Delissa and so many others actually looked to and in some cases, admired.

Shaking his head, Taylor hardly had the stomach to listen to the man's groans. Rowna was actually trying to speak through Taylor's firm telekinetic grip around both throat and body, but only mere sounds could make their way out.

"I will snap your neck in two if you don't shut the hell up!" Taylor said feverishly.

Tristan looked up at Rowna and could see that the man's head was being pulled to the side at an odd angle. *He might actually do it!* Tristan thought, and with this the noises Rowna was making became more panicked.

The boy at Taylor's side, though still in a great deal of pain as a result of his great-great-great-grandfather's actions, put his hand on Taylor's as a request for him to stop.

Taylor, though, only looked at Tristan with a slight grin and a wink. Pathically, he told the boy, "I'm just screwing around with him – relax!"

Tristan returned the grin with his own pained smile and he watched as Taylor took some tools out of his pockets and lined them on the bench. Some of these Tristan recognized; others, he didn't, but since their first meeting, Tristan knew he could trust Taylor to take care of him, and that was a kind of faith that the boy put in very few people.

Taylor grabbed the teen's arm and raised it to be examined. This forced Tristan to grimace in pain, and at this Taylor had to admire how well the boy was able to handle pain. Tears streaming down his face, Tristan uttered not a word as Taylor went to work.

First he put a small device on the boy's arm, and, with the tap of a button the unit lit up and it had the immediate effect of deadening all of Tristan's feeling in his arm. In fact, Tristan thought, he couldn't feel anything of his arm past where the unit was attached. Curiosity led him to want to play with the little unit, but a quick stare from Taylor told him that this wasn't a good idea.

"Now, don't get freaked out, but I have to set the bone!" Taylor said stiffly as he grabbed the broken arm with both hands and, feeling it firmly, he shifted and flexed it to a straight and proper position. Despite Taylor's words, Tristan's eyes widened at seeing this, for it did freak him out that his flesh and bones were being manipulated so easily, and yet he felt nothing – absolutely nothing by way of pain.

Grabbing another of his tools, Taylor used the ever familiar bone replicator to mend the break and as he did this he couldn't help but ask, "Ehh, Tris', isn't this the same arm..."

"Yeah!" the boy said, shaking his head, and Taylor did the same.

"Man – that's just – just..." Taylor couldn't think of the right words to describe this kind of coincidental injury.

"Whatever." Tristan said in a half bored, half irritated tone.

"Now," Taylor said with a stare straight into the boy's eyes, "I'm going to take this off, and when I do, you're going to feel a shock of pain. It'll be what you would've felt if I'd never put it on – so it's really – REALLY going to hurt!"

Taylor grabbed the unit between his fingers, and he watched as the boy bit his lip in expectation of the pain. With a pull it was removed, and the boy's arm flinched violently until it ended in a cradled position in his other arm.

"Eaahhhhhhh! Man – you weren't kidding!" Tristan yelled, but the pain subsided after a few seconds, and, with a little flexing and moving, Tristan was able to manipulate the twice broken arm as though he'd never had an injury.

Standing up, he and Taylor both walked up to and faced Rowna and without a word, Taylor turned his back on the man and faced the five craft in the hangar.

One by one Taylor then kinetically ripped them apart in large chunks, until he reached the last. This one, kept unharmed, was his and Tristan's ride to the city.

They both climbed into the craft in the same position's they were in before, and, with a new focus on the craft itself, Taylor was able to cyberly force commands into it despite the ship's bizarre design.

In the matter of a few seconds the hatch overhead was closed and the craft lifted itself from the hangar floor straight upward through a large circular hole in the ceiling that opened on approach. As they rose out of the hangar the last Taylor and Tristan saw of Rowna was the man falling hard to the concrete floor.

Rowna looked up at the craft in disgust and anger. Taylor, again, hoped that this would be the last he would see of Rowna, but something in his gut told him that he should know better.

Rising out of one of several large false sequoia tree trunks, Taylor couldn't help but almost laugh at how well camouflaged the hangar exits were in the dense forest. Without a moment's pause, he slowly forced the craft to rise above the trees, and at the first real onslaught of sunlight he immediately worried of satellite detection from the skies.

Being cautious, Taylor lowered the craft to back below the tree line, and slowly he made his way through the forest. He knew, quickly enough, that he wasn't making as good of time as he would like, and with the winter solstice forcing the day's to be much shorter, he was desperate to make it into the city before nightfall. This timing, as he had planned it, was crucial.

While navigating the ship through the trees Taylor's mind wandered to the contents of the hangar and the cloaking suits inside. Where did this technology come from, and this craft, while simple in design, was unlike anything he had ever seen. If it was built by the same people, why couldn't they have added the cloaking technology to it? Taylor imagined in his head how easy it would be, if the ship were cloaked, to just rise above the trees and skirt across the top of the forest right to the city's edge in the matter of a half hour or so.

Looking out into the dark thick forest, Taylor noticed something he hadn't seen before on the surface of the ship. It was something he was familiar with, and in surprise he sputtered, "Oh damn, you've got to be kidding!"

Tristan, from behind, snapped at attention with this bit of profanity.

"What?! What's wrong?!"

"Look out, over the side! Do you see what I see?" Taylor asked, and with these words the boy's eyes both looked and grew wide from what he had taken in. The craft did, indeed, have the same kind of brightly covered veins running over its surface as the familiar cloaking suits. Strangely, this wasn't perceptible before, and Taylor could only assume that his desire for this had somehow forced the cloaking of the craft to activate itself through his cyber powers.

Taylor immediately set the craft down under the cover of some large trees and focused on the control display before him. He drew up page after page of schematics and engineering drawings that were stored in the craft's memory until, "Aha!" he said aloud, and he saw that there were a few pages on the design and function of the cloaking system. Following the schematics and translating them to physical drawings of the craft, Taylor realized that there was a simple button to activate the cloaking device. But the button, strangely enough, it wasn't in front of him.

He grunted, "Tristan – look straight up, above your head. Now move your eyes a little to the left. Is there a big – green blinking button that says 'Cloaking On' on it?"

Tristan saw the button, and immediately felt awful that he hadn't noticed it before. "Uhhh – yeah!" He said softly.

Taylor, in almost a playfully irritated fashion made the simple request, "Could you please press the 'cloaking on' button so that we might be able to actually get somewhere today?" And with these words and the sound of the button click, Taylor watched as the view in front of him grew to a pitch black, then displayed a simple black-and-white image of the many trees in front of the craft.

"Thank you!" Taylor said shrilly as he immediately forced the craft into the air, high above the trees. He then directed it to make a straight line for the city and at their current speed he knew he would be able to get there sometime in the early afternoon.

Tristan seemed to grow ever anxious about entering the city. He had always been raised with such a negative view of the life and the people it contained, but since the arrival of Taylor and his students, that view had drastically changed. Taylor could tell that the children had filled his head with stories and images of what the city was like, and he had to laugh as he realized that not all of the stories were true.

"They were just pulling your leg on that one!" Taylor said almost with a laugh, for he had just heard Tristan say, "I can't wait to see Mutant-Town!"

Tristan looked down with almost a frown of disappointment at these words, "You mean there's no part of the city with all the mutants?"

Taylor had to shake his head and smile.

"I mean there are no mutants!" he said with a laugh, and instantly Tristan seemed even more upset.

The boy's irritation over this tall tale would've persisted had it not been for the view he got of the city, which was now only kilometers away. Taylor himself was a little surprised to see the city pop up so large on the screen, but he remembered that the cloaking technology didn't allow for very far distant visuals. Clarity of the city's buildings, therefore, only came when they were within a close range.

"Woahhh are those the..."

"Yes," Taylor said cutting him off, "those are the EduCorp Towers. The kids lived there for over five years, and I lived there nearly my whole life."

Indeed The Towers were large in the view of the craft, and Taylor veered away from them in favor of another direction. His focus pushed the craft toward another part of the city that, to Tristan, was obviously less interesting.

"What the – Hey – where are we going?" Tristan asked impatiently.

"What, you don't expect us to just land on the roof, break in, get what we need, and everything'll just be fine?"

"Uhhh – okay, no I guess not..." the boy said with disappointment as he felt the craft head toward a building that looked like so many others, and was therefore boring.

"So – eh, where are we going?" the teen asked curiously and Taylor could hear a tone in the child's voice that clearly gave the impression he'd much rather have gone to The Towers.

"We're not on a sight-seeing tour, kid. We're going to the one person I know who can help us get inside The Towers."

"Ohhh – Uh – Jay!" Tristan said with uncertainty, pulling the man's name out of his brain's memory with difficulty.

"Exactly. I would've gone straight there, but I'm not used to this thing or how it navigates, so I needed a point of reference: The Towers! Now that I know where they are, I know where I'm headed."

Within a few minutes Taylor landed the craft on the roof of Jay's residential building in lieu of using a landing pad. There, on the pad, he was certain the traffic would become a problem, but on the roof no one would be able to see the cloaked craft and as few people visit rooftops these days, he was fairly confident that it would be safe. He kept the craft on minimal power just to keep the cloaking device running and turned to Tristan voicing a readiness to leave.

"It would be best if we weren't seen." He said to Tristan, and he needed to say little else for the boy to understand and immediately both donned their cloaking hoods and quickly vanished in the cockpit. Opening the hatch to the craft, Taylor and Tristan made their way into the building through a service access door. The two found their way to Jay's front door, with Taylor having to pathically tell Tristan where to go as the boy couldn't see him. Taylor, without much thought pressed the call button, and waited for an answer.

Tristan and Taylor both felt that luck definitely wasn't on his side though, for a mere second before Jay answered a couple made their way into the corridor where Taylor and Tristan were standing, still hidden in their suits.

"Can I help you?" Jay asked of those walking through the hall.

The couple stared at Jay in confusion, shrugged their shoulders and walked on. Jay went back inside and Taylor had to, once again, push the call button.

What is it with these people? Taylor thought as, once again, when Jay answered the door, someone else came out into the hall.

Taylor and Tristan both took their places at the side of the hall and waited, again for this new person to make their way while, once again, Jay answered the door. He looked at the man in the hall with expectation. This man, however, actually noticed the call light and said quite plainly in response; "Wasn't me!" before continuing down the corridor.

Taylor would have thought it best to simply project thoughts into Jay's head, but he was afraid this would make the man feel he was going insane.

Instead, Taylor opted for a different idea. He reached into his pocket, pulled out a small tissue generator and, walking down the hall a few steps, he activated it and set it on the floor. The unit immediately started beeping; something it always did when there was no tissue to replicate when turned on. This beeping would last only about thirty seconds, so Taylor had to move fast.

He sprinted back to the door and pushed the call button again.

Several seconds went by, but Jay didn't answer the door. Panicking Taylor used his kinesis to force the door open and, looking inside, he could see that Jay was staring at the security screen just inside the door. To make matters more interesting, he was confused that the call button not only activated itself, but the door opened itself, and there seemed no reason as to why either had actually happened.

Jay quickly pushed the close button to the entrance, but Taylor opened it again, and it was at this, the fourth opening of the door that Jay heard, as Taylor had hoped, a beeping just outside the entrance.

"What's that?" Jay murmured as he stepped out to find, and eventually pick up the tissue replicator.

Confused and irritated, he made his way back into his apartment and closed the door holding the tissue generator in his hand. In his mind he was certain that this had something to do with his door's *malfunction*.

He turned to his living room, staring hard at the tissue generator, and when he finally thought to look up, his eyes were met with the familiar faces of both Tristan and Taylor.

"I was wondering how long it would take for you to move your big butt out of the way!" Taylor said with a smile, and Jay, his face lighting up with fantastic eagerness, greeted his new guests each with an excited handshake and hug.

PART FOUR

MINDS, MACHINES, AND MONSTERS

61 No Good Deed...

"SO – WHERE ARE THEY?" Jay asked, looking and feeling around the room quite awkwardly. "I gotta admit, I really do miss 'em!"

Taylor shook his head sorrowfully at these words. He knew that Jay was feeling about for the children, hoping that, like him, they were cloaked.

"They've been taken." Taylor worded miserably, but it seemed that Jay didn't absorb this new information, so Taylor repeated, "Jay – They've been taken. They're not here!"

Jay, still leaning to feel about the room, looked over his shoulder at Taylor, "What do you mean, 'Taken'?"

"I'll explain everything in time." Taylor said softly, "But they found us in the forest. Jay, they have the kids, and if..."

"Wait, wait, wait," Jay cut in, having completely and instantly lost his patience, "Who, at least tell me who it is that has them."

"It's the whole E-Crew, and – I don't know – they," Taylor paused and it was clear that he was very upset at saying each word. "They tricked me. I left them alone and," Taylor paused from his now clearly upset rhetoric and took a deep breath, "now they're gone."

Jay started pacing, "Gone! – you mean gone as in you have no idea where they are 'gone!'"

Taylor only nodded his head and added, "Jay, there's more. That vision, the sphere, they're all connected... the government has plans for the children, but if... if they don't cooperate – they'll be terminated"

Jay's face screwed itself up in anger, and with a reddening expression he turned to Taylor, "You didn't just come here to tell me all this good news did you. I assume you have some plan, some idea, of what to do now.

"I do, but it's going to be tricky, and we don't have much time!" Taylor glanced over at a clock on the wall of Jay's apartment, it read 4:37PM, and Taylor knew that sunset would be in just over two hours.

"Well what've you got – What's the plan?"

Taylor didn't feel he had the time to explain so, with his usual stare of concentration, he forced his plans and ideas into Jay's head, including the idea of using the sphere to boost his own powers so he could track the history and possibly the future of the man cloaked in green by using the cloth that was still folded neatly in his pocket.

"I'm not going to tell you I think you're crazy. I'm just *not* going to tell you that." Jay said shaking his head in disbelief at what he had just received.

"Good!" Taylor shouted, "Because it's the only way I can think of to find them."

Jay paced his living room, and it was clear that he wasn't comfortable with the plan Taylor had set forth.

"You've got nothing else? There's *nothing* else you can think of."

Taylor merely shook his head, offering an impatient stare to his friend.

Thinking it through and looking into Taylor's ever coercing eyes, Jay had come to the same conclusion Taylor did: that using the sphere was the only way of finding, and possibly saving the children.

Taylor turned to Tristan, who was walking around the living room, curious of the items it contained and, just as the boy reached out to grab something on a low table in the middle of the room, Taylor shouted at him, forcing a jolt of fear to rush through him.

"Don't touch anything!"

Tristan pulled his own hand to the center of his chest and held it close to his heart as though it had been injured, and as if the pain were real, the boy had a face to match.

"I was just looking!" he said innocently.

"Sorry Tris'. It's just – I don't want to leave any impressions behind – nothing they could use to follow us, or even know we were here."

The boy nodded his head and Taylor turned to Jay, "So – how are things with the company anyways?"

Jay shook his head. "You know, since you've left, they've increased security ten-fold. You now have to provide voice, print, and retinal scans just to get into the place. It's really become a fortress." Jay sounded desperately. It wasn't that he was trying to dissuade Taylor from his decision, but more that he should prepare his friend for a slightly different welcome on returning to formerly familiar grounds.

"I'll be on my toes then!" Taylor said, half relaxed and still offering an impatient and expectant stare for Jay to get moving.

"Are you sure about this?" Jay asked, and he only needed a forceful exhale of breath to accompany that stare from Taylor to answer the question without words.

"Alright, alright! Just give me a minute." Jay retorted and he quickly laced up his shoes and replicated a few extra layers of clothing to compete with the now cooler outside weather.

Taylor walked over to Tristan's side. He saw that the boy was staring at a framed picture of Taylor and Jay standing between six very young children. There were smiles from ear to ear on each face, and Taylor could only sigh in remembrance of such simple times. Here, as Taylor recalled, the children were only 7, and he would give anything to have the troubles of that past over those of the this present. He'd gladly take their rambunctious nature, their unreliable control over their powers, and their constant defiance – yes he would take it all any day over what he was having to deal with now... *simpler times indeed.*

Jay walked up to Tristan's other side and gave a little chuckle at seeing the picture. "I always liked that picture." He then stepped to the side, "And this one..."

Jay paused seeing that one of the frames on the shelf was turned over. "What the heck?" he barked irritation, for on turning up the frame he saw that the picture inside was missing.

"That picture was there just day before yesterday. I'm sure of it. What the hell happened to it?"

Raising an eyebrow, Taylor walked over to Jay and reached out to grab the frame. "May I?" He asked, and Jay knew that what his friend was up to. What Jay didn't know, though, was that Taylor had much more running through his mind than just simply trying to find a misplaced picture. He had suspicions that he'd rather not voice until they were confirmed.

Grabbing the frame, Taylor didn't get any immediate impressions. He held it in his hands, rubbed its wooden edges, and focused hard on an imagined image of Jay holding the frame in his hands.

Slowly the room grew dark and Taylor realized that his mind was moving in the right direction. He closed his eyes, and tried to hone in on the frame, the apartment, and Jay. With concentration he tried to work his mind back some two days ago.

The room had successfully gone completely black in Taylor's mind and after a moment it lit up again, as though nothing had changed. A difference, however, was the fact that Taylor was standing alone in the room where, before, Tristan and Jay were only a few feet away.

He turned and looked back on the shelf. He could, indeed, see the same picture frame, and how it did actually have a picture in it. Taylor smiled at this. He recognized the picture as one that he had on his desk in his office. It was a picture of the six children, Jay, and himself all sitting together on the grass of the LAM Park.

He reached out to grab it, but pulled his hand back at the last second, realizing that there was little point. This was only a vision of the past, and he couldn't touch the picture even if he wanted to; and in seeing the happy faces of his students, he desperately wanted to.

Taylor's head turned around quickly when he heard voices from another room in the apartment. He didn't have to move though, for he saw quickly enough that Jay had come into the living room in a rapid effort to get ready for work. He was followed almost immediately by a very familiar looking brunette.

"Shannon, I don't have time for this right now. They've called me in and I have to go. You know that! I've been in enough trouble at the office as it is."

"But it's a freaking Sunday for Christ's sake. You never go in on a Sunday, what could they possibly want that's so damned important?"

"I don't know – but things have changed, and if I want to keep my job I have to go – now!"

Taylor listened to the conversation with only a half interest. He felt as though he was intruding on their personal moments – especially considering the fact that Shannon was only half dressed, and he could only make an educated guess as to why they were coming from the bedroom.

Just the same, a sparkle on her hand did catch his attention. Was that a ring? Yes – yes it was – and it's on her left hand! Taylor looked up at Jay in surprise.

"You proposed! You actually proposed – I'm impressed. You're afraid of everything, and here you've gone and actually proposed to the girl."

He watched her hand reach behind Jay's head, and as she brought herself within an inch of his face she whispered to him.

"Fine – If you have to go – then take this with you." She offered him a kiss that Taylor felt extremely uncomfortable watching.

Shannon continued her playful game of seduction. "And there's more where that came from. Just try to get back as soon as you can. I had plans for today!"

Taylor watched as Jay was only barely able to pull himself away from Shannon's hold and make his way out of the apartment. The teen was impressed with how completely the two had fallen for each other, and he finally thought to himself that maybe, just maybe, she wasn't as bad as he had remembered from their first encounter at that club so long ago.

He watched as she made her way into the bedroom, and he was hoping that, soon, this vision would finish itself with a revelation of what happened to the missing picture in the frame. He had his suspicions and he wanted to have them confirmed or refuted soon as time was running short.

With this thought in mind, Taylor was relieved that he didn't have to wait but a few moments longer to see what he needed.

With a call light coming on over the front door, Taylor watched as Shannon made her way to the apartment entrance. Quite to his surprise, she collapsed only a few inches away from the door and immediately thereafter it opened. Taylor was confused. There was nothing to cause her to pass out like that. In fact, now that he thought about it, he's only seen that happen a few times in *his* life.

The door to Jay's apartment opened and Taylor watched as two familiar figures, and one that he didn't recognize, made their way into Jay's apartment.

The man cloaked in white, the woman cloaked in black, and another woman – what is it with the colored cloaks, Taylor thought, for she was covered in a deep blue – all walked into Jay's apartment.

The man of the group quickly scooped Shannon up into his arms and walked her into the bedroom where he laid her down gently with Taylor following to make sure that she remained unharmed. Then, to Taylor's expectation, they started rummaging through the apartment. Item by item the man in white and the woman in black started passing things between each other's bare hands very carefully.

"Nothing!" one would say, and then the other would repeat it.

"Come on – we haven't got all day!" The woman in blue said with a frown as she watched the two grab up practically everything in the apartment.

Taylor then watched as the woman in black approached Jay's shelf of pictures. She snatched the first of the two pictures on the shelf and put it back almost immediately. The second, however, she grabbed and held for a moment. She then took the frame apart and pulled out the picture inside.

"Yes – Yes – Here's something we can use!" She hissed and the man in white moved to her side and carefully pulled the picture from her fingers. She was still concentrating, her eyes closed, and even without the picture itself, Taylor could see that she was still able to hold onto the vision in her mind.

"Yes – I see him – he's lying in the forest – asleep – and there are people around him." She said softly as he recounted the vision in her mind.

"They're children. THE children. They're saying goodbye – and – wait – the girl – Caitlin – she's giving Jay this picture. Ahhhhhh – she must have brought it with her.

The man in white was apparently able to see enough into the future to know that she was right. "Yes," he said softly, "we'll use this to take us right to them. *This* is what we've been looking for." He quickly, decided to put it back into the hands of the woman in black.

"Come on, girl – push it back – go back further. If the girl had it with her in the forest then we use it to find out where. I've already seen it! Now push!"

The woman in black could hear these words in her mind and she furrowed her brow in deep concentration, gripping the picture tighter and tighter – flexing it harshly.

Taylor's mind was spinning as to what the woman was seeing. *Did she actually follow their path back to the elevated home? What kind of stupid question is that – of course she did! But why, why did Caitlin leave Jay this picture? The girl's a post-cog! She should know how dangerous that could be!*

Taylor started to fill with anger, but sighed and relaxed. Being angry at the girl would prove little point to him now.

He watched the woman in black and was now able to understand why the government had people like this doing their dirty work. They were very good at what they did.

Taylor then watched the woman in black slowly relax her grip on the picture. "They used the man as a decoy. They're nowhere near where we found him!

Taylor could hear a line of profane exclamations inside his head as he accepted that this is how they were, in fact, caught. He watched the woman in black put the picture delicately in a pocket of her cloak. She then patted the outside of it once it was in place, and smiled. "We have them!"

"So that's what you were grabbing outside the tree!" Taylor said to himself as he thought back to the moment when she had reached into her cloak. *That must've been why they decided to leave. She tracked the picture's history back to the home.*

Taylor was frustrated watching this rush of Black, White and Blue leave Jay's apartment. He tried to follow behind, hoping to get some clue to where they were headed, but as he moved to walk out of the apartment his path was blocked by yet another individual.

The man cloaked in green simply stood in the doorway and, with a focus on the disheveled room, brought it back to its original state of cleanliness. Placing the last item, the newly assembled, but now empty, picture frame back on its shelf, he decided to flip it forward to hide its vacant state.

Trying to again follow behind the man in Green, Taylor stepped quickly, moving away from the apartment, but with each step, his vision grew hazy and he realized that he was going beyond the scope of this particular postcog vision, which was based on his holding the frame, and not the picture itself. As expected, his view shifted to black, and when he opened his eyes he found himself staring at the anxious faces of Tristan and Jay.

He sighed, and, just like the many other times in his life that he had ever done it, he forced what he had seen into the minds of the two in front of him. Jay remained calm during this endeavor, but Tristan flinched and turned his head almost uncontrollably. Taylor had never projected a fluid series of active thoughts into the boy's brain before and it was clear that the child was having trouble adjusting to this new form of communication.

When Taylor had finished the boy showed total relax when he opened his eyes and saw Taylor standing nearby.

"So now you know!" he said to Jay. "And now we know," he added, looking at Tristan. With a turn to the clock his eyes grew large. "And we've got to go!"

Jay nodded and threw on the light jacket he had replicated before opening the door. Taylor and Tristan looked at each other and with the same thoughts running through each other's brains they both cloaked themselves before leaving. With Jay walking between them, they all made their way to the lift.

Jay was about to push the button to take them to the level of the lift pick-up station, but his hand was grabbed by an invisible one as Taylor said softly, "Take me to the roof – I've got something I have to do first."

Jay nodded, and to the top floor they went. When the doors opened, Taylor stepped out and went through the service door leading to the rooftop. He was back in a mere minute and, throwing the bag of supplies he had pulled from the river in the forest to Jay, Taylor was now ready to go.

Jay pushed the button for the level of the lift pick-up station, and the three were met by a standard transport within a few minutes.

It was quite an interesting predicament Taylor and Tristan were in because they, being unseen, had to be extra careful about their surroundings. To be bumped into or sat on at this point would create some very interesting panic in the transport; a panic that all three of them would much rather avoid.

Riding the transport to its final stop before The Towers, though, Taylor realized that they were alone and either out of sentiment, or out of anger, he had it in his mind that it was important he view The Towers once again with his own eyes.

Deactivating his cloaking suit, he took off his hood and stood beside Jay, staring at this building in all its fantastic glory against the bright westbound sun.

"Is it me, or does it look different now?" Taylor asked, but no one answered. And the instant these words fell from his mouth Taylor thought of how, for so long, this was his home, and there was a time when it had always welcomed him with open arms. Whether it looked different or not hardly mattered; he was trying to break into the landmark towers, and he felt at that moment that his welcome had completely worn itself out.

"It's definitely different now!" Jay finally replied with a sad and tired look to Taylor, it seemed he was making a statement and not answering Taylor's question. "A lot has changed in the way things are run there. I didn't want to tell you, but all the experiments have been forced to shift their focus. It's all about the department of evolutionary development now! The council didn't want it that way, but the government forced it on them."

"I'll bet," Taylor said as they rounded on the building to come to its first level entrance.

"Some of the council even resigned!" Jay voiced desolately. This was followed by a quick stare of concern from Taylor, and it seemed that Jay didn't need a telepathic message to hear what the man was thinking. "Don't worry – Dr. Young's still there – it would take more than a few memos and policy changes for her to abandon her post."

Taylor smiled at this with almost a sneer, and with a look at the massive building, now only a few feet away, Taylor put his cloaking hood back on and, with one hand on Jay's shoulder and the other activating the suit, Taylor disappeared into nothingness. Jay, at watching his friend's hand dissolve away, was filled with a pessimistic sense of foreboding. He took a deep nervous breath. Taylor, on seeing this, voiced a quick "relax, everything's going to be fine – like a walk in the park."

62 Cloaked and Dagger

TAYLOR AND TRISTAN walked beside Jay to the entrance of The Towers – completely committed to the task at hand. With Jay offering his hand-print, retinal scan, and voice identification, the door opened. Jay then dropped the bag he was carrying, thus allowing Tristan and Jay to enter.

The two were standing one straight in front of the other, and while the steps were awkward to move in quickly, the task was complete and after a few seconds the secondary door opened, offering the two an entry to the lobby.

Inside a large security guard was scrutinizing Jay's action, and, in seeing what he believed to be an honest fumble, he offered an override to allow Jay to enter the building.

Jay had informed Taylor that under the new security protocols, a person can only enter a doorway once with their own access code. In order to pass through it again, they would have to leave, and then come back again, unless, of course, they got an override.

Taylor watched carefully as the security guard entered the code on the inside pad. "Eight – Seven – Two – Seven – Four – Two – Seven."

With Jay walking past him closely, Taylor whispered these numbers into his friend's ear.

"What was that?" asked the security guard, hearing a voice in the air.

"Oh, nothing – just insulting my own clumsiness." Jay said as he continued through the lobby to the main lift for West Tower.

Fortunately, Jay had already discussed with Taylor and Tristan that if this little operation was going to work, that the two would have to stay close in front of him, otherwise long pauses and doors staying open too long might look suspicious. With the door to the lift opening, Jay stepped in and felt, with his toes, that he had actually stepped on Tristan's heel. A knee-jerk reaction would be to apologize for this, but Jay knew better. He only mouthed the word 'sorry' instead.

When the doors closed Jay looked down at the touch screen in front of him and, navigating through the EduCorp offices, he found the location of Dr. Hathaway's office. He quickly tapped the numbers 5-3-7 on the touch screen and, in pushing the go button, the lift accelerated. The numbers ascended quickly, telling all that they were moving fast. But between the three in the lift it was uncertain if the acceleration was what caused their stomachs to quiver and ache, or if it was the nervousness of what they were about to do.

Either way, the anticipation of what was sure to be total chaos made them all feel agitated. Tristan, as Taylor could sense, was the only one who had the extra excited emotions of riding in a lift for, now, the third time in his life, and for the first time the boy was going to take it to a fantastic new height.

With the last few floors being passed the trio could feel the lift decelerate until it came to a smooth stop at the 537th floor. A soft beep and the doors opening revealed a bright corridor fully bustling with activity.

Jay walked down the hall to Dr. Hathaway's office. He worried over whether someone might bump into Taylor or Tristan, but with any luck the two were right on his tail and he would act as their shield, keeping them from any physical contact. Jay slowed his walk as he approached Dr. Hathaway's office and, standing in front of it, he wasn't sure if she was in or not.

A quick telepathic message from Taylor told Jay the best action so that they could get into the room. As such he, Jay, pushed the call button and waited. If Dr. Hathaway answered, Jay would try to lead her away from her office while Taylor and Tristan went to work. If she didn't answer, then Taylor would use his cyber-kinesis to perform a little unauthorized locksmith work, allowing himself and Tristan to enter while Jay stood watch outside for any unexpected visitors.

Several seconds passed after Jay's request for entry and it was clear that Dr. Hathaway wasn't in her office. Taylor quickly forced the door open, making sure, of course, to show that the call light above the door had turned green to reflect an authorized entry.

Jay only popped his head into the office for a moment so as to not attract attention as to why he didn't enter the requested room and as he did this he could feel, with a slight brush of something unseen, that Taylor and Tristan had entered the room.

Jay pulled his head back. All Jay could do at point was watch and wait. It was decided that only Tristan and Taylor should be in the office so that, if Dr. Hathaway did return, Jay could slow her down, and if she still made it to her office, they would be unseen, regardless of the state of upturned room.

Inside the office, which Taylor was vaguely familiar with from his interrogation of Dr. Hathaway several months prior, he and Tristan started rummaging through desk drawers and storage containers looking for the memory module that parented the sphere. In this effort the room was turned upside down in no time. There was nothing left untouched. Nothing, that is, except for the framed diplomas and certificates on the wall behind her desk. Here, Taylor quickly realized, was the perfect hiding place for what they were seeking.

He scanned the certificates of merit and appreciation along with the diplomas of completed PhDs. His first guess, and apparently a good one at that, was to look under the certificate of appreciation from the GC for research and work that went above and beyond etc... etc... Taylor didn't care about the details. He quickly and carelessly pulled the frame off the wall. There was nothing on the wall behind it, but looking at the backside of the frame he saw, tickling him with delight, a memory module with the same markings as the one he had seen in his shared memory of her office.

"Bingo!" Taylor said, and he quickly shoved the memory module in a zip up pocket of his cloaking suit.

Taylor opened the entrance to Dr. Hathaway's office and he and Tristan exited the office as undetected as they had entered. They made their way down corridor, meeting a conversing Jay on the way.

"Uh, I never really apologized for what happened those months back. You know – you – tied to a table – me – standing there not doing anything. I'm really very, very sorry!"

Dr. Hathaway, who Jay was talking to, paused and smiled. "Are you saying that because you're really sorry, or because I've been promoted to head the new project you're on?"

"Ehhh – would it be wrong if I said it was a little bit of both?"

"Well, it would be honest." she said, making her way further down the corridor.

Taylor, noticing how close they were coming to her office, tugged on Jay's shirt as a signal that now would be a good time to cut off the ridiculous chit chat.

Jay took the hint quite well. "Ehhh – well, I am really sorry about all that and I hope you can just forget the whole thing ever happened. Oh – gosh, I just realized I'm late for a uh – meeting – yeah – a meeting." Jay said this in a rush as he pulled away from a distracted Dr. Hathaway.

Taylor cringed at this horrible impromptu acting and storytelling, but it seemed that what the teen noticed, Dr. Hathaway didn't and she finished the last few steps to her office while Jay practically bolted for the lift with Taylor and Tristan close behind.

"How long do you figure?" Jay asked of Taylor once the doors to the lift had closed and the three of them were headed down to the lobby.

Taylor whispered in response, "Three – two – one..." Taylor counted, and after the 'one' there was a lengthy pause. For that fleeting moment Taylor was curious if it was possible that Dr. Hathaway wouldn't contact EduCorp security over her office being left in shambles. The teen actually laughed inside at the thought of what her face would look like when she entered the room and saw the mess he had made.

If only she knew it was me.

With this thought he was about to tap Jay on the shoulder to share this friendly laugh. Unfortunately, this did not happen. With a red flashing of the alarm in the lift, Taylor and Jay were both sure that Dr. Hathaway had, indeed, notified security. Additionally, knowing her, Taylor figured she suspected that Jay, with his less than believable apology, was behind her office disarray.

Taylor checked the time on the display in the lift – it was 6:25. Sunset would be in exactly eighteen minutes, and unless they acted quickly, the three of them would miss their only opportunity for escape from The Towers.

With the alarms ringing, the answer of up or down was quickly ascertained and Jay quickly punched the 550th floor on the lift. This floor, having little else besides Dr. Isaac's main office, also had his private arboretum. Taylor himself had never been up there, but he remembered from his tour with Jay several years back that the arboretum was curtailed with a series metallic panels that, only at sunset, would close to transceive massive amounts of data through the night. This, *he had seen*, was their only option for escape.

With yet another ding and the opening of the lift doors, Taylor, Jay, and Tristan had actually, for the first time in all of their lives, stood on the top floor of The Towers. Here there was only a small reception area, and a large door to Dr. Isaac's office. None of the three standing in front of the office door knew if the EduCorp CEO was in or out, but Taylor was the only one who didn't care, and was forceful enough to act. He opened the man's office doors kinetically and in stepping into it he saw in an instant that he was face to face with the head of EduCorp.

It was amazing for Taylor to see the most powerful man in the company, here, and yet with the mere opening of the office doors amid the red glow of emergency lights, the man's face was latent with fear. Taylor was not seen as he was currently cloaked, but he concentrated hard on the man's projected and panicked thoughts. He knew if he focused on them hard enough, he could silence the man's brain forcing him to pass out like an entire floor of technicians some fifteen years before in this very building.

Taylor's effort had an immediate effect, for Dr. Isaacs barely had time to stand at his feet before he collapsed onto the desk in front of him. Tristan and Jay entered the office immediately after, and, with a quick look around the office, Taylor found an M-Gen nested in a nearby wall.

Thinking fast, he pulled out the memory module and shoved it roughly into the panel. Within a few seconds, just as Taylor had seen from Dr. Hathaway's projected memories, the M-Gen produced a case with the letters GCSD printed on it. He opened this case and could see the three items that were, to his expectation, supposed to be in the container. "Yes!" he said enthusiastically, but with this word he heard the door to Dr. Isaac's office open.

Taylor was expecting to see several security personnel walk in, but, to his surprise he was greeted with security robots instead.

He almost sneered at these, and stood in front of them with an instant arrogance.

"You must vacate this office immediately. Your entrance is not authorized." the robots said plainly as Taylor glared at them. He was still unseen and was already working hard to cyberly manipulate these robotic guards.

Nothing seemed to be happening. The robots were still advancing, and with a countdown of only a few seconds, they were taking their aim at both Tristan and Taylor, despite the fact that neither could be seen.

Was it possible that the robots were able to detect them?

Tristan was far too excited at watching these things work, and he had grown quite complacent with his stealthness to have any fear for himself, even though eminent danger was only a few seconds away. Taylor, only at the last moment turned around and realized that Jay, who had been standing behind himself and Tristan, was the actual target of the robots. He could see the panicked look on his friends face, and while pushing himself and Tristan apart, he also kinetically shoved Jay to the ground.

Tristan may have quickly lost his complacence, but it was Taylor who heaved a sigh in looking around the room and realizing how he had to watch everyone's butt, including his own. This thought was heightened when the blast from the Robot's plasma cannon caused both a fire and a good deal of smoke and, after a moment, the fire suppression system was activated.

It only took a few seconds for Taylor to realize that, with the falling water, he and Tristan were now visible.

"Ahhrgh – Great! Just great!"

He pulled his hood off quickly and with an onslaught of color, he was instantly impressed with Dr. Isaacs office. This appreciation, however, only lasted for a moment as, with his appearance, Taylor had become the newest and greatest threat in the office.

The security robots targeted their new enemy and with immediate aggression they fired. Taylor ducked and with a concentrated look the kinetically threw the two security robots through the walls of the office, creating a pair of new, albeit messy, ways to enter into Dr. Isaac's private space. Turning around, Taylor then jumped over the desk with the thought in mind that sunset must be only a few minutes away and that he and his friends had to hurry if they were going to make their escape.

Taylor jumped from where he was to the door behind the desk. Forcing it open with his telekinesis, he, Jay and Tristan made their way into Dr. Isaacs's private arboretum.

It was laid out simply, with several tall trees, plants, a park style bench and, with the glass allowing a greater than 180 degree view of the city skyline, Taylor had to take a fleeting moment to enjoy the fantastic view.

He turned his stare to the ceiling and with a focused concentration he pulled one of the plex panels from its hinge. It came down fast, almost crashing before Taylor held it firmly with a telekinetic grip and set it on the floor of the arboretum. He then looked out to the horizon and in the entire city he was at the only place where it could be seen that the last glint of sunlight was lost behind the Pacific waters. With his face, his hair, and his eyes losing that last bit of sunlight from view, Taylor held his breath.

All at once the arboretum started to grow dark. Taylor, Tristan, and Jay all looked around in panic at the sight of the giant metallic panels that were closing around the glass encased room. Taylor tried using his kinesis to keep the aperture open, but he realized instantly that each panel weighed several hundred tons, and he was unable to do much more than just slow them down. He knew better than to try anything cyberly, for the aperture itself was on a solar clock, set to close right at sunset and reopen just before sunrise – there were no wireless connections to speak of.

Shaking his head he turned to the others. “Come here, both of you, now!” he shouted, and as the two approached quickly, he stepped on the plex panel and pointed to the others that they should do the same.

Looking down at his feet he then concentrated on the plex panel and forced it to rise into the air. This was slow at first, but with an explosion of the arboretum entrance, Taylor decided it best to move things along.

So much was this speedy rise that Tristan fell when the panel was quickly nestled back into its proper place, and the boy started sliding down the sloped roof of the arboretum.

Taylor flinched, reached out his hand and with a surge of telekinesis he raised the boy high into the air and carefully set him down beside Jay.

“Honestly – and you used to live in the trees!” Taylor said in mild jest.

Jay and Tristan barely took in this comment. They were too focused in looking down at the a dozen or so security personnel making their way into the arboretum beneath them. Holding their breaths, they hoped that none of those below saw their escape into the air and wouldn’t think to check the ceiling. This proved mostly true as, for the first few seconds; none cast their eyes skyward.

When the first did, and spotted the three of them, that was all it took. They were firing relentlessly under the spot where Taylor, Tristan and Jay stood.

Fortunately for them, the enclosure over the arboretum was nearly sealed, and with Tristan and Taylor jumping to one side, and Jay jumping to the other, the three of them were now under – or rather over – the safety of nearly a foot of composite metal.

With the arboretum completely sealed off, the three of them were over a mile high in the air, and while they could feel slight vibrations beneath them, it tickled each of their spines to know that they were, at least for the next few moments, completely safe. Jay turned to Taylor, who was lying flat on his back, seemingly resting from the success of such a well oiled plan. He, Taylor, was patting the box that he had replicated, reveling in the satisfaction that he was actually able to get it out of the building. And for just a short moment he pulled the small green cloth from his pocket, rolled it in his fingers, and tucked it away again.

Just as he had seen glimpses of it out in the forest, what he had suspected would be his future, had actually come true. Here he was, at sunset, at the top of The Towers, he had what he needed, he was safe, and it was satisfying – his plan had finally come to completion.

“So this is great!” Tristan said in a disconcerted tone, “What now?”

Taylor cast his eyes skyward and, with the appearance of several streams of bright light blue veins, he had to giggle as one last minute change to his plan appeared in physical form.

Overhead the cloaked craft that Tristan and Taylor had taken into the city had revealed itself, and Jay, who was seeing it for the first time, cowered in absolute fear.

"Chin up!" Taylor said, and as the teen stood tall and firm, staring with admiration at the craft overhead, he couldn't help but arrogantly add, "She's mine! So – uh – Whaddaya think?"

Jay looked from under the hands covering his face, and he smiled at seeing that both Tristan and Taylor weren't the least bit frightened over the appearance of this – this thing.

"I'm not even going to ask!" Jay said shaking his head, and he raised himself up to a stand. He watched as, with concentration, Taylor forced the glowing craft to slowly tip its strangely shaped wing downward so that they could all easily walk on top of the craft to the overhead hatch.

Jay was all eyes and ears on entering this craft for he had never seen anything like it. He almost started laughing when he finally realized they were able to escape completely unscathed. So much for any pre-cognitive abilities he might have, he for his feelings of uneasiness and foreboding were completely misplaced.

"Sorry," Taylor said strapping himself in to the front seat in the cockpit, "but there's only seating for two – so you'll have to pull one of the jump-seats out.

"No problem!"

"So back to my place, right?" Jay half suggested with agitation.

"Uhhh – that's not such a good idea – I had something else in mind," Taylor replied suggestively, and he turned his head to look back at Jay with a half-pathic expression. He had offered a single word that made Jay cringe.

"Shannon's?"

At first Jay started shaking his head, completely unwilling to concede, but, with Taylor nodding his, and the compelling light blue stare of his eyes, eventually Jay's head started moving a new direction.

"Oh, fine – she's always looking for the next big story!"

"Story," Taylor questioned. "Story? Wait – your Shannon isn't – yes – now – oh wow – she's *that* Shannon – the newscaster for the late – late news!"

"Yeah – that's her – I didn't think anybody watched the news that late."

"I caught her that first morning when Johnny had *the vision*. Man the makeup they put on her makes her a completely different person." Taylor then paused and thought for a moment. "Well, then she'll be in for a really big treat now!"

Jay was curious about the makeup comment, but then realized that Taylor had just seen a vision of her when he grabbed the picture frame back at his apartment where she wasn't wearing any, and he had to admit, in that case, she definitely did look different.

Shifting his stare, Jay's eyes grew wide as he stared out the front window of the craft and he nodded forward for Taylor to look in the same direction. "We've got company!" Jay said, and as Taylor looked out, he could see some dozen or so police craft in front of him, and while his craft dwarfed theirs, they both knew it had little chance of winning a gun battle.

"Don't worry," Taylor said with a smile, "this bird comes with all the trimmings!"

Taylor then closed his eyes and with the instant bright glow of the craft's outer veins, he forced it into cloaking mode before diving down into the inner workings of the city. Not one craft dared follow him, for what would they follow. So, being completely unhampered in his travels through the city, the teen put as much distance between him and The Towers as possible.

Under Jay's direction Taylor headed straight for Shannon's residential building as fast as he could and, similar to the way he and Tristan entered Jay's building, the three of them did the same here, landing on the roof and using a service entrance.

With the call button being pressed at her entrance, she opened the door with uncertainty at seeing that Jay had company with him. Taylor, while only offering a smile, was keeping a firm hold on the case he had replicated back at The Towers.

"Hey, what's up? Who - who are they, and," she shifted to a whisper to end her rapid questions, "what in the world is with those outfits?"

"Is she always this nosy?" Taylor whispered loudly at Jay.

She offered a frown, pursed her lips and looked wide eyed at Jay, unwilling to budge, or let anyone enter her apartment until she got the answers she was looking for.

"This," Jay said motioning a hand to the friend at his side, "is my old, and dearest friend Taylor – Dr. Taylor, and this is Tristan – they've come back from the forest outside the city!"

Shannon's eyes lit up, "Oh, well then, in that case, come on in – where are my manners?!" She quickly opened the door wide, and despite the fact that she was clearly in the middle of watching some kind of online net program, she turned it off in lieu of having this unexpected company.

"I'm sorry I didn't call, this was kind of an emergency; very unexpected."

Taylor, and Tristan walked into the woman's living room, and the younger immediately started sniffing the air in appreciation of a strange flowery fragrance that made the room a delightfully different experience for him. Taylor put his hand on the boy's shoulder as a way to force him to sit on a small couch next to him as Jay and Shannon sat opposite.

"So what's going on?" Shannon asked of Taylor, her eyes clearly hungry for information.

"To put it simply," Taylor started, "the government found us, and they've taken the children."

"The children – you mean the..." an excitement grew in her that Taylor could actually appreciate, and as she spoke Jay put his hand on hers. "Yes, dear, the ones I used to work with – they've been taken."

The woman's face became wrought with concern, and Taylor could see in her behavior that Jay was right, she had, indeed, changed a good deal since the first time he had seen her.

She snapped her head and looked at the boy by Taylor's side. "So whose this little guy – Tristan is it?"

Tristan practically blushed from this attention while Taylor answered, "This *is*

Tristan. His mother was taken along with the children."

"And his father..." She started to ask.

"She's the only family he's got – other than me and the kids."

Tristan looked up at Taylor with a gratuitous smile.

"Anyways – let's get to the point. We're here just for a little while. I need a place to work for a few hours – then we'll be gone.

"Work – on what?" she asked.

"I'll let Jay explain that. Right now – I need to use your M-Gen."

She nodded, waved her hand in the direction of the unit, and started a private conversation with Jay, looking for the explanation she had been searching for.

Tristan was seemingly glued to Taylor's side, for the instant the older teen rose out of his seat, so did the younger. Taylor made his way to the M-Gen panel, and after his usual kinetic focus, he pulled out a large fold-up data display, and, a small stack of protobars.

"What are those for?" Tristan asked curiously.

"Here, try one," Taylor said, tossing one to the boy, and taking three for himself. Sitting down in front of Shannon and Jay, he opened them quickly so that he could devour them before beginning his work.

As Taylor practically inhaled the bars, and not without a few side comments from Shannon, the teen's mind started filling with thoughts of his children, and how much he missed them and watching them eat; David's own messy face at eating the bars, Orion and Aspen, who always took so much care in remaining spotless, Caitlin and Grace, who never really liked the taste of the bars but ate them anyways, and lastly, there was Johnny, who invariably would only eat a half a bar, and would scream with an "eaaack" as he absentmindedly stuck his hand in a now warm and mushy pocket full of soft chocolaty protobar that he had put there with the intent of eating later.

With a sigh, and welling tears, Taylor shoved the last bit of protobar into his mouth. He felt several eyes watching him as he did this. Looking across the table, he saw a bewildered trio whose expressions spoke volumes over what they thought of his emotional state, and the sympathy that they felt for him.

"Wha'?" Taylor said wiping his eyes, and thereafter his mouth.

"Man you're a pig!" Tristan said with almost a laugh in hopes of raising Taylor's spirits. "What's with all that anyways?"

"If I'm going to hook myself up to this thing, I'm going to need all the energy I can get."

Jay nodded before addressing both Tristan and Shannon. "When he hooks himself into this – this – power booster, all of his abilities – every one – is going to go absolutely nuts – So don't freak out!"

Tristan smiled at Jay, "Me – freak out! Yeah right. I don't freak out!"

Jay shook his head with a smile.

"First thing's first," Taylor mumbled, "I've got to get this thing reprogrammed. You and Jay need to help Shannon tie everything down that isn't and make sure that anything electronic is turned off – it'll be safer that way."

"What?" Shannon questioned, and as Taylor went to work with the sphere, Jay explained things to her. Jay then had Tristan help in doing as Taylor had asked.

"I wasn't kidding when I said his abilities are going to go nuts. His kinesis, his cyber, his pathic, and his cognitive powers – everything – crazy – you get it?" Jay said this while waving his arms around and Shannon both smiled, and looked around – "This is going to take some time – I've got all kinds of things that need to be protected!"

"I've got a better idea." Jay said with a smile. "Let's take anything small enough to fit in the M-Gen and break it down – that way we can store it in memory modules and have a lot less to deal with."

"Ehhh – alright. I guess that can work. She said apprehensively, and Jay, Shannon and Tristan quickly started running around the apartment grabbing all sorts of small items, knick-knacks and anything that could be taken apart to still fit in the panel.

Taylor, on the other hand was focused hard on the data display in front of him. He was reading line after line of code from the sphere, changing the protocols, and replacing all references to his children with references to himself.

He knew that the sphere wasn't designed to deal with his brain – or brain patterns. In fact, it was designed to shut down if it detected his presence. If he was going to make it work on him, practically every line of code had to be examined and changed to reflect him as a subject and not a threat.

With nearly an hour passing Taylor had just finished with the last few lines of code from the sphere, and Tristan, Jay and Shannon had all but emptied the entire apartment of its many smaller items and secured the larger ones.

To finalize his preparations, Taylor generated a neural reader for Jay before shutting the M-Gen panel down completely. He then looked at the room around him and closed his eyes. The other three were slowly filled with an eerie feeling as all the lights grew dark and with a deadening hum, everything in the apartment had turned itself off by Taylor's will.

Taylor looked around the room when he stood and he pointed at Tristan and Shannon. "You two, sit there!" he said pointing to the little couch that he himself had been sitting on just a moment before. He, though, sat in the middle of the empty floor and looked up at Jay, who was standing over him.

"I've got a few simple instructions: First – I want you to watch the neural reader constantly – I've removed its ability to take wireless commands, so it will function without interference. I've also rigged it to operate on a different frequency than the standard readers, so it won't interfere with the nanites. All that being said; if my patterns ever push over 15% in the red for more than a few seconds I want you to activate the sphere's emergency shutdown."

"That thing doesn't have an emergency shutdown?" Jay spewed.

Taylor smiled, "It does now!" Turning the sphere over, Taylor showed Jay an open panel on it that revealed a few exposed wires. "Pull these – that's the shutdown!"

Jay nodded and Taylor continued. "This shouldn't take longer than an hour according to what I've read in the programming protocols – so if it takes longer than that – by say – fifteen minutes, you'll need to shut it down!"

"I need you all to be on your toes – so when things start to happen you don't freak out on me."

Taylor then looked down at the sphere. He was about to push the activation button as he had remembered from his vision so long ago.

"Wait, wait, wait!" Jay said hastily, "One thing you haven't thought out – how are we going to get the nanites out of your head? We don't have the equipment here!"

Taylor sighed in appreciation over his friend's concern. "The nanites are benign – I'm not gonna worry about that until later. Remember – Their purpose is to improve the brain, not destroy it! Heck, they might just pass through my system naturally!"

With a deep breath, Taylor sat with his legs folded. He looked down at the sphere he was holding in his lap, and he pushed the activation button.

As Taylor had expected, the sphere's long tentacles slowly emerged and while some stayed in front of him, others seemed to wrap around him in an eerie embrace. Taylor felt a gripping nervousness as he watched the ends of the tentacles flower and prod the air with their sharp points.

Taylor had a mind to stay perfectly still, but, at the last moment he realized he had forgotten something. He, keeping his head in one place, quickly reached into his pocket. After feeling inside it for only a moment, he pulled out the small piece of green cloth and gripped it firmly with both hands.

Taylor's eyebrows rose as he watched the tentacles surround him before, with a split second of pain, they planted themselves firmly in different locations on his head.

63 Confined

OF THE SIX CHILDREN, only Johnny had ever really experienced a truly horrible headache, something that was completely foreign to the other children throughout their entire life. But as they were so young, this should be of little surprise. Taking this into consideration though, for each of these children it was quite a horrible first time experience to have as they slowly opened their eyes in a strange, small, metallic room with a very high ceiling.

Orion, with his own horribly aching head, sat stiffly upright gripping his forehead while groaning. Johnny and Aspen followed this example as, slowly, their heads also pounded more intensely by the second. Indeed, it took nearly a full minute for all of the children to come around each one offering a moan, grunt, or groan to reflect their discomfort. To add insult to injury, their bodies seemed strangely twisted, lying mismatched on top of each other so that the difficulty of trying to rise to their feet seemed to agitate the pain in their heads even further.

Johnny was the first to start smacking his lips as he got to his feet and looked around the room. The metallic taste in his mouth forced a sour look on his face as he stared at the shiny walls around him. If he could taste what he was seeing, he could be sure that this was where the flavor was coming from.

"Hey slugs, look – there's a door!" Grace said with finger pointed, and she walked to within a few inches of it and saw that it had some sort of security access panel at its side.

"'Rion, get over here!" she shouted.

The boy, still gripping his head, walked over to Grace's side. She gave him a wink and pointed at the panel.

"This's more your thing." she said with a smile.

He looked down at the panel and focused on it. "Nothing." He said sharply. This was followed by an uncertain "Maybe it's not wireless!"

Caitlin got wind of this, snapped her fingers at David, and pointed that he should check out what was going on. The boy, who was the only one that hadn't risen yet, groaned at the idea of having to get up when his head pained him so. Still, he slowly rolled over to his knees and stood with a wavering dizziness. "Woah – head rush!" He then made his way over to the door and panel. "Well, maybe we can just force it open!"

Grace and Orion split, allowing David to stand between them and take a firm stance in front of the door, focusing hard on its shiny metal surface. With a twitching of his head, the children knew that David was doing his best, but, to their amazement nothing was happening. He let out a deep breath, looked over at Aspen and waved for her to come to his side.

"Come on – together then!"

She took her place at his side, and between the two of them, they both pushed their focus to the limits, but with no avail.

A panic filled both their heads – was it possible that they were powerless.

As if the two had the same thought at the same time, David and Aspen turned to each other, and with a telekinetic blast, each one was shot across the room with fantastic force until they hit the walls on opposite sides.

"What the heck!" Johnny said making his way between the two of them – what was that for?"

The impact didn't make David or Aspen's headache feel any better and they groaned even further on getting back to their feet.

"Uhhhhggggg – Sorry Asp'."

"Likewise!" She responded rubbing her head, and with these words, Caitlin, Johnny and Grace all stood between the two of them trying to make some kind of protective wall to keep the two from hurting each other.

David stood and started making his way to the middle of the room – "Dudes, it's fine. I just wanted to see if my kinesis was still working. You know – we all have headaches – I mean hello – I just wanted to make sure *they* didn't do something to our brains!"

Aspen approached the middle of the room and added to this, "Yeah, I guess we were trying so hard on the door that we just overdid it on each other."

With the three in the middle of the room moving out of the way, David and Aspen offered each other a smile and a quick back-patted hug before looking to Orion. He, the tallest, and agreeably the smartest of the bunch, was staring at the wall where Aspen had fallen with his eyes in a concentrated focus.

All the others caught sight of this and walked up to him, wondering what had caught his attention so absolutely. Grace eventually waved her hand in front of the boy's eyes to make sure he was alright.

"Oh, don't be stupid!" he said pushing her hand out of his way.

He then walked quickly to where Aspen had made impact on the wall and pointed, "She never hit the wall. She just – well," and he made a fist and hit the wall with the side of his hand. The others watched as his hand seemingly hit an invisible layer that protected the wall, keeping him from making contact with it. The barrier only showed itself when he made contact, and with this, Orion exhaled a deep breath of understanding.

All of the other children were amazed at this, but the enthusiasm didn't last for long. In fact, it only took a few seconds of the children hitting the walls themselves to realize that they were trapped in this small room.

"This is some kind of containment field! Ahhhhgh we can't use our powers or anything!" He said hitting the wall with increasing frustration.

"That's right!" A familiar voice shouted through the air, and all of the children turned to see, opposite the door, high above them, that the face of Dr. Zeldin was staring down, looking at each of them.

"You know, you children really are quite amazing." He said, and the six of them all gathered close to each other and stared up in instant anger as they took in the fact that this was the man who nearly caused Caitlin to fall out of the transport several months back during their escape.

"I have to say," Dr. Zeldin continued, "I've seen all kinds of kinetics and cognitives like yourselves – but none were as – ummm – interesting, nor as entertaining as you guys!"

David grunted at this, stared down at his shoes, and with a deep breath, he focused on lifting himself into the air.

Dr. Zeldin almost laughed at seeing the boy rise up to his window to now stare at him at eye level.

"Very, very entertaining!" Dr. Zeldin said with almost a laugh, but David was not amused.

"Why are we here? Where are we, and what have you done with Taylor? What have you done with Delissa, and Tristan?" The boy shouted angrily.

"Well, I can't attest to your father's well being – but that wouldn't be our doing. The same goes for Tristan. But, Delissa – hmmm – she's safe – here." Dr. Zeldin waved his hand as a way of letting David know that Delissa was with them in this strange place.

"Now – to answer the most important question." Dr. Zeldin said with a voice shifting to the serious. "I and my colleagues have brought you here for two reasons. One which I can tell you, the other, I cannot.

"You are here, my children, to be trained. You are here to push yourselves to the limits. We want to see what you can really – really do with your gifts!"

"What if we don't want to?" Grace shouted upwards.

Dr. Zeldin didn't frown – he didn't smile – he merely looked down at a small panel in front of him and with the pressing of a few buttons a bright electric shock emanated from the ceiling hitting David. The boy screamed instantly, and fell from his high position, only being kept from a hard impact by the quick reaction of Aspen, who kinetically caught him only inches from the floor.

"Make no mistake my little ones – We have only two options here – work with us – or die! We aren't afraid to eliminate you from the bigger equation if we have to!"

Rushing around David, Orion, Grace, Caitlin and Johnny could see that the was actually steaming from the shock, but with a quick check, it was Grace that determined the boy to still be alive. They looked up at the glass window and started shouting vehemently in anger. This had little effect on Dr. Zeldin, who merely pushed a button to close the metallic cover over the window.

"You okay?" Johnny asked kneeling by the boy's side, pulling his brother's long blonde hair out of his face.

"Oh, I'm fine! Just a little – uhhhh sore – that's all!" David said with an aching sound to his voice, and while he was able to get to his feet, this didn't last for long as his legs gave way and he collapsed again, landing his weight on the shoulders of his two brothers.

"Easy big guy – you should stay down for a few minutes!" Orion said, letting him slowly rest to a seated position.

"Why is this happening to us?" Aspen shouted in the air, as though someone was still there to hear her.

"Like it's any surprise," Orion said loudly, "We are who we are because we were made this way – you've all heard the stories – this isn't a coincidence – It isn't their choice – it's follow up. I can feel it – there's more going on here than just an interest in kinetics and cognitives – we were made and now they want us back!"

"What are you talking about?" Aspen shouted in anger.

"Well think about it! Johnny has these weird visions of the future – the city destroyed and all. He's hooked up to this bizarre sphere that gives him extra abilities – and then, like idiots, we all take the bait."

"That couldn't have been part of any plan!" Caitlin hissed.

"Maybe not," Orion said weakly, "but if their idea was to test it out, then use it on the rest of us, we certainly made their job a lot easier didn't we?"

No one responded to this comment, and while Orion wanted to continue, all of the children were distracted by a small opening in one of the walls. The children slowly approached it with little fear, and much curiosity.

"What do you think it is?" Johnny asked, standing closest to it.

There was no time for an answer. Instead, the children were met with a quick spray of darts that flew across the room, hitting each one in the arm, leg or stomach.

They were all out cold in just a few seconds, with their last view being that of the cell's door opening and a person draped in black walking into the room.

Waking with more horrible headaches, the same terrible taste in their mouths, and the irritation of realizing they had just been knocked out again, the children woke to realize that several changes had been made to the room, and to themselves.

The clothes they had been wearing, those that they had since waking in their forest home, had been changed. Now they were in a strange set of white pajama-like outfits.

David seemed the most offended by this, patting himself up and down, vocalizing his irritation. "I've been changed – someone changed my clothes – uhhhhggg is nothing sacred anymore!"

The children also noticed a new object inside the metallic room with them. This, a large metal rectangular box that Orion quickly measured at two meters tall and one meter to each side, had a strange button on one face.

The boy sneered. He instantly had his suspicions about the nature of this object considering its size. As such, he walked up to the box, pushed its button, and, expectedly, one side of it opened to reveal a small lavatory.

Aspen looked in and turned up her nose instantly. "I'm not using that thi..."

She barely had time to get the words out before Johnny practically pushed her over in making his way inside the unit and pulling the door closed behind him.

"Apparently," Orion said with a smile, "some of us aren't as discriminating!"

"Apparently!" Aspen scoffed, and when Johnny had finished his visit to the new, though exceedingly small bathroom, each of the other children stared at it with an ever growing envy. Eventually, one by one, they each gave in to the call of their bodies and, with Aspen being the last, they each felt a sense of relief.

"Well, it's nice to have a bathroom and all," David said with a smile, "But I'm starving."

"What would you like?" asked a voice in the air, and as the children looked up, they could see that, once again, the window above them was exposed.

They could see that the woman inside, wearing a deep blue cloak, was speaking to them through a microphone and as such David made no haste in making demands over what he wanted to eat.

"Mmmmm – Cheeseburger – Fries, Pizza, and a chocolate Protobar!" He shouted; his appetite increasing with each called item.

The woman pushed a few buttons on the panel in front of her, which caused David to slowly well with fear, and, with a bright flash of color in the room, the boy practically fell backward in shock, but this was his own doing, for in front of him was a large plate with everything he had asked for.

"And to drink my boy?"

David, who, of the six, had the worst table manners looked up from the plate in front of him. "A Choglak Milg Pleashe"

The boy barely flinched the second time, and in front of him, his request appeared in another bright flash.

"Anyone else care to place an order?" She asked politely.

With a series of bright flashes and an onslaught of food appearing on the floor of the small room, the children were able to slowly get all the food they wanted. All, except for Grace, that is. She felt anger welling inside her over the fact that they were still being kept in this cell against their will.

"I don't want any friggin' food. I want to get the hell out of here!"

All of the other children looked up at her, amazed at her anger and her use of language.

"Grace, Behave!" Caitlin said looking up from her own plate of food.

"No! I will not behave. There's no reason for me to behave! I'm not going to eat when they say chow down, go to the bathroom when they say pee, or jump when they say jump. There's no reason for it. We've done nothing wrong – we're children – and we have rights!"

"Grace – you saw what happened to David! Now sit down and tell the woman what you want to eat!" Orion said firmly. With his words, the boy was voicing telepathic comments into Grace's mind to add to his rhetoric.

"If we cooperate – maybe we can find a way out of here – don't make it difficult – make them *think* they've won! We're powerful and we will find a way out! Now sit down – be pissed off – but be nice!"

Her eyebrow perked at this and she almost lit a smile. Orion was, indeed, the wiser, and his idea actually made sense. But with another quick message, from him her frown returned.

"Don't get happy for goodness sakes – you're supposed to be mad. Sit down in a huff, and work your way into it, otherwise you'll obvious!"

"Fine!" Grace huffed, and after marching harshly to a place between two of her brothers, she slumped to the floor.

"I'll have some burritos – beef – and a glass of milk."

When they all had finished their meal a bright flash took away the used plates and utensils, and with nothing to do children then started looking at each other in a curious expectation of what was going to happen next.

Aspen, who was sitting next to David though, had one observation to make. "David – you're a mess!" She said looking at the boy's food covered face and newly stained attire. "If you don't want them to keep *changing* you, you might want to keep yourself a little more – uh – tidy!"

"Fine!" The boy said, and he reached over to her, grabbed a loose bit of her sleeve, and wiped his mouth on it.

"Eaaaagh! Disgusting!" She squealed and she looked to her siblings for some kind of reprimand for this behavior. It was clear, though, that her other brothers and sisters got a huge kick out of it, and as far as reprimands, there were none.

While the children were, indeed, settling themselves down over their confinements, the many questions running through their minds helped keep them from getting too comfortable. Questions like where they were, how long they had been there, where Taylor was, and why he hadn't yet saved them from all of this.

64 Missing Taylor

WITH BOREDOM SLOWLY SETTING IN, the children perked to see that the door to their cell had opened. The blue-cloaked woman they had seen before had walked in with a bright shining smile on her face. Her light brown hair was down and free-flowing, and with a small nose and only a bit of make-up on her face she, indeed, looked quite beautiful.

She had a small pad in her hand that she tapped while standing at the doorway, and in the middle of the room, between all of the children, a chair appeared with a bright flash. She then pushed another button, and started walking into the room. The children were shocked and a bit dismayed to see that around this new guest, an electric type of shield slowly followed her until she sat down.

With this kind of entry, they knew that their boundaries were never turned off, and that, at least at this point, a way out had not easily presented itself.

The woman in blue tapped one button to force the field around her to release her and bounce back into the wall, and with one last button on the pad in front of her she turned the handheld unit off.

The children, standing around her quietly, all wondered if they should do anything to try and escape or not. Their thoughts were running rampant about how, with this tight security, they could ever get out.

"Hmmm – I do think it's a bit early to be thinking about that, don't you Orion! Escaping now – before you really find out all the truths you've been searching for – hmmm – maybe later – but not now!"

Orion frowned, "I wasn't – how did you – that's not possible."

"Why not?" She asked softly, giving him a smiling stare. "Dr. Taylor reads your stray thoughts all the time – he can even pick up some of those you'd like to keep from him. It's a gift that not many people have. But me, I can read everything – even more than he can – it's something you learn – with good practice..."

"So before you plan some elaborate escape again, Johnny," she said turning to the boy at her other side, "You might want to know how you could use this gift too."

"I don't," the boy muttered, but the woman in blue turned in her seat and interrupted his response.

"Oh but you do my child. Each of you, like Dr. Taylor, does. But yours is the strongest – I can tell."

She then turned to the group of children in front of her. "Anyways – Enough with the small talk, I've been sent here to answer any questions you might have. This, some hope, will help you feel more relaxed, become more trusting – and maybe, just maybe – you'll see that what we're trying to do here is actually for the greater good." The woman in blue was looking each child in the eye and, keeping her mind clear, she spoke with a paternal sound in her voice that made each of the children slowly reach some level of calm.

She turned her stare to Caitlin, and with a smile, she addressed and answered an unspoken question.

"My name, little Caitlin, is Elizabeth, or as I am known around here, Miss E." she paused at this answer, and on reading the girl's thoughts, she added. "Oh, just like your second middle name, that's alright. But I think it would be best if you just call me Miss E. like everyone else."

"Well my father says," Grace started arrogantly, but, as usual, the woman now known to the children Miss E., and who they all felt, just to annoy her, that they would never call her by that name, cut off her words.

"I know, I know, you want to know my age..."

She finished these words and the children, who seemed very receptive to Elizabeth at first, suddenly offered her a cold, almost angry stare.

"Quite right, quite right!" Elizabeth added in a high pitched voice, "It is rude of me not to let you at least finish your questions. Well, anyways – I am two hundred fourteen years old."

The children gasped at hearing this, and Johnny was the first to spurt out, "That's not possible – you're a fibber – nobody's ever lived that far past two hundred!"

"One might think so!" She said with a smile, and she let the accusation Johnny had made just roll off her without even a thought.

"I and the other members of the Evol Crew are the only ones in the world infected with a mutated version of the Methuselah virus that, as of yet, offers an indeterminably long lifespan."

There was a silence that overtook the room, and it was clear that the children were both digesting this information, and trying to determine for themselves if what they were hearing was true. Orion quickly responded with the first question of doubt.

"How come the rest of the world doesn't have this *version* of the virus?"

Elizabeth, who was now the center of attention for this half-circle of children that were all sitting on the floor, smirked and pointed her finger in Orion's direction. "Boy, you are the smart one aren't you? Well, this virus is too delicate to survive in the air, so it can't infect the rest of the planet's population. So, well, I guess I'm the lucky one."

"Indeed!" Aspen bellowed with a smile.

"On a serious note," Orion started as he made his way to his feet, "I have some very important questions to ask."

As Orion finished these words he could see that his brothers and sisters on either side all offered a wide eyed stare. *Why should he spoil such a simple and pleasant conversation with something serious?*

Caitlin, David, and Aspen all shook their heads at this and merely listened as the boy listed out what he wanted to know.

"What are we doing here? Why were we taken from *father?* Does this have anything to do with the fact that we're genetically engineered? Why not include him in whatever's going on, and will we ever see him again?" As Orion finished this last question he watched as his brothers and sisters were now nodding their head, agreeing to this line of questioning. Turning back to Elizabeth, Orion smiled and continued. "These are all questions that, I think, we are owed an answer to, and, if you're smart, you would think it strange if we didn't ask them."

Elizabeth. looked at Orion, who had counted his questions on one hand to make sure he asked each one, and she smiled in watching him sit down again.

"I will answer these questions as best I can, but you must realize that even I cannot give you all the answers you are looking for."

"Is that because you don't know the answers, or just because you don't want to give them?" Grace asked.

Elizabeth's eyebrows raised and she nodded her head, "A little bit of both really." She said high pitched and smiling. "But I'll tell you what I can." She turned and gave each of the children a quick look in the eye and started.

"You are here to be trained on how to use your abilities – and use them well. Even your new ones!"

"Father says we're not supposed to use our new abilities unless someone's there to help!" Johnny quickly interrupted.

"Ah yes," Elizabeth responded. "That's a very smart idea. But here, we'll be prepared for anything – so you can rest assured – we *want* to see what you can do, even if it's uncontrolled or considered dangerous." At these last words Elizabeth's voice grew dark and raspy as she leaned over to engage the children, who all turned amongst themselves and smiled while she continued.

"Now, I can't say why it was decided that your father couldn't join in assisting your training, but I can say that soon, very soon in fact, you will see him again. So relax – when the time comes – you'll be together again as a family!"

Johnny, of all of the children, felt his heart leap inside his chest with absolute joy from hearing these words, and while he nudged his siblings to see if they had the same reactions, it was clear that no one felt this emotion as strong as he. Elizabeth couldn't help but feel this overflowing emotion from the boy, and she offered him a wide smile in return. "That's right, Johnny, you'll all be back as a family in no time – but the easiest way for this to happen is if you just cooperate with us."

Elizabeth shifted in her seat as she looked around at the children and with a grabbing of her cloak she slowly stood and rewrapped herself in it.

"Well, I think it's about time that I take my leave. I've got other things I have to do. You know, busy, busy, busy, always very busy! But if you have any other questions – I'll be around." She smiled, looking up at the covered window above before glancing down at David. She offered him a quick scrubbing on the head. The boy returned this with a grinning stare before turning away in blushing embarrassment.

Elizabeth walked to the entrance of the small metallic room, and with the control panel in her hand; she pushed a few buttons and turned to walk out.

"Miss E.!" Orion said loudly across the room, calling her by the name she preferred. He then stood and made a short sprint in her direction. "Miss E. You didn't answer one of my questions?"

She turned around and looked down at the boy, "Oh, which question was that?"

"The one about our being 'engineered'. Our being here, is it because we were engineered – constructed for some purpose?"

"Oh sweetie – what makes you think you were *engineered?*"

"Honestly, like you'd even have to ask that question. There are six of us, all the same age. We've been genetically tested – were all brothers and sisters, that much is certain, but on top of that we were all gifted at an extraordinarily early age that didn't match our development, and, if that isn't enough for you, consider the fact that our gifts are very specific and defined. Of course we were engineered; no mother, no father, just some unknown lab somewhere, some concoction of biological matter. That's what we are!"

"Oh, my, this is the first I've heard of this." She said softly, and in watching the boy's face grow a look of sad distress, she reached out and touched him delicately on the cheek, then ran her fingers lightly through his raven black hair. "I wish I could give you an answer to that question, but I just - I don't know. I'll look into it though, and if I can, I'll tell you what I find out."

Orion smiled, rubbed his face on her fingers softly, and as he did this his eyes grew wide, as if almost with fear. After a few seconds he slowly pulled his face away from her hand. She didn't see this change in his expression, for she merely turned to the open exit and left without a word.

Orion, though, reached out to touch her on the shoulder and found that his fingers were met with the same strange electric field that ensured their confinement. Elizabeth could sense this effort, though, and she turned around to look at Orion.

The boy only smiled and offered a soft, "Thank you," to which Elizabeth simply nodded, turned around and walked out.

After the door behind her closed Orion quickly wiped his face of the touch of Elizabeth in what appeared to be anger and frustration. He then looked to his siblings and said only one softly spoken, yet daunting word to express the result of his short conversation with her at the doorway.

"Interesting!" he said rubbing his chin, his eyes closing to thin little slits, "very interesting."

"I know that look," Grace said as she approached her brother, "What's going on in that little head of yours?"

Orion looked at his brothers and sisters and with a telepathic focus he fed all of them the same message. He didn't want his words to be recorded, but he still wanted to offer what he had just discovered to them.

"I don't think I have to tell you this – but it's pretty obvious that she was lying when she said it was the first she had heard – you know – of us being engineered."

His brain was flooded with the telepathic voices of his siblings:

"Oh yeah!" – Aspen.

"Big Liar!" – David.

"I wouldn't trust a word she says!" – Caitlin.

"What a fibber!" – Johnny.

"She can't fool us!" – Grace.

"What she didn't know was that I was testing her," Orion transmitted, and he watched as all of the other's faces lit up. "That's right, testing her. I worked myself up all to an upset look and she touched me – actually touched me!"

"So she can touch you. Big deal, didn't you touch her too?" Grace queried?

"No, I didn't. I just tapped the field around her. She didn't feel a thing."

"So how did you keep her from knowing what you were doing – you know – testing her and all?" David asked.

"Didn't have to – she may be strong, but even she can't read thoughts through the field they've created to keep us under control."

"Dude, that's great and all, but what does it mean?" David asked shaking his head.

Orion would have responded, but he watched as the youngest, Johnny, made his way away from the group to sit in the corner of their small confinement. Lowering his head in frustration, the boy even went as far as to lean against the walls, causing a strange wave like flux to pulse across two of the room's surfaces.

Speaking verbally, Orion put his hand on his younger brother's shoulder. "What's up Johnny?"

"Nuthin'! Leamee alone!" the boy spewed telepathically.

Orion heard these words in his head and he could feel, as if they had tagged along, the emotions that came with them. Johnny was worried, upset even, over the possibility of messing things up. He already missed Taylor beyond words, and if cooperation would guarantee that he could see Taylor again, then he would play no part in a plot or plan that might threaten this.

Orion may not have picked up this much detail in the emotions he was reading from Johnny, but he inferred a good portion of it. He immediately reached out and with both hands he held his younger brother gently by the arms. Putting his forehead to the back of Johnny's head, he communicated telepathically.

"Johnny – again – you can't trust that woman as far as you could throw her." At this Orion could hear telepathic sneers, and he looked over his shoulder to see curious defiant stares from both Aspen and David. "Whatever," he retorted.

"She's only told you what you want to hear so you'll do what she wants. She can't be trusted. She just can't! You remember what you saw when you and Caity were pulled out of your sleep the morning before we were caught. Father can't be with us – it just wasn't possible – isn't that what you said they said?"

Johnny looked up from his knees, his face latent with tears. "I just want to go home. I want my father, and I want to get out of here that's all!" he said sadly.

"Aaarg" Orion grunted at seeing the boy's tears, "I know, I know, we all do, but crying won't get you there, so stop being such a baby!" At saying these words Orion felt a push at his side, making him fall over with a loud thud that echoed through the room.

"What's wrong with you?" Caitlin voiced harshly. "If the boy wants to cry, then let him cry. Like father says – he's got good reason to cry, so just let him!"

"Sorry," Orion transmitted, "I just think we all need to be strong right now – tears aren't going to help and we need to see if we can work out some kind of plan or something before we run out of time. That's all I'm saying!"

Caitlin stared at Orion, half with distaste, half with understanding. "No offense, 'Rion, but you've got the sensitivity of a rock! You need to lighten up. I mean, unless I'm mistaken – we've got nothing but time here!"

"Yeah, well, you didn't see what I did!"

"And what did you see?" Caitlin asked almost rudely.

"This place, these people, they're up to no good – They don't care if they practically kill us, as long as they get what they want! I'm not going to be specific, but if we don't get out of here soon, we may not make it out at all!"

"Stop it! Just stop it!" Caitlin said loudly at trying her best to calm her brother; a task that was becoming exceedingly difficult with Orion's words. She looked down at Johnny and starting humming a tune that was ever familiar to him. One that Taylor had hummed before, to help calm his nerves.

Slowly, her humming turned to words that Aspen joined in by singing, and as the soft lullaby came out, one by one the other children chimed in.

I love you
In the darkness of the night
You are safe.
Ah, yes, I adore you
Never leave my sight.
I assure you
I'll always be there by your side.

I love you
When you're lonely and alone
You'll be loved
Because I'm with you
You're always more than one
Your heart hides two,
Inside there's me and you!

I love you
When you think you can't go on
Just know that I am here
You've already won

My heart I fear
My dear
I'm here
I love you.

While the children were pausing, smiling almost to laughter and about to restart this simple song again, none seemed to notice the ever familiar opening at one side of the room. They had just started the first line, now with Johnny joining in, when a sharp and calculated prick at each one forced the song to stop immediately, and an unwelcome sleep took over the minds of each of the children.

65 Visions Inside Visions

"WHERE ARE THEY – where have you taken them!" David yelled.

He was the first to wake, and it seemed that his body was getting used to whatever drug it was that had knocked out all of the children. The headaches and metallic flavor were mild in comparison to previous experiences and it was for these reasons that David was actually able to get to his feet and immediately lift himself to the high, yet covered window near the top of the small room. He started hitting and hammering field that protected the metallic surface, despite the pain it inflicted on his hands, and he continued to yell.

"I know you can hear me. So open up! I wanna see my brother and sister now!"

David's ranting was quite purposeful, for on opening his eyes, he immediately accounted for, and realized the absence of Caitlin and Johnny.

"Your screaming isn't going to do any good!" Orion shouted, staring up at his brother while massaging his own temples. He too realized that he was missing a brother and a sister, but rather than panic, he rationalized what was happening.

"There's nothing to worry about!" Orion shouted. "They took 'em 'cause they're cognitives. They're safe – no harm can come to anybody through those gifts.

Aspen forced herself to rise by David's side. "Come on David, there's nothing you can do here. Just relax and wait it out! Everything's going to be fine!"

David offered his sister a stare that showed only the utmost of contempt that he had for their captors. Shaking his head, he lowered himself to the floor, took a firm stance in front of Orion, who was still making efforts to bring Grace out of her rest.

"You wanted to think up a plan – so let's think up a plan!" David said to Orion pathically.

Orion, however, was still distracted by Grace, who hadn't yet opened her eyes.

He sat with his legs folded in front of him and her head in his lap, trying with increasing panic to pathically wake her from inside her own mind. Closing his eyes he focused on her thoughts, trying hard to find what it was that was keeping her from coming out of this drug induced sleep.

He started to lower his forehead to hers when, quite unexpectedly, she opened her eyes and sat full upright, making her head smack hard into his.

"Oh man!" he shouted, and she did the same. Both were now rubbing what was sure to be the location of new healthy bumps on the noggins.

"Couldn't you have just smiled and sat up slowly or something like that!"

"Sorry!" Grace bellowed, and she finally brought herself, though quite unsteadily, to her feet. "One second I was with Caity and Johnny, and the next I was staring at you – no offense, but it kina scared the crap out of me."

"That's not possible!" Orion said loudly, and he waved his arms around the room. They're not here."

She shook her head, "I know what I saw. I saw Caity and Johnny."

Orion shook his head just the same. "If they're outside, then you can't communicate with them because they're out there and where in here!"

"I know what I saw, dork!" she retorted loudly. "They were," she paused and bit her lip. "They were in a vision with the rest of us – but we were back in the forest – and I saw them, I talked to them, and they..."

"It's just not possible!" Orion cut in, and he turned his stare to Aspen and David. "Could one of you please tell her that *that* is just not possible?"

Grace started pacing the room and thinking pathically aloud both for her and for her siblings to hear.

"You say it's not possible because of the barrier. But I say it is, so help me out here – if we can get that kind of communication from the outside – then there must be a leak."

"A leak?" David asked.

"Yeah, a leak!" Grace persisted, and she continued to pace the room, with Orion watching her every move.

Finally frustrated with entertaining the impossible idea of *a leak* in their room, Orion sat in front of David and with a concentrated stare he thought to himself that it would be best to take advantage of the time they had to actually work out some kind of escape plan, but the two weren't in their telepathic link for less than five seconds before the doors opened and Caitlin and Johnny were seen at the entrance, visibly tired and worn down. They were brought in by a familiar looking man wearing a green cloak.

The arriving brother and sister pair were clearly conscious, but were bound by a telekinetic hold that was obviously in place to keep them in line. With rough disregard, the man in green forced them into the center of the room, and after they had stumbled their way there, he released his kinetic hold.

The other children stared at the man cloaked in green with both anger, and fear, so it wasn't without a dropping feeling in their gut that David and Aspen, watched his finger point in their direction before firmly stating "You're next, let's go!"

Before David stood he cast a stare in Orion's direction.

The look told Orion enough of what David's ideas were, and with a quick return message of "now isn't the time," David knew that it wouldn't be appropriate to resist the man cloaked in green.

In walking past his sister, David looked at Caitlin, concerned that her weary state would explain at least to some degree, that whatever was about to happen to Aspen and himself, it would be exhausting. She noticed this stare, and with her own telepathic message, she spoke to him.

"Do whatever it takes – try to find out where we are – there's no field outside the door!"

David smiled at this, but his stare was interrupted by a kinetic push from the man in green. David turned with a frown, and in response he slowly, at a speed that highly irritated the man in green, made his way out of the small confining room with Aspen at his side. Just at exiting the room, the man in green held a firm grip on each of their shoulders as they walked. He wanted to push the pair at a faster pace, but David resisted. The boy had a habit that, anytime someone forced him to do something he didn't want to do, he would always take his time in doing it. He, for that reason, had his own little motto; one that he had no problem quoting.

"I have no reason to make you think I'm willing or enthusiastic. You might get the wrong idea – That I like it!" There were times that saying this horribly frustrated Taylor, but even he had to admire the logic, and David was sure he'd receive Taylor's approval in this case.

With one more step, the three of them finally, and not without gruff jeers from the man in green, made it outside the room, causing the door to the children's cell to close.

Orion rushed on Caitlin and Johnny. "Are you guys okay? What did they do?"

Caitlin sat slowly and looked in Grace's direction, "Why don't you ask her? She was there!"

Orion turned his head and offered an excited and yet apologetic stare at Grace, who stuck out her tongue and sassily offered an "I told you so!" to his absolute irritation. He then looked back at Caitlin and, shaking his head, he smiled, "I'm not asking *her*, I'm asking you – what happened – *show* me everything!"

She looked over at Johnny, who had fallen asleep in the matter of a few seconds. "He did most of the work – poor guy," She whispered, and with a nervous and unsteady glance, she shifted her eyes about the tiny room until she could no longer ignore the fact that Orion was staring at her quite expectantly.

"Come on. Show me!" the boy pressed.

"Oh, fine," Caitlin grunted before whispering, "I hate it when he's right – he's just as bad as father."

Orion looked confused and at this Caitlin sighed, "Johnny knew you'd be doing this – he told me." Orion himself was a little intrigued at hearing that his actions could be predicted. Orion shook his head of these thoughts quickly and watched in anticipation as Caitlin focused on him, trying to offer an account of what had happened outside their confinement.

Though he didn't close his eyes, Orion's vision grew slowly dark and, after a few seconds it lit up again. He could see himself staring upward at several passing lights. He was lying flat on his back. He tried moving his hands and legs, but there was no use – he realized with the pain of his struggles that they were tied down. He could also tell that, as Caitlin was offering him the vision of what had happened, she was doing it from a first person perspective. He wasn't looking down on Caitlin, observing her actions. No – he *was* Caitlin.

His eyes looked wildly around and he could see to either side of him a familiar looking woman in a black cloak, and a man that he hadn't seen before – this one dressed in a white cloak. Orion could at least make some sense of what they might be doing – Caitlin was, after all, a post cognitive and, with a little message sent by her from outside the vision, Orion was told that the man in white was actually a pre-cog.

He barely had time to take in the hall Caitlin was being wheeled through when, with a whirl of movement, she was placed inside a different room and, after a few seconds he saw that Johnny had been wheeled in by her side. On seeing this, two emotions overwhelmed Orion instantly. He knew that these were not his emotions, but that of his sister. In her place he felt her relief of knowing that she wasn't alone, and yet she was still afraid for her younger brother.

"Johnny! Johnny!" he heard his sister's voice call to his brother.

Johnny's head rolled to the side, "Hey 'Rion – glad you could make it!"

"What are you talking about," Orion heard his sister's voice say – "have you gone crazy?"

"Caity – I'm talking to 'Rion now – he's there," she turned her head and looked to her other side, but saw no one.

"No, no – he's there, inside your head – you're showing him what you see – or at least you will!"

Caitlin shook her head and offered a screwed up and overly perplexed expression. "What!" she said loudly, and with her voice echoing through the room they were in, Johnny offered a soft "shhhh!" as the man in white walked between the two of them.

"Hello Johnny – Caitlin how are you doing today?" the man in white asked politely.

Both instantly started struggling with their wrist and ankle straps. "We'd be doing a lot better," Caitlin said sternly, "if we weren't tied down."

"Ah yes!" The man in white said, and with a quick button on each of the different beds, the straps released themselves. Both Caitlin and Johnny sat up immediately and started rubbing their wrists from pain. Offering a scowling stare at the man in white, Caitlin felt her anger, and her telekinesis rise.

The man in white, whose back was turned on the pair, was opening some sort of container. As he did this he looked over his shoulder. "I may not have the telepathic abilities of Miss E., so I'll offer you little ones a simple warning. Don't even think of doing anything you might later regret. This place is being watched – eyes everywhere!" The man finished his words in a mysterious whispering tone, and after his words, he turned around. He was holding two strange objects that neither of the children recognized.

His words hadn't fallen on deaf ears, however, for Caitlin worked hard to suppress her anger and her eyes looked curiously at what the man in white was holding.

"This is the first of a series of tests for you two. Now I know, Caitlin, that you weren't originally a pre-cognitive. I know, however, that you, like your brother, should be predisposed to this talent. Together, I want to see what you can read from these objects."

Caitlin pulled herself away and stared up at the man in white with harshly questioning eyes.

"Name, and age?" She said stiffly, to which the man stared at her with a curious and confused expression.

"Excuse me?" he asked with a haughtily arrogant tone.

"We're not doing anything until you tell us what you're name is, and how old you are."

"Fine!" The man said with a deep irritated sigh, "I suppose that would only be proper." His eyes shifted between the two, who were sitting up on either side of him, "My name is Stewart, and I am 215 years old. I'm a pre-cog if want to know that too..."

Johnny turned to Stewart, "We already knew you were a pre-cog – remember – you pulled us out of our sleep!" The boy paused, then turned his head to Caitlin, "but I don't know if you knew that or not, 'Rion?" he pathically sent her, and while she shook her head in confusion at this message, Orion was tickled that Johnny could be so smart, and so confusing at the same time.

"Ah yes," Stewart responded nodding his head, "Well, now that we've got that out of the way. Let's see what you can do. This is strictly a test of your pre-cog abilities. We've had both of these pieces electromagnetically blocked for post-cog reading, so any efforts to move in the wrong direction won't work – you'll just see blackness. I want you to concentrate hard and see what you can do to predict what's in the future for these!"

He thrust out the strange objects to both Caitlin and Johnny. They stared at these, confused as to what they were. One of the objects looked like some kind of strange helmet – but it seemed far too large to be designed for a normal head. It was, in fact, twice the size of a normal human head, and when Johnny reached out to grab this, he could feel that it was exceedingly heavy. He placed it on the bed beside himself with a heaving breath as Stuart approached with several small wireless transmitters.

Caitlin, who had grabbed her own object of interest, a strange metallic rod with a series of odd and unrecognizable markings, felt it carefully, trying her best to see what the future of this strange thing might hold.

Johnny stared at his oversized helmet with a curious, almost playful expression. He was intrigued by the design of this helmet, with its large semi-rigid spikes that poked out in all direction. He also noticed what looked like a recognizable set of white veins that ran over it with a familiar design. More than anything, though, the boy was sure that if anyone actually put the thing on, they would definitely look very intimidating.

With a sigh of irritation, Johnny waited as Stuart hooked up the boy's head with several transmitters so as to record his neural activity, during which Johnny was careful not to touch the helmet until he was told.

Caitlin was far less patient. She kept feeling her piece, touching it carefully and intently, trying her best to see the future, to get an impression – something – anything.

Orion knew at one point that she thought she was channeling a vision, but when her view only revealed a strange black barrier, they both realized that she wasn't moving in the right direction. She grunted and when she opened her eyes she could see that Stuart had started connecting her with the same type of wireless neural readers that had been put on Johnny.

With grunts and heaves of frustration she tried again to concentrate on the large metal rod, but she couldn't help her own smiling or becoming instantly distracted by Johnny. Once he had been given the go ahead, the boy actually put the oversized helmet on his own head. She stood up, walked over to him, and with a giggle she waved a free hand in front of him. His eyes were not open, so she knew he couldn't see what she was doing. Or at least that's what she thought!

She turned her head when she heard a beeping come from a machine at Johnny's side, and she watched as a peak in his neural activity grew higher and higher. Stuart, the man in white, who was also focused on the display, looked to Caitlin when she let out a quick scream.

Johnny had reached up and grabbed her by the hand, and with almost a shock, she closed her eyes and rode a pathic wave into the boy's pre-cognitive vision of the future.

For Orion, who was still reliving the experiences of Caitlin through her pathic connection, this was a first. He actually followed her into a vision offered through Johnny. His view was clouded at first, but when it had finally become clear, he could see and feel the large, bright sun shining on his face.

Looking around, he could see that, as he was familiar with it, he was in the middle of the ruins of the Los Angeles Metroship. He looked across the barren, smoky rubble and could see his younger brother standing off in the distance.

"Johnny!" Orion could hear Caitlin's voice yell, and with this she ran toward the boy as fast as she could.

Her approach was immediately slowed when she was distracted by a large craft flying overhead, casting a dark, foreboding shadow over them. The speed of Caitlin's running again picked up in a rush, and when she reached her brother she held him close in an embrace, fearful for what was going to happen next.

Johnny looked up into her eyes, and while he could see a look of absolute terror on her face, his showed nothing but absolute calm.

"It's just a vision – remember – it's just a vision – take it in – there's no point in having them if we can't learn from them," the boy said calmly.

With the large craft drawing ever closer, Caitlin closed her eyes, giving Orion the inability to see what was going on around himself. Still, Orion could hear the crashing and thudding noises of something large impacting the ground all around him.

Out of terror, or out of curiosity, Caitlin finally opened her eyes. She looked around and could see nothing. The craft overhead was forcing a whirl of dirt and debris into the air, yet, the noises, which she continued to hear, seemed to have no source. She cast her eyes downward to look at her brother. She could see that Johnny hadn't closed his eyes at all. In fact, he was staring at the ground, thoroughly concentrating on something. Looking out to the ground herself, Caitlin, and thereby Orion, could see a strange series of impacted footprints – very large footprints – that were making their way ever closer to where they were standing.

Having seen a working cloaking technology before, Caitlin again closed her eyes and screamed with the realization that something large, something invisible, something that wasn't friendly, was approaching them from all sides. She held her brother even more tightly out of fear, and while he was struggling to free himself, both were quite surprised to hear – nothingness.

Indeed, the craft, the swirling windy noises it made, the thuds from the unseen things around them – it all went quiet.

With a gripping hand on her shoulder, Caitlin flinched and stiffened. She was absolutely terrified.

"Shhhh. Caity – it's me!" she heard a familiar voice say, and it was clear to all three; Caitlin, Johnny, and Orion, who the voice belonged to.

"Father!" Johnny shouted. "What are you doing here?"

Caitlin had opened her eyes, and smiled instantly at seeing Taylor's familiar face. "I thought you were..."

Johnny grabbed his sister by the shoulder and pulled her away from the newest member in this vision. His face had quickly frowned and he stared at Taylor, who was wearing the ever familiar cloaking suit.

"Is he from now – or is he from the future?" Johnny asked, and in response, Caitlin could only shrug her shoulders.

"Not that it makes a big difference, but I'm from now!" Taylor shouted.

"How do we know that?" Johnny replied sassily.

"Uh – two things – I wouldn't be answering your questions – and I just entered your vision a few seconds ago – I saw you both, in some lab – with a strange helmet on your head."

As Taylor said these words, he could see his children's faces light up with relief and happiness. Johnny, who had missed Taylor so much through their ordeal, rushed up to him offering a waist-high hug.

"I miss you!" the boy squealed pulling his tear covered face back, "we all mss you!"

"I know, I know. I'm trying to find you!" So tell me, where have they taken you?" Taylor asked firmly, kneeling down in front of both Johnny and Caitlin.

"We don't know father. They have some sort of energy field keeping us using any of our powers. No telepathy, no visions – nothing.

"Hmmm – well you're not in the field now – that much is true. You should do what you can to figure out where you are – you know – while you're out. If I can catch up with you later maybe you can give me some idea!" The boy nodded, and he watched as Taylor cast his eyes skyward with a flinch.

"Uh oh. I think they know I'm here. Time to make myself scarce!"

Johnny leaped forward and put his hands around Taylor's neck. "Don't go father! Don't go!"

These words did little to change Taylor's mind. But he looked between Johnny and Caitlin with an expression that neither had ever seen before it was almost sad, but still affectionate – but after a moment, the teen smiled.

"I'll be back soon – you just watch out for your brother!"

Taylor then took a double take at Caitlin. "Is - is that you 'Rion?" He asked curiously.

"No!" Caitlin said, but Orion, who was still watching all of this like some kind of first person spectator, was shouting inside his own head in the hopes that Taylor would hear his thoughts.

Taylor shook his head, reached out, and put his hand on the girl's forehead.

"I'm here, I'm here! I'm inside her head," Orion shouted. "I'm trying to see things and get some idea of where we are and what's going on."

After a few seconds Taylor pulled his hand back. "That's my boy! You just figure out everything you can – I'm counting on you! I'm counting on all of you!" he said shifting his stare to Johnny and back to Caitlin again, "any help is better than nothing – so do what you can!"

Taylor stood to full height and smiled at Johnny, "I will be back soon – for real – I promise! Oh, I love you all so much – let the others know I'll be seeing them too!"

Taylor then stood and, in a fleeting second, he was gone – vanished from the vision, and at that moment the noise from the vision that had paused itself recommenced. Caitlin now had little fear of the approaching, yet unseen and unknown that had surrounded them. Now she had fully taken in the fact that this was a vision, and like all visions, even if death came – it wasn't the end.

"I can't wait to tell the others!" She said smiling, though this seemed a bit odd considering their circumstance, for if it were real, there would be little to smile about.

Both Johnny and Caitlin felt nothing of pain by way of the ending of their vision, this was because, for some reason, whatever it was that was pounding their way around the children had absolutely no interest in them. *Of course!* In an instant they both rationalized that this vision was object oriented – so they were unseen in this version of the future – because they didn't exist.

Caitlin closed her eyes, and in thinking hard on what she was holding in her hands, she tried to pull herself into her own vision of the future. With any luck she'd be able to pull herself into a different vision that Taylor might be able to enter into. She thought hard, concentrated, even contorting her face in physical reality at the labors of trying, but she quickly realized that her efforts weren't working.

Frustrated, she let out a grunt, but the boy at her side only smiled. "Caity –

don't try so hard. Just relax – here – let me show you."

He put one hand on her forehead, and the other held her hand, the hand that, in reality, was still holding onto the strange rod she had been given. Caitlin closed her eyes – she wasn't sure what was happening, but with a swirl of white, she could feel her mind approaching some strange misty tunnel. Much to her surprise, she actually flew through this tunnel and found her vision completely lit up in white before, with a closing and opening of her eyes, she revealed a dark, familiar looking patch of forest. In the background she could hear water running, and she could smell freshly prepared food. Feeling a tight grip on her had, Caitlin realized that Johnny was still by her side.

"Good job. Good job!" the boy said.

With a laughing sound, the two quickly whirled around and felt overjoyed at seeing Taylor, Jay, and their other four siblings, along with future versions of themselves, all playing in the forest. Caitlin and Johnny approached the group and, in looking at themselves, the two couldn't help but playfully criticize their own appearance.

The children were happy amid the shadowed and dimly lit forest, and Caitlin felt someone staring at her from the group a bit differently than the rest. Yes – yes – Grace wasn't acting the same as the others, in fact, Grace was standing next to herself – *there were two of her!* Neither Johnny nor Caitlin admitted to seeing this before, and they immediately ran up to the two duplicates curious over what they were seeing.

"Grace – Grace is that you?" Caitlin asked, but she got a nudge in the side by Johnny. "What kind of a stupid question is that? – Of course it's her!" and he looked up at the version of Grace that was wearing the same attire as both of them, and with a deep breath, he was about to ask his own question of her.

Grace's hand reached out and covered the boy's mouth. "Where am I – one minute we were all in that freakin' cell – and now we're here! What the heck's going on?" she asked almost accusingly.

Orion noted that he would have to give Grace further apologies for his doubts that she had, indeed, seen both Johnny and Caitlin in her vision. Orion's mind instantly spun over how it was that she, Grace, could have pathically communicated with their brother and sister, all the while he listened as Caitlin and Johnny tried giving answers to her question.

In the middle of their words and conversations, trying to understand what was going on and how it was possible, they were quickly distracted by a splitting of the trees above their heads. No sunlight broke through when this happened though, because above the trees the same kind of craft as from the previous vision the two had experienced was hovering overhead. Caitlin and Johnny both sighed at the sight of this, but Grace was filled with fear, having never seen them before, and it was with absolute panic that she cowered and hid behind the other two.

The large craft continued to lower itself with Caitlin and Johnny watching it carefully. Johnny then pulled on Caitlin's shirt, and pointed out that all of the other children, Jay and Taylor included, were not reacting to the craft in a negative way at all. In fact, they waved and smiled at it happily.

All three of the children from the present shook their heads with Caitlin mumbling "I don't get it?"

As they waited, the craft stopped its descent a few feet from the ground. Then, with a strange hissing noise it opened some kind of loading door.

With a strange curiosity that hinged between confusion and entertainment, Caitlin and Johnny watched as a long rod, very similar if not the same one that Caitlin was holding in the testing room, actually walked itself down the ramp of the craft.

Taylor smiled, with the future version of Johnny standing in front of him, he gripped the boy's shoulders. "It's good to see you again – we have much to talk about!"

At finishing these words a strange howling filled the air, a noise that all four children; Caitlin, Johnny, Orion, and Grace had heard before.

Taylor's smile only widened at hearing this noise, and he turned his stare down at the future version of Johnny, who reached out to grab what could only be assumed as some invisible hand. The boy and whatever it was that was unseen and holding the rod, slowly walked away into the forest followed by Taylor and all the others from the future vision.

Johnny, Grace, and Caitlin moved to follow their now migrating family, but with a sharp pulling of their heads, as if they had been nearly ripped off their shoulders, both Caitlin and Johnny saw with a blur of color that their vision of the future disappeared, and gave way to a clear view of the testing room.

Johnny pulled the large helmet off his head, and threw up almost immediately onto the white lab floor. Caitlin, who was sitting by his side, quickly patted his back and looked around for someone to help. Her eyes were met by the bright colors of white and green.

"What's wrong with him?" She yelled, but her answer came from Johnny himself.

"I'm fine. Fine – just exhausted that's all."

Stewart, the man in the white cloak, smiled and turned to the man in green. "That boy's been holding them both in visions for nearly a half-hour – He's been doing the work of two pre-cogs. *That's* impressive."

With intermittent coughs Johnny spoke to Stewart arrogantly. "Father can do – ten times more and not even break a sweat! You just wait – 'til he finds us! – You'll see!"

Caitlin offered the boy a quick nudge as a signal for his silence, and the two sat and listened as Stewart spoke to the man in green.

"Well, I think it's time you get the other two!"

"Hmmm – I'll get the tranquilizers ready!"

"I don't think that's such a good idea." Stewart said cautiously, "They might wake up in a panic and cause some serious damage. Better to keep them awake the whole time."

The man in green nodded, "Fine, I'll take these two back to the cell."

Caitlin and Johnny hardly had time to respond before their bodies were telekinetically seized up and with barely the ability to walk, the two made their way out of the testing lab, down a long corridor to a lift at its end.

Both were on their toes, working hard to pick up any stray thoughts from the man in green and working even harder to pick up any visual clues as to where they were.

Once in the lift, the man in green pressed buttons for the 342nd floor, and Caitlin quickly looked up at the digital display on the lift. It showed the 340th floor – then the 341st – then the 342nd.

So they were two floors below our cell – Orion thought, as he was still hitching a ride on Caitlin's thoughts and images of the past.

The man in green then walked Johnny and Caitlin out into a long corridor that looked very similar to the one they had just come from. They walked down this corridor, and eventually made their way to what was the door to their confinement.

With its opening, Orion was able to, through the eyes of Caitlin, see and hear himself, arguing with Grace.

Orion blinked his eyes quickly as he came out of his telepathic link with Caitlin. After such a long pathic and cognitive link, the two were very hungry for proto-bars and in turning his look to his younger brother, Orion noticed that the boy's color was even worse than when he had come in.

"Hey!" Orion shouted, "We're starving – can we get some food down here?"

With a quick lightning zap, a small mound of proto-bars revealed themselves in the center of the cell.

Orion didn't even bother offering thanks. Instead, he grabbed one of the bars, ripped it open with his teeth, and broke off a chunk of it for his brother. The boy seemed almost too weak to chew, but, after a few minutes of coaxing, he could see that Johnny's effort and eventually his color was returning. With eager fingers, the boy finally grabbed the bar himself and started eating.

Orion, Caitlin, and Grace all started eating their own bar, and the three leaned up against the wall of the cell, almost mesmerized by the flow of electrostatic color that emanated from their contact with the containment field.

"I still don't get it!" Orion said in frustration.

"How did Grace get into your vision? How could she get past the field?"

Grace and Caitlin both shrugged their shoulders, "I don't know? Maybe I'm just gifted!" Grace said with a smile.

"No!" Orion dismissed, "It's not that – I'm missing something – There has to be something I'm not getting!"

Johnny, who was now standing in front of the group, looked upward and shouted, "How 'bout a ball, or something to play with – anything!"

Another zap revealed a small blue rubber ball that the boy immediately swiped up and started throwing.

Grace was still on a high, believing herself able to somehow penetrate the containment field. Caitlin was still frustrated that Johnny, her younger brother, could predict Orion's actions, and use his own abilities to carry both of them through two separate visions, eventually putting a strain on his own health.

Orion, on the other hand, was still perplexed at the intricacies of the visions he had just seen. But he was hopeful that, indeed, there was some hole in their containment; a way out that he hadn't thought about yet. Distracted, he watched Johnny throw the ball over and over again.

Throw - it the floor – hit the field – catch. Throw – hit the floor – hit the field – catch. Throw – hit the floor – hit the field – catch.

Orion's eyes grew wide. He ran up to the boy, snatched the ball from his hand and threw it in exactly the same way. Throw – HIT THE FLOOR – hit the field – catch!

"Heeeyyy!" Johnny protested.

"That's it!" He yelled, and he turned to his two sisters. "I've got it!"

Looking around the room, Orion quickly cast his eyes to the floor. Grabbing Grace and Caitlin both by the hands, he stood them in the middle of the room.

"There's no floor!" he whispered pointing downward, and at first the two didn't understand. Orion noticed the looks of confusion and he walked over to the side of the cell. He hit his hands on the wall several times, revealing the familiar electrostatic wave before he started stomping his foot on the floor – revealing nothing. Then he whispered again "NO FLOOR! We need to dig our way out!"

Caitlin and Grace merely looked at the metal floor in confusion – "We'll need David and Aspen for that!"

Growling in irritation, Orion realized these words to be truth, and he slumped to the ground, watching the cell's entryway, waiting for the time of their return, but Johnny was still so exhausted he put his head in Caitlin's lap where he slept soundly with a stomach appreciating it's new supply of food.

66 Chaos

SHANNON AND JAY were quite the nervous couple sitting on the floor of her apartment. They were holding hands and Jay's free hand was the neural reader, which he started at with unwavering dedication, carefully monitoring Taylor's vital signs.

Taylor had been out for nearly a minute, and there was nothing to suggest that he was doing more than just normal sleep. Nearby, Tristan loomed with a constant pacing on the other side of Taylor's body that Jay and he had carefully positioned to be straight and flat, lying on the floor. The boy was just as nervous as Jay and Shannon, but as the time passed, his nervousness slowly filled with irritation and frustration.

"What's going on? Do you see any change?"

"Not yet." Jay said optimistically, and with these words he could feel Shannon squeeze his hand firmly, offering him a sense of hope and faith.

Jay wasn't one to just sit and wait though. He stood, and as if to balance Tristan's efforts, he also started pacing around Taylor's body, watching it closely for any physical sign of change. As he looked over his friend, his eyes couldn't help but follow the wires attached to his friend's head. They weren't tangled or woven in any way. In fact, their paths went along parallel curves eventually leading up to their source: the enigmatic sphere that Jay had grown to both to fear and revere – though not necessarily in that order.

"Ahhh ahhh!" With a gasping breath, Shannon caught the attention of both Jay and Tristan.

"What – what's the matter?" Jay asked with curious anxiety.

The woman practically looked cross eyed at the pendant necklace she was wearing. The small jewel which Jay had given to her on her birthday earlier that year was actually levitating in front of her face.

"Is – is – is that *him*?" She asked half excited, half frightened.

"I don't know? I don't think so!" Jay said looking down at the neural reader. He shook his head, and hit the unit on the side, but the display clearly showed no peaks in any of the evolved areas. *If he's lifting the necklace, surely I'd see it on the reader* – Jay thought.

With a deep rumble and what Jay knew was a shift in the foundation of the whole building, all three were nearly knocked to the floor, then, the floor started shaking and rattling from what felt like an earthquake. Shannon looked at Jay with instant panic, and Tristan tried desperately to see if he could see anything by way of pulling the neural reader from the man's hands.

Shaking his head, the boy thrust the reader back at Jay. "I can't read that crap!"

"Of course you can't!" Jay scolded before looking at the unit himself and seeing that, to his expectation, there was a small peak in the telekinetic area of Taylor's neural readout. This in itself wasn't impressive, but the fact that the peak was, indeed, a small one, told Jay that Taylor was causing a huge amount of physical disturbance while the teen's brain was using very little effort.

Eventually the shaking vibrations and rattling noises subsided, and Taylor's neural peak disappeared with them. Jay sighed with relief at hearing the quietness of the room around him, but it only took the man a moment to realize that this release was premature. In seconds the shaking started again, this time, though, it was far worse. Looking at the neural reader, Jay was only just able to see that Taylor's telekinetic peak had returned, and this time it was larger – much larger.

The noise from the quake like rattling had completely engulfed the apartment and forced Shannon plug her ears and wince her eyes in fear. Tristan found it best just to sit on the floor rather than stand as keeping balance seemed far more difficult now. Jay, on the other hand, made a desperate attempt at keeping his stance near Taylor while he watched the peak maintain itself. With edgy nerves, the man snapped his eyes from the reader to the apartment window, which had shattered, despite its being made of near indestructible plex material. At that moment the apartment filled with a rush of noise as it had lost a good deal of air pressure, and as a result everyone's ears had popped. Jay leaned himself against a wall, staring at the body of his best friend and the attached sphere. He wasn't sure if he should be amazed or afraid.

Slowly the shaking had subsided. Jay wasn't trusting to hope that this would be the last he would see of the neural spike, or the quaking movement that accompanied it. He would have taken another look at the neural reader, but he was distracted by Tristan, who had made his way to the window to look out.

"He's destroying everything!" Tristan yelled, and with these words Jay quickly slid to the boy's side.

Looking out over the dark, dusky sky the two could see buildings from all around with shattered windows – cracked facades – some with bits of smoke bellowing from their tops and Jay's face couldn't even try to show the heartache he was feeling at looking out over this dark scene.

"Tha – that can't be him! There's just no way!" Shannon spewed.

With a roar unlike anything they had experienced yet, the quake returned, and with the shaking now at its most intense, Jay looked down at the reader and could only barely make out the fact that the unit was reading just a hair over the redline.

"Uh – it's definitely him!" Jay shouted through the din. Then, turning away from Shannon, he looked out the window and to his terror he could see that the many transports zooming around were having great difficulty keeping to their designated paths. Several times the transports would come to within inches of hitting each other or the city's buildings, and Jay cringed as he could see large bits of rubble and building material slowly crumble away from the sides of the tall structures all around, but before they would fall to the ground, Taylor's kinetic manipulation would grab them and shoot them off like missiles to either strike other buildings, or land mercilessly somewhere far off.

Whipping around, Jay started crawling on his knees. Slowly he made his way to the sphere. He had it full in his mind to de-activate the unit. What Taylor was doing – his power – a power that in his years of knowing him, Jay had never, ever seen used to that extent, was far too dangerous. He reached his arm up, wrapped his fingers around the wires and was ready to pull them with all his might.

With a swift movement Taylor's arm smacked Jay's hand hard forcing the man to release the wire, and as Jay reached for them again, Taylor, while still unconscious, was able to catch Jay's arm, keeping the man from deactivating the sphere.

Jay struggled, and tried to move, but Taylor's physical and now telekinetic grip was too strong. After struggling for nearly a minute Jay looked closely at the neural reader – slowly – too slowly by Jay's wishes, the kinetic neural peak subsided.

Taylor eased a release of Jay's hand and body. With it free, Shannon was screaming at him to deactivate the sphere. Jay, though, only shot up his hand, flat palmed, "One second!"

With the peace and quiet, and the release of his body, Jay had calmed himself, and with a close look at the neural reader he finally realized what was happening.

"It's shifting his focus!" Jay yelled, and these words confirmed themselves by showing a small peak in the cyberkinetic neural frequency.

"The quakes are done! Now all we have to worry about..."

Jay would have finished his words, but he could see that the lights in the room started to flicker – the wall inset plex-view turned itself on and off rapidly, and, to add to the craziness of activity, the doors in Shannon's apartment kept opening and closing over and over again.

"What's going on?" Tristan screamed.

"Everything's shifting – the sphere is moving through his higher neural frequencies."

"I don't speak geek – what does that mean!"

"Tristan, the five evolved talents operate on five closely linked neural frequencies – the lowest is telepathy – that's why nearly everybody in the world has it. Then there's telekinesis, cyberkinesis – what he's doing now – and post-cog, and pre-cog."

Knowing this order, Jay was certain he could expect the same kind of activity out of Taylor in cyber fashion as he saw for the kinetic kind.

Sure enough, the low peak of cyber ability subsided, and as it just so happened, the plex-view was left on.

Shannon, Tristan, and Jay all watched the screen in nervous fear. Reading the caption, it stated –

"FREAK EARTHQUAKE – 9.5 – STRIKES LAM!"

The scenes of damaged buildings – billowing smoke – and absolute chaos in the streets seemed to run from one end of the city to the other.

Watching the screen, a new caption rose.

"REPORTS OF MINOR DAMAGE IN SCM, SDM AND SFM"

"What's SCM, SDM and..." Tristan started to ask. He had lived on the outskirts of the Los Angeles Metroship long enough to know what LAM stood for, but he knew little outside of this small world.

"Sacramento, San Diego, and San Francisco!" Jay said to both answer Tristan's question, and evoke a sense of amazement at the fact that Taylor had used such an impressive, albeit dangerous and destructive amount of telekinetic power.

With the three watched the screen, their eyes quickly scattered as it, along with the lights, and doors started to go crazy once again. Jay looked down at the neural reader and could see, once again, that the peak had showed itself to be somewhere around sixty percent.

Not knowing how far reaching Taylor's cyber abilities could be, Jay went to the window again. He could see that the transport crafts were operating normally, and that there seemed to be little by way of a disturbance much beyond their own apartment building. Jay knew that there were all kinds of trouble *inside* the building because he could hear screams and yells through the many windows of apartments both above and below, and in his mind he could only imagine the chaos that his ears were reflecting.

Continuing to scan the scene outside, he noticed a transport that was on approach to their building. With a cringing, Jay watched the craft falter as it neared the rooftop. But, fortunately, as he could tell, it landed safely.

Tristan and Shannon joined Jay at the window, and in looking out, Tristan's heart was the one that now ached the most. The boy surely wasn't going to be able to see the city in any kind of respectable state now. It was absolutely devastated from what Taylor had done.

After a few more seconds Jay nervously watched the neural peak slowly subside, but before it reached bottom, it kicked right back up again, this time, as Jay could expect, straight to the one hundred percent mark and beyond.

The scene of transports moving normally about the city quickly changed. All around, Jay and Delissa gasped as these transports started falling to the ground like flies. Jay shifted his eyes the plex-screen on the wall as it once again started to waver, but unlike before, now there was only electrostatic snow when it was on.

Terrified Jay stepped beside Taylor's body. "Dude, you need to hurry this up!" he yelled, and reached out to the teen, shaking him. Jay was certain that this would do little good, but as felt a need to do something and his frustrations were getting the better of him, this made him feel loads better.

"Babe! Take a look at this!" Shannon said nervously.

Jay stood and sprinted back to the window. He watched as the many transports that had fallen out of the sky just a moment ago rose high into the air. In unison they seemed to flow in a single direction.

Curious of what was going on, Tristan tried to predict where they were all headed, but didn't fully absorb where they were going until Jay put his hand on the boy's shoulder with a deep sigh.

"He's going for The Towers!" Jay said with a deeply rooted panic in his voice. He could see that the transports were all indeed headed in that same direction at high speed. *Were they on a collision course?* Jay wondered, and he was curious if Taylor bore some ill will toward The Towers because of everything that had happened. *Maybe his anger translated into some kind of odd cyberkinetic focus.*

Jay moved to Taylor's side again. "Dude, you have to stop this – people's lives are at stake. Children's lives are at stake! Taylor, come on – you can't do this!" the man pleaded before running back to the window. While Jay didn't know if it was his shouts that did it or just the mere fact that the cyberkinetic peak had timed itself out, either way, he man was beyond relieved that Taylor's boosted cyber abilities worked through their final decline. With a hissing soothing exhale, Jay released an exhale of emotional reprieve.

"What's next?" Shannon screamed looking back from the window. "I don't know how much more the city can take!"

"It's fine now" Jay said before offering a bit of logical reassurance. "All he has left is to go through his post and pre-cog powers – that's easy-peasy stuff!"

Jay couldn't have been more right about this – for it turned out to be the least chaotic part of his watch over his friend, and with a glance at the neural scanner Jay could see that, unlike the trio of increasing peaks that had preceded, the neural reader was showing a slow and steady increase in Taylor's post-cog activity. Eventually the peak reached over a hundred percent, but still within Taylor's guidelines.

It was in the uneventful watching of his friend's stiff and still body that Jay noticed Taylor's hand squeezed the green cloth ever tighter. This combined with the peak coming from Taylor's brain gave Jay a sense of hope that all of the destruction and chaos of these past several minutes was for something worthwhile, and that with any luck Taylor was getting the answers he so desperately sought. As the seconds slowly passed Jay felt a burning curiosity grow inside himself. The longer he waited the more wanted to know about what Taylor was seeing and learning.

Within seconds after the post-cog peak had maxed out Taylor started sweating profusely. Jay couldn't help but show good bedside manner by replicating a small towel to wipe Taylor's forehead. It was in putting his hand so close to the most powerful brain on the planet, a now undisputed fact in Jay's mind, that the man was at his most anxious to know what was going on inside Taylor's mind. To learn the deepest secrets of the Evol Crew – to understand what had happened to the children. Keeping his hand on the cloth that had been placed on Taylor's forehead, Jay's curiosity, this anxiousness over the unknown, didn't last for long...

67 The Truths of the Past

TAYLOR OPENED HIS EYES and could see that he was still in Shannon's apartment and that he was still holding the green cloth lightly between his fingers. He offered it a firm squeeze. In that instant the teen closed his eyes and was immediately met with a massive black wall that stood in his way, As he looked in all directions he could see that the wall seemed unending – up, down, left, right – it didn't matter where he looked the wall was everywhere. Taylor felt his resolve build, and as he squeezed the cloth ever tighter, he could see that the wall was slowly growing more transparent. Eventually, as if it was nothing to do so, he moved past it, and in moving beyond the large dark surface he saw that all that was ahead of him was an unending blackness.

In this void Taylor started to hear voices – familiar voices he had heard less than a day before back in the forest.

"So what do you think of this whole idea?" the voice asked.

"I don't know – I just don't know."

"So you and I are going to be like the fathers?"

"You, me, and Stewart you mean!"

Taylor's vision slowly brightened up, and he could see two men sitting on examining beds. He recognized them immediately. One was Dr. Zeldin, one was the man that was usually cloaked in green. Taylor saw that they were not dressed in their usual colored robes. Instead, they were dressed in simple examination gowns.

Taylor looked around the room and, with its many displays, he could see that the main focus of whatever study was being done had a great deal to do with DNA manipulation.

"Did somebody say my name?" Taylor heard a third familiar voice before turning around and seeing the man typically cloaked in white, who was also wearing an examination robe.

"Eh, yeah – just havin' a little chat about how we're basically going to be like parents – fathers."

"I already am a father – this isn't parenting – this is an experiment – nothing more!"

With these words Taylor's mind started spinning.

"So where are the other two?" Dr. Zeldin asked curiously.

"*Who* are the other two?" the man usually in green interjected, "I haven't even met them. And besides – why two – we have Pre-cog – telekinetic and cyberkinetic all right here!"

The man that Taylor now knew as Stewart frowned at these words. "I know one is named Elizabeth, I didn't catch the other girl's name."

"Oh – girls! No wonder they're not here with us!" the man usually in green said with a widening smile.

"So what's their story?"

"Well, as I've met Elizabeth, I know why she's here – she's an *extremely* gifted telepath."

"We're all extremely gifted telepaths – big deal!" the man usually in green said.

"Yeah well – after I found out who she was I checked on her file – that's where I was just now – and let me tell you – I'm impressed!"

"Aaaaaand!" Dr. Zeldin pressed.

"And she could use your abilities to crack a top security network while making breakfast with your abilities," he continued, shifting his stare from Dr. Zeldin to the man usually cloaked in green before continuing, "she can do that – use your powers – and neither of you would even know she was *making* you do it!"

"NO WAY!" the man in green shouted.

"Yes Daniel, Yes. She's that good!"

Taylor was intrigued. This Elizabeth *was* a gifted telepath, Taylor thought, and as he mulled over this woman in his mind he had a quick realization. *She must've been the woman in blue at Jay's apartment.*

"So that must mean that the other girl's the post-cog." Dr. Zeldin said while looking down at his chest inside his robe.

"Man these things itch!" he said scratching the vital transmitters attached to his body.

Taylor started pacing the room. In his mind the teen was putting all of the pieces together. Two women, three men, five very powerful gifts – that's why they want the children – they're the *parents.*

It all seemed to make perfect sense. But then Taylor thought again – why would they be just as important dead – or alive. In fact he remembered the man in white – Stewart – telling him that if the children didn't cooperate they would have to be eliminated. That's not like any parent he knew.

Taylor replayed his own myriad of thoughts inside his head; what he knew, what he'd heard, what he remembered. No, now that he thought about it, this didn't make any sense at all.

With a small feeling of déjà vu Taylor heard the words he had just been thinking, and for this reason he tuned himself back in to the conversation that the other three were having.

"Two women, three men, five very powerful gifts, that's going to be one powerful kid!" Daniel said, and at this point Taylor was at least grateful to know the names of his enemies rather than having to think of the colored robes he had always seen them wearing – in this case green.

"Have they picked a gender?" Dr. Zeldin asked.

"Sure have – a boy!" Stewart said, "I just heard the project leaders talking outside.

Dr. Zeldin and Daniel gave each other a quick high five, but Taylor's brain was instantly confused. *Only one child?* He watched as Daniel and Dr. Zeldin turned back in Stewart's direction, but rather than look at him, they looked over his shoulder.

Stewart didn't turn around, but simply spoke with a broken pause, "Elizabeth – aaaand – Christine, what a beautiful name for a post-cog."

These two women, still wearing examination gowns, had entered into the room with the men.

"I'm glad to hear you like it. I am saddened, though, to hear you say that what we're doing is nothing more than just an experiment. There's so much more going on here – I can feel it – you have to feel it too?"

In between Christine's words Taylor felt a churning in his stomach – his mind was thinking thoughts that his heart desperately hoped were not true. He sat on the bench beside Dr. Zeldin and, turning his head to the room's entrance, he saw a man in a lab-coat, wave to the others and call them out.

"Hey guys – uh – girls – we've got a meeting in ten minutes. Just down the hall, third door on the left."

Daniel looked at this person with a smirk on his face, "What, should we go like this?" He said waving his hands over himself, thus declaring the inappropriateness of his attire.

"Actually – *yes*" the man in the labcoat said. "They want you like this – there's a little surprise waiting – for all of you." Despite the protests from others, Daniel left the room with only a wave and left the others to talk amongst themselves.

"Can you believe the nerve?" Elizabeth said with a scowl.

"What's the big deal?" Dr. Zeldin said with a smile, and after a moment he too walked out of the room and down the hall.

"Well, I guess we should all get going then." Stewart said, and with the door opened, he waved his hand, "Ladies first."

Both Elizabeth and Christine had walked over to a small supply cabinet, pulled out two extra gowns and put them on backwards and tied them in the front. "Whatever you say Stew." Elizabeth responded while tying the front of her gown. She then quickly made her way down the hall to the proper door with Christine, Daniel, Dr. Zeldin, Stewart, and an invisible Taylor all following closely behind. The teen was still digesting his own thoughts, his suspicions and his fears as he walked from one room of the corridor to the next.

It wasn't a moment after the group had taken their seats that this small meeting started by way of another man, whom Taylor instantly recognized, entering the room and taking position in front of the others.

This small round room, with its centered oblong wooden table, quickly grew dark. "Okay class. Let's get through the basics. My name, if any of you don't already know, is Seymour Andrews, President of the GC, and founder of this project. You are all here to contribute a bit of your DNA so that we might create an individual who, with any luck, will actually possess all of your talents."

"I know this isn't anything new to you. What is new, though, is the fact that the GC is prepared to make five new seats for each of you to become its newest members." President Andrews had to pause and allow a series of gasps and mumbles to pass themselves around the room. "We are creating these five new seats on the council, one for each of your talents, so that you can be, for all purposes, our liaison to those with your um – special gifts."

With "oohs" and "aahs" of understanding the small group had digested their surprise at hearing this and each one was further impressed as a series of small openings appeared in the table, one in front of each of them. Out of each opening a small box rose out. The boxes all had black bottom halves, but each of their lids was a different color; there was Blue, Green, Black, White, and Red.

Taylor felt he didn't even have to ask what was inside these boxes, but he listened as President Andrews explained just the same.

"We've tested thousands of people from around the world – from visions to object movement to machine control and mind control and we've found that you five are the best. Bar none! Your positions on the council will be – hmmm – how shall I put it – permanent and eternal. If you accept you will be responsible for representing your – uh – kind, but as this group of people is so very small you will also have the additional responsibility of policing them. It is for this reason it is an absolute that we keep your identities a secret."

"So open the boxes in front of you!" President Andrews ordered with a smile.

None around the table were truly eager about opening the boxes. They each smoothly pulled the lid from them and with a bland expression each found that inside was a color matched uniform, all of which were very familiar to Taylor's eyes. The teen had practically grown up watching and following the "Evol-Crew" as they were eventually called, and while the name and the people had lost a great deal of luster in his mind, it did intrigue him that he was able to watch this very secretive and quite historical first meeting of the five of them.

"These," President Andrews continued, "will be your uniforms. They can only be replaced by the GC as they have special encrypted trackers in them. You can't use an M-Gen to clean them – but then again – they've been designed to never need cleaning – so there you are. Also, they've been electromagnetically charged to block the cognitive tracing of any imprints left on them. So postcogs and precogs won't ever get a read on where you've been or where you're going – that's why you'll be required to wear the gloves that come with them."

If Taylor could've been seen by the group, he was sure that his smile would've been more than obvious – and he appreciated the irony of even hearing this statement, for in hearing it – he disproved it completely.

"Ahem – excuse me – but I thought we were just here to help with some little experiment. A little physical – a blood sample – a questionnaire and that's it – we get paid – we go home! What you're talking about is a – a job. Have you planned for the possibility that we might not accept your offer? And how – exactly – do you plan on our positions being 'permanent and eternal'?" Daniel voiced arrogantly.

"Ah – and here we will get to first things first! Your position will be permanent and eternal because of a mutated version of the Methuselah Virus that has been designed to keep you at your current state with, so far as we have tested, an unseen aging factor. You can decide to retire after four hundred or five hundred years – even consult the government if you want to end your own life – we have an anti-virus that can assist in these matters – but that is entirely your option."

"And pay – what about pay?" Daniel asked leaning far over the table.

"All GC reps make at least three times any of your salaries." At this point Andrews looked around the table and could see these uncertain faces suddenly grow excited. "Now listen – we wouldn't have done all this work if we didn't know we could provide you with the perfect offer. The paperwork is ready – the training is scheduled for Monday – but that's not the only reason we're here."

"Right!" Stewart said loudly, "The experiment, the boy. I've been getting impressions of this meeting all morning, but nothing concrete. Tell us a little about it and how we fit in."

President Andrews took a deep breath and smiled. "The GC has decided on a project to create what might be called the perfect human."

"And why a boy?" Christine questioned, half irritated.

"Oh that's easy," the president responded, "boys have the XY mix – girls have XX. If this goes well – then we have broader gender possibilities by starting with a boy and just using his genetics as a template."

Elizabeth nodded her head, "I'll buy that," but Christine looked confused.

"Now, other than your genetic contributions – we really don't expect much else from you."

"Not true!" Stewart whispered. "You want us on staff in case this boy, this experiment of yours, gets out of hand. Figure with a team like us – we can keep him under control if we have to."

"He is good, isn't he?" Andrews said completely put off by the fact that he just had his future preempted by one of his new subordinates.

"That's right – that's a small part of the reason why we've asked you to join the council. But trust me – as part of the GC that will be the least of your worries."

With a growing knot in the pit of his stomach Taylor wondered why any reference to this experiment always mentioned only one subject – he had six students – so this didn't make sense. *If they were the parent genetics for these six – why the reference to only one?*

"We are going to be training the child through EduCorp in Los Angeles, a place, as I have heard, Dr. Zeldin is familiar with. Anyways – here the boy will be trained under their newest project – a highly aggressive education program called *Prodigy...*"

Taylor nearly fell over. It was as if his stomach was ready to open itself up and swallow his heart from the inside. He instantly became nauseated, angry and frustrated. His ears started pounding. His head ached with the welling thoughts of the lie that was his life. With a shocked and accusing stare at all of those at the table, Taylor was furious at the whole lot. All at once, as if he had simply snapped his fingers to do it, Taylor forced the entire room to freeze to an absolute stillness.

He paced the room and lowered his head to gaze at the table in front of President Andrews. In it, the teen could looked over a reflection of himself. Lifting his head up, he glanced at each one of those that he might consider his parents and frowned.

They may have been his parents by blood, but in his mind Taylor considered a parent someone who actually worked hard to raise a child – made sure that the best of their own qualities shined in everything they did. Taylor didn't have one parent. He didn't even have five parents. Taylor had practically hundreds of parents, all working hard with his programming, protocols, and well – his lifestyle. He found that they, the staff and technicians of EduCorp, were the ones he considered his parents – not this small group of egocentrics.

Swallowing his emotions, Taylor stiffened his face to a simple boorish expression. In his bright blue eyes there was nothing to be read, no tears, no sadness – nothing. Inside his anger had all but dried up any other emotion. Instead, he was more concerned with the lie that was his life. Who else knew of this? Dr. Young, his mentor for so many years, was on the Education Council – did she know – and how could he not have seen it in some form or another – a vision – a telepathic transmission. Taylor's mind was spinning, and he realized that the best thing to do was to see the truth rather than speculate about it. With a wave of his hand, Taylor forced the vision to continue.

"When this child is a teenager, all of these powers are going blossom – and he's going to find out the truth – you know that right! I mean you can't cover everything up." Christine said with a tone of concern.

"Oh, come on, Christine! Get creative!" Andrews said with a wide smirk on his face, one that Taylor wished he could wipe off with a quick punch.

"When we drop the kid on their doorstep, he's going to come fully loaded with fabricated files."

"Let me guess," Stewart started in a sour tone, "geriatric mother gives birth to the kid before she dies. She was found in some remote area just outside Los Angeles – Let me know if I'm getting warm. You'll even plant a few files in the CESPA network, just in case anybody goes snooping around."

"Yes – Stewart – We all know you're a pre-cog – no need to show off!" Dr. Zeldin said with just as equally a droll tone.

"And man is he good!" President Andrews said excitedly, "You just saved me all kinds of time explaining. This boy will come with a story – and the only people who will know the truth are the six of us and a mere handful of GC technicians – all of whom possess only the highest of secret clearance."

Indeed, Taylor actually felt a rush of relief to know that everyone he had worked with over the years, everyone that trained him – they were all honest –

including Dr. Young – for none of them really knew the truth of how he had come to be, and if he had his way, they would never know. He liked the lie better, and if it truly made no difference in how anyone treated him, he wouldn't tell a soul.

He looked up at President Andrews, who, once again, addressed the group. "Now all I have left is three little things to cover. One – Let's see who's in. Can I have a show of hands?"

At this Elizabeth shot her arm up like a rocket – "I am 196, and I know you," she said looking at Stewart, "are practically the same age as I – so you have similar motivations to – uh – participate."

Stewart nodded to her, and slowly his hand ascended. Whether it was the thought of mortality or of immortality, or of the money, or the anonymity of using their powers, Taylor watched as one-by-one the other three lifted their hands into the air.

"Good! Now on to number two!" President Andrews proceeded, "Let's try on those cloaks and see how they fit – we'll have to get them altered if their too wide or too long – but we did the best with the information we had."

Everyone around the table rose and with a wave of colorful whirls they each donned their cloaks which, at first, seemed like little more than just hooded capes. Inside the capes, just at the neck clasp was small round plate no more than a few inches in any direction. The plate beeped with an ever increasing speed when the clasp was hooked around each of their necks. Then, these simple plates spouted full suits that slowly plastered themselves over each of the respective bodies.

With the exception of Daniel, who was too short for his suit, all the others seemed to fit fine, and Taylor had a strange feeling as he looked on this full team, together, in uniform for the first time. He couldn't put his finger on what this feeling was – if it was pride, he certainly didn't recognize it as such. If it was fear – Taylor shook his head, it definitely wasn't fear. No – it was the feeling of admiring your enemy – and the pride of realizing you were their equal.

"Ahh – look at you!" President Andrews said, "A Crew of Extra-Evolved for the GC – finally we've got people we can trust to get a handle on all those others out there. The Evol-Crew – that's what I'll call you – yes – has a nice ring to it I think."

At the end of his words President Andrews could hear Daniel offer a few soft whimpers over the improper size of his outfit. "You know – I used to wait tables – they couldn't get the uniform size right either, but man – wait 'til they hear about this!"

"No!" President Andrews shouted. "What part of having a secret identity didn't you understand? You can't tell anyone about your new job, and as we've got so much scheduled for you in the next few days you'll have to quit – immediately – call them right here if you have to – but you can't let anyone know about this!"

"But I have to give my boss a two week notice before I quit the firm!" Elizabeth said heatedly.

"Elizabeth?" President Andrews started with a tone of condescension. "Let me remind you that you're being given a job that is secure – for eternity – and as you've already pointed out, you're knocking on death's door here – this job has benefits you can't possibly imagine – worldwide travel – all expenses paid, and nearly complete anonymity from your actions – and you don't have to worry about that whole death thing – at least from age anyways! Is it so much to ask for you to give up one life to start a new one?"

"But I have a child!" Christine said firmly. The other's at the table looked at her in surprise, but she merely smiled, "I – I'm only seventy-three."

"And the youngest in this group," President Andrews added. "But don't worry – you don't have to give up your family – it's just – they can't know what your new job is. That's all." President Andrews finished his words and looked around the room at five very uneasy faces.

"Listen – are you guys in our out?" he asked firmly.

Slowly they all nodded their heads and sat at the table with inquiring stares at President Andrews.

"Good! Now for the last order of business," the man said as he stepped around and put his hand on Elizabeth's shoulder. "We need to go over your training schedules – you're going to have to learn when you can and cannot use your powers – and we have some computer, database, and well a lot of crash courses on where and how the GC operates – most of it is paperwork stuff. And we have a few courses that are designed to help you better understand your powers."

"What do you mean – better understand our powers – we've had them for years – we know all there is to know!" Dr. Zeldin said arrogantly, and at this President Andrews smiled. He stared down at Elizabeth for only a moment, and without saying a word, she picked up on what he wanted.

"Well – If I'm reading him right," Elizabeth started, "the GC has a group of scientists that have studied our natural born gifts and know them – apparently – better than we do – so –we *could* learn things we possibly don't even know about ourselves yet. It might be interesting."

"And who are you – the teacher's pet?" Daniel spewed.

At this, Elizabeth barely had to wink at the man to force him to sit down, and use his own kinetic abilities against himself. With a frown, he realized that he was not in control of his limbs. He grabbed the box that had been used to hold his uniform, picked it up and pulled it down on his head so hard that he punched a rough hole through it so that it made a very awkward head decoration.

"If I am the teacher's pet – then you are definitely the class clown!" she said with a smile and as President Andrews took his position back at the head of the table the room filled with both laughter and jeers directed at Daniel.

With a deep breath Taylor became overly tired of watching so many egos trapped in such a small room. He worried over his students and he was no closer to getting an answer as to where they were. Maybe – with any luck – he could force them into his mind with a little extra focus. He knew he was still holding the green cloth – he could feel it's now fraying edges working between his very real fingers, and he so thought hard of his children and of the man he knew now as Daniel.

With a blur of the five colors from the Evol Crew the vision of the conference room shifted into another, and, with a new set of voices, and an onslaught of color, Taylor again found himself in the company of several of those he had just tried to leave. With the thought to be patient, Taylor was hoping that maybe, just maybe, he was getting somewhere.

He could see Daniel looking over several displays in a small lab. On the displays was more genetic code.

What's this all about? Taylor wondered.

With a hissing noise, the door to this small room opened and Taylor watched with instant contempt as Dr. Zeldin entered.

"So – how'd everything go? Did you get him to show you what he's really got?" Daniel asked plainly.

"No! He attacked me – unprovoked and he attacked me!" Dr. Zeldin said frustratingly.

"That's not what I heard."

"Oh, and what did you hear?"

"I heard you tried to torture him into submission, and when that didn't work – you tried doing the same to his friend."

"Who said..."

"Does it matter?" Daniel said shortly. "Anyways, they're just happy you got him to use his powers at all – even if it was to knock your ass to the ground – but if he can't be coaxed willingly things could get complicated!"

Dr. Zeldin instantly became furious over this exchange, and Daniel knew it. The displays in the lab were all flickering with glitches and power surges.

"Oh, for heaven's sake – calm down! We need to get those samples to President Andrews – he's waiting for you."

The instant that Taylor eyed the vials that Dr. Zeldin pulled from his cloak, and pairing this with the conversation he had heard, he could identify the time that all of this was taking place. Back at The Towers Taylor was a few months from turning eight years old. Still, he was a little confused over what this had to do with the children. They weren't here – they weren't even born yet.

Taylor followed Dr. Zeldin out of the lab and down a long corridor with Daniel trailing closely behind. Eventually the three made their way to another room – ah – this looked very familiar – it was the same conference room he had just left in his previous vision.

"You know – there are times when I wonder about picking you!" spoke the familiar voice of President Andrews, who turned in his chair, his face hidden by a shroud of darkness before he leaned forward into the light. Indeed, the darkness about the man made him seem very sinister, despite the next part of what he was about to say.

"We've spent years developing that child and you're going to just torture him like he's some kind of dog. I wanted to see if you could convince him to demonstrate his talents – you know – for them. You – you – ahrghh – sometimes you just make me sick."

Dr. Zeldin stammered, trying to gain approval. "At the boy's last encounter with the GC, he was trying to convince them that he had no special ability at all. I was just trying to..."

"We know he has abilities – we know he can use them we've got mounds of data to prove it." President Andrews paused and heaved a low somber breath. "But he's our prize – if any of this was going to work we needed him to trust us.. You already messed up two years ago when the boy turned on you – I don't know what happened, but I know you lost his trust in an instant. And now – now you – YOU – ugh – give me those and get out of my sight!"

Taylor watched as President Andrews eyed the vials in Dr. Zeldin's cloak and he, that is to say Taylor, was overly pleased to hear the verbal reprimand.

Those many years ago, Taylor was uncertain if Dr. Zeldin was under orders to do what he did, or if he did it out of pure spite – now Taylor knew the truth – the government wasn't necessarily responsible for the man's actions, and, indeed, Dr. Zeldin had done what he did out of anger and malice.

"At least he remembered the samples?" President Andrews whispered sourly to Daniel.

"Here. Allow me!" Daniel said as he kinetically pulled the vials from Dr. Zeldin's hands and set them in the center of the conference table.

"Thank you!" President Andrews said in a praising voice to Daniel before pressing a small button inset just to his left at the table.

Instantly a bright white light flashed in the room and the two containers were gone. Within moments a holographic image was thrown up, and Taylor watched with scrutinizing detail as it revealed genetic code – his genetic code.

'Now that we're ready – we can start the second batch." President Andrews said softly.

"Second batch," Taylor whispered, "What second batch – did they make more of me – Am I just one of many – what the hell are you talking about?" Taylor uselessly voiced.

The teen watched the man eagerly stare at the holographic image. It was partially transparent and Taylor too looked up at this most basic of biological material – he was curious over what plans were in store for his DNA. What other horrible truths were out there that he didn't know about?

All at once his view of these helixes of code morphed away into something else – slowly more light started to pass through them, and with a shift and change in his perspective he could see – to his absolute amazement – two large glass cylindrical units, each one holding an infant – an unborn infant.

Taylor's surprise at this forced him to nearly fall backward. He wasn't certain what he was seeing, but he had a pretty good idea. In pulling away from the two units in front of him, his larger view revealed a total of six unborn infants. No – no – there were seven. Taylor just noticed, to his surprise, there were actually seven – one of the containers actually had – twins!

Taylor could hear voices again – and he listened intently at the words being spoken.

"So tell me again," Christine said walking right over and through Taylor's legs, "how is it you can get both girls and boys from the blood sample of little Robert."

"Oh that's basic genetics – you should know that!" Elizabeth responded, but Christine only smiled and shook her head.

"Just tell me, alright." Christine said with frustration.

"Touchy, touchy! Fine! Here's the simple version – In order to be a boy you need to have an X and Y chromosome. To be a girl you need an X and another X. With me so far?"

Christine nodded her head and Elizabeth continued, "In normal sex and birth – the Woman offers one of her X's and the man offers either an X or a Y – so you either end up with XX or XY – again – a boy or a girl – still with me?"

"Yeah yeah – go on!" She said excitedly as she was taking in the information being offered."

"Okay, well in the case of our subjects here - if it's a boy – then they have both X and Y from..." Elizabeth consulted her paperwork, "Robert. If it's a girl then the genetic coder just doubles the X and leaves out the Y. There's a little genetic manipulation that has to take place in order for it all to really work – but that's the basics of it."

Christine smiled – "Eight years old – and he's going to be a father."

Elizabeth started to laugh, "A father and a mother!"

Christine looked confused, but Elizabeth didn't feel the need to explain – she just continued laughing, making her way past the unborn infants to Daniel who had also come down to take a look at them.

"So – how's the grandkids?" He said jokingly, and at these words Taylor clenched his teeth.

Elizabeth smiled, "Nice one – but you can't make me feel old. I'm immortal!"

"Good point, good point! Daniel said, and at this he put his hand on the glass casing of one of the infants. "So have you heard – We don't have to demonstrate these – they're just going to take them – right after their telepathy starts – just like that."

"But there's seven – they only wanted six – what's going to happen to the extra one?"

"Oh – he's going into stasis – you know – just in case."

Taylor was listening to these words, but it was some time before that he started feeling his heart pound ever harder in his chest – his head was aching from the emotion he was feeling – his eyes welling with tears – tears of joy – tears of frustration – tears of absolute confusion over the life he was leading – and the children he was training. With one hand over his mouth, and the other over his heart, his eyes spewed more tears than he felt he had ever cried in his life – "They are mine – they're mine – no one can tell me any different – they're mine! Oh, God, they're mine!"

Taylor looked at the seven innocent infants, and while they were still not completely developed, he was able to see enough in their own characteristics to know who each child was.

"Orion – Grace – Aspen – Caitlin – David – Johnny – and his twin."

As Taylor looked at this last container, he could tell that the vision was progressing to some new part of the past where, now, one of the twins had been removed. Was this one Johnny – the one that was still with the other five? Putting two and two together, Taylor knew what was coming next. He watched as the children were born from their containment, but only five survived the inevitable infection of the Methuselah virus. The sixth infant – one of the twins – died after a difficult struggle that was much too long for Taylor to have to watch.

"The virus is just breaking down his code." Taylor heard one of the geneticists say, and he, Taylor, watched as months passed in seconds and eventually the child was gone.

Later, Taylor's view showed the other twin.

"That must be Johnny!" Taylor whispered in excitement. He was being pulled from stasis and, within a few months he was born. Unlike his identical predecessor, however, Johnny had been infected by another virus that rewrote his genetic code prior to his birth, and subsequently had only minor side effects after the Methuselah virus took its hold.

Taylor breathed a great relief and beamed with pride when Taylor he saw, for the first time, this baby open his eyes – his bright – light blue eyes – there could be little doubt that this child was one of Taylor's own.

Taylor was shaking – his head was filled with fantastic excitement. He and his children – no matter how they were conceived or created, were alive – were human – and they were HIS children. They had a right to live happy and free lives – nothing could tell him any different. He smiled as he watched the boy being placed near his older brother's and sisters for the first time, and with a sense of overwhelming pride the teen watched his children play for the first time.

With a deep inhale Taylor's vision grew instantly dark – pitch black in fact, and for a moment, he opened his eyes to see Jay sitting over him, pressing a towel to his forehead, but the man's eyes were closed. Jay was deep in concentration. *Did he see – could he have seen – those visions!*

Taylor felt a sharp shock inside his head. All at once his view went white, then, with the view of a massive white wall he knew what was happening, his hand gripped the green cloth in his hand ever tighter, ready to ride the wave of the future in an effort to find his kids, and now he knew – they were in fact, *his* children.

68 Finding the Future

ACHING WITH THE THOUGHT of seeing them again, Taylor filled with thoughts and memories of his children. He stared hard at the bright white wall in front of him. Again, with extra concentration, he forced its unending presence to slowly dissolve away, eventually leaving nothing but a bright white color that stretched across a massive expanse before him.

Slowly, this too dissolved away to reveal a much more confining space. Taylor sa Daniel, green cloak and all, walking down a long corridor. The man stopped, and made his way into a small room where Stewart was seen standing over two of the children.

"How's everything going?" Daniel asked curiously.

"Oh, fine, fine! I just got them started on these two items. They've got another fifteen minutes or so – then you can take 'em back and get the other two."

"Cute kids." Daniel said looking at Johnny through the helmet capped over his head. "I've heard he has your eyes!"

"He's got my eyes, jerk!" Taylor said testily, but after what he had seen he now knew that both were actually true. Just the same, he felt better letting out a little anger.

"Yeah – I've seen," Stewart said before adding, "Some of the GC scientists think those eyes could be the mark of a truly gifted pre-cog.

"Could be!" Daniel replied in half concurrence.

Taylor was frustrated at this useless conversation. He looked at several displays in the room, and one of them had a date and time stamp on it that told him it was sometime in the very early morning hours of the following day. Indeed, if there was just some way he could figure out where the kids were being held – if he could talk to them and know what they had seen.

Taylor kneeled to look at Johnny. The boy's eyes were closed. "If I could just get inside your head," Taylor muttered. Then his stare shifted. He moved his unseen body over Johnny's, eventually, his head was under the helmet too, and with a deep concentration, he hoped that having their two minds converge, there just might be a chance he could get through to the boy. He had never done anything like this before in a vision, but with his being wired to the sphere, and knowing that his powers were being pushed to their limits – he thought there just might be a chance...

Taylor rode Johnny's thoughts straight into the premonition he had seen several times before. In front of him, Taylor saw that the boy was gripping his sister tightly underneath the chaos of several craft over head. Now, from this perspective, Taylor smiled at these craft – they were of a very similar design to the one he had taken from the forest into the city. His mind thought on this for only a moment, but he found it hard to think amid all the noise and thuds from all around.

With a deep breath, and a deep concentration, Taylor hoped that the sphere would show how powerful it could really make him. He thought to stop everything – seize the moment and hold it in place.

Indeed, it took a mere second for everything around Taylor to go completely quiet and still. The teen had all at once lost his interest in the ships overhead – he noticed the still shaking Caitlin just a few feet away. With a gentle grip, he grabbed her shoulder. She flinched from fear, and he quickly cooed her. "Shhhh. Caity – it's me."

He could see that Johnny had looked up from her grip and with a word that now had new meaning to Taylor, the boy yelled out.

"Father – What are you doing here?" Oh how this word made Taylor's heart ache.

Caitlin opened her eyes, started to say something but stopped. She stared at Johnny in confusion and even the boy had to ask in seeing Taylor dressed in his full cloaking suit, "Is he from now – or is he from the future."

Taylor was instantly irritated at how this, his magic moment of being called father at a time when he knew it to be true, had been thwarted by the uncertainty of his presence. To make things worse – his two children were no longer addressing him directly – they were talking amongst each other like he wasn't even there.

"Not that it makes a big difference, but I'm from *now*!" Taylor shouted angrily, hoping to convince them by just talking with them.

"How do we know that?" Johnny shouted, and with these words Taylor grunted and explained himself into their confidence. When Taylor had finished, Johnny lit a huge smile, rushing upon the teen and hugging him around the middle. Whatever irritation Taylor had felt before was quickly washed away. In his mind he felt he could take no more of this emotion, this love – this happiness. And now, being held by one of his children, he felt as if it was for the first time.

Taylor took a deep breath and focused hard on not becoming a torrential downpour of tears. He looked down at Johnny, who cried while still holding him tightly.

"I miss you! We all do!" Johnny said this with tears streaming down his face, and Taylor had to now use everything in his power – *I'm not going to cry – I'm not, I'm not!* Taylor thought.

To distract himself from the emotion he instantly squatted down to their level and tried his best to talk to them calmly and, with a purpose in his voice, he started questioning the children.

"I know, I know. I'm trying to find you! So tell me, where have they taken you?"

Taylor listened to their comments regarding an energy field of sorts, and he was perplexed that the government had somehow developed a technology that blocks his children's ability to use their powers. *But they're using them now.*

"Hmmm – well you're not in the field now – that much is true." Then he thought about what he heard Daniel say before he entered this vision.

Fifteen minutes – then you can take 'em back and get the other two.

Caitlin and Johnny would be leaving in a few minutes and walking back to their confinement with Daniel. *Perfect!* With a purposeful voice he spoke to the two children.

"You should do what you can to figure out where you are now – you know – while you're out. With any luck I'll be able to follow you and see what you see. Maybe then I can figure things out!"

Taylor suddenly flinched – he watched as a glitch in what he was seeing slowly started to obscure his vision – he could hear voices in his head – voices from Johnny's physical ears.

"There's a huge spike in the boy's telepathic range – something weird's going on!" he could hear Stewart's voice say.

Taylor all at once filled with fear over the thought of anyone finding out what he was up to – or what they would do if they knew he was trying to get to the kids.

"Uh oh, I think they know I'm here. Time to make myself scarce!" Taylor said, quickly, and just as these words came out, Johnny jumped for him and hugged him firmly around the neck. "Don't go father! Don't go!"

Now we're back to this – *no tears – no tears* – Taylor thought. He turned to Caitlin, "I'll be back soon – you just watch out for your brother!"

But as Taylor stared at Caitlin he could see a different face when she moved. It was as if one was superimposed on hers – he hadn't noticed it before – but as she had just stood up – this movement made it much more apparent.

"Is that you 'Rion!" he asked, recognizing a few features from the face.

"No!" She shouted, but Taylor knew something was up. He put his hand on the girl's forehead and, with a quick focus he could read the thoughts of two distinct minds inside.

One of these thoughts was definitely Orion's. It was as if he was screaming at the top of his lungs - "It's me father – I'm here – inside her head – I want to see what she saw – we're trying to figure out a way to escape – I figured this could help!"

Taylor pulled his hand away, "That's my boy! Just figure out everything you can – I'm counting on you! I'm counting on all of you!" He said turning his face to Johnny, then back at Caitlin again.

Taylor then stood at full height, smiled down at Johnny, "I'll be back soon. I love you all so much – let the others know I'll be seeing them soon!" And with these words Taylor left Johnny's vision and found himself now staring down at the two children who were still locked in their vision.

He could see that Stewart was nearly ready to grab the helmet and could only assume that the man was going to make an effort to interject himself into the children's vision.

"Hold on!" Daniel said quickly, "he's flattened out – s'fine now!"

Stewart grunted – uncertain of what to make of the strange telepathic peak that had worked its way into his test. He moved over to the display, pushed a few buttons, shrugged his shoulders, and sat for several more minutes, simply allowing the test to finish.

Daniel, who had moved in and out of this room several times, noticed that Stewart's test was still progressing.

"You've got less than five minutes! I'm almost done here!" Stewart said quickly as Daniel made his way through one last time, with several boxes telekinetically following behind him.

"Yes, I know – I'm almost finished too!" Daniel said. With these words Stewart reached out, and slowly grabbed the helmet from the boy's head. Taylor watched as, slowly, his two children blinked themselves into reality. He both longed for the children and raged at their captors when he noticed how sever these tests were on his two children, especially Johnny, for Taylor could see that the boy all at once lost a great deal of his color.

Daniel kinetically grabbed the children and was ready to walk them out of the room, but Taylor was so angry he couldn't help but shout as loud and unheard as he could. "The boy need's some food you moron – get him some food – he's ready to pass out!"

These comments did little other than alleviate Taylor's anger as he watched Daniel take the children out of the room and walk them down the corridor. Taylor walked beside Daniel, but rather than look at this man, draped in green, or even stare at his children, Taylor was taking in everything he could to try and figure out where he was. Entering a lift, Taylor rode up two floors and on exiting he made his way to the children's cell.

Daniel pushed a quick series of buttons on the door, offered a retinal scan, voice print, *and a DNA sample* just to open the door. With a soft sliding noise from the opening entrance Taylor was filled with both joy and heartache to see his other children. They were on the other side of some strange, yet clearly visible pulsing field. Without a thought he tried to walk through it.

With an instant, sharp, horrific pain that Taylor knew would somehow be reflected in his physical body back in Shannon's apartment, Taylor felt his whole body seize, and with a surge, he was forced backward.

So hard was this push that Taylor actually went through the wall on the other side of the corridor. Quickly looking around, Taylor realized he was in another cell, this one obviously not equipped with the same containment field. It was small, with high ceilings like the other room, and as he took in all of its detail, he turned himself around quickly at the sound of something on the floor. Taylor, as a knee-jerk reaction, dropped down at the side of a very battered and bruised woman, a woman he instantly recognized. It was Delissa, and in seeing her abused body Taylor filled with an anger that boiled over as he clenched both his hands and his teeth.

Asleep, she rolled over slowly and in seeing her peaceful rest Taylor didn't want to wake her. Instead, he moved around and with his forehead touching hers, he was able to interject a few thoughts into an otherwise dreamless slumber.

He had hoped that she wouldn't wake through this effort, but the second he pulled his head away she opened her eyes and offered a wide smile.

"I'll be waiting for you!" She whispered, and at this Taylor knew his attempt to let her know he was coming was successful.

Taylor noticed his view growing hazy. Daniel must be on the move – Taylor thought to himself, and with a rush of movement he quickly stood and walked through the wall from where he had entered the room.

Indeed he had to run a good distance to catch up to Daniel, who was, pushing Aspen and David via his kinesis.

It was as the teen ran down the hall that he noticed someone else walking in the opposite direction. It was a woman – a scientist of sorts. She was wearing a badge – with a familiar logo – the GCSD logo and Taylor could see behind it the large WDC emblem behind it – denoting the Metroship they were in.

"Of course – of course!" Taylor said loudly, "ghhhaad I'm so stupid!"

Taylor, with the sight of something so small, had the realization of where the children were and the added benefit of riding in the lift provided him with the exact floor or floors where he could find them.

Taylor focused hard on trying to release himself from the vision he was in, but despite his best efforts, nothing happened. He concentrated harder – thought of the sphere – focused on making it release him – still nothing.

"Maybe if I let go of the cloth...!" Taylor thought, and with a focus on his physical hand, he was just barely able to force his fingers to slowly let go of the green fabric. His hope was that, with nothing to tie his mind to it, his vision would dissolve and he would be left with nothing to do but wake up.

Taylor realized the error in his judgment the moment the fabric fell from his fingers. With a quick change, as if everything around him had been consumed by fire, Taylor found himself standing in front of the giant PlexView screen of his old apartment. He looked all around to make sure of what he was seeing, and as his eyes shifted back to the screen he saw, with an eerie feeling of familiarity, the flashing green numbers from the clock in Johnny's window across the city.

It showed the date and time, as before, of the destruction of the city: 10:24AM March 23, 2458.

Taylor was about to take his eyes from the screen, certain of what was going to happen, but before he could, he noticed the clock change. It now showed 10:24AM March 22, 2458 – a full day earlier. This happened again – 10:24AM March 21, 2458 – and again 10:24AM March 20, 2458 – over and over again and Taylor watched with his nerves on edge as the clock moved all the way back, not through a few days, or even a few weeks, but months back – all the way to October 4th, 2457.

"What the hell's going on?" Taylor asked rhetorically, and with a focus on the screen in front of him, he took in the full skyline of the city.

As before, he could see the walls of the tall buildings with cracks, broken windows, and bits of billowing smoke rising into the air.

"Could it be?" Taylor asked himself, and just as the words fell out of his mouth, his question received its answer.

Once again a mass of clouds started billowing in the sky, and thereafter dipped into the city skyline. Taylor started pacing the room, looking up at the ceiling as if his talking in a certain direction would really make a difference.

"Jay! Jay! If you can hear me get me out – turn the sphere off! Jay – get me out of here!"

Taylor watched as a familiar bright dot slowly shot itself through the cyclone and made its way to the center of the city. On impact there was, as Taylor could have expected, a bright flash, but with this onslaught of light, Taylor felt a very strange pulling sensation in his brain.

When the white color had subsided, Taylor was taking in many things all at once. Jay still had the white towel pressed against the teen's forehead, a small beeping from the man's other wrist told him that the full hour had passed, and, in seeing Tristan's fingers wrapped around wires that were half pulled from the bottom of the sphere, Taylor knew that the boy had turned the unit off.

Taylor looked over at Shannon, who showed a look of great fear, and it wasn't directed at him, or Jay, but at the boy, who, in his other hand, had Delissa's sword drawn. Glancing back at Jay, he could see that his friend slowly blinking his way out of some trance and was also trying to get his bearings.

"I tried to get him to turn it off sooner" Shannon spewed fretfully, "but he wouldn't let me. He grabbed that green bit of cloth when you dropped it, then turned on me with that sword – said you had to find his mother or something!" She was speaking to Taylor, but her eyes were still locked on Tristan.

"Tristan – drop the sword!" Taylor yelled, "Everything's fine – I know where she is – but we haven't got much time!"

Taylor sat up, felt a great rush in his head, and he fell over nearly as fast as he got up. Slowly, he made the effort to rise again – this time using a wall for support.

Jay pressed him on his shoulder – "Stay – 'til you've had something to eat!"

Tristan turned his nose up at Shannon. "See I told you we shouldn't turn it off!"

Taylor's head snapped at Tristan, "You – you didn't pull the wires?"

Looking confused, Tristan replied in surprise, "I thought you knew. The wires were fine at the bottom of that thing... that's what Shannon was saying – I didn't pull the wires. I was protecting them. *She* was freaking out – tried to pull them herself – so I did what I had to!"

Taylor was half relieved to realize that the sphere had actually finished its job, mostly because he was unsure of any side effects on himself if, in fact, the strange device couldn't complete its tasks.

Taylor then felt his heart sink within him as he felt the need to ask a question that was wrought with deep emotion. He turned a cautious stare over to Jay.

"Were you – just now – you know – seeing everything I saw?" Taylor asked as he took a protobar and a glass of water from the man.

"Yeah – seeing and feeling." Jay said, not releasing the two items to Taylor until he could see a response to his answer.

"Oh man." Taylor said half embarrassed.

"What's the matter – Oh – you didn't want me to know you are – you know – what you are!"

Taylor nodded and put the cool glass of water to his head.

"Dude, who cares? Doesn't change how I look at you – you're still the coolest guy I know!" Jay then quickly offered Taylor, though now a grown man, another scrubbing on the head.

"But – now you know the truth – you know the truth about yourself – and you know the truth about those kids – *your kids*."

"Damn straight they're my kids!" Taylor said with a huge grin on his face.

Jay looked down at him, "Taylor – mind your language – you're a parent now!"

Taylor cast his eyes to Tristan with a smile, "sorry."

The boy shrugged his shoulders and watched as Taylor, while still weak, was still struggling to stand.

"We have to move – now!" Taylor said insistently, and with these words Jay helped Taylor to his feet and the two, with Tristan following closely behind, made their way for the door.

"You don't really think that the vision's going to come true do you? I mean – you're talkin' about tomorrow morning!" Jay asked.

Taylor's face darkened in response. "Let's put it this way. Remember what I told you a few months back. That you'd be the first to know... Consider yourself told! It's gone from possible – to definite! Right now it would take a miracle to pull things off course from where they're headed."

Jay's face stiffed and a few shades of color seemed to seep out of the man's cheeks. He quickly hit the button to open the door for the three of them to leave.

"What – where do you think you're going!" Shannon asked frantically.

Jay turned around, "We don't have much time, honey. As far as I can tell we only have about twelve hours..."

"Twelve hours for what?" Shannon shouted.

"D'you remember that vision I told about? The one Taylor had before he left – with the city completely destroyed?"

She nodded her head, but Taylor was taken by surprise at the mere thought of this man sharing Taylor's visions with her. He had always assumed, and wrongly so, that all of what he and Jay did at work would be kept just between the two of them. But with a deep breath, he actually appreciated that there was someone else, someone outside The Towers, who was in this tiny loop of knowledge.

"Well – something's happened – something's changed – now it's not a '*might happen in five months'* thing– it's now an *'ABSOLUTELY GONNA HAPPEN IN TWELVE HOURS'* thing."

"What should I do?" she asked as a look of fear took her over.

"You should get the hell out of here, that's what you should do!" Taylor said loudly, but Jay quickly corrected him.

"No – No – sweetie," he said firmly and with a calming and soothing voice, he let go of Taylor and held her firmly by the shoulders. "You need to warn everyone – get them out of the city – do whatever it takes – there are two billion people here – two billion people who are going to die if they aren't warned."

"But what – what should I do?" she asked nervously.

"Shannon – you're in the media world every day – think of something – anything that would get their full attention. Do whatever it takes!"

Jay pulled her close, "I love you!" he said softly, and he gave her a kiss that Taylor blushed at seeing. He turned away but saw that Tristan was simply gawking at the couple.

"Hmmm – you have an audience." Taylor said with a smile.

Jay pulled himself away from her, and offered an arm of support to Taylor.

Taylor focused on opening the lift doors down the corridor as a sign that they should get moving, and so, with his friend helping him down the hall, a young teen at his side, and a resolute purposefulness on his face Taylor walked down the corridor, leaving Jay's fiancée, a woman that he had a blossoming respect for, to make herself decent and find some way to warn the world of what could only be called a catastrophe on fast approach.

69 In the Skies and In Time

IT COULD EASILY BE SAID that Taylor's mind wasn't spinning. No, it was being crushed under the many thoughts he was having; all focused what he had learned about his life, and the lives of his students. Students that he now knew were his own flesh and blood. Knowing more than just the truth of his relationship to them, Taylor also knew where his children were, and he was filled with a determination to rescue them from their prison. Yes, knowing the future that was fast on approach, he was resolute in his mind that he would do anything – *absolutely anything* to get his children back and make sure that they were in his protection.

"Dude, I know what you're thinking, and just to let you know I haven't lost faith, man, but I have to ask, how you plan on getting' in there – that place is like a fortress?" Jay said with a cautious excitement. These words fell on Taylor's ears, and while he'd of rather not answered the question, he could tell that Jay's eyes were staring at him, expectant of some much needed reassurance.

"Well," Taylor started, wincing his eyes from a slight pain in his head, "I'm sure I have no idea how I'm going to get in, but whatever it takes, I will get in!" He then offered Jay an unmistakable stare of firmness that the man understood.

"What about my mother?" Tristan asked both nervous and fearful. The boy hadn't said anything until now because he knew that Taylor's attention would have been on his students, but the thought had been pressing on his brain with an ever increasing force, and he couldn't keep from asking any longer.

Taylor looked at the boy with a smile and he could see that Tristan's eyes were filled with uncertainty. "She's fine – she's in a cell just across the hall from the kids!"

Taylor said this with a wavering in his voice as another pain struck his head. He did his best to hide this from Jay, but the teen saw, with a sideways glance, that his best friend had indeed noticed the suffering.

Tristan, however, did not notice and continued asking questions.

"Why don't they break out – I mean – it's just a cell," he said quickly. "I've seen what they can do! You can't tell me that they're being held in one place by a..."

Taylor beamed at the confidence that this boy had in his children, "It's more than just a cell," Taylor interrupted, "they're trapped in some kind of energy field. It keeps them from using their powers and believe me, even now Orion will be working hard on a plan of escape!"

Tristan's eyes widened. "Oh!" he said in a half excited voice and through the rest of the ride up to the ceiling Taylor tried to reassure the boy at his side that everything was going to be fine; that they were going to find his mother, and that somehow, though he wasn't exactly sure how, he was going to stop this pressing cataclysmic vision of the future from coming true.

With a ding the lift stopped, opened, and the three of them quickly made their way to the service access door and out onto the building's rooftop. In the instant that Taylor could see the city skyline, his heart plummeted to the floor in a panic. *What on earth had happened to his beautiful city?*

He stood there, in awe of the wreckage that he could see, with lights pouring into the skies revealing plumes of smoke and tattered buildings all around. Jay took position beside him and heaved a deep sigh.

"I know you never meant to do any of that – but when you were under – that is what the sphere made you do!"

Taylor quickly recognized the city skyline as that of the dilapidated one he had always seen in his horrible vision of the future – yet another sign that what he knew as a possible vision – was definitely going to happen. Breathing deep, he felt his legs grow weak, and rather than collapse uncontrolled, he dropped to his knees. Jay, a little frightened by this, tried to help the teen stand again, but Taylor resisted.

Taylor's eyes looked carefully under the wing that was in front of him. Here, under the cover of night, Taylor found himself looking it over with a curious familiarity. He crept across its underside, rubbing the bottom of it, staring at a strange set of markings that looked all too familiar. While this craft wasn't exactly the same as those he had seen in his vision with Johnny and Caitlin, the similarities couldn't be ignored.

Being sharply grabbed on the shoulder by Jay, Taylor pulled himself from under the craft and at this all three climbed the wing and entered it as fast as possible.

Taylor, having become much more familiar with the workings of this ship, prepared it for takeoff in only a few seconds. He then concentrated, forcing it high into the air while turning it eastward.

Much to his apologies, Taylor had accelerated the craft so fast that Tristan didn't even have time to strap himself in properly. As a result, the boy fell onto Jay quite hard.

"Hey! Let's try to get there in one piece, why don't we!" Jay shouted as he sat Tristan upright again.

While Taylor may have heard these words, he promptly ignored them. He knew that time was short, and if he was going to get to the children, before the foreseen horrific end, he would have to move fast.

With a concentration on the displays in front of him, Taylor was able to view a readout that told him the craft was traveling fast, but not fast enough. At its current speed it would take somewhere around 5 hours just to get to the D.C. Metroship. Taylor frowned.

It was here, in this other massive city, one that only just edged out Los Angeles in population, that the GC headquarters was located. And in this building, holding the GC Science Division and many other departments, he was sure to find his children.

As Taylor thought about the distance, and the time it would take to get there, he felt his mind grow frustrated at the idea of waiting so long for this craft to make its way across the country.

"Come on – can't this heap go any faster?" Taylor grunted in frustration.

As if the craft could listen to his question and offer an answer, his eyes were met with a flashing image on the display – "what's that?" Taylor asked rhetorically, and with a strange arrow appearing on the display he was directed to a button that revealed itself just above where the arrow was pointing.

Taylor leaned over and pushed the button, uncertain of what it would do, yet somehow having a feeling that it would help rather than hinder their journey. With a quick click – he heard the engines power down, and, at this, he immediately spewed a line of profanity to which even Tristan couldn't help but reply, "Taylor – mind your language!"

"What happened?" Jay asked, "Why've the engines stopped?"

"Nothing – nothing – I'll get them back up in a second." Taylor pleaded in frustration and as he said these words he saw, from above his head, a strange object lower itself from the ceiling of the craft. As if like a mechanical budding flower, this object showed itself to be a helmet that grew from the ceiling and positioned itself right in front of Taylor.

"What's that?" Jay asked curiously.

"Hmmm – It's a – a - well I don't know what it is?" Taylor said with a confused look on his face. This uncertainty didn't keep him from trying the helmet on, though, and with a quick grabbing, he shoved it on his head.

The second he put the helmet in place Taylor could see a translucent virtual control in front of him that he could grab, though not in reality, with both his hands.

"Cool!" he said softly with a smile, and in reaching his hands up to grab nothing more than air he, Jay, and Tristan were all met with a high level G force that made their heads to whip back sharply. None of the three ever heard an engine fire, or any kind of electronic unit start up. So whatever propulsion the craft was using, it was deadly quiet. Taylor, in fact, could hear little more than his heart pounding as he saw the scenes around him move swiftly by.

Amazed at what he could see through the view of this helmet, Taylor was hardly able to believe his eyes. As he looked around, this headgear, which was still attached to the ceiling of the craft, offered him images of what he would have seen had the paneling and other structure from the ship not been in his way. Indeed, it was like seeing through the walls of the ship – he could clearly see all the buildings of the Los Angeles Metroship and thereby know everything that was going on all around him, with absolutely no blind spots. He could still see a half transparent view of everything around him, including Jay and Tristan, but somehow he could see through it all and be shown a complete and unobstructed view of the outside of the craft.

As Taylor shifted his hands forward, the tall buildings disappeared quickly, and he realized that he was no longer in the confines of the city, nor was he traveling at a crawling speed. Looking at the display again, and with a quick calculation in his head, he realized that they would now be able to reach the D.C. Metroship in just over twenty minutes. He quickly calculated that the speed they were traveling was somewhere close to Mach ten.

Taylor felt himself grow giddy over the possibility that he'd be able to see his kids in such a short time. That is, of course, if everything went as he hoped – not as he planned, but as he hoped. In fact Taylor really had no plans for what would happen once he got to that city. Other than his landing on the roof of the GC headquarters, he was completely unfamiliar with the building and the city, and with this in mind, he knew he would have to play everything by ear.

Taylor realized that this kind of break in and break out would require a great deal of his kinetic and possibly even cognitive use and was relieved that he and Jay both remembered to bring handfuls of proto-bars for extra energy and with that thought in mind he grabbed a few from his own side pocket and started eating them slowly. Much to his additional relief, as he started eating the bars, he could feel the pounding in his head slowly subside. With everything he had done – everything that Jay had pointed out to him on the rooftop – it all must've taken a great deal out of him, and surely that was why his head pained him so.

In eating the proto-bars Taylor's face was all at once met with the impact of a face full of chocolate and peanuts.

"What the hell?" Jay said turning he head from side to side, wondering what was going on with the craft.

While this action may have provided little for Jay to see, when Taylor did the same, he was able to see that, behind their ship, there was another craft, of the exact same design, flying behind them.

Taylor's mind was flooded with two quick questions – Who was in the craft that was chasing him – and why were they attacking?"

He watched as a quick blast came from the craft behind. With rapid mental reflexes he forced his own ship to roll out of the way of the attack, and, thereby, he released the manual controls and focused hard on the craft, cyberly controlling it rather than using his hands. He still kept the helmet on his head, knowing that this would provide him the best view of the outside world, and of course, a constant view of any attacker, but he had to disengage whatever advanced propulsion the craft was using in lieu of slower, much safer, speeds.

Moving the craft to a stable path, Taylor rolled the craft to avoid another attack, and only pulled out of the roll a few feet from the ground below. In seeing the square pattern of what was beneath along with a few cattle roaming the grounds, he realized that he had nearly crashed into one of the food pattern farms in the Great Plains.

Taylor pulled himself up to a better altitude, and with a series of explosions to either side, he could see that the other craft wasn't about to let up.

Turning around, he tried to both control his own craft while also focusing on the one behind. *If I could just work my mind into that ship, I could just make it land – disable it somehow!*

It only took Taylor a few seconds to realize that this effort was useless, and, with a second attempt at using his powers, he tried to telekinetically manipulate his attacker out of the air. Again though, this provided no result.

"Come on Taylor – knock him out of the sky!" Jay shouted in seeing Taylor's backward stare.

"I – I can't I don't know what's going on!"

Taylor turned his head forward and started rolling the craft again, doing his best to keep from getting hit by his attacker. As his forward stare showed little but the dark of night, his eyes quickly caught sight of the glowing display before him.

The ship, which apparently had ears, was showing him a graphic display of how it had different kinds of shields to protect it. Indeed, Taylor was able to see that clearly this ship had more bells and whistles than he was aware of.

"And is there an easy way to turn these on?" Taylor asked aloud.

While both Tristan and Jay were confused as to who Taylor was talking to and why, the ship itself responded with a blinking "YES!" on the display. The virtual controls in front of Taylor showed that there were two virtual buttons on each handle that were now glowing; one was red, the other was blue.

He reached out, grabbed the controls, and lifted his thumbs up on the handles. He pushed the blue buttons, which had the words "shield" floating beside them and for a split second he saw an energy field rapidly engulf the craft. Taylor recognized the look of this field, but only just – it was the same that had been used to confine the children and as such, it explained why his powers didn't work on the other ship.

Taylor focused hard on the ship's controls in front of him. With a seizing motion he forced the craft to slow down and quickly lower in altitude, allowing it to be passed up by their attacker.

Now, with his enemy in his sights, Taylor pressed the red buttons that the ship had simply labeled "weapons" for him to read. He expected to see the same kind of blast as had been directed at him, but instead all he got was the display flashing a red message.

"WEAPONS MALFUNCTION"

"What the?" Taylor said, and with a quick focus on the display he *felt* his way to a diagnostic screen that showed him the problem. The first hit they suffered had completely destroyed whatever weapons they had.

The ship before him, as if it could tell Taylor's was crippled, turned around and quickly started firing. Taylor frantically started shifting his ship around, side to side, up, down, rolling – any maneuver he could think of to keep himself from getting hit. Before he knew it he was turned around, going the wrong way and now headed further from his original destination.

Whoever it was that was trailing and attacking him was obviously not going to leave him be. Taylor thought hard and fast. He dove down again. With his altitude dropping fast, he came within a hundred feet of the flat ground before leveling out. His pursuer followed this move exactly.

"Crap!" Taylor said, aloud. It was his hope that the other ship might have crashed, unable to pull up in time.

Taylor continued to shift the craft from side to side over fields of different crops. In looking at these it was as if a wave of thought had hit him and his eyes lit up. All at once Taylor dropped the shields of his own craft and focused hard on the ground. With a surge of telekinetic effort far greater than he could possibly have expected, he forced a mass of vegetable, plant, and earth into the air behind him. If Taylor didn't know it was his own effort that was pulling the earth into the air, he would have thought it was some massive explosion he should try to outrun.

Jay, in not knowing what was happening, was panic stricken. Small bits of plant fall on the front of the craft's windshield, and with words to reflect his emotion, Jay spewed, "What's going on? What's going on? What's happening? Oh crap – Oh crap!"

He said this over and over again and Taylor turned around offering a hard silencing stare. When Jay saw this, the man immediately stopped his nonsensical words, but what the man didn't realize was that Taylor wasn't looking at him. Taylor was looking to see the results of his kinetic efforts.

To his amazement, the teen saw that this *moderate amount* of effort, which he hoped had pulled a few fields of vegetation from their roots, had actually excavated everything on the ground as far as his eyes could see in both directions and thrown it high into the air. To his satisfaction though, when everything had settled, Taylor saw that his follower was no longer behind him. Instantly Taylor turned his stare forward again, and with a grabbing of the virtual controls before him, he made his craft turn around.

"What happened?" Jay asked in an awe stricken voice at having taken in, for the first time, the scope and mass of the fields that had uprooted themselves and eventually landed back to the earth in a raining heap of dirt and debris.

Taylor moved through these fields slowly, eventually seeing the other craft, half buried in dirt, some short distance away.

Taylor forced his craft to land amid protests from both Tristan and Jay.

"What are you doing?" Jay asked.

"We don't have time for this?" Tristan spewed.

"Shut up you two. I just need to know who's inside that's all!" Taylor then opened the craft and ordered the other two to stay inside while he exited the ship.

With his feet hitting the soft ground, Taylor heard sparks by his head, and when he turned he could see the damage that the first blast had caused to their craft. In the place of where a gun turret might have been, only a small electrical stump with a few hanging wires existed, and a strange oozing material leaked out slowly from the craft at the same spot, slowly overtaking the wires; something that made Taylor nervous in worry of the safety of flying his ship. The teen shook his head, turned to the other craft and walked across the soft upturned soil.

His enemy's ship was fully upside-down and covered by tons of dirt, and he had it in his mind to turn around and walk back, thinking it impossible to get inside, even with his kinetic abilities. But with this doubt over his abilities, Taylor's mind started questioning – wondering – then doubting the doubts. With the thought of what he had just done with his telekinetic power – *throwing all of that earth into the air* – Taylor quickly turned around and stared at the tattered craft. With barely the thought to do so, he was able to lift the machine high into the air. Taylor was amazed – *that, certainly, should've taken a great deal more effort, if not been impossible.*

Turning the craft upright, Taylor watched as large chunks of soil fell to the ground.

"Amazing!" Jay said as he watched Taylor from inside the other craft. The man then looked side to side at the large fields of unearthed plants and realized quickly that Taylor had caused all of their surrounding chaos just to get the other ship out of the air. "He's all but unstoppable!" Jay whispered.

With the other craft set properly on the ground, Taylor climbed on top of it, opening its hatch slowly. Even with his newly boosted abilities, which Taylor had quickly attributed to the work of the mysterious sphere and the many microscopic nanites which were surely still working hard in his brain, his nerves were very much on edge. The darkness inside the broken vessel revealed little to his view, and with a slow stepping into the craft, he turned his cloaking suit on standby, letting the glowing veins illuminate the entire cockpit.

Sparks zapped at odd intervals all around, and the smell of ozone was the first to hit his nose. He could quickly see so much damage done to the inside of the ship, and yet, just the same as the underside of his own craft, there was an oozing material that seemed to exude itself from the walls of the craft. Indeed, it was as if the ship itself was bleeding. Then Taylor at once could feel a cool breeze blowing from the front of the craft. He realized quickly its front windshield had been shattered and the flow of the night air saturated his nose with the smell of the freshly turned soil. As he slowly walked to the front of the craft he felt bits of dirt, grass, and glass beneath his feet. He could only assume that before the ship had crashed the breaking of the glass had let in all sorts of debris.

He approached the front seat of the cockpit. Whoever it was in the chair still had their helmet on – exactly the same as the one Taylor was using to navigate with, and the teen, while apprehensive, walked around to stand in front of this individual – a man. Whoever he was, he had suffered a good amount of cuts from the shattering of the windshield and Taylor could see that he was wearing an extinguished and horribly damaged cloaking suit.

Taylor reached out and in pulling off the helmet he could identify who was underneath it with a reveal of bright red hair.

"Rowna." Taylor whispered, and with a feel for the man's pulse – he could tell that Rowna was still alive.

Taylor cringed with the thought that this man had the knowledge and ability to have repaired one of the ships that he, Taylor, had utterly destroyed before he left the forest. Shaking his head at this thought, Taylor knew that the man must have had some help. With this idea in mind, he placed his hand on Rowna's forehead in the hopes of gleaning the truth. He focused hard on entering the man's post-cognitive history, thinking hard of what happened back at the hangar in the forest.

With little change in what Taylor was seeing, his view grew dark to a pitch black – then, it shifted to a brighter image. Taylor relaxed and allowed himself to see the vision with no effort to interact. He was, after all, seeing the world through Rowna's eyes, so there was little he could do but watch.

Taylor could see that he was lifted high into the air, and, looking down, he could see, himself – that is – the past version of himself, working hard on Tristan's broken arm. As he took in this vision of the past, Taylor could feel Rowna's emotions of hatred slowly swell inside his own brain – it was as if he hated looking at himself – hated the sight of himself – and most of all, he hated the fact that he was being held in place; helpless and weak in comparison to this person that he detested so horribly.

Taylor flinched in reality as he could hear Tristan yell. With a familiar play of events he had just watched the past version of himself pull the Anesth-X from Tristan's arm.

Then, to Rowna's ultimate anger, an anger Taylor felt straight to his core, the Taylor of the past crushed each remaining craft well beyond repair.

Through Rowna's eyes, Taylor continued to watch himself and Tristan enter the only functional craft that was left. Eventually it rose into the air and, quite suddenly, Taylor's view through Rowna's eyes shifted rapidly as he was dropped from where he was being held. He felt the sharp pain in his legs as his feet hit the hard concrete floor. In reality Taylor's true legs almost buckled under the pain, but, he focused hard on not losing physical contact with the body of Rowna.

Inside the vision Taylor slowly, through Rowna's own movements, made his way to one of the damaged craft. Inside it, he sat patiently in the cockpit until he could see a message on the display screen at the front of the craft.

"Ship regeneration in progress: Time to complete – 7 hours 36 minutes."

"Ship regeneration!" Taylor thought with amazement. "What, these things can rebuild themselves?"

Taylor continued to watch as Rowna walked to the other crafts and, each one suffering a different degree of damage, found he was satisfied at waiting in one that had a little less than five hours to complete repair.

Taylor had never heard of this kind of technology and he would have loved to stay and watch how this was done, but as he knew that time was short, he needed to pull his mind from this vision. His thoughts quickly shifted to the true task at hand – finding his kids.

Just as this thought entered Taylor's mind, a dark shadow fell over his view, and he quickly realized that he was moving to another vision of the man's past.

Indeed, with this new image Taylor looked out at a view of the forest where several large sequoia stumps jutted from the ground, and he had a good idea of where he was. He watched as a craft rose out of one of the stumps and thus his assumption was confirmed. He was looking at the topside of the strange hangar that he had seen only a few moments before, but wait – the ship that was lifting itself out of the large stump was completely different – one he wasn't familiar with. It was larger – and clearly had a different shape than his.

Taylor watched the craft head toward the Los Angeles Metroship and was curious of what it's destination was. After a few seconds of looking off in the distance where the craft had flown, Taylor heard a large booming noise – an explosion of sorts must have just happened. Instantly he, or rather Rowna, started running in the direction that the ship had flown.

The vision seemed to sped itself up as the man made his way through the forest – a journey that clearly took him several hours – eventually forcing him to stop, and rest for the night.

The following morning, which appeared to Taylor after only a few seconds, Rowna rose again and continued his journey. Taylor could feel that Rowna knew he was close to the crash via the sight of damaged trees caused by the ship's demise.

Rowna was cautious – and as he made his way through the last few trees that separated him from viewing the ship, he and Taylor saw that the craft from the day before had just lifted high into the air – but beneath where it had taken off, there were six small children lying bruised and quite helpless in the middle of the leveled trees.

Rowna would have approached, but it seemed that the moment one craft was out of sight, another appeared. This one was a standard emergency transport from the city. It landed right next to where the children were and immediately two people, a man and a woman both of whom Taylor actually recognized, started tending to the unconscious children.

Taylor could only assume from what he had seen, that the first craft was trying to transport the children into the city, but, as Taylor remembered from once before, the little ones probably woke before the trip was finished, and in a panic, they, or rather Grace and Orion, probably forced the ship to crash. Taylor quickly rationalized the events he had seen.

An impact like that probably caused so much damage that whoever was flying it probably had to wait until morning before the ship had brought itself back into repair.

But why leave the children? Taylor questioned, and as he watched the emergency personnel load the toddlers into the transport, he knew from memory how the rest of the children's journey would pan out.

Inside Rowna's head, Taylor watched as the man walked toward the crash site after the others had gone. Taylor was, just as curious to investigate the site himself, but just as he had stepped into the clearing his view shifted again. This time Taylor knew it wasn't of his own doing or thought, and as if his view was pulled away in a backwards motion, everything went to blackness once again.

Getting frustrated, he was about to focus on breaking his vision when he saw – was that – it looked like Tristan. – But no – he's older than thirteen. Taylor was confused. He could see a grown man that looked exactly like Tristan, but with lighter, blonde hair. This person was sitting on a log, almost in the same place where Taylor had decided to build his family's home.

Taylor's heart pounded loud in his ears at what he witnessed. He could do nothing to stop the actions of Rowna, and with the rising of his hands, Rowna had pulled a bow and arrow from his back. With perfect aim, he pulled the arrow – and released.

The shot went straight through the man's chest. This man that looked like Tristan glanced down for only a moment, grabbing the arrow delicately in quick realization of what had caused his new pain, then, after only a second or two, the man's body slumped down and released the arrow from his loose grip.

Rowna had killed this man, a man that Taylor now recognized, in putting the pieces together, as Delissa's husband – Tristan's father.

Rowna walked up to the unmoving body. With the use of his foot he pushed the body over and could see that the man had been writing something.

Rowna picked up the piece of parchment-like paper. With Rowna's eyes and voice Rowna, Taylor was able to read and hear what Tristan's father had written.

My Dearest Delissa,

I am so sorry about leaving last night. I was afraid our argument might lead me to say things I shouldn't. It's just that sometimes you can be so stubborn! It's funny but, now that I think about it, I know that this was why I fell in love with you, and why I love you still!

About our discussion – if you don't want to go to the city – if you're afraid, afraid of losing Tristan – I will accept your decision. But at least let me say my peace and understand why I would have these thoughts. I am fearful that as our Tristan gets older - Rowna will taint him with a constant influence of anger and violence. I know that Rowna is family, and that his efforts help us survive. But at the same time, I feel like I'm losing my son. Its like I'm watching someone else take his place. This scares me more than words. I want him to grow up wit

The letter was unfinished, and in listening to the words through Rowna's sarcastic voice, Taylor felt his own real anger rise higher than any emotion of the man whose body he possessed.

Rowna dropped the letter on the man's dead body and pushed it into the stream. Whatever time of year it was, the stream was much higher, and there was little doubt that it could carry the man's body for miles before it would either wash out to sea, or be found by someone.

Taylor could now make sense of Delissa's emotions about her husband leaving. It was after a heated argument, one that was obviously a very delicate subject for Delissa as even Taylor had discovered. What she didn't know was that he hadn't permanently left – he was murdered.

Taylor felt his stomach sicken. Now, with the thought to do so, he pulled himself from Rowna's vision and when he opened his eyes from total darkness, he could see that under his hand a man was staring up at him in absolute terror.

70 Failing to Plan

TAYLOR PULLED HIS HAND BACK and he watched the man under his nose flinch uncontrollably. Walking away, Taylor was about to leave the ship, but he noticed, out of the corner of his eye, that there was a glow in the cockpit that wasn't there before. Turning full around, he saw that the main display was actually lit up and in his memories he *knew* that this screen was shattered before. On this display Taylor could read the familiar phrase, "Ship regeneration in progress: Time to complete – 2 hours 25 minutes."

Taylor walked up to the display – with a focused concentration he started editing the code in the computer's core. As Taylor was now more familiar with the programming of the craft, he started deleting, adding, and editing the displayed lines of programming at a very high speed. Eventually Taylor stopped, turned around, and made his way to leave the craft.

Rowna didn't move a muscle, but in reading the screen he knew that there was no way this ship would ever fly again. The display now read, "Ship degeneration in progress: Time to complete – 2 hours 36 minutes," and as the man looked around the craft, he could see that different parts of it were actually dissolving – melting away into a strange oozing dark material that slowly started to suck itself into the ship's walls.

Pulling himself out of the craft's open hatch, Taylor smirked at hearing Rowna wail. He then took the last few steps off the ship's wing and made his way gingerly to his own ship. As he slumped through the upturned soil, Taylor noticed that neither Jay nor Tristan was capable of following the simplest of instructions. Both had left the craft and were on their way across the tattered field of upturned crops.

"I thought I told you..." Taylor started.

"Yeah, yeah, whatever! You don't actually expect us to just sit there!" Jay shouted.

"Who was that anyway?" Jay asked.

"Oh, just an old enemy. A little too hard to explain!" Taylor said on thinking it too much to first tell Jay who Rowna was, then explain the history he had just seen. With these words to Jay, however, Taylor offered Tristan a wink and a smile. He passed Jay up and, with a smirk put a firm a hand on the boy's shoulder before walking back to the ship, keeping the boy at his side.

"So what happened?" Tristan asked.

"Rowna was out cold when I boarded the ship – so I used him to look into the past – see if I could figure out how he repaired one of the one's I had destroyed."

On walking up to the edge of his own craft, Taylor smiled. There were no more sparks underneath and the stump of wires that once sat uselessly under the ship's wing was now replaced by a fully functional gun turret.

"And?" Tristan pressed, not noticing Taylor's change in attention.

"And – when I got out of *this ship* that gun turret wasn't even there! It *grew* back!"

"Ships can't grow!" Tristan corrected, but after a moment a wash of doubt fell over him and he recanted his certainty to now question "Can they?"

"Well – I don't know about other ships, but this one does – and so did Rowna's. After I wrecked all the others back in the forest, he just waited for one of them to repair itself well enough to fly again. 'T's really quite amazing!"

Tristan half grinned with disbelief, hopped on the wing of the craft and quickly hopped inside. Taylor then waited for Jay to do the same, making sure that he himself would be the last to enter the ship. "This way there'll be no surprises," Taylor said to Jay on making him enter the craft first.

Just before lowering himself into the ship, Taylor looked across the field to the other ship. It had lost most of its wings now and Taylor was certain that the ship would actually short circuit before it could finish degenerating itself. His face twitched with anger though. This was the third time he had left Rowna alive – and now, more than ever, he would have liked nothing more than to have a good reason to get rid of him – for good!

Taylor's angry stare shifted to a smirk as he lowered himself into the craft. The look of fear, the flinches of Rowna at the sight of Taylor – it was all too funny for words – this powerful man had been reduced to nothing in the teen's eyes.

While readying his own craft for flight, Taylor thought on Rowna and what happened in the now disintegrated craft. *I wonder if Rowna's thoughts were the reason I saw that last vision. Yes, yes, he was probably afraid that I was looking into his past – he was afraid that I would see exactly what he showed me with his own fears.* Taylor shook his head – it was all too weird in his mind, and as he turned around to make sure that Jay and Tristan were both strapped in his heart ached for the day that the boy might learn the truth about his father – a truth that most certainly should be told by Delissa, his mother, and not by anyone else.

Turning to the front of the craft, Taylor forced it to raise high into the air and, putting on the familiar helmet again, he forced the it to continue its journey east. He had lost nearly an hour with everything that had just happened, but, with his current speed, Taylor was certain he would make it to the D.C. Metroship and thus have plenty of time to spare.

As the minutes passed Taylor appreciated the changing scenes of North America, and as the images shifted he thought to check on his passengers. With a quick glance Taylor could see that Jay was already fast asleep, relaxed by the light humming of the craft. In looking at Tristan, however, he heard the boy's thoughts inside his own head. The teen, barely able to see outside the forward windows, was growing ever more frustrated because of an inability to take in a world that, until now, he had seen so little of.

"It's too bad there isn't another seat up here, that way you could really get a good look at what's down below!"

"Great! Yeah – thanks for that!" Tristan said with a sneer. He thought Taylor was saying this just to increase his irritation. Taylor, though, wanted to offer a hint to the ship – maybe it could accommodate with an extra seat at Taylor's side.

Taylor grinned as the ship did so much more than this. He felt his own seat shift a few inches to the left, and watched as Tristan's made its way forward. The boy's face showed a wide grin – "Hey!" he said loudly offering Taylor a nervously excited stare.

Taylor's face lit a wide grin when he noticed that the boy's seat had pushed itself up several inches further than his own, offering Tristan an even better view out the front and side windows of the ship.

Taylor focused on the ship cyberly so he could pull the helmet off his head without the craft losing its speed. Getting up, he whispered in the boy's ear.

"The ship has ears!" he said softly, "It hears us, and if it can do what we ask – it does!"

Tristan turned and frowned – "Nuh-uh – no way!" he said almost playfully.

"Sure – watch!" Taylor said loudly, "Ship – please give the boy a helmet like mine – so he can see outside like I can?"

Just as these words left his mouth a second helmet sprouted from the ceiling, and Tristan looked at it with a wide ecstatic smile. "Wow!" the boy bellowed as he grabbed the helmet. Taylor also reached out and also gripped it firmly, and with a firm grin he countered the boy's efforts – "Yeah, right! Ahem – ship! Please remove all navigation controls from *this helmet* as *I* will be controlling the ship."

He could see Tristan's face offering a pouting yet playful frown as he pulled the helmet from the boy's hand and placed it on the boy's head.

Tristan's face lit up instantly once the helmet was activated and he couldn't help but voice his elation.

"This is so cool!"

Hearing these words, Taylor put on his own helmet and at that moment he felt a pounding ache inside his chest, it felt so good to see a happy child, and he only hoped that soon enough he would be in the company of his own children. He started to wonder what was going on with them at that very moment, but decided to quickly distract himself by pointing out different scenes to Tristan, who didn't really know anything of what was passing by outside the craft. On occasion as they traveled over different metroships at high speed Taylor would offer little bits of history and names to help educate Tristan on a world that the boy had never seen. Taylor was, after all, a teacher, and he felt that it would be remiss if he didn't at least make some small effort to improve the boy's knowledge.

In their trek across the country they passed over Denver, Kansas City, St. Louis, Chicago, and Cleveland before slowly descending into DC airspace. Taylor immediately concentrated on the craft's cloaking device, which activated on his willing it to, and he felt his stomach slowly churn as he realized that he was approaching their final destination – "Well – here we are!" Taylor said loudly, and at this Jay woke with a start, snapping himself to attention.

Taylor could see, in as much as the EduCorp Towers were the city-center of Los Angeles, that the GC Towers, with their massive well lit antennas, were the center for the D.C. Metroship. Of course they weren't as tall as the EduCorp Towers, but what they lacked in height, the certainly made up for in sheer volume. This singular building measured nearly a mile in each direction.

Taylor slowly pulled off his helmet, cyberly controlling the craft through its normal engines. He turned the ship around and, with its nose readily facing west, he slowly landed the ship down beside one of the massive GC communication antennas.

Taylor and Tristan both turned their cloaking suits to standby mode and, with a quick look at Jay, the two realized he wouldn't be able to get anywhere without a cloaking suit of his own.

"Ship – a cloaking suit for my friend?" Taylor asked, unsure if the ship would have the capability to supply what he requested.

"Look at that, service with a smile!" Jay said as a small storage cabinet opened itself on the side of the ship – it contained four different suits of different sizes, and Jay quickly found one that was a close fit.

"That's fine" Jay said, and he turned his nose upward, "what about weapons!"

Another cabinet opened itself up, revealing an assortment of guns that Jay was only just able to glance at before the cabinet slammed itself shut. Taylor quickly turned to Jay with a sneer – "No guns!"

"What do you mean no guns? Come on, dude. They're probably gonna have guns!" Jay said in a high pitched excited voice.

"No guns! Too dangerous – if we have to defend ourselves – well – leave that to me!" Taylor said this with a slight confidence as he tapped his own temple.

"Man – you get to have all the fun!" Jay said, and with this Taylor only half laughed and shook his head.

"I'll be the first to go." Taylor said firmly, "wait for my signal, then follow!"

Jay and Tristan nodded as they watched Taylor climb out of the hatch.

After several seemingly interminable seconds they heard a tapping noise on the side of the ship. One by one they each nervously made their way up the hatch and out on the wing.

Jumping down, Jay and Tristan were making their way to Taylor, who was standing beside the large GC antenna.

A few feet away, though, Jay could instantly tell that something was wrong. Taylor wasn't moving – he was standing upright – stiffly upright. Jay reached his arm out and held Tristan back.

"What?" Tristan asked quickly.

"Back to the ship!" Jay shouted and as the two turned around, they both felt a massive pounding in their heads that eventually pushed their minds into total darkness. They were out cold.

Taylor stepped, quite stiffly, from the side of the antenna and without seeing who had done it, he received a sharp shock on the side of his head. The pain was excruciating and as he fell over the last thing he could remember seeing was the deep color of blue cloth swirling over his head.

*****

Opening his eyes slowly, Taylor felt a pounding in his head that was only aggravated by the lights beaming down on him. As he looked around he saw that he was in a small metal room with a high ceiling. He instantly recognized this room – it was the same cell or the same type of cell that his children were in.

With a quick turn of his head, Taylor was sure he might find any one, or all six of his kids somewhere in sight. Instead, with a moment of panic, he saw that the room was empty. He stood up, feeling the drafty air of – *what the* – he was wearing some kind of thin clothed pajama like outfit – why, he was dressed just the way he remembered his children being dressed in their cells.

He started frantically looking around for a way out. He walked up to the side of the room – tapped it softly with his fingers. With a show of electrostatic pulses he knew he was in the same confinement as his children and that using any of his powers would prove useless. Useless, that is, unless there was a leak – some way of getting out.

Taylor's mind started to spin – he continued to stare around the room, but his attention was caught by a shift in the metal plates and surfaces high above that eventually revealed a window.

Taylor looked in this direction and found his mind completely distracted by the possibility of this being a way out. His stare grew wide, though, as his eyes met the appearance of five cloaked figures. They were all there, standing and staring at him; red, white, black, green, and blue, all with their hoods raised. Welling with anger, Taylor started shouting at them, demanding that he be able to see his children, his words half strung with profanity.

"Father – Language!" offered the voice of a child, and at this, Taylor's brain had to do a double take. He played the voice over again in his head and tried to make sense of what he had just heard. Unless he was mistaken – that sounded like – "Aspen, are you there?" He asked with uncertainty, completely confused, and a little embarrassed that he may have used such words in front of one of his children.

The hooded figures all raised their hands, small hands, children's hands, and at the same time, they all revealed themselves. Taylor's jaw might have dropped to the floor with a clang if it weren't attached. He was staring at Caitlin, Orion, Grace, David, and Aspen all standing high above him, each smiling.

"What!" Taylor said softly in shock, "What are you doing in those cloaks?

And where's your brother?" he added more forcefully, but as he stared at their young round faces, the children only smiled and laughed amongst each other.

"Don't you see, father?" Orion said softly, looking down into the metallic room. "We're being trained! We're going to be on the council!"

"Yeah, Dad," David started, "Isn't it cool – we're gonna be the youngest members on the council, once we're all trained up."

Taylor's brain was having trouble taking in his own thoughts on what he was seeing and hearing. *It can't be – it just can't be.*

"That's impossible – the others aren't going to die off – and I'm quite certain they're not going to retire." Taylor looked to the ground, then shot his eyes skyward – "They're lying to you! They're trying to turn you against me – that's all! Don't believe a word they say!"

"Oh, father," Aspen said softly with words t hat were quickly followed by those of Grace, "You just don't get it! They'd do anything for family – and who else would be perfect for the positions but us?"

Taylor shook his head at these words, "What have they told you! What do you *think* you know?"

"Come on, Dad," Caitlin said shaking her head, "What do you think we are, stupid? They've told us everything – we know about you, about them, and about us."

"Yeah – it all makes sense." Aspen said and in turn the children seemed to finish each other's thoughts, "You were their first project – we were their second – and, as there are five of us – it's only fitting that we should take their place – when we're ready."

"There are six of you!" Taylor shouted, and as he listened to the words of his children, his temper grew more heated. Had total strangers taken away his right to tell his children that he was, in fact, their father? Had they brainwashed his children into little mini-versions of themselves? Taylor grunted, but as a sense of purpose overtook him, he heaved a deep sigh and looked upward again, doing his best to keep calm.

"You're too young to understand what you're getting into! Now come down here so we can talk about all this."

"There's nothing else to talk about." Orion said firmly as it was his turn in rotation to speak before being followed by Grace, "We've made our decision – and we don't need you to help us anymore!"

Taylor felt himself growing more and more frustrated. He hit his hand on the side of the cell, offering an electrostatic wave that eventually made its way over the glass window. "You let me out of here now or so help me!" Taylor shouted, and as he looked up at the young faces of his children, he could see them stare back with – was that – pity?

In glowering at the children Taylor noticed others enter into view from the side of the window. Taylor recognized them immediately. They were much taller than the children, yet wore exactly matching cloaks.

"You!" Taylor shouted, his anger boiling over and he watched as the familiar faces of the cloaked GC representatives were revealed. Christine put her hand on Orion's shoulder and it was as if the boy was speaking at her command.

"You see, father, we don't need you anymore!" the boy said softly.

"Oh you just wait!" Taylor shouted, "When I get out of here you're going to get it – big time!"

"The children started laughing at him from their high positions, and Taylor was further angered to hear the children's voices overshadowed by the laughter of their older counterparts. He slowly stepped back from under the window and turned away. He felt as if his heart had been wrenched out from his chest. All at once he started feeling what he had told his children was the worst of emotions – despair!

In his stepping back, his heel hit something soft on the floor and looking down, he saw Johnny's curled up body in the corner of the cell. Taylor shook his head of his emotions and kneeled down to grab the boy who, he was certain, wasn't there before.

"Johnny – Johnny – what's going on?" Taylor asked frantically. "What's happened to your brothers and sisters? Nothing's making any sense!"

On seeing Taylor's face, the boy smiled. He reached up around Taylor's neck and gave him a soothing hug, putting his chin on Taylor's shoulder. This was something that, while Taylor didn't know it, he desperately needed. In an instant the man felt – perfect – and he couldn't explain why. As he pulled the small boy away and looked at him, bright blue eyes to bright blue eyes, he suddenly lost all his thoughts and all his words.

"Father," Johnny said softly, "sometimes a dream is just a dream."

Taylor took in these words with a wink from the boy, and he grinned to one side. Setting the boy upright, he held the child's hand, and after a moment of taking in the fact that the child was fine and that this reality wasn't that at all, they both stood to full height.

"So how's Orion doing with that escape plan?" Taylor asked with a smile. Johnny took a breath to answer, but his words were interrupted by a voice from above.

"Father – I'm up here!"

Taylor and Johnny both cast their eyes upward and saw a second version of Johnny. He was on the other side of the glass window, alone, and the other ten that were there before – were nowhere in sight.

Taylor shook his head, "Tricky – very tricky!"

"Orion thinks he's figured out a way to escape – but we're waiting for Aspen and David to come back."

Taylor nodded his head, "Ah! So, what's the boy got up his sleeve!" He asked Johnny almost playfully.

Johnny smiled and cast his eyes downward, stomping his foot.

Taylor tilted his head with an almost laughing grin, "Alright. Well, I guess we should stand back then."

"But father, this is just a dream." Johnny said with a voice of confused concern.

"Oh, I think it's a little more than that!" Taylor said, and with a grin he cast his stare upward at the observing room. The other five children and the Evol-Crew were back inside the room and the second image of Johnny was gone. Taylor shook his head and just before he cast his eyes downward, he saw ten small hands shoot out to the glass, smacking it with their flat palms.

"Nice try!" Taylor said, and with a focused glare he ripped open the floor beneath himself and Johnny. The room immediately went dark, and below, Taylor could see an image of himself sleeping. This surprised Taylor a little, for he was hoping that in escaping the cell he would wake up, but he didn't expect such a strange physical representation of re-entering his own body.

"Get the others to the edge of the cell – I'll be coming through the floor!" Taylor yelled amid the noise of sparks, venting air, and even plumbing that he had ripped open with his mind.

The boy at his side nodded before pleading, "don't let go!" as he tightened his grip on Taylor's hand.

"I'll try!"

At these words Taylor and Johnny both jumped through the hole in the floor and their ears heard the word "No!" being screamed by all those in the observation room overhead.

Taylor's stomach turned with the freefall feeling and while he tried to hold tight to Johnny's hand, the boy's grip lost continuity. Johnny's hand slipped right through his own, and in a panic, Taylor watched the boy slide away and through the wall of the cell. Taylor landed on himself with a bang, and in an instant he sat upright with a deep heaving breath.

71 Escape Reprised

IN THAT MOMENT WHEN HE SAT UP, Taylor wanted immediately to lie back down. His head – as now he wished he could detach it from the rest of his body – was still pounding with a horrible headache. Looking about, he took in his full bodied form and his surroundings. Indeed he *had* been changed into a pajama like outfit that was identical to the ones he remembered from his dream and his earlier vision, and he was in the same kind of cell that he had seen before. Tristan and Jay, who Taylor was happy to see, were in the cell with him, and he had to grin at the fact that they too were wearing the same odd attire.

Furrowing his brow in confusion, Taylor noticed that the other two were kneeled down, staring at one of the walls of the cell with a curious focus. He walked over to them, his feet making no sound at all, and with his first words he caused the both of them to jump with a fright.

"Hey guys – whatcha lookin' at?"

"Geeze!" Jay shouted, "Next time make a little noise or somethin' I hate it when you do crap like that."

Tristan just closed his eyes and took a deep breath, opened them again, and smiled at seeing Taylor on his feet. The teen's smile quickly soured though, and he started shouting at Taylor the instant he could speak the words in his mind.

"You attacked us! Why the heck did you attack us?" The boy bellowed across the room.

"It wasn't me, it was Elizabeth!" Taylor shouted, and while he could expect the next response, he looked to Jay for a little support.

"Elizabeth," Tristan shouted, "Who the heck's Elizabeth!"

Jay looked over at the boy, "She's a very powerful telepath – she can make people do things with their own powers that they don't want to do!"

"Right!" Taylor said looking down at the boy "I only realized she was there when she knocked me out. She seized control of me, but I don't know if she made me knock the two of you out, or if she did it herself – because I know that she and I share that. So it could've been her!"

Taylor bit his lip at the thought of his own words. "But what was she doing on the roof?" He questioned in a whisper. *She must have known we were coming; someone must have told her.* All at once his mind moved to his children and to

Delissa – of the two possibilities he knew it would be much easier to get the information out of the latter, who was in an unprotected cell, and if Elizabeth shared his talents, then she probably shared his ability to communicate with non-telepaths too. Thus getting this information from her would be relatively easy.

In having these thoughts Taylor's face shifted to a look of concern, but with Tristan tapping the side of the cell and causing large electrostatic waves to creep up its sides, Taylor was brought back to the issues at hand. He quickly looked down at Jay and the boy, "What are you two doing down there anyways?" he asked.

"Funny thing, this field we're in," Tristan started, "Over here, the wall kept pulsing constantly, even though it wasn't being touched or anything, then, just a few seconds ago – probably right when you woke up – it just stopped!"

"I know." Taylor said with a smirking smile. "Apparently it isn't a completely impenetrable barrier."

Jay looked at Taylor with wide eyes. Getting to his feet and looking all around the cell the man asked excitedly, "What do you mean by that?"

"Well," Taylor said speaking in a tone that told the others he wasn't completely sure of what he was saying, but that it was his best theory. "I know that for the most part the barrier does its job fine. But I think that Johnny and I have a lot more in common than anyone else seems to realize. I could be wrong – but I think our minds can – hmmm – *operate* on the same frequency or something like that. My guess is that's one of the reasons he's always standing out in my visions; I seem to know what he's thinking a lot more than the others – and were so closely bonded."

Jay looked at Taylor with a complete expression of doubt to which the teen responded, "Of course this is all just a theory."

Jay's smile diminished, "What's that got to do with the containment field?"

"Well," Taylor started again, but this time his voice shifted to one of a more definite tone. "While I was asleep, Johnny and I were – uh – communicating through that wall – that's probably why it was going all buggy."

"Really?" Jay said with a doubtful voice, and then persisted, "I don't suppose you'd know if they found a way out of this place yet."

Taylor stomped his foot, "Sure would and sure have!"

Jay didn't seem to get what Taylor was trying to show him, but with his arms spread wide Taylor forced both Jay and Tristan back to one of the walls of the cell, "Ahem – let me demonstrate." Taylor then hit the wall with his fist, revealing the electrostatic wave. He then stomped on the floor, revealing nothing.

"So! – What are you waiting for – rip it open! Let's get a move on!" Tristan said in realization of what Taylor was trying to show them.

"Before I do anything I want your word," Taylor said in a serious tone looking at his two companions. They returned the serious stare and Taylor continued. "I don't want either of you telling them the truth of things. *I'll* tell them when it's time."

Jay and Tristan nodded their heads, with Tristan adding, "That's your business, not ours!"

Jay on the other hand just simply shook his head, "I still can't believe that you and Johnny... the same *frequency*?" he said mockingly.

"After everything that you've seen, you can't believe?" Taylor responded in a half frustrated voice while shaking his head. "Well, my friend, believe it! That's all I have to say, just believe it!"

Taylor then cast his eyes downward. "I have to be careful about this – I don't want to make the whole building come down!" he said with concern and this caused Jay to remember the miles of upturned field, forcing the man to swell with worry.

Taylor focused hard on the floor beneath him. At first, Tristan and Jay thought nothing was going to happen, but after a few seconds of waiting, they realized that they were absolutely mistaken. With a rumbling of the floor, Taylor forced an almost earthquake like shaking to rattle the room. "That's some thick metal!" Taylor said with almost a grunt, and as these words passed over his lips, a huge booming crack resonated through the cell and the floor broke nearly in half. At the same time as this, the lights overhead started to flicker then go out completely, and Taylor watched as, beneath the thick plates that made up the floor, cables and pipes started ripping themselves apart.

Seemingly, the only thing that was still working was the red flashing lights and the audio alarms. Indeed, at that instant, everyone in the building knew there was an escape in progress.

Taylor continued to carefully focus as the two fractured pieces slowly lowered downward through the floor-line. Once he saw that they were separated enough and low enough, he stopped with a heavy exhale.

"Was it really that tough?" Jay asked with a look of concern.

"Not at all," Taylor said shaking his head.

Jay pulled back his head with a sense of disbelief, turned to Tristan and, with a firm grip on the boy's shoulder, the two slid down the now angled floor. On reaching bottom, it was Jay that noticed that the floor was constructed of twenty-four inch thick composite metal.

"Taylor!" Jay shouted, rubbing his hand along the blunt broken edge of the floor, "You must be joking! That must've taken everything you had!"

"Was nothing really – hard - ly even tried." Taylor said with a bump in his voice as he landed after sliding down. This was half a lie and half the truth for Taylor, but either way Jay didn't believe it. The truth was that Taylor hadn't used hardly any of his telekinetic ability, but it took all his concentration not to just rip the whole building in half.

Looking around their new room, Taylor quickly recognized that they were in another cell, this one was shorter, and, with a tapping on the wall – "Yup – no field!" Taylor said with a smile.

He then cast his eyes back upward and, trying to get his bearings, he looked at one of the walls of the cell with a half focused stare. It ripped itself open after only a second and in the teen's own mind his confidence was building over how well he could control his abilities.

With the new hole in the wall, Taylor caught sight of a slew of security ready for attack. They started firing and with a quick "Down!" and jumps in different directions, he, Jay and Tristan all moved out of the way of the hole.

Taylor rolled over on his back just in front of the hole he had created. He closed his eyes and, with the sound of several thuds and the clinking of guns hitting the floor, Taylor realized that he had, again, forced everyone he had focused on to simply pass out.

He stood up, surveyed the mass of strewn bodies, and stepped over them carefully. Making his way to the next wall, he again punched through it with little effort. Sparks were flying as he had pushed his way though more electrical conduits and wires. Stepping into the next room Taylor and Jay took in the thick odor of ozone that was filling the air from all the electrical chaos. Looking to the floor, the three had to, again, step carefully over the bodies of a second wave of security personnel that Taylor didn't even know he had knocked out.

Taylor was about to push though the next wall when, to his surprise, he heard voices inside his head.

"Father stop!" He recognized this as Caitlin's voice.

"Yeah, stop – we're here!" he heard now in Orion's voice

Taylor cast his eyes upward, "they must be just above us!" Taylor said, his heart pounding with fantastic euphoria.

"How do you know?" Jay asked.

"I can hear their thoughts." Taylor said, but he was met with an incredulous stare from Jay.

"Line of sight, remember!" Taylor said matter-of-factly as he very, very carefully started pulling at the ceiling overhead.

Jay nodded his head, but Tristan didn't understand. The boy tugged on Jay's pajama like shirt as the two shifted to the side of the cell, a place where, hopefully, they'd be safe.

"What's line of sight have to do with anything?" the boy asked confusedly.

"Line of sight," Jay started, "a term used in radio transmission and telepaths. It means that a telepath can only communicate with another telepath if there isn't any interference in their line of sight."

Tristan shook his head, still confused.

"It's like this!" Jay said using his hands to explain. "If the children are in the containment field, then we can't communicate with them because something is blocking us. But we know that the bottoms of those cells aren't protected. If the children can communicate with him – then they're in line of sight – right overhead!"

Jay had just finished the word 'overhead' when the light fixture above them and the supporting structure had pulled itself down. Taylor kept his eyes sharp, in case any children may have been directly above where he had opened the ceiling. Of course he would not want to injure his children by allowing them to drop to the level below, but fortunately his stare was not met with any raining children. In fact, his eyes weren't met with any children at all. He reached up and started climbing the slanted and overly slick surface of the now steeply angled floor. Pulling his body up by hanging wires and anything else he could get his hands on, Taylor eventually made his way high enough to see into the upper level, and, looking around quickly, he noticed that behind him, four familiar bodies; Orion, Grace, Caitlin and Johnny were all crouched in the corner.

"Come on guys, whatcha waitin' for?" Taylor shouted.

They pulled their heads from under the thin sleeves of their pajama outfits. Their faces quickly lit with bright smiles, and Taylor waved for them to slide down the slanted floor into his arms.

While no specific order had been determined as far as who would go first, Taylor could have predicted it and been exactly right. Johnny, the youngest, was first; then Caitlin, who was always more delicate and feminine, then Grace, who only went as a comment of Orion's, "ladies first," then, and last, was Orion himself.

Taylor caught each one of these children as they landed, offered them a quick hug, then handed them over to Jay, who accepted them quickly and forced them to crouch next to Tristan who, when Johnny saw him, gave him a quick high five.

"What're *you* doing here?" Johnny asked.

Tristan smiled, shaking his head, "You know, you weren't the only ones that were taken."

Johnny looked confused, "I thought you went to go look for him," he said nodding in Taylor's direction.

"You knew about that?" Tristan said with wide eyes.

"Course I did!" Johnny said with a smile and he, in a fashion that reminded everyone of Taylor, he tapped his own temple.

Tristan shook his head, "Yeah, I was gone, so *I* wasn't taken, but my mom was."

"Right!" Taylor said making his way between the children and Jay, "This way!"

He moved to the entrance of the cell that they were in and, with hardly a focus, he opened it cyberly, revealing a corridor that reminded Taylor, Johnny, and Caitlin of the one that, undoubtedly was just above it. Across from their current room, Taylor could see another door. This was obviously another cell which Taylor instantly opened.

Turning to those around him, Taylor spoke quickly and quietly. "Everyone stay here. I'll be back in a second!"

"Wait what do you mean stay here!" Tristan said nervously.

"I'll be right back – and I won't be alone!" he said offering the boy a quick wink. Tristan smiled at this and he knew that Taylor was going after his mother.

Taylor bolted across the corridor into the other cell. His eyes took in the fact that, all through the level, everything was very quiet. In fact, no one other than himself, Jay, and the children was moving about.

Standing in the doorway, Taylor cast his eyes upward. He spent a great effort focusing on the edges of the ceiling until, eventually, he pulled the entire upward surface downward as a whole. He concentrated on detaching wires and other utilities as the large flat surface slowly descended. Eventually it passed Taylor's eye level. With this he looked up into the newly revealed room to see a calm Delissa sitting with folded legs in the middle of the descending floor.

"What took you so lo-ong?" she asked with a jolt as the floor beneath her had finally settled.

"Do you have any idea where you are?" Taylor asked curiously.

She shook her head and he smiled, "You're over two thousand miles from where you were this morning – on the other side of the continent!"

She stood up as he spoke, walked toward him, and with a blood boiling closeness she offered him a kiss that, this time, he expected and reciprocated. They eventually pulled apart from each other and she spoke softly to him as he was only a few inches away.

"So – you came all this way just for me?" She asked playfully, but her words and the mood were quickly spoiled by a cough from Jay. Delissa looked over Taylor's shoulder, and saw that there was a young audience watching them, including her wide grinning son.

Delissa slowly pushed Taylor aside and moved across the corridor to the boy. She kneeled in front of him, pushing his face side to side, checking his every inch. "Are you okay? Where have you been? I looked all over for you when – when..."

"Mom! It's okay. I followed Taylor – it's a long story – but I've been with him the whole time."

She smiled, gave him a suffocating hug, and over his shoulder she could see the wide stares of the other four children. She reached up and patted each one on the head.

"'T's good to see you all!" she said softly, but realized immediately that two were missing from their ranks. "Where are the others?" she asked almost panicked.

"I can only guess that they're three levels down." Taylor said calmly, and he looked around at the group with waving hands, "I think it's about time we get them and get the hell out of here!"

With uproarious consent, they all ran down the corridor, carefully stepping over dozens of GC security. With focus, Taylor opened the lift doors and everyone entered it quickly, making for a tight fit. Taylor carefully edited the security protocols of the lift, which now seemed so much easier for him to do, and so absolutely simple for him to navigate. He allowed the lift, which had been locked into position to prevent escape, to operate normally, and instantly they all dropped levels where the lift stopped again.

Taylor was sure to relocate himself so that he was in front of the doors when they opened. He then cyberly forced it to stay at the same level and he took a deep breath with the thought in mind that he didn't know what to expect on the other side of the flat surface so close to his face. He was about to force them open cyberly when, to his surprise, they opened on their own.

Taylor was shocked to see David and Aspen standing in front of him, wide smiles bearing white teeth. He squatted and they both rushed in and gave him a quick hug. The teen almost laughed at this, and looked over their shoulders while enjoying the warm embrace.

It was this view that showed Taylor a man walking awkwardly down the corridor in the distance. It was Daniel, wearing his green cloak, stumbling with his hand on his forehead.

Taylor turned himself and the children around so that his back was to the long corridor. "You need to get to the roof as quick as you can – I'll be up in a minute – I've got some business to take care of!"

"Dad no!" all of the children, less Tristan, shouted in unison.

Taylor only smiled. "I'll be fine – trust me. I'll be just fine – now when you get up there, I want you all to get into the ship and I want you," he said turning to Tristan, "To put on *my* helmet and activate the shields. You'll be protected that way."

"But I don't know how to..." Tristan started, but his words were interrupted with a quick telepathic blast from Taylor – he was instructing the boy visually on how to at least activate the ship's power so he could do as he was told.

The boy nodded and, with a gasp and huge gaping eyes that looked over Taylor's, the child showed fear of something that caught his attention.

Taylor turned around and with an unnecessary wave of his hand, he forced the lift doors to close and in an instant the overstuffed lift ascended higher and higher, taking its load of nine passengers to the roof.

For Taylor, he saw that Daniel was no longer alone in the corridor. Now he had Dr. Zeldin at his side. Between the two of them, they both had their colored hoods raised and it was with the unnatural darkness that these hoods afforded that Taylor was unable to see their faces.

72 Red and Green

TAYLOR STOOD FIRM in front of the lift doors, with the two powerful individuals in front of him, he stared them down, unwavering in his otherwise quite exposed pajama latent stance. Had he been forced to face these two before, he might have felt ill equipped to handle them. Now, however, his confidence forced a smile to slowly widen on his face. He reveled with the thought of how much power he could harness if he needed to.

"I'm only going to ask you once." he said firmly. "Tell me why these children, *my children*, are so important. What does the GC want with them?" He stood and watched as the two hooded men turned to each other.

"Oh, aye. It must be surprising to hear, but I know about my connection to the children – my *genetic connection!* I even know about our connection!" Taylor said loudly pointing between himself and those he was facing.

He watched as Dr. Zeldin slowly lowered his hood and turned to Daniel, who followed his lead. After a moment's silence it was Dr. Zeldin who spoke first.

"You don't know the whole truth – there are reasons why we have to take the children – reasons you can't know!"

"Your cloak seems damaged there shorty! I wonder how that happened." Taylor said almost playfully as he pointed to the hole in Daniel's cloak. With wide eyes the two members of the Evol Crew pulled up at the garment, staring at the damage, all the while Taylor continued to speak with absolute confidence.

"And as far as what I know – I know enough. I know about *them.* You made certain of that! And if you're wondering how I got past your little cognitive blocks – well – let's just say I've grown more powerful in the last few hours; more powerful than you could possibly imagine."

He watched as Daniel carefully examined his cloak, running his finger through the hole. Dr. Zeldin, who hadn't thought of it until then, pulled a small piece of green cloth from a pocket inside his uniform. Daniel snatched it from the man's hand and focused on the two perfectly fitting opposites, and in staring at the hole in his uniform he was curious how Dr. Zeldin had come to have this piece of it in his possession. He glowered up at Dr. Zeldin with immediately questioning eyes.

"I found it on him – when they brought him in. But how..."

Daniel's eyes darkened to anger, and he looked up at Taylor with a fierce stare.

"Oh, don't worry, it wasn't me! It was that close shave you had with the end of Delissa's sword that offered that little clue; quite perfect if I do say so myself." Taylor was almost laughing with his words, but Dr. Zeldin dampened this high mood with his own rhetoric.

"You selfish little child! Those children are dangerous! In the wrong hands they'll cause the destruction of...

"Bull!" Taylor shouted, "And don't give a crap about your plans, your conspiracies, or your stupid little theory that my children – *my children* are NOT responsible for the future that we all know is coming – and I won't tolerate hearing otherwise!"

"Listen here, boy," Daniel shouted in frustration, "we don't have time for your immature ignorance. Those children are ours. They were ours to begin with, and they're ours still. You have no rights to them, none whatsoever!"

Taylor's lip curled in anger. All around the three of them the walls in the hall started to rattle and shake with Taylor's fury, his memories, his pain, and his growing irritation. He started to shout angrily at the two men before him. "You had no rights to my blood when you made them," Taylor said in a low accusing voice, "so I'm just taking back what was stolen from me to begin with!" At these words Taylor started to walk toward the two of them. He was sure that if they were aware of how truly powerful he had become, they would run away. But this was not the case – and Taylor still had more questions that needed answering.

"Taylor," Dr. Zeldin commanded, hoping his forceful voice would make his former friend back down, "Your blood was *ours* too, so in essence, you belong to us as much as the children do – and you'll have your time – when..."

"Shhht!" Daniel hissed at the doctor, forcing his words to stop.

"You might as well let him speak, *Daniel*!" Taylor said sourly, "Anything you offer me willingly will keep you from a torturous pathic linking later!"

"You pompous little..." Daniel growled – irritated at the fact that Taylor had somehow figured out his name. Daniel quickly tucked away the green cloth in a pocket under his cloak and, at that moment, the teen could see that the man was furrowing his brow with a focused look in his direction.

It was a strange thing for Taylor, having his improved telekinetic powers, for it was as if he could feel Daniel's efforts to force him backward – a hard push – a throw. Taylor reacted by cleaving this telekinetic force in half, raising his chin as he did this. He focused hard on what Daniel was trying to do, looking at the man with a firm almost one-eyed stare. Taylor didn't even flinch when he heard that the doors to the lift behind him had buckled with the telekinetic force Daniel had thrown in his direction.

"You're going to have to do better than that to get the best of me." Taylor said with amusement.

Daniel, while somewhat unnerved at the idea that his efforts did nothing to Taylor, but a great deal to the doors behind him, grunted and huffed angrily. "I'm just getting started, boy!"

Daniel looked harshly in Taylor's direction. Taylor took a deep breath, closed his eyes, and with Daniel forcing kinetic hits in all manners at Taylor, it seemed that nothing could hit the teen, who merely stood there as the many deflected blows caused damage to the walls, panels, and lights of the corridor in all directions.

Daniel shook his head slightly, his eyes rolling around in confusion.

"Well, doctor, you got any bright ideas?" he asked, turning to Dr. Zeldin.

"Only one!" he said while quickly moving behind Daniel and Taylor had neither the sight, nor the reflexes to react to Dr. Zeldin's reaching to a holster under his cloak.

He raised it up and fired, grazing Taylor through the top of the shoulder. The pain was brief as the wound was instantly cauterized, and Taylor moved quickly to avoid a second hit.

Focusing on the floor, Taylor lifted several tiles into the air. He moved them around, in a random pattern so that, as Dr. Zeldin fired, he was completely unable to hit Taylor a second time. Eventually Taylor simplified the situation by forcing one of the tiles to hit Dr. Zeldin's hand, making him drop the gun. The tile then struck the man hard under the chin.

Taylor tried to hit Daniel too, but the man used his telekinesis to keep himself safe from several efforts made by Taylor in this regard.

"I use my powers for a living – you're going to have to do better than that if you hope to bring me down - *teacher*."

Taylor smiled, "This teacher's about to take you to school!"

As these words fell out of his mouth, Taylor almost laughed at the situation in which he now found himself. It amused him beyond words how he once revered the Evol-Crew and their ability to *bring down the bad guy* – but as he was now on the receiving end of this effort at apprehension, he got to see, first-hand, what so many others had – and it was, for lack of a better word in the teen's mind – entertaining.

Daniel raised his hand, waving for Taylor to do his best.

Taylor smirked as he concentrated on the walls of the corridor. "Well – if we're going to do this – let's get a little room." He turned his head to one side of the corridor. It started to flex and eventually crushed against itself until, with a deafening boom he caused the wall and all the cells to compress themselves. Taylor then turned his head to the other side of the corridor to, again, do exactly the same. In his efforts, he was careful to make sure that he didn't damage the major structure that actually supported the building and the end result was an arena sized room latent with metal support pillars ready for a fight to take place.

With his eyes looking back at Daniel, and an obviously firghtened Dr. Zeldin, Taylor smiled. "It's not too late to change your mind – just relinquish your claim to the children – leave them alone – leave me alone – and let us live in peace!" he said, noticing the contagion of fear spread from Dr. Zeldin's face to that of Daniel, who was doing is best not to show it, and only making it so much more obvious.

"Just who do you think you are? Making demands!" Daniel shouted, fearfully swallowing his words as quick as he said them.

"Do you really think you can win here, Daniel." Dr. Zeldin half whispered as he took his place behind one of the pillars in the middle of the now large empty room. "I mean I've seen what this boy can do – you have no idea how..."

"Shut up – coward!" Daniel shouted, and with a look in the direction of Dr. Zeldin, he noticed over a dozen metal beams sticking out form the chaotic mess that Taylor had left in clearing out nearly the entire floor. He then turned to Taylor with a focus on using these metal beams as spears.

Taylor dropped himself to the floor quickly while kinetically deflecting all the approaching pieces of metal except for two that he had grabbed out of the air with his hands, partly slowing them with his powers.

Daniel grunted in anger. With a focus on the beams again, he used them in all sorts of directions in an effort to attack Taylor. He tried to hit the teenager from any angle, in any way, from all directions, using every bit of focus he had on swinging, throwing, and spinning the beams at his will.

Taylor worked diligently with his own metal beams, his shoulder paining with nearly every move. He countered or dodged each move Daniel forced and eventually realized that he could alleviate the pain in his arm by using his kinesis to control his second beam. With this thought, he let the beam go and, concentrating on it while using the other in the hand of his uninjured arm; he was able to keep all of Daniel's efforts at bay. Taylor, in fact, offered the man an unflinching stare as he physically and mentally did all the work needed to keep safe.

Daniel raised his eyebrows with a fearful look as if he knew what was coming! Taylor tipped his head, forcing a hard telekinetic hit that threw the man across the room, forcing him to hit one of the building's supports hard with his head. Daniel fell to the ground, out cold, and with a series of loud clanging noises all the beams Daniel had been controlling fell to the floor.

Taylor dropped his own beams and in looking around the room, he focused hard on locating Dr. Zeldin. He took a deep breath and while closing his eyes he thought of the man, trying to feel where he was. After only a moment Taylor sighed, and turned around.

"Don't you think that's quite enough?" He said as he opened his eyes and looking at Dr. Zeldin who was, again, holding the same plasma gun he had yielded a moment earlier. Taylor shook his head noticing the man's nervous quivering. Taylor felt perfectly safe in thinking that the doctor was unable to properly aim his weapon.

"Don't move or I will shoot!" Dr. Zeldin said, completely overcome with panic. It was interesting to see how much this man, who's ego was usually so inflated, had been torn down to almost nothing when he realized his powers were practically useless.

Taylor ripped the gun from Dr. Zeldin's hand in an instant, throwing it across the room. The doctor fell to the ground in fear and Taylor didn't say a word, he just concentrated on the bodies of the two men, forcing them both to their feet. Je put them together against a nearby support column, all the while hearing whimpers from Dr. Zeldin.

"Now – let's keep you two nice and cozy." Taylor said as Dr. Zeldin practically screamed at the sight several beams on fast approach. Taylor was now controlling all of them and, with the metallic squealing of their being bent, the teen wove an intricate circular cage around his two enemies, practically bonding them to the building's support at their backs. Dr. Zeldin then shrieked as he heard a loud crack, and a shift in the column behind him. Eventually Taylor had removed the entire body of the column, and left their circular cage in its place as support.

"Now – you might want to tell Daniel, when he wakes up that is, that if he tries to escape – if he tries to remove this cage – the entire roof is going to come tumbling down all on top of your little heads – so even now – the best advice I can give is – don't move!"

Taylor then reached down and pulled out the small piece of cloth from Daniel's uniform and tucked it in one of his own pockets with a wide grin – a token of this man's uniform, and possibly a way of finding more secrets.

"You might escape today, but we'll find you! We'll get the children – there's nothing you can do about it!" Dr. Zeldin shouted half terrified, half angry. Taylor might have left these two alone before this bit of rhetoric, but the moment these words fell on his ears, Taylor changed his mind and decided to stay for a moment.

He watched as Dr. Zeldin's head looked about the room in all sorts of directions, but Taylor was more interested in what was inside the man's head, not what it was doing. Why should he use a small bit of cloth when he has a perfectly good source of information right here.

The teen reached up, forcing the doctor to flinch, and with a calm delicate touch he put his palm on the man's forehead. He raised his other hand, painfully, to put it on Daniel's forehead as well.

Closing his eyes, Taylor actually felt nervousness well up inside him as he realized he was about to see and learn the secrets of both of these men, one of whom used to be his friend and mentor. Hopefully he might learn some truth about what, why, and how to avoid the massive destruction that seemed inevitable. He took a deep breath and focused on the thoughts and history that had been covered up so carefully.

Opening his eyes from total darkness, Taylor saw a pair of hands rolling a pen back and forth on a smooth table. Forcing his stare to look upward, he quickly realized that these hands belonged to Dr. Zeldin, a man with a very impatient and very annoyed look on his face. Taylor pulled his stare back and looked over others that were sitting at the same table. He could see Christine, Elizabeth, Stewart, and Daniel all offering their own eager gazes to the end of the table where President Andrews stood with a wide smile.

"I am so sorry to pull you from your assignments – but there's been a huge development the Prodigy project!"

Christine offered a concerned look and immediately vented her fears.

"Is Robert alright – is there something wrong – can we do anything...?"

Taylor winced at hearing his name yet listened to President Andrews's response.

"He's fine, fine – just fine!"

"Well then what's the big deal?" Daniel said sourly, "Chris and I were tracking a rogue telekinetic. Been wreaking havoc all through Johannesburg!"

"Eh – this is a little bigger than that!" The President said with a definitive stare.

"Sir," Daniel said respectfully, "We've been tracking this guy for days – he's killed over a hundred people so far – what's bigger than that?"

President Andrews paused and after a moment he turned to his side.

Daniel and the others at the table leaned back with gasps as, in front of them, a wide, yet dark figure appeared from out of nowhere. The figure glowed with veins of bright light that Taylor instantly recognized as the foundation for the cloaking technology he had now seen repeatedly. More than this, Taylor acknowledged the short figure as quite familiar. He had seen the same image, or rather felt it when he pulled Caitlin from a vision several months back. Indeed, getting a clear view of this – *thing*, Taylor felt that he was going to get more answers than he bargained for by diving into the history of Daniel and Dr. Zeldin.

The short figure, standing before the fully assembled Evol Crew, slipped off the cloaking suit from over his head, revealing a large helmet – a helmet that Taylor recognized as similar to the one Johnny was wearing to get his visions of the future when he was being tested by Stewart. Wasting no time, the figure pulled this helmet off to reveal its true self and immediately the thoughts and emotions of each member of the Evol Crew seemed obvious by the looks on their faces while each one at the table leaned in closer to get a good look at this newly revealed face. Some of the crew were in awe, some were actually afraid, and only Elizabeth alone seemed repulsed. Looking at the strange figure before him Taylor was filled with a little of all of this, but awe seemed to overwhelm him most. Inside, he felt he was witnessing something historic, and something he wouldn't *ever* forget.

With strange, scaly green skin and bright yellow eyes, one might have originally compared it to a lizard, but its absence of a nose left it with an almost perfectly round head that constantly displayed a gaping wide mouth of sharp white teeth. At the top of the head, this creature had a shock of white hair that ran from the top center of its forehead down to and beyond the back of its neck.

As Taylor took the time to absorb the appearance of this strange looking creature a chill ran up his spine when it opened its mouth even wider and offered a loud, deep, howling cry that was, in an instant, so familiar to Taylor's ears.

Everyone sitting around the table leaned backwards and President Andrews offered a mild smile. Taylor could see that the man was reading a short message that appeared on a data-pad in front of him.

"This is eh – well, I really can't pronounce his name – but as I'm sure I don't have to tell you, he's uh – he's not from around here."

Elizabeth leaned forward, "Just say it like it is – he's an alien!" she bellowed.

President Andrews nodded his head, "Right – right! He *is* an alien!"

With fast blinking and a shift in his expression, Stewart quickly leaned forward.

"I can't believe you!" he said angrily. "You'd cow bow to their threats – you tricked us – you bastard." He stood up and left the room with a rush of white cloth, leaving all but Elizabeth confused at what the man was talking about.

"Ah – well – about that..." President Andrews started, seeing a table of confused faces. He would have continued but Elizabeth interrupted.

"Listen – we could be here all day waiting for you to explain so if you don't mind – I'm going to speed things up a bit."

The others looked at her with either a smirk or a smile. "Is he really that transparent?" Daniel asked with an arrogant smile.

"Today he is – actually, it's the first time I've been able to get a read on him."

She nodded her head and started speaking. "Egg head lizard-boy here has an entire armada at his disposal, and they are ready to destroy our planet if we or I should say, President Andrews doesn't give in to his demands.

"And what demands are those?" Dr. Zeldin asked with a reserved curiosity.

Elizabeth offered the creature a dark frown, "He wants our powers."

"But we can't just give..." Daniel started to say, but Elizabeth interrupted again.

"No, no – let me correct – He wants people with our powers."

"And you've agreed to this!?" Daniel questioned angrily.

"I have no choice – they've given me the ultimatum. I give him people with your gifts or he'll destroy the planet."

"But why? I mean they've obviously got better technology." Christine rationalized.

"They consider our powers too much of a threat" Elizabeth said with almost a smirk, "we either help them *level the field* – or get eliminated."

The creature at the end of the table offered another horrific series of howls and grunts that caused a few to plug their ears, but Taylor listened intently as President Andrews translated. "You have no choice – either give us the child – or your planet will be destroyed!"

"You – you want Robert?" Christine asked fearfully.

The creature didn't respond, but Dr. Zeldin did. "There's no guarantee that he'll agree to go – he's very powerful, and he could resist. I know I would. I mean look at that thing!"

Dr. Zeldin's words were met with a loud howling noise as the creature jumped onto the table and growled down at him, forcing the man to sit low in his chair.

"Eh – he doesn't like to be called a 'thing.' If you're going to refer to him – call him – eh - Kashal – that's at least the first part of his name.

"Okay" Dr. Zeldin said stiffly, "Well you can tell Kashal that if the doesn't get his disgusting head away from me I'll have to make a huge mess by turning it into a pile of mush with the phase gun I have under his chin."

He nudged the gun into Kashal's jaw, and at that, the creature slowly pulled away and jumped from the table, returning to President Andrews' side.

There was an uncomfortable pause that was only broken when Elizabeth addressed the group softly.

"They plan on using Robert's DNA – to duplicate it – and make more of him –

that's what they have in mind. But you already knew that, didn't you President Andrews?"

He looked at Elizabeth in confusion, "How did you know?"

"I can hear that – eh – Kashal's thoughts!" She said softly, "But if these are his plans, then why do they need the boy at all – why not just take a sample of blood and work with it? And why bring us here – what's the point?"

"Well," President Andrews started, but his face was met with a hand from Elizabeth. She started speaking the instant she finished reading his thoughts, and the thoughts of Kashal.

"Hmmm – before you say another word, I need to speak with my colleagues for a minute – in private!"

Kashal grumbled and President Andrews seemed to respond similarly, "What's this all about? Are you forgetting who you're talking to? I called this meeting, and I say when there are to be private conversations."

"Maybe you're forgetting who you're talking to – if you don't leave willingly, I'll make you leave – the both of you!"

Taylor watched as President Andrews slowly closed his mouth and stood at the end of the table with a sour expression on his face. "Fine," he said soberly, "You have five minutes!"

He inched his way to the exit, and after a moment Kashal followed with a strange hobbling walk. The door closed behind them and Taylor was intent on hearing what was up Elizabeth's sleeve, but all at once there was a screaming voice inside the conference room – a scream that no one seemed to react to.

The screaming voice was instantly familiar and Taylor realized that it was his own that quickly drowned out all sound and seemingly drowned his vision away in a wash of color. With the ensuing wash of darkness Taylor had a sharp pain in his shoulder and on opening his eyes he saw that Daniel was awake and had somehow freed one of his arms, reached out, and grabbed Taylor's injured shoulder.

Daniel's thumb was half inside Taylor's wound and the pain was immeasurable. Taylor pulled himself back and with a telekinetic flinch, he blasted both Daniel and Dr. Zeldin across the room so hard that they practically flew through one of the far windows. Taylor was shocked at the force of his reaction and watched for only a split second as the two metal-strewn and rubble latent bodies crashed through the side of the building and fell out of sight. Taylor turned his eyes up immediately, focusing his attention to the noise overhead. The ceiling was starting to crumble.

Taylor kinetically kept the ceiling stable while he pulled more metal beams and placed them in the cage's former location. When he knew that he had kept the upper floor from collapsing, Taylor turned on his heel and sprinted to the lift, barely able to absorb the idea that he had just ended the life of two men – but not any two men, two members of the Evol-Crew – he could see the headlines now in his mind – and knew that, worldwide, his being a criminal would be undeniable.

He forced a lift squeal its way open with it's damaged entrance before cyberly commanding it to close and go straight up. On reaching the top floor Taylor used a combination of cyber and kinetic efforts to punch an opening straight through the roof of the building with the lift.

The doors opened and Taylor could see, only a few yards away, that his ship had been powered up and through the front windshield he saw Delissa and Tristan's staring out at this explosive topside exit that Taylor had created. Most unexpected to Taylor, though, was the face full of sunlight that washed over him when the doors opened. Whatever time it was, the sun had risen hours before and he was panicked over the hour, and how much time he had left before the foreseen attack.

Bringing his thoughts into focus, Taylor looked to the craft in front of him and to the woman and boy in the cockpit. They were focused on him, frantically waving their hands and shaking their heads.

Taylor was no idiot – he wasn't to spend another moment questioning what it was they were trying to tell him. He knew that someone was up there already – waiting – expecting him – an ambush.

Taylor focused hard on the ship, hoping he could kinetically bring it closer to him. It was no use – the ship's shields prevented any kind of kinesis from affecting it.

"Well," he whispered, "it's now or never!" and with this running through his mind, he bolted from the sparking and now completely dysfunctional lift to the ship that now seemed so very far away. He was only a few second's run from the wing. With any luck he could just jump on it, run to the hatch and get inside before anyone had a chance to react.

All at once Taylor stopped his run at the wingtip, and as he knew he didn't want his feet to stop moving, he felt his stomach plummet and churn with the realization of what was happening. He stared in anger as Elizabeth made her way from behind the ship. She was clapping a slow, solitary applause. Taylor looked down at his feet, but his muscles weren't responding. *She* had control of them now.

73 Rooftop Parley

HE WAS SO CLOSE – so very close – and yet with Elizabeth controlling his every action now, it seemed that there was no chance of his escape.

"I am so very, very impressed, Robert!" She said as she kept her eyes focused on him. "You *have* become quite powerful – you've gotten past the cognitive blocks, scared Dr. Zeldin into submission, and even bested Daniel with only minimal effort. All in all, I must say, you're something else."

Elizabeth started pacing around Taylor's completely immobile body. "And to think, you almost got away with stealing our children."

"My children!" Taylor shouted, and with these words he could feel Elizabeth forcing his mouth to stay closed.

"Don't interrupt dear. It's bad manners!" She said sourly.

Taylor would have turned his head with the sound of new footsteps; footsteps that didn't belong to Elizabeth, but he was unable to move. So he had to wait, and saw who was approaching only when they walked in his line of sight.

Taylor's eyes looked back up at the ship, he could see the panicked faces of Johnny, Grace, and David all staring out at him from the cockpit window. Delissa must have made way for them to see though he wished she hadn't.

The footsteps were finally coming around, and with the show of red and green cloth, Taylor's mouth would have gaped open if it could, for he saw a pair of scraped up and battered men that he had only a moment ago thought dead.

"Thought you got rid of us, didn't you?" Dr. Zeldin said angrily, "I can see it in your eyes – you thought you killed us! Well – it takes a little more than just a punk kid like you to get the better of us!"

Taylor should have known better – D*id Daniel force them to divert their fall and crash through the window of a lower level, or did Dr. Zeldin mentally hijack a nearby transport to catch them on their way down?* Either way it didn't matter – the two were, in fact, still alive. Taylor's heart started pumping faster and faster, now he knew he had his hands full.

"You know – it's too bad we can't kill him!" Daniel said angrily, "he certainly had no qualms about getting rid of us!"

Dr. Zeldin turned an angry stare on Daniel and with a flinching reaction he vented on the man.

"You stuck your finger in his shoulder! What the hell was he supposed to do – everything was fine until you screwed it all up - again!"

"He was going to see everything you idiot – he can't know the truth – you know that!" Daniel said in frustration.

Taylor was growing more irritated by the moment at the fact that he was being referred to in the third person As if he wasn't there, the two continued to argue, before, quite unexpectedly, they stopped quarrelling.

Elizabeth had turned her stare to the two of them, and had obviously forced their silence. "Now, now, boys – let's not argue – everything's fine, so just calm down," she said in an almost sing song manner.

Taylor heard more footsteps on approach. He had no choice but to wait, again, this time more impatient to see who was coming to watch his confinement, though he did have a pretty good idea who it might be.

"Chris, Stewart, good of you to join us," Elizabeth said with a smile.

"We got your message about meeting on the roof." Stewart said as he rounded on Taylor, "Had no idea you'd have such a wonderful surprise waiting up here."

Elizabeth stared at him with disbelief.

"Oh, okay, fine, I knew what was up here – I just wanted to act surprised, is that so bad?" he said happily.

He, Stewart, then looked up to the ship and saw the young faces staring out from the window. "Are they...?" He started to ask, and his question was immediately met with a nod from Elizabeth.

"Wow, so the whole family's here!" He said excitedly before turning to Dr. Zeldin.

Elizabeth seemed to intercept the message Stewart was sending to the doctor and she spoke very plainly in response, "There's no point in trying – the ship's shielded. I swear I can't go anywhere – I leave the city for just a few hours to help the President in Los Angeles, and when I get back – nothing but a mess. It's insane!"

"So what should we do with him?" Christine asked calmly. "It's clear he already knows more than he's supposed to."

"Hmmm," Elizabeth hummed, "This much is certain."

"But what's so wrong about him knowing the whole truth?" Christine asked softly. "If he knew – he might not resist."

"I think it's safe to say – you're not the brightest of us." Elizabeth responded insultingly, "If he knew the truth he'd never go along with it – think about it!" Elizabeth started pointing between the ship and Taylor, but Taylor was unable to figure out what exactly she meant.

"I think it would be best if we kept everyone here – let President Andrews figure it all out – he started this mess anyways!" Elizabeth said commandingly. "Daniel – send a message to Andrews – have him come back to DC and meet us here – shouldn't take him too long – and have him bring a full security detail."

Daniel stepped away from the group while the others stared calmly at Taylor. They weren't saying anything between each other, but Taylor knew that they were pathically communicating. They examined him, taking in his every detail. He could only imagine how he might look at a person in a similar situation. He was genetically the result of each of them, and if he was in their shoes; he might also want to fully take in each attribute of this manufactured offspring, to see which qualities came from whom.

The moment of him looking at them looking at him had waned though, and Taylor was growing irritated at his inability to control his own limbs. He stood, motionless as Stewart finally broke the silence.

"Well, I think it's pretty clear that he got his height and eyes from me – and definitely not Daniel."

There were a few consenting nods between three of the others, but Taylor noticed a concerned look from Stewart who cast his eye in Taylor's direction one last time.

"Hold on – there's something not right here," he whispered, looking at Taylor with an eye of scrutiny.

"He's hiding something." Stewart said, but Taylor had no idea what the man was talking about.

Much in the same fashion as Taylor had looked into the thoughts, future, and history of others, Stewart put his hand on Taylor's forehead, closed his eyes, and after a few seconds, he pulled away with a jerk.

Christine, Elizabeth, and Dr. Zeldin all looked at Stewart with concern as a show of fear washed over his face.

"It can't be! It can't be!"

"What? What's the matter?" Christine asked, seeing the panic stricken look on Stewart's face.

"We have to – we have to..."

Daniel walked up to the group having just put away his communicator. "President Andrews isn't coming – he's staying in LA – he – he said we should just..."

"Let them go." Stewart said finishing both his and Daniel's sentence at the same time.

"Man, I hate it when he does that!" Daniel said angrily.

"What!" Stewart said in surprise, "Why would he just want us to let them go?"

"But isn't that what you just said," Elizabeth questioned in confusion.

"Well yes but,"

"Listen," Daniel interrupted, "the President said he had everything under control – 'just let them go' he said."

"Maybe he already knows." Stewart said cautiously.

"Knows what?" Dr. Zeldin asked, completely perplexed.

"Robert here has seen the future – he's seen the destruction of our cities, and it isn't going to happen in a few months like we thought – it's going to happen in a few hours!"

"But how is that possible?" Christine asked.

"I, I don't know – something must have changed." Stewart said nervously.

"Well how do you know we should just let them go?" Elizabeth asked with a sneer before adding, "Maybe them escaping or your ridiculous idea of letting them go is what causes this whole damn thing in the first place!"

Dr. Zeldin and Christine looked confused, but it was quite clear that none were convinced of what would be the best action to take considering what was at stake.

Stewart and Elizabeth continued to argue the point back and forth with the occasional comment from Christine, Dr. Zeldin, or Daniel. It was clear that between all of them though, they felt it best that a definitive decision should be made in lieu of President Andrews' orders. Taylor, all the while, was thinking over and over in his head that he wasn't confused about the issues at all. Indeed, he knew exactly what he wanted, and it didn't matter to him what any vision told him about the future or the past. Those children were his and he was going to get them one way or another.

He grew more and more frustrated watching the arguing group, yet he was completely unable to do anything about it. Elizabeth's hold was unwavering even if her attention seemed to be diverted elsewhere. How is it – Taylor wondered – that she could do this to him despite how powerful he had become – what was it that she was doing – he himself had never tried to forcibly control someone else's actions through telepathy – especially against their will. He tried to move his feet again. Nothing! He looked at her and tried to use his telekinesis to push her over. Nothing there either – she must have found a way to take total control of his actions. It was obvious though, that she couldn't take control over everything. He was, after all, thinking on his own. And he was thinking how he would like nothing more than to just hop in the ship that was only a few feet away, and fly it as far away as possible, as fast as possible, and never return, but this seemed all but impossible.

Taylor continued to think amid the rising arguing voices of Stewart and Elizabeth. If only there was some way – maybe the children could help him. Hmm – no. It would be too dangerous – he'd rather keep them in the safety of the ship, no matter what, but time was running short.

Taylor stared at Dr. Zeldin, who had somehow retrieved another plasma gun. There's no way he could get it. He looked at Daniel, whose cloak still had its tale telling hole. Then his eyes moved back to Elizabeth. He was filling with more hatred for her by the second and as the time passed he was growing more desperate for escape

"On the count of three – go for the ship!" whispered a voice in Taylor's head. Was his mind deceiving him – he waited for a moment, and, sure enough, he heard the voice again.

"Ready – one – two..."

Taylor thought fast. He thought that if he had control of his legs he would jump and try his best to kinetically force this leap to push him right to the top of the ship. He waited for the word.

"three!"

With no unnatural sounds; no, just the grunts and yells of those in front of him, all five cloaks and those wearing them flew some thirty feet across the rooftop of the GC headquarters, eventually colliding with the massive transmitter towers. Taylor watched this and realized that the children had worked out some kind of plan to use their own powers to free him. With Elizabeth falling to the ground and slumping forward, her face smacking the pavement, Taylor found himself released from her mental hold and his legs reacted quickly with the thoughts planted in his own head.

Taylor leaped high into the air, eventually making his way over the craft and, with a bit of kinetic help, he fell right on top of the hatch, which he kinetically opened as soon as he got sight of it. Taylor then forced the hatch to close on his landing hard on his feet and he was sure that he had broken his ankle on impact.

"Tristan – put the shields back on!" Orion shouted.

Taylor blinked his eyes over and over again; unable to believe that he had done it. He had stolen his children back! He looked all around, taking in their young and happy faces and the nervous stare of Jay to accompany their carefree expressions.

"See I told you it would work!" Orion said to Jay before playfully punching the man on the shoulder.

"How did you – what did you...?" Taylor started asking, but he was simply overjoyed that, at that moment, the whole group of them was now safe and sound in the large, albeit now very cramped craft.

"Well," Orion started, "I had everybody time it just right – Johnny did the counting – you heard him in your head I'm sure, and Asp and Dave knocked those weirdoes around outside when Tristan dropped the shields."

Taylor smiled and gave the boy a wink.

"Brilliant! Now," he said with an aching foot, "can someone get me the bone and tissue replicators, I think I left them under the pilot's seat."

With no wait at all from his request, Delissa parted the children and tended to Taylor's foot and his wounded shoulder with the replicators she had found much earlier when she browsed around the craft. She offered him a wide smile, and he could feel her emotions as though they were his own. She was ecstatic over the fact that the whole group of them; the children, her son, he, and even Jay, were all together again. For her, this was an absolutely perfect moment.

The second she knew his shoulder was better she reached around Taylor's neck and offered him a much needed hug. On pulling herself away, she looked down at him with an almost devilish grin. "Nice threads!" she said reaching inside his shirt and poking her finger through the hole that Dr. Zeldin's plasma gun had made.

He looked around the craft and, seeing that everyone else was wearing the same thing, offered a light laugh, "Yeah, well, I've heard these are in style now. You know – everybody's wearing 'em!" He offered a smirk, looked over at Johnny, and scrubbed the boy's head. It was when he heard his children's laughter that now, for him, *this* was the perfect moment.

Moments like that, though, are often not meant to last for long, and with a bright flash Taylor's eyes shifted to the front of the craft.

He stood and was able to appreciate his fully working foot as he worked his way to the front of the ship. "Move over big guy. I've got 'er now!"

"What about the shields?" Tristan asked quickly with concern.

Taylor put his hand on the boy's shoulder. "I said I've got it. Don't worry!"

The boy pulled the control helmet from his head and Taylor, true to his word, cyberly made sure that the shields stayed up. Now, with Tristan getting out of the pilot's seat, Taylor took the boy's place and quickly donned the helmet himself. Turning his head he could see that Elizabeth had somehow taken the phase gun from Dr. Zeldin and was firing uncontrollably at the craft.

Taylor looked at the ship's main display and navigated to a screen that showed its shield strength. He almost laughed with the realization that the shots were useless. He reached up, grabbing the virtual handles for the craft. Immediately everyone could feel a small shake as the ship lifted itself from the roof of the building, and Taylor forced it westward.

"So, where are we headed?" Jay asked, stepping up to Taylor's side.

"We're going back to L.A."

"Wha' – What for?"

"Hello!" Taylor said arrogantly, "End of the world! Gotta figure this whole thing out!"

Jay's eyes grew wide, "You mean that's still going to happen?"

"Uh, not sure. But there's so much – oh God, so much more going on that I can't even begin to explain." the teen said excitedly, remembering the fact that aliens, actual *aliens* weren't a thing of fiction – they were a fact, a reality. "And there's still ton's more that I don't know about – I can feel it – there's still more secrets – and right now, to be honest, I'm a little tired of secrets."

Jay responded to these words with a look of patronizing sympathy that Taylor felt a need to respond to. "I - I don't know? All I have to figure out as much as possible if my kids'll ever be safe!"

"Right?!" Jay said with uncertainty. "So what? You plan on just going to the local GC office building and ask President Andrews to tell you everything! Oh, and of course they're going to welcome you with open arms."

"I could do without the sarcasm!" Taylor said in a frustrated tone as he turned his frowning face to Jay. Jay backed off immediately, having little else to say.

After a few minutes Taylor had it in mind to look at the clock of the craft, and saw that the time was 11:35AM. Initially the teen filled with panic, thinking he was far too late and that the destruction of Los Angeles had already occurred – but as he stared at the clock and saw that the hour had clicked back to 10:35AM. He quickly realized that DC was three hours earlier than Los Angeles, and as they had just passed the time zone, he was now only two hours ahead.

From this point on Taylor was of a mind to focus on flying the ship as fast as possible straight west with his only spoken words being to the ship.

"Can you give these people a place to sit or do you expect them to just stand the whole time?!" he said half irritated. He was still frustrated over not knowing what he was going to do once he had, again, traveled across the country.

From his request, Taylor watched as the two seats behind him quickly widened to form bench seats, and that the panels of the craft seemed to suck themselves outward to make room for this new seating.

"That's better!" He said, and he was at least satisfied in knowing that his children were able to sit comfortably through the journey.

Despite how short as the trip was, Taylor knew that his kids would grow restless after only a few minutes. To help alleviate this he turned and offered each one the opportunity to trade out the co-pilot's seat and see the fast moving countryside. To this end Tristan politely gave up his position and David, who was all too eager, was the first to go. Taylor felt his own heart leap as he watched his children's eyes explode wide with wonder. Following David was Grace, then Johnny, then Aspen, then Caitlin, and lastly, Orion. It wasn't until Orion took his seat that Taylor felt a sudden jerking in the motion of the craft.

"What are you doing?" he asked in irritation, looking to the boy. In his stare at the child, though, he saw that Orion had only touched the helmet, not at all putting it on, and the confused look on the child's face told him that the boy knew nothing of what Taylor was talking about.

Taylor turned his stare forward again, and with a firm concentration on the controls while also using his hands, he made every effort to turn and control the craft. His labors proved of little success, and while they were still headed in the right direction, Taylor's nerves were immediately tensed with the realization that the craft was no longer under his control.

74 To the Beginning

TAYLOR TURNED HIS HEAD AROUND. He could see, through the back of the craft, the horizon that he had been running from for nearly twenty minutes. Time was definitely not on his side this morning. He continued to struggle with the controls of the ship, completely unable force it in any direction. With Jay nudging Orion out of the co-pilot's seat, he spoke to Taylor with a whispering voice of concern.

"Wha – what's going on?"

"I – I just don't know. I've lost control of the ship!" Taylor whispered.

"Well if you don't have control – who does?"

Taylor's eyes opened wide in a panic. He stared down at the ship's main display and forced it through a series of screens until, with a look of surprise; he saw one that showed a map of where the control signal was coming from.

"It's The Towers!" Taylor said excitedly, but he could tell that Jay was far less enthused.

"Yeah so if it's a signal from the outside can't you interrupt it – you know – with your mind?" Jay said while waving his hands through the air.

"Sure I could – heck, practically any cyber could. The question is – do I want to?"

"Of course you do!"

"Not necessarily," Taylor said looking at Jay with a growing grin, "this could be those 'arms open wide' you were talking about."

"How can you be so sure?" Jay asked with disbelief.

"Well, I can't be *absolutely* certain. But when I was outside the ship, I heard Daniel, you know – green pea, say that President Andrews wanted them to just let us go... but why would he say that – unless the man had a plan to get us back."

Taylor watched as Jay thought hard for a moment.

"It's certainly not a very good plan – I mean we could escape in a heartbeat!"

"True, but I'm willing to bet that Andrews is betting on my curiosity. He hopes I'm curious enough to just ride this thing out – and I think we will. If what I think is happening is really happening – then it'll be worth the wait."

"And what if there's trouble?" Jay asked as he looked out over the horizon, barely able to make out the approaching brightly colored skyline of the Vegas

Metroship.

Taylor shook his head with a smile, "If there's trouble it won't be from them – it'll be from me."

"Should we tell the others?"

Taylor nodded. "Yeah," he said softly, turning his chair around, and letting the ship guide itself. "Okay, everybody – I think it's pretty clear that someone, or something has taken control of the ship!" Taylor said in full voice.

With these words a wave of worried faces fell over the young group in front of him, and Orion was the first to insist, "Just put the ship under your own control – what's the problem?"

"Sure, I could – but I just talked with Jay and – well – we're going to ride this one out. From what I can tell, it's going to take us back to The Towers."

The children all looked at each other, clearly feeling the mixed emotions of going back to a place that they had worked so hard to escape and yet appreciating the idea of returning to a place that they, for so much of their life, had called home.

Trying to decide on his own what would be the best information to share, Taylor spoke very carefully, "Listen kids, I think – No, I know there's a lot more going on here than I can figure out right now – there's a reason you were hunted down, and there's a reason why you're wanted so badly. Until I can figure out some way to keep that from happening – and figure out what this whole horrible vision is about, I don't think I could sleep wondering if I could've done something to make things right – and somehow keep you safe."

"Yeah, if we can even make it past today!" Johnny said with a wide eyed frown.

"So you've seen?" Taylor asked, surprised at these words.

"Of course I have – and I've seen a lot more than that!" the boy said pulling a small piece of green cloth from behind his back.

Taylor's eyes practically fell out of his head. "Where did you get that?" He asked almost in a panic.

Johnny offered a somber almost apologetic look, "You had it, but it fell out of your pocket when you jumped in the ship."

Instantly Taylor's eyes bulged. He looked in his shirt pocket, and saw that the small piece of green cloth was no longer there. He then stared up at the boy with a half apologetic stare. But the boy Johnny offered a strange smiling gaze in return.

"When I grabbed it I saw you, lying on the floor with that ball attached to your head – and I – I went inside your thoughts – I saw what you saw – I was gonna give it back – but I just. It all happened so fast and – well – I'm sorry."

Taylor sighed. "There's nothing to be sorry about!" he said sympathetically, staring into the child's bright blue eyes.

"What's that all about?" Caitlin asked, reaching for the green cloth herself. Taylor's hand shot up quickly and snatched it from Johnny's grip before the girl had a chance to touch it. Taylor looked at her with a grin – his daughter, oh how that thought sent chills up his spine – he was a father! He was instantly a father and six times over no less. He hadn't really thought about telling the children the truth until this moment, but he was hoping for better timing. Looking around the ship at the curious faces of his children – *really his children* – his heart sank. Should he tell them this news when everything could go so horribly wrong in just a few hours?

"It's – it's nothing." Taylor said gripping the cloth tightly.

"What!" Johnny said with an almost instant anger. "What're you talking about?"

"Johnny, stop! Now isn't the time!" Taylor said, his heart aching at the boy's persistence.

"'Now isn't the time.' Whatever! What if there isn't any other time! Hello – they have a right to know!"

With these words it seemed that however the children were preoccupied and whatever they were doing had ceased. They turned questioning stares up to either Taylor or Johnny. Taylor took a deep breath,\ and before the children started pressing either of them for the facts, the teen stared each one of them in the face and started to speak, his heart heavily dripping emotion over each spoken word.

"You're right! You're right – I know you're right." Taylor paused with his eyes landing on Johnny, searching for the right words. "I was just hoping to tell you under better circumstances – that's all" he said softly, rubbing a thumb on the boy's cheek.

Aspen reached out and grabbed Taylor's other hand. "Tell us what father?" Taylor, with this touch, felt his mind struggle for the right words to make them all understand. As he took a deep breath his brain seemed to pick the most obscure and least pleasant fact to bring up first.

"Those color coded weirdoes back there in DC – well – they're the source of all of your – um – powers."

"What?" Grace shouted, "I don't believe it."

Her face along with her siblings all turned very sour.

"Now, now – let me finish – just let me finish!" Taylor said forcefully trying to calm the children down. "Let me start from the beginning!"

"I – I was not born to a geriatric mother, like I had been lead to believe all my life." The teen started, and he watched as the children lost all want or need to interrupt him, and so he continued. "Just like you, I was created artificially by genetic manipulation. I was born from the genetic code of all five of those cloaked weirdoes. back in DC." With this the children all murmured a hum of discordance, but Taylor was unwavering in his telling of the facts.

"Their genetic code is what affords me all of my powers and gifts. I was designed as part of some plan – some government conspiracy – and while I don't know all the details – I do know that somewhere along the line – the government ordered that some of my blood be used to generate more just like me. So, about eleven years ago, samples of my blood were taken and used to generate other powerful – beautiful – children. Six to be exact – well actually seven..."

At this Taylor explained how it was that Johnny had a twin who did not survive, and detailed how, for a very understandable reason, the boy had a one year gap in age compared to his other siblings. But to the others, this detail seemed minor in comparison to the larger, more profound truth. Each seemed to understand perfectly, and while Aspen did too, it seemed that her brain was having trouble wrapping her brain around this new information and how to handle it appropriately.

"What does that mean?" she asked curiously.

"Don't you get it?" Johnny said standing up next to Taylor, staring at his brothers and sisters. "He's our father – he really – really is our dad!"

Orion, David, Grace, Caitlin, and Aspen all stared at Johnny and Taylor standing together. With slowly shifting and curious expressions it seemed that the children had come to realize the truth. With the two so close to each other and wearing exactly the same outfit, it dawned on them, as it never had before, how much the two looked like each other; from the eyes to the face, the hair, everything. With that kind of similarity, what they just heard – it just had to be true.

There was dead silence that was unbroken for over a minute. The children seemed to only want to look at Johnny, look at Taylor, look at each other, and with almost head-splitting thoughts, they each seemed to mist up with the emotions that were welling inside.

Behind the children Taylor could see Tristan looking over the children's heads curiously with Delissa rubbing his shoulders. She listened intently to what he said, and while she had her own intuitions on the matter – believing it a possibility – she was, herself, still ill prepared to hear the truth.

"Well," Tristan whispered, "isn't somebody gonna say something?"

There was a long and uncomfortable pause, which Taylor felt inappropriate to break himself, and he waited, for a short eternity, for one of his children to distract from the deafening hum of the craft's engines.

"This is so awesome!" David shouted, causing the other children to jump, and he finished his exclamation, "I've got the coolest dad on the planet!"

"'You've got the coolest dad'" Delissa repeated dismissively, shaking her head, "you've got a dad – period!"

Orion suddenly spoke up at her words though, curious of the thoughts in his own head. "But if what you've said is true," he asked, "then aren't you like – uh – our father *and* our mother?"

Taylor nodded his head, "Uh – yeah!" He said, and in his mind he couldn't help but recognize a similarity in the way Orion and Elizabeth had come to the same conclusion.

"Weird!" Caitlin said, and she stood up with a half grin on her face, "Whatever – I just want to give you a hug – as my father – for the first time!"

Her words were quickly met with the other four children standing, each wanting to repeat her sentiment. After a few seconds Taylor was drowning in the arms of his children and all he could do was smile.

"Tay, you'd better have a look at this!" Jay called from the front of the craft, ruining one of Taylor's few and perfect moments.

The teen worked to the front of the ship, and in looking out, he could see hundreds of transports all headed away from the Los Angeles Metroship.

"What the hell's going on – is everybody leaving the city?" Taylor asked.

He could tell that the ship's automated navigation had to slow down considerably as it was having trouble traveling in a straight path because, in front of it, so many other crafts were traveling in the opposite direction.

"I wonder." Jay questioned, and he looked at Taylor with a curious stare, "Can you make this display show normal radio frequencies?"

Taylor understood exactly what Jay was asking. He stared down at the screen. After a few moments of shifting from one image to another, Taylor was able to see a channel of sorts that displayed a woman who was reporting the news quite blandly.

"Numerous reports of electrical failure after the 9.5 earthquake that hit Los Angeles yesterday evening are still being reported. In related news, we have received three different accounts, which we have aired over the last two hours – All coming from the GC Geological Survey – one states that there has been a cataclysmic failure of the Tectonic Control System or TCS, the other reports that the GC Geological Survey is denouncing any equipment failure or wrongdoing for the cause of the earthquake, and still another states that there is evidence to show that another earthquake is imminent and that a Metrowide evacuation is underway."

Jay turned to Taylor with a wide grin, "Ghost messages – Shannon's great with sending ghost messages – she did it with me once."

Taylor nodded his head with the realization that Shannon was probably using the GC Geological Survey mailing infrastructure to send erroneous messages about the earthquakes and equipment failure, even if they weren't true. "With those kinds of reports, it's no wonder everyone's leaving!" Taylor said with a smile, happy that the woman's plan seemed to be working.

Now inside the wall of the city, Taylor could see the EduCorp Towers only occasionally through the mass of departing transports and billowing smoke. His eyes and head turned to watch a transport full of passengers and instantly his head filled with a horrible thought.

There aren't enough transports to get everybody out!

Taylor quickly calculated that it would take millions of transports to get the entire city to safety.

Taylor then stared down at the ship's data display – he made the news reporter flick off, forcing Jay to stare up at him in anger – "Hey I was watching that!"

Taylor paid no attention. He simply focused on the screen, navigating through communications and programming protocols. As Jay watched this he wasn't sure what was going on, but he knew that Taylor had a purpose for what he was doing.

"Orion – Grace – I need your help!" He shouted to the back of the craft, and with these words the two children snapped at attention and weaseled their way to Taylor's side – "Sorry Jay – they're going to have to take a back seat."

With the relatively tight and uncomfortable shifting of positions, the two children finally took their places with the ship actually figuring out on its own that it needed shrink the two seats to make room for a third.

"What's up, Dad?" The two asked in unison.

Taylor offered them a purposeful stare – "We don't have much time before we land, so we have to do this quickly. "Grace – I want you to pull up schematics of the different models of transports used throughout the world – I need you to find a way to tap into their navigation system – and somehow force all those with no passengers to divert from their normal path and to head straight for L.A."

"And what's my job?" Orion asked excitedly over such 'grown up' requests coming from his father.

"I need you to crack the L.A. Transportation system – Once you're in I need you to reprogram the mainframe to handle an almost infinite number of incoming craft – there aren't enough handles in the transportation network to deal with the number of incoming, so I need you to get creative – and I need you to be fast!" He then shifted a still serious stare to Grace, "Remember, only empty transports – there's no point in bringing more people into the city!"

"What are you going to be doing?" Grace asked curiously.

"I'm going to create a program that tells the ships what to do once they're here! When you guys are done I'll use our transmitter to send out my program to the LA Transportation System and Grace's into the World Transportation Network.

"Ship – I need two more displays if you please!"

The craft complied, growing two more main displays, and the three stared at the screens, unblinking, and feverishly loading changing code at high speed.

Jay looked over their shoulders and, in putting the three pieces together, he realized exactly was going on, though he was met with questions from the others in the ship.

"What's happening up there?" Delissa asked with wide eyed curiosity.

"Unless I miss my guess Taylor's trying to figure out a way to get transports to come into the city."

"But why?"

"There are only about a million transports throughout the entire L.A. Metroship – even if you could fit twenty people in each transport you'd still need about a hundred times that to clear the city. So right now there's just no way to get everybody out in time."

The word time forced Taylor to look at one of the three displays. It showed 9:02AM local time. He immediately went back to changing the code he had been looking at before, and within a few minutes he sealed up the program he had changed and clapped his hands in front of him. "Done!" he said, and with his eyes looking over at Grace he could see that she had just closed out her terminal. "Done!" she said.

Orion looked over at her in frustration. "How could you be done, that's some serious programming?"

"Actually it was pretty simple – just think less like a computer program and more like a computer virus."

Orion blinked his eyes rapidly. "Oh, wow, you're a genius!" he said with a wide grin and with his screen being the last to be active, Grace and Taylor stared at it curiously.

The boy explained as he deleted his hundreds of lines of generated code and opted for a different approach. "I'll just create a virus that will direct all crafts to return to their source cities once they've arrived at a pickup station and filled to capacity. That way I don't have to worry about how many handles the network has – it only has to talk to a ship for a second, transmit the virus, then move on to the next ship.

"But once they head back to their cities won't they be reprogrammed with my virus?" Grace said with a frown.

"Sure will, but – they won't be empty – so you're program can't send them away!" he said with a wink, and she smiled realizing the genius of his plan.

"Done!" Orion said energetically.

"Great! So let's do this!" Taylor said, and he turned his head up to stare at the ceiling of the ship. He hoped that his faith in his children was not misplaced. After a short prayer inside his mind, the teen stared back at his own screen and pushed the transmit button that had been blinking there for several seconds. He turned to Grace and told her to do the same then turned to Orion and told him to activate his virus on the L.A. Transportation Network.

Waiting for nearly a minute, all three were curious as to whether or not their programs worked.

Jay, looking at their blank expressions, was just as curious. "Hello – Did it work? Check the news!" he said behind their heads.

Taylor stared at his display. With a single blink the screen brought up the same news channel where the woman was still reporting on the earthquake.

"And in just a minute the GC Geological Survey will make a formal statement at an emergency press conference called just moments ago."

"Hold on – is – is that right?" Woman said pressing an earpiece harder into her ear, "Ladies and Gentlemen this just in – empty transports from around the world are all leaving their designated flight paths and are now headed – straight for Los Angeles; sounds like the Metro Evacuation System has just been activated."

"What!" Taylor said loudly, "There's an evacuation system – all we had to do was hit up an evacuation system!?"

"That's so wrong!" Orion said, realizing that he, Grace, and his father all worked so hard at devising a plan to evacuate the city when, in fact, there was already a system in place to do the same thing.

"Shhhhh," Jay said as the woman blinked off the screen and the GC Geological Survey press conference came up.

Some boorish looking man in a grey suit stepped in front of the camera, shadowing the emblem of the GC. His name was displayed just below his face; a Dr. Jerian K. Louis.

The man spoke firmly and softly. "I will not be taking any questions for this conference. No – at this time, we at Geological Survey division of the GC would like to make a few statements. Firstly – the phenomenon that occurred over twelve hours ago has now been classified as exactly that – a phenomenon. It was not – I repeat, NOT an earthquake. All seismic devices confirm that the vibrations that rattled the city were not ground based, and as of yet we are still trying to determine the source."

"Additionally, any reports that the Tectonic Control System, or TCS, has been compromised in any way – is completely false. No – this vibration was indeed caused by something else."

"Now I have just heard reports that the Metro Evacuation System has been activated – but as to this I have no comment and I defer to the GC Transportation Department to hold their own press conference on the matter."

Taylor forced the screen to blink off. "Arrrrgh – With reports like that people aren't going to want to leave!"

He then looked to The Towers that were now only a few hundred meters away. His eyes quickly shifted, offering a nervous stare as, in front of him, he could see that the main landing pad was full of GC security personnel. This, in itself, wouldn't have made Taylor fearful, but the fact that they, on catching sight of the ship, were all activating some kind of protective suit that offered each member the same shielding technology that protected his ship, this is what would and did make the teen a bit worried; worried that this government issued security might actually have the upper hand.

Slowly the ship landed, bringing the hundreds of GC security a little closer to eye level, and Taylor felt a growing pain in the pit of his stomach.

"Apparently I was right – they've been expecting us!" He said looking to the children at his side.

With a smooth landing the ship rested on the landing platform between the four high towers. Taylor willed the shields of the ship to drop. He stepped his way through his children and walked to the hatch, kinetically forcing it open.

"So – what's next?" Jay asked looking at his friend, expectant of an answer.

"Now, I go see what this is all about – you are all going to stay here!" Taylor said this firmly, and he could already hear the whimpers of protests from his children.

"NO – no arguing about this. You're all going to stay here – in the ship! If this vision comes true – or even comes close to coming true," Taylor said shifting his stare from his children to Jay, "I want you and the children to get the hell out of here as fast as you can."

He then kneeled down and offered all of his children, even Tristan, a huge warm hug. "I don't want you to worry. I can take care of myself – everything's going to be fine!" He said softly, "But no matter what – just don't forget that I love you all more than life itself!"

He spoke slowly, feeling his emotions getting the better of him. "Now Grace – I want you to take control of the ship once I've left. Raise the shields and keep her ready. If you have to – use the onboard weapons. I know you'll figure them out.

"Orion I've heard and I've seen what you can do – you're in charge of flying, if – IF it comes to that – and make sure you two don't cross systems – we don't need any more of *those* kinds of incidents!"

He watched their nods and smiled. He swelled with pride that he could offer such orders to his young children, and that he could just trust that they would know what to do. He prided himself on everything that they had done, that they had been through, that they had learned and had accomplished at such a young age, and, as if it was the first time he had ever told them, he, again, laid his emotions out for them to hear. "God, I love you all so much!"

He waited a moment, hearing the repeated 'I love you too's from his children before standing at full height. Turning to the exit ladder, he grabbed the first rung, but his face was quickly grabbed and kissed by Delissa. This was quite unexpected, but not unwanted, and on prematurely pulling away Delissa smiled, seeing Taylor's face. With another kiss, he could tell that she didn't want him to go.

"We'll finish that later!" she said with a smile as she watched him slowly pull himself up the ladder and out of the hatch.

In leaving the ship, and seeing her as the last face inside, he thought for only a moment that maybe now would be a good time to reveal the truth to her about her husband. This thought was instantly distracted by the sounds of hundreds of powering plasma guns.

So, with his arms raised, hoping not to provoke those outside the ship, Taylor walked out to the wingtip, ready to receive his warm welcome.

75 Unseen Enemy, Unseen Friend

"I'M UNARMED – I'M UNARMED!" Taylor said loudly, and he was met with words from someone other than the crowd of security in front of him.

"Everyone up here knows who you are, and they all know that you don't need a weapon to be dangerous!"

Taylor turned his stare. He saw that President Andrews was walking through the mass of security, weaving in and out of the mass of standard issue uniforms and helmets. The teen jumped off the wing and the second his feet hit the ground a strange flash and buzzing noise occurred for only a moment. Taylor realized that Grace raised the shields of the craft protecting it and those inside the instant he was off the ship. Taylor turned a smile and a wink to the girl, who he saw through the cockpit window.

President Andrews continued to approach Taylor, and with their being only a few feet apart, and an even shorter distance from the craft's wingtip, the man smiled and rubbed his hand on its lower surface, showing a wave of the shield that worked over the entire surface of the ship.

"Make no mistake – we don't want you, Taylor – we want them!" the President said, turning his eyes to the ship

"Dream on!" Taylor said walking up to the man, and with these words all of the security armed themselves with weapons of a design Taylor had never seen before. Some of these were aimed at Taylor, but most were aimed at the craft, and Taylor felt his nerves twitch while President Andrews continued to speak.

"I don't think you realize what you're up against!" he said firmly. "Everyone up here, myself included, are protected by the same shielding technology that is right now keeping your children safe. None of your powers will work on us! So, again, if you please – tell your children to drop the shields. After all, we don't want there to be an incident."

"Not going to happen! They've been told to leave if things get out of hand – and you'd better believe that they will and leave me behind long before they'd ever let you take them prisoner again!"

"Well, if that's the way you want it, then fine we'll take them by force – while you watch!" President Andrews said with thinning patience, and with a mere hand signal, he ordered those on the landing pad to start firing on the ship.

Taylor could see that after the first few shots the ship was, indeed, becoming damaged. His heart plummeted. *They must have some different kind of weapon that can break through the shield!*

Looking around quickly, he forced a telekinetic wave to hit the landing pad. This caused a shaking that eventually made all those who were attacking the ship fall hard on the concrete beneath their feet.

Taylor then forced the concrete to roll in waves, against the struggling crowd of security making it impossible for them to stand, much less get a decent shot off at Taylor or the craft.

"Your suits don't make you invincible – they just force me to get creative. Now, if you don't want me to peel the entire pad off and drop you and your entire entourage to the ground below, you'd better listen up!"

President Andrews, the most powerful man in the world by position, offered a sour look that seemed to grow more rancid with each second that he had to watch his security being so easily manipulated by a teenager. He was further annoyed over the fact that he had to actually listen to the demands of this eighteen year old; someone that, in his eyes, was still a child. But he couldn't ignore that, in the background, the concrete was still rolling, cracking, and moving constantly, except where he, Taylor, and the ship stood.

Taylor looked at the man in front of him with an unblinking stare. "*We're* going to go to the council chambers and *you're* going to explain to me, and to *them* exactly what's been going on – and you're going to explain to them why it is that I've been denied rights to my own children."

"Fine then, let's go!" the president said arrogantly with a grin that Taylor couldn't seem to decipher.

"Oh, not so fast, before I leave sight of this ship, I want a pad that's tied in to the surveillance cameras. I want to see the ship and my children at all times. If I see these lemmings attack or the screen waver or go blank for even a second, I'll tell them to take off in a heartbeat!"

President Andrews smile, "Now I know you're bluffing! With the shield around the ship there's no way you can communicate with anyone inside!"

Taylor merely tilted his head back for a moment, and with a telepathic effort to communicate with Johnny, it only took a moment for the craft to lift into the air some ten feet or so and President Andrews started waving his hand in a panic. "Okay, okay fine! I get it!"

Taylor cast his eyes at the President with a malicious grin. "Good!" He said with a purposeful arrogance before looking over at the mass of bodies that were still clamoring over each other, trying to get their footing. With a quick flick of his head and a skyward stare, his eyes followed a small mass of concrete that had lifted high into the air with Taylor's head movement. When the block had finally come down, Taylor and President Andrews could both see that one of the security was lying atop the block. The man was terrified, gripping it tightly with his hands.

When the block finally settled on the landing pad President Andrews immediately commanded. "Son – You got a pad on you?"

Taylor almost felt bad for the guy; his face scrunched in fear, and had only opened his eyes at hearing President Andrew's voice, and realizing that he had finally landed safely. Slowly he crawled off the block and got to his feet. "P – Pad – sir. A data-pad? I – I do sir!"

"Good – if you would be so kind – hand it to Mr. Taylor over there."

Taylor forced his face to offer a menacing stare at the man, but inside he wanted to laugh at how afraid this guy was of him – his hand was shaking so horribly that Taylor had to steady it with his kinesis just so he could take what was being offered.

President Andrews looked at Taylor with an expectant stare, "Are you satisfied Mr. Tayl..."

Taylor held up his hand as he stared at the data-pad, using its wireless capabilities and his cyber abilities to tie in to the security system. After a few seconds he saw exactly what he was looking for. A four way split showing views from the four different security cameras mounted at the four corners of the landing pad.

"There! Now I'm satisfied – and it's Doctor Taylor, if you please!"

"Good," President Andrews said shortly, "now – do you think you can give my team here a break?"

"Oh, certainly!" Taylor said, and without a moment's wait the rolling and shaking concrete ceased its movement.

Taylor offered a quick pathic message to the entire mass of individuals on the pad, letting them know that they were under the President's orders not to attack, that the two of them were leaving for a while, and that, should any of them break this 'cease fire' order, he'd have no problem throwing the entire concrete pad down to the street below. After this message was sent, Taylor watched as every member of the GC security team knelt down in front of the craft and merely watched it, as if expecting it to do something interesting, or worshipping it as some kind of deity. Nonetheless, Taylor was satisfied and he slowly made his way with President Andrews to the lifts of East Tower. He willed the doors open in his usual manner, and just to put the president on edge, he released the safety interlocks of the lift and forced it to ascend over one hundred levels to the council chambers in just a few seconds.

"So how much do you really know about what's really going on here?" President Andrews asked with a nervous stare at watching the numbers ascend so quickly.

"I know enough to know that I need to know more!" Taylor said with a smile and he watched as the president shook his head.

"Well, you can't force me to tell you a single word – you forget, I'm the president of the GC."

"Hmmm – You might think you're right – but then again, here we are, in a small lift – together – and alone... Something I thought impossible. Just like the idea of the President negotiating with alien races, offering genetics in exchange for – well – we'll discuss that later."

"Well – you know a lot more than I thought!" The President said almost testily as the lift passed the 400th floor.

Taylor glanced down at the data pad, noticing that the four screens were still intact, and while the ship was many floors below them and completely surrounded by the president's security team, Taylor could see that these men and women were all still kneeling patiently, waiting for some word of what they were to do next.

"By the way, how'd you like my earthquake last night?" Taylor asked with a grin as he saw President Andrews' eyes grow wide with fear and confusion.

"Oh yes, that was me – I reprogrammed the sphere. You know – little snaky arms – made just for my children. Yeah – it's got a few side effects though – but then again I'm sure you knew that!"

"That wasn't designed for you!" the president said with biting anger.

As the lift slowed on approach to the 450th floor Taylor cast the man a look of distaste.

"Lemmie tell you something right now – and I want to make sure it's perfectly clear." Taylor worded slowly taking a deep breath. "Those children down there," He said pointing to the floor of the lift, "I love each and every one of them with all my heart. Now I know you have children of your own, but I don't really *know* how you feel for them. I can only hope that you realize that I love my children *at least* as much as you love your own, if not more."

"Freaks." He heard President Andrews whisper.

Furious and frustrated, Taylor grabbed the president by the neck and practically threw the man across the lift and pinned him against the wall. "I and my children are only freaks because you made us this way you pompous prick!"

Taylor took a deep breath, calming his nerves. "And we're not freaks – there's nothing wrong with us. If anything, there's something wrong with you! That you would sell the lives of innocent children to some alien race – it's just disgusting!"

"It's to save the planet you moron!" President Andrews said in a scratchy voice.

"Fine!" Taylor said dropping the man to his feet. "If that's the reason I can accept it – but you've got to accept the fact that I *will* always stay with my children – no matter what."

With a ding the lift reached the 450th floor and while Taylor was hoping he could get more out of the President before the two left their confined space, the president had other ideas. The man swiftly departed the lift and walked to the center of the council chambers – "I hold you all responsible for the piss poor attitude of this man. He was yours to rear and this is what you've done – I hand pick him and...!"

Taylor lifted one of the marble floors of the council chambers forcing the President to trip on its uneven surface, and thus forcing him to stop his insulting rhetoric.

"I am so sorry for that little outburst," Taylor said calmly looking into the faces of Dr. Ellington and Dr. Young, all the while though, he was taking in a bird's eye view of the damage that he himself had caused several hours before. He took in the tattered city and his heart ached. Even the room he was in, with several cracked plex panels and a show of debris on the floor, had signs of weathering Taylor's kinetic side effects. Then, with the head of the council trying to speak, the teen's attention was finally pulled away from his horrible view of the outside world.

"I – I – What do I say – what do I say?" Dr. Ellington stuttered, and he looked to Dr. Young for a little support.

"Taylor, honey, now isn't the best time – we're – uh – in the middle of a meeting. Wait – isn't that President Andrews. Oh you shouldn't be here!"

Taylor's mind was analyzing the words he had just heard from Dr. Young. She hadn't seen him for nearly three months and considering the circumstances surrounding how he left, her response was a little less than what he expected.

"Yeah, that's the president." he said with a quick, albeit apprehensive answer to her comment. "I was hoping we could take a little of your time to discuss..."

"Taylor," Dr. Young said with concerned stares around the room, "like I said, now isn't the best time."

What was she looking at? Taylor wondered as he glanced around the room. He couldn't see anyone other than himself and President Andrews, but he knew that somehow, someone else was there – or maybe it was *something!* He stared back at Dr. Young with a furrowed brow. Her face showed a look of fear, he only wondered about this for a moment before walking full up to the council table and turning around.

Curiously, the council was quiet and patient over his movements, and Taylor's suspicions increased every second. Normally they would've called security by now. No, there was something else going on.

He looked at Dr. Young and quickly sent her a telepathic question. "Where are they? I know they're here!"

She offered a confused look and responded, "I don't know what you're talking about."

"Oh, come on! I know about the aliens," Taylor transmitted with growing impatience, "I've seen them – they're obviously cloaked – so where are they?"

Dr. Young's eyebrows rose with a look of great surprise. "I – I don't know – it's been so long – they've probably moved, but how do you...?"

Taylor turned his head quickly, ending his attention to Dr. Young's message. He walked up to President Andrews, who was trying to deal with the bloodied nose he had just received from his fall.

"Come on Mr. President – you sent them here – *here* – to the chambers! Must've thought you'd have the children by now. Well, I'm here to tell you, the council – *and anyone else that's listening* that the children aren't coming! They and I are going to leave and there's nothing – absolutely nothing you can do about it!"

Taylor waited for only a moment, and with a series of loud growling howls, he looked around the room as several short, stout, and very menacing looking creatures revealed themselves. Taylor could have frowned. He could have offered a horrible look of disgust or of anger, but instead he simply smiled.

Taylor recognized one of the strange alien creatures as having the same uniform markings as he had seen in a prior vision.

"Ah – nice to finally meet you Kashal!" he said with an air of friendship that most certainly didn't fit their relationship or the mood in the room.

Kashal, who had obviously growled words of anger, stopped quite abruptly. He looked at Taylor through his cloaking hood and, with yet another series of loud noises, he disappeared.

Taylor was certain that the creature was going to attack. He let President Andrews go, and the man immediately ran around the council table, filled with fear and trepidation.

"There's no way you can beat something you can't see!" President Andrews said arrogantly, but Taylor knew better. The teenager looked with fierce concentration at the large empty space in front of him. With some kind of telekinetic sonar, something he'd never really done before, he could feel the movements of his unseen opponent.

He pointed his finger at the invisible Kashal, and moved his pointing finger to show that he knew exactly where the creature was through all of its movements. Taylor's finger pointed left – right – then left again. Then, quite unexpectedly, he pointed his finger in an upward direction.

"Oh!" Taylor said with surprise, and with a telekinetic push, he forced Kashal backward from what would have obviously been a landing directly on top of him.

Kashal, who was now at the far end of the chambers, was growling and howling. Then Taylor heard what he couldn't mistake for anything else – a laugh – a deep gurgling laugh that resonated throughout the chamber, and sent a chill up the teen's spine. He watched with wide eyes as Kashal revealed himself again.

The creature then growled a series of grumbles and howls to President Andrews that Taylor didn't understand – but he could see that the man was holding a mini-pad, staring at it with concentration.

"Hey!" the president said in anger as the small pad flew from his hands into Taylor's, who immediately looked down to read what was printed on the small screen.

IF THIS IS WHO YOU HAD TRAINING THE
CHILDREN - THEN I CANNOT WAIT TO GET
MY HANDS ON THEM!

Taylor absorbed these complimenting words and looked up at Kashal with a smile. "I must say, I'm quite impressed with your technology – I suppose the children *would* be a fair trade, but as they are my own – and I am quite attached to them – So you can't have them without taking me!"

Kashal started growling and almost angry series of growls, and Taylor looked down at the display in front of him, reading the words as they printed on the screen.

THE CHILDREN WE WANT ARE MUCH BETTER THAN YOU - THEY CAN HAVE ALL THE GIFTS THAT YOU DO NOT - AND YOU ARE ONLY THEIR TEACHER - THEY DO NOT BELONG TO YOU!

Kashal must have thought that he only had the one gift, telekinesis, and maybe he didn't understand what Taylor meant when he said that the children were his. He immediately clarified.

"I have all five gifts, Kashal – I was born with them – and when I say that those children are mine – I am referring to the fact that I am their father!"

Taylor could hear murmurs from the council table, but his attention was strictly focused on the creature in front of him.

Kashal offered only a low growl before laughing with his gurgling chuckle. Taylor listened to this with a light heart, and he thought to himself that while he would have to struggle to get information out of President Andrews, Kashal might be more forthcoming – even if he did have to read every single word.

Taylor turned his head as he felt a soft hand grab his shoulder. It was Dr. Young, who had made her way to the teen's side and asked gently of him, "What is that thi..."

"Shhhhtt!" Taylor hissed, "He doesn't like to be called 'that thing.' Just call him by his name – Kashal."

"Oh, fine," she whispered, "What is Kashal saying?" she asked. Taylor merely lifted the pad so she could read the words on the screen as the alien, again, grumbled and howled out another sequence of words.

IF YOU ARE BETTER THAN THE OTHERS - WELL - I'LL HAVE TO RE-NEGOTIATE. I MUST HAVE YOU.

Taylor cringed at the idea of being someone's property, but he slowly shook this feeling off with the realization that neither he, nor his children could ever *really* be someone's property without their own consent. He re-read the statement from Kashal, looked up at the creature then offered an almost evil stare to President Andrews.

"You don't need to re-negotiate anything – I'm going of my own free will!" He said this purposefully for both Kashal and President Andrews to hear.

President Andrews offered a nervous stare at Taylor while Kashal gurgled and grumbled. The teen looked down at the pad in his hand and textual chaos came up on the screen.

"What's that?" Dr. Young asked curiously.

"Hmm – He must be speaking a different language." Taylor said in a whisper. Dr. Young nodded her head with the realization that this species, like humans, probably had several well developed languages and dialects, but the pad in Taylor's hand was only capable of translating one of these.

"This is probably the only way he can talk with the others without President Andrews being able to translate.

Kashal looked up at Taylor and offered more loud howling and growls. Taylor snapped at attention realizing that the pad, again, started showing words that made sense.

WE WILL OFFER CONSESSIONS FOR YOU - BUT YOU ALREADY HAVE OUR SHIP DESIGN, SHIELD AND CLOAKING TECHNOLOGY - WHAT ELSE IS THERE?

Taylor read the pad aloud and looked at President Andrews, who was biting his lip, nervous, and hesitant to respond. The man's thoughts inside his head were obvious though, and Taylor responded for him in an instant. "How 'bout your faster that light drive? Apparently his team of scientists aren't anywhere near finding or designing a suitable engine?"

There was a brief pause before Kashal started to howl and growl both loudly and angrily.

It was clear that he wasn't going to agree to these terms, and Taylor held his hand up quickly, thinking of the best way to meet a happy middle ground.

"That's fine! Fine! If you can't give us the technology, maybe you can look at our designs – tell us where we're messing up and how we could improve on what we have – help us to do better!"

Kashal's angry words immediately subsided and he offered what Taylor could clearly see as a smile before, again, laughing.

"I thought you might find that alright!" Taylor said with a grin.

Taylor looked over at President Andrews with a snide smile as Kashal hobbled over, offering a scaly clawed hand to Taylor. It seemed he was trying to offer the human version of a handshake. The teen reached out and it was clear that, pending some details of course, the agreement was now binding.

Taylor looked over at the large clock in the chambers – it now showed 10:15AM, and his heart seemed to skip a beat with the thought that maybe – just maybe – his efforts helped avoid the inevitable from coming true.

He looked at President Andrews, though, still unsure of the man's uneasiness – his nervousness – it didn't make sense – and it certainly didn't make sense that, if he had a desire for something that this species could offer, why he didn't negotiate it in the first place. It just didn't make sense.

With a booming echo Taylor's head snapped over to the side of the chambers where the doors swung open quickly, and with a rush of bright colors five cloaked individuals stormed into the room.

"Oh, good, we're not too late!" Stewart said. He was holding the same helmet that Johnny had once worn back in DC, and in seeing it Kashal immediately snatched it up with a loud horrific growl.

Taylor looked down at the small pad, realizing that the grumbles were more words that could be translated.

THAT'S MINE YOU LITTLE THEIF!

Stewart jumped back, not noticing the creature until the helmet was well out of his reach.

Dr. Ellington stood up in the middle of this rush of chaos, and finally, as if he had wanted to do it all morning, he hammered down his fist on the table, "Will someone tell me what the hell is going on here? Dr. Zeldin, what the hell are you doing here? President – you knew about these aliens, and you were going to barter off our students. Taylor – where the hell have you been, and – oh – I'm getting a damned headache just..." The man was ranting to the point where he started heaving his words, but Taylor walked up to him slowly, offering the sober stare with his bright blue eyes.

"Sir, I'll explain everything – or at least what I know, maybe President Andrews can confirm things and fill in some of the blanks, but I think I've got most of this figured out."

Taylor was about to speak, but his mouth suddenly held itself shut, and he knew instantly that Elizabeth was keeping him from talking.

"Well, come on!" Dr. Ellington said impatiently but Taylor was unable to move a single muscle.

Kashal, who was standing behind him, hobbled to a position in front of Taylor. With a loud booming voice the teen could hear the creature howl and garble words, but Taylor did not respond. He couldn't even lift his hand to read what the creature was saying. Kashal's eyes grew large with a stare in Elizabeth's direction – the creature garbled more words, but Taylor did nothing. Inside his head the teen was screaming at the top of his mental lungs over frustration that, again, Elizabeth had found a way to control him.

Kashal paced to Taylor's side. He offered a loud shouting howl, turned quickly, and with an arm that was clearly three times longer than he had thought was hiding inside the creature's uniform, Kashal reached out and hit Elizabeth so hard she flew across the room some twenty feet, hitting her back on a large pillar before falling to the hard marble floor.

Taylor turned his head and looked to Kashal with a smile – "Thank you!"

He reached out his hand and looked at the pad in his fingers.

WHAT IS WRONG WITH YOU? WHY AREN'T
YOU TALKING?

I SEE. SHE HAS YOU. EMPTY YOUR MIND
BOY EMPTY YOUR MIND GIVE HER NOTHING
TO READ...

Taylor was grateful that Kashal had become so frustrated that he decided to take matters into his own hands – his very far reaching hands.

"Empty my mind?" Taylor asked curiously, and President Andrews responded with an almost bored voice.

"Not many people can do it – it takes a great deal of focus – but that's the only way to keep her from taking control – if you empty your thoughts then she has nothing to read – nothing to ride into your brain."

"How does he know about that?" Taylor asked with a nod to Kashal.

"Ah – Kashal wouldn't continue negotiations unless I told him how to break her control. Later it didn't matter much – when we found that the shielding technology blocked all mentally evolved powers, he protected himself with constant shielding. Either way it's pretty obvious – he doesn't like her very much."

Taylor looked at Kashal with a smile and offered a false whisper, "I don't like any of them!"

Kashal gurgled another laugh before calling out to one of his own. Within seconds a small unit was thrown to him, and he put it in Taylor's hand. The teen looked down at the strange small device, barely the size of a bioelastic polymer unit. It had a small blinking green light and an elastic band just large enough to put over his arm.

Taylor put on the small unit and pressed the green button – with a flash of electrostatic blue, he realized that he was completely covered with the same shielding technology as his ship and the squad of security that were now waiting around it.

Snapping to attention, Taylor pulled the data pad from the elastic band of his pajama like pants and looked at the display with a defined concentration. The ship was still sitting quietly on the pad, but beside it there was another craft. Obviously the one that the Evol Crew had rode in on. Taylor breathed a sigh of relief, realizing that he was still getting a live feed.

He put the pad back in his waistband and turned to Dr. Ellington, now ready to again reveal what truth he knew of this government conspiracy that had overshadowed his entire life and the lives of his children.

76 Mystery Mostly Solved

"NOW – AS I WAS ABOUT TO SAY," Taylor voiced with a fierce stare at Elizabeth, who had just been revived by Daniel.

"As I understand it, President Andrews made an agreement with Kashal some ten or eleven years ago to give him children that had the same gifts as I possess. Right so far?" He asked looking at President Andrews, who was actually smiling and nodding.

"That wasn't what Kashal wanted, but it's what we eventually agreed on." President Andrews voiced with a nod to Elizabeth.

Taylor remembered the last part of the vision he had before finding a thumb in his shoulder and understood that Elizabeth had actually worked with the rest of the Evol Crew to change the negotiations.

"So, when an agreement had been made for a trade you had a team take some of my blood; blood that, I know for a fact, was used to create the six beautiful children that are now in a ship on the landing pad below."

President Andrews continued to nod – "that's almost right."

Dr. Ellington leaned forward, "So those children are really, *really* yours?"

"Indeed, I was a father at 8 years old, even if I didn't know it, and best of all, you can't charge me with having kids without a license because it wasn't my decision!" Taylor said arrogantly in President Andrew's direction.

"But those kids are mine!" He said turning back to the council. "The one thing I can't figure out though, is why you didn't give them the same abilities that I had?"

"Hmmm" President Andrews interrupted, "Their gifts were supposed to be completely dormant – but, well, our genetics department wasn't completely perfect. They tried creating genetic variations for look and gender, but there were other variations we hadn't planned on."

Taylor offered a stare to President Andrews, waiting for an explanation. "They were going to be normal kids – we were going to – eh – activate their gifts later – when the time was right – say *ten* years old."

"Indeed, that makes even more sense now that I think about it!" Taylor interrupted. "So you trained the kids up for five years – and let me guess – you used the same protocols as Prodigy."

President Andrews shook his head.

"NO!" Taylor responded in surprise. "But why, when they were so young did they have fully developed powers?"

"Ah! Well, apparently, it is a part of your and their genetic code to develop those gifts early, not part of *Prodigy*. It's something we haven't yet been able to isolate. I suppose you could say that it was actually a problem that these kids weren't raised by the Prodigy standards. They were very violent with their powers – they weren't like you, you know – well maturated and behaved. No, they were very hard to control, and it made things very difficult for us – there were injuries and lots of damage. We had to watch the youngest – uh – Johnny and – uh Caitlin – constantly too because their visions would be so intense sometimes that they'd wake up with severe night terrors – it was a very stressful time for them."

Taylor shook his head, "I suppose you finally realized you were playing with fire!"

President Andrews nodded, "Indeed. We tried to wipe them of their powers before we handed them over. The powers could then be reactivated later."

"But there isn't a perfected method to do that yet!" Taylor voiced heatedly, and then a realization washed over him – "Ah, but you figured you'd try the latest theory and instead of wiping their gifts, you wiped their memories – all of their memories."

"Exactly, and we were panicked. We told Kashal of the news and he thought it would be best if his team raised the children. They would obviously have better technology to manage them, so we just handed them over – you know – finished our half of the deal."

"But they woke up with the minds of infants, were terrified, and crashed the ship that was supposed to transport them. How lucky for me!"

President Andrews nodded, "Yes, and Kashal thought I was trying to – uh – sell them a lemon or a trap. It felt like we were back to square one with our negotiations. He had already shared the cloaking and shielding technology with us – but now we had nothing to offer him and he didn't want any part of these children until they were better trained – maybe a bit older. We sat for hours thinking of the best course of action to take; then it came to me."

"Ahhh," Taylor said with a smile, "I could train them – I'd already developed the perfect program – and I could control them a lot better than any of you."

"Exactly! I examined your program and told Kashal that in another five years he'd have the children – 10 years old as promised – and much easier to reason with."

"Yeah – but then the kids came here, crashed the ship that brought them, and I had to work for hours to get them stable."

President Andrews shrugged his shoulders, "I was going to arrange for a transport with a whole team of people, but the first crash site outside the city had already been spotted. There was nothing I could do. Kashal's ship got out of there just in time to keep everybody from finding out the truth! We even had to close down our training facility in case anyone tried to investigate where the children might have come from. It was all just too risky."

Taylor shook his head. He felt that this answer was unacceptable, but as it was a matter of history, and was so long ago, it hardly mattered. In thinking further, he turned to Dr. Ellington. "So, with my project so close to being finished, the president here, was about to hand over the children, but they still each only had their one gift. This wasn't the agreement – No – these children were supposed to each have all five gifts."

Dr. Ellington, who was listening to Taylor and President Andrews intently, offered a wide eyed stare, "That – that sphere!"

"Right you are Dr. Ellington – the sphere was to be used to re-program the children's brains and bring their powers out of dormancy. It was first tried on Johnny, but I interfered. Still though, the damage was done and the nanites were in place re-programming his brain."

"Eventually I was able to extract the nanites the first time, and then again when all six children had decided for themselves that they liked the idea of being just like their father."

"So are they all now just like you?" President Andrews asked anxiously.

"Uh, no – Johnny was the closest – but as I've watched them over the past few months, I can tell that they're losing those extra talents that they didn't already have."

President Andrews gritted his teeth. "So CTP2 didn't work." He said softly. Instantly Kashal howled in anger at these words. Taylor raised his hands on both sides quickly, though, and started to speak between the two of them.

"Ah – wait, wait. The only reason why it didn't work was because I extracted the nanites before they could finish their job. If they could be allowed to finish, the neural connections would be permanent – especially with trained and constant use." Taylor then turned to Kashal. "Maybe later – when the time is right – we can use the sphere – uh – the CTP2 – and let the nanites run their course."

President Andrews nodded his head, as did Kashal, and Taylor turned to Dr. Ellington. "Now, about these visions of the future... They are the biggest confusing mystery of this whole thing."

"Not really," interjected Stewart, a man that had been biting his tongue – listening and allowing President Andrews reveal this conspiracy to a worthy audience.

"No matter what," Stewart shouted loudly in the chambers, "that *Kashal,* is going to kill us all, even if we give him what he wants!"

President Andrews and Taylor looked at Stewart with surprise and shock.

"How can you be so sure?" Taylor asked snidely as his eyes took in the beaming bright white of the man's cloak.

"I've seen it!" Stewart said firmly, "with that damn helmet; I've seen it!"

Taylor turned his stare to Kashal. "Hmmm, but why would you do that?"

Taylor's answer didn't come from the creature in front of him, who was slowly grumbling in anger. Instead President Andrews' face started telling the tale.

"Well," President Andrews said stiffly, "If Kashal doesn't want our inborn gifts to be used against him or his people, he might get rid of all of us, even if we made an agreement." By the end of his words President Andrews tone shifted to one of an accusing nature.

Kashal's growling turned to angry howls yet again, and Taylor looked down, reading aloud quickly as the words came up on his small data pad.

MY THREATS ON YOUR PLANET HAVE ALWAYS BEEN HOLLOW. MY PEOPLE ARE DESPERATE. BILLIONS HAVE DIED TRYING TO PROTECT YOUR PART OF THE GALAXY - YOU WOULD NEVER EVEN UTTER SUCH DOUBTS IF YOU KNEW THE TRUTH!

"Protect our galaxy?" Taylor questioned. "From who – I don't understand."

Taylor looked around the room with his mind spinning. This was more information that he had to, again, fit into what he knew. He tried to make sense of everything and, slowly, an idea came into his head.

He turned to Stewart, "You said war – before – when you showed me the vision – you said the word war – but you weren't talking about humans fighting humans, or even humans fighting aliens – you were talking about two alien species fighting each other.

Stewart's eyes widened, but he didn't say a word.

"And earlier," Taylor said turning on Elizabeth, "You said that if I knew the whole truth I would never agree to *it* – whatever it was. – And it doesn't make sense that I couldn't just be part of the exchange between Kashal and President Andrews if it meant *this* much trouble... No – no – there's more, so much more! I was the first – I was made for a reason," Taylor said with an arrogant air, "so who else has been looking? Who else is willing to buy our powers – our gifts?"

Taylor looked at President Andrews, whose accusing attitude to Kashal had retracted.

"You! You've made a deal – with both sides!" Taylor said accusingly, and at this President Andrews looked over at Kashal, his human face trying to offer an expression of innocence. Apparently this expression did nothing for Kashal, who began, again, howling angrily.

Slowly, either out of panic, or just a need to clear everything up, President Andrews dropped his shield and the man's brain started leaking thoughts that Taylor was able to read.

"You – you made a deal with the other alien race – you – you made it before you ever met Kashal – that's why I was created – that's why I was made. You were going to give them me – then Kashal came along and – and he was going to get me too – but – but Elizabeth was the only one who could read your thoughts – she knew about the double deal – so she – she penned the deal for my children."

"You – You don't know what you're talking about!" President Andrews recanted nervously, but, at least among the humans, everyone in the room quickly realized that Taylor had hit a nerve – and had revealed even more of the truth. The teen looked over at Elizabeth, who, with her desperate stare, was wishing that she could do something to keep Taylor from saying another word.

"You didn't actually expect that we, my children and I, would fight on opposite sides of this war did you?" Taylor asked, almost entertained at the lunacy of such an idea.

President Andrews did not respond, he just offered a wandering stare at the council to see if he could read which side they believed, then, with a realization that he was President Andrews – he stiffened his posture and removed all care from his mind on the matter.

"But it's him that does it – it's him that levels our cities – I'm telling you!" Stewart bellowed at Taylor.

"Hmmm – No, I don't think so!" Taylor said cautiously as he walked up to Kashal. "If I may," he said holding out his hand.

Kashal looked at Taylor with his massive yellow eyes, and after a few grumbles he shot out the helmet from under his arm and handed it to Taylor.

The teen grabbed the overly large headgear and, with his eyes closed, he focused hard on the future of what the helmet might hold. Quickly enough, the darkness that was his view under closed eyelids suddenly lit up in a bright white glow. Taylor then looked out and saw, with the reveal of the oncoming vision that he was in a craft that seemed similar to, but much larger than the one he had parked on the EduCorp landing pad. The teen looked all through the cockpit, hoping to get some idea of what ship this was, or when exactly he was in time.

It was clear that among all the symbols he could see, nothing was printed in any discernible Earth language. No – the markings that made little sense to him, but just the same, he did notice one display that counted in a constant interval, and he made a strong effort to memorize the symbols he saw on it.

As Taylor took the time to absorb this display, he was distracted by a flashing in front of him. He looked out the front window of the craft and, as if he hadn't noticed it before, he saw a view of blackness was slowly being overtaken by the huge blue swirling image of Earth. Taylor quickly realized that he was actually in space, and he was descending toward Earth.

But what was that flash?

As he looked out, Taylor could see another bright flash overwhelm his view of the outside. This time, however, the flash was followed by a rattling of the floor. Taylor felt his heart leap into his chest as, behind him, he could hear a strange yet beautiful songlike sound come from some unknown source. The teen, staring in all directions, was almost mesmerized by how beautiful the sound was, but was shocked when he realized its source.

When he whirled himself around, Taylor saw, in some kind of pilot's chair, a tall thin white figure whose skin glowed with a whitish blue luminescence. Indeed his mind was thinking that the sounds from this creature were as beautiful to the ear as its appearance was to the eye. But Taylor quickly put his mind in check with the realization that this must be the other alien species; the one Kashal was at war with.

These thoughts seemed to be confirmed instantly when Taylor looked just to the side of the thin glowing creature. Here he could see that the long skinny glowing fingers were massaging the helmet that Taylor knew, in reality, he was holding. Taylor could tell that there was another flash at the front of the ship, and with the shaking of the craft the Taylor could hear the strange, thin, alien creature speak more words in a high pitched song-like voice. He watched the creature hold up its hand and make a shaking fist into the air.

Was that – frustration? Taylor wondered, but as he stared at the alien, he could see that it was concentrating hard on something in front of him.

Taylor turned around, and saw that in front of the ship there was a series of small dots that were moving quite fast, but one dot in particular was being tracked with some sort of holographic set of arrows. The creature offered another songlike series of words but Taylor ignored them in his efforts of trying to focus on the small dot. It zigzagged fiercely as the ship tried to attack it with relentless fire.

As this constantly shifting motion continued, the dot got bigger and bigger, eventually getting large enough for Taylor to determine what it was.

Taylor wasn't at all surprised to realize that it was another ship, but it wasn't just any other ship – it was *his* ship, Taylor's ship – there was no mistaking the markings – and Taylor could see that the craft was weaving in and out rapidly, making it extremely difficult for the thin glowing creature to land any hits.

Taylor shook his head with a smile, he was about to turn back to the glowing alien behind him but his eyes were distracted by the changing view in front of him. He saw and felt that the ship he was in made a nose dive, eventually heading itself directly toward the Los Angeles Metroship. The city showed itself as one of several shiny sections on the Pacific coast.

Taylor's stomach lurched. He watched the ship zap a series of strange electrostatic charges into the atmosphere, causing it to cloud up almost instantly.

The teen heaved a sigh. This was practically the hundredth time that he had seen this vision, but no matter how many times he took in the same series of events from different perspectives – it terrified him to even think that this had any chance of becoming a reality. So, again, he watched the dark clouds grow more detailed in their puffy churning nature, and with a sense of familiarity he noticed a hole that swirled and formed directly in front of the ship. He looked up at the strange foreign counter that he had tried to memorize before – some of the characters were different – but if this was the moment of truth, he would want to know exactly when it was.

He turned to the bright glowing creature and, nearly pulled his hand from the real helmet in the chambers when he saw, to his surprise, himself – no, no, a future version of himself standing behind the alien. Taylor had to do a double take – he saw that this wide eyed future version of himself was holding a large metal pipe, or something like a metal pipe, over the creature's head and with a high hold, preparing for a very hard hit, Taylor was ready to strike. But the Taylor of now, the one with his hand on the helmet in the EduCorp Council Chambers, noticed a bright flash that illuminated his future face; a face of anger and fear that Taylor didn't know he could ever force his face to express. The Taylor of the future swung the pipe down After the hit, and after the flash, he turned his head and watched the light slowly diminish as his eyes followed a bright dot that pushed its way through the clouds.

Taylor turned back to his future self and couldn't help but feel a growing anger over his own hesitation. If he hadn't waited, he would've been able to stop that last shot. He heaved heated words at himself as he watched the future him grab the helmet from beside the unconscious and now dimming creature that was sitting in the pilot's chair.

Future Taylor looked up for several seconds, focusing on a data panel with hard concentration and, with a bright electrostatic bubble forming around him, he was gone in an instant.

Taylor's view immediately washed away with a bright whiteness before coming back to a deep brownish orange. With the salty, fishy smell in the air he automatically knew where he was. With the sight of rising smoke, the odor, and the ruins before him, he knew that he was viewing the aftermath of the city's destruction.

With a whirling of wind and dust, he looked up to see, again, the same crafts that had haunted his visions before. But on thinking back to them, he was far less afraid. Now, as the ships drew closer, and the ground continued to shake, he almost welcomed the overhead visitors with open arms.

Taylor looked to his side and saw his future self, holding the helmet, and instantly he frowned. Every other time he had been in this part of the vision he didn't have a helmet in his hands... *But then again – the original vision wasn't supposed to happen for another 5 months.* Things change – and this is only one small detail that he could overlook.

Knowing that he had seen this before, Taylor knew what to expect. He watched as, again, hands reached up and out of the dirt to pull him under. The instant that this happened several loud booming thuds could be heard from all around and Taylor could see that some of these had crashed into caverns below the earth.

Taylor then noticed that one of the ships actually landed rather than have its loading door open for an alien trooper emerge, and from this ship's upper hatch a short, stout, familiar alien made his way onto the dirt. It was Kashal, who looked down to the ground and grumbled. He stomped once with his wide foot and the earth trembled from its weakened state – he stomped again, and this time he fell through to the cave beneath.

Taylor would have leaned over to see him, but another alien, very similar in appearance to Kashal, de-cloaked and looked in on the subterranean chamber. This alien pulled out a small weapon of sorts, and with a quick blast, Taylor watched as the creature shot Kashal through the shoulder and through the helmet that the alien had just picked up from the underground chamber.

Kashal let out a loud howling growl that seemed to resonate through Taylor's own chest before one final shot penetrated him through the eye and the back of the head. Taylor turned and looked at the alien that had fired the weapon. This creature was one of Kashal's own. A traitor. Taylor looked at the assassin and took in his appearance fully and with a concentrated effort he forced himself to release the helmet that he was holding in his own hands.

The wash of white that came over him was somewhat inviting, but the image that followed forced Taylor to jump. When he opened his eyes, their light blue color was met in contrast with two large yellow ones that were framed by a green scaly face that frightened Taylor, even if it was only for an instant. The teenager flinched and jumped back. He looked around the chambers at each of Kashal's crew with a narrow eyed stare. He didn't say a word of what he saw – he was far too focused and determined to offer any details until he finished looking each member of Kashal's crew over. He was hoping that he could identify the assassin from this last vision of the future.

With a raised finger he pointed – "Kashal – that one is not your friend." Taylor said firmly.

Kashal, who was listening to a quick translation of Taylor's words, turned his head to the alien that Taylor was pointing to. Then Kashal growled and gurgled a phrase that Taylor read in shuffling the alien's helmet with that of the pad between his fingers.

RAFASHIL-GILKIRNIKI-SHKIAN!
BUT - HE IS NOTHING - A MERE
BOY - WHY WOULD YOU SAY SUCH
THINGS ABOUT A BOY.

"Raf – Rafash," Taylor shook his head at such a complicated name, "Rafash will kill you when he gets the chance – I've seen it – he's the one – he's the reason that *the others* are here. You know, the one's made of light!"

Taylor realized that this description sounded a little juvenile the moment it left his lips, but after a moment, he knew that he had successfully conveyed the point across to Kashal. With a quick spin the creature turned on the alien that Taylor now knew as Rafash. With harsh booming voices the two argued.

Taylor watched the pad as it displayed their words, but he was also concerned with getting the pad from his own waistband again. With a focus on it, he forced the surveillance images to disappear and he mentally drew the characters and images that he remembered from his vision in the ship.

He walked up to Kashal, reading as he went.

BOY. HE SAY'S YOU ARE A TRAITOR. HE
SAY'S HE HAS SEEN YOU TRY TO KILL ME.

THE HUMAN IS LYING. HE DOES NOT KNOW
WHAT HE SAW.

HE KNOWS ENOUGH FOR ME TO BELIEVE HIM AND FOR YOU THAT IS NOT A GOOD THING.

HOW CAN YOU BELIEVE ANY OF THEM? THEY ALL SPEAK NOTHING BUT LIES.

HE KNOWS ABOUT THEM. HE KNOWS WHAT THEY LOOK LIKE. HE KNOWS BECAUSE YOU BROUGHT THEM HERE.

Taylor watched as all of Kashal's troops turned on Rafash, and Kashal himself raised his weapon and pointed it at this traitor in his midst.

Taylor pulled Kashal's arm for a moment and handed him the data pad, "Whatever you're going to do, do it fast 'cause we don't have much time!" he said firmly.

Kashal, who paused only a moment for translation, reached up. Not taking his eyes off Rafash, he grabbed the pad and looked at it for a split second before looking at a timing unit that was on the back of his hand.

Taylor had to plug his ears as Kashal's screams were the loudest he had heard yet, and he could swear that the plex-panels in the ceiling would shatter if the creature didn't' quiet down. The alien was obviously furious, but once he had vented his anger and his voice died down, another sound, one of alien laughter, could be heard rising through the chambers.

Taylor, the council, the Evol-Crew, and the President all looked at Rafash with growing concern as the alien continued his deep gurgling laugh. This made Taylor very nervous, and with hardly any movement, the alien clicked a button between his fingers that caused a series of beeping noises that distracted everyone's attention.

Taylor watched as a strange electrostatic bubble formed around Rafash and instantly the creature disappeared with a flash. With all the electrostatic noise, what Taylor and the others didn't seem to realize was that he, Taylor, was also beeping.

He looked around himself and realized that the beeping was coming from his armband.

"What the hell?" He said loudly, and in that instant a large electrostatic ball engulfed him. He looked over at Dr. Young, whose face showed a look of both shock and surprise.

"Get everybody out of the city! Get out...!" Taylor shouted, but with a similar bright flash, he too was gone before finishing his words and all at once the large room fell silent. This quietness did not last for long. Kashal, who was clearly frustrated beyond words, bellowed loudly in the chambers a terrifying wail that made every human present cringe.

The creature pointed at President Andrews and offered a series of gurgling and howling expressions that no one had any means of understanding. The alien then tapped a series of buttons on his wristband and each of his comrades did the same.

Noises of electric sparks and bubbles filled the room until, with bright flashes, the chamber was emptied of any alien presence.

"You know, you have some nerve!" Dr. Ellington said angrily at President Andrews, "Making deals – selling children – and putting us in the middle of some interstellar war – what – are you insane?"

"I had no choice!" the president shouted in return.

"Of course you did! You could've at least told us what was going..."

"We don't have time for this!" Dr. Young screamed above the both of them, while casting a scowling stare at Dr. Ellington, "We have to clear out the children – we have to clear out the city – everybody!"

President Andrews turned in the direction of the Evol-Crew, but his eyes were focused downward. The man was staring at the floor and showed an almost apologetic expression before looking up at all of them with a somber stare. With a deep sigh he started voicing several instructions.

77 Into the Unknown

TAYLOR, FROM INSIDE the buzzing electrostatic bubble, could see that his outside world was quickly changing. With a morphing of color and images he saw that the large, beautiful council chambers had quickly changed, and that the face of Dr. Young dissolved away. In place of these familiar and mostly friendly surroundings, Taylor saw a small room measuring only a few square feet appear and close in around him.

The teen watched with curiosity as the glowing bubble around him quickly disappeared into a small bright dot before popping out of sight. *Had he been moved from one place to another electronically? Where am I?* He wondered, but as quick as these words entered his brain, he remembered the vision that he had just experienced. He stared down at the helmet in his hands. *Yes – yes – this all made sense now.* He must have been brought to a ship that's in orbit.

"Eaaaaah!" Taylor shrieked as he felt a harsh zapping pain at the ends of his fingertips. He released the helmet that he had been holding – and while it floated in the air only momentarily, Taylor saw, by the object's surrounding bubble, that it was being taken from him with the same device that had brought him to his cell.

With the helmet gone Taylor took a deep breath and closed his eyes. He could see in his mind that the helmet was probably sitting beside the pilot of this ship. Taylor almost grinned with the thought that his vision was slowly coming full circle from how he remembered it – and maybe – just maybe – he would be able to act fast enough and prevent that final devastating shot to the city below.

Feeling a resolute determination, he looked around, and it was with a heaving sigh that he realized how confined and completely restricted he really was. As he stepped to what would be the entrance of his cell, he noticed that his feet pulsed on the floor with a familiar electrostatic throb. Clearly he wouldn't be able to break through the floor of this cell the way he had done before, and, considering his possible location, it's not like he would want to – after all, just inches beneath his feet could be the full exposure of space – breaking through that kind of barrier wouldn't necessarily be a good thing.

He stepped up to the control panel and carefully looked it over. He smiled. He could read symbols and see patterns that were definitely of no language that he recognized. Without a doubt he was definitely on the alien ship he had seen before.

It only took a moment for Taylor to become restless though, and he wondered how it was that he had escaped from this cell so that he would eventually stand right behind the alien pilot of this craft. He looked around, but indeed there was nothing for him to use to escape. Curiosity got the better of him, and, reaching his hand out, he knew the moment that he tried to touch the control panel his fingers would be met with the cell's confining shield – but he still felt that he had to try!

Taylor closed his eyes for a moment in concentration. Trying to remember his most recent vision – how would he be able to escape. Thinking back he focused on what he could remember. After rolling broken memories in his head for nearly a minute, he opened his eyes with a deep sigh – nothing he could remember would work in getting him out of this mess, but as his eyes stared down at the pulsing floor beneath his feet – he was reminded of the bright flashes that kept washing over the ship – flashes that were caused by an attacking ship – *his ship!*

Of course! Of course! Duh! He thought before slumping to the floor.

He took a deep breath, hesitating only for a moment, reserved about bringing his children into this conflict – but in remembering the vision, he realized that they would be better off in space than in the city. *Yes – this is the only way!* Taylor reassured himself.

He then slowed his breathing as he concentrated on creating a telepathic link between himself and Johnny. After a moment Taylor lit a smile with the realization that his efforts must be working. This was because he could see a pulsing on the wall of his cell; a pulsing that obviously didn't come from any physical contact. No, this disturbance was definitely from his telepathically reaching out to connect with his son. *Come on Taylor – Come on! Focus on your son – Focus!*

***

"How long are we going to wait out here?" voiced an impatient David, sitting in the pilot's chair.

"Johnny – have you gotten any word?" Jay asked. On the surface the man was ignoring David's question, yet he wanted to voice his own worries over this idling.

Johnny shook his head. He was sitting in the middle of the ship, between Aspen and Caitlin.

"Wait – what's that?" Tristan said looking out the front of the craft from his side chair.

Jay immediately popped his head between the two boys in the pilot and co-pilot's seats and saw that Dr. Zeldin and Daniel were rushing out of West Tower's lift to the ship that they had flown in on. This ship, which was practically identical to theirs, took off after only a moment.

Jay walked back talk to the others, and in telling them what he saw, each became even more curious and nervous over what was happening.

"But why just the two of them?" Aspen questioned.

"I don't know." Jay said softly, and in his mind he knew that this couldn't be a good thing.

Jay turned and tried to work his way to the front of the ship, but his movements were immediately stalled.

"Oh my God! Johnny – Johnny!" Delissa shouted.

"What's going on?" Jay spewed.

"Johnny – Johnny!" Delissa repeated over the boy, shaking him lightly.

Jay moved between the other children and squatted in front of the youngest. He offered a curious stare at the child and as he did this Delissa reached to shake him again, but Jay raised his hand with a cautioned look. "Wait – don't!" he said stiffly, and slowly the boy's eyes opened. All at once the child stiffened and sat upright. "We have to go – now!" He said offering a fearfully wide blue eyed stare.

"What's going on? Tell me Johnny – What's happened? What's going on?" Jay was frantic after seeing the expression on the child's face, but Orion and Grace didn't wait. They immediately replaced David and Tristan in the front seats, started up the ship and prepared it for takeoff.

"He's not here – he's gone!" Johnny said in a panic.

"What? What do you mean gone!" asked Jay, echoed by several of the other children in the cabin.

Johnny sighed, "It would take too long to explain just trust me. We have to go now or it'll be too late!"

Slowly the other's faces all changed to show a look of understanding with Jay being the only one to still be filled with apprehension.

"Orion – get us out of here! Now!" Johnny half shouted, and at this, the craft quickly lifted off the pad.

"No, wait! How do we know..." Jay questioned, but this did little good amid the commotion up front.

"I don't need to be told twice." Orion said enthusiastically, and within moments they were lifting high above the four towers of EduCorp. As he took off Orion smiled at seeing the security team below stumble and climb over each other wondering what was going on. Their faces were confused, and it was clear that the boy pilot didn't want to wait for them to figure anything out. He started flying over the city of Los Angles completely devoid of any real direction.

"So where are we headed?" Orion asked with his head tilted back to the cabin of the ship.

Johnny, with closed eyes, offered a wide smile for all others to see. He pointed straight up. The smile seemed to comfort Jay to some degree, but when the boy pointed straight up confusion filled the man's brain. Namely, Jay was grasping at straws trying to figure out what was going on. He watched the boy with a curious sense of irritation. Then, with the boy closing his eyes, Johnny seemed in some kind of telepathic trance, but still able to hear and feel the world around him.

"Go up! Straight up!" Caitlin shouted realizing that Orion didn't notice his brother's pointing.

"Okaaaay!" Orion said with a confused uncertainty as he pointed the ship's nose skyward. When he did this both his and Grace's face seemed to light up with a strange wavering color.

"What the?" she said curiously, "What's going on?"

Their attention, and that of the entire ship, seemed to be focused on a strange pulsing of the shields that had slowly revealed itself directly in front of the craft.

"There's something wrong with the shields!" Orion shouted nervously, but Tristan popped his head beside the boy and smiled. He knew without any doubt, what was happening.

"No – NO! It's Taylor!"

Jay, who at first was just as confused as Orion, came to realize what Tristan was thinking the instant the words fell from the child's mouth.

"Orion, fly straight toward the shield disturbance! Use it as your guide!" Jay instructed purposefully.

"I don't understand,"

"Your brother and your father," Jay said referencing Taylor as their true father for the first time "they're communicating telepathically!"

"Yeah, aaand!" Orion pressed.

Jay hadn't thought that it was entirely possible for Orion not to know of the shield disturbance caused by Johnny and Taylor's connection. With an instant pathic link the he explained to the boy what he knew before finishing with a verbal phrase.

"The shield fluctuations are caused by their telepathic connection – Like a connecting string between the two of them." Jay said using his hands to express what he was saying.

Orion's eyes grew wide with his understanding of the truth "Oh, that's going to come in handy!" he said with a smile, all the while guiding the ship directly into the shield disturbance, yet never really reaching it.

After a few seconds of this Orion's face grew a beguiling smile. In his mind, the boy was reminded of an archaic image of how a horse might be motivated to move by hanging a carrot in front of its face.

Eagerly watching as the bright blue sky slowly shifted to a deep darkness at reaching the highest levels of the atmosphere, all of the children were in awe over going into space for the first time in their lives. Tristan and Delissa shared this emotion as well, but Jay, having traveled to both moon and mars based colonies on prior occasions, was not nearly as taken with the event.

As the final shades of blue slowly died away into the blackness of the universe, Orion quickly realized that in front of him, he could see little else but stars.

"I – I can't see anything out there – are you sure he's all the way up here."

"Certain!" Johnny said with his eyes closed.

"Wait, wait – it's moving!" Orion said as he watched the pulsing of the shield slowly shift from the center of his view.

"Johnny – tell him he's moving?!

The boy, eyes still closed, paused for a moment, before responding, with a question. "Where's he headed?"

"Back down - to the city!" Orion replied.

Johnny must have sent this message, but as Caitlin and Aspen both watched his face shift and contort, it was clear that the boy was uneasy with what was going on. He shook his head, and then started nodding before shaking it again.

"Shoot him! Shoot him!" the boy screamed fearfully, completely uncertain of what he was saying.

"What?" Orion shouted!

"Shoot him down – he's going to attack the city!"

"Are you sure?"

"Yes – do it! Do it now!" Johnny shouted, but Jay and a few others thought, in looking at the boy's face, there was a chance that Johnny wasn't speaking for himself, and that maybe, just maybe, Taylor was speaking for him.

Orion, feeling he didn't have the luxury to question orders in such a dire situation, immediately obeyed this command. He directed the ship to point in the direction of the shield disturbance and Grace started firing as soon as she felt he had it square in her sights.

While not all of the shots hit their target, one did, and this forced the unseen ship to suddenly de-cloak and reveal its much larger self. Indeed, Orion had to quickly change his course to keep from hitting the enemy craft, which had stopped itself dead in its path of decline and started pulling back into space once again.

"Oh no you don't!" Orion said as he made hard efforts to keep the enemy ship in sight. He started firing again, and realized immediately that his hits were having little effect as his enemy's shields were now up, preventing any major damage.

"The shields are up – what does he want me to do?" Orion shouted, keeping a keen and focused eye in front of him, working hard not to let the enemy craft get away.

"Just keep attacking – you'll eventually wear the shields out!" Johnny shouted in response, and Orion had to quickly force the ship to move in and out of the enemy fire that was now directed at him.

With hard focus, concentrated, and even frustrating stares, Grace worked hard on targeting the alien craft. This was exceedingly difficult as two things were keeping her from getting a good shot. Orion was weaving in and out of the enemy fire so fast, it was nearly impossible for Grace to keep track of the enemy ship, and when she was able to see it, often her view was be obscured by the strange shield fluctuation caused by Johnny and Taylor's telepathic link.

"Johnny, you have to drop your link with dad – it's blocking my view – I can't get a decent shot off!"

"But – but – but no!" Johnny said in a whining and whimpering voice. "No - no - no!" He said again, face welling with tears.

All at once the shield fluctuation had stopped and Grace looked back to see that Johnny, whose body started heaving sobs of sadness, had curled up into a small fetal ball in his seat.

It was clear to everyone that Johnny wasn't the one to terminate the connection. Taylor must have picked up on Grace's words and did it himself.

"Don't worry Johnny," Delissa said in a calming motherly tone. She reached over and slowly patted his head, "When the time comes – he'll talk to you. Don't worry; everything's going to be fine!" These words sounded definite and reassuring, but in Delissa's mind, she was nervous and on edge over the fact that she was in a ship being flown and gunned by two ten year old children.

At the front of the ship, Grace was immediately able to hit her enemy with better accuracy now that she could clearly see what she was doing. As she focused relentlessly on disabling the shields of the other craft, Orion zigzagged quickly to avoid being hit by oncoming fire.

Orion turned the ship toward the alien craft. He had put a great deal of distance between himself and his enemy, and he felt that a direct attack might be the last thing the pilot of the other ship would expect.

His eyes thinned offering a sideways grin to his sister, and with a focus on the space in front of him he made their ship head straight for their enemy, with only minor changes in course as necessary to avoid being hit. Grace complimented this maneuver with a constant stream of fire where nearly every one hit their target.

Finally, both could see a faltering of their enemy's shields and with the last few shots just as their craft flew past the target, Orion and Grace saw explosions – the result of direct hits.

Orion offered his sister a high five, and the two knew that they now had an edge – a fighting chance to keep this craft from destroying the city below.

But it was in their congratulations to each other that neither Grace nor Orion could have expected what would happen next. Their faces lit up with fear as they had turned around and could see a series of shots fired directly at them. Orion tried to force his ship to move – put the spread of fire from the alien craft was too wide – there was no escaping a direct hit.

Orion only glanced at the shield strength of the ship – it was still at minimum from the shots the ship had taken on the EduCorp rooftop. He closed his eyes before spiraling the ship but full expecting a hard, if not devastating impact. A seconds passed by, but there was nothing; no shifting of the craft, no loud noises, nothing. *Did every shot actually miss?*

Opening his eyes, Orion lit a quick smile, he found himself staring at another ship that was engaging in the fight. It had intercepted the onslaught of firing had taken a few of the hits that were meant for his ship.

It only took Orion and Grace a moment to realize that this craft was the exact same design as theirs. Brother and sister glanced at each other with almost a smirk. *Dr. Zeldin?* Each questioned to themselves.

"What are you kids doing here?" They could hear his voice coming through their speakers.

"We could ask you the same question?" Orion responded, still steering the ship into positions of attack. He didn't know if he had to push any buttons to communicate, but he hoped that maybe this living ship would do the work for him.

"We're here to – uh – disable that ship. What's your excuse?"

"We're trying to save our father – and stop the ship!"

"I'm sorry," Dr. Zeldin said stiffly, "Did you say 'save your father?'"

"Well – uh – yeah – he's there – on that ship!" Orion said with an air of arrogance and impatience.

Orion and Grace sat patiently for a moment through the radio silence, but in seeing that the alien craft was making a straight line for the city, they decided to intervene as quickly as possible.

"I'll come in from below, try and see if you can knock out its weapons!"

With the alien ship growing ever larger as they approached, Grace was firing shots at it, working diligently to refine her target to only the weapons of the ship while Orion was simply focused on reaching it as fast as he could.

"What the?!"

Grace and Orion's attention was distracted by shots that were clearly coming from behind.

From the ceiling of the craft Orion forced the overhead helmet to lower itself. He put it on and could see that the craft that had just saved their necks now seemed to be targeting them from behind.

"What are you doing?" Orion shouted as he spun his craft, doing his best to dodge the oncoming blasts.

"I don't know how you found him out here, but I'm ordering you to disengage!"

"Order – we're ten years old – we don't take orders." Grace said with a laugh, but Orion responded more harshly. "What! What are you talking about?"

"It's too complicated!" Dr. Zeldin said impatiently, "Your father belongs to them now – we can't take him back!"

"What!" Grace shouted, "Screw you!"

The two then offered each other a coinciding grin and continued to force their descent, growing ever closer to the hovering alien ship that was now zapping the earth's atmosphere, forcing clouds to form underneath.

"I've got an idea!" Orion voiced with a sly air of deviousness.

Grace, who was at this point simply a spectator watching the many missed shots being fired from behind, only offered her brother a concerned stare.

Orion slightly veered the course of his ship to come in on the side of the alien craft. Turning his head he could see that Dr. Zeldin's ship was following closely behind. "Perfect"

The boy turned and focused straight forward, and with a focused concentration he made his own craft head straight for the front of the alien ship. Seemingly unconcerned with any other activity, the alien craft was still zapping the atmosphere with high energy charges – charges that Orion was forcing himself straight into.

"Are you crazy – what are you doing!" Grace shouted as her and her brother's face both lit up in strange colors from the high energy charges in front of the ship.

Unwavering his focused stare, Orion just hissed, "Shhht – Trust me!"

78 Attack in Perspectives

TAYLOR WAITED PATIENTLY INSIDE HIS CELL, hoping that there might come a time when his escape would be possible. It had been nearly two minutes since he terminated his contact with Johnny, and with each passing second he grew ever more anxious and nervous of what was going on outside the ship.

Pacing, he started to doubt his decisions. Was it a bad idea for him to involve his children? Was there a better way to solve this complex problem without them? His mind was churning ideas, but his stomach was churning more from nerves.

Then, it hit. Taylor wasn't sure what *it* was – but it hit! He felt the entire room shake with a jarring motion and he braced himself with the wall at his side. With a loud explosion that sounded like it was just outside the door, the room shook again. Something was happening; of this much Taylor was certain.

He looked down at his feet and immediately realized with the lack of pulsing electrostatics that his confining shield was disabled. With the ship stabilizing, he looked at small control panel on the wall. With no shield there was a chance he could cyberly or kinetically escape from his confines. Looking over the small control panel there was only one small button that, with a push, revealed a display screen and a keypad, neither of which showed a language Taylor could use.

He reached into his pocket and pulled out the mini pad that had been transported with him from the council chambers. Staring at it for a moment, he hoped that it might be able to bridge this linguistic barrier.

As fast as his eyes and his cyber abilities would allow, Taylor transcribed the strange characters that took up two whole lines on the display into the pad in his hands.

Sure enough the little unit translated the complicated series of characters into one simple phrase, "Password Please:"

Taylor grunted, "I don't have time for this!"

He stood back from the door, and after a mere second and a loud crushing noise, he forced the doors to crumple, offering him a coarse, but adequate exit. Stepping out into a very short corridor, he looked up and saw that a panel had blown itself out from the ceiling. Several wires and conduits were dangling, disconnected and torn. Amid the sparking noises, the smoke in the air, and smell of burning materials, the familiar sound of a strange high pitched songlike voice forced Taylor to look to one end of the hall. There he saw a small circular pad on the floor, and judging by the tiny panel on its side and the hole that was above it, this pad looked like it might be some kind of short lift. *But a lift to where,* Taylor wondered.

Hearing more soothing singsong noises, Taylor walked toward the pad. With an awkward stumble due to the craft's constant shifts he slipped on something under his feet and would have had a face full of metal grating were it not for his quick kinetic reflexes. Heaving a breath of relief and rolling over, he looked to see what had caused his fall.

Taylor smirked when he glanced to his feet. There, in plain view, was a long thin metal pole. *Probably used for structure*, Taylor thought, but in grabbing it, he knew instantly that he would have to use it for something else.

Amid more high pitched noises that now sent chills down Taylor's spine, he stepped on the small circular pad, and in pushing what he considered the 'logical' up button, he started to lift to the next level. He looked up into the hole above and saw several flashes that seemed ever familiar. *Must be the cockpit* – he thought.

When the pad reached the upper level Taylor cautiously stepped forward to a position that was seemingly exactly where he was in his earlier vision. This gave him a strange sense of déjà vu that he shook off immediately as he realized he was standing only inches from the pilot's seat.

Strange – Taylor thought, *the alien should be right here –Right Here!* Yet, in positioning himself right behind the chair, he could see that there was no glow, no brightly colored skin, thus no tall thin alien offering a clear target for Taylor to attack. No – none other than he was in the cockpit.

Taylor looked out into the space in front of the ship – he could see the familiar appearance of the California coastline as the craft made its dive straight into the Earth's atmosphere, yet with no one piloting the craft, he was unsure of how this was happening.

The craft started to shake and rattle with more attacks and Taylor felt his nerves on edge over the fact that this ship was still on its path to destroy the city.

Should I do something – he asked himself, and just as this thought left his brain he saw, appearing before him, the alien that he had seen in his vision. It appeared in a way that was quite familiar to Taylor – as if it had been cloaked by the same technology he was now so familiar with.

With a moment's thought the teen rationalized that the alien must have some sort of built in cloaking – right into its skin.

That would explain the glow – Taylor thought, and as the craft continued to descend, Taylor tightly gripped the pipe in his hands, ready to strike.

He glanced out the window for a split second, and watched as the ship started zapping the Los Angeles skies. These zaps quickly forced billowing clouds to form in the atmosphere and instantly Taylor's stomach started turning.

Now, finally, after seeing it so many different times from so many different perspectives, this vision was playing itself out in reality – he was finally living it.

And now, without question, Taylor was where he needed to be to stop the attack.

The ship wavered with an unexpected attack and Taylor stumbled behind the alien's seat. He caught himself on a nearby panel, making great efforts to keep quiet, and stood himself up quickly to watch as missed shots whizzed past the craft and into view.

Taylor's nerves were on edge. He was tossing between the idea of using his kinesis to knock the alien from its chair, or using the pole in his hands. Not wanting to waste any time, he quickly decided that using the pole was his best option in case the alien had the same kind of personal shielding technology as the other alien race.

Raising the pole high above his head, he looked in front of himself for only a second with the thought of staring through the spot where he had been standing in his vision.

His face lit up with a blast and all at once the large explosion rattled the ship. Taylor's face lost all its color as it changed to show a look of disbelief and terror. His heart and mind could have exploded at that very moment.

With a single electrostatic zap, the alien craft had destroyed his own ship.

"NOOOOOOOOOOOO!" He screamed as if his mouth could pour out his soul.

The alien in front of him turned in surprise, and Taylor stared down at the creature with a hard blue-eyed gaze of cold hatred. The creature offered a horrible high pitched shriek before turning forward just as Taylor started to swing.

Taylor did not see the alien do anything that would lend to its taking aim or firing a shot, but at the impact of the pole in his hand to the alien's head, his face was lit up in a ghastly look of anger as the ship ejected its final devastating shot.

The alien was out cold and Taylor seemed uncontrolled in his swinging again and again at the creature out of total anger. He looked out at the clouds in front of the ship. In the middle of his view he could see the descending glowing dot. He swung the pole, once again hitting the alien on its already battered head, and in doing so he realized that he had broken any similarities between the vision he had seen before and the reality in which he was living now.

His face was pouring with tears. This wasn't supposed to happen. He shook his head not knowing what went wrong. Was there anything left for him now that he had just watched his children killed before his very eyes?

Slowly the glowing dot pushed its way through the earth's upper atmosphere and it was in staring at this, through the haze of his anger, sorrow, and tears, that Taylor could hardly believe his eyes over what was happening.

***

Heading straight for the electrostatic zaps emanating from his enemy's craft, Orion quickly forced his ship to cloak, and with a rapid change in direction he pulled himself out of a path that would have taken him straight into the line of fire. Unfortunately Dr. Zeldin's reflexes were not as quick.

Orion stopped his ship and leaned forward, watching as the other ship exploded in a bright fiery blaze.

"Woah! They just got blown up!" Orion shouted to a cabin filled with wide eyed children, a terrified Jay, and Delissa, who was preoccupied by offering all attentions to Johnny.

"Who just blew up? Who?" Jay shouted as he stuck his head between Orion and Grace.

"Dr. Zeldin and that other guy!"

"Daniel," Jay corrected, and the sound in his voice seemed almost relieved, but he realized quickly that with that ship gone, it was solely up to them to take out the alien craft. "We have to do something! That – that ship could still destroy the city!"

"Yeah and it could destroy us too!" Orion shouted."

"Uh – too late!" Grace said as she pointed to a bright shining speck that was descending into Los Angeles.

Orion, not really thinking, bit his lip and forced the ship after the bright white dot. He told Grace over and over again to shoot at it, even though she was already firing.

She was relentless in her attack, and while she blasted it with what seemed like hundreds of hits, they each seem to have missed every time. With grunts and groans her frustration was becoming more and more apparent.

Was it possible that, rather than missing, she had hit the twinkling dot hundreds of times but it had no effect? Did the tiny speck consume her attacks with its insatiable appetite? Either way, it was clear that there seemed little the children could do to change the course of what was going to happen.

Orion was unwilling to give up though, and in still wearing the pilot's helmet he quickly slipped his ship in front of the alien's craft. He looked behind himself with focused attention. He was hoping against hope that if the alien craft had fired at him with something more powerful, he could move out of the way fast enough to allow the shot to hit the descending dot below. This was a long shot for sure, and with the glowing speck, the children's ship, and the alien craft all descending lower and lower into the atmosphere, Orion's nerves were wearing thin.

"Come on – shoot! Shoot!" He shouted looking through the back of the ship, but the alien craft didn't fire – in fact it started to shift off course form its approach to the city and as Orion took a moment to look below – he decided it was time to do the same. He thereby watched the glowing dot penetrate the clouds and decided, finally, that there was nothing he could do. Stopping his own ship dead in its tracks, Orion swerved carefully, making sure that the alien craft, which was apparently still descending to the city, did not hit his own.

"What're you doing?" Johnny shouted – "Dad is in that ship – you can't just leave him behind!"

"Yeah – well what am I supposed to do?"

"We have to go after him!" Johnny retorted at the top of his lungs.

"If we go down there we'll get sucked in like everything else. You remember what happens when that thing hits!" Orion reasoned.

Johnny's face grew red and heated with anger, it was clear to both Caitlin and Aspen that their brother was more than just upset – he was furious and devastated. They wanted to say something to comfort him, but there were no words that came to the surface. Not when their emotions were just as mixed on the issue. In their minds saving their father was just as important as saving themselves.

It was Delissa that slowly shifted to sit next to the boy, "Come on Johnny, you know there's nothing we can do" she said softly, tears welling in her own eyes, "there's nothing we can do!"

Johnny didn't say a word, he merely closed his eyes and focused on his father – tried to send a message to him – let him know – in his last moments – that he loved him more than life itself.

Delissa wasn't sure if it was her touch or the bright flash of light that washed through the entire cabin that caused the boy's uncontrollable sobs, but just the same, she pulled him into a closer embrace. Speaking softly she tried her best to comfort him. Tristan, on the other side, tried to console him silently with his own wrapping embrace, but this did little to quell the boy.

"I'm so sorry," she said with tears trickling slowly down her own face, "There's nothing we can do!" She whispered over and over again, "There's nothing we can do!"

She started rocking him gently with David, Caitlin and Aspen all starting to cry. They each watched Delissa's face, which offered just a hint of how much she had fallen for their father. The children each were torn in seeing Delissa and Johnny. In their tears, it was clear that they could no longer control their own emotions.

Jay, on the other hand, was stoic, hiding his emotions and while he stared out the front of the craft, he wanted to just wipe his mind of everything. The destruction of Los Angeles was inevitable, like the loss of his friend, and he did not have a brain or a heart big enough to handle his emotions, so he had somehow resorted to showing none.

Delissa's mournful eyes opened wide as she suddenly felt a vibration shake the craft. She turned around and could see that her fear was shared by all those in the cabin. Jay, whose face finally showed an emotion – something that was far more than worried, quickly shot to the front of the craft.

"What's happening?" He shouted.

Orion, who had decided to use the virtual controls through his helmet, was shaking his hands in an effort to steer the craft, but they were making no headway. The ship was pointed straight up, but they didn't seem to be going anywhere – or worse – they were going the wrong way!

Grace, Orion, and Jay all felt their blood run cold as they could see that their ship was slowly lowering through the clouds. Despite all efforts they were being pulled into the city.

"Come on 'Rion – you have to do something!" Grace shouted to her brother in a terrified voice.

"I'm doing everything I can!" He said. But it was clear, with the appearance of the top of the EduCorp Towers in their sight, that the craft was still descending ever lower. Orion's efforts weren't enough.

Orion's virtual view of the controls started flashing red – the ship displayed a message that caused the boy to heave a frightened grunting breath.

"ENGINE OVERHEAT – EMERGENCY SHUTDOWN IN PROGRESS"

"The engines are overheated – they're shutting down!" He repeated to Grace.

With a low and deadening noise, the vibration of the ship had died, but then again so had the engines and once they turned themselves off the ship started rotating so that its nose eventually pointed toward the bright disturbance in the center of the city. Both brother and sister in the cockpit had to cover their eyes from the instant bright light.

"David – Aspen – Get up here now!" Grace said to the back of the ship.

Partially covering their own eyes, the two had to carefully crawl to the front of the ship nervously asking what they could possibly do.

"We're a sinking ship – keep us in the air!" Grace shouted.

Feeling a purpose and confidence rush through them, David and Aspen instantly held hands, remembering several months back when they had saved themselves under similar circumstances.

If the vibration from the work of the engines wasn't bad enough, the contorting of the ship under high gravity and telekinetic forces seemed to rattle it nearly twice as much.

Grace started manipulating the controls of the craft – she saw that the ship had a set of reverse thrusters which she immediately activated. While this reduced the vibration, the children watched as the craft slowly made it past the landing pad of The Towers.

"Why aren't The Towers coming down?" Grace asked on seeing this – If we're getting sucked in then why aren't The Towers coming down?"

The ship suddenly shook hard as it hit an outcropping stemming from The Towers. But all those who could see them knew that the structure of The Towers was completely uncompromised.

"Wait – look there!" David said staring almost directly into the bright light of the weapon!"

The children all almost smiled as they looked out amid the bright white light – elated and ecstatic over what was right in front of them.

***

Taylor wiped his tears away quickly as he saw that someone or something else was attacking the descending dot – there was someone else out in space with him.

Their aim seemed dead on, yet with hundreds of hits this glowing weapon was still dropping fatefully into the city.

Taylor heaved a sorrowful sigh, not sure of what to think until, quite to his surprise, the attacking ship came into view.

"What the hell?" He questioned seeing that the ship looked exactly like his own. His heart pounded in his ears with fear, confusion, but most of all – hope.

Taylor watched in curiosity as the ship seemed to get itself right in the line of fire. He would hate to think that his kids would be that stupid, but somewhere inside he still hoped that it was them that he was seeing. His attention sharpened on the view in front of him as he realized that it was slowly shifting.

No one's piloting the ship, he thought in a panic, and in staring at what displays he could see, he tried his best to communicate with the craft electronically – maybe see if he could recognize the structure – the code – anything.

Unable to comprehend a single character he was seeing, or mentally understand what his cyber abilities could *feel*, Taylor pulled out the small pad from his pocket.

With every ounce of concentration he had, he forced the translation program of the pad to infiltrate the ship. If he did things just right, his life might be made a lot easier in just a few seconds.

Still changing lines of code and interpreting every inch of what he could see from the mini pad, his ears suddenly perked – "Dad– It's Johnny – I'm here – I'm here!"

Taylor's emotions exploded with this voice in his head – *They're alive – they're alive!* He wailed in his own brain.

But who was in that other ship, he wondered.

Rapidly slipping past the EduCorp Towers, Taylor quickly realized that his time was very short – he looked down at the pad, not wanting to waste any energy responding to the message from his son.

"Come on – Come on – Yes!" He said aloud, and after skimming through one display screen after another that was now printed in ENGLISH, Taylor was able to see something – the only thing that offered him a hope of escape.

He stared at the display screen for a few seconds, then, with an upward gaze he noticed that all around him an electrostatic bubble started to form.

The craft around him dissolved away and in his last seconds in this ship Taylor turned his stare to the unconscious alien in the pilot's chair – the slowly dimming glow gave way to the darkness of the city streets in front of the EduCorp Towers.

Taylor grew nauseated as he looked up to see that he was standing only a few hundred yards from where the weapon was going to impact. He whipped his head around in all directions for only a few seconds realizing that the city's sidewalks – streets and skies were almost completely clear – it seemed that the city was nearly deserted. Then, with a loud crashing noise and a huge explosion to match, Taylor watched the impact of his captor's craft on the city streets some distance away. Indeed, he had made it to safety only a few seconds before impact. But there was a greater distraction for him to worry about.

Widening his gleaming bright blue eyes, Taylor watched the illuminating weapon slowly descend overhead and with a great effort he kinetically focused on keeping it from impact.

No use! The weapon was impervious to his efforts. He held his breath as it slowed and settled right in front of him on the street.

Taylor had to admire its beauty of it, but as the silence of the streets offered little to hear, he could sense a high pitched whistling noise emanate from the bright object when it had finally stopped.

Taylor covered his eyes, and rightfully so, for the object offered its expected bright flash that seemed to glow through Taylor's fingers and his eyelids affording a bright red flash under Taylor's efforts to protect his eyes.

In looking around – he could see that the explosion of light did absolutely no damage, but with a sudden lurching in his stomach he knew that the weapon was just getting started.

"Oh crap!" He shouted as he realized that the tiny dot was doing its job of creating the equivalent of an artificial black hole.

The teen heaved a panicked breath. He was now living in the nightmare that he had envisioned so many times – but he never thought he would've been this close! From the empty city to the swirling clouds, it was nothing less than amazing to him to truly feel with all of his senses, the world around him finally existing in a fashion that he had seen so many times.

When he first saw the vision, Taylor was sure that the only way to beat something like this weapon was to simply stay as far away as possible. Now, though, Taylor felt that he had within him the power to do something – the power to stop his beloved city from being destroyed. With solid determination he planted his feet on the concrete and focused hard on himself and on the city around him.

"Oh, I don't think so!" he said resolutely as he plucked what must have been one of the last departing transports from the air.

He set it gently on the street beside him; its panicked passengers certain they were about to perish, and with a cyber-kinetic effort he forced the door to the craft to open wide.

"Everyone, get inside – take cover now!" Taylor shouted with his hands waving to one of the nearby buildings.

The teen then listened as the buildings themselves started to ache with the increased gravity that was pulling at their base. He turned to these and focused, but while he did this the other buildings behind him started to crack and give way. *There's no way I can focus on every object in the city. It's simply impossible.*

Turning his stare back to the glowing light, he covered its center with his hands and continued to focus on it. If it worked through gravity, then maybe he could just focus on it and keep it from doing its job.

He concentrated, focusing harder and harder – feeling his head ache with his efforts. To his surprise though, his ears took in the fact all the movement, all sounds, everything around him had stopped.

What he was doing seemed to be working. But how long could he keep this up

– and to what purpose? He couldn't just stand there forever.

Then, as if Taylor could sense it, he felt the glowing orb in front of him strengthen its gravitational pull, and in return, he forced his telekinetic efforts to match, dropping to his knees with his efforts. His eyes closed and, with his hands at his side, this was one of the few times that he didn't use a false gesture to direct his efforts, and as he sat there, one on one fighting this gravitational weapon, he felt his brain slowly throb with a pain that pulsed harder and harder.

Not letting it deter his efforts, Taylor watched as smaller bits of debris still inched toward the light. He clenched his fists and forced his newly improved kinesis into full swing. It was clear that his efforts had an immediate effect as all of the central movement had stopped.

Panting with hard and heavy breaths, Taylor winced and raised a hand to his temple – the pain inside was immeasurable. He knew, without a doubt that he couldn't keep this up for long.

Is there no end to this thing? Taylor wondered, but then he realized that in all of his other visions he could see the aftermath and destruction that was left behind – that would, of course, mean that it eventually had to stop – maybe it was on some kind of timer. What an archaic and foolish thought – but then again – maybe it was.

Taylor's side thoughts were immediately distracted. Above him he could see a ship struggling to fight the gravitational force of this weapon.

Oh my God! My children!

His children were inside and the ship was fighting every step of the way and Taylor watched as the engines of the craft suddenly cut off and it slowly rotated, continuing to fall inward toward the bright light.

"But why?" Taylor wondered – he could see that one or two other crafts were moving freely about the city picking up even more evacuees that were hopeful to leave before it was too late – even if it was too late! So if he was doing his job of keeping this weapon at bay, why is it that this craft, his craft, was still struggling so hard against the forces of this weapon?

Taylor focused even harder on the glowing weapon in front of him, but this had little effect on the ship above. This didn't make sense.

Taylor panicked as he saw that the craft was inching ever closer to the ground – now it was only a few hundred meters or so above his head. He had to think of something – there had to be an answer – a solution to what was going on?

He could see his children's happy and excited faces – he tried to telekinetically force the craft away – throw it if he had to – but its shields must have been on – nothing he could do would change where it was headed.

With a change in his children's faces, Taylor could see that they were now concerned, fearful, and terrified.

Then, with a loud crack, Taylor watched as the ship hit an outcropped ledge from The Towers – this caused the shield to show itself with a wave of electrostatic glow – and there it was – the answer he was looking for, and Taylor practically fell over with the realization of what was happening.

The shield, in its showing itself, offered to Taylor the fact that it was deformed from the normal shape of the craft. It was stretched and distorted – like it was being pulled by a hook toward the glowing light.

Seeing this, Taylor suddenly made sense of this alien weapon. With its affect on gravity and a ship's shields it would be the perfect weapon to attack any alien craft – with or without shields there would be no way to escape.

Taylor looked into the cockpit above and could tell by the focused stares of Aspen and David that the two were trying desperately to push themselves, or rather the ship, as far away as possible. This would account for the ship's slow decline – and even with the reverse thrusters being active – the ship was still descending.

Taylor thought for a moment and shifted some of his focus to the ship above, ever increasing the pounding in his head, but no matter how hard he concentrated, his efforts had no effect on the craft. Of course! Telekinetic efforts can only control gravitational attraction. This wasn't gravity – it was something else.

He watched and listened in terror as the ship above slowly started to crumple at the nose – it was being sucked in – and there was nothing Taylor could do about it. He concentrated harder and harder – but it seemed no use. He could see, clearly, that the shield was pulling itself and the ship deeper and deeper into the light, and he could see the screaming, terrified faces of Daivd, Aspen, Grace, and Orion.

With a wavering flash the shield suddenly blinked out of existence. Apparently the damage to the ship was too much, forcing the shield to fail. Taylor looked up with a heaving exhale of relief. Now that the shields were gone the craft was open to his kinetic efforts. He, for just a fraction of a second, put what he had into a kinetic push, forcing the ship away. This made the craft practically throw itself high into the air.

Quickly, though, Taylor had to re-focus back on the weapon before him. His brain pained him so horrible, yet his heart felt so good. He wanted to revel in their safety, but at that moment, danger seemed to lurk over his shoulder.

His ears perked. He could hear metal streetlights slowly ache and bend inward under the increasing gravity that he wasn't able to control, and slowly, he felt his knees and toes drag against the pavement – he, too, was being forced into the light.

After everything he had done, all of his efforts, all of his strengths, and everything that he had seen, this couldn't be how it would end. It just couldn't be! He had saved his children, and though he was out of breath, and seemingly out of effort, and his heart was pounding painfully in his aching brain, his determination was present now more than ever. Grunting, Taylor stood to his feet again and screamed in pain at the weapon in front of him. Using all the energy he had, he closed his telekinetic hold on the bright light. As he did this his mind slowly started to grow dark – as if he was blacking out from his efforts. Concentrate – Concentrate!

Taylor turned his head. All at once he felt a sense of relief as he watched the poles around him stop their inward lean.

Staring back at the bright light, he could see that it started to dim. "Come on!

Hold on!" He said loudly, "Hold on!"

But with the dimming of the light in front of him, Taylor's own vision suddenly grew very dark and his sweat-covered body grew very weak. It was as if he had nothing left. He collapsed, and with his release of the weapon he could feel the instant force of gravity pull his body. But it wasn't a hard pull – it was light and simple. So, with is body offering total release, his eyes rolled freely in his head and he knew that he was about to hit the hard concrete.

With a shift in his perspective, he expected the impact, but for some reason his head never touched the pavement. He was confused. He rolled over and could see the feet and legs of several approaching children. With the darkness that washed over him, Taylor hissed a shallow breath and smiled almost to the point of laughter.

79 Truth and Silence

SOMETIMES PEOPLE CAN WAKE, and wish that their sleep had been never-ending. Most of the time this is just because the labors of the day are too difficult, and the life that they drudge their feet through on a daily basis offers them no solace or comfort, especially when they realize that their hard working lives can last for nearly two hundred years.

Taylor, who by all accounts, was very diligent and hard working – almost never felt this way. Sure, when he slept he would welcome happy dreams, but when he woke, no matter what falsities were running through his brain, he was excited to start each and every day. His love for his students – his children, made sure of that.

This feeling – this emotion was never more present in Taylor's brain than when he woke in the recovery room of The Towers, and for the first time he was surrounded by the six beautiful and smiling faces of his children, with him waking up and not the reverse. Jay, Delissa, and Tristan were there, of course, but they were secondary to him as his most important worry was seeing that Johnny, Caitlin, David, Aspen, Grace, and Orion all were okay. In fact – they were better than okay. Seeing that Taylor was awake, they were bounding with energy and love – ready to attack.

So, with bleary eyes, and amazingly – no headache to speak of, Taylor was in an absolute utopia when he gained consciousness, and he was eager to start not just the day, but the rest of his life with *his* children.

"Well, it's about time!" Jay said from the foot of the bed with half a smirk on his face.

Not waiting for Taylor to give him attention, Johnny leaped forward onto Taylor, and forced a hug that made the man ache with the pains of love.

Eventually Delissa helped to pull the boy off and the rest of the newly forged clan made their love known with a hug, or a kiss. Even Tristan joined in the affection, offering Taylor a simple "thanks" through a shallow breath and instantly the room was filled with smiles and laughter.

"How – how long have I...?" Taylor asked.

Not too long – 'bout six hours."

Taylor nodded his head, and with a strange feeling that he was being watched, Taylor looked out, trying to find another set of prying eyes that he could feel were looking at him and the family that was sstill working hard to dote on him and make sure that he was comfortable, had no needs, and was absolutely happy.

To be honest with himself, Taylor was a little embarrassed from all the attention he was receiving from everyone, and as he looked to the side, his eyes caught what he had sensed, another person being treated in the recovery room off in the distance who was staring at Taylor and his visitors. The man himself had no one to speak of to offer him any kind of attention and was probably one of the many casualties that resulted either from the damage Taylor had inflicted on the city, or from what little damage the mostly averted weapon had caused afterward. Either way, it was clear that, having suffered a broken leg and arm, and a horrible hit on the head, this other patient had no one to give him any attention. And despite his relatively minor injuries, he was clearly jealous of Taylor, offering a look that embarrassed the teen even further because both inwardly and outwardly Taylor was seemingly fine.

If all this private and personal attention didn't irritate the other patient across the room enough, what happened next certainly did.

With a soft hissing noise, the doors to the recovery room opened, and Taylor watched with a mixture of anger and irritation as President Andrews entered, flanked by three members of the Evol-Crew. What Taylor thought truly odd was the fact that Stewart, Elizabeth, and Christine were not wearing their colored cloaks. Instead, they were dressed in civilian clothes that Taylor instantly decided did not suit them.

Turning to the physician on duty, President Andrews instantly started barking orders. "I want you, that man over there, and everybody else out of here – *now!*"

The physician on duty, a man that Taylor hadn't ever seen before, walked up to president Andrews, offering stiffly spoken words. This forced Taylor to instantly admire the man for his steadfast dedication.

"I am the head physician in this recovery room. I give the orders here and..."

"Don't you recognize me – BOY," a word that Taylor thought was funny considering the fact that the two of them looked the same age, and for all President Andrews knew – this physician was actually older than he. But the physician showed a confused look to which the President responded, "I'm GC President Andrews you idiot!"

"I don't care who you are. I'm in charge here, and I don't take orders from yo..."

The physician's words were cut short and Taylor, in noticing Elizabeth's controlling stare at the man, knew exactly what was happening. Taylor didn't interfere, and everyone; the children, Delissa, Jay, Tristan and the other patient in the recovery room were all staring at either President Andrews or the physician in charge, hoping that some sense would be made of this grand entrance.

With the physician not saying a word, he walked over to the patient at the other end of the recovery room and wheeled him out quietly. While the physician was moving slowly, Taylor couldn't help but be distracted by the screen above the entryway, which, being turned to a news channel, was showing pictures and scenes of two individuals whose red and green cloaks were instantly recognizable. Taylor was in awe at the caption beneath these images. "GC mourns the death of two of its own."

No one else seemed to see this as all eyes were on the physician and the man he was moving. It was the blank stare on the man's face that told Jay what was going on. Taylor, however, shifted his attention to eye President Andrews with a solid confidence; an arrogance in fact.

"And that goes for the rest of you too!" President Andrews said glancing around at everyone but Taylor.

While all those around Taylor's bed glowered at the President in defiance, and certainly not moving a muscle, Taylor waited until the telepathically controlled physician had wheeled out the only other patient and the door had closed before taking any action. Once gone, Taylor cyberly locked the doors to the recovery room and offered a single purposefully directed stare at Elizabeth – and, as if it was as simple as flicking a switch, he turned her thoughts off.

She collapsed there, on the floor, instantly, and Taylor slowly pulled hisemlf to sit up and stare at President Andrews, who now only had a precog and a postcog for protection. It was like asking ants to protect their queen from a little boy with a big foot. Just the same, it was clear to everyone in the room that President Andrews was growing more nervous by the second, and considering what Taylor had just done, both cognitives knew better than to provoke the teen.

"I assume that Elizabeth was your only real means of protection here. Huh, now that I think about it, with Daniel and Dr. Zeldin gone, you're going to be in a world of hurt to find someone to help you with your evolved criminals.

"Don't underestimate how easily I can drum up others to take their place!" President Andrews said with an obvious sense of arrogance.

"I suppose – but that's not why you came here, is it?"

"No, it isn't... the fact of the matter is – you and I have some things that we need to discuss – things that you should know – things that only I can tell you. But know this – I am prepared to tell you and no-one else."

"Well, now, you see that's not going to work for me – and as I now have this room locked down, and am, by far, the most powerful person here – you're kinda stuck – until I say you can go. So now I'm calling the shots – get it!"

President Andrews hesitated, but after a moment's thought, he offered a deep sigh before nodding as a way for Taylor to recognize the concession.

"Good!" Taylor said softly. "Now – kids," Taylor said looking at the seven youngsters before him, "I want you to go wait outside. The president and I have some talking to do."

"But daaaaaddddd"

"Come oooonnnnnnn"

"Whatever!"

Taylor couldn't have expected anything less from his children, and he totally understood their negativity to his request, but he wanted to filter any information that President Andrews was about to offer – even if the president didn't know he was about to offer it.

"I said go – and I mean it – I'll fill you in later," he retorted with a laugh before shoot a devilish smile to Johnny. "And don't even think of trying to read what's going on in here – I can tell when you're watching me – and I can block it too – so – just – just don't!"

Taylor unlocked the door to the recovery room and slowly, with a sluggish drag in their steps, the seven children each made their way out of the recovery room, the last being Tristan who had received a small nod from Delissa that everything was going to be fine.

Then, with an almost evil grin, Taylor turned to both Christine and Stewart. "Oh, and you two can leave too. You can figure out what he's told me after the fact, or in your case, before." Taylor then looked to the passed out woman on the floor, "And, uh, on your way out – take her with you. I'll admit it – she still makes me nervous." Taylor said nodding to the limp body of Elizabeth.

Not saying a word, Christine and Stewart both offered a simple glance to President Andrews, who reluctantly nodded his head, pathically telling them to do as Taylor requested.

"And those two?" President Andrews queried, referring to Delissa and Jay.

"Let me be clear about this," Taylor started, speaking in a condescending tone to the man. "Jay is the only man in the world that I would ever trust with my life – 't's been that way for nearly ten years – you might remember why."

President Andrews grumbled a bit in response to this, but Taylor continued. "Anyways – he stays – there's no question – and Delissa here has been imprisoned by your people, and taken from her son without any due process, and I think she's owed a complete..."

"Okay, fine – fine – whatever!" President Andrews said hastily raising his hand. Taylor had, in fact, noticed that the man was pacing in front of his bed, constantly staring at his watch, and was clearly becoming more impatient as the seconds passed.

"Good." Taylor said with a smirk. "Now I don't want to control the whole conversation – I mean you came here – right?"

Jay and Taylor both widened their grin as President Andrews flexed the muscles in his jaw. Clearly the man was wrought with irritation – how insulting it was that *he* should be dictated to by an eighteen year old. *A child that he was responsible for in the first place!*

Shaking his head, the President stood firmly at the foot of Taylor's bed, and with Delissa on one side of Taylor, and Jay on the other, all three listened as the man spoke.

"You know – it's hard for me to say this, what with your cocky attitude and all, but I came here to say it, and I'm going to say it, because it needs to be said."

President Andrews then gripped the railing at the end of Taylor's bed, and with a deep breath he slipped out words that none in the room could have ever expected.

"Thank you." He said softly – almost so low that Taylor wanted him to repeat it, but didn't want to cause the man any more anguish than was necessary. Even still, all three at one end of the bed looked at the president with a curious, if not perplexed set of expressions.

"You helped to save billions of lives today – and, though I still can't figure it out, and neither can Stewart, you have averted an absolute chaos that only three people in the world have seen and predicted."

Taylor looked confused at this "three people," reference, and so President Andrews explained. "Ahem, that would be Stewart, you, and Johnny, of course. I mean no other pre-cog in the world ever saw the coming of that attack, or us being placed smack in the middle of this war the way we have."

Taylor wanted to interject at this point – he wanted to say something about the fact that this whole situation was started because of what this man had done and the deals that he had made, but an argument like that would lead up to only one inevitable conclusion; that without President Andrews' efforts, neither Taylor, nor any of his children would have been born. So Taylor kept his thoughts and his comments guarded and let the President continue.

"So I say thank you, again for what you have done – and regardless of how I feel right now, or what I have told you – I am grateful for you and your children."

Instantly Taylor remembered being in a lift with this man and being called a freak – but he guessed that averting an absolute catastrophe was probably good enough to change the man's mind – for now.

With a soft hiss, everyone turned their attention to the door of the recovery room. It had opened, and Tristan poked his head in for a brief moment, offering an impatient gaze about the room.

"Just checking!" the teen said before pulling his head back and letting the door close again.

Taylor almost laughed aloud, but in turning a stare to President Andrews, he found himself hungry for more answers.

"So that's it? You just came here to say 'thanks'? I don't think so – there has to be more – I can feel it – I can hear it wanting to come out."

"Hmmm," the president groaned, "right you are – and there is no easy way to tell you this."

"Well – out with it – before I squeeze it out of you myself." Taylor said playfully, casting a smile to Delissa who had been holding his hand for the past several minutes, though he was too distracted to really notice until now.

"You saved the city today, but I've received word from Kashal that the Aurorians, that's what we've named them, are moving in to our part of the galaxy – and yes – and are apparently adding us to the list of planet's with which they are at war."

"Aaaaaand?"

"Robert – uh – Taylor," the President continued, "Kashal intercepted a communiqué between his traitor and the Aurorian fleet. The Aurorians think that we're siding with the Takashians. They think that we're going to give them the advantage of our genetics – our powers. And they'll do anything they can to keep that from happening."

Jay shook his head and held his hand up between Taylor and President Andrews. "Hold on – hold on! Who's who in all this – I don't get it!"

"Jay," Taylor clarified, "I'm gonna make this simple – the Takashians are the good guys that look bad – the Aurorians are the bad guys that – well – they look beautiful."

With a nodding of his friend's head, Taylor grinned at President Andrews as a way for the man to continue.

"Well, I can't really say who are the good guys and the bad guys here. All I can say is – both species are much more technologically advanced – and we can't afford a war with them."

"Well, what do they want?" Taylor asked, quickly impatient for an answer.

President Andrews took a deep breath, "They want you, Taylor. They know now, that you are the only thing – the only *one* that can stop their *singularity* device."

"But you were supposed to give me to them anyways – that was part of your deal with them, wasn't it – so why did they attack in the first place?"

"I – I don't know. That doesn't make any sense. We agreed to wait until sometime next year to hand you over – that way the children would be out of your care and you'd be practically desperate to get away from all this."

Taylor at least made some logical sense of what the president was saying about his expected emotional state, his willingness to participate, and what would have been the final fitting piece to this otherwise extremely complex puzzle.

Once again the doors to the recovery room opened, and Tristan popped his head in, thus forcing everyone to stare in his direction.

"Oh, sorry – still checking."

Delissa waved a hand at the boy to stay out of the room and, with the teen pulling his head back and the door closing, Taylor forced the next topic to be covered.

"What about my students – my children. You were just going to hand them over to the other side? What the hell was that all about?"

"Taylor, you have to understand. I was getting threats from both sides. I had to do something. I had to come up with something to make both sides happy. You – eh – you all just got caught in the middle."

"We were born in the middle," Taylor corrected, and with a snap he redirected the conversation again. "Listen. Let's just cut to the chase, shall we! What do *you* think is going to happen now? I mean both of these races haven't got what they wanted, and we're considered a threat by at least one of them... so what's next?!"

President Andrews paced at the end of Taylor's bed, it was clear that the man was thinking – whether he was trying to come up with a plan – or trying to come up with words to explain his plan, Taylor was unsure, but the teen's irritation was mounting with each passing second. Then, the man spoke.

"Taylor – the truth is, even with Stewart by my side looking to the future, we - we don't know what to do. We can't see anything past the chaos that's about to rush on us in a few hours. But I know that if the Aurorians are about to exterminate us because of our participation in this war – I'm asking, no – I am begging." At this the man offered a somber expression to match his words before pleading again, "*begging* you to work for us at the GC – we *need* you."

"Dude. You must be joking!" Jay instantly retorted, not even offering Taylor a chance to consider the request, or think of his own answer. "You botch this whole thing up, try to sell off this man's whole life to some alien race – he cleans it all up, and now you expect him to work for you? What are you? Insane!"

Taylor held up his hand and Jay silenced his angry words.

"What of my children – what would happen to them?" Taylor asked.

"They would stay here – at The Towers. You can visit them any time you like, when you're not on assignment of course, and we'll make sure that your custody is definitive – no questions – on the books – everything in black and white."

In a flash Taylor was falling victim to the easy bait that President Andrews had laid in front of him. *Permanent custody, no questions – that's quite an offer* – he thought. Then, slowly other questions filled the teen's brain.

"Why couldn't they just come with me?" Taylor asked.

"'T's too dangerous – we'd rather have them in our protection – in case we – eh – we need them."

Taylor's stare darkened. "I see."

Once again the doors to the recovery room opened, and with all eyes looking in the direction of the door, everyone expected to see Tristan pop his head in again, but the boy wasn't there, and after a short second the door closed.

Taylor sat, still thinking. He wasn't sure if this offer was something he considered acceptable or not, and as he turned his many thoughts, options, desires, and needs over in his brain, his eyes were again distracted by the door of the recovery room hissing its way open again.

"Sorry – just checking – are you guys ever gonna let us back in?"

"Not yet Tris!" Delissa bellowed, "Now get back out there!"

With Tristan leaving yet again, the doors closed, and with a slightly confused look Taylor sat up in his bed, curious of what he had just seen. No one in the room seemed to notice this increase in the Taylor's attention, and probably assumed he was just shifting himself about in his bed to make himself more comfortable. But Taylor felt something – something in the future. Something wasn't right!

The truth was that Taylor was instantly suspicious. With his newfound telekinetic sonar, Taylor scanned the room.

"We are not alone!" Taylor said in a low and soft voice looking between Jay and Delissa.

"What – what do you mean?" Jay questioned, but Delissa, having been around cloaking technology long enough, knew exactly what Taylor was saying.

Taylor, however, didn't want there to be any confusion – so, with a focus on those in the room, he pathically told them what he meant, and where he knew the intruder was. Now Taylor knew that none of his children or any member of the Evol-Crew had cloaking suits – so he knew that the visitor he sensed couldn't be any of them. And it was this, and this alone that made Taylor nervous.

"We know you're in here – you might as well show yourself." Taylor said, raising his hand and pointing his finger where he detected the newest member in the room. It only took a few seconds for Taylor's request to be met with the slow morphing of a cloaking suit deactivating.

While Taylor expected this, he didn't expect it to be in the form of a Takashian traitor.

"Rafash! I wasn't expecting you!" Taylor said in loud surprise.

While both President Andrews and Taylor were calm in watching the alien as it removed its cloaking hood, both Delissa and Jay were terrified. They had never seen anything like what was in front of them, at least in person, and while the conversations about aliens was easy enough to absorb, neither was ready for the full shock of actually seeing one in person.

Taylor closed his eyes for a fraction of a second and took a deep breath. With no effort to do so, Taylor could feel and see the future. As if it wasn't there before, but it was now, he could feel death coming fast and he knew that the creature was there for only one purpose – and that was to assassinate President Andrews. So it was with little surprise that the alien raised up some kind of weapon and aimed it directly at the man.

President Andrews quickly jumped and ducked away, and while Taylor tried to kinetically push the alien, it was clear that the creature was under a protective shield.

There was a blast that lit up the entire room, and Taylor watched in horror as the alien fired at the President.

Taylor tore computer units, floor tiles, ceiling panels, and just about anything else he could find from where they sat and piled them on Rafash until, when covered with a mound of chaos, the teen was convinced that the alien was either dead, or unconscious. And with bits of smoke, the zapping of electrical ends, and the deadening noise of settling masses of equipment, Taylor jumped off his bed and sprinted to the mound in the center of the room.

"Taylor! Taylor!" Delissa shouted, forcing him to turn around in excitement.

She was holding a simple lab-coat, and a button shirt, and Taylor could see the panicked look in her face. It didn't take Taylor but a moment to realize that the coat and shirt belonged to Jay – but in looking to where he once stood and glancing around the room quickly, he couldn't see his friend anywhere.

Taylor could feel the tears in his eyes well up even if his senseless questions came at the same time. "Where's Jay – What happened to Jay – Wha...?"

At that instant, the horrible feeling in the pit of Taylor's stomach completely drained whatever strength he had in his legs. So, with a collapse, the teen watched as Delissa rushed upon him with the last clothes that Jay would ever wear.

Taylor could feel a panic in his chest that he couldn't hold back, and with a deep heaving breath, he slowly stood with Delissa's help.

With a flinching stare, Taylor saw that the doors to the recovery room started to open, and he cyberly slammed them closed in an instant, locking them. He could feel that President Andrews was about to say something – but with a fierce stare, the teen forced the man to understand that he wanted nothing but absolute silence.

Turning to the pile of strewn equipment, Taylor removed just enough to see the gloved hand of Rafash. He quickly pulled off the glove and grabbed the bare, scaly hand of the creature, hard focused on anything that he might be able to pick up, past, present, or future.

Whether it was that the nanites had completely finished their job of improving his powers, or his anger, frustration, or despair forcing a perfect focus, Taylor didn't care, but in grabbing the alien hand, Taylor was able to see and experience much of the alien's life from just this simple touch. In the span of less than a minute, he learned about the Takashian race, their culture, and about the war between the Takasians and the Aurorians.

Taylor could feel Rafash's anger and frustration over the constant threat of attack, and the great losses that war always brought home with the many warriors when they returned. But mostly Taylor could feel the absence of peace in the alien's life. And so, with as much hatred as he bore for the Aurorians, Rafash armed himself with just as much against the leaders of his own people. Thus his treachery began.

Taylor watched as this alien met several times secretly with one Aurorian who, Taylor could only guess, was the same that Taylor himself had beaten when he was in space. And so he listened as Rafash was ordered to make sure that, one way or another, Taylor himself was to be captured. Then, in sequence, the President was to be killed and the city of Los Angeles destroyed, hopefully at the same time by the Aurorian himself. This would put the entire planet in chaos, and offer the Aurorian fleet a perfect opportunity for attack.

Taylor listened through Rafash's ears, and his understanding of the language as the Aurorian continued by stating that the entire race of humans should be eliminated – because they pose far too great a threat in the war.

"What of the children?" Rafash howled and gurgled.

"They are nothing – let them be destroyed with the rest of the planet."

Then, with a flash, Taylor watched as his entire environment changed. He was now in a ship very similar to Taylor's. But this one was piloted by Rafash, and was being pursued by Kashal's entire fleet. Rafash only found refuge by cloaking himself and hiding his ship in the forest just north of the San Francisco Metroship.

It was here that Taylor watched Rafash send a message to the Aurorian fleet, and after several hours, the alien received a message telling him that the attack on Los Angeles did not work, and that he *must* make another attempt to assassinate President Andrews and re-acquire Taylor.

Pulling himself from the vision, Taylor was washed over in darkness before seeing the bright lights of the recovery room. And when his eyes opened, he saw the sad, expectant faces of his children, the unexpected eyes of Dr. Young staring down at him and the mass of chaotic equipment by his side.

With her security access as a council member Dr. Young had let herself and the children into the recovery room while Taylor was in his vision, and it was clear that she had been talking to President Andrews, and Delissa – so she knew exactly what had happened.

Even at that moment, somewhere deep inside, while in clearing his still bleary vision, Taylor hoped, for a fleeting moment, that he was just coming out of a bad dream, and there might have been a possibility that Jay's death was a part of that – *a bad but untrue dream.*

"Dad," Taylor heard, and as if it were a new, built-in reaction, his eyes shot over to Johnny, "yes Son" he said in a weak voice.

"'Lissa says that Jay's – gone – that he's d – dead!"

Taylor didn't want to respond in the affirmative – and he really didn't have to – for it was his lack of any real answer, and the tears filling his eyes that told his children the answer and the truth that they were looking for.

Their saddened faces offered little by way of noise, or vocal crying. Instead, they crowded around Taylor, reaching out and touching the lab-coat or shirt that the teen was holding. And so, this whole family, who had suffered so much, now had to endure the loss of their best of friends. And together they wept in silence from their aching hearts, sharing quick pathic memories of their history, and trying their best to cycle from crying to consoling – to crying again with each other. But Taylor, amid his tears, was full of thought, full of anger, and fully ready to do what he needed to protect his children and his home.

80 A New Beginning

WITH A SOFT AND DELICATE TOUCH, Delissa was the first to try and break apart the small family that was still carefully handling the clothing that woefully smelled like Jay.

"Taylor, honey, we've got other things to worry about."

The teen pulled his head up through the mass of hair that had formed when his children had surrounded him.

"I – what – huh?" Taylor asked, half confused, and still trying to comfort his family.

"Taylor – the Aurorians – they're still going to attack. Stewart has told me they're going to attack – and soon."

Wiping his face quickly, Taylor stood at full height. He then grabbed the hands of Grace and Orion, and pathically told them to help keep everyone else back while he uncovered the body of Rafash – the alien underneath.

"Alien?" Grace whispered, and for the first time, she looked down to see the hand that Taylor had at one time been holding to get his last vision.

She gasped, and Taylor cupped her cheeks in his hands and offered her a forceful stare so she might calm down.

"Don't worry – don't worry – just help me – and keep everybody back!"

Orion, who had taken Taylor's words in stride, and seemed ready to accept just about anything happening at this point, pulled all of his brothers and sisters aside, while Grace barely managed to pull herself off the floor and walk to Delissa, offering a simple "stay back" which she didn't even need to hear.

Quite rapidly the mound that sat atop Rafash threw itself to either side, and revealed, without a doubt, that the creature had been crushed and killed. And knowing that Taylor had done it, that he had killed someone – or rather something, it didn't faze him at all. He was far too concentrated on the alien's equipment, quickly looking over a handful of devices that were nearly impossible to figure out. But with each one that he touched, he pushed any and all buttons he could find, hoping desperately that he could find something anything that would do what he needed.

And then it happened.

A strange buzzing noise surrounded Taylor and the children, and with a brilliant glow of color, Taylor saw a series of swelling electrostatic balls. Then, with the fresh smell of ozone piercing the nose and the dimming glow of the chaos around, Taylor saw the familiar face of Kashal as well as those of his comrades.

It was clear that the creature was ready to attack, but in looking down at the broken body of Rafash, Kashal knew that there was nothing left to satisfy his own vengeful satisfaction. So, with a loud gurgling howl that Taylor was just starting to get used to, the creature belted out his own vocal angers.

"Kashal – I know you can understand me, but I can't understand you, so I'm asking you to just listen. We're running out of time – and I know the Aurorians are readying for an attack. I've seen enough, and I know enough to know that the only way our planet is going to survive is if I work with you. They aren't interested in our survival – all they wanted was me – and the rest of the planet, my kids – well – none of that matters to them – but it matters to me – and they matter to me!"

Kashal offered a low gurgling noise that Taylor only paused a moment to hear, but couldn't understand.

"Yeah – you wanted me – you got me! And my kids. I know they can help."

Kashal let out a loud grunt, followed by a howl, then a series of awkward expressions, but it was clear that he wasn't talking to Taylor, or to anyone human in the room at all for that matter, and after a few seconds, he could hear the unmistakable sounds of laughter echoing from those that Kashal had brought with him.

"Believe me – they are more powerful, and more dangerous than you could possibly imagine. I'd much rather have them by my side, doing what they can, than even think of what might happen if they stick around down here.

With everything that was going on, the children had been offering terrified looks at the creatures in front of them. They hadn't seen anything so bizarre in all their lives, and their looks of fear didn't waver or change until Taylor had referred to them as powerful and dangerous. Then and only then did each of the children realize that, despite their unattractive exteriors, these aliens were nothing to be afraid of and that, with a little effort, even Caitlin and Johnny could muster up enough telekinetic ability to keep these creatures at bay. So, with slowly changing outward expression, the children each adopted their own relaxed, and in the cases of David and Grace, aggressive faces; faces that didn't waver even when they were clearly being laughed at.

Kashal turned to Taylor and shoved a small unit into his hand. It was a translator and the teen knew instantly that Kashal wanted to say something. So with his eyes focused on the small unit, and his ears listening to the harsh noises coming from the creature in front of him, Taylor started deciphering and communicating with the alien.

YOU HAVE MADE DEALS WITH THE ENEMY.
WHY SHOULD WE HELP YOU?

Taylor read the message, and his brain was running on empty for how to convince this alien to help.

"I – I don't know what to tell you. I don't work with them – they tried to sell me – TO THE ENEMY – and they were going to give my children to you. I haven't made any deals with anyone. I'm just trying to fix this thing. And that – that piece of crap over there just killed my best friend. I need your help. I have to set things right!" Taylor's expression was desperate, and Kashal could definitely see this. So, with the creature listening to Taylor's words being translated inside its helmet, the instant the words came out the alien started howling and garbling again, but this phrase was short, and had repetitions in it that Taylor could almost pick out – yet he still needed the translator to understand.

YOU NEED US. WE NEED YOU.

"Fine!" Taylor shouted, "We'll help you – you can have us – ALL OF US! We are yours to do with as you please. I don't care. Trust me – we'll be worth it!"

"No! You can't..." President Andrews shouted, but before he could even try finishing his words, Taylor snapped at him in a deep and desperate growl.

"Don't even think about telling me what I can and cannot do! You're the reason for this whole mess!" Taylor said, and in that instant he at least said half of the argument he wanted to, even if it wasn't complete. "And right now – you really *really* don't want to say no to me – or to them!"

Turning around with a jerk, Taylor heard Kashal laugh and with a gesture that Taylor was surprised to see, the alien forced out its arm to nearly three times its visible length, and while Taylor was confused at first, he eventually figured out what Kashal was trying to do.

Reaching out, Taylor actually shook the alien's hand and watched as the hand shifted to each of his other children. He watched with a lightened heart as his children stared at the long outstretched hand with apprehension, but after a bit of playful smiles, they each shook it carefully. In an instant Taylor realized that his whole life, his whole universe, and everything he had ever seen, would be nothing compared to what he was about to see and do from this point on. Then, with a few grumbling comments, the teen looked down at the translator as the aliens disappeared with electrostatic fervor. Kashal's parting comments:

BE READY IN AN HOUR!

*****

Taylor did what he could to ready himself and his children for this unknown journey that had suddenly landed before him. Yet, no matter how hard he tried, his mind kept gravitating to the loss of his best friend. His memories clouded his vision with tears, weighted his heart, and made his hands move with an uneasy weakness as he pulled mounds of clothes, medical devices, MREs, and other items that he deemed necessary to satisfy his and his children's basic needs from an M-Gen panel inside the recovery room.

Memories of Jay working with him, having fun with him and the kids kept rushing on Taylor constantly. Deeper memories of his own early childhood, when he was alone and Jay was the only soul he seemed bonded to. His first meeting with the teen when he was a young boy, that virtual encounter, while awkward, still made Taylor smile to this very day, but in mere seconds it also filled him with sorrow of loss again.

With the finality of closing up a few of the bags and packs that he had just prepared, Taylor slumped down onto the bed in the recovery room. He so horribly wanted to do nothing but mourn. With a soft hissing noise the nearby door opened, and Taylor saw Johnny standing at the entrance. His face was latent with tears and while Taylor might usually have to ask what it was that was bothering the boy, now, he knew exactly what it was.

Taylor patted the bed and, following this lead, Johnny walked in and sat beside the teen. Taylor quickly reached around and pulled the boy close, but the child quickly leaned over and put his head in Taylor's lap. Taylor knew that the child needed a great deal of comforting, but to say anything at this point would invite either a sobbing voice, or uncontrollable heaves of anguish that Taylor didn't think he could handle, so instead he just ran his fingers through the child's hair, and patted his head lightly. Hopefully this small degree of physical affection and Taylor's pathic emotion of love would be enough to help the child feel better.

Deep inside, though, Taylor was wishing that someone would make *him* feel better. In the last day his emotions had gone from one extreme to another so quickly that it was a wonder to him his skull didn't either implode or explode from all the activity. Either way – he'd welcome such an event if it meant that he didn't have to feel this empty hollowness in his heart. Taylor ached not only for himself, but for his children too. He knew that they would all now have to face a great deal of emotional suffering from their loss, and despite how quickly he might ask them to put their emotions aside considering the tasks ahead, he knew that they would eventually have to contend with the simmering grief that would have to let itself out over a long period of time.

Taylor looked at the clock. He and his children would have to meet Kashal's crew on the tower's landing pad in ten minutes. But he didn't feel ready for anything right now. He let the emotions inside him slowly consume his will, and all he wanted to do was to love and be loved by his children – this, in fact, seemed the only remedy for his aching heart.

With the hissing of the door opening again, Taylor saw that Grace was standing at the door this time, and as she stared in on the sullen pair in front of her – her face hardened even more than when she first looked in.

"Come on! We've got some alien butt to kick and I for one want to get me a piece – so let's get moving," she said angrily, and Taylor, for the first time, was happy that it wasn't Johnny who brought him into the reality of the world around him – it was Grace – who clearly let her anger and her frustrations guide her into purpose. She would be, Taylor knew, one of the hardest to fall when she did finally come down and grieve for Jay. But for now – he let her face, her fuming attitude, and her forceful nature guide him into action.

He lifted the boy's head from his lap, offered the child just as angry of a stare as the one Grace had offered him, and with the spark of this emotion igniting the gas of his emptiness and loss, Johnny filled with the rage needed to get moving.

With the three marching into the hall, they were met by David, Orion, Aspen and Caitlin, who all saw the angry expressions that the three shared. As if it were an instantaneous infection, the anger spread to each of the other children – and pathically they enhanced each other's frustrations.

The seven of them made their way to the lift and quickly ascended to the main landing pad where, much to Taylor's surprise a handful of people were there to see him and the children off.

In line, he could see Dr. Young and Dr. Ellington, President Andrews flanked by what was left of his Evol Crew, and the one person that Taylor wanted to see the least, but knew he needed to the most – Shannon.

While he and the children walked past the others with handshakes, hugs, and a few angry stares, they each seemed to lose purpose when they approached this woman. And Taylor, for one, could feel the anger he had been shielding himself with melt away as he stared into her mournful face.

"Shannon – I – I am so sorry. I don't know what to say."

With these words Taylor could feel his weaker emotions rise to the surface, and Shannon could see this in Taylor's misting eyes.

"I will tell you this, because I know it," the teen said with a sober stare before adding, "He loved you so very, very much. He gave up his best friend and seeing these children just to be with you – you know that don't you."

She smiled, tears still streaming down her face. "I know he loved me. And he loved you – all of you too. You were all he ever talked about, and even though it made me sooooooo angry sometimes – I can tell why just by looking at you. You are amazing – and I want you to do whatever it takes to make sure he didn't die for nothing."

Taylor could hear anger well in Shannon's voice, and all at once his face stiffened. Her words and her tone had again swung him into purpose, and with an outward stare to the Los Angeles skyline, he noticed another pair of individuals standing at the edge of the pad.

He looked around at his children, and with a nodding of his chin, Taylor let them run ahead of him while he offered Shannon a warm embrace; a final token of the grief that they shared, and the only thing they could offer each other in hoping to find peace.

After allowing this moment of sympathy and shared emotion to pass, Taylor turned a strange and beguiling stare to President Andrews. He spoke to the man with a calm arrogance. "Did you bring what I asked you?"

From his hip the President pulled a data pad which he presented with a simple response of "here."

Taylor grabbed the pad, and he could tell that the president was reluctant in handing it over. The teen scanned it over carefully, and after being satisfied with what he read, he pressed his thumb to it with a deep breathing sigh, and a wide smile.

"What is that?" Shannon asked, which was quickly echoed by Caitlin, and immediately the other children surrounded Taylor. It wasn't the question so much that got their attention, but the smile and tears that were much more enigmatic.

"It's official!" Taylor shouted with an exited tone that did nothing to express how the teen really felt inside. He then passed the pad to Caitlin, who stared at it with a bit of confusion and quickly handed it to Orion, who, she assumed, would be able to make sense of what it said.

The boy scanned it over, and just as quick as Taylor, he looked up with a smile. "This is – it's – we're – we're his! The adoption's final – we're his!" Orion worded almost breathlessly, and in that instant the other children snatched the pad up from Orion's hands.

But when the pad reached Johnny, the boy looked up at it with almost a frown, and David couldn't help but ask, "hey bro, what's the problem?"

"Well," Johnny started, and it was clear that the boy was looking for the right words to say so that his feelings were not misunderstood. "It's just that father's thumbprint's on here, and it's just his!"

David shook his head with a "huh?!" and Johnny persisted.

"His print's on here because *he wants us,* but I want my print on here. I want to make sure that *they* know *I want him!*"

The other children's faces lit up at this simple but deeply thought comment and Taylor quickly walked up to Johnny and put his hand on the boy's shoulder. With a reaching of his hand, Taylor pulled the pad from Grace's light grip. He scanned the page on the screen, and after a quick focus, he held out the pad in front of the boy.

Johnny read the page, and saw, at the bottom of the page, an addendum which read that the children, willing and able, would apply their own thumb prints to show that they agree to the adoption. Johnny smiled and quickly pressed his finger to the pad before passing it to his brothers and sisters who all did the same. Once finished, Taylor looked at the finished product, a single large print with 6 smaller ones, all representing the bonds of a newly formed family, and he smiled. He focused on the pad for a few hard seconds, concentrating deeply before finally passing it back to President Andrews.

"And it's not that I don't trust you," he said to the President, "or that I do, but I've just made triplicate copies of this document and sent them to CESPA, my own secure DataVault on the WSN, and to the EduCorp mainframe." At this point he turned a smile and a wink to Dr. Young, who had been listening, and she smiled in knowing that she had just played witness to a simple and crucial event if, in fact, it were ever questioned.

As the pad left Taylor's fingers he turned and smiled to his children, all of whom offered him a hug that he was thrilled to receive. In his heart he realized that finally, after all this time, after all these struggles, he was the father of these children in absolutely every sense of the word. He took a deep and quickly saddened breath. The only thing that would've or could've made this moment more perfect was if Jay could've been witness to it. He was, after all, the one man that knew how much this was something that Taylor wanted. After such a heartfelt conversation with Shannon, who had watched the whole affair of the data-pad with a sympathetic and aching expression of pride that she could witness this moment, Taylor felt the pangs of missing his friend, and wishing him to be there to see this life changing event.

Then, with a bit of distraction, Taylor's brain went in a completely different direction. He turned his head and saw in the distance that Tristan and Delissa had been waiting for them quite patiently at the far end of the pad. So far off, in fact that they hadn't heard what just happened. But the instant that the children and he caught sight of them, the mood had completely changed.

It was pretty obvious when all the children ran up to the mother-son pair that Aspen's attention would be focused on the latter and she offered him a hug around the neck that almost made him want to push her way from embarrassment. But when she finally let him go they stared at each other. The boy had a smirk on his face that she couldn't yet decipher.

"Mom's gonna see if we can come with you!"

"Huh?" she replied, looking over at Delissa – who was being showered with attention by Aspen's courteously avoiding siblings.

With an eventual swapping of the attentive, Orion, Grace, David, Johnny, and Caitlin all rushed on Tristan as Aspen made her way through her siblings to Delissa.

"Is that true – Are you going to come with us?" she asked, running up to the woman, giving her a hug.

"Well, I'm going to see what I can do – but really, I think it's up to your father."

"What's up to me?" Taylor asked, but before he could get an answer, the whole of the EduCorp landing pad lit up with a bright electrostatic light show. Kashal and his usual entourage of other Takashians appeared in that instant, and the leader wasted no time in handing a bundle of arm bands for Taylor and the children, and while all of the little ones were still apprehensive about even being in the presence of these creatures, Taylor's confidence helped them to be more comfortable. So Taylor handed out the bands, and instructed the children to put them on, but he himself did not put his armband on until he was ready to leave.

He turned to Delissa, and with her smile, green eyes, and red hair framed by a silhouette of the now setting sun in the city sky, Taylor could think of nothing better to do than take her in his arms and kiss her the way he had been wanting to kiss her when they first looked at each other with admiration and desire those months ago while huddled over her son. And when he pulled himself away she had a smile on her face that didn't wane when she heaved out her words of excitement.

"Wow! I – Oh, wow! I hope you know that wasn't a goodbye kiss – because whether you like it or not, Tris and I are coming with you?"

Taylor shook his head in disapproval.

"No – no way. You two are staying here – at least for now. Besides – out there – there's nothing you can do."

"Taylor, honey – you don't have to protect me! Remember, I'm twice your age!"

"Are you sure about this?" Taylor pressed. She answered without words, just energetic shaking of her head, and her wonderful red hair, forcing Taylor to smile. He held her close and in doing so, whispered in her ear.

"Here, take this!" Taylor said putting a small ring in her hands, "I made it just for you. I love you Delissa. I really do! So don't think I'm gonna just leave you here. If we get out of this thing alive – you'd better believe that I'm coming back to get you - and this will make sure I can find you, wherever you are.

When he pulled himself away, he could see a fantastic glint in Delissa's eyes as she delighted in his words. So, with another kiss, the two showed, again, no fear of showing affection in front of their respective children.

"Ahem!" Orion interrupted, "Tristan says they're coming with us! Is that true?"

Taylor heard, behind Orion's words, an excitement over the possibility that Tristan and Delissa would be joining them on this journey, but Taylor's instant show of disapproval told him otherwise.

"No children – we'll have to come back and get them when we're *done*."

Amazingly, all six of Taylor's kids weren't upset at these words. Instead, they had an understanding that when Taylor said the word done, he referenced the fact that they had work to do – work that did not require the distractions of a friend, or of a girlfriend. And more importantly, that this was not a sightseeing trip – it wasn't a vacation. No – this was war – whether the children had thought about it or not, and whether they were prepared for something that hadn't happened on earth in nearly 400 years or not. More than all of this, Taylor knew that he and his children were the only chance for Earth's survival and this was a burden he knew that they would never *ever* understand.

Kashal quickly separated the small group on the landing pad and barked a few growls that Taylor had to translate in order to understand.

IT IS TIME TO LEAVE - THE AURORIANS
ARE ADVANCING IN YOUR SYSTEM!

Taylor wanted to stall – he wanted to give Delissa one more hug, and scrub Tristan on the head one more time. But instead, he slipped the band over his arm, and stared Kashal in the eyes.

"I'm ready – we're all ready." Then, with barely a focus, he pulled the bags that he had left at the lift to slide along the pad and rest beside him. "Okay kids –

grab a bag – Each one has the same thing – so there's one for each of you. It should have everything you need."

The children did as they were told, all the while either looking at Taylor, Kashal, Tristan, Delissa, Dr. Ellington or Dr. Young. They each offered simple stare and smile as a gesture of saying goodbye. Taylor, on the other hand, had his eyes transfixed on Delissa, and with his mouthing of the words "I love you!" He and the children were engulfed in a series of electrostatic bubbles before being transported out of sight.

Eventually, Delissa and Tristan were the last ones on the landing pad. President Andrews left almost immediately after the departure, flanked by his last three members of the Evol-Crew. Shannon left with Dr. Young and Dr. Ellington – who did their best to comfort her with memories of the man that she loved, and doing their best to reassure that he was in a better place.

But the last two standing on the pad stared up at the now darkened skies of Los Angeles through the four massive columns that stood so very tall on all sides. From the forest, staring at the stars in this way wasn't always the easiest for them, and so they marveled at the wide open sky, their hearts filled with love and hope for their friends' safe return.

But below them, quiet and calm, in the massive EduCorp Towers, in the center of the city of Los Angeles sat the desolate office of Jaylen Wess, and in this office, on a shelf, leaning against one of the many white walls, was a picture of eight happy souls who, for a moment in their complicated lives, were intertwined in love, peace and tranquility. And while clearly one of them was gone forever, the future of the history of these young and beautiful souls would never again, through their journeys to come, hold such a moment of peace.

www.ingramcontent.com/pod-product-compliance
Lightning Source LLC
Chambersburg PA
CBHW030823310726
48980CB00006B/617/J
* 9 7 8 0 6 1 5 1 7 1 3 9 5 *